Agatha Christie is known throughout the world as the Queen of Crime. Her books have sold over a billion copies in English with another billion in foreign languages. She is the most widely published author of all time and in any language, outsold only by the Bible and Shakespeare. She is the author of 80 crime novels and short story collections, 20 plays, and six novels written under the name of Mary Westmacott.

Agatha Christie's first novel, *The Mysterious Affair at Styles*, was written towards the end of the First World War, in which she served as a VAD. In it she created Hercule Poirot, the little Belgian detective who was destined to become the most popular detective in crime fiction since Sherlock Holmes. It was eventually published by The Bodley Head in 1920.

In 1926, after averaging a book a year, Agatha Christie wrote her masterpiece. *The Murder of Roger Ackroyd* was the first of her books to be published by Collins and marked the beginning of an author–publisher relationship which lasted for 50 years and well over 70 books. *The Murder of Roger Ackroyd* was also the first of Agatha Christie's books to be dramatized – under the name *Alibi* – and to have a successful run in London's West End. *The Mousetrap*, her most famous play of all, opened in 1952 and is the longest-running play in history.

Agatha Christie was made a Dame in 1971. She died in 1976, since when a number of books have been published posthumously: the bestselling novel *Sleeping Murder* appeared later that year, followed by her autobiography and the short story collections *Miss Marple's Final Cases*, *Problem at Pollensa Bay* and *While the Light Lasts*. In 1998 *Black Coffee* was the first of her plays to be novelized by another author, Charles Osborne.

THE AGATHA CHRISTIE COLLECTION

The Man in the Brown Suit
The Secret of Chimneys
The Seven Dials Mystery
The Mysterious Mr Quin
The Sittaford Mystery
The Hound of Death
The Listerdale Mystery
Why Didn't They Ask Evans?
Parker Pyne Investigates
Murder is Easy
And Then There Were None
Towards Zero
Death Comes as the End
Sparkling Cyanide
Crooked House
They Came to Baghdad
Destination Unknown
Ordeal by Innocence
The Pale Horse
Endless Night
Passenger to Frankfurt
Problem at Pollensa Bay
While the Light Lasts

Poirot
The Mysterious Affair at Styles
The Murder on the Links
Poirot Investigates
The Murder of Roger Ackroyd
The Big Four
The Mystery of the Blue Train
Peril at End House
Lord Edgware Dies
Murder on the Orient Express
Three-Act Tragedy
Death in the Clouds
The ABC Murders
Murder in Mesopotamia
Cards on the Table
Murder in the Mews
Dumb Witness
Death on the Nile
Appointment With Death
Hercule Poirot's Christmas
Sad Cypress
One, Two, Buckle My Shoe
Evil Under the Sun
Five Little Pigs
The Hollow
The Labours of Hercules
Taken at the Flood
Mrs McGinty's Dead
After the Funeral
Hickory Dickory Dock

Dead Man's Folly
Cat Among the Pigeons
The Adventure of the Christmas Pudding
The Clocks
Third Girl
Hallowe'en Party
Elephants Can Remember
Poirot's Early Cases
Curtain: Poirot's Last Case

Marple
The Murder at the Vicarage
The Thirteen Problems
The Body in the Library
The Moving Finger
A Murder is Announced
They Do It With Mirrors
A Pocket Full of Rye
4.50 from Paddington
The Mirror Crack'd from Side to Side
A Caribbean Mystery
At Bertram's Hotel
Nemesis
Sleeping Murder
Miss Marple's Final Cases

Tommy & Tuppence
The Secret Adversary
Partners in Crime
N or M?
By the Pricking of My Thumbs
Postern of Fate

Published as Mary Westmacott
Giant's Bread
Unfinished Portrait
Absent in the Spring
The Rose and the Yew Tree
A Daughter's a Daughter
The Burden

Memoirs
An Autobiography
Come, Tell Me How You Live

Play Collections
The Mousetrap and Selected Plays
Witness for the Prosecution
and Selected Plays

Play Adaptations by Charles Osborne
Black Coffee (Poirot)
Spider's Web
The Unexpected Guest

Agatha Christie

POIROT

THE COMPLETE
ARIADNE OLIVER

VOLUME I

•

CARDS ON THE TABLE

•

MRS MCGINTY'S DEAD

•

DEAD MAN'S FOLLY

•

PLUS TWO SHORT STORIES

•

HarperCollins*Publishers*

HarperCollins*Publishers*
77–85 Fulham Palace Road,
Hammersmith, London W6 8JB
www.harpercollins.co.uk

This edition first published 2005
1

ISBN 0 00 719067 0

Typeset in Plantin Light and Gill Sans by
Palimpsest Book Production Limited,
Polmont, Stirlingshire

Printed and bound in Great Britain by
Clays Ltd, St Ives plc

CONTENTS

CARDS ON THE TABLE

There is an idea prevalent that a detective story is rather like a big race – a number of starters – likely horses and jockeys. 'You pays your money and you takes your choice!' The favourite is by common consent the opposite of a favourite on the race-course. In other words he is likely to be a complete outsider! Spot the least likely person to have committed the crime and in nine times out of ten your task is finished.

Since I do not want my faithful readers to fling away this book in disgust, I prefer to warn them beforehand *that this is not that kind of book*. There are only *four* starters and any one of them, *given the right circumstances*, might have committed the crime. That knocks out forcibly the element of surprise. Nevertheless there should be, I think, an equal interest attached to four persons, each of whom has committed murder and is capable of committing further murders. They are four widely divergent types, the motive that drives each one of them to crime is peculiar to that person, and each one would employ a different method. The deduction must, therefore, be entirely *psychological*, but it is none the less interesting for that, because when all is said and done it is the *mind* of the murderer that is of supreme interest.

I may say, as an additional argument in favour of this story, that it was one of Hercule Poirot's favourite cases. His friend, Captain Hastings, however, when Poirot described it to him, considered it very dull! I wonder with which of them my readers will agree.

Agatha Christie

....
MR SHAITANA

'My dear M. Poirot!'

It was a soft purring voice – a voice used deliberately as an instrument – nothing impulsive or premeditated about it.

Hercule Poirot swung round.

He bowed.

He shook hands ceremoniously.

There was something in his eye that was unusual. One would have said that this chance encounter awakened in him an emotion that he seldom had occasion to feel.

'My dear Mr Shaitana,' he said.

They both paused. They were like duellists *en garde*.

Around them a well-dressed languid London crowd eddied mildly. Voices drawled or murmured.

'Darling – exquisite!'

'Simply divine, aren't they, my dear?'

It was the Exhibition of Snuff-Boxes at Wessex House. Admission one guinea, in aid of the London hospitals.

'My dear man,' said Mr Shaitana, 'how nice to see you! Not hanging or guillotining much just at present? Slack season in the criminal world? Or is there to be a robbery here this afternoon – that would be too delicious.'

'Alas, Monsieur,' said Poirot. 'I came here in a purely private capacity.'

Mr Shaitana was diverted for a moment by a Lovely Young Thing with tight poodle curls up one side of her head and three cornucopias in black straw on the other.

He said:

'My *dear* – *why* didn't you come to my party? It really was a marvellous party! Quite a lot of people actually *spoke* to me! One woman even said, "How do you do," and "Goodbye" and "Thank you so much" – but of course she came from a Garden City, poor dear!'

While the Lovely Young Thing made a suitable reply, Poirot allowed himself a good study of the hirsute adornment on Mr Shaitana's upper lip.

A fine moustache – a *very* fine moustache – the only moustache in London, perhaps, that could compete with that of M. Hercule Poirot.

'But it is *not* so luxuriant,' he murmured to himself. 'No, decidedly it is inferior in every respect. *Tout de même*, it catches the eye.'

The whole of Mr Shaitana's person caught the eye – it was designed to do so. He deliberately attempted a Mephistophelian effect. He was tall and thin, his face was long and melancholy, his eyebrows were heavily accented and jet black, he wore a moustache with stiff waxed ends and a tiny black imperial. His clothes were works of art – of exquisite cut – but with a suggestion of bizarre.

Every healthy Englishman who saw him longed earnestly and fervently to kick him! They said, with a singular lack of originality, 'There's that damned Dago, Shaitana!'

Their wives, daughters, sisters, aunts, mothers, and even grandmothers said, varying the idiom according to their generation, words to this effect: 'I know, my dear. Of course, he is *too* terrible. But *so* rich! And such marvellous parties! And he's always got something amusing and spiteful to tell you about people.'

Whether Mr Shaitana was an Argentine, or a Portuguese, or a Greek, or some other nationality rightly despised by the insular Briton, nobody knew.

But three facts were quite certain:

He existed richly and beautifully in a super flat in Park Lane.

He gave wonderful parties – large parties, small parties, *macabre* parties, respectable parties and definitely 'queer' parties.

He was a man of whom nearly everybody was a little afraid.

Why this last was so can hardly be stated in definite words. There was a feeling, perhaps, that he knew a little too much about everybody. And there was a feeling, too, that his sense of humour was a curious one.

People nearly always felt that it would be better not to risk offending Mr Shaitana.

It was his humour this afternoon to bait that ridiculous-looking little man, Hercule Poirot.

'So even a policeman needs recreation?' he said. 'You study the arts in your old age, M. Poirot?'

Poirot smiled good-humouredly.

'I see,' he said, 'that you yourself have lent three snuff-boxes to the Exhibition.'

Mr Shaitana waved a deprecating hand.

'One picks up trifles here and there. You must come to my flat one day. I have some interesting pieces. I do not confine myself to any particular period or class of object.'

'Your tastes are catholic,' said Poirot smiling.

'As you say.'

Suddenly Mr Shaitana's eyes danced, the corners of his lips curled up, his eyebrows assumed a fantastic tilt.

'I could even show you objects in your own line, M. Poirot!'

'You have then a private "Black Museum".'

'Bah!' Mr Shaitana snapped disdainful fingers. 'The cup used by the Brighton murderer, the jemmy of a celebrated burglar – absurd childishness! I should never burden myself with rubbish like that. I collect only the best objects of their kind.'

'And what do you consider the best objects, artistically speaking, in crime?' inquired Poirot.

Mr Shaitana leaned forward and laid two fingers on Poirot's shoulder. He hissed his words dramatically.

'The human beings who commit them, M. Poirot.'

Poirot's eyebrows rose a trifle.

'Aha, I have startled you,' said Mr Shaitana. 'My dear, dear man, you and I look on these things as from poles apart! For you crime is a matter of routine: a murder, an investigation, a clue, and ultimately (for you are undoubtedly an able fellow) a conviction. Such banalities would not interest me! I am not interested in poor specimens of any kind. And the caught murderer is necessarily one of the failures. He is second-rate. No, I look on the matter from the artistic point of view. I collect only the best!'

'The best being –?' asked Poirot.

'My dear fellow – *the ones who have got away with it!* The successes! The criminals who lead an agreeable life which no breath of suspicion has ever touched. Admit that is an amusing hobby.'

'It was another word I was thinking of – not amusing.'

'An idea!' cried Shaitana, paying no attention to Poirot. 'A little dinner! A dinner to meet my exhibits! Really, that is a most amusing thought. I cannot think why it has never occurred to me before. Yes – yes, I see it exactly . . . You must give me a little time – not next week – let us say the week after next. You are free? What day shall we say?'

'Any day of the week after next would suit me,' said Poirot with a bow.

'Good – then let us say Friday. Friday the 18th, that will be. I will write it down at once in my little book. Really, the idea pleases me enormously.'

'I am not quite sure if it pleases me,' said Poirot slowly. 'I do not mean that I am insensible to the kindness of your invitation – no – not that –'

Shaitana interrupted him.

'But it shocks your *bourgeois* sensibilities? My dear fellow, you *must* free yourself from the limitations of the policeman mentality.'

Poirot said slowly:

'It is true that I have a thoroughly *bourgeois* attitude to murder.'

'But, my dear, *why*? A stupid, bungled, butchering business – yes, I agree with you. But murder can be an *art*! A murderer can be an artist.'

'Oh, I admit it.'

'Well then?' Mr Shaitana asked.

'But he is still a murderer!'

'Surely, my dear M. Poirot, to do a thing supremely well is a *justification*! You want, very unimaginatively, to take every murderer, handcuff him, shut him up, and eventually break his neck for him in the early hours of the morning. In my opinion a really successful murderer should be granted a pension out of the public funds and asked out to dinner!'

Poirot shrugged his shoulders.

'I am not as insensitive to art in crime as you think. I can admire the perfect murder – I can also admire a tiger – that splendid tawny-striped beast. But I will admire him from outside his cage. I will not go inside. That is to say, not unless it is my duty to do so. For you see, Mr Shaitana, the tiger might spring . . .'

Mr Shaitana laughed.

'I see. And the murderer?'

'Might murder,' said Poirot gravely.

'My dear fellow – what an alarmist you are! Then you will not come to meet my collection of – tigers?'

'On the contrary, I shall be enchanted.'

'How brave!'

'You do not quite understand me, Mr Shaitana. My words were in the nature of a warning. You asked me just now to admit that your idea of a collection of murderers was amusing. I said I could think of another word other than amusing. That word was dangerous. I fancy, Mr Shaitana, that your hobby might be a dangerous one!'

Mr Shaitana laughed, a very Mephistophelian laugh.

He said:

'I may expect you, then, on the 18th?'

Poirot gave a little bow.

'You may expect me on the 18th. *Mille remerciments*.'

'I shall arrange a little party,' mused Shaitana. 'Do not forget. Eight o'clock.'

He moved away. Poirot stood a minute or two looking after him.

He shook his head slowly and thoughtfully.

CHAPTER 2
DINNER AT MR SHAITANA'S

The door of Mr Shaitana's flat opened noiselessly. A grey-haired butler drew it back to let Poirot enter. He closed it equally noiselessly and deftly relieved the guest of his overcoat and hat.

He murmured in a low expressionless voice:

'What name shall I say?'

'M. Hercule Poirot.'

There was a little hum of talk that eddied out into the hall as the butler opened a door and announced:

'M. Hercule Poirot.'

Sherry-glass in hand, Shaitana came forward to meet him. He was, as usual, immaculately dressed. The Mephistophelian suggestion was heightened tonight, the eyebrows seemed accentuated in their mocking twist.

'Let me introduce you – do you know Mrs Oliver?'

The showman in him enjoyed the little start of surprise that Poirot gave.

Mrs Ariadne Oliver was extremely well-known as one of the foremost writers of detective and other sensational stories. She wrote chatty (if not particularly grammatical) articles on *The Tendency of the Criminal; Famous Crimes Passionnels; Murder for Love v. Murder for Gain.* She was also a hot-headed feminist, and when any murder of importance was occupying space in the Press there was sure to be an interview with Mrs Oliver, and it was mentioned that Mrs Oliver had said, 'Now if a *woman* were the head of Scotland Yard!' She was an earnest believer in woman's intuition.

For the rest she was an agreeable woman of middle age, handsome in a rather untidy fashion with fine eyes, substantial shoulders and a large quantity of rebellious grey hair with which she was continually experimenting. One day her appearance would be highly intellectual – a brow with the hair scraped back from it and coiled in a large bun in the neck – on another Mrs Oliver would suddenly appear with Madonna loops, or large masses of slightly untidy curls. On this particular evening Mrs Oliver was trying out a fringe.

She greeted Poirot, whom she had met before at a literary dinner, in an agreeable bass voice.

'And Superintendent Battle you doubtless know,' said Mr Shaitana.

A big, square, wooden-faced man moved forward. Not only did an onlooker feel that Superintendent Battle was carved out of wood – he also managed to convey the impression that the wood in question was the timber out of a battleship.

Superintendent Battle was supposed to be Scotland Yard's best representative. He always looked stolid and rather stupid.

'I know M. Poirot,' said Superintendent Battle.

And his wooden face creased into a smile and then returned to its former unexpressiveness.

'Colonel Race,' went on Mr Shaitana.

Poirot had not previously met Colonel Race, but he knew something about him. A dark, handsome, deeply bronzed man of fifty, he was usually to be found in some outpost of empire – especially if there were trouble brewing. Secret Service is a melodramatic term, but it described pretty accurately to the lay mind the nature and scope of Colonel Race's activities.

Poirot had by now taken in and appreciated the particular essence of his host's humorous intentions.

'Our other guests are late,' said Mr Shaitana. 'My fault, perhaps. I believe I told them 8.15.'

But at that moment the door opened and the butler announced: 'Dr Roberts.'

The man who came in did so with a kind of parody of a brisk bedside manner. He was a cheerful, highly-coloured individual of middle age. Small twinkling eyes, a touch of baldness, a tendency to *embonpoint* and a general air of well-scrubbed and disinfected medical practitioner. His manner was cheerful and confident. You felt that his diagnosis would be correct and his treatments agreeable and practical – 'a little champagne in convalescence perhaps.' A man of the world!

'Not late, I hope?' said Dr Roberts genially.

He shook hands with his host and was introduced to the others. He seemed particularly gratified at meeting Battle.

'Why, you're one of the big noises at Scotland Yard, aren't you? This *is* interesting! Too bad to make you talk shop but I warn you I shall have a try at it. Always been interested in crime. Bad thing for a doctor, perhaps. Mustn't say so to my nervous patients – ha ha!'

Again the door opened.

'Mrs Lorrimer.'

Mrs Lorrimer was a well-dressed woman of sixty. She had finely-cut features, beautifully arranged grey hair, and a clear, incisive voice.

'I hope I'm not late,' she said, advancing to her host.

She turned from him to greet Dr Roberts, with whom she was acquainted.

The butler announced:

'Major Despard.'

Major Despard was a tall, lean, handsome man, his face slightly marred by a scar on the temple. Introductions completed, he gravitated naturally to the side of Colonel Race – and the two men were soon talking sport and comparing their experiences on *safari*.

For the last time the door opened and the butler announced: 'Miss Meredith.'

A girl in the early twenties entered. She was of medium height and pretty. Brown curls clustered in her neck, her grey eyes were large and wide apart. Her face was powdered but not made up. Her voice was slow and rather shy.

She said:

'Oh dear, am I the last?'

Mr Shaitana descended on her with sherry and an ornate and complimentary reply. His introductions were formal and almost ceremonious.

Miss Meredith was left sipping her sherry by Poirot's side.

'Our friend is very punctilious,' said Poirot with a smile.

The girl agreed.

'I know. People rather dispense with introductions nowadays. They just say "I expect you know everybody" and leave it at that.'

'Whether you do or you don't?'

'Whether you do or don't. Sometimes it makes it awkward – but I think this is more awe-inspiring.'

She hesitated and then said:

'Is that Mrs Oliver, the novelist?'

Mrs Oliver's bass voice rose powerfully at that minute, speaking to Dr Roberts.

'You can't get away from a woman's instinct, doctor. Women know these things.'

Forgetting that she no longer had a brow she endeavoured to sweep her hair back from it but was foiled by the fringe.

'That is Mrs Oliver,' said Poirot.

'The one who wrote *The Body in the Library*?'

'That identical one.'

Miss Meredith frowned a little.

'And that wooden-looking man – a *superintendent* did Mr Shaitana say?'

'From Scotland Yard.'

'And you?'

'And me?'

'I know all about you, M. Poirot. It was you who really solved the A.B.C. crimes.'

'Madamoiselle, you cover me with confusion.'

Miss Meredith drew her brows together.

'Mr Shaitana,' she began and then stopped. 'Mr Shaitana –'

Poirot said quietly:

'One might say he was "crime-minded". It seems so. Doubtless he wishes to hear us dispute ourselves. He is already egging on Mrs Oliver and Dr Roberts. They are now discussing untraceable poisons.'

Miss Meredith gave a little gasp as she said:

'What a queer man he is!'

'Dr Roberts?'

'No, Mr Shaitana.'

She shivered a little and said:

'There's always something a little frightening about him, I think. You never know what would strike him as amusing. It might – it might be something *cruel*.'

'Such as fox-hunting, eh?'

Miss Meredith threw him a reproachful glance.

'I meant – oh! something *Oriental*!'

'He has perhaps the tortuous mind,' admitted Poirot.

'Torturer's?'

'No, no tortuous, I said.'

'I don't think I like him frightfully,' confided Miss Meredith, her voice dropping.

'You will like his dinner, though,' Poirot assured her. 'He has a marvellous cook.'

She looked at him doubtfully and then laughed.

'Why,' she exclaimed, 'I believe you are quite human.'

'But certainly I am human!'

'You see,' said Miss Meredith, 'all these celebrities are rather intimidating.'

'Mademoiselle, you should not be intimidated – you should be thrilled! You should have all ready your autograph book and your fountain-pen.'

'Well, you see, I'm not really terribly interested in crime. I don't think women are: it's always men who read detective stories.'

Hercule Poirot sighed affectedly.

'Alas!' he murmured. 'What would I not give at this minute to be even the most minor of film stars!'

The butler threw the door open.

'Dinner is served,' he murmured.

Poirot's prognostication was amply justified. The dinner was delicious and its serving perfection. Subdued light, polished wood, the blue gleam of Irish glass. In the dimness, at the head of the table, Mr Shaitana looked more than ever diabolical.

He apologized gracefully for the uneven number of the sexes.

Mrs Lorrimer was on his right hand, Mrs Oliver on his left. Miss Meredith was between Superintendent Battle and Major Despard. Poirot was between Mrs Lorrimer and Dr Roberts.

The latter murmured facetiously to him.

'You're not going to be allowed to monopolize the only pretty girl all the evening. You French fellows, you don't waste your time, do you?'

'I happen to be Belgian,' murmured Poirot.

'Same thing where the ladies are concerned, I expect, my boy,' said the doctor cheerfully.

Then, dropping the facetiousness, and adopting a professional tone, he began to talk to Colonel Race on his other side about the latest developments in the treatment of sleeping sickness.

Mrs Lorrimer turned to Poirot and began to talk of the latest plays. Her judgements were sound and her criticisms apt. They drifted on to books and then to world politics. He found her a well-informed and thoroughly intelligent woman.

On the opposite side of the table Mrs Oliver was asking Major Despard if he knew of any unheard-of-out-of-the-way poisons.

'Well, there's *curare.*'

'My *dear* man, *vieux jeu*! That's been done hundreds of times. I mean something *new*!'

Major Despard said drily:

'Primitive tribes are rather old-fashioned. They stick to the good old stuff their grandfathers and great-grandfathers used before them.'

'Very tiresome of them,' said Mrs Oliver. 'I should have thought they were always experimenting with pounding up herbs and things. Such a chance for explorers, I always think. They could come home and kill off all their rich old uncles with some new drug that no one's ever heard of.'

'You should go to civilization, not to the wilds for that,' said Despard. 'In the modern laboratory, for instance. Cultures of innocent-looking germs that will produce bona fide diseases.'

'That wouldn't do for *my* public,' said Mrs Oliver. 'Besides one is so apt to get the names wrong – staphylococcus and streptococcus and all those things – so difficult for my secretary and anyway rather dull, don't you think so? What do *you* think, Superintendent Battle?'

'In real life people don't bother about being too subtle, Mrs Oliver,' said the superintendent. 'They usually stick to arsenic because it's nice and handy to get hold of.'

'Nonsense,' said Mrs Oliver. 'That's simply because there are lots of crimes you people at Scotland Yard never find out. Now if you had a woman there –'

'As a matter of fact we have –'

'Yes, those dreadful policewomen in funny hats who bother people in parks! I mean a woman at the head of things. Women *know* about crime.'

'They're usually very successful criminals,' said Superintendent Battle. 'Keep their heads well. It's amazing how they'll brazen things out.'

Mr Shaitana laughed gently.

'Poison is a woman's weapon,' he said. 'There must be many secret women poisoners – never found out.'

'Of course there are,' said Mrs Oliver happily, helping herself lavishly to a *mousse* of *foie gras*.

'A doctor, too, has opportunities,' went on Mr Shaitana thoughtfully.

'I protest,' cried Dr Roberts. 'When we poison our patients it's entirely by accident.' He laughed heartily.

'But if I were to commit a crime,' went on Mr Shaitana.

He stopped, and something in that pause compelled attention. All faces were turned to him.

'I should make it very simple, I think. There's always an

accident – a shooting accident, for instance – or the domestic kind of accident.'

Then he shrugged his shoulders and picked up his wine-glass.

'But who am I to pronounce – with so many experts present . . .'

He drank. The candlelight threw a red shade from the wine on to his face with its waxed moustache, its little imperial, its fantastic eyebrows . . .

There was a momentary silence.

Mrs Oliver said:

'Is it twenty-to or twenty-past? An angel passing . . . My feet aren't crossed – it must be a black angel!'

CHAPTER 3

A GAME OF BRIDGE

I

When the company returned to the drawing-room a bridge table had been set out. Coffee was handed round.

'Who plays bridge?' asked Mr Shaitana. 'Mrs Lorrimer, I know. And Dr Roberts. Do you play, Miss Meredith?'

'Yes. I'm not frightfully good, though.'

'Excellent. And Major Despard? Good. Supposing you four play here.'

'Thank goodness there's to be bridge,' said Mrs Lorrimer in an aside to Poirot. 'I'm one of the worst bridge fiends that ever lived. It's growing on me. I simply will *not* go out to dinner now if there's no bridge afterwards! I just fall asleep. I'm ashamed of myself, but there it is.'

They cut for partners. Mrs Lorrimer was partnered with Anne Meredith against Major Despard and Dr Roberts.

'Women against men,' said Mrs Lorrimer as she took her seat and began shuffling the cards in an expert manner. 'The blue cards, don't you think, partner? I'm a forcing two.'

'Mind you win,' said Mrs Oliver, her feminist feelings rising. 'Show the men they can't have it all their own way.'

'They haven't got a hope, the poor dears,' said Dr Roberts cheerfully as he started shuffling the other pack. 'Your deal, I think, Mrs Lorrimer.'

Major Despard sat down rather slowly. He was looking at Anne Meredith as though he had just made the discovery that she was remarkably pretty.

'Cut, please,' said Mrs Lorrimer impatiently. And with a start of apology he cut the pack she was presenting to him.

Mrs Lorrimer began to deal with a practised hand.

'There is another bridge table in the other room,' said Mr Shaitana.

He crossed to a second door and the other four followed him into a small comfortably furnished smoking-room where a second bridge table was set ready.

'We must cut out,' said Colonel Race.

Mr Shaitana shook his head.

'I do not play,' he said. 'Bridge is not one of the games that amuse me.'

The others protested that they would much rather not play, but he overruled them firmly and in the end they sat down. Poirot and Mrs Oliver against Battle and Race.

Mr Shaitana watched them for a little while, smiled in a Mephistophelian manner as he observed on what hand Mrs Oliver declared Two No Trumps, and then went noiselessly through into the other room.

There they were well down to it, their faces serious, the bids coming quickly. 'One heart.' 'Pass.' 'Three clubs.' 'Three spades.' 'Four diamonds.' 'Double.' 'Four hearts.'

Mr Shaitana stood watching a moment, smiling to himself.

Then he crossed the room and sat down in a big chair by the fireplace. A tray of drinks had been brought in and placed on an adjacent table. The firelight gleamed on the crystal stoppers.

Always an artist in lighting, Mr Shaitana had simulated the appearance of a merely firelit room. A small shaded lamp at his elbow gave him light to read by if he so desired. Discreet floodlighting gave the room a subdued look. A slightly stronger light shone over the bridge table, from whence the monotonous ejaculations continued.

'One no trump' – clear and decisive – Mrs Lorrimer.

'Three hearts' – an aggressive note in the voice – Dr Roberts.

'No bid' – a quiet voice – Anne Meredith's.

A slight pause always before Despard's voice came. Not so much a slow thinker as a man who liked to be sure before he spoke.

'Four hearts.'

'Double.'

His face lit up by the flickering firelight, Mr Shaitana smiled.

He smiled and he went on smiling. His eyelids flickered a little . . .

His party was amusing him.

II

'Five diamonds. Game and rubber,' said Colonel Race. 'Good for you, partner,' he said to Poirot. 'I didn't think you'd do it. Lucky they didn't lead a spade.'

'Wouldn't have made much difference, I expect,' said Superintendent Battle, a man of gentle magnanimity.

He had called spades. His partner, Mrs Oliver, had had a spade, but 'something had told her' to lead a club – with disastrous results.

Colonel Race looked at his watch.

'Ten-past-twelve. Time for another?'

'You'll excuse me,' said Superintendent Battle. 'But I'm by way of being an "early-to-bed" man.'

'I, too,' said Hercule Poirot.

'We'd better add up,' said Race.

The result of the evening's five rubbers was an overwhelming victory for the male sex. Mrs Oliver had lost three pounds and seven shillings to the other three. The biggest winner was Colonel Race.

Mrs Oliver, though a bad bridge player, was a sporting loser. She paid up cheerfully.

'Everything went wrong for me tonight,' she said. 'It is like that sometimes. I held the most beautiful cards yesterday. A hundred and fifty honours three times running.'

She rose and gathered up her embroidered evening bag, just refraining in time from stroking her hair off her brow.

'I suppose our host is next door,' she said.

She went through the communicating door, the others behind her.

Mr Shaitana was in his chair by the fire. The bridge players were absorbed in their game.

'Double five clubs,' Mrs Lorrimer was saying in her cool, incisive voice.

'Five No Trumps.'

'Double five No Trumps.'

Mrs Oliver came up to the bridge table. This was likely to be an exciting hand.

Superintendent Battle came with her.

Colonel Race went towards Mr Shaitana, Poirot behind him.

'Got to be going, Shaitana,' said Race.

Mr Shaitana did not answer. His head had fallen forward, and he seemed to be asleep. Race gave a momentary whimsical glance at Poirot and went a little nearer. Suddenly he uttered a muffled exclamation, bent forward. Poirot was beside him in a minute, he, too, looking where Colonel Race was pointing – something that might have been a particularly ornate shirt stud – but was not . . .

Poirot bent, raised one of Mr Shaitana's hands, then let it fall. He met Race's inquiring glance and nodded. The latter raised his voice.

'Superintendent Battle, just a minute.'

The superintendent came over to them. Mrs Oliver continued to watch the play of Five No Trumps doubled.

Superintendent Battle, despite his appearance of stolidity, was a very quick man. His eyebrows went up and he said in a low voice as he joined them:

'Something wrong?'

With a nod Colonel Race indicated the silent figure in the chair.

As Battle bent over it, Poirot looked thoughtfully at what he could see of Mr Shaitana's face. Rather a silly face it looked now, the mouth drooping open – the devilish expression lacking . . .

Hercule Poirot shook his head.

Superintendent Battle straightened himself. He had examined, without touching, the thing which looked like an extra stud in Mr Shaitana's shirt – and it was not an extra stud. He had raised the limp hand and let it fall.

Now he stood up, unemotional, capable, soldierly – prepared to take charge efficiently of the situation.

'Just a minute, please,' he said.

And the raised voice was his official voice, so different that all the heads at the bridge table turned to him, and Anne Meredith's hand remained poised over an ace of spades in dummy.

'I'm sorry to tell you all,' he said, 'that our host, Mr Shaitana, is dead.'

Mrs Lorrimer and Dr Roberts rose to their feet. Despard stared and frowned. Anne Meredith gave a little gasp.

'Are you sure, man?'

Dr Roberts, his professional instincts aroused, came briskly across the floor with a bounding medical 'in-at-the-death' step.

Without seeming to, the bulk of Superintendent Battle impeded his progress.

'Just a minute, Dr Roberts. Can you tell me first who's been in and out of this room this evening?'

Roberts stared at him.

'In and out? I don't understand you. Nobody has.'

The superintendent transferred his gaze.

'Is that right, Mrs Lorrimer?'

'Quite right.'

'Not the butler nor any of the servants?'

'No. The butler brought in that tray as we sat down to bridge. He has not been in since.'

Superintendent Battle looked at Despard.

Despard nodded in agreement.

Anne said rather breathlessly, 'Yes – yes, that's right.'

'What's all this, man,' said Roberts impatiently. 'Just let me examine him; may be just a fainting fit.'

'It isn't a fainting fit, and I'm sorry – *but nobody's going to touch him until the divisional surgeon comes. Mr Shaitana's been murdered, ladies and gentlemen.*'

'Murdered?' A horrified incredulous sigh from Anne.

A stare – a very blank stare – from Despard.

A sharp incisive 'Murdered?' from Mrs Lorrimer.

'A "Good God!" from Dr Roberts.

Superintendent Battle nodded his head slowly. He looked rather like a Chinese porcelain mandarin. His expression was quite blank.

'Stabbed,' he said. 'That's the way of it. Stabbed.'

Then he shot out a question:

'Any of you leave the bridge table during the evening?'

He saw four expressions break up – waver. He saw fear – comprehension – indignation – dismay – horror; but he saw nothing definitely helpful.

'Well?'

There was a pause, and then Major Despard said quietly (he had risen now and was standing like a soldier on parade, his narrow, intelligent face turned to Battle):

'I think every one of us, at one time or another, moved from the bridge table – either to get drinks or to put wood on the fire. I did both. When I went to the fire Shaitana was asleep in the chair.'

'Asleep?'

'I thought so – yes.'

'He may have been,' said Battle. 'Or he may have been dead then. We'll go into that presently. I'll ask you now to go into the room next door.' He turned to the quiet figure at his elbow: 'Colonel Race, perhaps you'll go with them?'

Race gave a quick nod of comprehension.

'Right, Superintendent.'

The four bridge players went slowly through the doorway.

Mrs Oliver sat down in a chair at the far end of the room and began to sob quietly.

Battle took up the telephone receiver and spoke. Then he said:

'The local police will be round immediately. Orders from headquarters are that I'm to take on the case. Divisional surgeon will be here almost at once. How long should you say he'd been dead, M. Poirot? I'd say well over an hour myself.'

'I agree. Alas, that one cannot be more exact – that one cannot say, "This man has been dead one hour, twenty-five minutes and forty seconds."'

Battle nodded absently.

'He was sitting right in front of the fire. That makes a slight difference. Over an hour – not more than two and a half: that's what our doctor will say, I'll be bound. And nobody heard anything and nobody saw anything. Amazing! What a desperate chance to take. He might have cried out.'

'But he did not. The murderer's luck held. As you say, *mon ami*, it was a very desperate business.'

'Any idea, M. Poirot, as to motive? Anything of that kind?'

Poirot said slowly:

'Yes, I have something to say on that score. Tell me, M. Shaitana – he did not give you any hint of what kind of a party you were coming to tonight?'

Superintendent Battle looked at him curiously.

'No, M. Poirot. He didn't say anything at all. Why?'

A bell whirred in the distance and a knocker was plied.

'That's our people,' said Superintendent Battle. 'I'll go and let 'em in. We'll have your story presently. Must get on with the routine work.'

Poirot nodded.

Battle left the room.

Mrs Oliver continued to sob.

Poirot went over to the bridge table. Without touching anything, he examined the scores. He shook his head once or twice.

'The stupid little man! Oh, the stupid little man,' murmured Hercule Poirot. 'To dress up as the devil and try to frighten people. *Quel enfantillage!*'

The door opened. The divisional surgeon came in, bag in hand. He was followed by the divisional inspector, talking to Battle. A camera man came next. There was a constable in the hall.

The routine of the detection of crime had begun.

CHAPTER 4
....
FIRST MURDERER?

Hercule Poirot, Mrs Oliver, Colonel Race and Superintendent Battle sat round the dining-room table.

It was an hour later. The body had been examined, photographed and removed. A fingerprint expert had been and gone.

Superintendent Battle looked at Poirot.

'Before I have those four in, I want to hear what you've got to tell me. According to you there was something behind this party tonight?'

Very deliberately and carefully Poirot retold the conversation he had held with Shaitana at Wessex House.

Superintendent Battle pursed his lips. He very nearly whistled.

'Exhibits – eh? Murderers all alive oh! And you think he *meant* it? You don't think he was pulling your leg?'

Poirot shook his head.

'Oh, no, he meant it. Shaitana was a man who prided himself on his Mephistophelian attitude to life. He was a man of great vanity. He was also a stupid man – that is why he is dead.'

'I get you,' said Superintendent Battle, following things out in his mind. 'A party of eight and himself. Four "sleuths", so to speak – and four murderers!'

'It's impossible!' cried Mrs Oliver. 'Absolutely impossible. None of those people can be *criminals*.'

Superintendent Battle shook his head thoughtfully.

'I wouldn't be so sure of that, Mrs Oliver. Murderers look and behave very much like everybody else. Nice, quiet, well-behaved, reasonable folk very often.'

'In that case, it's Dr Roberts,' said Mrs Oliver firmly. 'I felt instinctively that there was something wrong with that man as soon as I saw him. My instincts never lie.'

Battle turned to Colonel Race.

Race shrugged his shoulders. He took the question as referring to Poirot's statment and not to Mrs Oliver's suspicions.

'It could be,' he said. 'It could be. It shows that Shaitana was right in *one* case at least! After all, he can only have *suspected* that these people were murderers – he can't have been *sure*. He may have been right in all four cases, he may have been right in only one case – but he was right in *one* case; his death proved that.'

'One of them got the wind up. Think that's it, M. Poirot?'

Poirot nodded.

'The late Mr Shaitana had a reputation,' he said. 'He had a dangerous sense of humour, and was reputed to be merciless. The victim thought that Shaitana was giving himself an evening's amusement, leading up to a moment when he'd hand the victim over to the police – *you*! He (or she) must have thought that Shaitana had definite evidence.'

'Had he?'

Poirot shrugged his shoulders.

'That we shall never know.'

'Dr Roberts!' repeated Mrs Oliver firmly. 'Such a hearty

man. Murderers are often hearty – as a disguise! If I were you, Superintendent Battle, I should arrest him at once.'

'I dare say we would if there was a Woman at the Head of Scotland Yard,' said Superintendent Battle, a momentary twinkle showing in his unemotional eye. 'But, you see, mere men being in charge, we've got to be careful. We've got to get there slowly.'

'Oh, men – men,' sighed Mrs Oliver, and began to compose newspaper articles in her head.

'Better have them in now,' said Superintendent Battle. 'It won't do to keep them hanging about too long.'

Colonel Race half rose.

'If you'd like us to go –'

Superintendent Battle hesitated a minute as he caught Mrs Oliver's eloquent eye. He was well aware of Colonel Race's official position, and Poirot had worked with the police on many occasions. For Mrs Oliver to remain was decidedly stretching a point. But Battle was a kindly man. He remembered that Mrs Oliver had lost three pounds and seven shillings at bridge, and that she had been a cheerful loser.

'You can all stay,' he said, 'as far as I'm concerned. But no interruptions, please (he looked at Mrs Oliver), and there mustn't be a hint of what M. Poirot has just told us. That was Shaitana's little secret, and to all intents and purposes it died with him. Understand?'

'Perfectly,' said Mrs Oliver.

Battle strode to the door and called the constable who was on duty in the hall.

'Go to the little smoking-room. You'll find Anderson there with four guests. Ask Dr Roberts if he'll be so good as to step this way.'

'I should have kept him to the end,' said Mrs Oliver. 'In a book, I mean,' she added apologetically.

'Real life's a bit different,' said Battle.

'I know,' said Mrs Oliver. 'Badly constructed.'

Dr Roberts entered with the springiness of his step slightly subdued.

'I say, Battle,' he said. 'This is the devil of a business! Excuse me, Mrs Oliver, but it is. Professionally speaking, I could hardly have believed it! To stab a man with three other people a few yards away.' He shook his head. 'Whew! I wouldn't like to have done it!' A slight smile twitched up the corners of his mouth. 'What can I say or do to convince you that I *didn't* do it?'

'Well, there's motive, Dr Roberts.'

The doctor nodded his head emphatically.

'That's all clear. I hadn't the shadow of a motive for doing away with poor Shaitana. I didn't even know him very well. He amused me – he was such a fantastic fellow. Touch of the Oriental about him. Naturally, you'll investigate my relations with him closely – I expect that. I'm not a fool. But you won't find anything. I'd no reason for killing Shaitana, and I didn't kill him.'

Superintendent Battle nodded woodenly.

'That's all right, Dr Roberts. I've got to investigate as you know. You're a sensible man. Now, can you tell me anything about the other three people?'

'I'm afraid I don't know very much. Despard and Miss Meredith I met for the first time tonight. I knew of Despard before – read his travel book, and a jolly good yarn it is.'

'Did you know that he and Mr Shaitana were acquainted?'

'No. Shaitana never mentioned him to me. As I say, I'd heard of him, but never met him. Miss Meredith I've never seen before. Mrs Lorrimer I know slightly.'

'What do you know about her?'

Roberts shrugged his shoulders.

'She's a widow. Moderately well off. Intelligent, well-bred woman – first-class bridge player. That's where I've met her, as a matter of fact – playing bridge.'

'And Mr Shaitana never mentioned her, either?'

'No.'

'H'm – that doesn't help us much. Now, Dr Roberts, perhaps you'll be so kind as to tax your memory carefully and tell me how often you yourself left your seat at the bridge table, and all you can remember about the movements of the others.'

Dr Roberts took a few minutes to think.

'It's difficult,' he said frankly. 'I can remember my own movements, more or less. I got up three times – that is, on three occasions when I was dummy I left my seat and made myself useful. Once I went over and put wood on the fire. Once I brought drinks to the two ladies. Once I poured out a whisky and soda for myself.'

'Can you remember the times?'

'I could only say very roughly. We began to play about nine-thirty, I imagine. I should say it was about an hour later that I stoked the fire, quite a short time after that I fetched the drinks (next hand but one, I think), and perhaps half-past eleven when I got myself a whisky and soda – but those times are quite approximate. I couldn't answer for their being correct.'

'The table with the drinks was beyond Mr Shaitana's chair?'

'Yes. That's to say, I passed quite near him three times.'

'And each time, to the best of your belief, he was asleep?'

'That's what I thought the first time. The second time I didn't even look at him. Third time I rather fancy the thought just passed through my mind: "How the beggar does sleep." But I didn't really look closely at him.'

'Very good. Now, when did your fellow-players leave their seats?'

Dr Roberts frowned.

'Difficult – very difficult. Despard went and fetched an extra ash-tray, I think. And he went for a drink. That was before me, for I remember he asked me if I'd have one, and I said I wasn't quite ready.'

'And the ladies?'

'Mrs Lorrimer went over to the fire once. Poked it, I think. I rather fancy she spoke to Shaitana, but I don't know. I was playing a rather tricky no trump at the time.'

'And Miss Meredith?'

'She certainly left the table once. Came round and looked at my hand – I was her partner at the time. Then she looked at the other people's hands, and then she wandered round the room. I don't know what she was doing exactly. I wasn't paying attention.'

Superintendent Battle said thoughtfully:

'As you were sitting at the bridge table, no one's chair was directly facing the fireplace?'

'No, sort of sideways on, and there was a big cabinet between – Chinese piece, very handsome. I can see, of course, that it would be perfectly *possible* to stab the old boy. After all, when you're playing bridge, you're playing bridge. You're not looking round you, and noticing what is going on. The only person who's likely to be doing that is dummy. And in this case –'

'In this case, undoubtedly, dummy was the murderer,' said Superintendent Battle.

'All the same,' said Dr Roberts, 'it wanted nerve, you know. After all, who is to say that somebody won't look up just at the critical moment?'

'Yes,' said Battle. 'It was a big risk. The motive must have been a strong one. I wish we knew what it was,' he added with unblushing mendacity.

'You'll find out, I expect,' said Roberts. 'You'll go through his papers, and all that sort of thing. There will probably be a clue.'

'We'll hope so,' said Superintendent Battle gloomily.

He shot a keen glance at the other.

'I wonder if you'd oblige me, Dr Roberts, by giving me a personal opinion – as man to man.'

'Certainly.'

'Which do you fancy yourself of the three?'

Dr Roberts shrugged his shoulders.

'That's easy. Off-hand, I'd say Despard. The man's got plenty of nerve; he's used to a dangerous life where you've got to act quickly. He wouldn't mind taking a risk. It doesn't seem to me likely the women are in on this. Take a bit of strength, I should imagine.'

'Not so much as you might think. Take a look at this.'

Rather like a conjurer, Battle suddenly produced a long thin instrument of gleaming metal with a small round jewelled head.

Dr Roberts leaned forward, took it, and examined it with rich professional appreciation. He tried the point and whistled.

'What a tool! What a tool! Absolutely made for murder, this little boy. Go in like butter – absolutely like butter. Brought it with him, I suppose.'

'No. It was Mr Shaitana's. It lay on the table near the door with a good many other knick-knacks.'

'So the murderer helped himself. A bit of luck finding a tool like that.'

'Well, that's one way of looking at it,' said Battle slowly.

'Well, of course, it wasn't luck for Shaitana, poor fellow.'

'I didn't mean that, Dr Roberts. I meant that there was another angle of looking at the business. It occurs to me that it was noticing this weapon that put the idea of murder into our criminal's mind.'

'You mean it was a sudden inspiration – that the murder wasn't premeditated? He conceived the idea after he got here? Er – anything to suggest that idea to you?'

He glanced at him searchingly.

'It's just an idea,' said Superintendent Battle stolidly.

'Well, it might be so, of course,' said Dr Roberts slowly.

Superintendent Battle cleared his throat.

'Well, I won't keep you any longer, doctor. Thank you for your help. Perhaps you'll leave your address.'

'Certainly. 200 Gloucester Terrace, W. 2. Telephone No. Bayswater 23896.'

'Thank you. I may have to call upon you shortly.'

'Delighted to see you any time. Hope there won't be too much in the papers. I don't want my nervous patients upset.'

Superintendent Battle looked round at Poirot.

'Excuse me, M. Poirot. If you'd like to ask any questions, I'm sure the doctor wouldn't mind.'

'Of course not. Of course not. Great admirer of yours, M. Poirot. Little grey cells – order and method. I know all about it. I feel sure you'll think of something most intriguing to ask me.'

Hercule Poirot spread out his hands in his most foreign manner.

'No, no. I just like to get all the details clear in my mind. For instance, how many rubbers did you play?'

'Three,' said Roberts promptly. 'We'd got to one game all, in the fourth rubber, when you came in.'

'And who played with who?'

'First rubber, Despard and I against the ladies. They beat us, God bless 'em. Walk over; we never held a card.

'Second rubber, Miss Meredith and I against Despard and Mrs Lorrimer. Third rubber, Mrs Lorrimer and I against Miss Meredith and Despard. We cut each time, but it worked out like a pivot. Fourth rubber, Miss Meredith and I again.'

'Who won and who lost?'

'Mrs Lorrimer won every rubber. Miss Meredith won the first and lost the next two. I was a bit up and Miss Meredith and Despard must have been down.'

Poirot said, smiling, 'The good superintendent has asked you your opinion of your companions as candidates for murder. I now ask you for your opinion of them as bridge players.'

'Mrs Lorrimer's first class,' Dr Roberts replied promptly. 'I'll bet she makes a good income a year out of bridge. Despard's a good player, too – what I call a *sound* player – long-headed chap. Miss Meredith you might describe as quite a safe player. She doesn't make mistakes, but she isn't brilliant.'

'And you yourself, doctor?'

Roberts' eyes twinkled.

'I overcall my hand a bit, or so they say. But I've always found it pays.'

Poirot smiled.

Dr Roberts rose.

'Anything more?'

Poirot shook his head.

'Well, goodnight, then. Goodnight, Mrs Oliver. You ought to get some copy out of this. Better than your untraceable poisons, eh?'

Dr Roberts left the room, his bearing springy once more. Mrs Oliver said bitterly as the door closed behind him:

'Copy! Copy indeed! People are so unintelligent. I could invent a better murder *any* day than anything *real*. I'm *never* at a loss for a plot. And the people who read my books *like* untraceable poisons!'

CHAPTER 5

SECOND MURDERER?

Mrs Lorrimer came into the dining-room like a gentlewoman. She looked a little pale, but composed.

'I'm sorry to have to bother you,' Superintendent Battle began.

'You must do your duty, of course,' said Mrs Lorrimer quietly. 'It is, I agree, an unpleasant position in which to be placed, but there is no good shirking it. I quite realize that one of the four people in that room must be guilty. Naturally, I can't expect you to take my word that I am not the person.'

She accepted the chair that Colonel Race offered her and sat down opposite the superintendent. Her intelligent grey eyes met his. She waited attentively.

'You knew Mr Shaitana well?' began the superintendent.

'Not very well. I have known him over a period of some years, but never intimately.'

'Where did you meet him?'

'At a hotel in Egypt – the Winter Palace at Luxor, I think.'

'What did you think of him?'

Mrs Lorrimer shrugged her shoulders slightly.

'I thought him – I may as well say so – rather a charlatan.'

'You had – excuse me for asking – no motive for wishing him out of the way?'

Mrs Lorrimer looked slightly amused.

'Really, Superintendent Battle, do you think I should admit it if I had?'

'You might,' said Battle. 'A really intelligent person might know that a thing was bound to come out.'

Mrs Lorrimer inclined her head thoughtfully.

'There is that, of course. No, Superintendent Battle, I had no motive for wishing Mr Shaitana out of the way. It is really a matter of indifference to me whether he is alive or dead. I thought him a *poseur*, and rather theatrical, and sometimes he irritated me. That is – or rather was – my attitude towards him.'

'That is that, then. Now, Mrs Lorrimer, can you tell me anything about your three companions?'

'I'm afraid not. Major Despard and Miss Meredith I met for the first time tonight. Both of them seem charming people. Dr Roberts I know slightly. He's a very popular doctor, I believe.'

'He is not your own doctor?'

'Oh, no.'

'Now, Mrs Lorrimer, can you tell me how often you got up from your seat tonight, and will you also describe the movements of the other three?'

Mrs Lorrimer did not take any time to think.

'I thought you would probably ask me that. I have been trying to think it out. I got up once myself when I was dummy. I went over to the fire. Mr Shaitana was alive then. I mentioned to him how nice it was to see a wood fire.'

'And he answered?'

'That he hated radiators.'

'Did anyone overhear your conversation?'

'I don't think so. I lowered my voice, not to interrupt the players.' She added dryly: 'In fact, you have only my word for it that Mr Shaitana *was* alive and spoke to me.'

Superintendent Battle made no protest. He went on with his quiet methodical questioning.

'What time was that?'

'I should think we had been playing a little over an hour.'

'What about the others?'

'Dr Roberts got me a drink. He also got himself one – that was later. Major Despard also went to get a drink – at about 11.15, I should say.'

'Only once?'

'No – twice, I think. The men moved about a fair amount – but I didn't notice what they did. Miss Meredith left her seat once only, I think. She went round to look at her partner's hand.'

'But she remained near the bridge table?'

'I couldn't say at all. She may have moved away.'

Battle nodded.

'It's all very vague,' he grumbled.

'I am sorry.'

Once again Battle did his conjuring trick and produced the long delicate stiletto.

'Will you look at this, Mrs Lorrimer?'

Mrs Lorrimer took it without emotion.

'Have you ever seen that before?'

'Never.'

'Yet it was lying on a table in the drawing-room.'

'I didn't notice it.'

'You realize, perhaps, Mrs Lorrimer, that with a weapon like that a woman could do the trick just as easily as a man.'

'I suppose she could,' said Mrs Lorrimer quietly.

She leaned forward and handed the dainty little thing back to him.

'But all the same,' said Superintendent Battle, 'the woman

would have to be pretty desperate. It was a long chance to take.'

He waited a minute, but Mrs Lorrimer did not speak.

'Do you know anything of the relations between the other three and Mr Shaitana?'

She shook her head.

'Nothing at all.'

'Would you care to give me an opinion as to which of them you consider the most likely person?'

Mrs Lorrimer drew herself up stiffly.

'I should not care to do anything of the kind. I consider that a most improper question.'

The superintendent looked like an abashed little boy who has been reprimanded by his grandmother.

'Address, please,' he mumbled, drawing his notebook towards him.

'111 Cheyne Lane, Chelsea.'

'Telephone number?'

'Chelsea 45632.'

Mrs Lorrimer rose.

'Anything you want to ask, M. Poirot?' said Battle hurriedly.

Mrs Lorrimer paused, her head slightly inclined.

'Would it be a *proper* question, madame, to ask you your opinion of your companions, not as potential murderers but as bridge players?'

Mrs Lorrimer answered coldly:

'I have no objection to answering that – if it bears upon the matter at issue in any way – though I fail to see how it can.'

'I will be the judge of that. Your answer, if you please, madame.'

In the tone of a patient adult humouring an idiot child, Mrs Lorrimer replied:

'Major Despard is a good sound player. Dr Roberts overcalls, but plays his hand brilliantly. Miss Meredith is quite a nice little player, but a bit too cautious. Anything more?'

In his turn doing a conjuring trick, Poirot produced four crumpled bridge scores.

'These scores, madame, is one of these yours?'

She examined them.

'This is my writing. It is the score of the third rubber.'

'And this score?'

'That must be Major Despard's. He cancels as he goes.'

'And this one?'

'Miss Meredith's. The first rubber.'

'So this unfinished one is Dr Roberts'?'

'Yes.'

'Thank you, madame, I think that is all.'

Mrs Lorrimer turned to Mrs Oliver.

'Goodnight, Mrs Oliver. Goodnight, Colonel Race.'

Then, having shaken hands with all four of them, she went out.

CHAPTER 6

THIRD MURDERER?

'Didn't get any extra change out of her,' commented Battle. 'Put me in my place, too. She's the old-fashioned kind, full of consideration for others, but arrogant as the devil! I can't believe she did it, but you never know! She's got plenty of resolution. What's the idea of the bridge scores, M. Poirot?'

Poirot spread them on the table.

'They are illuminating, do you not think? What do we want in this case? A clue to character. And a clue not to one character, but to four characters. And this is where we are most likely to find it – in these scribbled figures. Here is the first rubber, you see – a tame business, soon over. Small neat figures – careful addition and subtraction – that is Miss Meredith's score. She was playing with Mrs Lorrimer. They had the cards, and they won.

'In this next one it is not so easy to follow the play, since it is kept in the cancellation style. But it tells us perhaps something about Major Despard – a man who likes the whole time to know at a glance where he stands. The figures are small and full of character.

'This next score is Mrs Lorrimer's – she and Dr Roberts against the other two – a Homeric combat – figures mounting up above the line each side. Overcalling on the doctor's part, and they go down; but, since they are both first-class players, they never go

WE	THEY		WE	THEY
(Mrs LORRIMER v Miss MEREDITH)	(MAJOR DESPARD v DR ROBERTS)		(MAJOR DESPARD v Mrs LORRIMER)	(DR ROBERTS v Miss MEREDITH)
			⑪	
			1060	
			~~450~~	
			~~410~~	
			~~440~~	
			~~540~~	
700			~~440~~	
300			~~560~~	
50			~~500~~	
50			~~50~~	
30				
HONOURS			**HONOURS**	
TRICKS			**TRICKS**	
120			~~60~~	~~120~~
120			~~100~~	
1370			70	30
			80	

1st RUBBER			2nd RUBBER	
Score kept by MISS MEREDITH			Score kept by MAJOR DESPARD	

WE	THEY		WE	THEY
DR ROBERTS v MRS LORRIMER	MAJOR DESPARD v MISS MEREDITH		DR ROBERTS v MISS MEREDITH	MAJOR DESPARD v MRS LORRIMER
500				
1500	200			
100	100		50	
100	200		100	
300	100		100	
500	100		50	
200	50		200	100
200	50		50	50
30	50		50	100
			50	50

| | HONOURS | | | |

	TRICKS			TRICKS
	30		30	70
	120			
100				
280				
3810	1000			

(28)

3rd RUBBER
Score kept by Mrs LORRIMER

4th (Unfinished) RUBBER
Score kept by DR ROBERTS

down very much. If the doctor's overcalling induces rash bidding on the other side there is the chance seized of doubling. See – these figures here are doubled tricks gone down. A characteristic handwriting, graceful, very legible, firm.

'Here is the last score – the unfinished rubber. I collected one score in each person's handwriting, you see. Figures rather flamboyant. Not such high scores as the preceding rubber. That is probably because the doctor was playing with Miss Meredith, and she is a timid player. His calling would make her more so!

'You think, perhaps, that they are foolish, these questions that I ask? But it is not so. I want to get at the characters of these four players, and when it is only about bridge I ask, everyone is ready and willing to speak.'

'I never think your questions foolish, M. Poirot,' said Battle. 'I've seen too much of your work. Everyone's got their own ways of working. I know that. I give my inspectors a free hand always. Everyone's got to find out for themselves what method suits them best. But we'd better not discuss that now. We'll have the girl in.'

Anne Meredith was upset. She stopped in the doorway. Her breath came unevenly.

Superintendent Battle was immediately fatherly. He rose, set a chair for her at a slightly different angle.

'Sit down, Miss Meredith, sit down, Now, don't be alarmed. I know all this seems rather dreadful, but it's not so bad, really.'

'I don't think anything could be worse,' said the girl in a low voice. 'It's so awful – so *awful* – to think that *one* of us – that one of *us* –'

'You let me do the thinking,' said Battle kindly. 'Now, then, Miss Meredith, suppose we have your address first of all.'

'Wendon Cottage, Wallingford.'

'No address in town?'

'No, I'm staying at my club for a day or two.'

'And your club is?'

'Ladies' Naval and Military.'

'Good. Now, then, Miss Meredith, how well did you know Mr Shaitana?'

'I didn't know him well at all. I always thought he was a most frightening man.'

'Why?'

'Oh, well he *was*! That awful smile! And a way he had of bending over you. As though he might bite you.'

'Had you known him long?'

'About nine months. I met him in Switzerland during the winter sports.'

'I should never have thought he went in for winter sports,' said Battle, surprised.

'He only skated. He was a marvellous skater. Lots of figures and tricks.'

'Yes, that sounds more like him. And did you see much of him after that?'

'Well – a fair amount. He asked me to parties and things like that. They were rather fun.'

'But you didn't like him himself?'

'No, I thought he was a shivery kind of man.'

Battle said gently:

'But you'd no special reason for being afraid of him?'

Anne Meredith raised wide limpid eyes to his.

'Special reason? Oh, no.'

'That's all right, then. Now about tonight. Did you leave your seat at all?'

'I don't think so. Oh, yes, I may have done once. I went round to look at the others' hands.'

'But you stayed by the bridge table all the time?'

'Yes.'

'Quite sure, Miss Meredith?'

The girl's cheeks flamed suddenly.

'No – no, I think I walked about.'

'Right. You'll excuse me, Miss Meredith, but try and speak the truth. I know you're nervous, and when one's nervous one's apt to – well, to say the thing the way you want it to be. But that doesn't really pay in the end. You walked about. Did you walk over in the direction of Mr Shaitana?'

The girl was silent for a minute, then she said:

'Honestly – *honestly* – I don't remember.'

'Well, we'll leave it that you may have done. Know anything about the other three?'

The girl shook her head.

'I've never seen any of them before.'

'What do you think of them? Any likely murderers amongst them?'

'I can't believe it. I just can't believe it. It couldn't be Major Despard. And I don't believe it could be the doctor – after all, a doctor could kill anyone in much easier ways. A drug – or something like that.'

'Then, if it's anyone, you think it's Mrs Lorrimer.'

'Oh, I *don't*. I'm sure she wouldn't. She's so charming – and so kind to play bridge with. She's so good herself, and yet she doesn't make one feel nervous, or point out one's mistakes.'

'Yet you left her name to the last,' said Battle.

'Only because stabbing seems somehow more like a woman.'

Battle did his conjuring trick. Anne Meredith shrank back.

'Oh, horrible. Must I – take it?'

'I'd rather you did.'

He watched her as she took the stiletto gingerly, her face contracted with repulsion.

'With this tiny thing – with this –'

'Go in like butter,' said Battle with gusto. 'A child could do it.'

'You mean – you mean' – wide, terrified eyes fixed themselves on his face – 'that *I* might have done it? But I didn't. Why should I?'

'That's just the question we'd like to know,' said Battle. 'What's the motive? Why did anyone want to kill Shaitana? He was a picturesque person, but he wasn't dangerous, as far as I can make out.'

Was there a slight indrawing of her breath – a sudden lifting of her breast?

'Not a blackmailer, for instance, or anything of that sort?' went on Battle. 'And anyway, Miss Meredith, you don't look the sort of girl who's got a lot of guilty secrets.'

For the first time she smiled, reassured by his geniality.

'No, indeed I haven't. I haven't got any secrets at all.'

'Then don't worry, Miss Meredith. We shall have to come round and ask you a few more questions, I expect, but it will be all a matter of routine.'

He got up.

'Now off you go. My constable will get you a taxi; and don't you lie awake worrying yourself. Take a couple of aspirins.'

He ushered her out. As he came back Colonel Race said in a low, amused voice:

'Battle, what a really accomplished liar you are! Your fatherly air was unsurpassed.'

'No good dallying about with her, Colonel Race. Either the poor kid is dead scared – in which case it's cruelty, and I'm not a cruel man; I never have been – or she's a highly accomplished little actress, and we shouldn't get any further if we were to keep her here half the night.'

Mrs Oliver gave a sigh and ran her hands freely through her fringe until it stood upright and gave her a wholly drunken appearance.

'Do you know,' she said, 'I rather believe now that she did it! It's lucky it's not in a book. They don't really like the young and beautiful girl to have done it. All the same, I rather think she did. What do *you* think, M. Poirot?'

'Me, I have just made a discovery.'

'In the bridge scores again?'

'Yes, Miss Anne Meredith turns her score over, draws lines and uses the back.'

'And what does that mean?'

'It means she has the habit of poverty or else is of a naturally economical turn of mind.'

'She's expensively dressed,' said Mrs Oliver.

'Send in Major Despard,' said Superintendent Battle.

CHAPTER 7

FOURTH MURDERER?

Despard entered the room with a quick springing step – a step that reminded Poirot of something or some one.

'I'm sorry to have kept you waiting all this while, Major Despard,' said Battle. 'But I wanted to let the ladies get away as soon as possible.'

'Don't apologize. I understand.'

He sat down and looked inquiringly at the superintendent.

'How well did you know Mr Shaitana?' began the latter.

'I've met him twice,' said Despard crisply.

'Only twice?'

'That's all.'

'On what occasions?'

'About a month ago we were both dining at the same house. Then he asked me to a cocktail party a week later.'

'A cocktail party here?'

'Yes.'

'Where did it take place – this room or the drawing-room?'

'In all the rooms.'

'See this little thing lying about?'

Battle once more produced the stiletto.

Major Despard's lip twisted slightly.

'No,' he said. 'I didn't mark it down on that occasion for future use.'

'There's no need to go ahead of what I say, Major Despard.'

'I beg your pardon. The inference was fairly obvious.'

There was a moment's pause, then Battle resumed his inquiries.

'Had you any motive for disliking Mr Shaitana?'

'Every motive.'

'Eh?' The superintendent sounded startled.

'For disliking him – not for killing him,' said Despard. 'I hadn't the least wish to kill him, but I would thoroughly have enjoyed kicking him. A pity. It's too late now.'

'Why did you want to kick him, Major Despard?'

'Because he was the sort of Dago who needed kicking badly. He used to make the toe of my boot fairly itch.'

'Know anything about him – to his discredit, I mean?'

'He was too well dressed – he wore his hair too long – and he smelt of scent.'

'Yet you accepted his invitation to dinner,' Battle pointed out.

'If I were only to dine in houses where I thoroughly approved of my host I'm afraid I shouldn't dine out very much, Superintendent Battle,' said Despard drily.

'You like society, but you don't approve of it?' suggested the other.

'I like it for very short periods. To come back from the wilds to lighted rooms and women in lovely clothes, to dancing and good food and laughter – yes, I enjoy that – for a time. And then the insincerity of it all sickens me, and I want to be off again.'

'It must be a dangerous sort of life that you lead, Major Despard, wandering about in these wild places.'

Despard shrugged his shoulders. He smiled slightly.

'Mr Shaitana didn't lead a dangerous life – but he is dead, and I am alive!'

'He may have led a more dangerous life than you think,' said Battle meaningly.

'What do you mean?'

'The late Mr Shaitana was a bit of a Nosey Parker,' said Battle.

The other leaned forward.

'You mean that he meddled with other people's lives – that he discovered – what?'

'I really meant that perhaps he was the sort of man who meddled – er – well, with women.'

Major Despard leant back in his chair. He laughed, an amused but indifferent laugh.

'I don't think women would take a mountebank like that seriously.'

'What's your theory of who killed him, Major Despard?'

'Well, I know I didn't. Little Miss Meredith didn't. I can't imagine Mrs Lorrimer doing so – she reminds me of one of my more God-fearing aunts. That leaves the medical gentleman.'

'Can you describe your own and other people's movements this evening?'

'I got up twice – once for an ash-tray, and I also poked the fire – and once for a drink –'

'At what times?'

'I couldn't say. First time might have been about half-past ten, the second time eleven, but that's pure guesswork. Mrs Lorrimer went over to the fire once and said something to Shaitana. I didn't actually hear him answer, but, then, I wasn't paying attention. I couldn't swear he didn't. Miss Meredith wandered about the room a bit, but I don't think she went over near the fireplace. Roberts was always jumping up and down – three or four times at least.'

'I'll ask you M. Poirot's question,' said Battle with a smile. 'What did you think of them as bridge players?'

'Miss Meredith's quite a good player. Roberts overcalls his hand disgracefully. He deserves to go down more than he does. Mrs Lorrimer's damned good.'

Battle turned to Poirot.

'Anything else, M. Poirot?'

Poirot shook his head.

Despard gave his address as the Albany, wished them goodnight and left the room.

As he closed the door behind him, Poirot made a slight movement.

'What is it?' demanded Battle.

'Nothing,' said Poirot. 'It just occurred to me that he walked like a tiger – yes, just so – lithe, easy, does the tiger move along.'

'H'm!' said Battle. 'Now, then' – his eyes glanced round at his three companions – '*which of 'em did it*?'

CHAPTER 8

WHICH OF THEM?

Battle looked from one face to another. Only one person answered his question. Mrs Oliver, never averse to giving her views, rushed into speech.

'The girl or the doctor,' she said.

Battle looked questioningly at the other two. But both the men were unwilling to make a pronouncement. Race shook his head. Poirot carefully smoothed his crumpled bridge scores.

'One of 'em did it,' said Battle musingly. 'One of 'em's lying like hell. But which? It's not easy – no, it's not easy.'

He was silent for a minute or two, then he said:

'If we're to go by what they *say*, the medico thinks Despard did it, Despard thinks the medico did it, the girl thinks Mrs Lorrimer did it – and Mrs Lorrimer won't say! Nothing very illuminating there.'

'Perhaps not,' said Poirot.

Battle shot him a quick glance.

'You think there is?'

Poirot waved an airy hand.

'A *nuance* – nothing more! Nothing to go upon.'

Battle continued:

'You two gentlemen won't say what you think –'

'No evidence,' said Race curtly.

'Oh, you *men*!' sighed Mrs Oliver, despising such reticence.

'Let's look at the rough possibilities,' said Battle. He considered a minute. 'I put the doctor first, I think. Specious sort of customer. Would know the right spot to shove the dagger in. But there's not much more than that to it. Then take Despard. There's a man with any amount of nerve. A man accustomed to quick decisions and a man who's quite at home doing dangerous things. Mrs Lorrmier? She's got any amount of nerve, too, and she's the sort of woman who might have a secret in her life. She looks as though she's known trouble. On the other hand, I'd say she's what I call a high-principled woman – sort of woman who might be headmistress of a girls' school. It isn't easy to think of her sticking a knife into anyone. In fact, I don't think she did. And lastly, there's little Miss Meredith. We don't know anything about her. She seems an ordinary good-looking, rather shy girl. But one doesn't know, as I say, anything about her.'

'We know that Shaitana believed she had committed murder,' said Poirot.

'The angelic face masking the demon,' mused Mrs Oliver.

'This getting us anywhere, Battle?' asked Colonel Race.

'Unprofitable speculation, you think, sir? Well, there's bound to be speculation in a case like this.'

'Isn't it better to find out something about these people?'

Battle smiled.

'Oh, we shall be hard at work on that. I think you could help us there.'

'Certainly. How?'

'As regards Major Despard. He's been abroad a lot – in South America, in East Africa, in South Africa – you've means of knowing those parts. You could get information about him.'

Race nodded.

'It shall be done. I'll get all available data.'

'Oh,' cried Mrs Oliver. 'I've got a plan. There are four of us – four sleuths, as you might say – and four of *them*! How would it be if we each took one. Backed our fancy! Colonel Race takes Major Despard, Superintendent Battle takes Dr Roberts, I'll take Anne Meredith, and M. Poirot takes Mrs Lorrimer. Each of us to follow our own line!'

Superintendent Battle shook his head decisively.

'Couldn't quite do that, Mrs Oliver. That is official, you see. I'm in charge. I've got to investigate *all* lines. Besides, it's all very well to say back your fancy. Two of us might want to back the same horse! Colonel Race hasn't said he suspects Major Despard. And M. Poirot mayn't be putting his money on Mrs Lorrimer.'

Mrs Oliver sighed.

'It was such a good plan,' she sighed regretfully. 'So *neat.*' Then she cheered up a little. 'But you don't mind me doing a little investigating on my own, do you?'

'No,' said Superintendent Battle slowly. 'I can't say I object to that. In fact, it's out of my power to object. Having been at this party tonight, you're naturally free to do anything your own curiosity or interest suggests. But I'd like to point out to you, Mrs Oliver, that you'd better be a little careful.'

'Discretion itself,' said Mrs Oliver. 'I shan't breathe a word of – of anything –' she ended a little lamely.

'I do not think that was quite Superintendent Battle's meaning,' said Hercule Poirot. 'He meant that you will be dealing with a person who has already, to the best of our belief, killed twice. A person, therefore, who will not hesitate to kill a third time – if he considers it necessary.'

Mrs Oliver looked at him thoughtfully. Then she smiled – an agreeable engaging smile, rather like that of an impudent small child.

'YOU HAVE BEEN WARNED,' she quoted. 'Thank you, M. Poirot. I'll watch my step. But I'm not going to be out of this.'

Poirot bowed gracefully.

'Permit me to say – you are the sport, madame.'

'I presume,' said Mrs Oliver, sitting up very straight and speaking in a business-like committee-meeting manner, 'that all information we receive will be pooled – that is that we will not keep any knowledge to ourselves. Our own deductions and impressions, of course, we are entitled to keep up our sleeves.'

Superintendent Battle sighed.

'This isn't a detective story, Mrs Oliver,' he said.

Race said:

'Naturally, all information must be handed over to the police.'

Having said this in his most 'Orderly Room' voice, he added with a slight twinkle in his eye: 'I'm sure you'll play fair, Mrs Oliver – the stained glove, the fingerprint on the tooth-glass, the fragment of burnt paper – you'll turn them over to Battle here.'

'You may laugh,' said Mrs Oliver. 'But a woman's intuition –'

She nodded her head with decision.

Race rose to his feet.

'I'll have Despard looked up for you. It may take a little time. Anything else I can do?'

'I don't think so, thank you, sir. You've no hints? I'd value anything of that kind.'

'H'm. Well – I'd keep a special lookout for shooting or poison or accidents, but I expect you're on to that already.'

'I'd made a note of that – yes, sir.'

'Good man, Battle. You don't need me to teach you your job. Goodnight, Mrs Oliver. Goodnight, M. Poirot.'

And with a final nod to Battle, Colonel Race left the room.

'Who is he?' asked Mrs Oliver.

'Very fine Army record,' said Battle. 'Travelled a lot, too. Not many parts of the world he doesn't know about.'

'Secret Service, I suppose,' said Mrs Oliver. 'You can't tell me so – I know; but he wouldn't have been asked otherwise this evening. The four murderers and the four sleuths – Scotland Yard. Secret Service. Private. Fiction. A clever idea.'

Poirot shook his head.

'You are in error, madame. It was a very *stupid* idea. The tiger was alarmed – and the tiger sprang.'

'The tiger? Why the tiger?'

'By the tiger I mean the murderer,' said Poirot.

Battle said bluntly:

'What's *your* idea of the right line to take, M. Poirot? That's one question. And I'd also like to know what you think of the psychology of these four people. You're rather hot on that.'

Still smoothing his bridge scores, Poirot said:

'You are right – psychology is very important. We know the *kind* of murder that has been committed, the *way* it was committed. If we have a person who from the psychological point of view could not have committed that particular type of murder, then we can dismiss that person from our calculations. We know *something* about these people. We have our own impression of them, we know the line that each has elected to take, and we know something about their minds and their characters from what we have learned about them as card players and from the study of their handwriting and of these scores. But alas! it is not too easy to give a definite pronouncement. This murder required audacity and nerve – a person who was willing to take a risk. Well, we have Dr Roberts – a bluffer – an overcaller of his hand – a man with complete confidence in his own powers to pull off a risky thing. His psychology fits very well with the crime. One might say, then, that that automatically wipes out Miss Meredith. She is timid, frightened of over-calling her hand, careful, economical, prudent and lacking in self-confidence. The last type of person to carry out a bold and risky coup. But a timid person will murder out of fear. A frightened nervous person can be made desperate, can turn like a rat at bay if driven into a corner. If Miss Meredith had committed a crime in the past, and if she believed that Mr Shaitana knew the circumstances of that crime and was about to deliver her up to justice she would be wild with terror – she would stick at nothing to save herself. It would be the same result, though brought about through a different reaction – not cool nerve and daring, but desperate panic. Then take Major Despard – a cool, resourceful man willing to try a long shot if he believed it absolutely necessary. He would weigh the pros and cons and might decide that there was a sporting chance in his favour – and he is the type of man to prefer action to inaction, and a man who would never shrink from taking the dangerous way if he believed there was a reasonable chance of success. Finally, there is Mrs Lorrimer, an elderly woman, but a woman in full possession of her wits and faculties. A cool woman. A woman with a mathematical brain. She has probably the best brain of the four. I confess that if Mrs Lorrimer committed a crime, I should expect it to be a *premeditated* crime. I can see her planning a crime slowly and carefully, making sure that there were no flaws in her scheme. For that reason she seems to me slightly more unlikely than the other three. She is, however, the most dominating personality, and whatever she undertook she would probably carry through without a flaw. She is a thoroughly efficient woman.'

He paused:

'So you see, that does not help us much. No – there is only one way in this crime. We must go back into the past.'

Battle sighed.

'You've said it,' he murmured.

'In the opinion of Mr Shaitana, each of those four people had committed murder. Had he evidence? Or was it a guess? We cannot tell. It is unlikely, I think, that he could have had actual evidence in all four cases –'

'I agree with you there,' said Battle, nodding his head. 'That would be a bit too much of a coincidence.'

'I suggest that it might come about this way – murder or a certain form of murder is mentioned, and Mr Shaitana surprised a look on someone's face. He was very quick – very sensitive to expression. It amuses him to experiment – to probe gently in the course of apparently aimless conversation – he is alert to notice a wince, a reservation, a desire to turn the conversation. Oh, it is easily done. If you suspect a certain secret, nothing is easier than to confirm your suspicion. Every time a word goes home you notice it – *if you are watching for such a thing.*'

'It's the sort of game that would have amused our late friend,' said Battle, nodding.

'We may assume, then, that such was the procedure in one or more cases. He may have come across a piece of actual evidence in another case and followed it up. I doubt whether, in any of the cases, he had sufficient actual knowledge with which, for instance, to have gone to the police.'

'Or it mayn't have been the kind of case,' said Battle. 'Often enough there's a fishy business – we suspect foul play, but we can't ever prove it. Anyway, the course is clear. We've got to go through the records of all these people – and note any deaths that may be significant. I expect you noticed, just as the Colonel did, what Shaitana said at dinner.'

'The black angel,' murmured Mrs Oliver.

'A neat little reference to poison, to accident, to a doctor's opportunities, to shooting accidents. I shouldn't be surprised if he signed his death-warrant when he said those words.'

'It was a nasty sort of pause,' said Mrs Oliver.

'Yes,' said Poirot. 'Those words went home to one person at least – that person probably thought that Shaitana knew far more than he really did. That listener thought that they were the prelude to the end – that the party was a dramatic entertainment arranged by Shaitana leading up to arrest for murder as its climax! Yes, as you say, he signed his death-warrant when he baited his guests with those words.'

There was a moment's silence.

'This will be a long business,' said Battle with a sigh. 'We can't find out all we want in a moment – and we've got to be careful. We don't want any of the four to suspect what we're doing. All our questioning and so on must seem to have to do with *this* murder. There mustn't be a suspicion that we've got any idea of the motive for the crime. And the devil of it is we've got to check up on four possible murders in the past, not one.'

Poirot demurred.

'Our friend Mr Shaitana was not infallible,' he said. 'He may – it is just possible – have made a mistake.'

'About all four?'

'No – he was more intelligent than that.'

'Call it fifty-fifty?'

'Not even that. For me, I say one in four.'

'One innocent and three guilty? That's bad enough. And the devil of it is, even if we get at the truth it mayn't help us. Even if somebody did push their great-aunts down the stairs in 1912, it won't be much use to us in 1937.'

'Yes, yes, it will be of use to us.' Poirot encouraged him. 'You know that. You know it as well as I do.'

Battle nodded slowly.

'I know what you mean,' he said. 'Same hall-mark.'

'Do you mean,' said Mrs Oliver, 'that the former victim will have been stabbed with a dagger too?'

'Not quite as crude as that, Mrs Oliver,' said Battle turning to her. 'But I don't doubt it will be essentially the same *type* of crime. The *details* may be different, but the essentials underlying them will be the same. It's odd, but a criminal gives himself away every time by that.'

'Man is an unoriginal animal,' said Hercule Poirot.

'Women,' said Mrs Oliver, 'are capable of infinite variation. I should never commit the same type of murder twice running.'

'Don't you ever write the same plot twice running?' asked Battle.

'*The Lotus Murder*,' murmured Poirot. '*The Clue of the Candle Wax.*'

Mrs Oliver turned on him, her eyes beaming appreciation.

'That's clever of you – that's really very clever of you. Because, of course, those two are exactly the same plot – but nobody else has seen it. One is stolen papers at an informal weekend party of the Cabinet, and the other's a murder in Borneo in a rubber planter's bungalow.'

'But the essential point on which the story turns is the same,' said Poirot. 'One of your neatest tricks. The rubber planter arranges his own murder – the Cabinet Minister arranges the robbery of his own papers. At the last minute the third person steps in and turns deception into reality.'

'I enjoyed your last, Mrs Oliver,' said Superintendent Battle kindly. 'The one where all the Chief Constables were shot simultaneously. You just slipped up once or twice on official details. I know you're keen on accuracy, so I wondered if –'

Mrs Oliver interrupted him.

'As a matter of fact I don't care two pins about accuracy. Who is accurate? Nobody nowadays. If a reporter writes that a beautiful girl of twenty-two dies by turning on the gas after looking out over the sea and kissing her favourite labrador, Bob, goodbye, does anybody make a fuss because the girl was twenty-six, the room faced inland, and the dog was a Sealyham terrier called Bonnie? If a journalist can do that sort of thing, I don't see that it matters if I mix up police ranks and say a revolver when I mean an automatic, and a dictograph when I mean a phonograph, and use a poison that just allows you to gasp one dying sentence and no more. What really matters is plenty of *bodies*! If the thing's getting a little dull, some more blood cheers it up. Somebody is going to tell something – and then they're killed first. That always goes down well. It comes in all my books – camouflaged different ways, of course. And people *like* untraceable poisons, and idiotic police inspectors and girls tied up in cellars with sewer gas or water pouring in (such a troublesome way of killing anyone really) and a hero who can dispose of anything from three to seven villains single-handed. I've written thirty-two books by now – and of course they're all exactly the same really, as M. Poirot seems to have noticed – but nobody else has – and I only regret one thing – making my detective a Finn. I don't really know anything about Finns and I'm always getting letters from Finland pointing out something impossible that he's said or done. They seem to read detective stories a good deal in Finland. I suppose it's the long winters with no daylight. In Bulgaria and Romania they don't seem to read at all. I'd have done better to have made him a Bulgar.'

She broke off.

'I'm so sorry. I'm talking shop. And this is a real murder.' Her face lit up. 'What a good idea it would be if none of them had murdered him. If he'd asked them all, and then quietly committed suicide just for the fun of making a schemozzle.'

Poirot nodded approvingly.

'An admirable solution. So neat. So ironic. But, alas, Mr Shaitana was not that sort of man. He was very fond of life.'

'I don't think he was really a nice man,' said Mrs Oliver slowly.

'He was not nice, no,' said Poirot. 'But he was alive – and now he is dead, and as I told him once, I have a *bourgeois* attitude to murder, I disapprove of it.'

He added softly:

'And so – I am prepared to go inside the tiger's cage . . .'

CHAPTER 9

DR ROBERTS

'Good morning, Superintendent Battle.'

Dr Roberts rose from his chair and offered a large pink hand smelling of a mixture of good soap and faint carbolic.

'How are things going?' he went on.

Superintendent Battle glanced round the comfortable consulting-room before answering.

'Well, Dr Roberts, strictly speaking, they're not going. They're standing still.'

'There's been nothing much in the papers, I've been glad to see.'

'*Sudden death of the well-known Mr Shaitana at an evening party in his own home*. It's left at that for the moment. We've had the autopsy – I brought a report of the findings along – thought it might interest you –'

'That's very kind of you – it would – h'm – h'm. Yes, very interesting.'

He handed it back.

'And we've interviewed Mr Shaitana's solicitor. We know the terms of his will. Nothing of interest there. He has relatives in Syria, it seems. And then, of course, we've been through all his private papers.'

Was it fancy or did that broad, clean-shaven countenance look a little strained – a little wooden?

'And?' said Dr Roberts.

'Nothing,' said Superintendent Battle, watching him. There wasn't a sigh of relief. Nothing so blatant as that. But the doctor's figure seemed to relax just a shade more comfortably in his chair.

'And so you've come to me?'

'And so, as you say, I've come to you.'

The doctor's eyebrows rose a little and his shrewd eyes looked into Battle's.

'Want to go through *my* private papers – eh?'

'That was my idea.'

'Got a search warrant?'

'No.'

'Well; you could get one easily enough, I suppose. I'm not going to make difficulties. It's not very pleasant being suspected of murder but I suppose I can't blame you for what's obviously your duty.'

'Thank you, sir,' said Superintendent Battle with real gratitude. 'I appreciate your attitude, if I may say so, very much. I hope all the others will be as reasonable, I'm sure.'

'What can't be cured must be endured,' said the doctor good-humouredly.

He went on:

'I've finished seeing my patients here. I'm just off on my

rounds. I'll leave you my keys and just say a word to my secretary and you can rootle to your heart's content.'

'That's all very nice and pleasant, I'm sure,' said Battle. 'I'd like to ask you a few more questions before you go.'

'About the other night? Really, I told you all I know.'

'No, not about the other night. About yourself.'

'Well, man, ask away, what do you want to know?'

'I'd just like a rough sketch of your career, Dr Roberts. Birth, marriage, and so on.'

'It will get me into practice for *Who's Who*,' said the doctor dryly. 'My career's a perfectly straightforward one. I'm a Shropshire man, born at Ludlow. My father was in practice there. He died when I was fifteen. I was educated at Shrewsbury and went in for medicine like my father before me. I'm a St Christopher's man – but you'll have all the medical details already, I expect.'

'I looked you up, yes, sir. You an only child or have you any brothers or sisters?'

'I'm an only child. Both my parents are dead and I'm unmarried. Will that do to get on with? I came into partnership here with Dr Emery. He retired about fifteen years ago. Lives in Ireland. I'll give you his address if you like. I live here with a cook, a parlourmaid and a housemaid. My secretary comes in daily. I make a good income and I only kill a reasonable number of my patients. How's that?'

Superintendent Battle grinned.

'That's fairly comprehensive, Dr Roberts. I'm glad you've got a sense of humour. Now I'm going to ask you one more thing.'

'I'm a strictly moral man, superintendent.'

'Oh, that wasn't my meaning. No, I was going to ask you if you'd give me the names of four friends – people who've known you intimately for a number of years. Kind of references, if you know what I mean.'

'Yes, I think so. Let me see now. You'd prefer people who are actually in London now?'

'It would make it a bit easier, but it doesn't really matter.'

The doctor thought for a minute or two, then with his fountain pen he scribbled four names and addresses on a sheet of paper and pushed it across the desk to Battle.

'Will those do? They're the best I can think of on the spur of the moment.'

Battle read carefully, nodded his head in satisfaction and put the sheet of paper away in an inner pocket.

'It's just a question of elimination,' he said. 'The sooner I can get one person eliminated and go on to the next, the better it is for every one concerned. I've got to make perfectly certain that you weren't on bad terms with the late Mr Shaitana, that you had no private connections or business dealings with him, that there was no question of his having injured you at any time and your bearing resentment. *I* may believe you when you say you only knew him slightly – but it isn't a question of *my* belief. I've got to say I've made *sure.*'

'Oh, I understand perfectly. You've got to think everybody's a liar till he's proved he's speaking the truth. Here are my keys, superintendent. That's the drawers of the desk – that's the bureau – that little one's the key of the poison cupboard. Be sure to lock it up again. Perhaps I'd better just have a word with my secretary.'

He pressed a button on his desk.

Almost immediately the door opened and a competent-looking young woman appeared.

'You rang, doctor?'

'This is Miss Burgess – Superintendent Battle from Scotland Yard.'

Miss Burgess turned a cool gaze on Battle. It seemed to say:

'Dear me, what sort of an animal is this?'

'I should be glad, Miss Burgess, if you will answer any questions Superintendent Battle may put to you, and give him any help he may need.'

'Certainly, if you say so, doctor.'

'Well,' said Roberts, rising, 'I'll be off. Did you put the morphia in my case? I shall need it for the Lockheart case.'

He bustled out, still talking, and Miss Burgess followed him.

'Will you press that button when you want me, Superintendent Battle?'

Superintendent Battle thanked her and said he would do so. Then he set to work.

His search was careful and methodical, though he had no

great hopes of finding anything of importance. Roberts' ready acquiescence dispelled the chance of that. Roberts was no fool. He would realize that a search would be bound to come and he would make provisions accordingly. There was, however, a faint chance that Battle might come across a hint of the information he was really after, since Roberts would not know the real object of his search.

Superintendent Battle opened and shut drawers, rifled pigeon-holes, glanced through a chequebook, estimated the unpaid bills – noted what those same bills were for, scrutinized Roberts' passbook, ran through his case notes and generally left no written document unturned. The result was meagre in the extreme. He next took a look through the poison cupboard, noted the wholesale firms with which the doctor dealt, and the system of checking, relocked the cupboard and passed on to the bureau. The contents of the latter were of a more personal nature, but Battle found nothing germane to his search. He shook his head, sat down in the doctor's chair and pressed the desk button.

Miss Burgess appeared with commendable promptitude.

Superintendent Battle asked her politely to be seated and then sat studying her for a moment, before he decided which way to tackle her. He had sensed immediately her hostility and he was uncertain whether to provoke her into unguarded speech by increasing that hostility or whether to try a softer method of approach.

'I suppose you know what all this is about, Miss Burgess?' he said at last.

'Dr Roberts told me,' said Miss Burgess shortly.

'The whole thing's rather delicate,' said Superintendent Battle.

'Is it?' said Miss Burgess.

'Well, it's rather a nasty business. Four people are under suspicion and one of them must have done it. What I want to know is whether you've ever seen this Mr Shaitana?'

'Never.'

'Ever heard Dr Roberts speak of him?'

'Never – no, I am wrong. About a week ago Dr Roberts told me to enter up a dinner appointment in his engagement-book. Mr Shaitana, 8.15, on the 18th.'

'And that is the first you ever heard of this Mr Shaitana?'

'Yes.'

'Never seen his name in the papers? He was often in the fashionable news.'

'I've got better things to do than reading the fashionable news.'

'I expect you have. Oh, I expect you have,' said the superintendent mildly.

'Well,' he went on. 'There it is. All four of these people will only admit to knowing Mr Shaitana slightly. But one of them knew him well enough to kill him. It's my job to find out which of them it was.'

There was an unhelpful pause. Miss Burgess seemed quite uninterested in the performance of Superintendent Battle's job. It was her job to obey her employer's orders and sit here listening to what Superintendent Battle chose to say and answer any direct questions he might choose to put to her.

'You know, Miss Burgess,' the superintendent found it uphill work but he persevered, 'I doubt if you appreciate half the difficulties of our job. People say things, for instance. Well, we mayn't believe a word of it, but we've got to take notice of it all the same. It's particularly noticeable in a case of this kind. I don't want to say anything against your sex but there's no doubt that a woman, when she's rattled, is apt to lash out with her tongue a bit. She makes unfounded accusations, hints this, that and the other, and rakes up all sorts of old scandals that have probably nothing whatever to do with the case.'

'Do you mean,' demanded Miss Burgess, 'that one of these other people has been saying things against the doctor?'

'Not exactly *said* anything,' said Battle cautiously. 'But all the same, I'm bound to take notice. Suspicious circumstances about the death of a patient. Probably all a lot of nonsense. I'm ashamed to bother the doctor with it.'

'I suppose someone's got hold of that story about Mrs Graves,' said Miss Burgess wrathfully. 'The way people talk about things they know nothing whatever about is disgraceful. Lots of old ladies get like that – they think everybody is poisoning them – their relations and their servants and even their doctors. Mrs Graves had had three doctors before she came to Dr Roberts and then when she got the same fancies about him he was quite willing for her to have Dr Lee instead. It's the only thing to do in these cases, he said. And after Dr Lee she had Dr Steele, and then Dr Farmer – until she died, poor old thing.'

'You'd be surprised the way the smallest thing starts a story,' said Battle. 'Whenever a doctor benefits by the death of a patient somebody has something ill-natured to say. And yet why shouldn't a grateful patient leave a little something, or even a big something to her medical attendant.'

'It's the relations,' said Miss Burgess. 'I always think there's nothing like death for bringing out the meanness of human nature. Squabbling over who's to have what before the body's cold. Luckily, Dr Roberts has never had any trouble of that kind. He always says he hopes his patients won't leave him anything. I believe he once had a legacy of fifty pounds and he's had two walking sticks and a gold watch, but nothing else.'

'It's a difficult life, that of a professional man,' said Battle with a sigh. 'He's always open to blackmail. The most innocent occurrences lend themselves sometimes to a scandalous appearance. A doctor's got to avoid even the appearance of evil – that means he's got to have his wits about him good and sharp.'

'A lot of what you say is true,' said Miss Burgess. 'Doctors have a difficult time with hysterical women.'

'Hysterical women. That's right. I thought in my own mind, that that was all it amounted to.'

'I suppose you mean that dreadful Mrs Craddock?'

Battle pretended to think.

'Let me see, was it three years ago? No, more.'

'Four or five, I think. She was a *most* unbalanced woman! I was glad when she went abroad and so was Dr Roberts. She told her husband the most frightful lies – they always do, of course. Poor man, he wasn't quite himself – he'd begun to be ill. He died of anthrax, you know, an infected shaving brush.'

'I'd forgotten that,' said Battle untruthfully.

'And then she went abroad and died not long afterwards. But I always thought she was a nasty type of woman – man-mad, you know.'

'I know the kind,' said Battle. 'Very dangerous, they are. A doctor's got to give them a wide berth. Whereabouts did she die abroad – I seem to remember.'

'Egypt, I think it was. She got blood-poisoning – some native infection.'

'Another thing that must be difficult for a doctor,' said Battle, making a conversational leap, 'is when he suspects that one of his patients is being poisoned by one of their relatives. What's he to do? He's got to be sure – or else hold his tongue. And if he's done the latter, then it's awkward for him if there's talk of foul play afterwards. I wonder if any case of that kind has ever come Dr Roberts' way?'

'I really don't think it has,' said Miss Burgess, considering. 'I've never heard of anything like that.'

'From the statistical point of view, it would be interesting to know how many deaths occur among a doctor's practice per year. For instance now, you've been with Dr Roberts some years –'

'Seven.'

'Seven. Well, how many deaths have there been in that time off-hand?'

'Really, it's difficult to say.' Miss Burgess gave herself up to calculation. She was by now quite thawed and unsuspicious. 'Seven, eight – of course, I can't remember exactly – I shouldn't say more than thirty in the time.'

'Then I fancy Dr Roberts must be a better doctor than most,' said Battle genially. 'I suppose, too, most of his patients are upper-class. They can afford to take care of themselves.'

'He's a very popular doctor. He's so good at diagnosis.'

Battle sighed and rose to his feet.

'I'm afraid I've been wandering from my duty, which is to find out a connection between the doctor and this Mr Shaitana. You're quite sure he wasn't a patient of the doctor's?'

'Quite sure.'

'Under another name, perhaps?' Battle handed her a photograph. 'Recognize him at all?'

'What a very theatrical-looking person. No, I've never seen him here at any time.'

'Well, that's that.' Battle sighed. 'I'm much obliged to the doctor, I'm sure, for being so pleasant about everything. Tell him from me, will you? Tell him I'm passing on to No. 2. Goodbye, Miss Burgess, and thank you for your help.'

He shook hands and departed. Walking along the street he took a small notebook from his pocket and made a couple of entries in it under the letter R.

> *Mrs Graves? Unlikely.*
> *Mrs Craddock?*
> *No legacies.*
> *No wife. (Pity.)*
> *Investigate deaths of patients. Difficult.*

He closed the book and turned into the Lancaster Gate branch of the London and Wessex Bank.

The display of his official card brought him to a private interview with the manager.

'Good morning, sir. One of your clients is a Dr Geoffrey Roberts, I understand.'

'Quite correct, superintendent.'

'I shall want some information about that gentleman's account going back over a period of years.'

'I will see what I can do for you.'

A complicated half-hour followed. Finally Battle, with a sigh, tucked away a sheet of pencilled figures.

'Got what you want?' inquired the bank manager curiously.

'No, I haven't. Not one suggestive lead. Thank you all the same.'

At that same moment, Dr Roberts, washing his hands in his consulting-room, said over his shoulder to Miss Burgess:

'What about our stolid sleuth, eh? Did he turn the place upside down and you inside out?'

'He didn't get much out of me, I can tell you,' said Miss Burgess, setting her lips tightly.

'My dear girl, no need to be an oyster. I told you to tell him all he wanted to know. What did he want to know, by the way?'

'Oh, he kept harping on your knowing that man Shaitana – suggested even that he might have come here as a patient under a different name. He showed me his photograph. Such a theatrical-looking man!'

'Shaitana? Oh, yes, fond of posing as a modern Mephistopheles.

It went down rather well on the whole. What else did Battle ask you?'

'Really nothing very much. Except – oh, yes, somebody had been telling him some absurd nonsense about Mrs Graves – you know the way she used to go on.'

'Graves? Graves? Oh, yes, old Mrs Graves. That's rather funny!' The doctor laughed with considerable amusement. 'That's really very funny indeed.'

And in high good humour he went in to lunch.

CHAPTER 10
DR ROBERTS (*CONTINUED*)

Superintendent Battle was lunching with M. Hercule Poirot.

The former looked downcast, the latter sympathetic.

'Your morning, then, has not been entirely successful,' said Poirot thoughtfully.

Battle shook his head.

'It's going to be uphill work, M. Poirot.'

'What do you think of him?'

'Of the doctor? Well, frankly, I think Shaitana was right. He's a killer. Reminds me of Westaway. And of that lawyer chap in Norfolk. Same hearty, self-confident manner. Same popularity. Both of them were clever devils – so's Roberts. All the same, it doesn't follow that Roberts killed Shaitana – and as a matter of fact I don't think he did. He'd know the risk too well – better than a layman would – that Shaitana might wake and cry out. No, I don't think Roberts murdered him.'

'But you think he has murdered someone?'

'Possibly quite a lot of people. Westaway had. But it's going to be hard to get at. I've looked over his bank account – nothing suspicious there – no large sums suddenly paid in. At any rate, in the last seven years he's not had any legacy from a patient. That wipes out murder for direct gain. He's never married – that's a pity – so ideally simple for a doctor to kill his own wife. He's well-to-do, but then he's got a thriving practice among well-to-do people.'

'In fact he appears to lead a thoroughly blameless life – and perhaps does do so.'

'Maybe. But I prefer to believe the worst.'

He went on:

'There's the hint of a scandal over a woman – one of his patients – name of Craddock. That's worth looking up, I think. I'll get someone on to that straightaway. Woman actually died out in Egypt of some local disease so I don't think there's anything in that – but it might throw a light on his general character and morals.'

'Was there a husband?'

'Yes. Husband died of anthrax.'

'Anthrax?'

'Yes, there were a lot of cheap shaving brushes on the market just then – some of them infected. There was a regular scandal about it.'

'Convenient,' suggested Poirot.

'That's what I thought. If her husband were threatening to kick up a row – But there, it's all conjecture. We haven't a leg to stand upon.'

'Courage, my friend. I know your patience. In the end, you will have perhaps as many legs as a centipede.'

'And fall into the ditch as a result of thinking about them,' grinned Battle.

Then he asked curiously:

'What about you, M. Poirot? Going to take a hand?'

'I, too, might call on Dr Roberts.'

'Two of us in one day. That ought to put the wind up him.'

'Oh, I shall be very discreet. I shall not inquire into his past life.'

'I'd like to know just exactly what line you'll take,' said Battle curiously, 'but don't tell me unless you want to.'

'*Du tout – du tout.* I am most willing. I shall talk a little of bridge, that is all.'

'Bridge again. You harp on that, don't you, M. Poirot?'

'I find the subject very useful.'

'Well, every man to his taste. I don't deal much in the fancy approaches. They don't suit my style.'

'What is your style, superintendent?'

The superintendent met the twinkle in Poirot's eyes with an answering twinkle in his own.

'A straightforward, honest, zealous officer doing his duty in the most laborious manner – that's my style. No frills. No fancy work. Just honest perspiration. Stolid and a bit stupid – that's my ticket.'

Poirot raised his glass.

'To our respective methods – and may success crown our joint efforts.'

'I expect Colonel Race may get us something worth having about Despard,' said Battle. 'He's got a good many sources of information.'

'And Mrs Oliver?'

'Bit of a toss-up there. I rather like that woman. Talks a lot of nonsense, but she's a sport. And women get to know things about other women that men can't get at. She may spot something useful.'

They separated. Battle went back to Scotland Yard to issue instructions for certain lines to be followed up. Poirot betook himself to 200 Gloucester Terrace.

Dr Roberts' eyebrows rose comically as he greeted his guest.

'Two sleuths in one day,' he asked. 'Handcuffs by this evening, I suppose.'

Poirot smiled.

'I can assure you, Dr Roberts, that my attentions are being equally divided between all four of you.'

'That's something to be thankful for, at all events. Smoke?'

'If you permit, I prefer my own.'

Poirot lighted one of his tiny Russian cigarettes.

'Well, what can I do for you?' asked Roberts.

Poirot was silent for a minute or two puffing, then he said:

'Are you a keen observer of human nature, doctor?'

'I don't know. I suppose I am. A doctor has to be.'

'That was exactly my reasoning. I said to myself, "A doctor has always to be studying his patients – their expressions, their colour, how fast they breathe, any signs of restlessness – a doctor notices these things automatically almost without noticing he notices! Dr Roberts is the man to help me.'

'I'm willing enough to help. What's the trouble?'

Poirot produced from a neat little pocket-case three carefully folded bridge scores.

'These are the first three rubbers the other evening,' he explained. 'Here is the first one – in Miss Meredith's handwriting. Now can you tell me – with this to refresh your memory – exactly what the calling was and how each hand went?'

Roberts stared at him in astonishment.

'You're joking, M. Poirot. How can I possibly remember?'

'Can't you? I should be very grateful if you could. Take this first rubber. The first game must have resulted in a game call in hearts or spades, or else one or other side must have gone down fifty.'

'Let me see – that was the first hand. Yes, I think they went out in spades.'

'And the next hand?'

'I suppose one or other of us went down fifty – but I can't remember which or what it was in. Really, M. Poirot, you can hardly expect me to do so.'

'Can't you remember any of the calling or the hands?'

'I got a grand slam – I remember that. It was doubled too. And I also remember going down a nasty smack – playing three no trumps, I think it was – went down a packet. But that was later on.'

'Do you remember with whom you were playing?'

'Mrs Lorrimer. She looked a bit grim, I remember. Didn't like my overcalling, I expect.'

'And you can't remember any other of the hands or the calling?'

Roberts laughed.

'My dear M. Poirot, did you really expect I could. First there was the murder – enough to drive the most spectacular hands out of one's mind – and in addition I've played at least half a dozen rubbers since then.'

Poirot sat looking rather crestfallen.

'I'm sorry,' said Roberts.

'It does not matter very much,' said Poirot slowly. 'I hoped that you might remember one or two, at least, of the hands, because I thought they might be valuable landmarks in remembering other things.'

'What other things?'

'Well you might have noticed, for instance, that your partner made a mess of playing a perfectly simple no trumper, or that an opponent, say, presented you with a couple of unexpected tricks by failing to lead an obvious card.'

Dr Roberts became suddenly serious. He leaned forward in his chair.

'Ah,' he said. 'Now I see what you're driving at. Forgive me. I thought at first you were talking pure nonsense. You mean that the murder – the successful accomplishment of the murder – might have made a definite difference in the guilty party's play?'

Poirot nodded.

'You have seized the idea correctly. It would be a clue of the first excellence if you had been four players who knew each other's game well. A variation, a sudden lack of brilliance, a missed opportunity – that would have been immediately noticed. Unluckily, you were all strangers to each other. Variation in play would not be so noticeable. But think, M. le docteur, I beg of you to *think*. Do you remember any inequalities – any sudden glaring mistakes – in the play of anyone?'

There was silence for a minute or two, then Dr Roberts shook his head.

'It's no good. I can't help you,' he said frankly. 'I simply don't remember. All I can tell you is what I told you before: Mrs Lorrimer is a first-class player – she never made a slip that I noticed. She was brilliant from start to finish. Despard's play was uniformly good too. Rather a conventional player – that is, his bidding is strictly conventional. He never steps outside the rules. Won't take a long chance. Miss Meredith –' He hesitated.

'Yes? Miss Meredith?' Poirot prompted him.

'She did make mistakes – once or twice – I remember – towards the end of the evening, but that may simply have been because she was tired – not being a very experienced player. Her hand shook, too –'

He stopped.

'When did her hand shake?'

'When was it now? I can't remember . . . I think she was just nervous. M. Poirot, you're making me imagine things.'

'I apologize. There is another point on which I seek your help.'

'Yes?'

Poirot said slowly:

'It is difficult. I do not, you see, wish to ask you a leading question. If I say, did you notice so and so – well, I have put the thing into your head. Your answer will not be so valuable. Let me try to get at the matter another way. If you will be so kind, Dr Roberts, describe to me the contents of the room in which you played.'

Roberts looked thoroughly astonished.

'The contents of the room?'

'If you will be so good.'

'My dear fellow, I simply don't know where to begin.'

'Begin anywhere you choose.'

'Well, there was a good deal of furniture –'

'*Non, non, non*, be precise, I pray of you.'

Dr Roberts sighed.

He began facetiously after the manner of an auctioneer.

'One large settee upholstered in ivory brocade – one ditto in green ditto – four or five large chairs. Eight or nine Persian rugs – a set of twelve small gilt Empire chairs. William and Mary bureau. (I feel just like an auctioneer's clerk.) Very beautiful Chinese cabinet. Grand piano. There was other furniture but I'm afraid I didn't notice it. Six first-class Japanese prints. Two Chinese pictures on looking-glass. Five or six very beautiful snuff-boxes. Some Japanese ivory netsuke figures on a table by themselves. Some old silver – Charles I tazzas, I think. One or two pieces of Battersea enamel –'

'Bravo, bravo!' Poirot applauded.

'A couple of old English slipware birds – and, I think, a Ralph Wood figure. Then there was some Eastern stuff – intricate silver work. Some jewellery, I don't know much about that. Some Chelsea birds, I remember. Oh, and some miniatures in a case – pretty good ones, I fancy. That's not all by a long way – but it's all I can think of for the minute.'

'It is magnificent,' said Poirot with due appreciation. 'You have the true observer's eye.'

The doctor asked curiously:

'Have I included the object you had in mind?'

'That is the interesting thing about it,' said Poirot. 'If you had mentioned the object I had in mind it would have been extremely surprising to me. As I thought, you could not mention it.'

'Why?'

Poirot twinkled.

'Perhaps – because it was not there to mention.'

Roberts stared.

'That seems to remind me of something.'

'It reminds you of Sherlock Holmes, does it not? The curious incident of the dog in the night. The dog did not howl in the night. That is the curious thing! Ah, well, I am not above stealing the tricks of others.'

'Do you know, M. Poirot, I am completely at sea as to what you are driving at.'

'That is excellent, that. In confidence, that is how I get my little effects.'

Then, as Dr Roberts still looked rather dazed, Poirot said with a smile as he rose to his feet:

'You may at least comprehend this, what you have told me is going to be very helpful to me in my next interview.'

The doctor rose also.

'I can't see how, but I'll take your word for it,' he said.

They shook hands.

Poirot went down the steps of the doctor's house, and hailed a passing taxi.

'111 Cheyne Lane, Chelsea,' he told the driver.

CHAPTER 11
MRS LORRIMER

111 Cheyne Lane was a small house of very neat and trim appearance standing in a quiet street. The door was painted black and the steps were particularly well whitened, the brass of the knocker and handle gleamed in the afternoon sun.

The door was opened by an elderly parlourmaid with an immaculate white cap and apron.

In answer to Poirot's inquiry she said that her mistress was at home.

She preceded him up the narrow staircase.

'What name, sir?'

'M. Hercule Poirot.'

He was ushered into a drawing-room of the usual L shape. Poirot looked about him, noting details. Good furniture, well polished, of the old family type. Shiny chintz on the chairs and settees. A few silver photograph frames about in the old-fashioned manner. Otherwise an agreeable amount of space and light, and some really beautiful chrysanthemums arranged in a tall jar.

Mrs Lorrimer came forward to meet him.

She shook hands without showing any particular surprise at seeing him, indicated a chair, took one herself and remarked favourably on the weather.

There was a pause.

'I hope, madame,' said Hercule Poirot, 'that you will forgive this visit.'

Looking directly at him, Mrs Lorrimer asked:

'Is this a professional visit?'

'I confess it.'

'You realize, I suppose, M. Poirot, that though I shall naturally give Superintendent Battle and the official police any information and help they may require, I am by no means bound to do the same for any unofficial investigator?'

'I am quite aware of that fact, madame. If you show me the door, me, I march to that door with complete submission.'

Mrs Lorrimer smiled very slightly.

'I am not yet prepared to go to those extremes, M. Poirot. I can give you ten minutes. At the end of that time I have to go out to a bridge party.'

'Ten minutes will be ample for my purpose. I want you to describe to me, madame, the room in which you played bridge the other evening – the room in which Mr Shaitana was killed.'

Mrs Lorrimer's eyebrows rose.

'What an extraordinary question! I do not see the point of it.'

'Madame, if when you were playing bridge, someone were to say to you – why do you play that ace or why do you put on the knave that is taken by the queen and not the king which would take the trick? If people were to ask you such questions, the answers would be rather long and tedious, would they not?'

Mrs Lorrimer smiled slightly.

'Meaning that in this game you are the expert and I am the novice. Very well.' She reflected a minute. 'It was a large room. There were a good many things in it.'

'Can you describe some of those things?'

'There were some glass flowers – modern – rather beautiful . . . And I think there were some Chinese or Japanese pictures. And there was a bowl of tiny red tulips – amazingly early for them.'

'Anything else?'

'I'm afraid I didn't notice anything in detail.'

'The furniture – do you remember the colour of the upholstery?'

'Something silky, I think. That's all I can say.'

'Did you notice any of the small objects?'

'I'm afraid not. There were so many. I know it struck me as quite a collector's room.'

There was silence for a minute. Mrs Lorrimer said with a faint smile:

'I'm afraid I have not been very helpful.'

'There is something else.' He produced the bridge scores. 'Here are the first three rubbers played. I wondered if you could help me with the aid of these scores to reconstruct the hands.'

'Let me see.' Mrs Lorrimer looked interested. She bent over the scores.

'That was the first rubber. Miss Meredith and I were playing against the two men. The first game was played in four spades. We made it and an over trick. Then the next hand was left at two diamonds and Dr Roberts went down one trick on it. There was quite a lot of bidding on the third hand, I remember. Miss Meredith passed. Major Despard went a heart. I passed. Dr Roberts gave a jump bid of three clubs. Miss Meredith went three spades. Major Despard bid four diamonds. I doubled. Dr Roberts took it into four hearts. They went down one.'

'*Epatant*,' said Poirot. 'What a memory!'

Mrs Lorrimer went on, disregarding him:

'On the next hand Major Despard passed and I bid a no trump. Dr Roberts bid three hearts. My partner said nothing. Despard put his partner to four. I doubled and they went down two tricks. Then I dealt and we went out on a four-spade call.'

She took up the next score.

'It is difficult, that,' said Poirot. 'Major Despard scores in the cancellation manner.'

'I rather fancy both sides went down fifty to start with – then Dr Roberts went to five diamonds and we doubled and got him down to three tricks. Then we made three clubs, but immediately after the others went game in spades. We made the second game in five clubs. Then we went down a hundred. The others made one heart, we made two no trumps and we finally won the rubber with a four-club call.'

She picked up the next score.

'This rubber was rather a battle, I remember. It started tamely. Major Despard and Miss Meredith made a one-heart call. Then we went down a couple of fifties trying for four hearts and four spades. Then the others made game in spades – no use trying to stop them. We went down three hands running after that but undoubled. Then we won the second game in no trumps. Then a battle royal started. Each side went down in turn. Dr Roberts overcalled but though he went down badly once or twice, his calling paid, for more than once he frightened Miss Meredith out of bidding her hand. Then he bid an original two spades, I gave him three diamonds, he bid four no trumps, I bid five spades and he suddenly jumped to seven diamonds. We were doubled, of course. He had no business to make such a call. By a kind of miracle we got it. I never thought we should when I saw his hand go down. If the others had led a heart we would have been three tricks down. As it was they led the king of clubs and we got it. It was really very exciting.'

'*Je crois bien* – a Grand Slam Vulnerable doubled. It causes the emotions, that! Me, I admit it, I have not the nerve to go for the slams. I content myself with the game.'

'Oh, but you shouldn't,' said Mrs Lorrimer with energy. 'You must play the game properly.'

'Take risks, you mean?'

'There is no risk if the bidding is correct. It should be a mathematical certainty. Unfortunately, few people really bid well. They know the opening bids but later they lose their heads. They cannot distinguish between a hand with winning cards in it and a hand without losing cards – but I mustn't give you a lecture on bridge, or on the losing count, M. Poirot.'

'It would improve my play, I am sure, madame.'

Mrs Lorrimer resumed her study of the score.

'After that excitement the next hands were rather tame. Have you the fourth score there? Ah, yes. A ding-dong battle – neither side able to score below.'

'It is often like that as the evening wears on.'

'Yes, one starts tamely and then the cards get worked up.'

Poirot collected the scores and made a little bow.

'Madame, I congratulate you. Your card memory is magnificent – but magnificent! You remember, one might say, every card that was played!'

'I believe I do!'

'Memory is a wonderful gift. With it the past is never the past – I should imagine, madame, that to you the past unrolls itself, every incident clear as yesterday. Is that so?'

She looked at him quickly. Her eyes were wide and dark.

It was only for a moment, then she had resumed her woman-of-the-world manner, but Hercule Poirot did not doubt. That shot had gone home.

Mrs Lorrimer rose.

'I'm afraid I shall have to leave now. I am so sorry – but I really mustn't be late.'

'Of course not – of course not. I apologize for trespassing on your time.'

'I'm sorry I haven't been able to help you more.'

'But you have helped me,' said Hercule Poirot.

'I hardly think so.'

She spoke with decision.

'But yes. You have told me something I wanted to know.'

She asked no question as to what that something was.

He held out his hand.

'Thank you, madame, for your forbearance.'

As she shook hands with him she said:

'You are an extraordinary man, M. Poirot.'

'I am as the good God made me, madame.'

'We are all that, I suppose.'

'Not all, madame. Some of us have tried to improve on His pattern. Mr Shaitana, for instance.'

'In what way do you mean?'

'He had a very pretty taste in *objets de vertu* and *bric-à-brac* – he should have been content with that. Instead, he collected other things.'

'What sort of things?'

'Well – shall we say – sensations?'

'And don't you think that was *dans son caractère*?'

Poirot shook his head gravely.

'He played the part of the devil too successfully. But he was not the devil. *Au fond*, he was a stupid man. And so – he died.'

'Because he was stupid?'

'It is the sin that is never forgiven and always punished, madame.'

There was a silence. Then Poirot said:

'I take my departure. A thousand thanks for your amiability, madame. I will not come again unless you send for me.'

Her eyebrows rose.

'Dear me, M. Poirot, why should I send for you?'

'You might. It is just an idea. If so, I will come. Remember that.'

He bowed once more and left the room.

In the street he said to himself:

'I am right . . . I am sure I am right . . . It *must* be that!'

CHAPTER 12

ANNE MEREDITH

Mrs Oliver extricated herself from the driving-seat of her little two-seater with some difficulty. To begin with, the makers of modern motor-cars assume that only a pair of sylph-like knees will ever be under the steering wheel. It is also the fashion to sit low. That being so, for a middle-aged woman of generous proportions it requires a good deal of superhuman wriggling to get out from under the steering wheel. In the second place, the seat next to the driving-seat was encumbered by several maps, a handbag, three novels and a large bag of apples. Mrs Oliver was partial to apples and had indeed been known to eat as many as five pounds straight off whilst composing the complicated plot of *The Death in the Drain Pipe* – coming to herself with a start and an incipient stomach-ache an hour and ten minutes after she was due at an important luncheon party given in her honour.

With a final determined heave and a sharp shove with a knee against a recalcitrant door, Mrs Oliver arrived a little too suddenly on the sidewalk outside the gate of Wendon Cottage, showering apple cores freely round her as she did so.

She gave a deep sigh, pushed back her country hat to an unfashionable angle, looked down with approval at the tweeds she had remembered to put on, frowned a little when she saw that she had absent-mindedly retained her London high-heeled patent leather shoes, and pushing open the gate of Wendon Cottage walked up the flagged path to the front door. She rang the bell and executed a cheerful little rat-a-tat-tat on the knocker – a quaint conceit in the form of a toad's head.

As nothing happened she repeated the performance.

After a further pause of a minute and a half, Mrs Oliver stepped briskly round the side of the house on a voyage of exploration.

There was a small old-fashioned garden with Michaelmas daisies and straggling chrysanthemums behind the cottage, and beyond it a field. Beyond the field was the river. For an October day the sun was warm.

Two girls were just crossing the field in the direction of the cottage. As they came through the gate into the garden, the foremost of the two stopped dead.

Mrs Oliver came forward.

'How do you do, Miss Meredith? You remember me, don't you?'

'Oh – oh, of course.' Anne Meredith extended her hand hurriedly. Her eyes looked wide and startled. Then she pulled herself together.

'This is my friend who lives with me – Miss Dawes. Rhoda, this is Mrs Oliver.'

The other girl was tall, dark, and vigorous-looking. She said excitedly:

'Oh, are you the Mrs Oliver? Ariadne Oliver?'

'I am,' said Mrs Oliver, and she added to Anne, 'Now let us sit down somewhere, my dear, because I've got a lot to say to you.'

'Of course. And we'll have tea –'

'Tea can wait,' said Mrs Oliver.

Anne led the way to a little group of deck and basket chairs, all rather dilapidated. Mrs Oliver chose the strongest-looking with some care, having had various unfortunate experiences with flimsy summer furniture.

'Now, my dear,' she said briskly. 'Don't let's beat about the bush. About this murder the other evening. We've got to get busy and do something.'

'Do something?' queried Anne.

'Naturally,' said Mrs Oliver. 'I don't know what *you* think, but I haven't the least doubt who did it. That doctor. What was his name? Roberts. That's it! Roberts. A Welsh name! I never trust the Welsh! I had a Welsh nurse and she took me to Harrogate one day and went home having forgotten all about me. Very unstable. But never mind about her. Roberts did it – that's the point and we must put our heads together and prove he did.'

Rhoda Dawes laughed suddenly – then she blushed.

'I beg your pardon. But you're – you're so different from what I would have imagined.'

'A disappointment, I expect,' said Mrs Oliver serenely. 'I'm used to that. Never mind. What we must do is prove that Roberts did it!'

'How can we?' said Anne.

'Oh, don't be so defeatist, Anne,' cried Rhoda Dawes. 'I think Mrs Oliver's splendid. Of course, she knows all about these things. She'll do just as Sven Hjerson does.'

Blushing slightly at the name of her celebrated Finnish detective, Mrs Oliver said:

'It's got to be done, and I'll tell you why, child. You don't want people thinking *you* did it?'

'Why should they?' asked Anne, her colour rising.

'You know what people are!' said Mrs Oliver. 'The three who didn't do it will come in for just as much suspicion as the one who did.'

Anne Meredith said slowly:

'I still don't quite see why you come to *me*, Mrs Oliver?'

'Because in my opinion the other two don't matter! Mrs Lorrimer is one of those women who play bridge at bridge clubs all day. Women like that *must* be made of armourplating

– they can look after themselves all right! And anyway she's old. It wouldn't matter if anyone thought she'd done it. A girl's different. She's got her life in front of her.'

'And Major Despard?' asked Anne.

'Pah!' said Mrs Oliver. 'He's a man! I never worry about men. Men can look after themselves. Do it remarkably well, if you ask me. Besides, Major Despard enjoys a dangerous life. He's getting his fun at home instead of on the Irrawaddy – or do I mean the Limpopo? You know what I mean – that yellow African river that men like so much. No, I'm not worrying my head about either of those two.'

'It's very kind of you,' said Anne slowly.

'It was a beastly thing to happen,' said Rhoda. 'It's broken Anne up, Mrs Oliver. She's awfully sensitive. And I think you're quite right. It would be ever so much better to do something than just to sit here thinking about it all.'

'Of course it would,' said Mrs Oliver. 'To tell you the truth, a real murder has never come my way before. And, to continue telling the truth, I don't believe real murder is very much in my line. I'm so used to loading the dice – if you understand what I mean. But I wasn't going to be out of it and let those three men have all the fun to themselves. I've always said that if a woman were the head of Scotland Yard –'

'Yes?' said Rhoda, leaning forward with parted lips. 'If you were head of Scotland Yard, what would you do?'

'I should arrest Dr Roberts straight away –'

'Yes?'

'However, I'm not the head of Scotland Yard,' said Mrs Oliver, retreating from dangerous ground. 'I'm a private individual –'

'Oh, you're not that,' said Rhoda, confusedly complimentary.

'Here we are,' continued Mrs Oliver, 'three private individuals – all women. Let us see what we can do by putting our heads together.'

Anne Meredith nodded thoughtfully. Then she said:

'Why do you think Dr Roberts did it?'

'He's that sort of man,' replied Mrs Oliver promptly.

'Don't you think, though –' Anne hesitated. 'Wouldn't a doctor –? I mean something like poison would be so much easier for him.'

'Not at all. Poison – drugs of any kind would point straight to a doctor. Look how they are always leaving cases of dangerous drugs in cars all over London and getting them stolen. No, just because he *was* a doctor he'd take special care not to use anything of a medical kind.'

'I see,' said Anne doubtfully.

Then she said:

'But why do you think he wanted to kill Mr Shaitana? Have you any idea?'

'Idea? I've got any amount of ideas. In fact, that's just the difficulty. It always is my difficulty. I can never think of even one plot at a time. I always think of at least five, and it's agony to decide between them. I can think of six beautiful reasons for the murder. The trouble is I've no earthly means of knowing which is right. To begin with, perhaps Shaitana was a moneylender. He had a very oily look. Roberts was in his clutches, and killed him because he couldn't get the money to repay the loan. Or perhaps Shaitana ruined his daughter or his sister. Or perhaps Roberts is a bigamist, and Shaitana knew it. Or possibly Roberts married Shaitana's second cousin, and will inherit all Shaitana's money through her. Or – How many have I got to?'

'Four,' said Rhoda.

'Or – and this is a really good one – suppose Shaitana knew some secret in Roberts' past. Perhaps you didn't notice, my dear, but Shaitana said something rather peculiar at dinner – just before a rather queer pause.'

Anne stooped to tickle a caterpillar. She said, 'I don't think I remember.'

'What did he say?' asked Rhoda.

'Something about – what was it? – an accident and poison. Don't you remember?'

Anne's left hand tightened on the basketwork of her chair.

'I do remember something of the kind,' she said composedly.

Rhoda said suddenly, 'Darling, you ought to have a coat. It's not summer, remember. Go and get one.'

Anne shook her head.

'I'm quite warm.'

But she gave a queer little shiver as she spoke.

'You see my theory,' went on Mrs Oliver. 'I dare say one of

the doctor's patients poisoned himself by accident; but, of course, really, it was the doctor's own doing. I dare say he's murdered lots of people that way.'

A sudden colour came into Anne's cheeks. She said, 'Do doctors usually want to murder their patients wholesale? Wouldn't it have rather a regrettable effect on their practice?'

'There would be a reason, of course,' said Mrs Oliver vaguely.

'I think the idea is absurd,' said Anne crisply. 'Absolutely absurdly melodramatic.'

'Oh, Anne!' cried Rhoda in an agony of apology. She looked at Mrs Oliver. Her eyes, rather like those of an intelligent spaniel, seemed to be trying to say something. 'Try and understand. Try and understand,' those eyes said.

'I think it's a splendid idea, Mrs Oliver,' Rhoda said earnestly. 'And a doctor could get hold of something quite untraceable, couldn't he?'

'Oh!' exclaimed Anne.

The other two turned to look at her.

'I remember something else,' she said. 'Mr Shaitana said something about a doctor's opportunities in a laboratory. He must have meant something by that.'

'It wasn't Mr Shaitana who said that.' Mrs Oliver shook her head. 'It was Major Despard.'

A footfall on the garden walk made her turn her head.

'Well!' she exclaimed. 'Talk of the devil!'

Major Despard had just come round the corner of the house.

CHAPTER 13

SECOND VISITOR

At the sight of Mrs Oliver, Major Despard looked slightly taken aback. Under his tan his face flushed a rich brick red. Embarrassment made him jerky. He made for Anne.

'I apologize, Miss Meredith,' he said. 'Been ringing your bell. Nothing happened. Was passing this way. Thought I might just look you up.'

'I'm so sorry you've been ringing,' said Anne. 'We haven't got a maid – only a woman who comes in the mornings.'

She introduced him to Rhoda.

Rhoda said briskly:

'Let's have some tea. It's getting chilly. We'd better go in.'

They all went into the house. Rhoda disappeared into the kitchen. Mrs Oliver said:

'This is quite a coincidence – our all meeting here.'

Despard said slowly, 'Yes.'

His eyes rested on her thoughtfully – appraising eyes.

'I've been telling Miss Meredith,' said Mrs Oliver, who was thoroughly enjoying herself, 'that we ought to have a plan of campaign. About the murder, I mean. Of course, that doctor did it. Don't you agree with me?'

'Couldn't say. Very little to go on.'

Mrs Oliver put on her 'How like a man!' expression.

A certain air of constraint had settled over the three. Mrs Oliver sensed it quickly enough. When Rhoda brought in tea she rose and said she must be getting back to town. No, it was ever so kind of them, but she wouldn't have any tea.

'I'm going to leave you my card,' she said. 'Here it is, with my address on it. Come and see me when you come up to town, and we'll talk everything over and see if we can't think of something ingenious to get to the bottom of things.'

'I'll come out to the gate with you,' said Rhoda.

Just as they were walking down the path to the front gate, Anne Meredith ran out of the house and overtook them.

'I've been thinking things over,' she said.

Her pale face looked unusually resolute.

'Yes, my dear?'

'It's extraordinarily kind of you, Mrs Oliver, to have taken all this trouble. But I'd really rather not do anything at all. I mean – it was all so horrible. I just want to forget about it.'

'My dear child, the question is, will you be *allowed* to forget about it?'

'Oh, I quite understand that the police won't let it drop. They'll probably come here and ask me a lot more questions. I'm prepared for that. But privately, I mean, I don't want to think about it – or be reminded of it in any way. I dare say I'm a coward, but that's how I feel about it.'

'Oh, Anne!' cried Rhoda Dawes.

'I can understand your feeling, but I'm not at all sure that you're wise,' said Mrs Oliver. 'Left to themselves, the police will probably never find out the truth.'

Anne Meredith shrugged her shoulders.

'Does that really matter?'

'Matter?' cried Rhoda. 'Of course it matters. It *does* matter, doesn't it, Mrs Oliver?'

'I should certainly say so,' said Mrs Oliver dryly.

'I don't agree,' said Anne obstinately. 'Nobody who knows me would ever think I'd done it. I don't see any reason for interfering. It's the business of the police to get at the truth.'

'Oh, Anne, you *are* spiritless,' said Rhoda.

'That's how I feel, anyway,' said Anne. She held out her hand. 'Thank you very much, Mrs Oliver. It's very good of you to have bothered.'

'Of course, if you feel that way, there's nothing more to be said,' said Mrs Oliver cheerfully. 'I, at any rate, shall not let the grass grow under my feet. Goodbye, my dear. Look me up in London if you change your mind.'

She climbed into the car, started it, and drove off, waving a cheerful hand at the two girls.

Rhoda suddenly made a dash after the car and leapt on the running-board.

'What you said – about looking you up in London,' she said breathlessly. 'Did you only mean Anne, or did you mean me, too?'

Mrs Oliver applied the brake.

'I meant both of you, of course.'

'Oh, thank you. Don't stop. I – perhaps I might come one day. There's something – No, don't stop. I can jump off.'

She did so and, waving a hand, ran back to the gate, where Anne was standing.

'What on earth –?' began Anne.

'Isn't she a duck?' asked Rhoda enthusiastically. 'I do like her. She had on odd stockings, did you notice? I'm sure she's frightfully clever. She must be – to write all those books. What fun if she found out the truth when the police and everyone were baffled.'

'Why did she come here?' asked Anne.

Rhoda's eyes opened wide.

'Darling – she told you –'

Anne made an impatient gesture.

'We must go in. I forgot. I've left him all alone.'

'Major Despard? Anne, he's frightfully good-looking, isn't he?'

'I suppose he is.'

They walked up the path together.

Major Despard was standing by the mantelpiece, tea-cup in hand.

He cut short Anne's apologies for leaving him.

'Miss Meredith, I want to explain why I've butted in like this.'

'Oh – but –'

'I said that I happened to be passing – that wasn't strictly true. I came here on purpose.'

'How did you know my address?' asked Anne slowly.

'I got it from Superintendent Battle.'

He saw her shrink slightly at the name.

He went on quickly:

'Battle's on his way here now. I happened to see him at Paddington. I got my car out and came down here. I knew I could beat the train easily.'

'But why?'

Despard hesitated just a minute.

'I may have been presumptuous – but I had the impression that you were, perhaps, what is called "alone in the world".'

'She's got me,' said Rhoda.

Despard shot a qhick glance at her, rather liking the gallant boyish figure that leant against the mantelpiece and was following his words so intensely. They were an attractive pair, these two.

'I'm sure she couldn't have a more devoted friend than you, Miss Dawes,' he said courteously; 'but it occurred to me that, in the peculiar circumstances, the advice of someone with a good dash of world wisdom might not be amiss. Frankly, the situation is this: Miss Meredith is under suspicion of having committed murder. The same thing applies to me and to the two other people who were in the room last night. Such a situation is not agreeable – and it has its own peculiar difficulties and dangers which someone as young and inexperienced as you are, Miss Meredith, might not recognize. In my opinion, you ought to put yourself in the hands of a thoroughly good solicitor. Perhaps you have already done so?'

Anne Meredith shook her head.

'I never thought of it.'

'Exactly as I suspected. Have you got a good man – a London man, for choice?'

Again Anne shook her head.

'I've hardly ever needed a solicitor.'

'There's Mr Bury,' said Rhoda. 'But he's about a hundred-and-two, and quite gaga.'

'If you'll allow me to advise you, Miss Meredith, I recommend your going to Mr Myherne, my own solicitor. Jacobs, Peel & Jacobs is the actual name of the firm. They're first-class people, and they know all the ropes.'

Anne had got paler. She sat down.

'Is it really necessary?' she asked in a low voice.

'I should say emphatically so. There are all sorts of legal pitfalls.'

'Are these people very – expensive?'

'That doesn't matter a bit,' said Rhoda. 'That will be *quite* all right, Major Despard. I think everything you say is quite true. Anne ought to be protected.'

'Their charges will, I think, be quite reasonable,' said Despard. He added seriously: 'I really do think it's a wise course, Miss Meredith.'

'Very well,' said Anne slowly. 'I'll do it if you think so.'

'Good.'

Rhoda said warmly.

'I think it's awfully nice of you, Major Despard. Really fright-fully nice.'

Anne said, 'Thank you.'

She hesitated, and then said:

'Did you say Superintendent Battle was coming here?'

'Yes. You mustn't be alarmed by that. It's inevitable.'

'Oh, I know. As a matter of fact, I've been expecting him.'

Rhoda said impulsively:

'Poor darling – it's nearly killing her, this business. It's such a shame – so frightfully unfair.'

Despard said:

'I agree – it's a pretty beastly business – dragging a young girl into an affair of this kind. If anyone wanted to stick a knife into Shaitana, they ought to have chosen some other place or time.'

Rhoda asked squarely:

'Who do you think did it? Dr Roberts or that Mrs Lorrimer?'

A very faint smile stirred Despard's moustache.

'May have done it myself, for all you know.'

'Oh, no,' cried Rhoda. 'Anne and I know *you* didn't do it.'

He looked at them both with kindly eyes.

A nice pair of kids. Touchingly full of faith and trust. A timid little creature, the Meredith girl. Never mind, Myherne would see her through. The other was a fighter. He doubted if she would have crumpled up in the same way if she'd been in her friend's place. Nice girls. He'd like to know more about them.

These thoughts passed through his mind. Aloud he said: 'Never take anything for granted, Miss Dawes. I don't set as much value on human life as most people do. All this hysterical fuss about road deaths, for instance. Man is always in danger – from traffic, from germs, from a hundred-and-one things. As well be killed one way as another. The moment you begin being careful of yourself – adopting as your motto "Safety First" – you might as well be dead, in my opinion.'

'Oh, I do agree with you,' cried Rhoda. 'I think one ought to live frightfully dangerously – if one gets the chance that is. But life, on the whole, is terribly tame.'

'It has its moments.'

'Yes, for *you*. You go to out-of-the-way places and get mauled by tigers and shoot things and jiggers bury themselves in your toes and insects sting you, and everything's terribly uncomfortable but frightfully thrilling.'

'Well, Miss Meredith has had her thrill, too. I don't suppose it often happens that you've actually *been in the room* while a murder was committed –'

'Oh, don't!' cried Anne.

He said quickly:

'I'm sorry.'

But Rhoda said with a sigh:

'Of course it was awful – but it was exciting, too! I don't think Anne appreciates that side of it. You know, I think that Mrs Oliver is thrilled to the core to have been there that night.'

'Mrs –? Oh, your fat friend who writes the books about the unpronounceable Finn. Is she trying her hand at detection in real life?'

'She wants to.'

'Well, let's wish her luck. It would be amusing if she put one over on Battle and Co.'

'What is Superintendent Battle like?' asked Rhoda curiously.

Major Despard said gravely:

'He's an extraordinarily astute man. A man of remarkable ability.'

'Oh!' said Rhoda. 'Anne said he looked rather stupid.'

'That, I should imagine, is part of Battle's stock-in-trade. But we mustn't make any mistakes. Battle's no fool.'

He rose.

'Well, I must be off. There's just one other thing I'd like to say.'

Anne had risen also.

'Yes?' she said, as she held out her hand.

Despard paused a minute, picking his words carefully. He took her hand and retained it in his. He looked straight into the wide, beautiful grey eyes.

'Don't be offended with me,' he said. 'I just want to say this: It's humanly possible that there may be some feature of your acqaintanceship with Shaitana that you don't want to come out. If so – don't be angry, please' (he felt the instinctive pull of her hand) – 'you are perfectly within your rights in refusing to answer any questions Battle may ask unless your solicitor is present.'

Anne tore her hand away. Her eyes opened, their grey darkening with anger.

'There's nothing – *nothing* . . . I hardly knew the beastly man.'

'Sorry,' said Major Despard. 'Thought I ought to mention it.'

'It's quite true,' said Rhoda. 'Anne barely knew him. She didn't like him much, but he gave frightfully good parties.'

'That,' said Major Despard grimly, 'seems to have been the only justification for the late Mr Shaitana's existence.'

Anne said in a cold voice:

'Superintendent Battle can ask me anything he likes. I've nothing to hide – *nothing*.'

Despard said very gently, 'Please forgive me.'

She looked at him. Her anger dwindled. She smiled – it was a very sweet smile.'

'It's all right,' she said. 'You meant it kindly, I know.'

She held out her hand again. He took it and said:

'We're in the same boat, you know. We ought to be pals . . .'

It was Anne who went with him to the gate. When she came back Rhoda was staring out of the window and whistling. She turned as her friend entered the room.

'He's frightfully attractive, Anne.'

'He's nice, isn't he?'

'A great deal more than nice . . . I've got an absolute passion for him. Why wasn't I at that damned dinner instead of you? I'd have enjoyed the excitement – the net closing round me – the shadow of the scaffold –'

'No, you wouldn't. You're talking nonsense, Rhoda.'

Anne's voice was sharp. Then it softened as she said:

'It was nice of him to come all this way – for a stranger – a girl he's only met once.'

'Oh, he fell for you. Obviously. Men don't do purely disinterested kindnesses. He wouldn't have come toddling down if you'd been cross-eyed and covered with pimples.'

'Don't you think so?'

'I do not, my good idiot. Mrs Oliver's a *much* more disinterested party.'

'I don't like her,' said Anne abruptly. 'I had a sort of feeling about her . . . I wonder what she really came for?'

'The usual suspicions of your own sex. I dare say Major Despard had an axe to grind if it comes to that.'

'I'm sure he hadn't,' cried Anne hotly.

Then she blushed as Rhoda Dawes laughed.

CHAPTER 14

THIRD VISITOR

Superintendent Battle arrived at Wallingford about six o'clock. It was his intention to learn as much as he could from innocent local gossip before interviewing Miss Anne Meredith.

It was not difficult to glean such information as there was. Without committing himself definitely to any statement, the superintendent nevertheless gave several different impressions of his rank and calling in life.

At least two people would have said confidently that he was a London builder come down to see about a new wing to be added to the cottage, from another you would have learned that he was 'one of these weekenders wanting to take a furnished cottage,' and two more would have said they knew positively, and for a fact, that he was a representative of a hard-court tennis firm.

The information that the superintendent gathered was entirely favourable.

'Wendon Cottage – Yes, that's right – on the Marlbury Road. You can't miss it. Yes, two young ladies. Miss Dawes and Miss Meredith. Very nice young ladies, too. The quiet kind.

'Here for years? Oh, no, not that long. Just over two years. September quarter they come in. Mr Pickersgill they bought it from. Never used it much, he didn't, after his wife died.'

Superintendent Battle's informant had never heard they came from Northumberland. London, *he* thought they came from. Popular in the neighbourhood, though some people were old-fashioned and didn't think two young ladies ought to be living alone. But very quiet, they were. None of this cocktail-drinking weekend lot. Miss Rhoda, she was the dashing one. Miss Meredith was the quiet one. Yes, it was Miss Dawes what paid the bills. She was the one had got the money.

The superintendent's researches at last led him inevitably to Mrs Astwell – who 'did' for the ladies at Wendon Cottage.

Mrs Astwell was a locquacious lady.

'Well, no, sir. I hardly think they'd want to sell. Not so soon. They only got in two years ago. I've done for them from the beginning, yes, sir. Eight o'clock till twelve – those are my hours.

Very nice, lively young ladies, always ready for a joke or a bit of fun. Not stuck up at all.

'Well, of course, I couldn't say if it's the same Miss Dawes *you* knew, sir – the same *family*, I mean. It's my fancy her home's in Devonshire. She gets the cream sent her now and again, and says it reminds her of home; so I think it must be.

'As you say, sir, it's sad for so many young ladies having to earn their living nowadays. These young ladies aren't what you'd call rich, but they have a very pleasant life. It's Miss Dawes has got the money, of course. Miss Anne's her companion, in a manner of speaking, I suppose you might say. The cottage belongs to Miss Dawes.

'I couldn't really say what part Miss Anne comes from. I've heard her mention the Isle of Wight, and I know she doesn't like the North of England; and she and Miss Rhoda were together in Devonshire, because I've heard them joke about the hills and talk about the pretty coves and beaches.'

The flow went on. Every now and then Superintendent Battle made a mental note. Later, a cryptic word or two was jotted down in his little book.

At half-past eight that evening he walked up the path to the door of Wendon Cottage.

It was opened to him by a tall, dark girl wearing a frock of orange cretonne.

'Miss Meredith live here?' inquired Superintendent Battle.

He looked very wooden and soldierly.

'Yes, she does.'

'I'd like to speak to her, please. Superintendent Battle.'

He was immediately favoured with a piercing stare.

'Come in,' said Rhoda Dawes, drawing back from the doorway.

Anne Meredith was sitting in a cosy chair by the fire, sipping coffee. She was wearing embroidered crêpe-de-chine pyjamas.

'It's Superintendent Battle,' said Rhoda, ushering in the guest.

Anne rose and came forward with outstretched hand.

'A bit late for a call,' said Battle. 'But I wanted to find you in, and it's been a fine day.'

Anne smiled.

'Will you have some coffee, Superintendent? Rhoda, fetch another cup.'

'Well, it's very kind of you, Miss Meredith.'

'We think we make rather good coffee,' said Anne.

She indicated a chair, and Superintendent Battle sat down. Rhoda brought a cup, and Anne poured out his coffee. The fire crackled and the flowers in the vases made an agreeable impression upon the superintendent.

It was a pleasant homey atmosphere. Anne seemed self-possessed and at her ease, and the other girl continued to stare at him with devouring interest.

'We've been expecting you,' said Anne.

Her tone was almost reproachful. 'Why have you neglected me?' it seemed to say.

'Sorry, Miss Meredith. I've had a lot of routine work to do.'

'Satisfactory?'

'Not particularly. But it all has to be done. I've turned Dr Roberts inside out, so to speak. And the same for Mrs Lorrimer. And now I've come to do the same for you, Miss Meredith.'

Anne smiled.

'I'm ready.'

'What about Major Despard?' asked Rhoda.

'Oh, he won't be overlooked. I can promise you that,' said Battle.

He set down his coffee-cup and looked towards Anne. She sat up a little straighter in her chair.

'I'm quite ready, superintendent. What do you want to know?'

'Well, roughly, all about yourself, Miss Meredith.'

'I'm quite a respectable person,' said Anne, smiling.

'She's led a blameless life, too,' said Rhoda. 'I can answer for that.'

'Well, that's very nice,' said Superintendent Battle cheerfully. 'You've known Miss Meredith a long time, then?'

'We were at school together,' said Rhoda. 'What ages ago, it seems, doesn't it, Anne?'

'So long ago, you can hardly remember it, I suppose,' said Battle with a chuckle. 'Now, then, Miss Meredith, I'm afraid I'm going to be rather like those forms you fill up for passports.'

'I was born –' began Anne.

'Of poor but honest parents,' Rhoda put in.

Superintendent Battle held up a slightly reproving hand.

'Now, now, young lady,' he said.

'Rhoda, darling,' said Anne gravely. 'It's serious, this.'

'Sorry,' said Rhoda.

'Now, Miss Meredith, you were born – where?'

'At Quetta, in India.'

'Ah, yes. Your people were Army folk?'

'Yes – my father was Major John Meredith. My mother died when I was eleven. Father retired when I was fifteen and went to live in Cheltenham. He died when I was eighteen and left practically no money.'

Battle nodded his head sympathetically.

'Bit of a shock to you, I expect.'

'It was, rather. I always knew that we weren't well off, but to find there was practically nothing – well, that's different.'

'What did you do, Miss Meredith?'

'I had to take a job. I hadn't been particularly well educated and I wasn't clever. I didn't know typing or shorthand, or anything. A friend in Cheltenham found me a job with friends of hers – two small boys home in the holidays, and general help in the house.'

'Name, please?'

'That was Mrs Eldon, The Larches, Ventnor. I stayed there for two years, and then the Eldons went abroad. Then I went to a Mrs Deering.'

'My aunt,' put in Rhoda.

'Yes, Rhoda got me the job. I was very happy. Rhoda used to come and stay sometimes, and we had great fun.'

'What were you there – companion?'

'Yes – it amounted to that.'

'More like under-gardener,' said Rhoda.

She explained:

'My Aunt Emily is just mad on gardening. Anne spent most of her time weeding or putting in bulbs.'

'And you left Mrs Deering?'

'Her health got worse, and she had to have a regular nurse.'

'She's got cancer,' said Rhoda. 'Poor darling, she has to have morphia and things like that.'

'She had been very kind to me. I was very sorry to go,' went on Anne.

'I was looking about for a cottage,' said Rhoda, 'and wanting someone to share it with me. Daddy's married again – not my sort at all. I asked Anne to come here with me, and she's been here ever since.'

'Well, that certainly seems a most blameless life,' said Battle. 'Let's just get the dates clear. You were with Mrs Eldon two years, you say. By the way, what is her address now?'

'She's in Palestine. Her husband has some Government appointment out there – I'm not sure what.'

'Ah, well, I can soon find out. And after that you went to Mrs Deering?'

'I was with her three years,' said Anne quickly. 'Her address is Marsh Dene, Little Hembury, Devon.'

'I see,' said Battle. 'So you are now twenty-five, Miss Meredith. Now, there's just one thing more – the name and address of a couple of people in Cheltenham who knew you and your father.'

Anne supplied him with these.

'Now, about this trip to Switzerland – where you met Mr Shaitana. Did you go alone there – or was Miss Dawes here with you?'

'We went out together. We joined some other people. There was a party of eight.'

'Tell me about your meeting with Mr Shaitana.'

Anne crinkled her brows.

'There's really nothing to tell. He was just there. We knew him in the way you know people in a hotel. He got first prize at the fancy dress ball. He went as Mephistopheles.'

Superintendent Battle sighed.

'Yes, that always was his favourite effect.'

'He really was marvellous,' said Rhoda. 'He hardly had to make up at all.'

The superintendent looked from one girl to the other.

'Which of you two young ladies knew him best?'

Anne hesitated. It was Rhoda who answered.

'Both the same to begin with. Awfully little, that is. You see, our crowd was the ski-ing lot, and we were off doing runs most days and dancing together in the evenings. But then Shaitana seemed to take rather a fancy to Anne. You know, went out of his way to pay her compliments, and all that. We ragged her about it, rather.'

'I just think he did it to annoy me,' said Anne. 'Because I didn't like him. I think it amused him to make me feel embarrassed.'

Rhoda said laughing:

'We told Anne it would be a nice rich marriage for her. She got simply wild with us.'

'Perhaps,' said Battle, 'you'd give me the names of the other people in your party?'

'You aren't what I call a trustful man,' said Rhoda. 'Do you think that every word we're telling you is downright lies?'

Superintendent Battle twinkled.

'I'm going to make sure it isn't, anyway,' he said.

'You *are* suspicious,' said Rhoda.

She scribbled some names on a piece of paper and gave it to him.

Battle rose.

'Well, thank you very much, Miss Meredith,' he said. 'As Miss Dawes says, you seem to have led a particularly blameless life. I don't think you need worry much. It's odd the way Mr Shaitana's manner changed to you. You'll excuse my asking, but he didn't ask you to marry him – or – er – pester you with attentions of another kind?'

'He didn't try to seduce her,' said Rhoda helpfully. 'If that's what you mean.'

Anne was blushing.

'Nothing of the kind,' she said. 'He was always most polite and – and – formal. It was just his elaborate manners that made me uncomfortable.'

'And little things he said or hinted?'

'Yes – at least – no. He never hinted things.'

'Sorry. These lady-killers do sometimes. Well, good-night, Miss Meredith. Thank you very much. Excellent coffee. Goodnight, Miss Dawes.'

'There,' said Rhoda as Anne came back into the room after shutting the door after Battle. 'That's over, and not so very terrible. He's a nice fatherly man, and he evidently doesn't suspect you in the least. It was all ever so much better than I expected.'

Anne sank down with a sigh.

'It was really quite easy,' she said. 'It was silly of me to work myself up so. I thought he'd try to browbeat me – like K.C.s on the stage.'

'He looks sensible,' said Rhoda. 'He'd know well enough you're not a murdering kind of female.'

She hesitated and then said:

'I say, Anne, you didn't mention being at Croftways. Did you forget?'

Anne said slowly:

'I didn't think it counted. I was only there a few months. And there's no one to ask about me there. I can write and tell him if you think it matters; but I'm sure it doesn't. Let's leave it.'

'Right, if you say so.'

Rhoda rose and turned on the wireless.

A raucous voice said:

'You have just heard the Black Nubians play "Why do you tell me lies, Baby?"'

CHAPTER 15

MAJOR DESPARD

Major Despard came out of the Albany, turned sharply into Regent Street and jumped on a bus.

It was the quiet time of day – the top of the bus had very few seats occupied. Despard made his way forward and sat down on the front seat.

He had jumped on the bus while it was going. Now it came to a halt, took up passengers and made its way once more up Regent Street.

A second traveller climbed the steps, made his way forward and sat down in the front seat on the other side.

Despard did not notice the newcomer, but after a few minutes a tentative voice murmured:

'It is a good view of London, is it not, that one gets from the top of a bus?'

Despard turned his head. He looked puzzled for a moment, then his face cleared.

'I beg your pardon, M. Poirot. I didn't see it was you. Yes as you say, one has a good bird's eye view of the world from here. It was better, though, in the old days, when there wasn't all this caged-in glass business.'

Poirot sighed.

'*Tout de même*, it was not always agreeable in the wet weather when the inside was full. And there is much wet weather in this country.'

'Rain? Rain never did any harm to anyone.'

'You are in error,' said Poirot. 'It leads often to a *fluxion de poitrine.*'

Despard smiled.

'I see you belong to the well-wrapped-up school, M. Poirot.'

Poirot was indeed well equipped against any treachery of an autumn day. He wore a greatcoat and a muffler.

'Rather odd, running into you like this,' said Despard.

He did not see the smile that the muffler concealed. There was nothing odd in this encounter. Having ascertained a likely hour for Despard to leave his rooms, Poirot had been waiting for him. He had prudently not risked leaping on the bus, but he had trotted after it to its next stopping-place and boarded it there.

'True. We have not seen each other since the evening at Mr Shaitana's,' he replied.

'Aren't you taking a hand in the business?' asked Despard.

Poirot scratched his ear delicately.

'I reflect,' he said. 'I reflect a good deal. To run to and fro, to make the investigations, that, no. It does not suit my age, my temperament, or my figure.'

Despard said unexpectedly:

'Reflect, eh? Well, you might do worse. There's too much rushing about nowadays. If people sat tight and thought about a thing before they tackled it, there'd be less mess-ups than there are.'

'Is that your procedure in life, Major Despard?'

'Usually,' said the other simply. 'Get your bearings, figure out your route, weigh up the pros and cons, make your decision – stick to it.'

His mouth set grimly.

'And, after that, nothing will turn you from your path, eh?' asked Poirot.

'Oh, I don't say that. No use in being pig-headed over things. If you've made a mistake, admit it.'

'But I imagine that you do not often make a mistake, Major Despard.'

'We all make mistakes, M. Poirot.'

'Some of us,' said Poirot with a certain coldness, possibly due to the pronoun the other had used, 'make less than others.'

Despard looked at him, smiled slightly and said:

'Don't you ever have a failure, M. Poirot?'

'The last time was twenty-eight years ago,' said Poirot with dignity. 'And even then, there were circumstances – but no matter.'

'That seems a pretty good record,' said Despard.

He added: 'What about Shaitana's death? That doesn't count, I suppose, since it isn't officially your business.'

'It is not my business – no. But, all the same, it offends my *amour propre*. I consider it an impertinence, you comprehend, for a murder to be committed under my very nose – by someone who mocks himself at my ability to solve it!'

'Not under *your* nose only,' said Despard drily. 'Under the nose of the Criminal Investigation Department also.'

'That was probably a bad mistake,' said Poirot gravely. 'The good Superintendent Battle, he may look wooden, but he is not wooden in the head – not at all.'

'I agree,' said Despard. 'That stolidity is a pose. He's a very clever and able officer.'

'And I think he is very active in the case.'

'Oh, he's active enough. See a nice quiet soldierly-looking fellow on one of the back seats?'

Poirot looked over his shoulder.

'There is no one here now but ourselves.'

'Oh, well, he's inside, then. He never loses me. Very efficient fellow. Varies his appearance, too, from time to time. Quite artistic about it.'

'Ah, but that would not deceive you. You have the very quick and accurate eye.'

'I never forget a face – even a black one – and that's a lot more than most people can say.'

'You are just the person I need,' said Poirot. 'What a chance, meeting you today! I need someone with a good eye and a good memory. *Malheureusement* the two seldom go together. I have asked the Dr Roberts a question, without result, and the same with Madame Lorrimer. Now, I will try you and see if I get what I want. Cast your mind back to the room in which you played cards at Mr Shaitana's, and tell me what you remember of it.'

Despard looked puzzled.

'I don't quite understand.'

'Give me a description of the room – the furnishings – the objects in it.'

'I don't know that I'm much of a hand at that sort of thing,' said Despard slowly. 'It was a rotten sort of room – to my mind. Not a man's room at all. A lot of brocade and silk and stuff. Sort of room a fellow like Shaitana would have.'

'But to particularize –'

Despard shook his head.

'Afraid I didn't notice . . . He'd got some good rugs. Two Bokharas and three or four really good Persian ones, including a Hamadan and a Tabriz. Rather a good eland head – no, that was in the hall. From Rowland Ward's, I expect.'

'You do not think that the late Mr Shaitana was one to go out and shoot wild beasts?'

'Not he. Never potted anything but sitting game, I'll bet. What else was there? I'm sorry to fail you, but I really can't help much. Any amount of knick-knacks lying about. Tables were thick with them. Only thing I noticed was a rather jolly idol. Easter Island, I should say. Highly polished wood. You don't see many of them. There was some Malay stuff, too. No, I'm afraid I can't help you.'

'No matter,' said Poirot, looking slightly crestfallen.

He went on:

'Do you know, Mrs Lorrimer, she has the most amazing card memory! She could tell me the bidding and play of nearly every hand. It was astonishing.'

Despard shrugged his shoulders.

'Some women are like that. Because they play pretty well all day long, I suppose.'

'You could not do it, eh?'

The other shook his head.

'I just remember a couple of hands. One where I could have got game in diamonds – and Roberts bluffed me out of it. Went down himself, but we didn't double him, worse luck. I remember a no trumper, too. Tricky business – every card wrong. We went down a couple – lucky not to have gone down more.'

'Do you play much bridge, Major Despard?'

'No, I'm not a regular player. It's a good game, though.'

'You prefer it to poker?'

'I do personally. Poker's too much of a gamble.'

Poirot said thoughtfully:

'I do not think Mr Shaitana played any game – any card game, that is.'

'There's only one game that Shaitana played consistently,' said Despard grimly.

'And that?'

'A lowdown game.'

Poirot was silent for a minute, then he said:

'Is it that you *know* that? Or do you just *think* it?'

Despard went brick red.

'Meaning one oughtn't to say things without giving chapter and verse? I suppose that's true. Well, it's accurate enough. I happen to *know*. On the other hand, I'm not prepared to give chapter and verse. Such information as I've got came to me privately.'

'Meaning a woman or women are concerned?'

'Yes. Shaitana, like the dirty dog he was, preferred to deal with women.'

'You think he was a blackmailer? That is interesting.'

Despard shook his head.

'No, no, you've misunderstood me. In a way, Shaitana was a blackmailer, but not the common or garden sort. He wasn't after money. He was a spiritual blackmailer, if there can be such a thing.'

'And he got out of it – what?'

'He got a kick out of it. That's the only way I can put it. He got a thrill out of seeing people quail and flinch. I suppose it made him feel less of a louse and more of a man. And it's a very effective pose with women. He'd only got to hint that he knew everything – and they'd start telling him a lot of things that perhaps he didn't know. That would tickle his sense of humour. Then he'd strut about in his Mephistophelian attitude of "I know everything! I am the great Shaitana!" The man was an ape!'

'So you think that he frightened Miss Meredith that way,' said Poirot slowly.

'Miss Meredith?' Despard stared. 'I wasn't thinking of her. She isn't the kind to be afraid of a man like Shaitana.'

'*Pardon.* You meant Mrs Lorrimer.'

'No, no, no. You misunderstand me. I was speaking generally. It wouldn't be easy to frighten Mrs Lorrimer. And she's not the kind of woman who you can imagine having a guilty secret. No, I was not thinking of anyone in particular.'

'It was the general method to which you referred?'

'Exactly.'

'There is no doubt,' said Poirot slowly, 'that what you call a Dago often has a very clever understanding of women. He knows how to approach them. He worms secrets out of them –'

He paused.

Despard broke in impatiently:

'It's absurd. The man was a mountebank – nothing really dangerous about him. And yet women were afraid of him. Ridiculously so.'

He started up suddenly.

'Hallo, I've overshot the mark. Got too interested in what we were discussing. Goodbye, M. Poirot. Look down and you'll see my faithful shadow leave the bus when I do.'

He hurried to the back and down the steps. The conductor's bell jangled. But a double pull sounded before it had time to stop.

Looking down to the street below, Poirot noticed Despard striding back along the pavement. He did not trouble to pick out the following figure. Something else was interesting him.

'No one in particular,' he murmured to himself. 'Now, I wonder.'

CHAPTER 16

THE EVIDENCE OF ELSIE BATT

Sergeant O'Connor was unkindly nicknamed by his colleagues at the Yard: 'The Maidservant's Prayer.'

There was no doubt that he was an extremely handsome man. Tall, erect, broad-shouldered, it was less the regularity of his features than the roguish and daredevil spark in his eye which made him so irresistible to the fair sex. It was indubitable that Sergeant O'Connor got results, and got them quickly.

So rapid was he, that only four days after the murder of Mr Shaitana, Sergeant O'Connor was sitting in the three-and-sixpenny seats at the *Willy Nilly Revue* side by side with Miss Elsie Batt, late parlourmaid to Mrs Craddock of 117 North Audley Street.

Having laid his line of approach carefully, Sergeant O'Connor was just launching the great offensive.

'– Reminds me,' he was saying, 'of the way one of my old governors used to carry on. Name of Craddock. He was an old cuss, if you like.'

'Craddock,' said Elsie. 'I was with some Craddocks once.'

'Well, that's funny. Wonder whether they were the same?'

'Lived in North Audley Street, they did,' said Elsie.

'My lot were going to London when I left them,' said O'Connor promptly. 'Yes, I believe it *was* North Audley Street. Mrs Craddock was rather a one for the gents.'

Elsie tossed her head.

'I'd no patience with her. Always finding fault and grumbling. Nothing you did right.'

'Her husband got some of it, too, didn't he?'

'She was always complaining he neglected her – that he didn't understand her. And she was always saying how bad her health was and gasping and groaning. Not ill at all, if you ask *me*.'

O'Connor slapped his knee.

'Got it. Wasn't there something about her and some doctor? A bit too thick or something?'

'You mean Dr Roberts? He was a nice gentleman, he was.'

'You girls, you're all alike,' said Sergeant O'Connor. 'The

moment a man's a bad lot, all the girls stick up for him. I know his kind.'

'No, you don't, and you're all wrong about him. There wasn't anything of that kind about him. Wasn't his fault, was it, if Mrs Craddock was always sending for him? What's a doctor to do? If you ask me, he didn't think nothing of her at all, except as a patient. It was all her doing. Wouldn't leave him alone, she wouldn't.'

'That's all very well, Elsie. Don't mind me calling you Elsie, do you? Feel as though I'd known you all my life.'

'Well, you haven't! Elsie, indeed.'

She tossed her head.

'Oh, very well, Miss Batt.' He gave her a glance. 'As I was saying, that's all very well, but the husband, he cut up rough, all the same, didn't he?'

'He was a bit ratty one day,' admitted Elsie. 'But, if you ask me, he was ill at the time. He died just after, you know.'

'I remember – died of something queer, didn't he?'

'Something Japanese, it was – all from a new shaving brush, he'd got. Seems awful, doesn't it, that they're not more careful? I've not fancied anything Japanese since.'

'Buy British, that's my motto,' said Sergeant O'Connor sententiously. 'And you were saying he and the doctor had a row?'

Elsie nodded, enjoying herself as she re-lived past scandals.

'Hammer and tongs, they went at it,' she said. 'At least, the master did. Dr Roberts was ever so quiet. Just said, "Nonsense." And, "What have you got into your head?"'

'This was at the house, I suppose?'

'Yes. She'd sent for him. And then she and the master had words, and in the middle of it Dr Roberts arrived, and the master went for him.'

'What did he say exactly?'

'Well, of course, I wasn't supposed to hear. It was all in the Missus's bedroom. I thought something was up, so I got the dustpan and did the stairs. I wasn't going to miss anything.'

Sergeant O'Connor heartily concurred in this sentiment, reflecting how fortunate it was that Elsie was being approached unofficially. On interrogation by Sergeant O'Connor of the Police, she would have virtuously protested that she had not overheard anything at all.

'As I say,' went on Elsie, 'Dr Roberts, he was very quiet – the master was doing all the shouting.'

'What was he saying?' asked O'Connor, for the second time approaching the vital point.

'Abusing of him proper,' said Elsie with relish.

'How do you mean?'

Would the girl never come to actual words and phrases?

'Well, I don't understand a lot of it,' admitted Elsie. 'There were a lot of long words, "unprofessional conduct," and "taking advantage," and things like that – and I heard him say he'd get Dr Roberts struck off the – Medical Register, would it be? Something like that.'

'That's right,' said O'Connor. 'Complain to the Medical Council.'

'Yes, he said something like that. And the Missus was going on in sort of hysterics, saying "You never cared for me. You neglected me. You left me alone." And I heard her say that Dr Roberts had been an angel of goodness to her.

'And then the doctor, he came through into the dressing-room with the master and shut the door of the bedroom – and he said quite plain:

'"My good man, don't you realize your wife's hysterical? She doesn't know what she's saying. To tell you the truth, it's been a very difficult and trying case, and I'd have thrown it up long ago if I'd thought it was con – con – some long word; oh, yes, consistent – that was it – consistent with my duty." That's what he said. He said something about not over-stepping a boundary, too – something between doctor and patient. He got the master quietened a bit, and then he said:

'"You'll be late at the office, you know. You'd better be off. Just think things over quietly. I think you'll realize that the whole business is a mare's nest. I'll just wash my hands here before I go on to my next case. Now, you think it over, my dear fellow. I can assure you that the whole thing arises out of your wife's disordered imagination."

'And the master, he said, "I don't know what to think."

'And he come out – and, of course, I was brushing hard –

but he never even noticed me. I thought afterwards he looked ill. The doctor, he was whistling quite cheerily and washing his hands in the dressing-room, where there was hot and cold laid on. And presently he came out, with his bag, and he spoke to me very nicely and cheerily, as he always did, and he went down the stairs, quite cheerful and gay and his usual self. So you see, I'm quite sure as he hadn't done anything wrong. It was all her.'

'And then Craddock got this anthrax?'

'Yes, I think he'd got it already. The mistress, she nursed him very devoted, but he died. Lovely wreaths there was at the funeral.'

'And afterwards? Did Dr Roberts come to the house again?'

'No, he didn't, Nosey! You've got some grudge against him. I tell you there was nothing in it. If there were he'd have married her when the master was dead, wouldn't he? And he never did. No such fool. He'd taken her measure all right. She used to ring him up, though, but somehow he was never in. And then she sold the house, and we all got our notices, and she went abroad to Egypt.'

'And you didn't see Dr Roberts in all that time?'

'No. *She* did, because she went to him to have this – what do you call it? – 'noculation against the typhoid fever. She came back with her arm ever so sore with it. If you ask me, he made it clear to her then that there was nothing doing. She didn't ring him up no more, and she went off very cheerful with a lovely lot of new clothes – all light colours, although it was the middle of winter, but she said it would be all sunshine and hot out there.'

'That's right,' said Sergeant O'Connor. 'It's too hot sometimes, I've heard. She died out there. You know that, I suppose?'

'No, indeed I didn't. Well, fancy that! She may have been worse than I thought, poor soul.'

She added with a sigh:

'I wonder what they did with all that lovely lot of clothes. They're blacks out there, so they couldn't wear them.'

'You'd have looked a treat in them, I expect,' said Sergeant O'Connor.

'Impudence,' said Elsie.

'Well, you won't have my impudence much longer,' said Sergeant O'Connor. 'I've got to go away on business for my firm.'

'You going for long?'

'May be going abroad,' said the Sergeant.

Elsie's face fell.

Though unacquainted with Lord Byron's famous poem, 'I never loved a dear gazelle,' etc., its sentiments were at that moment hers. She thought to herself:

'Funny how all the really attractive ones never come to anything. Oh, well, there's always Fred.'

Which is gratifying, since it shows that the sudden incursion of Sergeant O'Connor into Elsie's life did not affect it permanently. 'Fred' may even have been the gainer!

CHAPTER 17

THE EVIDENCE OF RHODA DAWES

Rhoda Dawes came out of Debenham's and stood meditatively upon the pavement. Indecision was written all over her face. It was an expressive face; each fleeting emotion showed itself in a quickly varying expression.

Quite plainly at this moment Rhoda's face said: 'Shall I or shan't I? I'd like to . . . But perhaps I'd better not . . .'

The commissionaire said, 'Taxi, Miss?' to her hopefully.

Rhoda shook her head.

A stout woman carrying parcels with an eager 'shopping early for Christmas' expression on her face, cannoned into her severely, but still Rhoda stood stock-still, trying to make up her mind.

Chaotic odds and ends of thoughts flashed through her mind.

'After all, why shouldn't I? She asked me to – but perhaps it's just a thing she says to everyone . . . She doesn't mean it to be taken seriously . . . Well, after all, Anne didn't want me. She made it quite clear she'd rather go with Major Despard to the solicitor man alone . . . And why shouldn't she? I mean, three *is* a crowd . . . And it isn't really any business of mine . . . It isn't as though I particularly *wanted* to see Major Despard . . . He is nice, though . . . I think he must have fallen for Anne. Men don't take a lot of trouble unless they have . . . I mean, it's never just kindness . . .'

A messenger boy bumped into Rhoda and said, 'Beg pardon, Miss,' in a reproachful tone.

'Oh, dear,' thought Rhoda. 'I can't go on standing here all day. Just because I'm such an idiot that I can't make up my mind . . . I think that coat and skirt's going to be awfully nice. I wonder if brown would have been more useful than green? No, I don't think so. Well, come on, shall I go or shan't I? Half-past three, it's quite a good time – I mean, it doesn't look as though I'm cadging a meal or anything. I might just go and look, anyway.'

She plunged across the road, turned to the right, and then to the left, up Harley Street, finally pausing by the block of flats always airily described by Mrs Oliver as 'all among the nursing homes.'

'Well, she can't eat me,' thought Rhoda, and plunged boldly into the building.

Mrs Oliver's flat was on the top floor. A uniformed attendant whisked her up in a lift and decanted her on a smart new mat outside a bright green door.

'This is awful,' thought Rhoda. 'Worse than dentists. I must go through with it now, though.'

Pink with embarrassment, she pushed the bell.

The door was opened by an elderly maid.

'Is – could I – is Mrs Oliver at home?' asked Rhoda.

The maid drew back, Rhoda entered, she was shown into a very untidy drawing-room. The maid said:

'What name shall I say, please?'

'Oh – eh – Miss Dawes – Miss Rhoda Dawes.'

The maid withdrew. After what seemed to Rhoda about a hundred years, but was really exactly a minute and forty-five seconds, the maid returned.

'Will you step this way, Miss?'

Pinker than ever, Rhoda followed her. Along a passage, round a corner, a door was opened. Nervously she entered into what seemed at first to her startled eyes to be an African forest!

Birds – masses of birds, parrots, macaws, birds unknown to ornithology, twined themselves in and out of what seemed to be a primeval forest. In the middle of this riot of bird and vegetable life, Rhoda perceived a battered kitchen-table with a typewriter on it, masses of typescript littered all over the floor and Mrs Oliver, her hair in wild confusion, rising from a somewhat rickety-looking chair.

'My dear, how nice to see you,' said Mrs Oliver, holding out a carbon-stained hand and trying with her other hand to smooth her hair, a quite impossible proceeding.

A paper bag, touched by her elbow, fell from the desk, and apples rolled energetically all over the floor.

'Never mind, my dear, don't bother, someone will pick them up some time.'

Rather breathless, Rhoda rose from a stooping position with five apples in her grasp.

'Oh, thank you – no, I shouldn't put them back in the bag. I think it's got a hole in it. Put them on the mantelpiece. That's right. Now, then, sit down and let's talk.'

Rhoda accepted a second battered chair and focussed her eyes on her hostess.

'I say, I'm terribly sorry. Am I interrupting, or anything?' she asked breathlessly.

'Well, you are and you aren't,' said Mrs Oliver. 'I *am* working, as you see. But that dreadful Finn of mine has got himself terribly tangled up. He did some awfully clever deduction with a dish of French beans, and now he's just detected deadly poison in the sage-and-onion stuffing of the Michaelmas goose, and I've just remembered that French beans are over by Michaelmas.'

Thrilled by this peep into the inner world of creative detective fiction, Rhoda said breathlessly, 'They might be tinned.'

'They might, of course,' said Mrs Oliver doubtfully. 'But it would rather spoil the point. I'm always getting tangled up in horticulture and things like that. People write to me and say I've got the wrong flowers all out together. As though it mattered – and anyway, they are all out together in a London shop.'

'Of course it doesn't matter,' said Rhoda loyally. 'Oh, Mrs Oliver, it must be marvellous to write.'

Mrs Oliver rubbed her forehead with a carbonny finger and said:

'Why?'

'Oh,' said Rhoda, a little taken aback. 'Because it must. It must be wonderful just to sit down and write off a whole book.'

'It doesn't happen exactly like that,' said Mrs Oliver. 'One actually has to *think*, you know. And thinking is always a bore. And you have to plan things. And then one gets stuck every now and then, and you feel you'll never get out of the mess – but you do! Writing's not particularly enjoyable. It's hard work like everything else.'

'It doesn't seem like work,' said Rhoda.

'Not to *you*,' said Mrs Oliver, 'because you don't have to do it! It feels very like work to me. Some days I can only keep going by repeating over and over to myself the amount of money I might get for my next serial rights. That spurs you on, you know. So does your bankbook when you see how much overdrawn you are.'

'I never imagined you actually typed your books yourself,' said Rhoda. 'I thought you'd have a secretary.'

'I did have a secretary, and I used to try and dictate to her, but she was so competent that it used to depress me. I felt she knew so much more about English and grammar and full stops and semi-colons than I did, that it gave me a kind of inferiority complex. Then I tried having a thoroughly incompetent secretary, but, of course, that didn't answer very well, either.'

'It must be so wonderful to be able to think of things,' said Rhoda.

'I can always think of things,' said Mrs Oliver happily. 'What is so tiring is writing them down. I always think I've finished, and then when I count up I find I've only written thirty thousand words instead of sixty thousand, and so then I have to throw in another murder and get the heroine kidnapped again. It's all very boring.'

Rhoda did not answer. She was staring at Mrs Oliver with the reverence felt by youth for celebrity – slightly tinged by disappointment.

'Do you like the wallpaper?' asked Mrs Oliver waving an airy hand. 'I'm frightfully fond of birds. The foliage is supposed to be tropical. It makes me feel it's a hot day, even when it's freezing. I can't do anything unless I feel very, very warm. But Sven Hjerson breaks the ice on his bath every morning!'

'I think it's all marvellous,' said Rhoda. 'And it's awfully nice of you to say I'm not interrupting you.'

'We'll have some coffee and toast,' said Mrs Oliver. 'Very black coffee and very hot toast. I can always eat that any time.'

She went to the door, opened it and shouted. Then she returned and said:

'What brings you to town – shopping?'

'Yes, I've been doing some shopping.'

'Is Miss Meredith up, too?'

'Yes, she's gone with Major Despard to a solicitor.'

'Solicitor, eh?'

Mrs Oliver's eyebrows rose inquiringly.

'Yes. You see, Major Despard told her she ought to have one. He's been awfully kind – he really has.'

'I was kind, too,' said Mrs Oliver, 'but it didn't seem to go down very well, did it? In fact, I think your friend rather resented my coming.'

'Oh, she didn't – really she didn't.' Rhoda wriggled on her chair in a paroxysm of embarrassment. 'That's really one reason why I wanted to come today – to explain. You see, I saw you had got it all wrong. She did seem very ungracious, but it wasn't that, really. I mean, it wasn't your coming. It was something you said.'

'Something I *said*?'

'Yes. You couldn't tell, of course. It was just unfortunate.'

'What did I say?'

'I don't expect you remember, even. It was just the way you put it. You said something about an accident and poison.'

'Did I?'

'I knew you'd probably not remember. Yes. You see, Anne had a ghastly experience once. She was in a house where a woman took some poison – hat paint, I think it was – by mistake for something else. And she died. And, of course, it was an awful shock to Anne. She can't bear thinking of it or speaking of it. And your saying that reminded her, of course, and she dried up and got all stiff and queer like she does. And I saw you noticed it. And I couldn't say anything in front of her. But I did want you to know that it wasn't what you thought. She wasn't ungrateful.'

Mrs Oliver looked at Rhoda's flushed eager face. She said slowly:

'I see.'

'Anne's awfully sensitive,' said Rhoda. 'And she's bad about – well, facing things. If anything's upset her, she'd just rather not talk about it, although that isn't any good, really – at least, I don't think so. Things are there just the same – whether you talk about them or not. It's only running away from them to pretend they don't exist. I'd rather have it all out, however painful it would be.'

'Ah,' said Mrs Oliver quietly. 'But you, my dear, are a soldier. Your Anne isn't.'

Rhoda flushed.

'Anne's a darling.'

Mrs Oliver smiled.

She said, 'I didn't say she wasn't. I only said she hadn't got your particular brand of courage.'

She sighed, then said rather unexpectedly to the girl:

'Do you believe in the value of truth, my dear, or don't you?'

'Of course I believe in the truth,' said Rhoda staring.

'Yes, you say that – but perhaps you haven't thought about it. The truth hurts sometimes – and destroys one's illusions.'

'I'd rather have it, all the same,' said Rhoda.

'So would I. But I don't know that we're wise.'

Rhoda said earnestly:

'Don't tell Anne, will you, what I've told you? She wouldn't like it.'

'I certainly shouldn't dream of doing any such thing. Was this long ago?

'About four years ago. It's odd, isn't it, how the same things happen again and again to people. I had an aunt who was always in shipwrecks. And here's Anne mixed up in two sudden deaths – only, of course, this one is much worse. Murder's rather awful, isn't it?'

'Yes, it is.'

The black coffee and the hot buttered toast appeared at this minute.

Rhoda ate and drank with childish gusto. It was very exciting to her thus to be sharing an intimate meal with a celebrity.

When they had finished she rose and said:

'I do hope I haven't interrupted you too terribly. Would you mind – I mean, would it bother you awfully – if I sent one of your books to you, would you sign it for me?'

'Mrs Oliver laughed.

'Oh, I can do better than that for you.' She opened a cupboard at the far end of the room. 'Which would you like? I rather fancy *The Affair of the Second Goldfish* myself. It's not quite such frightful tripe as the rest.'

A little shocked at hearing an authoress thus describe the children of her pen, Rhoda accepted eagerly. Mrs Oliver took the book, opened it, inscribed her name with a superlative flourish and handed it to Rhoda.

'There you are.'

'Thank you very much. I have enjoyed myself. Sure you didn't mind my coming?'

'I wanted you to,' said Mrs Oliver.

She added after a moment's pause:

'You're a nice child. Goodbye. Take care of yourself, my dear.'

'Now, why did I say that?' she murmured to herself as the door closed behind her guest.

She shook her head, ruffled her hair, and returned to the masterly dealings of Sven Hjerson with the sage-and-onion stuffing.

CHAPTER 18

TEA INTERLUDE

Mrs Lorrimer came out of a certain door in Harley Street.

She stood for a minute at the top of the steps, and then she descended them slowly.

There was a curious expression on her face – a mingling of grim determination and of strange indecision. She bent her brows a little, as though to concentrate on some all-absorbing problem.

It was just then that she caught sight of Anne Meredith on the opposite pavement.

Anne was standing staring up at a big block of flats just on the corner.

Mrs Lorrimer hesitated a moment, then she crossed the road.

'How do you do, Miss Meredith?'

Anne started and turned.

'Oh, how do you do?'

'Still in London?' said Mrs Lorrimer.

'No. I've only come up for the day. To do some legal business.'

Her eyes were still straying to the big block of flats.

Mrs Lorrimer said:

'Is anything the matter?'

Anne started guiltily.

'The matter? Oh, no, what should be the matter?'

'You were looking as though you had something on your mind.'

'I haven't – well, at least I have, but it's nothing important, something quite silly.' She laughed a little.

She went on:

'It's only that I thought I saw my friend – the girl I live with – go in there, and I wondered if she'd gone to see Mrs Oliver.'

'Is that where Mrs Oliver lives? I didn't know.'

'Yes. She came to see us the other day and she gave us her address and asked us to come and see her. I wondered if it was Rhoda I saw or not.'

'Do you want to go up and see?'

'No, I'd rather not do that.'

'Come and have tea with me,' said Mrs Lorrimer. 'There is a shop quite near here that I know.'

'It's very kind of you,' said Anne, hesitating.

Side by side they walked down the street and turned into a side street. In a small pastry-cook's they were served with tea and muffins.

They did not talk much. Each of them seemed to find the other's silence restful.

Anne asked suddenly:

'Has Mrs Oliver been to see you?'

Mrs Lorrimer shook her head.

'No one has been to see me except M. Poirot.'

'I didn't mean –' began Anne.

'Didn't you? I think you did,' said Mrs Lorrimer.

The girl looked up – a quick, frightened glance. Something she saw in Mrs Lorrimer's face seemed to reassure her.

'He hasn't been to see me,' she said slowly.

There was a pause.

'Hasn't Superintendent Battle been to see you?' asked Anne.

'Oh, yes, of course,' said Mrs Lorrimer.

Anne said hesitatingly:

'What sort of things did he ask you?'

Mrs Lorrimer sighed wearily.

'The usual things, I suppose. Routine inquiries. He was very pleasant over it all.'

'I suppose he interviewed everyone?'

'I should think so.'

There was another pause.

Anne said:

'Mrs Lorrimer, do you think – they will ever find out who did it?'

Her eyes were bent on her plate. She did not see the curious expression in the older woman's eyes as she watched the downcast head.

Mrs Lorrimer said quietly:

'I don't know . . .'

Anne murmured:

'It's not – very nice, is it?'

There was that same curious appraising and yet sympathetic look on Mrs Lorrimer's face, as she asked:

'How old are you, Anne Meredith?'

'I – I?' the girl stammered. 'I'm twenty-five.'

'And I'm sixty-three,' said Mrs Lorrimer.

She went on slowly:

'Most of your life is in front of you . . .'

Anne shivered.

'I might be run over by a bus on the way home,' she said.

'Yes, that's true. And I – might not.'

She said it in an odd way. Anne looked at her in astonishment.

'Life is a difficult business,' said Mrs Lorrimer. 'You'll know that when you come to my age. It needs infinite courage and a lot of endurance. And in the end one wonders: "Was it worth while?"'

'Oh, *don't*,' said Anne.

Mrs Lorrimer laughed, her old competent self again.

'It's rather cheap to say gloomy things about life,' she said.

She called the waitress and settled the bill.

As they got to the shop door a taxi crawled past, and Mrs Lorrimer hailed it.

'Can I give you a lift?' she asked. 'I am going south of the park.'

Anne's face had lighted up.

'No, thank you. I see my friend turning the corner. Thank you so much, Mrs Lorrimer. Goodbye.'

'Goodbye. Good luck,' said the older woman.

She drove away and Anne hurried forward.

Rhoda's face lit up when she saw her friend, then changed to a slightly guilty expression.

'Rhoda, have you been to see Mrs Oliver?' demanded Anne.

'Well, as a matter of fact, I have.'

'And I just caught you.'

'I don't know what you mean by caught. Let's go down here and take a bus. You'd gone off on your own ploys with the boy friend. I thought at least he'd give you tea.'

Anne was silent for a minute – a voice ringing in her ears.

'Can't we pick up your friend somewhere and all have tea together?'

And her own answer – hurried, without taking time to think:

'Thanks awfully, but we've got to go out to tea together with some people.'

A lie – and such a silly lie. The stupid way one said the first thing that came into one's head instead of just taking a minute or two to think. Perfectly easy to have said 'Thanks, but my friend has got to go out to tea.' That is, if you didn't, as she hadn't, wanted to have Rhoda too.

Rather odd, that, the way she hadn't wanted Rhoda. She had wanted, definitely, to keep Despard to herself. She had felt jealous. Jealous of Rhoda. Rhoda was so bright, so ready to talk, so full of enthusiasm and life. The other evening Major Despard had looked as though he thought Rhoda nice. But it was her, Anne Meredith, he had come down to see. Rhoda was like that. She didn't mean it, but she reduced you to the background. No, definitely she hadn't wanted Rhoda there.

But she had managed it very stupidly, getting flurried like that. If she'd managed better, she might be sitting now having tea with Major Despard at his club or somewhere.

She felt definitely annoyed with Rhoda. Rhoda was a nuisance. And what had she been doing going to see Mrs Oliver?

Out loud she said:

'Why did you go and see Mrs Oliver?'

'Well, she asked us to.'

'Yes, but I didn't suppose she really meant it. I expect she always has to say that.'

'She did mean it. She was awfully nice – couldn't have been nicer. She gave me one of her books. Look.'

Rhoda flourished her prize.

Anne said suspiciously:

'What did you talk about? Not me?'

'Listen to the conceit of the girl!'

'No, but did you? Did you talk about the – the murder?'

'We talked about her murders. She's writing one where there's poison in the sage and onions. She was frightfully human – and said writing was awfully hard work and how she got into tangles with plots, and we had black coffee and hot buttered toast,' finished Rhoda in a triumphant burst.

Then she added:

'Oh, Anne, you want your tea.'

'No, I don't. I've had it. With Mrs Lorrimer.'

'Mrs Lorrimer? Isn't that the one – the one who was there?'

Anne nodded.

'Where did you come across her? Did you go and see her?'

'No. I ran across her in Harley Street.'

'What was she like?'

Anne said slowly:

'I don't know. She was – rather queer. Not at all like the other night.'

'Do you still think she did it?' asked Rhoda.

Anne was silent for a minute or two. Then she said:

'I don't know. Don't let's talk of it, Rhoda! You know how I hate talking of things.'

'All right, darling. What was the solicitor like? Very dry and legal?'

'Rather alert and Jewish.'

'Sounds all right.' She waited a little and then said:

'How was Major Despard?'

'Very kind.'

'He's fallen for you, Anne. I'm sure he has.'

'Rhoda, don't talk nonsense.'

'Well, you'll see.'

Rhoda began humming to herself. She thought:

'Of course he's fallen for her. Anne's awfully pretty. But a bit wishy-washy . . . She'll never go on treks with him. Why, she'd scream if she saw a snake . . . Men always do take fancies to unsuitable women.'

Then she said aloud.

'That bus will take us to Paddington. We'll just catch the 4.48.'

CHAPTER 19

CONSULTATION

The telephone rang in Poirot's room and a respectful voice spoke.

'Sergeant O'Connor. Superintendent Battle's compliments and would it be convenient for Mr Hercule Poirot to come to Scotland Yard at 11.30?'

Poirot replied in the affirmative and Sergeant O'Connor rang off.

It was 11.30 to the minute when Poirot descended from his taxi at the door of New Scotland Yard – to be at once seized upon by Mrs Oliver.

'M. Poirot. How splendid! Will you come to my rescue?'

'*Enchanté*, madame. What can I do?'

'Pay my taxi for me. I don't know how it happened but I brought out the bag I keep my going-abroad money in and the man simply won't take francs or liras or marks!'

Poirot gallantly produced some loose change, and he and Mrs Oliver went inside the building together.

They were taken to Superintendent Battle's own room. The superintendent was sitting behind a table and looking more wooden than ever. 'Just like a little piece of modern sculpture,' whispered Mrs Oliver to Poirot.

Battle rose and shook hands with them both and they sat down.

'I thought it was about time for a little meeting,' said Battle. 'You'd like to hear how I've got on, and I'd like to hear how you've got on. We're just waiting for Colonel Race and then –'

But at that moment the door opened and the colonel appeared.

'Sorry I'm late, Battle. How do you do, Mrs Oliver. Hallo, M. Poirot. Very sorry if I've kept you waiting. But I'm off tomorrow and had a lot of things to see to.'

'Where are you going to?' asked Mrs Oliver.

'A little shooting trip – Baluchistan way.'

Poirot said, smiling ironically:

'A little trouble, is there not, in that part of the world? You will have to be careful.'

'I mean to be,' said Race gravely – but his eyes twinkled.

'Got anything for us, sir?' asked Battle.

'I've got you your information re Despard. Here it is –'

He pushed over a sheaf of papers.

'There's a mass of dates and places there. Most of it quite irrelevant, I should imagine. Nothing against him. He's a stout fellow. Record quite unblemished. Strict disciplinarian. Liked and trusted by the natives everywhere. One of their cumbrous names for him in Africa, where they go in for such things, is "The man who keeps his mouth shut and judges fairly." General opinion of the white races that Despard is a Pukka Sahib. Fine shot. Cool head. Generally long-sighted and dependable.'

Unmoved by this eulogy, Battle asked:

'Any sudden deaths connected with him?'

'I laid special stress on that point. There's one fine rescue to his credit. Pal of his was being mauled by a lion.'

Battle sighed.

'It's not rescues I want.'

'You're a persistent fellow, Battle. There's only one incident I've been able to rake up that might suit your book. Trip into the interior in South America. Despard accompanied Professor Luxmore, the celebrated botanist, and his wife. The professor died of fever and was buried somewhere up the Amazon.'

'Fever – eh?'

'Fever. But I'll play fair with you. One of the native bearers (who was sacked for stealing, incidentally) had a story that the professor didn't die of fever, but was shot. The rumour was never taken seriously.'

'About time it was, perhaps.'

Race shook his head.

'I've given you the facts. You asked for them and you're entitled to them, but I'd lay long odds against its being Despard who did the dirty work the other evening. He's a white man, Battle.'

'Incapable of murder, you mean?'

Colonel Race hesitated.

'Incapable of what I'd call murder – yes,' he said.

'But not incapable of killing a man for what would seem to him good and sufficient reasons, is that it?'

'If so, they *would* be good and sufficient reasons!'

Battle shook his head.

'You can't have human beings judging other human beings and taking the law into their own hands.'

'It happens, Battle – it happens.'

'It shouldn't happen – that's my point. What do you say, M. Poirot?'

'I agree with you, Battle. I have always disapproved of murder.'

'What a delightfully droll way of putting it,' said Mrs Oliver. 'Rather as though it were fox-hunting or killing ospreys for hats. Don't you think there are people who ought to be murdered?'

'That, very possibly.'

'Well then!'

'You do not comprehend. It is not the victim who concerns me so much. It is the effect on the character of the slayer.'

'What about war?'

'In war you do not exercise the right of private judgement. *That* is what is so dangerous. Once a man is imbued with the idea that he knows who ought to be allowed to live and who ought not – then he is halfway to becoming the most dangerous killer there is – the arrogant criminal who kills not for profit – but for an idea. He has usurped the functions of *le bon Dieu*.'

Colonel Race rose:

'I'm sorry I can't stop with you. Too much to do. I'd like to see the end of this business. Shouldn't be surprised if there never was an end. Even if you find out who did it, it's going to be next to impossible to prove. I've given you the facts you wanted, but in my opinion Despard's not the man. I don't believe he's ever committed murder. Shaitana may have heard some garbled rumour of Professor Luxmore's death, but I don't believe there's more to it than that. Despard's a white man, and I don't believe he's ever been a murderer. That's my opinion. And I know something of men.'

'What's Mrs Luxmore like?' asked Battle.

'She lives in London, so you can see for yourself. You'll find the address among those papers. Somewhere in South Kensington. But I repeat, Despard isn't the man.'

Colonel Race left the room, stepping with the springy noiseless tread of a hunter.

Battle nodded his head thoughtfully as the door closed behind him.

'He's probably right,' he said. 'He knows men, Colonel Race does. But all the same, one can't take anything for granted.'

He looked through the mass of documents Race had deposited on the table, occasionally making a pencil note on the pad beside him.

'Well, Superintendent Battle,' said Mrs Oliver. 'Aren't you going to tell us what you have been doing?'

He looked up and smiled, a slow smile that creased his wooden face from side to side.

'This is all very irregular, Mrs Oliver. I hope you realize that.'

'Nonsense,' said Mrs Oliver. 'I don't suppose for a moment you'll tell us anything you don't want to.'

Battle shook his head.

'No,' he said decidedly. 'Cards on the table. That's the motto for this business. I mean to play fair.'

Mrs Oliver hitched her chair nearer.

'Tell us,' she begged.

Superintendent Battle said slowly:

'First of all, I'll say this. As far as the actual murder of Mr Shaitana goes, I'm not a penny the wiser. There's no hint or clue of any kind to be found in his papers. As for the four others, I've had them shadowed, naturally, but without any tangible result. No, as M. Poirot said, there's only one hope – the past. Find out what crime exactly (if any, that is to say – after all, Shaitana may have been talking through his hat to make an impression on M. Poirot) these people have committed – and it may tell you who committed this crime.'

'Well, have you found out anything?'

'I've got a line on one of them.'

'Which?'

'Dr Roberts.'

Mrs Oliver looked at him with thrilled expectation.

'As M. Poirot here knows, I tried out all kinds of theories. I established the fact pretty clearly that none of his immediate family had met with a sudden death. I've explored every alley as well as I could, and the whole thing boils down to one possibility – and rather an outside possibility at that. A few years ago Roberts must have been guilty of indiscretion, at least, with one of his lady patients. There may have been nothing in it – probably wasn't. But the woman was the hysterical, emotional kind who likes to make a scene, and either the husband got wind of what was going on, or his wife "confessed". Anyway, the fat was in the fire as far as the doctor was concerned. Enraged husband threatening to report him to the General Medical Council – which would probably have meant the ruin of his professional career.'

'What happened?' demanded Mrs Oliver breathlessly.

'Apparently Roberts managed to calm down the irate gentleman temporarily – and he died of anthrax almost immediately afterwards.'

'Anthrax? But that's a cattle disease?'

The superintendent grinned.

'Quite right, Mrs Oliver. It isn't the untraceable arrow poison of the South American Indians! You may remember that there was rather a scare about infected shaving brushes of cheap make about that time. Craddock's shaving brush was proved to have been the cause of infection.'

'Did Dr Roberts attend him?'

'Oh, no. Too canny for that. Dare say Craddock wouldn't have wanted him in any case. The only evidence I've got – and that's precious little – is that among the doctor's patients there *was* a case of anthrax at the time.'

'You mean the doctor infected the shaving brush?'

'That's the big idea. And mind you, it's only an idea. Nothing whatever to go on. Pure conjecture. But it could be.'

'He didn't marry Mrs Craddock afterwards?'

'Oh, dear me, no, I imagine the affection was always on the lady's side. She tended to cut up rough, I hear, but suddenly went off to Egypt quite happily for the winter. She died there. A case of some obscure blood-poisoning. It's got a long name, but I don't expect it would convey much to you. Most uncommon in this country, fairly common among the natives in Egypt.'

'So the doctor couldn't have poisoned her?'

'I don't know,' said Battle slowly. 'I've been chatting to a bacteriologist friend of mine – awfully difficult to get straight answers out of these people. They never can say yes or no. It's always "that might be possible under certain conditions" – "it would depend on the pathological condition of the recipient" – "such cases have been known" – "a lot depends on individual idiosyncrasy" – all that sort of stuff. But as far as I could pin my friend down I got at this – the germ, or germs, I suppose, might have been introduced into the blood before leaving England. The symptoms would not make their appearance for some time to come.'

Poirot asked:

'Was Mrs Craddock inoculated for typhoid before going to Egypt? Most people are, I fancy.'

'Good for you, M. Poirot.'

'And Dr Roberts did the inoculation?'

'That's right. There you are again – we can't prove anything. She had the usual two inoculations – and they may have been typhoid inoculations for all we know. Or one of them may have been typhoid inoculation and the other – something else. We don't know. We never shall know. The whole thing is pure hypothesis. All we can say is: it might be.'

Poirot nodded thoughtfully.

'It agrees very well with some remarks made to me by Mr Shaitana. He was exalting the successful murderer – the man against whom his crime could never be brought home.'

'How did Mr Shaitana know about it, then?' asked Mrs Oliver. Poirot shrugged his shoulders.

'That we shall never learn. He himself was in Egypt at one time. We know that, because he met Mrs Lorrimer there. He may have heard some local doctor comment on curious features of Mrs Craddock's case – a wonder as to how the infection arose. At some other time he may have heard gossip about Roberts and Mrs Craddock. He might have amused himself by making some cryptic remark to the doctor and noted the startled awareness in his eye – all that one can never know. Some people have an uncanny gift of divining secrets. Mr Shaitana was one of those people. All that does not concern us. We have only to say – he guessed. Did he guess right?'

'Well, I think he did,' said Battle. 'I've a feeling that our cheerful, genial doctor wouldn't be too scrupulous. I've known one or two like him – wonderful how certain types resemble each other. In my opinion he's a killer all right. He killed Craddock. He may have killed Mrs Craddock if she was beginning to be a nuisance and cause a scandal. *But did he kill Shaitana?* That's the real question. And comparing the crimes, I rather doubt it. In the case of the Craddocks he used medical methods each time. The deaths appeared to be due to natural causes. In my opinion if he had killed Shaitana, he would have done so in a medical way. He'd have used the germ and not the knife.'

'I never thought it was him,' said Mrs Oliver. 'Not for a minute. He's too obvious, somehow.'

'Exit Roberts,' murmured Poirot. 'And the others?'

Battle made a gesture of impatience.

'I've pretty well drawn blank. Mrs Lorrimer's been a widow for twenty years now. She's lived in London most of the time, occasionally going abroad in the winter. Civilized places – the Riviera, Egypt, that sort of thing. Can't find any mysterious death associated with her. She seems to have led a perfectly normal, respectable life – the life of a woman of the world. Everyone seems to respect her and to have the highest opinion of her character. The worst that they can say about her is that she doesn't suffer fools gladly! I don't mind admitting I've been beaten all along the line there. And yet there must be *something*! Shaitana thought there was.'

He sighed in a dispirited manner.

'Then there's Miss Meredith. I've got her history taped out quite clearly. Usual sort of story. Army officer's daughter. Left with very little money. Had to earn her living. Not properly trained for anything. I've checked up on her early days at Cheltenham. All quite straightforward. Everyone very sorry for the poor little thing. She went first to some people in the Isle of Wight – kind of nursery-governess and mother's help. The woman she was with is out in Palestine but I've talked with her sister and she says Mrs Eldon liked the girl very much. Certainly no mysterious deaths nor anything of that kind.

'When Mrs Eldon went abroad, Miss Meredith went to Devonshire and took a post as companion to an aunt of a school friend. The school friend is the girl she is living with now – Miss Rhoda Dawes. She was there over two years until Miss Dawes got too ill and she had to have a regular trained nurse. Cancer, I gather. She's alive still, but very vague. Kept under morphia a good deal, I imagine. I had an interview with her. She remembered "Anne," said she was a nice child. I also talked to a neighbour of hers who would be better able to remember the happenings of the last few years. No deaths in the parish except one or two of the older villagers, with whom, as far as I can make out, Anne Meredith never came into contact.

'Since then there's been Switzerland. Thought I might get on the track of some fatal accident there, but nothing doing. And there's nothing in Wallingford either.'

'So Anne Meredith is acquitted?' asked Poirot.

Battle hesitated.

'I wouldn't say that. There's *something* . . . There's a scared look about her that can't quite be accounted for by panic over Shaitana. She's too watchful. Too much on the alert. I'd swear there was *something*. But there it is – she's led a perfectly blameless life.'

Mrs Oliver took a deep breath – a breath of pure enjoyment.

'And yet,' she said, 'Anne Meredith was in the house when a woman took poison by mistake and died.'

She had nothing to complain of in the effect her words produced.

Superintendent Battle spun round in his chair and stared at her in amazement.

'Is this true, Mrs Oliver? How do you know?'

'I've been sleuthing,' said Mrs Oliver. 'I get on with girls. I went down to see those two and told them a cock-and-bull story about suspecting Dr Roberts. The Rhoda girl was friendly – oh, and rather impressed by thinking I was a celebrity. The little Meredith hated my coming and showed it quite plainly. She was suspicious. Why should she be if she hadn't got anything to hide? I asked either of them to come and see me in London. The Rhoda girl did. And she blurted the whole thing out. How Anne had been rude to me the other day because something I'd said had reminded her of a painful incident, and then she went on to describe the incident.'

'Did she say when and where it happened?'

'Three years ago in Devonshire.'

The superintendent muttered something under his breath and scribbled on his pad. His wooden calm was shaken.

Mrs Oliver sat enjoying her triumph. It was a moment of great sweetness to her.

'I take off my hat to you, Mrs Oliver,' he said. 'You've put one over on us this time. That is very valuable information. And it just shows how easily you can miss a thing.'

He frowned a little.

'She can't have been there – wherever it was – long. A couple of months at most. It must have been between the Isle of Wight and going to Miss Dawes. Yes, that could be it right enough. Naturally Mrs Eldon's sister only remembers she went off to a place in Devonshire – she doesn't remember exactly who or where.'

'Tell me,' said Poirot, 'was this Mrs Eldon an untidy woman?'

Battle bent a curious gaze upon him.

'It's odd your saying that, M. Poirot. I don't see how you could have known. The sister was rather a precise party. In talking I remember her saying "My sister is so dreadfully untidy and slapdash." But how did you know?'

'Because she needed a mother's-help,' said Mrs Oliver.

Poirot shook his head.

'No, no, it was not that. It is of no moment. I was only curious. Continue, Superintendent Battle.'

'In the same way,' went on Battle, 'I took it for granted that she went to Miss Dawes straight from the Isle of Wight. She's sly, that girl. She deceived me all right. Lying the whole time.'

'Lying is not always a sign of guilt,' said Poirot.

'I know that, M. Poirot. There's the natural liar. I should say she was one, as a matter of fact. Always says the thing that sounds best. But all the same it's a pretty grave risk to take, suppressing facts like that.'

'She wouldn't know you had any idea of past crimes,' said Mrs Oliver.

'That's all the more reason for not suppressing that little piece of information. It must have been accepted as a bona fide case of accidental death, so she'd nothing to fear – *unless she were guilty.*'

'Unless she were guilty of the Devonshire death, yes,' said Poirot.

Battle turned to him.

'Oh, I know. Even if that accidental death turns out to be not so accidental, *it doesn't follow that she killed Shaitana.* But these other murders are murders too. I want to be able to bring home a crime to the person responsible for it.'

'According to Mr Shaitana, that is impossible,' remarked Poirot.

'It is in Roberts' case. It remains to be seen if it is in Miss Meredith's. I shall go down to Devon tomorrow.'

'Will you know where to go?' asked Mrs Oliver. 'I didn't like to ask Rhoda for more details.'

'No, that was wise of you. I shan't have much difficulty. There must have been an inquest. I shall find it in the coroner's records. That's routine police work. They'll have it all typed out for me by tomorrow morning.'

'What about Major Despard?' asked Mrs Oliver. 'Have you found out anything about him?'

'I've been waiting for Colonel Race's report. I've had him shadowed, of course. One rather interesting thing, he went down to see Miss Meredith at Wallingford. You remember he said he'd never met her until the other night.'

'But she is a very pretty girl,' murmured Poirot.

Battle laughed.

'Yes, I expect that's all there is to it. By the way, Despard's taking no chances. He's already consulted a solicitor. That looks as though he's expecting trouble.'

'He is a man who looks ahead,' said Poirot. 'He is a man who prepares for every contingency.'

'And therefore not the kind of man to stick a knife into a man in a hurry,' said Battle with a sigh.

'Not unless it was the only way,' said Poirot. 'He can act quickly, remember.'

Battle looked across the table at him.

'Now, M. Poirot, what about your cards? Haven't seen your hand down on the table yet.'

Poirot smiled.

'There is so little in it. You think I conceal facts from you? It is not so. I have not learned many facts. I have talked with Dr Roberts, with Mrs Lorrimer, with Major Despard (I have still to talk to Miss Meredith) and what have I learnt? This! That Dr Roberts is a keen observer, that Mrs Lorrimer on the other hand has a most remarkable power of concentration but is, in consequence, almost blind to her surroundings. But she is fond of flowers. Despard notices only those things which appeal to him – rugs, trophies of sport. He has neither what I call the outward vision (seeing details all around you – what is called an observant person) nor the inner vision – concentration, the focusing of the mind on one object. He has a purposefully limited vision. He sees only what blends and harmonizes with the bent of his mind.'

'So those are what you call facts – eh?' said Battle curiously.

'They *are* facts – very small fry – perhaps.'

'What about Miss Meredith?'

'I have left her to the end. But I shall question her too as to what she remembers in that room.'

'It's an odd method of approach,' said Battle thoughtfully. 'Purely psychological. Suppose they're leading you up the garden path?'

Poirot shook his head with a smile.

'No, that would be impossible. Whether they try to hinder or to help, they necessarily reveal their *type of mind*.'

'There's something in it, no doubt, said Battle thoughtfully. 'I couldn't work that way myself, though.'

Poirot said, still smiling:

'I feel I have done very little in comparison with you and with Mrs Oliver – and with Colonel Race. My cards, that I place on the table, are very low ones.'

Battle twinkled at him.

'As to that, M. Poirot, the two of trumps is a low card but it can take any one of three aces. All the same, I'm going to ask you to do a practical job of work.'

'And that is?'

'I want you to interview Professor Luxmore's widow.'

'Why do you not do that yourself?'

'Because, as I said just now, I'm off to Devonshire.'

'Why do you not do that yourself?' repeated Poirot.

'Won't be put off, will you? Well, I'll speak the truth. I think you'll get more out of her than I shall.'

'My methods being less straightforward?'

'You can put it that way if you like,' said Battle grinning. 'I've heard Inspector Japp say that you've got a tortuous mind.'

'Like the late Mr Shaitana?'

'You think he would have been able to get things out of her?'

Poirot said slowly:

'I rather think he *did* get things out of her!'

'What makes you think so?' asked Battle sharply.

'A chance remark of Major Despard's.'

'Gave himself away, did he? That sounds unlike him.'

'Oh, my dear friend, it is impossible *not* to give oneself away – unless one never opens one's mouth! Speech is the deadliest of revealers.'

'Even if people tell lies?' asked Mrs Oliver.

'Yes, madame, because it can be seen at once that you tell *a certain kind of lie*.'

'You make me feel quite uncomfortable,' said Mrs Oliver, getting up.

Superintendent Battle accompanied her to the door and shook her by the hand.

'You've been the goods, Mrs Oliver,' he said. 'You're a much better detective than that long lanky Laplander of yours.'

'Finn,' corrected Mrs Oliver. 'Of course he's idiotic. But people like him. Goodbye.'

'I, too, must depart,' said Poirot.

Battle scribbled an address on a piece of paper and shoved it into Poirot's hand.

'There you are. Go and tackle her.'

Poirot smiled.

'And what do you want me to find out?'

'The truth about Professor Luxmore's death.'

'*Mon cher* Battle! Does anybody know the truth about anything?'

'I'm going to about this business in Devonshire,' said the superintendent with decision.

Poirot murmured:

'I wonder.'

CHAPTER 20

THE EVIDENCE OF MRS LUXMORE

The maid who opened the door at Mrs Luxmore's South Kensington address looked at Hercule Poirot with deep disapproval. She showed no disposition to admit him into the house.

Unperturbed, Poirot gave her a card.

'Give that to your mistress. I think she will see me.'

It was one of his more ostentatious cards. The words 'Private Detective' were printed in one corner. He had had them specially engraved for the purpose of obtaining interviews with the so-called fair sex. Nearly every woman, whether conscious of innocence or not, was anxious to have a look at a private detective and find out what he wanted.

Left ignominiously on the mat, Poirot studied the door-knocker with intense disgust at its unpolished condition.

'Ah! for some Brasso and a rag,' he murmured to himself.

Breathing excitedly the maid returned and Poirot was bidden to enter.

He was shown into a room on the first floor – a rather dark room smelling of stale flowers and unemptied ashtrays. There were large quantities of silk cushions of exotic colours all in need of cleaning. The walls were emerald green and the ceiling was of pseudo copper.

A tall, rather handsome woman was standing by the mantelpiece. She came forward and spoke in a deep husky voice.

'M. Hercule Poirot?'

Poirot bowed. His manner was not quite his own. He was not only foreign but ornately foreign. His gestures were positively baroque. Faintly, very faintly, it was the manner of the late Mr Shaitana.

'What did you want to see me about?'

Again Poirot bowed.

'If I might be seated? It will take a little time –'

She waved him impatiently to a chair and sat down herself on the edge of a sofa.

'Yes? Well?'

'It is, madame, that I make the inquiries – the private inquiries, you understand?'

The more deliberate his approach, the greater her eagerness.

'Yes – yes?'

'I make inquiries into the death of the late Professor Luxmore.'

She gave a gasp. Her dismay was evident.

'But why? What do you mean? What has it got to do with you?'

Poirot watched her carefully before proceeding.

'There is, you comprehend, a book being written. A life of your eminent husband. The writer, naturally, is anxious to get all his facts exact. As to your husband's death, for instance –'

She broke in at once:

'My husband died of fever – on the Amazon.'

Poirot leaned back in his chair. Slowly, very, very slowly, he shook his head to and fro – a maddening, monotonous motion.

'Madame – madame –' he protested.

'But I know! I was there at the time.'

'Ah, yes, certainly. You were *there*. Yes, my information says so.'

She cried out:

'What information?'

Eyeing her closely Poirot said:

'Information supplied to me by the late Mr Shaitana.'

She shrank back as though flicked with a whip.

'Shaitana?' she muttered.

'A man,' said Poirot, 'possessed of vast stores of knowledge. A remarkable man. That man knew many secrets.'

'I suppose he did,' she murmured, passing a tongue over her dry lips.

Poirot leaned forward. He achieved a little tap on her knee.

'He knew, for instance, that your husband did not die of fever.'

She stared at him. Her eyes looked wild and desperate.

He leaned back and watched the effect of his words.

She pulled herself together with an effort.

'I don't – I don't know what you mean.'

It was very unconvincingly said.

'Madame,' said Poirot, 'I will come out into the open. I will,' he smiled, 'place my cards upon the table. Your husband did not die of fever. *He died of a bullet!*'

'Oh!' she cried.

She covered her face with her hands. She rocked herself to and fro. She was in terrible distress. But somewhere, in some remote fibre of her being, she was enjoying her own emotions. Poirot was quite sure of that.

'And therefore,' said Poirot in a matter-of-fact tone, 'you might just as well tell me the whole story.'

She uncovered her face and said:

'It wasn't in the least the way you think.'

Again Poirot leaned forward – again he tapped her knee.

'You misunderstand me – you misunderstand me utterly,' he said. 'I know very well that it was not you who shot him. It was Major Despard. But you were the cause.'

'I don't know. I don't know. I suppose I was. It was all too terrible. There is a sort of fatality that pursues me.'

'Ah, how true that is,' cried Poirot. 'How often have I not seen it? There are some women like that. Wherever they go, tragedies follow in their wake. It is not their fault. These things happen in spite of themselves.'

Mrs Luxmore drew a deep breath.

'You understand. I see you understand. It all happened so naturally.'

'You travelled together into the interior, did you not?'

'Yes. My husband was writing a book on various rare plants.

Major Despard was introduced to us as a man who knew the conditions and would arrange the necessary expedition. My husband liked him very much. We started.'

There was a pause. Poirot allowed it to continue for about a minute and a half and then murmured as though to himself.

'Yes, one can picture it. The winding river – the tropical night – the hum of the insects – the strong soldierly man – the beautiful woman . . .'

Mrs Luxmore sighed.

'My husband was, of course, years older than I was. I married as a mere child before I knew what I was doing . . .'

Poirot shook his head sadly.

'I know. I know. How often does that not occur?'

'Neither of us would admit what was happening,' went on Mrs Luxmore. 'John Despard never said anything. He was the soul of honour.'

'But a woman always knows,' prompted Poirot.

'How right you are . . . Yes, a woman knows . . . But I never showed him that I knew. We were Major Despard and Mrs Luxmore to each other right up to the end . . . We were both determined to play the game.'

She was silent, lost in admiration of that noble attitude.

'True,' murmured Poirot. 'One must play the cricket. As one of your poets so finely says, "I could not love thee, dear, so much, loved I not cricket more."'

'Honour,' corrected Mrs Luxmore with a slight frown.

'Of course – of course – honour. "Loved I not honour more."'

'Those words might have been written for us,' murmured Mrs Luxmore. 'No matter what it cost us, we were both determined never to say the fatal word. And then –'

'And then –' prompted Poirot.

'That ghastly night.' Mrs Luxmore shuddered.

'Yes?'

'I suppose they must have quarrelled – John and Timothy, I mean. I came out of my tent . . . I came out of my tent . . .'

'Yes – yes?'

Mrs Luxmore's eyes were wide and dark. She was seeing the scene as though it were being repeated in front of her.

'I came out of my tent,' she repeated. 'John and Timothy

were – Oh!' she shuddered. 'I can't remember it all clearly. I came between them . . . I said "No – no, it isn't *true!*" Timothy wouldn't listen. He was threatening John. John had to fire – in self-defence. Ah!' she gave a cry and covered her face with her hands. 'He was dead – stone dead – shot through the heart.'

'A terrible moment for you, madame.'

'I shall never forget it. John was noble. He was all for giving himself up. I refused to hear of it. We argued all night. "For my sake," I kept saying. He saw that in the end. Naturally he couldn't let me suffer. The awful publicity. Think of the headlines. *Two Men and a Woman in the Jungle. Primeval Passions.*

'I put it all to John. In the end he gave in. The boys had seen and heard nothing. Timothy had been having a bout of fever. We said he had died of it. We buried him there beside the Amazon.'

A deep, tortured sigh shook her form.

'And then – back to civilization – and to part for ever.'

'Was it necessary, madame?'

'Yes, yes. Timothy dead stood between us just as Timothy alive had done – more so. We said goodbye to each other – for ever. I meet John Despard sometimes – out in the world. We smile, we speak politely – no one would ever guess that there was anything between us. But I see in his eyes – and he in mine – that we will never forget . . .'

There was a long pause. Poirot paid tribute to the curtain by not breaking the silence.

Mrs Luxmore took out a vanity case and powdered her nose – the spell was broken.

'What a tragedy,' said Poirot, but in a more everyday tone.

'You can see, M. Poirot,' said Mrs Luxmore earnestly, 'that the truth must never be told.'

'It would be painful –'

'It would be impossible. This friend, this writer – surely he would not wish to blight the life of a perfectly innocent woman?'

'Or even to hang a perfectly innocent man?' murmured Poirot.

'You see it like that? I am glad. He *was* innocent. A *crime passionnel* is not really a crime. And in any case it was self-defence. He *had* to shoot. So you do understand, M. Poirot, that the world must continue to think Timothy died of fever?'

Poirot murmured.

'Writers are sometimes curiously callous.'

'Your friend is a woman-hater? He wants to make us suffer? But you must not allow that. I shall not allow it. If necessary I shall take the blame on myself. I shall say *I* shot Timothy.'

She had risen to her feet. Her head was thrown back.

Poirot also rose.

'Madame,' he said as he took her hand, 'such splendid self-sacrifice is unnecessary. I will do my best so that the true facts shall never be known.'

A sweet womanly smile stole over Mrs Luxmore's face. She raised her hand slightly, so that Poirot, whether he had meant to do so or not, was forced to kiss it.

'An unhappy woman thanks you, M. Poirot,' she said.

It was the last word of a persecuted queen to a favoured courtier – clearly an exit line. Poirot duly made his exit.

Once out in the street, he drew a long breath of fresh air.

CHAPTER 21

MAJOR DESPARD

'*Quelle femme*,' murmured Hercule Poirot. '*Ce pauvre Despard! Ce qu'il a dû souffrir! Quel voyage épouvantable!*'

Suddenly he began to laugh.

He was now walking along the Brompton Road. He paused, took out his watch, and made a calculation.

'But yes, I have the time. In any case to wait will do him no harm. I can now attend to the other little matter. What was it that my friend in the English police force used to sing – how many years – forty years ago? "A little piece of sugar for the bird."'

Humming a long-forgotten tune, Hercule Poirot entered a sumptuous-looking shop mainly devoted to the clothing and general embellishment of women and made his way to the stocking counter.

Selecting a sympathetic-looking and not too haughty damsel he made known his requirements.

'Silk stockings? Oh, yes, we have a very nice line here. Guaranteed pure silk.'

Poirot waved them away. He waxed eloquent once more.

'French silk stockings? With the duty, you know, they are very expensive.'

A fresh lot of boxes was produced.

'Very nice, mademoiselle, but I had something of a finer texture in mind.'

'These are a hundred gauge. Of course, we have some extra fine, but I'm afraid they come out at about thirty-five shillings a pair. And no durability, of course. Just like cobwebs.'

'*C'est ça. C'est ça, exactement.*'

A prolonged absence of the young lady this time.

She returned at last.

'I'm afraid they are actually thirty-seven and sixpence a pair. But beautiful, aren't they?'

She slid them tenderly from a gauzy envelope – the finest, gauziest wisps of stockings.

'*Enfin* – that is it exactly!'

'Lovely, aren't they? How many pairs, sir?'

'I want – let me see, nineteen pairs.'

The young lady very nearly fell down behind the counter, but long training in scornfulness just kept her erect.

'There would be a reduction on two dozen,' she said faintly.

'No, I want nineteen pairs. Of slightly different colours, please.'

The girl sorted them out obediently, packed them up and made out the bill.

As Poirot departed with his purchase, the next girl at the counter said:

'Wonder who the lucky girl is? Must be a nasty old man. Oh, well, she seems to be stringing him along good and proper. Stockings at thirty-seven and sixpence indeed!'

Unaware of the low estimate formed by the young ladies of Messrs Harvey Robinson's upon his character, Poirot was trotting homewards.

He had been in for about half an hour when he heard the door-bell ring. A few minutes later Major Despard entered the room.

He was obviously keeping his temper with difficulty.

'What the devil did you want to go and see Mrs Luxmore for?' he asked.

Poirot smiled.

'I wished, you see, for the true story of Professor Luxmore's death.'

'True story? Do you think that woman's capable of telling the truth about anything?' demanded Despard wrathfully.

'*Eh bien*, I did wonder now and then,' admitted Poirot.

'I should think you did. That woman's crazy.'

Poirot demurred.

'Not at all. She is a romantic woman, that is all.'

'Romantic be damned. She's an out-and-out liar. I sometimes think she even believes her own lies.'

'It is quite possible.'

'She's an appalling woman. I had the hell of a time with her out there.'

'That also I can well believe.'

Despard sat down abruptly.

'Look here, M. Poirot, I'm going to tell you the truth.'

'You mean you are going to give me your version of the story?'

'My version will be the true version.'

Poirot did not reply.

Despard went on drily:

'I quite realize that I can't claim any merit in coming out with this now. I'm telling the truth because it's the only thing to be done at this stage. Whether you believe me or not is up to you. I've no kind of proof that my story is the correct one.'

He paused for a minute and then began.

'I arranged the trip for the Luxmores. He was a nice old boy quite batty about mosses and plants and things. She was a – well, she was what you've no doubt observed her to be! That trip was a nightmare. I didn't care a damn for the woman – rather disliked her, as a matter of fact. She was the intense, soulful kind that always makes me feel prickly with embarrassment. Everything went all right for the first fortnight. Then we all had a go of fever. She and I had it slightly. Old Luxmore was pretty bad. One night – now you've got to listen to this carefully – I was sitting outside my tent. Suddenly I saw Luxmore in the distance staggering off into the bush by the river. He was absolutely delirious and quite unconscious of what he was doing. In another minute he would be in the river – and at that particular spot it would have been the end of him. No chance of a rescue. There wasn't time to rush after him – only one thing to be done. My rifle was beside me as usual. I snatched it up. I'm a pretty accurate shot. I was quite sure I could bring the old boy down – get him in the leg. And then, just as I fired, that idiotic fool of a woman flung herself from somewhere upon me, yelping out, "Don't shoot. For God's sake, don't shoot." She caught my arm and jerked it ever so slightly just as the rifle went off – with the result that the bullet got him in the back and killed him dead!

'I can tell you that was a pretty ghastly moment. And that damned fool of a woman still didn't understand what she'd done. Instead of realizing that she'd been responsible for her husband's death, she firmly believed that I'd been trying to shoot the old boy in cold blood – for the love of her, if you please! We had the devil of a scene – she insisting that we should say he died of fever. I was sorry for her – especially as I saw she didn't realize what she'd done. But she'd have to realize it if the truth came out! And then her complete certainty that I was head over heels in love with her gave me a bit of a jar. It was going to be a pretty kettle of fish if she went about giving that out. In the end I agreed to do what she wanted – partly for the sake of peace, I'll admit. After all, it didn't seem to matter much. Fever or accident. And I didn't want to drag a woman through a lot of unpleasantness – even if she was a damned fool. I gave it out next day that the professor was dead of fever and we buried him. The bearers knew the truth, of course, but they were all devoted to me and I knew that what I said they'd swear to if need be. We buried poor old Luxmore and got back to civilization. Since then I've spent a good deal of time dodging the woman.'

He paused, then said quietly:

'That's my story, M. Poirot.'

Poirot said slowly:

'It was to that incident that Mr Shaitana referred, or so you thought, at dinner that night?'

Despard nodded.

'He must have heard it from Mrs Luxmore. Easy enough to get the story out of her. That sort of thing would have amused him.'

'It might have been a dangerous story – to you – in the hands of a man like Shaitana.'

Despard shrugged his shoulders.

'I wasn't afraid of Shaitana.'

Poirot didn't answer.

Despard said quietly:

'That again you have to take my word for. It's true enough, I suppose, that I had a kind of motive for Shaitana's death. Well, the truth's out now – take it or leave it.'

Poirot held out a hand.

'I will take it, Major Despard. I have no doubt at all that things in South America happened exactly as you have described.'

Despard's face lit up.

'Thanks,' he said laconically.

And he clasped Poirot's hand warmly.

<hr>

CHAPTER 22

EVIDENCE FROM COMBEACRE

Superintendent Battle was in the police station of Combeacre.

Inspector Harper, rather red in the face, talked in a slow, pleasing Devonshire voice.

'That's how it was, sir. Seemed all as right as rain. The doctor was satisfied. Everyone was satisfied. Why not?'

'Just give me the facts about the two bottles again. I want to get it quite clear.'

'Syrup of Figs – that's what the bottle was. She took it regular, it seems. Then there was this hat paint she'd been using – or rather the young lady, her companion, had been using for her. Brightening up a garden hat. There was a good deal left over, and the bottle broke, and Mrs Benson herself said, "Put it in that old bottle – the Syrup of Figs bottle." That's all right. The servants heard her. The young lady, Miss Meredith, and the housemaid and the parlourmaid – they all agree on that. The paint was put into the old Syrup of Figs bottle and it was put up on the top shelf in the bathroom with other odds and ends.'

'Not re-labelled?'

'No. Careless, of course; the coroner commented on that.'

'Go on.'

'On this particular night the deceased went into the bathroom, took down a Syrup of Figs bottle, poured herself out a good dose and drank it. Realized what she'd done and they sent off at once for the doctor. He was out on a case, and it was some time before they could get at him. They did all they could, but she died.'

'She herself believed it to be an accident?'

'Oh, yes – everyone thought so. It seems clear the bottles must have got mixed up somehow. It was suggested the housemaid did it when she dusted, but she swears she didn't.'

Superintendent Battle was silent – thinking. Such an easy business. A bottle taken down from an upper shelf, put in place of the other. So difficult to trace a mistake like that to its source. Handled with gloves, possibly, and anyway, the last prints would be those of Mrs Benson herself. Yes, so easy – so simple. But, all the same, murder! The perfect crime.

But why? That still puzzled him – why?

'This young lady-companion, this Miss Meredith, she didn't come into money at Mrs Benson's death?' he asked.

Inspector Harper shook his head.

No. She'd only been there about six weeks. Difficult place, I should imagine. Young ladies didn't stay long as a rule.'

Battle was still puzzled. Young ladies didn't stay long. A difficult woman, evidently. But if Anne Meredith had been unhappy, she could have left as her predecessors had done. No need to kill – unless it were sheer unreasoning vindictiveness. He shook his head. That suggestion did not ring true.

'Who did get Mrs Benson's money?'

'I couldn't say, sir, nephews and nieces, I believe. But it wouldn't be very much – not when it was divided up, and I heard as how most of her income was one of these annuities.'

Nothing there then. But Mrs Benson had died. And Anne Meredith had not told him that she had been at Combeacre.

It was all profoundly unsatisfactory.

He made diligent and painstaking inquiries. The doctor was quite clear and emphatic. No reason to believe it was anything but an accident. Miss – couldn't remember her name – nice girl but rather helpless – had been very upset and distressed. There was the vicar. He remembered Mrs Benson's last companion – a nice modest-looking girl. Always came to church with Mrs Benson. Mrs Benson had been – not difficult – but a trifle severe towards young people. She was the rigid type of Christian.

Battle tried one or two other people but learned nothing of value. Anne Meredith was hardly remembered. She had lived among them a few months – that was all – and her personality was not sufficiently vivid to make a lasting impression. A nice little thing seemed to be the accepted description.

Mrs Benson loomed out a little more clearly. A self-righteous grenadier of a woman, working her companions hard and changing her servants often. A disagreeable woman – but that was all.

Nevertheless Superintendent Battle left Devonshire under the firm impression that, for some reason unknown, Anne Meredith had deliberately murdered her employer.

CHAPTER 23

THE EVIDENCE OF A PAIR OF SILK STOCKINGS

As Superintendent Battle's train rushed eastwards through England, Anne Meredith and Rhoda Dawes were in Hercule Poirot's sitting-room.

Anne had been unwilling to accept the invitation that had reached her by the morning's post, but Rhoda's counsel had prevailed.

'Anne – you're a coward – yes, a coward. It's no good going on being an ostrich, burying your head in the sand. There's been a murder and you're one of the suspects – the least likely one perhaps –'

'That would be the worst,' said Anne with a touch of humour. 'It's always the least likely person who did it.'

'But you are one,' continued Rhoda, undisturbed by the interruption. 'And it's no use putting your nose in the air as though murder was a nasty smell and nothing to do with you.'

'It *is* nothing to do with me,' Anne persisted. 'I mean, I'm quite willing to answer any questions the police want to ask me, but this man, this Hercule Poirot, he's an outsider.'

'And what will he think if you hedge and try to get out of it? He'll think you're bursting with guilt.'

'I'm certainly not bursting with guilt,' said Anne coldly.

'Darling, I know that. You couldn't murder anybody if you tried. But horrible suspicious foreigners don't know that. I think we ought to go nicely to his house. Otherwise he'll come down here and try to worm things out of the servants.'

'We haven't got any servants.'

'We've got Mother Astwell. She can wag a tongue with anybody! Come on, Anne, let's go. It will be rather fun really.'

'I don't see why he wants to see me.' Anne was obstinate.

'To put one over on the official police, of course,' said Rhoda impatiently. 'They always do – the amateurs, I mean. They make out that Scotland Yard are all boots and brainlessness.'

'Do you think this man Poirot is clever?'

'He doesn't look a Sherlock,' said Rhoda. 'I expect he has been quite good in his day. He's gaga now, of course. He must be at least sixty. Oh, come on, Anne, let's go and see the old boy. He may tell us dreadful things about the others.'

'All right,' said Anne, and added, 'You do *enjoy* all this so, Rhoda.'

'I suppose because it isn't my funeral,' said Rhoda. 'You were a noddle, Anne, not just to have looked up at the right minute. If only you had, you could live like a duchess for the rest of your life on blackmail.'

So it came about that at three o'clock of that same afternoon, Rhoda Dawes and Anne Meredith sat primly on their chairs in Poirot's neat room and sipped blackberry *sirop* (which they disliked very much but were too polite to refuse) from old-fashioned glasses.

'It was most amiable of you to accede to my request, mademoiselle,' Poirot was saying.

'I'm sure I shall be glad to help in any way I can,' murmured Anne vaguely.

'It is a little matter of memory.'

'Memory?'

'Yes, I have already put these questions to Mrs Lorrimer, to Dr Roberts and to Major Despard. None of them, alas, have given me the response that I hoped for.'

Anne continued to look at him inquiringly.

'I want you, mademoiselle, to cast your mind back to that evening in the drawing-room of Mr Shaitana.'

A weary shadow passed over Anne's face. Was she never to be free of that nightmare?'

Poirot noticed the expression.

'*C'est pénible, n'est ce pas?* That is very natural. You, so young as you are, to be brought in contact with horror for the first time. Probably you have never known or seen a violent death.'

Rhoda's feet shifted a little uncomfortably on the floor.

'Well?' said Anne

'Cast your mind back. I want you to tell me what you remember of that room?'

Anne stared at him suspiciously.

'I don't understand?'

'But yes. The chairs, the tables, the ornaments, the wallpaper, the curtains, the fire-irons. You saw them all. Can you not then describe them?'

'Oh, I see.' Anne hesitated, frowning. 'It's difficult. I don't really think I remember. I couldn't say what the wallpaper was like. I think the walls were painted – some inconspicuous colour. There were rugs on the floor. There was a piano.' She shook her head. 'I really couldn't tell you any more.'

'But you are not trying, mademoiselle. You must remember some object, some ornament, some piece of bric-à-brac?'

'There was a case of Egyptian jewellery, I remember,' said Anne slowly. 'Over by the window.'

'Oh, yes, at the extreme other end of the room from the table on which lay the little dagger.'

Anne looked at him.

'I never heard which table that was on.'

'*Pas si bête,*' commented Poirot to himself. 'But then, no more is Hercule Poirot! If she knew me better she would realize I would never lay a *piège* as gross as that!'

Aloud he said:

'A case of Egyptian jewellery, you say?'

Anne answered with some enthusiasm.

'Yes – some of it was lovely. Blues and red. Enamel. One or two lovely rings. And scarabs – but I don't like them so much.'

'He was a great collector, Mr Shaitana,' murmured Poirot.

'Yes, he must have been,' Anne agreed. 'The room was full of stuff. One couldn't begin to look at it all.'

'So that you cannot mention anything else that particularly struck your notice?'

Anne smiled a little as she said:

'Only a vase of chrysanthemums that badly wanted their water changed.'

'Ah, yes, servants are not always too particular about that.'

Poirot was silent for a moment or two.

Anne asked timidly.

'I'm afraid I didn't notice – whatever it is you wanted me to notice.'

Poirot smiled kindly.

'It does not matter, *mon enfant*. It was, indeed, an outside chance. Tell me, have you seen the good Major Despard lately?'

He saw the delicate pink colour come up in the girl's face. She replied:

'He said he would come and see us again quite soon.'

Rhoda said impetuously:

'*He* didn't do it, anyway! Anne and I are quite sure of that.'

Poirot twinkled at them.

'How fortunate – to have convinced two such charming young ladies of one's innocence.'

'Oh, dear,' thought Rhoda. 'He's going to be French, and it does embarrass me so.'

She got up and began examining some etchings on the wall.

'These are awfully good,' she said.

'They are not bad,' said Poirot.

He hesitated, looking at Anne.

'Mademoiselle,' he said at last. 'I wonder if I might ask you to do me a great favour – oh, nothing to do with the murder. This is an entirely private and personal matter.'

Anne looked a little surprised. Poirot went on speaking in a slightly embarrassed manner.

'It is, you understand, that Christmas is coming on. I have to buy presents for many nieces and grand-nieces. And it is a little difficult to choose what young ladies like in this present time. My tastes, alas, are rather old-fashioned.'

'Yes?' said Anne kindly.

'Silk stockings, now – are silk stockings a welcome present to receive?'

'Yes, indeed. It's always nice to be given stockings.'

'You relieve my mind. I will ask my favour. I have obtained some different colours. There are, I think, about fifteen or sixteen pairs. Would you be so amiable as to look through them and set aside half a dozen pairs that seem to you the most desirable?'

'Certainly I will,' said Anne, rising, with a laugh.

Poirot directed her towards a table in an alcove – a table whose contents were strangely at variance, had she but known it, with the well-known order and neatness of Hercule Poirot. There were stockings piled up in untidy heaps – some fur-lined gloves – calendars and boxes of bonbons.

'I send off my parcels very much *à l'avance*,' Poirot explained. 'See, mademoiselle, here are the stockings. Select me, I pray of you, six pairs.'

He turned, intercepting Rhoda, who was following him.

'As for mademoiselle here, I have a little treat for her – a treat that would be no treat to you, I fancy, Mademoiselle Meredith.'

'What is it?' cried Rhoda.

He lowered his voice.

'A knife, mademoiselle, with which twelve people once stabbed a man. It was given to me as a souvenir by the Compagnie Internationale des Wagons Lits.'

'Horrible,' cried Anne.

'Ooh! Let me see,' said Rhoda.

Poirot led her through into the other room, talking as he went.

'It was given me by the Compagnie Internationale des Wagons Lits because –'

They passed out of the room.

They returned three minutes later. Anne came towards them.

'I think these six are the nicest, M. Poirot. Both these are very good evening shades, and this lighter colour would be nice when summer comes and it's daylight in the evening.'

'*Mille remercîments, mademoiselle.*'

He offered them more *sirop*, which they refused, and finally accompanied them to the door, still talking genially.

When they had finally departed he returned to the room and went straight to the littered table. The pile of stockings still lay in a confused heap. Poirot counted the six selected pairs and then went on to count the others.

He had bought nineteen pairs. There were now only seventeen.

He nodded his head slowly.

CHAPTER 24

ELIMINATION OF THREE MURDERERS?

On arrival in London, Superintendent Battle came straight to Poirot. Anne and Rhoda had then been gone an hour or more.

Without more ado, the superintendent recounted the result of his researches in Devonshire.

'We're on to it – not a doubt of it,' he finished. 'That's what Shaitana was aiming at – with his "domestic accident" business. But what gets me is the motive. Why did she want to kill the woman?'

'I think I can help you there, my friend.'

'Go ahead, M. Poirot.'

'This afternoon I conducted a little experiment. I induced mademoiselle and her friend to come here. I put to them my usual questions as to what there was in the room that night.'

Battle looked at him curiously.

'You're very keen on that question.'

'Yes, it's useful. It tells me a good deal. Mademoiselle Meredith was suspicious – very suspicious. She takes nothing for granted, that young lady. So that good dog, Hercule Poirot, he does one of his best tricks. He lays a clumsy amateurish trap. Mademoiselle mentions a case of jewellery. I say was not that at the opposite end of the room from the table with the dagger. Mademoiselle does not fall into the trap. She avoids it cleverly. And after that she is pleased with herself, and her vigilance relaxes. So that is the object of this visit – to get her to admit that she knew where the dagger was, and that she noticed it! Her spirits rise when she has, as she thinks, defeated me. She talked quite freely about the jewellery. She has noticed many details of it. There is nothing else in the room that she remembers – except that a vase of chrysanthemums needed its water changing.'

'Well?' said Battle.

'Well, it is significant, that. Suppose we knew nothing about this girl. Her word would give us a clue to her character. She notices flowers. She is, then, fond of flowers? No, since she does not mention a very big bowl of early tulips which would at once have attracted the attention of a flower lover. No, it is the paid companion who speaks – the girl whose duty it has been to put fresh water in the vases – and, allied to that, there is a girl who loves and notices jewellery. Is not that, at least, suggestive?'

'Ah,' said Battle. 'I'm beginning to see what you're driving at.'

'Precisely. As I told you the other day, I place my cards on the table. When you recounted her history the other day, and Mrs Oliver made her startling announcement, my mind went at once to an important point. The murder could not have been committed for gain, since Miss Meredith had still to earn her living after it happened. Why, then? I considered Miss Meredith's temperament as it appeared superficially. A rather timid young girl, poor, but well-dressed, fond of pretty things . . . The temperament, is it not, of a *thief*, rather than a murderer. And I asked immediately if Mrs Eldon had been a tidy woman. You replied that no, she had not been tidy. I formed a hypothesis. Supposing that Anne Meredith was a girl with a weak streak in her character – the kind of girl who takes little things from the big shops. Supposing that, poor, and yet loving pretty things, she helped herself once or twice to things from her employer. A brooch, perhaps, an odd half-crown or two, a string of beads. Mrs Eldon, careless, untidy, would put down these disappearances to her own carelessness. She would not suspect her gentle little mother's-help. But, now, suppose a different type of employer – an employer who *did* notice – accused Anne Meredith of theft. That would be a possible motive for murder. As I said the other evening, Miss Meredith would only commit a murder through fear. She knows that her employer will be able to prove the theft. There is only one thing that can save her: her employer must die. And so she changes the bottles, and Mrs Benson dies – ironically enough convinced that the mistake is her own, and not suspecting for a minute that the cowed, frightened girl has had a hand in it.'

'It's possible,' said Superintendent Battle. 'It's only a hypothesis, but it's possible.'

'It is a little more than possible, my friend – it is also probable. For this afternoon I laid a little trap nicely baited – the real trap – after the sham one had been circumvented. If what I suspect is true, Anne Meredith will never, never be able to resist a really expensive pair of stockings! I ask her to aid me. I let her know carefully that I am not sure exactly how many stockings there are, I go out of the room, leaving her alone – and the result, my friend, is that I have now seventeen pairs of stockings, instead of nineteen, and that two pairs have gone away in Anne Meredith's handbag.'

'Whew!' Superintendent Battle whistled. 'What a risk to take, though.'

'*Pas du tout*. What does she think I suspect her of? Murder. What is the risk, then, in stealing a pair, or two pairs, of silk stockings? I am not looking for a thief. And, besides, the thief, or the kleptomaniac, is always the same – convinced that she can get away with it.'

Battle nodded his head.

'That's true enough. Incredibly stupid. The pitcher goes to the well time after time. Well, I think between us we've arrived fairly clearly at the truth. Anne Meredith was caught stealing. Anne Meredith changed a bottle from one shelf to another. We know that was murder – but I'm damned if we could ever prove it. Successful crime No. 2. Roberts gets away with it. Anne Meredith gets away with it. But what about Shaitana? Did Anne Meredith kill Shaitana?'

He remained silent for a moment or two, then he shook his head.

'It doesn't work out right,' he said reluctantly. 'She's not one to take a risk. Change a couple of bottles, yes. She knew no one could fasten that on her. It was absolutely safe – because anyone might have done it! Of course, it mightn't have worked. Mrs Benson might have noticed before she drank the stuff, or she mightn't have died from it. It was what I call a *hopeful* kind of murder. It might work or it mightn't. Actually, it did. But

Shaitana was a very different pair of shoes. That was deliberate, audacious, purposeful murder.'

Poirot nodded his head.

'I agree with you. The two types of crime are not the same.'

Battle rubbed his nose.

'So that seems to wipe her out as far as he's concerned. Roberts and the girl, both crossed off our list. What about Despard? Any luck with the Luxmore woman?'

Poirot narrated his adventures of the preceding afternoon.

Battle grinned.

'I know that type. You can't disentangle what they remember from what they invent.'

Poirot went on. He described Despard's visit, and the story the latter had told.

'Believe him?' Battle asked abruptly.

'Yes, I do.'

Battle sighed.

'So do I. Not the type to shoot a man because he wanted the man's wife. Anyway, what's wrong with the divorce court? Everyone flocks there. And he's not a professional man; it wouldn't ruin him, or anything like that. No, I'm of the opinion that our late lamented Mr Shaitana struck a snag there. Murderer No. 3. wasn't a murderer, after all.'

He looked at Poirot.

'That leaves –'

'Mrs Lorrimer,' said Poirot.

The telephone rang. Poirot got up and answered it. He spoke a few words, waited, spoke again. Then he hung up the receiver and returned to Battle.

His face was very grave.

'That was Mrs Lorrimer speaking,' he said. 'She wants me to come round and see her – now.'

He and Battle looked at each other. The latter shook his head slowly.

'Am I wrong?' he said. 'Or were you expecting something of the kind?'

'I wondered,' said Hercule Poirot. 'That was all. I wondered.'

'You'd better get along,' said Battle. 'Perhaps you'll manage to get at the truth at last.'

CHAPTER 25

MRS LORRIMER SPEAKS

The day was not a bright one, and Mrs Lorrimer's room seemed rather dark and cheerless. She herself had a grey look, and seemed much older than she had done on the occasion of Poirot's last visit.

She greeted him with her usual smiling assurance.

'It is very nice of you to come so promptly, M. Poirot. You are a busy man, I know.'

'At your service, madame,' said Poirot with a little bow.

Mrs Lorrimer pressed the bell by the fireplace.

'We will have tea brought in. I don't know what you feel about it, but I always think it's a mistake to rush straight into confidences without any decent paving of the way.'

'There are to be confidences, then, madame?'

Mrs Lorrimer did not answer, for at that moment her maid answered the bell. When she had received the order and gone again, Mrs Lorrimer said dryly:

'You said, if you remember, when you were last here, that you would come if I sent for you. You had an idea, I think, of the reason that should prompt me to send.'

There was no more just then. Tea was brought. Mrs Lorrimer dispensed it, talking intelligently on various topics of the day.

Taking advantage of a pause, Poirot remarked:

'I hear you and little Mademoiselle Meredith had tea together the other day.'

'We did. Have you seen her lately?'

'This very afternoon.'

'She is in London, then, or have you been down to Wallingford?'

'No. She and her friend were so amiable as to pay me a visit.'

'Ah, the friend. I have not met her.'

Poirot said, smiling a little:

'This murder – it has made for me a *rapprochement*. You and Mademoiselle Meredith have tea together. Major Despard, he, too, cultivates Miss Meredith's acquaintance. The Dr Roberts, he is perhaps the only one out of it.'

'I saw him out at bridge the other day,' said Mrs Lorrimer. 'He seemed quite his usual cheerful self.'

'As fond of bridge as ever?'

'Yes – still making the most outrageous bids – and very often getting away with it.'

She was silent for a moment or two, then said:

'Have you seen Superintendent Battle lately?'

'Also this afternoon. He was with me when you telephoned.'

Shading her face from the fire with one hand, Mrs Lorrimer asked:

'How is he getting on?'

Poirot said gravely:

'He is not very rapid, the good Battle. He gets there slowly, but he does get there in the end, madame.'

'I wonder.' Her lips curved in a faintly ironical smile.

She went on:

'He has paid me quite a lot of attention. He has delved, I think, into my past history right back to my girlhood. He has interviewed my friends, and chatted to my servants – the ones I have now and the ones who have been with me in former years. What he hoped to find I do not know, but he certainly did not find it. He might as well have accepted what I told him. It was the truth. I knew Mr Shaitana very slightly. I met him at Luxor, as I said, and our acquaintanceship was never more than an acquaintanceship. Superintendent Battle will not be able to get away from these facts.'

'Perhaps not,' said Poirot.

'And you, M. Poirot? Have not you made any inquiries?'

'About you, madame?'

'That is what I meant.'

Slowly the little man shook his head.

'It would have been to no avail.'

'Just exactly what do you mean by that, M. Poirot?'

'I will be quite frank, madame. I have realized from the beginning that, of the four persons in Mr Shaitana's room that night, the one with the best brains, with the coolest, most logical head, was you, madame. If I had to lay money on the chance of one of those four planning a murder and getting away with it successfully, it is on you that I should place my money.'

Mrs Lorrimer's brows rose.

'Am I expected to feel flattered?' she asked drily.

Poirot went on, without paying any attention to her interruption:

'For a crime to be successful, it is usually necessary to think every detail of it out beforehand. All possible contingencies must be taken into account. The *timing* must be accurate. The *placing* must be scrupulously correct. Dr Roberts might bungle a crime through haste and overconfidence; Major Despard would probably be too prudent to commit one; Miss Meredith might lose her head and give herself away. You, madame, would do none of these things. You would be clear-headed and cool, you are sufficiently resolute of character, and could be sufficiently obsessed with an idea to the extent of overruling prudence, you are not the kind of woman to lose her head.'

Mrs Lorrimer sat silent for a minute or two, a curious smile playing round her lips. At last she said:

'So that is what you think of me, M. Poirot. That I am the kind of woman to commit an ideal murder.'

'At least you have the amiability not to resent the idea.'

'I find it very interesting. So it is your idea that I am the only person who could successfully have murdered Shaitana?'

Poirot said slowly:

'There is a difficulty there, madame.'

'Really? Do tell me.'

'You may have noticed that I said just now a phrase something like this: "For a crime to be successful it is usually necessary to plan every detail of it carefully beforehand." "Usually" is the word to which I want to draw your attention. For there *is* another type of successful crime. Have you ever said suddenly to any one, "Throw a stone and see if you can hit that tree," and the person obeys quickly, without thinking – and surprisingly often he *does* hit the tree? But when he comes to repeat the throw it is not so easy – for he has begun to *think*. 'So hard – no harder – a little more to the right – to the left.' The first was an almost unconscious action, the body obeying the mind as the body of an animal does. *Eh bien*, madame, there is a type of crime like that, a crime committed on the spur of the moment – an inspiration – a flash of genius – without time to pause or think. And that, madame, was the kind of crime that killed Mr Shaitana. A sudden dire necessity, a flash of inspiration, rapid execution.'

He shook his head.

'And that, madame, is not your type of crime at all. If you killed Mr Shaitana, it should have been a premeditated crime.'

'I see.' Her hand waved softly to and fro, keeping the heat of the fire from her face. 'And, of course, it wasn't a premeditated crime, so I couldn't have killed him – eh, M. Poirot?'

Poirot bowed.

'That is right, madame.'

'And yet –' She leaned forward, her waving hand stopped. '*I did kill Shaitana, M. Poirot . . .*'

CHAPTER 26
THE TRUTH

There was a pause – a very long pause.

The room was growing dark. The firelight leaped and flickered.

Mrs Lorrimer and Hercule Poirot looked not at each other, but at the fire. It was as though time was momentarily in abeyance.

Then Hercule Poirot sighed and stirred.

'So it was that – all the time . . . *Why* did you kill him, madame?'

'I think you know why, M. Poirot.'

'Because he knew something about you – something that had happened long ago?'

'Yes.'

'And that something was – another death, madame?'

She bowed her head.

Poirot said gently:

'Why did you tell me? What made you send for me today?'

'You told me once that I should do so some day.'

'Yes – that is, I hoped . . . I knew, madame, that there was only one way of learning the truth as far as you were concerned – and that was by your own free will. If you did not choose to speak, you would not do so, and you would never give yourself away. But there was a chance – that you yourself might *wish* to speak.'

Mrs Lorrimer nodded.

'It was clever of you to foresee that – the weariness – the loneliness –'

Her voice died away.

Poirot looked at her curiously.

'So it has been like that? Yes, I can understand it might be . . .'

'Alone – quite alone,' said Mrs Lorrimer. 'No one knows what that means unless they have lived, as I have lived, with the knowledge of what one has done.'

Poirot said gently:

'Is it an impertinence, madame, or may I be permitted to offer my sympathy?'

She bent her head a little.

'Thank you, M. Poirot.'

There was another pause, then Poirot said, speaking in a slightly brisker tone:

'Am I to understand, madame, that you took the words Mr Shaitana spoke at dinner as a direct menace aimed at you?'

She nodded.

'I realized at once that he was speaking so that one person should understand him. That person was myself. The reference to a woman's weapon being poison was meant for me. He *knew*. I had suspected it once before. He had brought the conversation round to a certain famous trial, and I saw his eyes watching me. There was a kind of uncanny knowledge in them. But, of course, that night I was quite sure.'

'And you were sure, too, of his future intentions?'

Mrs Lorrimer said drily:

'It was hardly likely that the presence of Superintendent Battle and yourself was an accident. I took it that Shaitana was going to advertise his own cleverness by pointing out to you both that he had discovered something that no one else had suspected.'

'How soon did you make up your mind to act, madame?'

Mrs Lorrimer hesitated a little.

'It is difficult to remember exactly when the idea came into my mind,' she said. 'I had noticed the dagger before going into dinner. When we returned to the drawing-room I picked it up and slipped it into my sleeve. No one saw me do it. I made sure of that.'

'It would be dexterously done, I have no doubt, madame.'

'I made up my mind then exactly what I was going to do. I had only to carry it out. It was risky, perhaps, but I considered that it was worth trying.'

'That is your coolness, your successful weighing of chances, coming into play. Yes, I see that.'

'We started to play bridge,' continued Mrs Lorrimer. Her voice cool and unemotional. 'At last an opportunity arose. I was dummy. I strolled across the room to the fireplace. Shaitana had dozed off to sleep. I looked over at the others. They were all intent on the game. I leant over and – and did it –'

Her voice shook just a little, but instantly it regained its cool aloofness.

'I spoke to him. It came into my head that that would make a kind of alibi for me. I made some remark about the fire, and then pretended he had answered me and went on again, saying something like: "I agree with you. I do not like radiators, either."'

'He did not cry out at all?'

'No. I think he made a little grunt – that was all. It might have been taken for words from a distance.'

'And then?'

'And then I went back to the bridge table. The last trick was just being played.'

'And you sat down and resumed play?'

'Yes.'

'With sufficient interest in the game to be able to tell me nearly all the calling and the hands two days later?'

'Yes,' said Mrs Lorrimer simply.

'*Epatant!*' said Hercule Poirot.

He leaned back in his chair. He nodded his head several times. Then, by way of a change, he shook it.

'But there is still something, madame, that I do not understand.'

'Yes?'

'It seems to me that there is some factor that I have missed. You are a woman who considers and weighs everything carefully. You decide that, for a certain reason, you will run an enormous risk. You do run it – successfully. And then, not two weeks later, you change your mind. Frankly, madame, that does not seem to me to ring true.'

A queer little smile twisted her lips.

'You are quite right, M. Poirot, there is one factor that you do not know. Did Miss Meredith tell you where she met me the other day?'

'It was, I think she said, near Mrs Oliver's flat.'

'I believe that is so. But I meant the actual name of the street. Anne Meredith met me in Harley Street.'

'Ah!' He looked at her attentively. 'I begin to see.'

'Yes, I thought you would. I had been to see a specialist there. He told me what I already half suspected.'

Her smile widened. It was no longer twisted and bitter. It was suddenly sweet.

'I shall not play very much more bridge, M. Poirot. Oh, he didn't say so in so many words. He wrapped up the truth a little. With great care, etc., etc., I might live several years. But I shall not take any great care. I am not that kind of a woman.'

'Yes, yes, I begin to understand,' said Poirot.

'It made a difference, you see. A month – two months, perhaps – not more. And then, just as I left the specialist, I met Miss Meredith. I asked her to have tea with me.'

She paused, then went on:

'I am not, after all, a wholly wicked woman. All the time we were having tea I was thinking. By my action the other evening I had not only deprived the man Shaitana of life (that was done, and could not be undone), I had also, to a varying degree, affected unfavourably the lives of three other people. Because of what I had done, Dr Roberts, Major Despard and Anne Meredith, none of whom had injured me in any way, were passing through a very grave ordeal, and might even be in danger. That, at least, I could undo. I don't know that I felt particularly moved by the plight of either Dr Roberts or Major Despard – although both of them had presumably a much longer span of life in front of them than I had. They were men, and could, to a certain extent, look after themselves. But when I looked at Anne Meredith –'

She hesitated, then continued slowly:

'Anne Meredith was only a girl. She had the whole of her life in front of her. This miserable business might ruin that life . . .

'I didn't like the thought of that . . .

'And then, M. Poirot, with these ideas growing in my mind, I realized that what you had hinted had come true. I was not going to be able to keep silence. This afternoon I rang you up . . .'

Minutes passed.

Hercule Poirot leaned forward. He stared, deliberately stared through the gathering gloom, at Mrs Lorrimer. She returned that intent gaze quietly and without any nervousness.

He said at last:

'Mrs Lorrimer, are you sure – are you *positive* (you will tell me the truth, will you not?) – *that the murder of Mr Shaitana was not premeditated*? Is it not a fact that you planned the crime *beforehand* – that you went to that dinner with the murder already mapped out in your mind?'

Mrs Lorrimer stared at him for a moment, then she shook her head sharply.

'No,' she said.

'You did not plan the murder beforehand?'

'Certainly not.'

'Then – then . . . Oh, you are lying to me – you must be lying! . . .'

Mrs Lorrimer's voice cut into the air like ice.

'Really, M. Poirot, you forget yourself.'

The little man sprang to his feet. He paced up and down the room, muttering to himself, uttering ejaculations.

Suddenly he said:

'Permit me.'

And, going to the switch, he turned on the electric lights.

He came back, sat down in his chair, placed both hands on his knees and stared straight at his hostess.

'The question is,' he said, 'can Hercule Poirot possibly be wrong?'

'No one can always be right,' said Mrs Lorrimer coldly.

'I am,' said Poirot. 'Always I am right. It is so invariable that it startles me. But now it looks, it very much looks, as though I am wrong. And that upsets me. Presumably, you know what you are saying. It is your murder! Fantastic, then, that Hercule Poirot should know better than you do how you committed it.'

'Fantastic and very absurd,' said Mrs Lorrimer still more coldly.

'I am, then, mad. Decidedly I am mad: No – *sacré nom d'un petit bonhomme* – I am *not* mad! I am right. I *must* be right. I am willing to believe that you killed Mr Shaitana – *but you cannot have killed him in the way you say you did*. No one can do a thing that is not *dans son charactère!*'

He paused. Mrs Lorrimer drew in an angry breath and bit her lips. She was about to speak, but Poirot forestalled her.

'Either the killing of Shaitana was planned beforehand – *or you did not kill him at all!*'

Mrs Lorrimer said sharply:

'I really believe you *are* mad, M. Poirot. If I am willing to admit I committed the crime, I should not be likely to lie about the way I did it. What would be the point of such a thing?'

Poirot got up again and took one turn round the room. When he came back to his seat his manner had changed. He was gentle and kindly.

'You did not kill Shaitana,' he said softly. 'I see that now. I see everything. Harley Street. And little Anne Meredith standing forlorn on the pavement. I see, too, another girl – a very long time ago, a girl who has gone through life always alone – terribly alone. Yes, I see all that. But one thing I do not see – why are you so certain that Anne Meredith did it?'

'Really, M. Poirot –'

'Absolutely useless to protest – to lie further to me, madame. *I tell you, I know the truth.* I know the very emotions that swept over you that day in Harley Street. You would not have done it for Dr Roberts – oh, no! You would not have done it for Major Despard, *non plus*. But Anne Meredith is different. You have compassion for her, *because she has done what you once did*. You do not know even – or so I imagine – what *reason* she had for the crime. But you are quite sure she did it. You were sure that first evening – the evening it happened – when Superintendent Battle invited you to give your views on the case. Yes, I know it all, you see. It is quite useless to lie further to me. You see that, do you not?'

He paused for an answer, but none came. He nodded his head in satisfaction.

'Yes, you are sensible. That is good. It is a very noble action that you perform there, madame, to take the blame on yourself and to let this child escape.'

'You forget,' said Mrs Lorrimer in a dry voice, 'I am not an innocent woman. Years ago, M. Poirot, I killed my husband . . .'

There was a moment's silence.

'I see,' said Poirot. 'It is justice. After all, only justice. You have the logical mind. You are willing to suffer for the act you committed. Murder is murder – it does not matter who the victim is. Madame, you have courage, and you have clear-sightedness. But I ask of you once more: *How can you be so sure?* How do you *know* that it was Anne Meredith who killed Mr Shaitana?'

A deep sigh broke from Mrs Lorrimer. Her last resistance had gone down before Poirot's insistence. She answered his question quite simply like a child.

'Because,' she said, 'I saw her.'

CHAPTER 27

THE EYE-WITNESS

Suddenly Poirot laughed. He could not help it. His head went back, and his high Gallic laugh filled the room.

'*Pardon, madame,*' he said, wiping his eyes. 'I could not help it. Here we argue and we reason! We ask questions! We invoke the psychology – and all the time *there was an eye-witness of the crime.* Tell me, I pray of you.'

'It was fairly late in the evening. Anne Meredith was dummy. She got up and looked over her partner's hand, and then she moved about the room. The hand wasn't very interesting – the conclusion was inevitable. I didn't need to concentrate on the cards. Just as we got to the last three tricks I looked over towards the fireplace. Anne Meredith was bent over Mr Shaitana. As I watched, she straightened herself – her hand had been actually on his breast – a gesture which awakened my surprise. She straightened herself, and I saw her face and her quick look over towards us. Guilt and fear – that is what I saw on her face. Of course, I didn't know what had happened then. I only wondered what on earth the girl could have been doing. Later – I knew.'

Poirot nodded.

'But *she* did not know that you knew. *She* did not know that you had seen her?'

'Poor child,' said Mrs Lorrimer. 'Young, frightened – her way to make in the world. Do you wonder that I – well, held my tongue?'

'No, no, I do not wonder.'

'Especially knowing that I – that I myself –' She finished the sentence with a shrug. 'It was certainly not my place to stand accuser. It was up to the police.'

'Quite so – but today you have gone further than that.'

Mrs Lorrimer said grimly:

'I've never been a very soft-hearted or compassionate woman, but I suppose these qualities grow upon one in one's old age. I assure you, I'm not often actuated by pity.'

'It is not always a very safe guide, madame. Mademoiselle Anne is young, she is fragile, she looks timid and frightened – oh, yes, she seems a very worthy subject for compassion. But I, *I do not agree*. Shall I tell you, madame, why Miss Anne Meredith killed Mr Shaitana. It was because he knew that she had previously killed an elderly lady to whom she was companion – because that lady had found her out in a petty theft.'

Mrs Lorrimer looked a little startled.

'Is that true, M. Poirot?'

'I have no doubt of it, whatsoever. She is so soft – so gentle – one would say. Pah! She is dangerous, madame, that little Mademoiselle Anne! Where her own safety, her own comfort, is concerned, she will strike wildly – treacherously. With Mademoiselle Anne *those two crimes will not be the end*. She will gain confidence from them . . .'

Mrs Lorrimer said sharply:

'What you say is horrible, M. Poirot. Horrible!'

Poirot rose.

'Madame, I will now take my leave. Reflect on what I have said.'

Mrs Lorrimer was looking a little uncertain of herself. She said with an attempt at her old manner:

'If it suits me, M. Poirot, I shall deny this whole conversation. You have no witnesses, remember. What I have just told you that I saw on that fatal evening is – well, private between ourselves.'

Poirot said gravely:

'Nothing shall be done without your consent, madame. And be at peace; I have my own methods. Now that I know what I am driving at –'

He took her hand and raised it to his lips.

'Permit me to tell you, madame, that you are a most remarkable woman. All my homage and respect. Yes, indeed, a woman in a thousand. Why, you have not even done what nine hundred and ninety-nine women out of a thousand could not have resisted doing.'

'What is that?'

'Told me just why you killed your husband – and how entirely justified such a proceeding really was.'

Mrs Lorrimer drew herself up.

'Really, M. Poirot,' she said stiffly. 'My reasons were entirely my own business.'

'*Magnifique!*' said Poirot, and, once more raising her hand to his lips, he left the room.

It was cold outside the house, and he looked up and down for a taxi, but there was none in sight.

He began to walk in the direction of King's Road.

As he walked he was thinking hard. Occasionally he nodded his head; once he shook it.

He looked back over his shoulder. Someone was going up the steps of Mrs Lorrimer's house. In figure it looked very like Anne Meredith. He hesitated for a minute, wondering whether to turn back or not, but in the end he went on.

On arrival at home, he found that Battle had gone without leaving any message.

He proceeded to ring the superintendent up.

'Hallo.' Battle's voice came through. 'Got anything?'

'*Je crois bien. Mon ami*, we must get after the Meredith girl – and quickly.'

'I'm getting after her – but why quickly?'

'Because, my friend, she may be dangerous.'

Battle was silent for a minute or two. Then he said:

'I know what you mean. But there's no one . . . Oh, well, we mustn't take chances. As a matter of fact, I've written her. Official note, saying I'm calling to see her tomorrow. I thought it might be a good thing to get her rattled.'

'It is a possibility, at least. I may accompany you?'

'Naturally. Honoured to have your company, M. Poirot.'

Poirot hung up the receiver with a thoughtful face.

His mind was not quite at rest. He sat for a long time in front of his fire, frowning to himself. At last, putting his fears and doubts aside, he went to bed.

'We will see in the morning,' he murmured.

But of what the morning would bring he had no idea.

CHAPTER 28

SUICIDE

The summons came by telephone at the moment when Poirot was sitting down to his morning coffee and rolls.

He lifted the telephone receiver, and Battle's voice spoke:

'That M. Poirot?'

'Yes, it is. *Qu'est ce qu'il y a?*'

The mere inflection of the superintendent's voice had told him that something had happened. His own vague misgivings came back to him.

'But quickly, my friend, tell me.'

'It's Mrs Lorrimer.'

'Lorrimer – yes?'

'What the devil did you say to her – or did she say to you – yesterday? You never told me anything; in fact, you let me think that the Meredith girl was the one we were after.'

Poirot said quietly:

'What has happened?'

'Suicide.'

'Mrs Lorrimer has committed suicide?'

'That's right. It seems she has been very depressed and unlike herself lately. Her doctor had ordered her some sleeping stuff. Last night she took an overdose.'

Poirot drew a deep breath.

'There is no question of – accident?'

'Not the least. It's all cut and dried. She wrote to the three of them.'

'Which three?'

'The other three. Roberts, Despard and Miss Meredith. All fair and square – no beating about the bush. Just wrote that she would like them to know that she was taking a short-cut out of all the mess – that it was she who had killed Shaitana – and that she apologized – apologized – to all three of them for the inconvenience and annoyance they had suffered. Perfectly calm, business-like letter. Absolutely typical of the woman. She was a cool customer all right.'

For a minute or two Poirot did not answer.

So this was Mrs Lorrimer's final word. She had determined, after all, to shield Anne Meredith. A quick painless death instead of a protracted painful one, and her last action an altruistic one – the saving of the girl with whom she felt a secret bond of sympathy. The whole thing planned and carried out with quite ruthless efficiency – a suicide carefully announced to the three interested parties. What a woman! His admiration quickened. It was like her – like her clear-cut determination, her insistence on what she had decided being carried out.

He had thought to have convinced her – but evidently she had preferred her own judgement. A woman of very strong will.

Battle's voice cut into his meditations.

'What the devil did you say to her yesterday? You must have put the wind up her, and this is the result. But you implied that the result of your interview was definite suspicion of the Meredith girl.'

Poirot was silent a minute or two. He felt that, dead, Mrs Lorrimer constrained him to her will, as she could not have done if she were living.

He said at last slowly:

'I was in error . . .'

They were unaccustomed words on his tongue, and he did not like them.

'You made a mistake, eh?' said Battle. 'All the same, she must have thought you were on to her. It's a bad business – letting her slip through our fingers like this.'

'You could not have proved anything against her,' said Poirot.

'No – I suppose that's true . . . Perhaps it's all for the best. You – er – didn't mean this to happen, M. Poirot?'

Poirot's disclaimer was indignant. Then he said:

'Tell me exactly what has occurred.'

'Roberts opened his letter just before eight o'clock. He lost no time, dashed off at once in his car, leaving his parlourmaid to communicate with us, which she did. He got to the house to find that Mrs Lorrimer hadn't been called yet, rushed up to her bedroom – but it was too late. He tried artificial respiration, but there was nothing doing. Our divisional surgeon arrived soon after and confirmed his treatment.'

'What was the sleeping stuff?'

'Veronal, I think. One of the barbituric group, at any rate. There was a bottle of tablets by her bed.'

'What about the other two? Did they not try to communicate with you?'

'Despard is out of town. He hasn't had this morning's post.'

'And – Miss Meredith?'

'I've just rung her up.'

'*Eh bien?*'

'She had just opened the letter a few moments before my call came through. Post is later there.'

'What was her reaction?'

'A perfectly proper attitude. Intense relief decently veiled. Shocked and grieved – that sort of thing.'

Poirot paused a moment, then he said:

'Where are you now, my friend?'

'At Cheyne Lane.'

'*Bien.* I will come round immediately.'

In the hall at Cheyne Lane he found Dr Roberts on the point of departure. The doctor's usual florid manner was rather in abeyance this morning. He looked pale and shaken.

'Nasty business this, M. Poirot. I can't say I'm not relieved – from my own point of view – but, to tell you the truth, it's a bit of a shock. I never really thought for a minute that it was Mrs Lorrimer who stabbed Shaitana. It's been the greatest surprise to me.'

'I, too, am surprised.'

'Quiet, well-bred, self-contained woman. Can't imagine her

doing a violent thing like that. What was the motive, I wonder? Oh, well, we shall never know now. I confess I'm curious, though.'

'It must take a load off your mind – this occurrence.'

'Oh, it does, undoubtedly. It would be hypocrisy not to admit it. It's not very pleasant to have a suspicion of murder hanging over you. As for the poor woman herself – well, it was undoubtedly the best way out.'

'So she thought herself.'

Roberts nodded.

'Conscience, I suppose,' he said as he let himself out of the house.

Poirot shook his head thoughtfully. The doctor had misread the situation. It was not remorse that had made Mrs Lorrimer take her life.

On his way upstairs he paused to say a few words of comfort to the elderly parlourmaid, who was weeping quietly.

'It's so dreadful, sir. So very dreadful. We were all so fond of her. And you having tea with her yesterday so nice and quiet. And now today she's gone. I shall never forget this morning – never as long as I live. The gentleman pealing at the bell. Rang three times, he did, before I could get to it. And, "Where's your mistress?" he shot out at me. I was so flustered, I couldn't hardly answer. You see, we never went in to the mistress till she rang – that was her orders. And I just couldn't get out anything. And the doctor he says, "Where's her room?" and ran up the stairs, and me behind him, and I showed him the door, and he rushes in, not so much as knocking, and takes one look at her lying there, and, "Too late," he says. She was dead, sir. But he sent me for brandy and hot water, and he tried desperate to bring her back, but it couldn't be done. And then the police coming and all – it isn't – it isn't – decent, sir. Mrs Lorrimer wouldn't have liked it. And why the police? It's none of their business, surely, even if an accident has occurred and the poor mistress did take an overdose by mistake.'

Poirot did not reply to her question.

He said:

'Last night, was your mistress quite as usual? Did she seem upset or worried at all?'

'No, I don't think so, sir. She was tired – and I think she was in pain. She hasn't been well lately, sir.'

'No, I know.'

The sympathy in his tone made the woman go on.

'She was never one for complaining, sir, but both cook and I had been worried about her for some time. She couldn't do as much as she used to do, and things tired her. I think, perhaps, the young lady coming after you left was a bit too much for her.'

With his foot on the stairs, Poirot turned back.

'The young lady? Did a young lady come here yesterday evening?'

'Yes, sir. Just after you left, it was. Miss Meredith, her name was.'

'Did she stay long?'

'About an hour, sir.'

Poirot was silent for a minute or two, then he said:

'And afterwards?'

'The mistress went to bed. She had dinner in bed. She said she was tired.'

Again Poirot was silent; then he said:

'Do you know if your mistress wrote any letters yesterday evening?'

'Do you mean after she went to bed? I don't think so, sir.'

'But you are not sure?'

'There were some letters on the hall table ready to be posted, sir. We always took them last thing before shutting up. But I think they had been lying there since earlier in the day.'

'How many were there?'

'Two or three – I'm not quite sure, sir. Three, I think.'

'You – or cook – whoever posted them – did not happen to notice to whom they were addressed? Do not be offended at my question. It is of the utmost importance.'

'I went to the post myself with them, sir. I noticed the top one – it was to Fortnum and Mason's. I couldn't say as to the others.'

The woman's tone was earnest and sincere.

'Are you sure there were not more than three letters?'

'Yes, sir, I'm quite certain of that.'

Poirot nodded his head gravely. Once more he started up the staircase. Then he said:

'You knew, I take it, that your mistress took medicine to make her sleep?'

'Oh, yes, sir, it was the doctor's orders. Dr Lang.'

'Where was this sleeping medicine kept?'

'In the little cupboard in the mistress's room.'

Poirot did not ask any further questions. He went upstairs. His face was very grave.

On the upper landing Battle greeted him. The superintendent looked worried and harassed.

'I'm glad you've come, M. Poirot. Let me introduce you to Dr Davidson.'

The divisional surgeon shook hands. He was a tall, melancholy man.

'The luck was against us,' he said. 'An hour or two earlier, and we might have saved her.'

'H'm,' said Battle. 'I mustn't say so officially, but I'm not sorry. She was a – well, she was a lady. I don't know what her reasons were for killing Shaitana, but she may just conceivably have been justified.'

'In any case,' said Poirot, 'it is doubtful if she would have lived to stand her trial. She was a very ill woman.'

The surgeon nodded in agreement.

'I should say you were quite right. Well, perhaps it is all for the best.'

He started down the stairs.

Battle moved after him.

'One minute, doctor.'

Poirot, his hand on the bedroom door, murmured, 'I may enter – yes?'

Battle nodded over his shoulder. 'Quite all right. We're through.' Poirot passed into the room, closing the door behind him . . .

He went over to the bed and stood looking down at the quiet, dead face.

He was very disturbed.

Had the dead woman gone to the grave in a last determined effort to save a young girl from death and disgrace – or was there a different, a more sinister explanation?

There were certain facts . . .

Suddenly he bent down, examining a dark, discoloured bruise on the dead woman's arm.

He straightened himself up again. There was a strange, cat-like gleam in his eyes that certain close associates of his would have recognized.

He left the room quickly and went downstairs. Battle and a subordinate were at the telephone. The latter laid down the receiver and said:

'He hasn't come back, sir.'

Battle said:

'Despard. I've been trying to get him. There's a letter for him with the Chelsea postmark all right.'

Poirot asked an irrelevant question.

'Had Dr Roberts had his breakfast when he came here?'

Battle stared.

'No,' he said, 'I remember he mentioned that he'd come out without it.'

'Then he will be at his house now. We can get him.'

'But why –?'

But Poirot was already busy at the dial. Then he spoke:

'Dr Roberts? It is Dr Roberts speaking? *Mais oui*, it is Poirot here. Just one question. Are you well acquainted with the hand-writing of Mrs Lorrimer?'

'Mrs Lorrimer's handwriting? I – no, I don't know that I'd ever seen it before.'

'*Je vous remercie.*'

Poirot laid down the receiver quickly.

Battle was staring at him.

'What's the big idea, M. Poirot?' he asked quietly.

Poirot took him by the arm.

'Listen, my friend. A few minutes after I left this house yesterday Anne Meredith arrived. I actually saw her going up the steps, though I was not quite sure of her identity at the time. Immediately after Anne Meredith left Mrs Lorrimer went to bed. As far as the maid knows, *she did not write any letters then*. And, for reasons which you will understand when I recount to you our interview, *I do not believe that she wrote those three letters before my visit*. When did she write them, then?'

'After the servants had gone to bed?' suggested Battle. 'She got up and posted them herself.'

'That is possible, yes, but there is another possibility – *that she did not write them at all.*'

Battle whistled.

'My God, you mean –'

The telephone trilled. The sergeant picked up the receiver. He listened a minute, then turned to Battle.

'Sergeant O'Connor speaking from Despard's flat, sir. There's reason to believe that Despard's down at Wallingford-on-Thames.'

Poirot caught Battle by the arm.

'Quickly, my friend. We, too, must go to Wallingford. I tell you, I am not easy in my mind. This may not be the end. I tell you again, my friend, this young lady, she is dangerous.'

CHAPTER 29

ACCIDENT

'Anne,' said Rhoda.

'Mmm?'

'No, really, Anne, don't answer with half your mind on a crossword puzzle. I want you to attend to me.'

'I am attending.'

Anne sat bolt upright and put down the paper.

'That's better. Look here, Anne.' Rhoda hesitated. 'About this man coming.'

'Superintendent Battle?'

'Yes, Anne, I wish you'd tell him – about being at the Bensons'.'

Anne's voice grew rather cold.

'Nonsense. Why should I?'

'Because – well, it might look – as though you'd been keeping something back. I'm sure it would be better to mention it.'

'I can't very well now,' said Anne coldly.

'I wish you had in the first place.'

'Well, it's too late to bother about that now.'

'Yes.' Rhoda did not sound convinced.

Anne said rather irritably:

'In any case, I can't see *why*. It's got nothing to do with all this.'

'No, of course not.'

'I was only there about two months. He only wants these things as – well – references. Two months doesn't count.'

'No, I know. I expect I'm being rather foolish, but it does worry me rather. I feel you ought to mention it. You see, if it came out some other way, it might look rather bad – your keeping dark about it, I mean.'

'I don't see how it can come out. Nobody knows but you.'

'N-no?'

Anne pounced on the slight hesitation in Rhoda's voice.

'Why, who does know?'

'Well, everyone at Combeacre,' said Rhoda after a moment's silence.

'Oh, that!' Anne dismissed it with a shrug. 'The superintendent isn't likely to come up against anyone from there. It would be an extraordinary coincidence if he did.'

'Coincidences happen.'

'Rhoda, you're being extraordinary about this. Fuss, fuss, fuss.'

'I'm terribly sorry, darling. Only you know what the police might be like if they thought you were – well – hiding things.'

'They won't know. Who's to tell them? Nobody knows but you.'

It was the second time she had said those words. At this second repetition her voice changed a little – something queer and speculative came into it.

'Oh, dear, I wish you would,' sighed Rhoda unhappily.

She looked guiltily at Anne, but Anne was not looking at her. She was sitting with a frown on her face, as though working out some calculation.

'Rather fun, Major Despard turning up,' said Rhoda.

'What? Oh, yes.'

'Anne, he *is* attractive. If you don't want him, *do, do, do* hand him over to me!'

'Don't be absurd, Rhoda. He doesn't care tuppence for me.'

'Then why does he keep on turning up? Of course he's keen on you. You're just the sort of distressed damsel that he'd enjoy rescuing. You look so beautifully helpless, Anne.'

'He's equally pleasant to both of us.'

'That's only his niceness. But if you don't want him, I could do the sympathetic friend act – console his broken heart, etc., etc., and in the end I might get him. Who knows?' Rhoda concluded inelegantly.

'I'm sure you're quite welcome to him, my dear,' said Anne, laughing.

'He's got such a lovely back to his neck,' sighed Rhoda. 'Very brick red and muscular.'

'Darling, must you be so mawkish?'

'Do you like him, Anne?'

'Yes, very much.'

'Aren't we prim and sedate? I think he likes me a little – not as much as you, but a little.'

'Oh, but he does like you,' said Anne.

Again there was an unusual note in her voice, but Rhoda did not hear it.

'What time is our sleuth coming?' she asked.

'Twelve,' said Anne. She was silent for a minute or two, then she said, 'It's only half-past ten now. Let's go out on the river.'

'But isn't – didn't – didn't Despard say he'd come round about eleven?'

'Why should we wait in for him? We can leave a message with Mrs Astwell which way we've gone, and he can follow us along the towpath.'

'In fact, don't make yourself cheap, dear, as mother always said!' laughed Rhoda. 'Come on, then.'

She went out of the room and through the garden door. Anne followed her.

Major Despard called at Wendon Cottage about ten minutes later. He was before his time, he knew, so he was a little surprised to find both girls had already gone out.

He went through the garden and across the fields, and turned to the right along the towpath.

Mrs Astwell remained a minute or two looking after him, instead of getting on with her morning chores.

'Sweet on one or other of 'em, he is,' she observed to herself. 'I think it's Miss Anne, but I'm not certain. He don't give much away by his face. Treats 'em both alike. I'm not sure they ain't both sweet on him, too. If so, they won't be such dear friends so much longer. Nothing like a gentleman for coming between two young ladies.'

Pleasurably excited by the prospect of assisting at a budding romance, Mrs Astwell turned indoors to her task of washing up the breakfast things, when once again the door-bell rang.

'Drat that door,' said Mrs Astwell. 'Do it on purpose, they do. Parcel, I suppose. Or might be a telegram.'

She moved slowly to the front door.

Two gentlemen stood there, a small foreign gentleman and an exceedingly English, big, burly gentleman. The latter she had seen before, she remembered.

'Miss Meredith at home?' asked the big man.

Mrs Astwell shook her head.

'Just gone out.'

'Really? Which way? We didn't meet her.'

Mrs Astwell, secretly studying the amazing moustache of the other gentleman, and deciding that they looked an unlikely pair to be friends, volunteered further information.

'Gone out on the river,' she explained.

The other gentleman broke in:

'And the other lady? Miss Dawes?'

'They've both gone.'

'Ah, thank you,' said Battle. 'Let me see, which way does one get to the river?'

'First turning to the left, down the lane,' Mrs Astwell replied promptly. 'When you get to the towpath, go right. I heard them say that's the way they were going,' she added helpfully. 'Not above a quarter of an hour ago. You'll soon catch 'em up.'

'And I wonder,' she added to herself as she unwillingly closed the front door, having stared inquisitively at their retreating backs, 'who you two might be. Can't place you, somehow.'

Mrs Astwell returned to the kitchen sink, and Battle and Poirot duly took the first turning to the left – a straggling lane which soon ended abruptly at the towpath.

Poirot was hurrying along, and Battle eyed him curiously.

'Anything the matter, M. Poirot? You seem in a mighty hurry.'

'It is true. I am uneasy, my friend.'

'Anything particular?'

Poirot shook his head.

'No. But there are possibilities. You never know . . .'

'You've got something in your head,' said Battle. 'You were urgent that we should come down here this morning without losing a moment – and, my word, you made Constable Turner step on the gas! What are you afraid of? The girl's shot her bolt.'

Poirot was silent.

'What are you afraid of?' Battle repeated.

'What is one always afraid of in these cases?'

Battle nodded.

'You're quite right. I wonder –'

'You wonder what, my friend?'

Battle said slowly:

'I'm wondering if Miss Meredith knows that her friend told Mrs Oliver a certain fact.'

Poirot nodded his head in vigorous appreciation.

'Hurry, my friend,' he said.

They hastened along the river bank. There was no craft visible on the water's surface, but presently they rounded a bend, and Poirot suddenly stopped dead. Battle's quick eyes saw also.

'Major Despard,' he said.

Despard was about two hundred yards ahead of them, striding along the river bank.

A little farther on the two girls were in view in a punt on the water, Rhoda punting – Anne lying and laughing up at her. Neither of them were looking towards the bank.

And then – *it happened*. Anne's hand outstretched, Rhoda's stagger, her plunge overboard – her desperate grasp at Anne's sleeve – the rocking boat – then an overturned punt and two girls struggling in the water.

'See it?' cried Battle as he started to run. 'Little Meredith caught her round the ankle and tipped her in. My God, that's her fourth murder!'

They were both running hard. But someone was ahead of them. It was clear that neither girl could swim, but Despard had run quickly along the path to the nearest point, and now he plunged in and swam towards them.

'*Mon Dieu*, this is interesting,' cried Poirot. He caught Battle's arm. 'Which of them will he go for first?'

The two girls were not together. About twelve yards separated them.

Despard swam powerfully towards them – there was no check in his stroke. He was making straight for Rhoda.

Battle, in his turn, reached the nearest bank and went in. Despard had just brought Rhoda successfully to shore. He hauled her up, flung her down and plunged in again, swimming towards the spot where Anne had just gone under.

'Be careful,' called Battle. 'Weeds.'

He and Battle got to the spot at the same time, but Anne had gone under before they reached her.

They got her at last and between them towed her to the shore.

Rhoda was being ministered to by Poirot. She was sitting up now, her breath coming unevenly.

Despard and Battle laid Anne Meredith down.

'Artificial respiration,' said Battle. 'Only thing to do. But I'm afraid she's gone.'

He set to work methodically. Poirot stood by, ready to relieve him.

Despard dropped down by Rhoda.

'Are you all right?' he asked hoarsely.

She said slowly:

'You saved me. You saved *me* . . .' She held out her hands to him, and as he took them she burst suddenly into tears.

He said, 'Rhoda . . .'

Their hands clung together . . .

He had a sudden vision – of African scrub, and Rhoda, laughing and adventurous, by his side . . .

CHAPTER 30

MURDER

I

'Do you mean to say,' said Rhoda incredulously, 'that Anne *meant* to push me in? I know it felt like it. And she knew I can't swim. But – but was it *deliberate*?'

'It was quite deliberate,' said Poirot.

They were driving through the outskirts of London.

'But – but – why?'

Poirot did not reply for a minute or two. He thought he knew one of the motives that had led Anne to act as she had done, and that motive was sitting next to Rhoda at the minute.

Superintendent Battle coughed.

'You'll have to prepare yourself, Miss Dawes, for a bit of a shock. This Mrs Benson your friend lived with, her death wasn't quite the accident that it appeared – at least, so we've reason to suppose.'

'What do you mean?'

'We believe,' said Poirot, 'that Anne Meredith changed two bottles.'

'Oh, no – no, how horrible! It's *impossible*. Anne? Why should she?'

'She had her reasons,' said Superintendent Battle. 'But the point is, Miss Dawes, that, as far as Miss Meredith knew, *you were the only person who could give us a clue to that incident.* You didn't tell her, I suppose, that you'd mentioned it to Mrs Oliver?'

Rhoda said slowly:

'No. I thought she'd be annoyed with me.'

'She would. Very annoyed,' said Battle grimly. 'But she thought that the only danger could come from *you*, and that's why she decided to – er – eliminate you.'

'Eliminate? *Me?* Oh, how beastly! It *can't* be all true.'

'Well, she's dead now,' said Superintendent Battle, 'so we might as well leave it at that; but she wasn't a nice friend for you to have, Miss Dawes – and that's a fact.'

The car drew up in front of a door.

'We'll go in to M. Poirot's,' said Superintendent Battle, 'and have a bit of a talk about it all.'

In Poirot's sitting-room they were welcomed by Mrs Oliver, who was entertaining Dr Roberts. They were drinking sherry. Mrs Oliver was wearing one of her new horsy hats and a velvet dress with a bow on the chest on which reposed a large piece of apple core.

'Come in. Come in,' said Mrs Oliver hospitably and quite as though it were her house and not Poirot's.

'As soon as I got your telephone call I rang up Dr Roberts, and we came round here. And all his patients are dying, but he doesn't care. They're probably getting better, really. We want to hear all about everything.'

'Yes, indeed, I'm thoroughly fogged,' said Roberts.

'*Eh bien*,' said Poirot. 'The case is ended. The murderer of Mr Shaitana is found at last.'

'So Mrs Oliver told me. That pretty little thing, Anne Meredith. I can hardly believe it. A most unbelievable murderess.'

'She was a murderess all right,' said Battle. 'Three murders to her credit – and not her fault that she didn't get away with a fourth one.'

'Incredible!' murmured Roberts.

'Not at all,' said Mrs Oliver. 'Least likely person. It seems to work out in real life just the same as in books.'

'It's been an amazing day,' said Roberts. 'First Mrs Lorrimer's letter. I suppose that was a forgery, eh?'

'Precisely. A forgery written in triplicate.'

'She wrote one to herself, too?'

'Naturally. The forgery was quite skilful – it would not deceive an expert, of course – but, then, it was highly unlikely that an expert would have been called in. All the evidence pointed to Mrs Lorrimer's having committed suicide.'

'You will excuse my curiosity, M. Poirot, but what made you suspect that she had not committed suicide?'

'A little conversation that I had with a maidservant at Cheyne Lane.'

'She told you of Anne Meredith's visit the former evening?'

'That among other things. And then, you see, I had already come to a conclusion in my own mind as to the identity of the guilty person – that is, the person who killed Mr Shaitana. That person was not Mrs Lorrimer.'

'What made you suspect Miss Meredith?'

Poirot raised his hand.

'A little minute. Let me approach this matter in my own way. Let me, that is to say, eliminate. The murderer of Mr Shaitana was not Mrs Lorrimer, nor was it Major Despard, and, curiously enough, it was not Anne Meredith . . .'

He leaned forward. His voice purred, soft and cat-like.

'You see, Dr Roberts, *you were the person who killed Mr Shaitana*; and you also killed Mrs Lorrimer . . .'

II

There was at least three minutes' silence. Then Roberts laughed a rather menacing laugh.

'Are you quite mad, M. Poirot? I certainly did not murder Mr Shaitana, and I could not possibly have murdered Mrs Lorrimer. My dear Battle' – he turned to the Scotland Yard man – 'are *you* standing for this?'

'I think you'd better listen to what M. Poirot has to say,' said Battle quietly.

Poirot said:

'It is true that though I have known for some time that you – and only you – could have killed Shaitana, it would not be an easy matter to prove it. But Mrs Lorrimer's case is quite different.' He leaned forward. 'It is not a case of my knowing. It is much simpler than that – for we have *an eye-witness who saw you do it.*'

Roberts grew very quiet. His eyes glittered. He said sharply:

'You are talking rubbish!'

'Oh, no, I am not. It was early in the morning. You bluffed your way into Mrs Lorrimer's room, where she was still heavily asleep under the influence of the drug she had taken the night before. You bluff again – pretend to see at a glance that she is dead! You pack the parlourmaid off for brandy – hot water – all the rest of it. You are left alone in the room. The maid has only had the barest peep. And then what happens?

'You may not be aware of the fact, Dr Roberts, *but certain firms of window cleaners specialize in early morning work.* A window cleaner with his ladder arrived at the same time as you did. He placed his ladder against the side of the house and began his work. The first window he tackled was that of Mrs Lorrimer's room. When, however, he saw what was going on, he quickly retired to another window, *but he had seen something first*. He shall tell us his own story.'

Poirot stepped lightly across the floor, turned a door handle, called:

'Come in, Stephens,' and returned.

A big awkward-looking man with red hair entered. In his hand he held a uniformed hat bearing the legend 'Chelsea Window Cleaners' Association' which he twirled awkwardly.

Poirot said:

'Is there anybody you recognize in this room?'

The man looked round, then gave a bashful nod of the head towards Dr Roberts.

'Him,' he said.

'Tell us when you saw him last and what he was doing.'

'This morning it was. Eight o'clock job at a lady's house in Cheyne Lane. I started on the windows there. Lady was in bed. Looked ill she did. She was just turning her head round on the pillow. This gent I took to be a doctor. He shoved her sleeve up and jabbed something into her arm about here –' He gestured. 'She just dropped back on the pillow again. I thought I'd better hop it to another window, so I did. Hope I didn't do wrong in any way?'

'You did admirably, my friend,' said Poirot.

He said quietly:

'*Eh bien*, Dr Roberts?'

'A – a simple restorative –' stammered Roberts. 'A last hope of bringing her round. It's monstrous –'

Poirot interrupted him.

'A simple restorative? – N-methyl – cyclo – hexenyl – methyl – malonyl urea,' said Poirot. He rolled out the syllables unctuously. 'Known more simply as Evipan. Used as an anaesthetic for short operations. Injected intravenously in large doses it produces instant unconsciousness. It is dangerous to use it after veronal or any barbiturates have been given. I noticed the bruised place on her arm where something had obviously been injected into a vein. A hint to the police surgeon and the drug was easily discovered by no less a person than Sir Charles Imphery, the Home Office Analyst.'

'That about cooks your goose, I think,' said Superintendent Battle. 'No need to prove the Shaitana business, though, of course, if necessary we can bring a further charge as to the murder of Mr Charles Craddock – and possibly his wife also.'

The mention of those two names finished Roberts.

He leaned back in his chair.

'I throw in my hand,' he said. 'You've got me! I suppose that sly devil Shaitana put you wise before you came that evening. And I thought I'd settled his hash so nicely.'

'It isn't Shaitana you've got to thank,' said Battle. 'The honours lie with M. Poirot here.'

He went to the door and two men entered.

Superintendent Battle's voice became official as he made the formal arrest.

As the door closed behind the accused man Mrs Oliver said happily, if not quite truthfully:

'I always *said* he did it!'

CHAPTER 31

CARDS ON THE TABLE

It was Poirot's moment, every face was turned to his in eager anticipation.

'You are very kind,' he said, smiling. 'You know, I think, that I enjoy my little lecture. I am a prosy old fellow.

'This case, to my mind, has been one of the most interesting cases I have ever come across. There was *nothing*, you see, to go upon. There were four people, one of whom *must* have committed the crime but which of the four? Was there anything to tell one? In the material sense – no. There were no tangible clues – no fingerprints – no incriminating papers or documents. There were only – the people themselves.

'And one tangible clue – the bridge scores.

'You may remember that from the beginning I showed a particular interest in those scores. They told me something about the various people who had kept them and they did more. They gave me one valuable hint. I noticed at once, in the third rubber, the figure of 1500 above the line. That figure could only represent one thing – a call of grand slam. Now if a person were to make up their minds to commit a crime under these somewhat unusual circumstances (that is, during a rubber game of bridge) that person was clearly running two serious risks. The first was that the victim might cry out and the second was that even if the victim did not cry out some one of the other three might chance to look up at the psychological moment and *actually witness the deed.*

'Now as to the first risk, nothing could be done about it. It was a matter of gambler's luck. But something could be done about the second. It stands to reason that during an interesting or an exciting hand the attention of the three players would be wholly on the game, whereas during a dull hand they were more likely to be looking about them. Now a bid of grand slam is always exciting. It is very often (as in this case it was) doubled. Every one of the three players is playing with close attention – the declarer to get his contract, the adversaries to discard correctly and to get him down. It was, then, a distinct possibility that the murder was committed during this particular hand and I determined to find out, if I could, exactly how the bidding had gone. I soon discovered that dummy during this particular hand had been Dr Roberts. I bore that in mind and approached the matter from my second angle – psychological probability. Of the four suspects Mrs Lorrimer struck me as by far the most likely to plan and carry out a successful murder – but I could not see her as committing any crime that had to be improvised on the spur of the moment. On the other hand her manner that first evening puzzled me. It suggested either that she had committed the murder herself or that she knew who had committed it. Miss Meredith, Major Despard and Dr Roberts were all psychological possibilities, though, as I have already mentioned, each of them would have committed the crime from an entirely different *angle.*

'I next made a second test. I got everyone in turn to tell me just what they remembered of the room. From that I got some very valuable information. First of all, by far the most likely person to have noticed the dagger was Dr Roberts. He was a natural observer of trifles of all kinds – what is called an observant man.

Of the bridge hands, however, he remembered practically nothing at all. I did not expect him to remember much, but his complete forgetfulness looked as though he had had something else on his mind all the evening. Again, you see, Dr Roberts was indicated.

'Mrs Lorrimer I found to have a marvellous card memory, and I could well imagine that with anyone of her powers of concentration a murder could easily be committed close at hand and she would never notice anything. She gave me a valuable piece of information. The grand slam was bid by Dr Roberts (quite unjustifiably) – and he bid it in her suit, not his own, so that she necessarily played the hand.

'The third test, the test on which Superintendent Battle and I built a good deal, was the discovery of the earlier murders so as to establish a similarity of method. Well, the credit for those discoveries belongs to Superintendent Battle, to Mrs Oliver and to Colonel Race. Discussing the matter with my friend Battle, he confessed himself disappointed because there were no points of similarity between any of the three earlier crimes and that of the murder of Mr Shaitana. But actually that was not true. The two murders attributed to Dr Roberts, when examined closely, *and from the psychological point of view and not the material one,* proved to be *almost exactly the same.* They, too, had been what I might describe as *public* murders. A shaving brush boldly infected in the victim's own dressing-room while the doctor officially washes his hands after a visit. The murder of Mrs Craddock under cover of a typhoid inoculation. Again done quite openly – in the sight of the world, as you might say. And the reaction of the man is the same. Pushed into a corner, he seizes a chance and acts at once – sheer bold audacious bluff – exactly like his play at bridge. As at bridge, so in the murder of Shaitana, he took a long chance and played his cards well. The blow was perfectly struck and at exactly the right moment.

'Now just at the moment that I had decided quite definitely that Dr Roberts was the man, Mrs Lorrimer asked me to come and see her – and quite convincingly accused herself of the crime! I nearly believed her! For a minute or two I *did* believe her – and then my little grey cells reasserted their mastery. It could not be – so it was not!

'But what she told me was more difficult still.

'She assured me that she had actually *seen* Anne Meredith commit the crime.

'It was not till the following morning – when I stood by a dead woman's bed – that I saw how I could still be right and Mrs Lorrimer still have spoken the truth.

'Anne Meredith went over to the fireplace – *and saw that Mr Shaitana was dead!* She stooped over him – perhaps stretched out her hand to the gleaming head of the jewelled pin.

'Her lips part to call out, but she does not call out. She remembers Shaitana's talk at dinner. Perhaps he had left some record. She, Anne Meredith, has a motive for desiring his death. Everyone will say that she has killed him. She dare not call out. Trembling with fear and apprehension she goes back to her seat.

'So Mrs Lorrimer is right, since she, as she thought, saw the crime committed – but I am right too, for actually she did not see it.

'If Roberts had held his hand at this point, I doubt if we could have ever brought his crimes home to him. We *might* have done so – by a mixture of bluff and various ingenious devices. I would at any rate have *tried.*

'But he lost his nerve and once again overbid his hand. And this time the cards lay wrong for him and he came down heavily.

'No doubt he was uneasy. He knew that Battle was nosing about. He foresaw the present situation going on indefinitely, the police still searching – and perhaps, by some miracle – coming on traces of his former crimes. He hit upon the brilliant idea of making Mrs Lorrimer the scapegoat for the party. His practised eye guessed, no doubt, that she was ill, and that her life could not be very much prolonged. How natural in those circumstances for her to choose a quick way out, and before taking it, confess to the crime! So he manages to get a sample of her handwriting – forges three identical letters and arrives at the house hot-foot in the morning with his story of the letter he has just received. His parlourmaid quite correctly is instructed to ring up the police. All he needs is a start. And he gets it. By the time the police surgeon arrives it is all over. Dr Roberts is ready with his story of artificial respiration that has failed. It is all perfectly plausible – perfectly straightforward.

'In all this he has no idea of throwing suspicion on Anne Meredith. He does not even know of her visit the night before. It is suicide and security only that he is aiming at.

'It is in fact an awkward moment for him when I ask if he is acquainted with Mrs Lorrimer's handwriting. If the forgery has been detected he must save himself by saying that he has never seen her handwriting. His mind works quickly, but not quickly enough.

'From Wallingford I telephone to Mrs Oliver. She plays her part by lulling his suspicions and bringing him here. And then when he is congratulating himself that all is well, though not exactly the way he has planned, the blow falls. Hercule Poirot springs! And so – the gambler will gather in no more tricks. He has thrown his cards upon the table. *C'est fini.*'

There was silence. Rhoda broke it with a sigh.

'What amazing luck that window cleaner happened to be there,' she said.

'Luck? Luck? That was not luck, mademoiselle. That was the grey cells of Hercule Poirot. And that reminds me –'

He went to the door.

'Come in – come in, my dear fellow. You acted your part *à merveille.*'

He returned accompanied by the window cleaner, who now held his red hair in his hand and who looked somehow a very different person.

'My friend Mr Gerald Hemmingway, a very promising young actor.'

'Then there was no window cleaner?' cried Rhoda. 'Nobody saw him?'

'I saw,' said Poirot. 'With the eyes of the mind one can see more than with the eyes of the body. One leans back and closes the eyes –'

Despard said cheerfully:

'Let's stab him, Rhoda, and see if his ghost can come back and find out who did it.'

•

THE CASE OF THE
DISCONTENTED SOLDIER

•

I

Major Wilbraham hesitated outside the door of Mr Parker Pyne's office to read, not for the first time, the advertisement from the morning paper which had brought him there. It was simple enough:

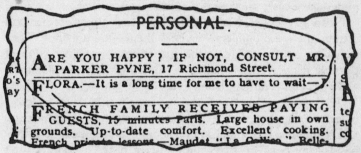

PERSONAL

ARE YOU HAPPY? IF NOT, CONSULT MR. PARKER PYNE, 17 Richmond Street.

FLORA.—It is a long time for me to have to wait—

FRENCH FAMILY RECEIVES PAYING GUESTS, 15 minutes Paris. Large house in own grounds. Up-to-date comfort. Excellent cooking. French private lessons.—Maudet "La Colline" Belle.

The major took a deep breath and abruptly plunged through the swing door leading to the outer office. A plain young woman looked up from her typewriter and glanced at him inquiringly.

'Mr Parker Pyne?' said Major Wilbraham, blushing.

'Come this way, please.'

He followed her into an inner office – into the presence of the bland Mr Parker Pyne.

'Good-morning,' said Mr Pyne. 'Sit down, won't you? And now tell me what I can do for you.'

'My name is Wilbraham –' began the other.

'Major? Colonel?' said Mr Pyne.

'Major.'

'Ah! And recently returned from abroad? India? East Africa?'

'East Africa.'

'A fine country, I believe. Well, so you are home again – and you don't like it. Is that the trouble?'

'You're absolutely right. Though how you knew –'

Mr Parker Pyne waved an impressive hand. 'It is my business to know. You see, for thirty-five years of my life I have been engaged in the compiling of statistics in a government office. Now I have retired and it has occurred to me to use the experience I have gained in a novel fashion. It is all so simple. Unhappiness can be classified under five main heads – no more I assure you. Once you know the cause of a malady, the remedy should not be impossible.

'I stand in the place of the doctor. The doctor first diagnoses the patient's disorder, then he recommends a course of treatment. There are cases where no treatment can be of any avail. If that is so, I say quite frankly that I can do nothing about it. But if I undertake a case, the cure is practically guaranteed.

'I can assure you, Major Wilbraham, that ninety-six per cent of retired empire builders – as I call them – are unhappy. They exchange an active life, a life full of responsibility, a life of possible danger, for – what? Straitened means, a dismal climate and a general feeling of being a fish out of water.'

'All you've said is true,' said the major. 'It's the boredom I object to. The boredom and the endless tittle-tattle about petty village matters. But what can I do about it? I've got a little money besides my pension. I've a nice cottage near Cobham. I can't afford to hunt or shoot or fish. I'm not married. My neighbours are all pleasant folk, but they've no ideas beyond this island.'

'The long and short of the matter is that you find life tame,' said Mr Parker Pyne.

'Damned tame.'

'You would like excitement, possibly danger?' asked Mr Pyne.

The soldier shrugged. 'There's no such thing in this tinpot country.'

'I beg your pardon,' said Mr Pyne seriously. 'There you are wrong. There is plenty of danger, plenty of excitement, here in London if you know where to go for it. You have seen only the surface of our English life, calm, pleasant. But there is another side. If you wish it, I can show you that other side.'

Major Wilbraham regarded him thoughtfully. There was something reassuring about Mr Pyne. He was large, not to say fat; he had a bald head of noble proportions, strong glasses and little twinkling eyes. And he had an aura – an aura of dependability.

'I should warn you, however,' continued Mr Pyne, 'that there is an element of risk.'

The soldier's eye brightened. 'That's all right,' he said. Then, abruptly: 'And – your fees?'

'My fee,' said Mr Pyne, 'is fifty pounds, payable in advance. If in a month's time you are still in the same state of boredom, I will refund your money.'

Wilbraham considered. 'Fair enough,' he said at last. 'I agree. I'll give you a cheque now.'

The transaction was completed. Mr Parker Pyne pressed a buzzer on his desk.

'It is now one o'clock,' he said. 'I am going to ask you to take a young lady out to lunch.' The door opened. 'Ah, Madeleine, my dear, let me introduce Major Wilbraham, who is going to take you out to lunch.'

Wilbraham blinked slightly, which was hardly to be wondered at. The girl who entered the room was dark, languorous, with wonderful eyes and long black lashes, a perfect complexion and a voluptuous scarlet mouth. Her exquisite clothes set off the swaying grace of her figure. From head to foot she was perfect.

'Er – delighted,' said Major Wilbraham.

'Miss de Sara,' said Mr Parker Pyne.

'How very kind of you,' murmured Madeleine de Sara.

'I have your address here,' announced Mr Parker Pyne. 'Tomorrow morning you will receive my further instructions.'

Major Wilbraham and the lovely Madeleine departed.

It was three o'clock when Madeleine returned.

Mr Parker Pyne looked up. 'Well?' he demanded.

Madeleine shook her head. 'Scared of me,' she said. 'Thinks I'm a vamp.'

'I thought as much,' said Mr Parker Pyne. 'You carried out my instructions?'

'Yes. We discussed the occupants of the other tables freely. The type he likes is fair-haired, blue-eyed, slightly anaemic, not too tall.'

'That should be easy,' said Mr Pyne. 'Get me Schedule B and let me see what we have in stock at present.' He ran his finger down a list, finally stopping at a name. 'Freda Clegg. Yes, I think Freda Clegg will do excellently. I had better see Mrs Oliver about it.'

II

The next day Major Wilbraham received a note, which read:

On Monday morning next at eleven o'clock go to Eaglemont, Friars Lane, Hampstead, and ask for Mr Jones. You will represent yourself as coming from the Guava Shipping Company.

Obediently on the following Monday (which happened to be Bank Holiday), Major Wilbraham set out for Eaglemont, Friars Lane. He set out, I say, but he never got there. For before he got there, something happened.

All the world and his wife seemed to be on their way to Hampstead. Major Wilbraham got entangled in crowds, suffocated in the tube and found it hard to discover the whereabouts of Friars Lane.

Friars Lane was a cul-de-sac, a neglected road full of ruts, with houses on either side standing back from the road. They were largish houses which had seen better days and had been allowed to fall into disrepair.

Wilbraham walked along peering at the half-erased names on the gate-posts, when suddenly he heard something that made him stiffen to attention. It was a kind of gurgling, half-choked cry.

It came again and this time it was faintly recognizable as the word 'Help!' It came from inside the wall of the house he was passing.

Without a moment's hesitation, Major Wilbraham pushed open the rickety gate and sprinted noiselessly up the weed-covered drive. There in the shrubbery was a girl struggling in the grasp of two enormous Negroes. She was putting up a brave fight, twisting and turning and kicking. One Negro held his hand over her mouth in spite of her furious efforts to get her head free.

Intent on their struggle with the girl, neither of the blacks had noticed Wilbraham's approach. The first they knew of it was when a violent punch on the jaw sent the man who was covering the girl's mouth reeling backwards. Taken by surprise, the other man relinquished his hold of the girl and turned. Wilbraham was ready for him. Once again his fist shot out, and the Negro reeled backwards and fell. Wilbraham turned on the other man, who was closing in behind him.

But the two men had had enough. The second one rolled over, sat up; then, rising, he made a dash for the gate. His companion followed suit. Wilbraham started after them, but changed his mind and turned towards the girl, who was leaning against a tree, panting.

'Oh, thank you!' she gasped. 'It was terrible.'

Major Wilbraham saw for the first time who it was he had rescued so opportunely. She was a girl of about twenty-one or two, fair-haired and blue-eyed, pretty in a rather colourless way.

'If you hadn't come!' she gasped.

'There, there,' said Wilbraham soothingly. 'It's all right now. I think, though, that we'd better get away from here. It's possible those fellows might come back.'

A faint smile came to the girl's lips. 'I don't think they will – not after the way you hit them. Oh, it was splendid of you!'

Major Wilbraham blushed under the warmth of her glance of admiration. 'Nothin' at all,' he said indistinctly. 'All in day's work. Lady being annoyed. Look here, if you take my arm, can you walk? It's been a nasty shock, I know.'

'I'm all right now,' said the girl. However, she took the proffered arm. She was still rather shaky. She glanced behind her at the house as they emerged through the gate. 'I can't understand it,' she murmured. 'That's clearly an empty house.'

'It's empty, right enough,' agreed the major, looking up at the shuttered windows and general air of decay.

'And yet it *is* Whitefriars.' She pointed to a half-obliterated name on the gate. 'And Whitefriars was the place I was to go.'

'Don't worry about anything now,' said Wilbraham. 'In a minute or two we'll be able to get a taxi. Then we'll drive somewhere and have a cup of coffee.'

At the end of the lane they came out into a more frequented street, and by good fortune a taxi had just set down a fare at one of the houses. Wilbraham hailed it, gave an address to the driver and they got in.

'Don't try to talk,' he admonished his companion. 'Just lie back. You've had a nasty experience.'

She smiled at him gratefully.

'By the way – er – my name is Wilbraham.'

'Mine is Clegg – Freda Clegg.'

Ten minutes later, Freda was sipping hot coffee and looking gratefully across a small table at her rescuer.

'It seems like a dream,' she said. 'A bad dream.' She shuddered. 'And only a short while ago I was wishing for something to happen – anything! Oh, I don't like adventures.'

'Tell me how it happened.'

'Well, to tell you properly I shall have to talk a lot about myself, I'm afraid.'

'An excellent subject,' said Wilbraham, with a bow.

'I am an orphan. My father – he was a sea captain – died when I was eight. My mother died three years ago. I work in the city. I am with the Vacuum Gas Company – a clerk. One evening last week I found a gentleman waiting to see me when I returned to my lodgings. He was a lawyer, a Mr Reid from Melbourne.

'He was very polite and asked me several questions about my family. He explained that he had known my father many years ago. In fact, he had transacted some legal business for him. Then he told me the object of his visit. "Miss Clegg," he said, "I have reason to suppose that you might benefit as the result of a financial transaction entered into by your father several years before he died." I was very much surprised, of course.

'"It is unlikely that you would ever have heard anything of the matter," he explained. "John Clegg never took the affair seriously, I fancy. However, it has materialized unexpectedly, but I am afraid any claim you might put in would depend on your ownership of certain papers. These papers would be part of your father's estate, and of course it is possible that they have been destroyed as worthless. Have you kept any of your father's papers?"

'I explained that my mother had kept various things of my father's in an old sea chest. I had looked through it cursorily, but had discovered nothing of interest.

'"You would hardly be likely to recognize the importance of these documents, perhaps," he said, smiling.

'Well, I went to the chest, took out the few papers it contained and brought them to him. He looked at them, but said it was impossible to say off-hand what might or might not be connected with the matter in question. He would take them away with him and would communicate with me if anything turned up.

'By the last post on Saturday I received a letter from him in which he suggested that I come to his house to discuss the matter. He gave me the address: Whitefriars, Friars Lane, Hampstead. I was to be there at a quarter to eleven this morning.

'I was a little late finding the place. I hurried through the gate and up towards the house, when suddenly those two dreadful men sprang at me from the bushes. I hadn't time to cry out. One man put his hand over my mouth. I wrenched my head free and screamed for help. Luckily you heard me. If it hadn't been for you –' She stopped. Her looks were more eloquent than further words.

'Very glad I happened to be on the spot. By Gad, I'd like to get hold of those two brutes. You'd never seen them before, I suppose?'

She shook her head. 'What do you think it means?'

'Difficult to say. But one thing seems pretty sure. There's something someone wants among your father's papers. This man Reid told you a cock-and-bull story so as to get the opportunity of looking through them. Evidently what he wanted wasn't there.'

'Oh!' said Freda. 'I wonder. When I got home on Saturday I thought my things had been tampered with. To tell you the truth, I suspected my landlady of having pried about in my room out of curiosity. But now –'

'Depend upon it, that's it. Someone gained admission to your room and searched it, without finding what he was after. He suspected that you knew the value of this paper, whatever it was, and that you carried it about on your person. So he planned this ambush. If you had it with you, it would have been taken from you. If not, you would have been held prisoner while he tried to make you tell where it was hidden.'

'But what can it possibly *be*?' cried Freda.

'I don't know. But it must be something pretty good for him to go to this length.'

'It doesn't seem possible.'

'Oh, I don't know. Your father was a sailor. He went to

out-of-the-way places. He might have come across something the value of which he never knew.'

'Do you really think so?' A pink flush of excitement showed in the girl's pale cheeks.

'I do indeed. The question is, what shall we do next? You don't want to go to the police, I suppose?'

'Oh, no, please.'

'I'm glad you say that. I don't see what good the police could do, and it would only mean unpleasantness for you. Now I suggest that you allow me to give you lunch somewhere and that I then accompany you back to your lodgings, so as to be sure you reach them safely. And then, we might have a look for the paper. Because, you know, it must be somewhere.'

'Father may have destroyed it himself.'

'He may, of course, but the other side evidently doesn't think so, and that looks hopeful for us.'

'What do you think it can be? Hidden treasure?'

'By jove, it might be!' exclaimed Major Wilbraham, all the boy in him rising joyfully to the suggestion. 'But now, Miss Clegg, lunch!'

They had a pleasant meal together. Wilbraham told Freda all about his life in East Africa. He described elephant hunts, and the girl was thrilled. When they had finished, he insisted on taking her home in a taxi.

Her lodgings were near Notting Hill Gate. On arriving there, Freda had a brief conversation with her landlady. She returned to Wilbraham and took him up to the second floor, where she had a tiny bedroom and sitting-room.

'It's exactly as we thought,' she said. 'A man came on Saturday morning to see about laying a new electric cable; he told her there was a fault in the wiring in my room. He was there some time.'

'Show me this chest of your father's,' said Wilbraham.

Freda showed him a brass-bound box. 'You see,' she said, raising the lid, 'it's empty.'

The soldier nodded thoughtfully. 'And there are no papers anywhere else?'

'I'm sure there aren't. Mother kept everything in here.'

Wilbraham examined the inside of the chest. Suddenly he uttered an exclamation. 'Here's a slit in the lining.' Carefully he inserted his hand, feeling about. A slight crackle rewarded him. 'Something's slipped down behind.'

In another minute he had drawn out his find. A piece of dirty paper folded several times. He smoothed it out on the table; Freda was looking over his shoulder. She uttered an exclamation of disappointment.

'It's just a lot of queer marks.'

'Why, the thing's in Swahili. *Swahili*, of all things!' cried Major Wilbraham. 'East African native dialect, you know.'

'How extraordinary!' said Freda. 'Can you read it, then?'

'Rather. But what an amazing thing.' He took the paper to the window.

'Is it anything?' asked Freda tremulously. Wilbraham read the thing through twice, and then came back to the girl. 'Well,' he said, with a chuckle, 'here's your hidden treasure, all right.'

'Hidden treasure? Not *really*? You mean Spanish gold – a sunken galleon – that sort of thing?'

'Not quite so romantic as that, perhaps. But it comes to the same thing. This paper gives the hiding-place of a cache of ivory.'

'Ivory?' said the girl, astonished.

'Yes. Elephants, you know. There's a law about the number you're allowed to shoot. Some hunter got away with breaking that law on a grand scale. They were on his trail and he cached the stuff. There's a thundering lot of it – and this gives fairly clear directions how to find it. Look here, we'll have to go after this, you and I.'

'You mean there's really a lot of money in it?'

'Quite a nice little fortune for you.'

'But how did that paper come to be among my father's things?'

Wilbraham shrugged. 'Maybe the Johnny was dying or something. He may have written the thing down in Swahili for protection and given it to your father, who possibly had befriended him in some way. Your father, not being able to read it, attached no importance to it. That's only a guess on my part, but I dare say it's not far wrong.'

Freda gave a sigh. 'How frightfully exciting!'

'The thing is – what to do with the precious document,' said

Wilbraham. 'I don't like leaving it here. They might come and have another look. I suppose you wouldn't entrust it to me?'

'Of course I would. But – mightn't it be dangerous for you?' she faltered.

'I'm a tough nut,' said Wilbraham grimly. 'You needn't worry about me.' He folded up the paper and put it in his pocket-book. 'May I come to see you tomorrow evening?' he asked. 'I'll have worked out a plan by then, and I'll look up the places on my map. What time do you get back from the city?'

'I get back about half-past six.'

'Capital. We'll have a powwow and then perhaps you'll let me take you out to dinner. We ought to celebrate. So long, then. Tomorrow at half-past six.'

Major Wilbraham arrived punctually on the following day. He rang the bell and enquired for Miss Clegg. A maid-servant had answered the door.

'Miss Clegg? She's out.'

'Oh!' Wilbraham did not like to suggest that he come in and wait. 'I'll call back presently,' he said.

He hung about in the street opposite, expecting every minute to see Freda tripping towards him. The minutes passed. Quarter to seven. Seven. Quarter-past seven. Still no Freda. A feeling of uneasiness swept over him. He went back to the house and rang the bell again.

'Look here,' he said, 'I had an appointment with Miss Clegg at half-past six. Are you sure she isn't in or hasn't – er – left any message?'

'Are you Major Wilbraham?' asked the servant.

'Yes.'

'Then there's a note for you. It come by hand.'

Dear Major Wilbraham, – Something rather strange has happened. I won't write more now, but will you meet me at Whitefriars? Go there as soon as you get this.
 Yours sincerely,
 Freda Clegg

Wilbraham drew his brows together as he thought rapidly. His hand drew a letter absent-mindedly from his pocket. It was to his tailor. 'I wonder,' he said to the maid-servant, 'if you could let me have a stamp.'

'I expect Mrs Parkins could oblige you.'

She returned in a moment with the stamp. It was paid for with a shilling. In another minute Wilbraham was walking towards the tube station, dropping the envelope in a box as he passed.

Freda's letter had made him most uneasy. What could have taken the girl, alone, to the scene of yesterday's sinister encounter?

He shook his head. Of all the foolish things to do! Had Reid appeared? Had he somehow or other prevailed upon the girl to trust him? What had taken her to Hampstead?

He looked at his watch. Nearly half-past seven. She would have counted on his starting at half-past six. An hour late. Too much. If only she had had the sense to give him some hint.

The letter puzzled him. Somehow its independent tone was not characteristic of Freda Clegg.

It was ten minutes to eight when he reached Friars Lane. It was getting dark. He looked sharply about him; there was no one in sight. Gently he pushed the rickety gate so that it swung noiselessly on its hinges. The drive was deserted. The house was dark. He went up the path cautiously, keeping a look out from side to side. He did not intend to be caught by surprise.

Suddenly he stopped. Just for a minute a chink of light had shone through one of the shutters. The house was not empty. There was someone inside.

Softly Wilbraham slipped into the bushes and worked his way round to the back of the house. At last he found what he was looking for. One of the windows on the ground floor was unfastened. It was the window of a kind of scullery. He raised the sash, flashed a torch (he had bought it at a shop on the way over) around the deserted interior and climbed in.

Carefully he opened the scullery door. There was no sound. He flashed the torch once more. A kitchen – empty. Outside the kitchen were half a dozen steps and a door evidently leading to the front part of the house.

He pushed open the door and listened. Nothing. He slipped through. He was now in the front hall. Still there was no sound. There was a door to the right and a door to the left. He chose the right-hand door, listened for a time, then turned the handle. It gave. Inch by inch he opened the door and stepped inside.

Again he flashed the torch. The room was unfurnished and bare.

Just at that moment he heard a sound behind him, whirled round – too late. Something came down on his head and he pitched forward into unconsciousness . . .

How much time elapsed before he regained consciousness Wilbraham had no idea. He returned painfully to life, his head aching. He tried to move and found it impossible. He was bound with ropes.

His wits came back to him suddenly. He remembered now. He had been hit on the head.

A faint light from a gas jet high up on the wall showed him that he was in a small cellar. He looked around and his heart gave a leap. A few feet away lay Freda, bound like himself. Her eyes were closed, but even as he watched her anxiously, she sighed and they opened. Her bewildered gaze fell on him and joyous recognition leaped into them.

'You, too!' she said. 'What has happened?'

'I've let you down badly,' said Wilbraham. 'Tumbled headlong into the trap. Tell me, did you send me a note asking me to meet you here?'

The girl's eyes opened in astonishment. '*I*? But you sent *me* one.'

'Oh, I sent you one, did I?'

'Yes. I got it at the office. It asked me to meet you here instead of at home.'

'Same method for both of us,' he groaned, and he explained the situation.

'I see,' said Freda. 'Then the idea was –?'

'To get the paper. We must have been followed yesterday. That's how they got on to me.'

'And – have they got it?' asked Freda.

'Unfortunately, I can't feel and see,' said the soldier, regarding his bound hands ruefully.

And then they both started. For a voice spoke, a voice that seemed to come from the empty air.

'Yes, thank you,' it said. 'I've got it, all right. No mistake about that.'

The unseen voice made them both shiver.

'Mr Reid,' murmured Freda.

'Mr Reid is one of my names, my dear young lady,' said the voice. 'But only one of them. I have a great many. Now, I am sorry to say that you two have interfered with my plans – a thing I never allow. Your discovery of this house is a serious matter. You have not told the police about it yet, but you might do so in the future.

'I very much fear that I cannot trust you in the matter. You might promise – but promises are seldom kept. And, you see, this house is very useful to me. It is, you might say, my clearing house. The house from which there is no return. From here you pass on – elsewhere. You, I am sorry to say, are so passing on. Regrettable – but necessary.'

The voice paused for a brief second, then resumed: 'No bloodshed. I abhor bloodshed. My method is much simpler. And really not too painful, so I understand. Well, I must be getting along. Good-evening to you both.'

'Look here!' It was Wilbraham who spoke. 'Do what you like to me, but this young lady has done nothing – nothing. It can't hurt you to let her go.'

But there was no answer.

At that moment there came a cry from Freda. 'The water – the water!'

Wilbraham twisted himself painfully and followed the direction of her eyes. From a hole up near the ceiling a steady trickle of water was pouring in.

Freda gave a hysterical cry. 'They're going to drown us!'

The perspiration broke out on Wilbraham's brow. 'We're not done yet,' he said. 'We'll shout for help. Surely somebody will hear us. Now, both together.'

They yelled and shouted at the tops of their voices. Not until they were hoarse did they stop.

'No use, I'm afraid,' said Wilbraham sadly. 'We're too far underground and I expect the doors are muffled. After all, if we could be heard, I've no doubt that brute would have gagged us.'

'Oh,' cried Freda. 'And it's all my fault. I got you into this.'

'Don't worry about that, little girl. It's you I'm thinking about. I've been in tight corners before now and got out of them. Don't you lose heart. I'll get you out of this. We've plenty of time. At the rate that water's flowing in, it will be hours before the worst happens.'

'How wonderful you are!' said Freda. 'I've never met anybody like you – except in books.'

'Nonsense – just common sense. Now, I've got to loosen those infernal ropes.'

At the end of a quarter of an hour, by dint of straining and twisting, Wilbraham had the satisfaction of feeling that his bonds were appreciably loosened. He managed to bend his head down and his wrists up till he was able to attack the knots with his teeth.

Once his hands were free, the rest was only a matter of time. Cramped, stiff, but free, he bent over the girl. A minute later she was also free.

So far the water was only up to their ankles.

'And now,' said the soldier, 'to get out of here.'

The door of the cellar was up a few stairs. Major Wilbraham examined it.

'No difficulty here,' he said. 'Flimsy stuff. It will soon give at the hinges.' He set his shoulders to it and heaved.

There was a cracking of wood – a crash, and the door burst from its hinges.

Outside was a flight of stairs. At the top was another door – a very different affair – of solid wood, barred with iron.

'A bit more difficult, this,' said Wilbraham. 'Hallo, here's a piece of luck. It's unlocked.'

He pushed it open, peered round it, then beckoned the girl to come on. They emerged into a passage behind the kitchen. In another moment they were standing under the stars in Friars Lane.

'Oh!' Freda gave a little sob. 'Oh, how dreadful it's been!'

'My poor darling.' He caught her in his arms. 'You've been so wonderfully brave. Freda – darling angel – could you ever – I mean, would you – I love you, Freda. Will you marry me?'

After a suitable interval, highly satisfactory to both parties, Major Wilbraham said, with a chuckle:

'And what's more, we've still got the secret of the ivory cache.'

'But they took it from you!'

The major chuckled again. 'That's just what they didn't do! You see, I wrote out a spoof copy, and before joining you here tonight, I put the real thing in a letter I was sending to my tailor and posted it. They've got the spoof copy – and I wish them joy of it! Do you know what we'll do, sweetheart! We'll go to East Africa for our honeymoon and hunt out the cache.'

III

Mr Parker Pyne left his office and climbed two flights of stairs. Here in a room at the top of the house sat Mrs Oliver, the sensational novelist, now a member of Mr Pyne's staff.

Mr Parker Pyne tapped at the door and entered. Mrs Oliver sat at a table on which were a typewriter, several notebooks, a general confusion of loose manuscripts and a large bag of apples.

'A very good story, Mrs Oliver,' said Mr Parker Pyne genially.

'It went off well?' said Mrs Oliver. 'I'm glad.'

'That water-in-the-cellar business,' said Mr Parker Pyne. 'You don't think, on a future occasion, that something more original – perhaps?' He made the suggestion with proper diffidence.

Mrs Oliver shook her head and took an apple from her bag. 'I think not, Mr Pyne. You see, people are used to reading about such things. Water rising in a cellar, poison gas, et cetera. Knowing about it beforehand gives it an extra thrill when it happens to oneself. The public is conservative, Mr Pyne; it likes the old well-worn gadgets.'

'Well, you should know,' admitted Mr Parker Pyne, mindful of the authoress's forty-six successful works of fiction, all best sellers in England and America, and freely translated into French, German, Italian, Hungarian, Finnish, Japanese and Abyssinian. 'How about expenses?'

Mrs Oliver drew a paper towards her. 'Very moderate, on the whole. The two darkies, Percy and Jerry, wanted very little. Young Lorrimer, the actor, was willing to enact the part of Mr Reid for five guineas. The cellar speech was a phonograph record, of course.'

'Whitefriars has been extremely useful to me,' said Mr Pyne.

'I bought it for a song and it has already been the scene of eleven exciting dramas.'

'Oh, I forgot,' said Mrs Oliver. 'Johnny's wages. Five shillings.'

'Johnny?'

'Yes. The boy who poured the water from the watering cans through the hole in the wall.'

'Ah yes. By the way, Mrs Oliver, how did you happen to know Swahili?'

'I didn't.'

'I see. The British Museum perhaps?'

'No. Delfridge's Information Bureau.'

'How marvellous are the resources of modern commerce!' he murmured.

'The only thing that worries me,' said Mrs Oliver, 'is that those two young people won't find any cache when they get there.'

'One cannot have everything in this world,' said Mr Parker Pyne. 'They will have had a honeymoon.'

Mrs Wilbraham was sitting in a deck-chair. Her husband was writing a letter. 'What's the date, Freda?'

'The sixteenth.'

'The sixteenth. By jove!'

'What is it, dear?'

'Nothing. I just remembered a chap named Jones.'

However happily married, there are some things one never tells.

'Dash it all,' thought Major Wilbraham. 'I ought to have called at that place and got my money back.' And then, being a fair-minded man, he looked at the other side of the question. 'After all, it was I who broke the bargain. I suppose if I'd gone to see Jones something would have happened. And, anyway, as it turns out, if I hadn't been going to see Jones, I should never have heard Freda cry for help, and we might never have met. So, indirectly, perhaps they have a right to the fifty pounds!'

Mrs Wilbraham was also following out a train of thought. 'What a silly little fool I was to believe in that advertisement and pay those people three guineas. Of course, they never did anything for it and nothing ever happened. If I'd only known what was coming – first Mr Reid, and then the queer, romantic way that Charlie came into my life. And to think that but for pure chance *I might never have met him!*'

She turned and smiled adoringly at her husband.

•

MRS MCGINTY'S DEAD

•

To Peter Saunders
in gratitude for his kindness
to authors

Hercule Poirot came out of the *Vieille Grand'mère* restaurant into Soho. He turned up the collar of his overcoat through prudence, rather than necessity, since the night was not cold. 'But at my age, one takes no risks,' Poirot was wont to declare.

His eyes held a reflective sleepy pleasure. The *Escargots de la Vieille Grand'mère* had been delicious. A real find, this dingy little restaurant. Meditatively, like a well fed dog, Hercule Poirot curled his tongue round his lips. Drawing his handkerchief from his pocket, he dabbed his luxuriant moustaches.

Yes, he had dined well . . . And now what?

A taxi, passing him, slowed down invitingly. Poirot hesitated for a moment, but made no sign. Why take a taxi? He would in any case reach home too early to go to bed.

'Alas,' murmured Poirot to his moustaches, 'that one can only eat three times a day . . .'

For afternoon tea was a meal to which he had never become acclimatized. 'If one partakes of the five o'clock, one does not,' he explained, 'approach the dinner with the proper quality of expectant gastric juices. And the dinner, let us remember, is the supreme meal of the day!'

Not for him, either, the mid-morning coffee. No, chocolate and *croissants* for breakfast, *Déjeuner* at twelve-thirty if possible but certainly not later than one o'clock, and finally the climax: *Le Dîner*!

These were the peak periods of Hercule Poirot's day. Always a man who had taken his stomach seriously, he was reaping his reward in old age. Eating was now not only a physical pleasure, it was also an intellectual research. For in between meals he spent quite a lot of time searching out and marking down possible sources of new and delicious food. *La Vieille Grand'mère* was the result of one of these quests and *La Vieille Grand'mère* had just received the seal of Hercule Poirot's gastronomic approval.

But now, unfortunately, there was the evening to put in.

Hercule Poirot sighed.

'If only,' he thought, '*ce cher Hastings* were available . . .'

He dwelt with pleasure on his remembrances of his old friend.

'My first friend in this country – and still to me the dearest friend I have. True, often and often did he enrage me. But do I remember that now? No. I remember only his incredulous wonder, his open-mouthed appreciation of my talents – the ease with which I misled him without uttering an untrue word, his bafflement, his stupendous astonishment when he at last perceived the truth that had been clear to me all along. *Ce cher, cher ami!* It is my weakness, it has always been my weakness, to desire to show off. That weakness, Hastings could never understand. But indeed it is very necessary for a man of my abilities to admire himself – and for that one needs stimulation from outside. I cannot, truly I cannot, sit in a chair all day reflecting how truly admirable I am. One needs the human touch. One needs – as they say nowadays – the *stooge*.'

Hercule Poirot sighed. He turned into Shaftesbury Avenue.

Should he cross it and go on to Leicester Square and spend the evening at a cinema? Frowning slightly, he shook his head. The cinema, more often than not, enraged him by the looseness of its plots – the lack of logical continuity in the argument – even the photography which, raved over by some, to Hercule Poirot seemed often no more than the portrayal of scenes and objects so as to make them appear totally different from what they were in reality.

Everything, Hercule Poirot decided, was too artistic nowadays. Nowhere was there the love of order and method that he himself prized so highly. And seldom was there any appreciation of subtlety. Scenes of violence and crude brutality were the fashion, and as a former police officer, Poirot was bored by brutality. In his early days, he had seen plenty of crude brutality. It had been more the rule than the exception. He found it fatiguing, and unintelligent.

'The truth is,' Poirot reflected as he turned his steps homeward, 'I am not in tune with the modern world. And I am, in a superior way, a slave as other men are slaves. My work has enslaved me just as their work enslaves them. When the hour of leisure arrives, they have nothing with which to fill their leisure. The retired financier takes up golf, the little merchant puts bulbs in his garden, me, I eat. But there it is, I come round to it again. *One can only eat three times a day*. And in between are the gaps.'

He passed a newspaper-seller and scanned the bill.

'Result of McGinty Trial. Verdict.'

It stirred no interest in him. He recalled vaguely a small paragraph in the papers. It had not been an interesting murder. Some wretched old woman knocked on the head for a few pounds. All part of the senseless crude brutality of these days.

Poirot turned into the courtyard of his block of flats. As always his heart swelled in approval. He was proud of his home. A splendid symmetrical building. The lift took him up to the third floor where he had a large luxury flat with impeccable chromium fittings, square armchairs, and severely rectangular ornaments. There could truly be said not to be a curve in the place.

As he opened the door with his latchkey and stepped into the square, white lobby, his manservant, George, stepped softly to meet him.

'Good evening, sir. There is a – gentleman waiting to see you.'

He relieved Poirot deftly of his overcoat.

'Indeed?' Poirot was aware of that very slight pause before the word *gentleman*. As a social snob, George was an expert.

'What is his name?'

'A Mr Spence, sir.'

'Spence.' The name, for the moment, meant nothing to Poirot. Yet he knew that it should do so.

Pausing for a moment before the mirror to adjust his moustaches to a state of perfection, Poirot opened the door of the sitting-room and entered. The man sitting in one of the big square armchairs got up.

'Hallo, M. Poirot, hope you remember me. It's a long time . . . Superintendent Spence.'

'But of course.' Poirot shook him warmly by the hand.

Superintendent Spence of the Kilchester Police. A very interesting case that had been . . . As Spence had said, a long time ago now . . .

Poirot pressed his guest with refreshments. A *grenadine? Crème de Menthe? Benedictine? Crème de Cacao?* . . .

At this moment George entered with a tray on which was a whisky bottle and a siphon. 'Or beer if you prefer it, sir?' he murmured to the visitor.

Superintendent Spence's large red face lightened.

'Beer for me,' he said.

Poirot was left to wonder once more at the accomplishments of George. He himself had had no idea that there was beer in the flat and it seemed incomprehensible to him that it could be preferred to a sweet liqueur.

When Spence had his foaming tankard, Poirot poured himself out a tiny glass of gleaming green *crème de menthe.*

'But it is charming of you to look me up,' he said. 'Charming. You have come up from –?'

'Kilchester. I'll be retired in about six months. Actually, I was due for retirement eighteen months ago. They asked me to stop on and I did.'

'You were wise,' said Poirot with feeling. 'You were very wise . . .'

'Was I? I wonder. I'm not so sure.'

'Yes, yes, you were wise,' Poirot insisted. 'The long hours of *ennui*, you have no conception of them.'

'Oh, I'll have plenty to do when I retire. Moved into a new house last year, we did. Quite a bit of garden and shamefully neglected. I haven't been able to get down to it properly yet.'

'Ah yes, you are one of those who garden. Me, once I decided to live in the country and grow vegetable marrows. It did not succeed. I have not the temperament.'

'You should have seen one of my marrows last year,' said Spence with enthusiasm. 'Colossal! And my roses. I'm keen on roses. I'm going to have –'

He broke off.

'That's not what I came to talk about.'

'No, no, you came to see an old acquaintance – it was kind. I appreciate it.'

'There's more to it than that, I'm afraid, M. Poirot. I'll be honest. I want something.'

Poirot murmured delicately:

'There is a mortgage, possibly, on your house? You would like a loan –'

Spence interrupted in a horrified voice:

'Oh, good Lord, it's not *money*! Nothing of that kind.'

Poirot waved his hands in graceful apology.

'I demand your pardon.'

'I'll tell you straight out – it's damned cheek what I've come for. If you send me away with a flea in my ear I shan't be surprised.'

'There will be no flea,' said Poirot. 'But continue.'

'It's the McGinty case. You've read about it, perhaps?'

Poirot shook his head.

'Not with attention. Mrs McGinty – an old woman in a shop or a house. She is dead, yes. How did she die?'

Spence stared at him.

'Lord!' he said. 'That takes me back. Extraordinary. And I never thought of it until now.'

'I beg your pardon?'

'Nothing. Just a game. Child's game. We used to play it when we were kids. A lot of us in a row. Question and answer all down the line. *"Mrs McGinty's dead!" "How did she die?" "Down on one knee just like I."* And then the next question, *"Mrs McGinty's dead." "How did she die?" "Holding her hand out just like I."* And there we'd be, all kneeling and our right arms held out stiff. And then you *got* it! *"Mrs McGinty's dead." "How did she die?" "Like THIS!"* Smack, the top of the row would fall sideways and down we all went like a pack of ninepins!' Spence laughed uproariously at the remembrance. 'Takes me back, it does!'

Poirot waited politely. This was one of the moments when, even after half a lifetime in the country, he found the English incomprehensible. He himself had played at *Cache Cache* in his childhood, but he felt no desire to talk about it or even to think about it.

When Spence had overcome his own amusement, Poirot repeated with some slight weariness, 'How *did* she die?'

The laughter was wiped off Spence's face. He was suddenly himself again.

'She was hit on the back of her head with some sharp, heavy implement. Her savings, about thirty pounds in cash, were taken after her room had been ransacked. She lived alone in a small cottage except for a lodger. Man of the name of Bentley. James Bentley.'

'Ah yes, Bentley.'

'The place wasn't broken into. No signs of any tampering with the windows or locks. Bentley was hard up, had lost his job, and owed two months' rent. The money was found hidden under a loose stone at the back of the cottage. Bentley's coat sleeve had blood on it and hair – same blood group and the right hair. According to his first statement he was never near the body – so it couldn't have come there by accident.'

'Who found her?'

'The baker called with bread. It was the day he got paid. James Bentley opened the door to him and said he'd knocked at Mrs McGinty's bedroom door, but couldn't get an answer. The baker suggested she might have been taken bad. They got the woman from next door to go up and see. Mrs McGinty wasn't in the bedroom, and hadn't slept in the bed, but the room had been ransacked and the floorboards had been prised up. Then they thought of looking in the parlour. She was there, lying on the floor, and the neighbour fairly screamed her head off. Then they got the police, of course.'

'And Bentley was eventually arrested and tried?'

'Yes. The case came on at the Assizes. Yesterday. Open and shut case. The jury were only out twenty minutes this morning. Verdict: Guilty. Condemned to death.'

Poirot nodded.

'And then, after the verdict, you got in a train and came to London and came here to see me. Why?'

Superintendent Spence was looking into his beer glass. He ran his finger slowly round and round the rim.

'Because,' he said, 'I don't think he did it . . .'

CHAPTER 2

There was a moment or two of silence.

'You came to me –'

Poirot did not finish the sentence.

Superintendent Spence looked up. The colour in his face was deeper than it had been. It was a typical countryman's face, unexpressive, self-contained, with shrewd but honest eyes. It was the face of a man with definite standards who would never be bothered by doubts of himself or by doubts of what constituted right and wrong.

'I've been a long time in the Force,' he said. 'I've had a good deal of experience of this, that and the other. I can judge a man as well as any other could do. I've had cases of murder during my service – some of them straightforward enough, some of them not so straightforward. One case *you* know of, M. Poirot –'

Poirot nodded.

'Tricky, that was. But for you, we mightn't have seen clear. But we did see clear – and there wasn't any doubt. The same with the others you don't know about. There was Whistler, he got his – *and* deserved it. There were those chaps who shot old Guterman. There was Verall and his arsenic. Tranter got off – but he did it all right. Mrs Courtland – she was lucky – her husband was a nasty perverted bit of work, and the jury acquitted her accordingly. Not justice – just sentiment. You've got to allow for that happening now and again. Sometimes there isn't enough evidence – sometimes there's sentiment, sometimes a murderer manages to put it across the jury – that last doesn't happen often, but it can happen. Sometimes it's a clever bit of work by defending counsel – or a prosecuting counsel takes the wrong tack. Oh yes, I've seen a lot of things like that. But – but –'

Spence wagged a heavy forefinger.

'I haven't seen – not in *my* experience – an innocent man hanged for something he didn't do. It's a thing, M. Poirot, that I don't *want* to see.

'Not,' added Spence, 'in *this* country!'

Poirot gazed back at him.

'And you think you are going to see it now. But why –'

Spence interrupted him.

'I know some of the things you're going to say. I'll answer them without you having to ask them. I was put on this case. I was put on to get evidence of what happened. I went into the whole business very carefully. I got the facts, all the facts I could. All those facts pointed one way – pointed to one person. When I'd got all the facts I took them to my superior officer. After that it was out of my hands. The case went to the Public Prosecutor and it was up to him. He decided to prosecute – he couldn't have done anything else – not on the evidence. And so James Bentley was arrested and committed for trial, and was duly tried and has been found guilty. They couldn't have found him anything else, not on the evidence. And evidence is what a jury have to consider. Didn't have any qualms about it either, I should say. No, I should say they were all quite satisfied he *was* guilty.'

'But you – are not?'

'No.'

'Why?'

Superintendent Spence sighed. He rubbed his chin thoughtfully with his big hand.

'I don't know. What I mean is, I can't give a reason – a concrete reason. To the jury I dare say he looked like a murderer – to me he didn't – and I know a lot more about murderers than they do.'

'Yes, yes, you are an expert.'

'For one thing, you know, he wasn't *cocky*. Not cocky at all. And in my experience they usually are. Always so damned pleased with themselves. Always think they're stringing you along. Always sure they've been so clever about the whole thing. And even when they're in the dock and must know they're for it, they're still in a queer sort of way getting a kick out of it all. They're in the lime-light. They're the central figure. Playing the star part – perhaps for the first time in their lives. They're – well – you know – *cocky!*'

Spence brought out the word with an air of finality.

'You'll understand what I mean by that, M. Poirot.'

'I understand very well. And this James Bentley – he was not like that?'

'No. He was – well, just scared stiff. Scared stiff from the start. And to some people that would square in with his being guilty. But not to me.'

'No, I agree with you. What is he like, this James Bentley?'

'Thirty-three, medium height, sallow complexion, wears glasses –'

Poirot arrested the flow.

'No, I do not mean his physical characteristics. What sort of a personality?'

'Oh – that.' Superintendent Spence considered. 'Unprepossessing sort of fellow. Nervous manner. Can't look you straight in the face. Has a sly sideways way of peering at you. Worst possible sort of manner for a jury. Sometimes cringing and sometimes truculent. Blusters in an inefficient kind of way.'

He paused and added in a conversational tone:

'Really a shy kind of chap. Had a cousin rather like that. If anything's awkward they go and tell some silly lie that hasn't a chance of being believed.'

'He does not sound attractive, your James Bentley.'

'Oh, he isn't. Nobody could *like* him. But I don't want to see him hanged for all that.'

'And you think he will be hanged?'

'I don't see why not. His counsel may lodge an appeal – but if so it will be on very flimsy grounds – a technicality of some kind, and I don't see that it will have a chance of success.'

'Did he have a good counsel?'

'Young Graybrook was allotted to him under the Poor Persons' Defence Act. I'd say he was thoroughly conscientious and put up the best show he could.'

'So the man had a fair trial and was condemned by a jury of his fellow-men.'

'That's right. A good average jury. Seven men, five women – all decent reasonable souls. Judge was old Stanisdale. Scrupulously fair – no bias.'

'So – according to the law of the land – James Bentley has nothing to complain of?'

'If he's hanged for something he didn't do, he's got something to complain of!'

'A very just observation.'

'And the case against him was *my* case – *I* collected the facts and put them together – and it's on that case and those facts that he's been condemned. And I don't like it, M. Poirot, I don't like it.'

Hercule Poirot looked for a long time at the red agitated face of Superintendent Spence.

'*Eh bien*,' he said. 'What do you suggest?'

Spence looked acutely embarrassed.

'I expect you've got a pretty good idea of what's coming. The Bentley case is closed. I'm on another case already – embezzlement. Got to go up to Scotland tonight. I'm not a free man.'

'And I – am?'

Spence nodded in a shame-faced sort of way.

'You've got it. Awful cheek, you'll think. But I can't think of anything else – of any other way. I did all I could at the time, I examined every possibility I could. And I didn't get anywhere. I don't believe I ever would get anywhere. But who knows, it may be different for you. You look at things in – if you'll pardon me for saying so – in a funny sort of way. Maybe that's the way you've got to look at them in this case. Because if James Bentley didn't kill her, then somebody else did. She didn't chop the back of her head in herself. You may be able to find something that I missed. There's no reason why you should do anything about this business. It's infernal cheek my even suggesting such a thing. But there it is. I came to you because it was the only thing I could think of. But if you don't want to put yourself out – and why should you –'

Poirot interrupted him.

'Oh, but indeed there are reasons. I have leisure – too much leisure. And you have intrigued me – yes, you have intrigued me very much. It is a challenge – to the little grey cells of my brain. And then, I have a regard for you. I see you, in your garden in six months' time, planting, perhaps, the rose bushes – and as you plant them it is not with the happiness you should be feeling, because behind everything there is an unpleasantness in your brain, a recollection that you try to push away, and I would not have you feel that, my friend. And finally –' Poirot sat upright and nodded his head vigorously, 'there is the principle of the thing. If a man has not committed murder, he should not be hanged.' He paused and then added, 'But supposing that after all, he did kill her?'

'In that case I'd be only too thankful to be convinced of it.'

'And two heads are better than one? *Voilà*, everything is settled.

I precipitate myself upon the business. There is, that is clear, no time to be lost. Already the scent is cold. Mrs McGinty was killed – when?'

'Last November, 22nd.'

'Then let us at once get down to the brass tacks.'

'I've got my notes on the case which I'll pass over to you.'

'Good. For the moment, we need only the bare outline. If James Bentley did not kill Mrs McGinty, who did?'

Spence shrugged his shoulders and said heavily:

'There's nobody, so far as I can see.'

'But that answer we do not accept. Now, since for every murder there must be a motive, what, in the case of Mrs McGinty, could the motive be? Envy, revenge, jealousy, fear, money? Let us take the last and the simplest? Who profited by her death?'

'Nobody very much. She had two hundred pounds in the Savings Bank. Her niece gets that.'

'Two hundred pounds is not very much – but in certain circumstances it could be enough. So let us consider the niece. I apologize, my friend, for treading in your footsteps. You too, I know, must have considered all this. But I have to go over with you the ground already traversed.'

Spence nodded his large head.

'We considered the niece, of course. She's thirty-eight, married. Husband is employed in the building and decorating trade – a painter. He's got a good character, steady employment, sharp sort of fellow, no fool. She's a pleasant young woman, a bit talkative, seemed fond of her aunt in a mild sort of way. Neither of them had any urgent need for two hundred pounds, though quite pleased to have it, I dare say.'

'What about the cottage? Do they get that?'

'It was rented. Of course, under the Rent Restriction Act the landlord couldn't get the old woman out. But now she's dead, I don't think the niece could have taken over – anyway she and her husband didn't want to. They've got a small modern council house of their own of which they are extremely proud.' Spence sighed. 'I went into the niece and her husband pretty closely – they seemed the best bet, as you'll understand. But I couldn't get hold of anything.'

'*Bien*. Now let us talk about Mrs McGinty herself. Describe her to me – and not only in physical terms, if you please.'

Spence grinned.

'Don't want a police description? Well, she was sixty-four. Widow. Husband had been employed in the drapery department of Hodges in Kilchester. He died about seven years ago. Pneumonia. Since then, Mrs McGinty has been going out daily to various houses round about. Domestic chores. Broadhinny's a small village which has lately become residential. One or two retired people, one of the partners in an engineering works, a doctor, that sort of thing. There's quite a good bus and train service to Kilchester, and Cullenquay which, as I expect you know, is quite a large summer resort, is only eight miles away, but Broadhinny itself is still quite pretty and rural – about a quarter of a mile off the main Drymouth and Kilchester road.'

Poirot nodded.

'Mrs McGinty's cottage was one of four that form the village proper. There is the post office and village shop, and agricultural labourers live in the others.'

'And she took in a lodger?'

'Yes. Before her husband died, it used to be summer visitors, but after his death she just took one regular. James Bentley had been there for some months.'

'So we come to – James Bentley?'

'Bentley's last job was with a house agent's in Kilchester. Before that, he lived with his mother in Cullenquay. She was an invalid and he looked after her and never went out much. Then she died, and an annuity she had died with her. He sold the little house and found a job. Well educated man, but no special qualifications or aptitudes, and, as I say, an unprepossessing manner. Didn't find it easy to get anything. Anyway, they took him on at Breather & Scuttle's. Rather a second-rate firm. I don't think he was particularly efficient or successful. They cut down staff and he was the one to go. He couldn't get another job, and his money ran out. He usually paid Mrs McGinty every month for his room. She gave him breakfast and supper and charged him three pounds a week – quite reasonable, all things considered. He was two months behind in paying her, and he was nearly at the end of his resources.

He hadn't got another job and she was pressing him for what he owed her.'

'And he knew that she had thirty pounds in the house? Why did she have thirty pounds in the house, by the way, since she had a Savings Bank account?'

'Because she didn't trust the Government. Said they'd got two hundred pounds of her money, but they wouldn't get any more. She'd keep that where she could lay her hands on it any minute. She said that to one or two people. It was under a loose board in her bedroom floor – a very obvious place. James Bentley admitted he knew it was there.'

'Very obliging of him. And did niece and husband know that too?'

'Oh yes.'

'Then we have now arrived back at my first question to you. How did Mrs McGinty die?'

'She died on the night of November 22nd. Police surgeon put the time of death as being between 7 and 10 p.m. She'd had her supper – a kipper and bread and margarine, and according to all accounts, she usually had that about half-past six. If she adhered to that on the night in question, then by the evidence of digestion she was killed about eight-thirty or nine o'clock. James Bentley, by his own account, was out walking that evening from seven-fifteen to about nine. He went out and walked most evenings after dark. According to his own story he came in at about nine o'clock (he had his own key) and went straight upstairs to his room. Mrs McGinty had had wash-basins fixed in the bedrooms because of summer visitors. He read for about half an hour and then went to bed. He heard and noticed nothing out of the way. Next morning he came downstairs and looked into the kitchen, but there was no one there and no signs of breakfast being prepared. He says he hesitated a bit and then knocked on Mrs McGinty's door, but got no reply.

'He thought she must have overslept, but didn't like to go on knocking. Then the baker came and James Bentley went up and knocked again, and after that, as I told you, the baker went next door and fetched in a Mrs Elliot, who eventually found the body and went off the deep end. Mrs McGinty was lying on the parlour floor. She'd been hit on the back of the head with something rather in the nature of a meat chopper with a very sharp edge. She'd been killed instantaneously. Drawers were pulled open and things strewn about, and the loose board in the floor in her bedroom had been prised up and the *cache* was empty. All the windows were closed and shuttered on the inside. No signs of anything being tampered with or of being broken into from outside.'

'Therefore,' said Poirot, 'either James Bentley must have killed her, or else she must have admitted her killer herself whilst Bentley was out?'

'Exactly. It wasn't any hold-up or burglar. Now who would she be likely to let in? One of the neighbours, or her niece, or her niece's husband. It boils down to that. We eliminated the neighbours. Niece and her husband were at the pictures that night. It is possible – just possible, that one or other of them left the cinema unobserved, bicycled three miles, killed the old woman, hid the money outside the house, and got back into the cinema unnoticed. We looked into that possibility, but we didn't find any confirmation of it. And why hide the money outside McGinty's house if so? Difficult place to pick it up later. Why not somewhere along the three miles back? No, the only reason for hiding it where it was hidden –'

Poirot finished the sentence for him.

'Would be because you were living in that house, but didn't want to hide it in your room or anywhere inside. In fact: James Bentley.'

'That's right. Everywhere, every time, you came up against Bentley. Finally there was the blood on his cuff.'

'How did he account for that?'

'Said he remembered brushing up against a butcher's shop the previous day. Baloney! It wasn't animal blood.'

'And he stuck to that story?'

'Not likely. At the trial he told a completely different tale. You see, there was a hair on the cuff as well – a blood-stained hair, and the hair was identical with Mrs McGinty's hair. That had got to be explained away. He admitted then that he had gone into the room the night before when he came back from his walk. He'd gone in, he said, after knocking, and found her there, on the floor, dead. He'd bent over and touched her, he said, to make sure. And then he'd lost his head. He'd always been very much affected by the sight of blood, he said. He went to his room in a state of collapse and more or less fainted. In the morning he couldn't bring himself to admit he knew what had happened.'

'A very fishy story,' commented Poirot.

'Yes, indeed. And yet, you know,' said Spence thoughtfully, 'it might well be true. It's not the sort of thing that an ordinary man – or a jury – can believe. But I've come across people like that. I don't mean the collapse story. I mean people who are confronted by a demand for responsible action and who simply can't face up to it. Shy people. He goes in, say, and finds her. He knows that he ought to do something – get the police – go to a neighbour – do the right thing whatever it is. And he funks it. He thinks "I don't need to know anything about it. I needn't have come in here tonight. I'll go to bed just as if I hadn't come in here at all . . ." Behind it, of course, there's fear – fear that he may be suspected of having a hand in it. He thinks he'll keep himself out of it as long as possible, and so the silly juggins goes and puts himself into it – up to his neck.'

Spence paused.

'It *could* have been that way.'

'It could,' said Poirot thoughtfully.

'Or again, it may have been just the best story his counsel could think up for him. But I don't know. The waitress in the café in Kilchester where he usually had lunch said that he always chose a table where he could look into a wall or a corner and not see people. He was that kind of a chap – just a bit screwy. But not screwy enough to be a killer. He'd no persecution complex or anything of that kind.'

Spence looked hopefully at Poirot – but Poirot did not respond – he was frowning.

The two men sat silent for a while.

CHAPTER 3

At last Poirot roused himself with a sigh.

'*Eh bien*,' he said. 'We have exhausted the motive of money. Let us pass to other theories. Had Mrs McGinty an enemy? Was she afraid of anyone?'

'No evidence of it.'

'What did her neighbours have to say?'

'Not very much. They wouldn't to the police, perhaps, but I don't think they were holding anything back. She kept herself to herself, they said. But that's regarded as natural enough. Our villages, you know, M. Poirot, aren't friendly. Evacuees found that during the war. Mrs McGinty passed the time of day with the neighbours but they weren't intimate.'

'How long had she lived there?'

'Matter of eighteen or twenty years, I think.'

'And the forty years before that?'

'There's no mystery about her. Farmer's daughter from North Devon. She and her husband lived near Ilfracombe for a time, and then moved to Kilchester. Had a cottage the other side of it – but found it damp, so they moved to Broadhinny. Husband seems to have been a quiet, decent man, delicate – didn't go to the pub much. All very respectable and above board. No mysteries anywhere, nothing to hide.'

'And yet she was killed?'

'And yet she was killed.'

'The niece didn't know of anyone who had a grudge against her aunt?'

'She says not.'

Poirot rubbed his nose in an exasperated fashion.

'You comprehend, my dear friend, it would be so much easier if Mrs McGinty was *not* Mrs McGinty, so to speak. If she could be what is called a Mystery Woman – a woman with a past.'

'Well, she wasn't,' said Spence stolidly. 'She was just Mrs McGinty, a more or less uneducated woman, who let rooms and went out charring. Thousands of them all over England.'

'But they do not all get murdered.'

'No. I grant you that.'

'So why should Mrs McGinty get murdered? The obvious answer we do not accept. What remains? A shadowy and improbable niece. An even more shadowy and improbable stranger. Facts? Let us stick to facts. What are the facts? An elderly charwoman is murdered. A shy and uncouth young man is arrested and convicted of the murder. Why was James Bentley arrested?'

Spence stared.

'The evidence against him. I've told you –'

'Yes. Evidence. But tell me, my Spence, was it real evidence or was it contrived?'

'Contrived?'

'Yes. Granted the premise that James Bentley is innocent, two possibilities remain. The evidence was manufactured, deliberately, to throw suspicion upon him. Or else he was just the unfortunate victim of circumstances.'

Spence considered.

'Yes. I see what you're driving at.'

'There is nothing to show that the former was the case. But again there is nothing to show that it was not so. The money was taken and hidden outside the house in a place easily found. To have actually hidden it in his room would have been a little too much for the police to swallow. The murder was committed at a time when Bentley was taking a lonely walk, as he often did. Did the bloodstain come on his sleeve as he said it did at his trial, or was that, too, contrived? Did someone brush against him in the darkness and smear tell-tale evidence on his sleeve?'

'I think that's going a bit far, M. Poirot.'

'Perhaps, perhaps. But we have got to go far. I think that in this case we have got to go so far that the imagination cannot as yet see the path clearly . . . For, you see, *mon cher Spence*, if Mrs McGinty is just an ordinary charwoman – it is the *murderer* who must be extraordinary. Yes – that follows clearly. It is in the murderer and not the murdered that the interest of this case lies. That is not the case in most crimes. Usually it is in the personality of the murdered person that the crux of the situation lies. It is the silent dead in whom I am usually interested. Their hates, their loves, their actions. And when you really know the murdered victim, then the victim speaks, and those dead lips utter a name – the name you want to know.'

Spence looked rather uncomfortable.

'Those foreigners!' he seemed to be saying to himself.

'But here,' continued Poirot, 'it is the opposite. Here we guess at a veiled personality – a figure still hidden in darkness. How did Mrs McGinty die? Why did she die? The answer is not to be found in studying the life of Mrs McGinty. The answer is to be found in the personality of the murderer. You agree with me there?'

'I suppose so,' said Superintendent Spence cautiously.

'Someone who wanted – what? To strike down Mrs McGinty? *Or to strike down James Bentley?*'

The Superintendent gave a doubtful 'H'm!'

'Yes – yes, that is one of the first points to be decided. Who is the real victim? Who was intended to be the victim?'

Spence said incredulously: 'You really think someone would bump off a perfectly inoffensive old woman in order to get someone else hanged for murder?'

'One cannot make an omelette, they say, without breaking eggs. Mrs McGinty, then, may be the egg, and James Bentley is the omelette. So let me hear, now, what you know of James Bentley.'

'Nothing much. Father was a doctor – died when Bentley was nine years old. He went to one of the smaller public schools, unfit for the Army, had a weak chest, was in one of the Ministries during the war and lived with a possessive mother.'

'Well,' said Poirot, 'there are certain possibilities there . . . More than there are in the life history of Mrs McGinty.'

'Do you seriously believe what you are suggesting?'

'No, I do not believe anything as yet. But I say that there are two distinct lines of research, and that we have to decide, very soon, which is the right one to follow.'

'How are you going to set about things, M. Poirot? Is there anything I can do?'

'First, I should like an interview with James Bentley.'

'That can be arranged. I'll get on to his solicitors.'

'After that and subject, of course, to the result, if any – I am not hopeful – of that interview, I shall go to Broadhinny. There, aided by your notes, I shall, as quickly as possible, go over that same ground where you have passed before me.'

'In case I've missed anything,' said Spence with a wry smile.

'In case, I would prefer to say, that some circumstance should strike me in a different light to the one in which it struck you. Human reactions vary and so does human experience. The resemblance of a rich financier to a soap boiler whom I had known in Liège once brought about a most satisfactory result. But no need to go into that. What I should like to do is to eliminate one or other of the trails I indicated just now. And to eliminate the Mrs McGinty trail – trail No. 1 – will obviously be quicker and easier than to attack trail No. 2. Where, now, can I stay in Broadhinny? Is there an inn of moderate comfort?'

'There's the Three Ducks – but it doesn't put people up. There's the Lamb in Cullavon three miles away – or there is a kind of a Guest House in Broadhinny itself. It's not really a Guest House, just a rather decrepit country house where the young couple who own it take in paying guests. I don't think,' said Spence dubiously, 'that it's very comfortable.'

Hercule Poirot closed his eyes in agony.

'If I suffer, I suffer,' he said. 'It has to be.'

'I don't know what you'll go there as,' continued Spence doubtfully as he eyed Poirot. 'You might be some kind of an opera singer. Voice broken down. Got to rest. That might do.'

'I shall go,' said Hercule Poirot, speaking with accents of royal blood, 'as myself.'

Spence received this pronouncement with pursed lips.

'D'you think that's advisable?'

'I think it is *essential*! But yes, essential. Consider, *cher ami*, it is *time* we are up against. What do we know? Nothing. So the hope, the best hope, is to go pretending that I know a great deal. I am Hercule Poirot. I am the great, the unique Hercule Poirot. And I, Hercule Poirot, am not satisfied about the verdict in the McGinty case. I, Hercule Poirot, have a very shrewd suspicion of *what really happened*. There is a circumstance that I, alone, estimate at its true value. You see?'

'And then?'

'And then, having made my effect, I observe the reactions. For there should be reactions. Very definitely, there should be reactions.'

Superintendent Spence looked uneasily at the little man.

'Look here, M. Poirot,' he said. 'Don't go sticking out your neck. I don't want anything to happen to you.'

'But if it does, you would be proved right beyond the shadow of doubt, is it not so?'

'I don't want it proved the hard way,' said Superintendent Spence.

CHAPTER 4

With great distaste, Hercule Poirot looked round the room in which he stood. It was a room of gracious proportions but there its attraction ended. Poirot made an eloquent grimace as he drew a suspicious finger along the top of a book case. As he had suspected – dust! He sat down gingerly on a sofa and its broken springs sagged depressingly under him. The two faded armchairs were, as he knew, little better. A large fierce-looking dog whom Poirot suspected of having mange growled from his position on a moderately comfortable fourth chair.

The room was large, and had a faded Morris wallpaper. Steel engravings of unpleasant subjects hung crookedly on the walls with one or two good oil paintings. The chair-covers were both faded and dirty, the carpet had holes in it and had never been of a pleasant design. A good deal of miscellaneous bric-à-brac was scattered haphazard here and there. Tables rocked dangerously owing to absence of castors. One window was open, and no power on earth could, apparently, shut it again. The door, temporarily shut, was not likely to remain so. The latch did not hold, and with every gust of wind it burst open and whirling gusts of cold wind eddied round the room.

'I suffer,' said Hercule Poirot to himself in acute self-pity. 'Yes, I suffer.'

The door burst open and the wind and Mrs Summerhayes came in together. She looked round the room, shouted 'What?' to someone in the distance and went out again.

Mrs Summerhayes had red hair and an attractively freckled face and was usually in a distracted state of putting things down, or else looking for them.

Hercule Poirot sprang to his feet and shut the door.

A moment or two later it opened again and Mrs Summerhayes reappeared. This time she was carrying a large enamel basin and a knife.

A man's voice from some way away called out:

'Maureen, that cat's been sick again. What shall I do?'

Mrs Summerhayes called: 'I'm coming, darling. Hold everything.'

She dropped the basin and the knife and went out again.

Poirot got up again and shut the door. He said:

'Decidedly, I suffer.'

A car drove up, the large dog leaped from the chair and raised its voice in a crescendo of barking. He jumped on a small table by the window and the table collapsed with a crash.

'*Enfin*,' said Hercule Poirot. '*C'est insupportable!*'

The door burst open, the wind surged round the room, the dog rushed out, still barking. Maureen's voice came, upraised loud and clear.

'Johnnie, why the hell did you leave the back door open! Those bloody hens are in the larder.'

'And for this,' said Hercule Poirot with feeling, 'I pay seven guineas a week!'

The door banged to with a crash. Through the window came the loud squawking of irate hens.

Then the door opened again and Maureen Summerhayes came in and fell upon the basin with a cry of joy.

'Couldn't think where I'd left it. Would you mind frightfully, Mr Er – hum – I mean, would it bother you if I sliced the beans in here? The smell in the kitchen is too frightful.'

'Madame, I should be enchanted.'

It was not, perhaps, the exact phrase, but it was near enough. It was the first time in twenty-four hours that Poirot had seen any chance of a conversation of more than six seconds' duration.

Mrs Summerhayes flung herself down in a chair and began slicing beans with frenzied energy and considerable awkwardness.

'I do hope,' she said, 'that you're not too frightfully uncomfortable? If there's anything you want altered, do say so.'

Poirot had already come to the opinion that the only thing in Long Meadows he could even tolerate was his hostess.

'You are too kind, madame,' he replied politely. 'I only wish it were within my powers to provide you with suitable domestics.'

'Domestics!' Mrs Summerhayes gave a squeal. 'What a hope! Can't even get hold of a *daily*. Our really good one was murdered. Just my luck.'

'That would be Mrs McGinty,' said Poirot quickly.

'Mrs McGinty it was. God, how I miss that woman! Of course it was all a big thrill at the time. First murder we've ever had right in the family, so to speak, but as I told Johnnie, it was a downright bit of bad luck for us. Without McGinty I just can't cope.'

'You were attached to her?'

'My dear man, she was *reliable*. She *came*. Monday afternoons and Thursday mornings – just like a clock. Now I have that Burp woman from up by the station. Five children and a husband. Naturally she's never here. Either the husband's taken queer, or the old mother, or the children have some foul disease or other. With old McGinty, at least it was only she herself who came over queer, and I must say she hardly ever did.'

'And you found her always reliable and honest? You had trust in her?'

'Oh, she'd never pinch anything – not even food. Of course she snooped a bit. Had a look at one's letters and all that. But one expects that sort of thing. I mean they must live such awfully drab lives, mustn't they?'

'Had Mrs McGinty had a drab life?'

'Ghastly, I expect,' said Mrs Summerhayes vaguely. 'Always on your knees scrubbing. And then piles of other people's washing-up waiting for you on the sink when you arrive in the morning. If I had to face that every day, I'd be positively relieved to be murdered. I really would.'

The face of Major Summerhayes appeared at the window. Mrs Summerhayes sprang up, upsetting the beans, and rushed across to the window, which she opened to the fullest extent.

'That damned dog's eaten the hens' food again, Maureen.'

'Oh damn, now *he*'ll be sick!'

'Look here,' John Summerhayes displayed a colander full of greenery, 'is this enough spinach?'

'Of course not.'

'Seems a colossal amount to me.'

'It'll be about a teaspoonful when it's cooked. Don't you know by now what spinach is like?'

'Oh Lord!'

'Has the fish come?'

'Not a sign of it.'

'Hell, we'll have to open a tin of something. You might do that, Johnnie. One of the ones in the corner cupboard. That one we thought was a bit bulged. I expect it's quite all right really.'

'What about the spinach?'

'I'll get that.'

She leaped through the window, and husband and wife moved away together.

'*Nom d'un nom d'un nom!*' said Hercule Poirot. He crossed the room and closed the window as nearly as he could. The voice of Major Summerhayes came to him borne on the wind.

'What about this new fellow, Maureen? Looks a bit peculiar to me. What's his name again?'

'I couldn't remember it just now when I was talking to him. Had to say Mr Er-um. Poirot – that's what it is. He's French.'

'You know, Maureen, I seem to have seen that name somewhere.'

'Home Perm, perhaps. He looks like a hairdresser.' Poirot winced.

'N-no. Perhaps it's pickles. I don't know. I'm sure it's familiar. Better get the first seven guineas out of him, quick.'

The voices died away.

Hercule Poirot picked up the beans from the floor where they had scattered far and wide. Just as he finished doing so, Mrs Summerhayes came in again through the door.

He presented them to her politely:

'*Voici, madame.*'

'Oh, thanks awfully. I say, these beans look a bit black. We store them, you know, in crocks, salted down. But these seem to have gone wrong. I'm afraid they won't be very nice.'

'I, too, fear that . . . . You permit that I shut the door? There is a decided draught.'

'Oh yes, do. I'm afraid I always leave doors open.'

'So I have noticed.'

'Anyway, that door never stays shut. This house is practically falling to pieces. Johnnie's father and mother lived here and they were badly off, poor dears, and they never did a thing to it. And then when we came home from India to live here, we couldn't afford to do anything either. It's fun for the children in the holidays, though, lots of room to run wild in, and the garden and everything. Having paying guests here just enables us to keep going, though I must say we've had a few rude shocks.'

'Am I your only guest at present?'

'We've got an old lady upstairs. Took to her bed the day she came and has been there ever since. Nothing the matter with her that I can see. But there she is, and I carry up four trays a day. Nothing wrong with her appetite. Anyway, she's going tomorrow to some niece or other.'

Mrs Summerhayes paused for a moment before resuming in a slightly artificial voice.

'The fishman will be here in a minute. I wonder if you'd mind – er – forking out the first week's rent. You are staying a week, aren't you?'

'Perhaps longer.'

'Sorry to bother you. But I've not got any cash in the house and you know what these people are like – always dunning you.'

'Pray do not apologize, madame.' Poirot took out seven pound notes and added seven shillings. Mrs Summerhayes gathered the money up with avidity.

'Thanks a lot.'

'I should, perhaps, madame, tell you a little more about myself. *I am Hercule Poirot.*'

The revelation left Mrs Summerhayes unmoved.

'What a lovely name,' she said kindly. 'Greek, isn't it?'

'I am, as you may know,' said Poirot, 'a detective.' He tapped his chest. 'Perhaps the most famous detective there is.'

Mrs Summerhayes screamed with amusement.

'I see you're a great practical joker, M. Poirot. What are you detecting? Cigarette ash and footprints?'

'I am investigating the murder of Mrs McGinty,' said Poirot. 'And I do not joke.'

'Ouch,' said Mrs Summerhayes, 'I've cut my hand.'

She raised a finger and inspected it.

Then she stared at Poirot.

'Look here,' she said. 'Do you mean it? What I mean is, it's all over, all that. They arrested that poor half-wit who lodged there and he's been tried and convicted and everything. He's probably been hanged by now.'

'No, madame,' said Poirot. 'He has not been hanged – yet. And it is not "over" – the case of Mrs McGinty. I will remind you of the line from one of your poets. "A question is never settled until it is settled – right."'

'Oo,' said Mrs Summerhayes, her attention diverted from Poirot to the basin in her lap. 'I'm bleeding over the beans. Not too good as we've got to have them for lunch. Still it won't matter really because they'll go into boiling water. Things are always all right if you boil them, aren't they? Even tins.'

'I think,' said Hercule Poirot quietly, 'that I shall not be in for lunch.'

CHAPTER 5

'I don't know, I'm sure,' said Mrs Burch.

She had said that three times already. Her natural distrust of foreign-looking gentlemen with black moustaches, wearing large fur-lined coats was not to be easily overcome.

'Very unpleasant, it's been,' she went on. 'Having poor auntie murdered and the police and all that. Tramping round everywhere, and ferreting about, and asking questions. With the neighbours all agog. I didn't feel at first we'd ever live it down. And my husband's mother's been downright nasty about it. Nothing of that kind ever happened in *her* family, she kept saying. And "poor Joe" and all that. What about poor me? She was *my* aunt, wasn't she? But really I did think it was all over now.'

'And supposing that James Bentley is innocent, after all?'

'Nonsense,' snapped Mrs Burch. 'Of course he isn't innocent. He did it all right. I never did like the looks of him. Wandering about muttering to himself. Said to auntie, I did: "You oughtn't to have a man like that in the house. Might go off his head," I said. But she said he was quiet and obliging and didn't give trouble. No drinking, she said, and he didn't even smoke. Well, she knows better now, poor soul.'

Poirot looked thoughtfully at her. She was a big, plump woman with a healthy colour and a good-humoured mouth. The small house was neat and clean and smelt of furniture polish and Brasso. A faint appetizing smell came from the direction of the kitchen.

A good wife who kept her house clean and took the trouble to cook for her man. He approved. She was prejudiced and obstinate but, after all, why not? Most decidedly, she was not the kind of woman one could imagine using a meat chopper on her aunt, or conniving at her husband's doing so. Spence had not thought her that kind of woman, and rather reluctantly, Hercule Poirot agreed with him. Spence had gone into the financial background of the Burches and had found no motive there for murder, and Spence was a very thorough man.

He sighed, and persevered with his task, which was the breaking down of Mrs Burch's suspicion of foreigners. He led the conversation away from murder and focused on the victim of it. He asked questions about 'poor auntie', her health, her habits, her preferences in food and drink, her politics, her late husband, her attitude to life, to sex, to sin, to religion, to children, to animals.

Whether any of this irrelevant matter would be of use, he had no idea. He was looking through a haystack to find a needle. But, incidentally, he was learning something about Bessie Burch.

Bessie did not really know very much about her aunt. It had been a family tie, honoured as such, but without intimacy. Now and again, once a month or so, she and Joe had gone over on a Sunday to have midday dinner with auntie, and more rarely, auntie had come over to see them. They had exchanged presents at Christmas. They'd known that auntie had a little something put by, and that they'd get it when she died.

'But that's not to say we were needing it,' Mrs Burch explained with rising colour. 'We've got something put by ourselves. And we buried her beautiful. A real nice funeral it was. Flowers and everything.'

Auntie had been fond of knitting. She didn't like dogs, they messed up a place, but she used to have a cat – a ginger. It strayed away and she hadn't had one since, but the woman at the post office had been going to give her a kitten. Kept her house very neat and didn't like litter. Kept brass a treat and washed down the kitchen floor every day. She made quite a nice thing of going out to work. One shilling and tenpence an hour – two shillings from Holmeleigh, that was Mr Carpenter's of the Works' house. Rolling in money, the Carpenters were. Tried to get auntie to come more days in the week, but auntie wouldn't disappoint her other ladies because she'd gone to them before she went to Mr Carpenter's, and it wouldn't have been right.

Poirot mentioned Mrs Summerhayes at Long Meadows.

Oh yes, auntie went to her – two days a week. They'd come back from India where they'd had a lot of native servants and Mrs Summerhayes didn't know a thing about a house. They tried to market-garden, but they didn't know anything about that, either. When the children came home for the holidays, the house was just pandemonium. But Mrs Summerhayes was a nice lady and auntie liked her.

So the portrait grew. Mrs McGinty knitted, and scrubbed floors and polished brass, she liked cats and didn't like dogs. She liked children, but not very much. She kept herself to herself.

She attended church on Sunday, but didn't take part in any church activities. Sometimes, but rarely, she went to the pictures. She didn't hold with goings on – and had given up working for an artist and his wife when she discovered they weren't properly married. She didn't read books, but she enjoyed the Sunday paper and she liked old magazines when her ladies gave them to her. Although she didn't go much to the pictures, she was interested in hearing about film stars and their doings. She wasn't interested in politics, but voted Conservative like her husband had always done. Never spent much on clothes, but got quite a lot given her from her ladies, and was of a saving disposition.

Mrs McGinty was, in fact, very much the Mrs McGinty that Poirot had imagined she would be. And Bessie Burch, her niece, was the Bessie Burch of Superintendent Spence's notes.

Before Poirot took his leave, Joe Burch came home for the lunch hour. A small, shrewd man, less easy to be sure about than his wife. There was a faint nervousness in his manner. He showed less signs of suspicion and hostility than his wife. Indeed he seemed anxious to appear cooperative. And that, Poirot reflected, was very faintly out of character. For why should Joe Burch be anxious to placate an importunate foreign stranger? The reason could only be that the stranger had brought with him a letter from Superintendent Spence of the County Police.

So Joe Burch was anxious to stand in well with the police? Was it that he couldn't afford, as his wife could, to be critical of the police?

A man, perhaps, with an uneasy conscience. Why was that conscience uneasy? There could be so many reasons – none of them connected with Mrs McGinty's death. Or was it that, somehow or other, the cinema alibi had been cleverly faked, and that it was Joe Burch who had knocked on the door of the cottage, had been admitted by auntie and who had struck down the unsuspecting old woman? He would pull out the drawers and ransack the rooms to give the appearance of robbery, he might hide the money outside, cunningly, to incriminate James Bentley, the money that was in the Savings Bank was what he was after. Two hundred pounds coming to his wife which, for some reason unknown, he badly needed. The weapon, Poirot remembered, had never been found. Why had that not also been found on the scene of the crime? Any moron knew enough to wear gloves or rub off fingerprints. Why then had the weapon, which must have been a heavy one with a sharp edge, been removed? Was it because it could easily be identified as belonging to the Burch ménage? Was that same weapon, washed and polished, here in the house now? Something in the nature of a meat chopper, the police surgeon had said – but not, it seemed, actually a meat chopper. Something, perhaps a little unusual . . . a little out of the ordinary, easily identified. The police had hunted for it, but not found it. They had searched woods, dragged ponds. There was nothing missing from Mrs McGinty's kitchen, and nobody could say that James Bentley had had anything of that kind in his possession. They had never traced any purchase of a meat chopper or any such implement to him. A small, but negative point in his favour. Ignored in the weight of other evidence. But still a point . . .

Poirot cast a swift glance round the rather over-crowded little sitting-room in which he was sitting.

Was the weapon here, somewhere, in this house? Was that why Joe Burch was uneasy and conciliatory?

Poirot did not know. He did not really think so. But he was not absolutely sure . . .

CHAPTER 6

I

In the offices of Messrs Breather & Scuttle, Poirot was shown, after some demur, into the room of Mr Scuttle himself.

Mr Scuttle was a brisk, bustling man, with a hearty manner.

'Good morning. Good morning.' He rubbed his hands. 'Now, what can we do for you?'

His professional eye shot over Poirot, trying to place him, making, as it were, a series of marginal notes.

Foreign. Good quality clothes. Probably rich. Restaurant proprietor? Hotel manager? Films?

'I hope not to trespass on your time unduly. I wanted to talk to you about your former employee, James Bentley.'

Mr Scuttle's expressive eyebrows shot up an inch and dropped.

'James Bentley. James Bentley?' He shot out a question. 'Press?'

'No.'

'And you wouldn't be police?'

'No. At least – not of this country.'

'Not of this country.' Mr Scuttle filed this away rapidly as though for future reference. 'What's it all about?'

Poirot, never hindered by a pedantic regard for truth, launched out into speech.

'I am opening a further inquiry into James Bentley's case – at the request of certain relatives of his.'

'Didn't know he had any. Anyway, he's been found guilty, you know, and condemned to death.'

'But not yet executed.'

'While there's life, there's hope, eh?' Mr Scuttle shook his head. 'Should doubt it, though. Evidence was strong. Who are these relations of his?'

'I can only tell you this, they are both rich and powerful. Immensely rich.'

'You surprise me.' Mr Scuttle was unable to help thawing slightly. The words 'immensely rich' had an attractive and hypnotic quality. 'Yes, you really do surprise me.'

'Bentley's mother, the late Mrs Bentley,' explained Poirot,

'cut herself and her son off completely from her family.'

'One of these family feuds, eh? Well, well. And young Bentley without a farthing to bless himself with. Pity these relations didn't come to the rescue before.'

'They have only just become aware of the facts,' explained Poirot. 'They have engaged me to come with all speed to this country and do everything possible.'

Mr Scuttle leaned back, relaxing his business manner.

'Don't know what you can do. I suppose there's insanity? A bit late in the day – but if you got hold of the big medicos. Of course I'm not up in these things myself.'

Poirot leaned forward.

'Monsieur, James Bentley worked here. You can tell me about him.'

'Precious little to tell – precious little. He was one of our junior clerks. Nothing against him. Seemed a perfectly decent young fellow, quite conscientious and all that. But no idea of salesmanship. He just couldn't put a project over. That's no good in this job. If a client comes to us with a house he wants to sell, we're there to sell it for him. And if a client wants a house, we find him one. If it's a house in a lonely place with no amenities, we stress its antiquity, call it a period piece – and don't mention the plumbing! And if the house looks straight into the gasworks, we talk about amenities and facilities and don't mention the view. Hustle your client into it – that's what you're here to do. All sorts of little tricks there are. "We advise you, madam, to make an immediate offer. There's a Member of Parliament who's very keen on it – very keen indeed. Going out to see it again this afternoon." They fall for that every time – a Member of Parliament is always a good touch. Can't think why! No member ever lives away from his constituency. It's just the good solid sound of it.' He laughed suddenly, displayed gleaming dentures. 'Psychology – that's what it is – just psychology.'

Poirot leapt at the word.

'Psychology. How right you are. I see that you are a judge of men.'

'Not too bad. Not too bad,' said Mr Scuttle modestly.

'So I ask you again what was your impression of James Bentley?

Between ourselves – strictly between ourselves – you think he killed the old woman?'

Scuttle stared.

'Of course.'

'And you think, too, that it was a likely thing for him to do – psychologically speaking?'

'Well – if you put it like that – no, not really. Shouldn't have thought he had the guts. Tell you what, if you ask me, he was barmy. Put it that way, and it works. Always a bit soft in the head, and what with being out of a job and worrying and all that, he just went right over the edge.'

'You had no special reason for discharging him?'

Scuttle shook his head.

'Bad time of year. Staff hadn't enough to do. We sacked the one who was least competent. That was Bentley. Always would be, I expect. Gave him a good reference and all that. He didn't get another job, though. No pep. Made a bad impression on people.'

It always came back to that, Poirot thought, as he left the office. James Bentley made a bad impression on people. He took comfort in considering various murderers he had known whom most people had found full of charm.

II

'Excuse me, do you mind if I sit down here and talk to you for a moment?'

Poirot, ensconced at a small table in the Blue Cat, looked up from the menu he was studying with a start. It was rather dark in the Blue Cat, which specialized in an old-world effect of oak and leaded panes, but the young woman who had just sat down opposite to him stood out brightly from her dark background.

She had determinedly golden hair, and was wearing an electric blue jumper suit. Moreover, Hercule Poirot was conscious of having noticed her somewhere only a short time previously.

She went on:

'I couldn't help, you see, hearing something of what you were saying to Mr Scuttle.'

Poirot nodded. He had realized that the partitions in the offices of Breather & Scuttle were made for convenience rather than privacy. That had not worried him, since it was chiefly publicity that he desired.

'You were typing,' he said, 'to the right of the back window.'

She nodded. Her teeth shone white in an acquiescing smile. A very healthy young woman, with a full buxom figure that Poirot approved. About thirty-three or four, he judged, and by nature dark-haired, but not one to be dictated to by nature.

'About Mr Bentley,' she said.

'What about Mr Bentley?'

'Is he going to appeal? Does it mean that there's new evidence? Oh, I'm so glad. I couldn't – I just couldn't believe he did it.'

Poirot's eyebrows rose.

'So you never thought he did it,' he said slowly.

'Well, not at first. I thought it must be a mistake. But then the evidence –' She stopped.

'Yes, the evidence,' said Poirot.

'There just didn't seem anyone else who could have done it. I thought perhaps he'd gone a little mad.'

'Did he ever seem to you a little – what shall I say – queer?'

'Oh no. Not queer in that way. He was just shy and awkward as anyone might be. The truth was, he didn't make the best of himself. He hadn't confidence in himself.'

Poirot looked at her. She certainly had confidence in herself. Possibly she had enough confidence for two.

'You liked him?' he asked.

She flushed.

'Yes, I did. Amy – that's the other girl in the office – used to laugh at him and call him a drip, but I liked him very much. He was gentle and polite – and he knew a lot really. Things out of books, I mean.'

'Ah yes, things out of books.'

'He missed his mother. She'd been ill for years, you know. At least, not really ill, but not strong, and he'd done everything for her.'

Poirot nodded. He knew those mothers.

'And of course she'd looked after him, too. I mean taken care of his health and his chest in winter and what he ate and all that.'

Again he nodded. He asked:

'You and he were friends?'

'I don't know – not exactly. We used to talk sometimes. But after he left here, he – I – I didn't see much of him. I wrote to him once in a friendly way, but he didn't answer.'

Poirot said gently:

'But you like him?'

She said rather defiantly:

'Yes, I do . . .'

'That is excellent,' said Poirot.

His mind switched back to the day of his interview with the condemned prisoner . . . He saw James Bentley clearly. The mouse-coloured hair, the thin awkward body, the hands with their big knuckles and wrists, the Adam's apple in the lean neck. He saw the furtive, embarrassed – almost sly glance. Not straightforward, not a man whose word could be trusted – a secretive, sly deceitful fellow with an ungracious, muttering way of talking . . . That was the impression James Bentley would give to most superficial observers. It was the impression he had given in the dock. The sort of fellow who would tell lies, and steal money, and hit an old woman over the head . . .

But on Superintendent Spence, who knew men, he had not made that impression. Nor on Hercule Poirot . . . And now here was this girl.

'What is your name, mademoiselle?' he asked.

'Maude Williams. Is there anything I could do – to help?'

'I think there is. There are people who believe, Miss Williams, that James Bentley is innocent. They are working to prove that fact. I am the person charged with that investigation, and I may tell you that I have already made considerable progress – yes, considerable progress.'

He uttered that lie without a blush. To his mind it was a very necessary lie. Someone, somewhere, had got to be made uneasy. Maude Williams would talk, and talk was like a stone in a pond, it made a ripple that went on spreading outwards.

He said: 'You tell me that you and James Bentley talked together. He told you about his mother and his home life. Did he ever mention anyone with whom he, or perhaps his mother, was on bad terms?'

Maude Williams reflected.

'No – not what you'd call bad terms. His mother didn't like young women much, I gather.'

'Mothers of devoted sons never like young women. No, I mean more than that. Some family feud, some enmity. Someone with a grudge?'

She shook her head.

'He never mentioned anything of that kind.'

'Did he ever speak of his landlady, Mrs McGinty?'

She shivered slightly.

'Not by name. He said once that she gave him kippers much too often – and once he said his landlady was upset because she had lost her cat.'

'Did he ever – you must be honest, please – mention that he knew where she kept her money?'

Some of the colour went out of the girl's face, but she threw up her chin defiantly.

'Actually, he did. We were talking about people being distrust-ful of banks – and he said his old landlady kept her spare money under a floorboard. He said: "I could help myself any day to it when she's out." Not quite as a joke, he didn't joke, more as though he were really worried by her carelessness.'

'Ah,' said Poirot. 'That is good. From my point of view, I mean. When James Bentley thinks of stealing, it presents itself to him as an action that is done behind someone's back. He might have said, you see, "Some day someone will knock her on the head for it."'

'But either way, he wouldn't be meaning it.'

'Oh no. But talk, however light, however idle, gives away, inevitably, the sort of person you are. The wise criminal would never open his mouth, but criminals are seldom wise and usually vain and they talk a good deal – and so most criminals are caught.'

Maude Williams said abruptly:

'But *someone* must have killed the old woman.'

'Naturally.'

'Who did? Do you know? Have you any idea?'

'Yes,' said Hercule Poirot mendaciously. 'I think I have a very good idea. But we are only at the beginning of the road.'

The girl glanced at her watch.

'I must get back. We're only supposed to take half an hour. One-horse place, Kilchester – I've always had jobs in London before. You'll let me know if there's anything I can do – really *do*, I mean?'

Poirot took out one of his cards. On it he wrote Long Meadows and the telephone number.

'That is where I am staying.'

His name, he noted with chagrin, made no particular impression on her. The younger generation, he could not but feel, were singularly lacking in knowledge of notable celebrities.

III

Hercule Poirot caught a bus back to Broadhinny feeling slightly more cheerful. At any rate there was one person who shared his belief in James Bentley's innocence. Bentley was not so friendless as he had made himself out to be.

His mind went back again to Bentley in prison. What a dispiriting interview it had been. There had been no hope aroused, hardly a stirring of interest.

'Thank you,' Bentley had said dully, 'but I don't suppose there is anything anyone can do.'

No, he was sure he had not got any enemies.

'When people barely notice you're alive, you're not likely to have any enemies.'

'Your mother? Did she have an enemy?'

'Certainly not. Everyone liked and respected her.'

There was a faint indignation in his tone.

'What about your friends?'

And James Bentley had said, or rather muttered, 'I haven't any friends . . .'

But that had not been quite true. For Maude Williams was a friend.

'What a wonderful dispensation it is of Nature's,' thought Hercule Poirot, 'that every man, however superficially unattractive, should be some woman's choice.'

For all Miss Williams's sexy appearance, he had a shrewd suspicion that she was really the maternal type.

She had the qualities that James Bentley lacked, the energy, the drive, the refusal to be beaten, the determination to succeed.

He sighed.

What monstrous lies he had told that day! Never mind – they were necessary.

'For somewhere,' said Poirot to himself, indulging in an absolute riot of mixed metaphors, 'there is in the hay a needle, and among the sleeping dogs there is one on whom I shall put my foot, and by shooting the arrows into the air, one will come down and hit a glass-house!'

CHAPTER 7

I

The cottage where Mrs McGinty had lived was only a few steps from the bus stop. Two children were playing on the doorstep. One was eating a rather wormy-looking apple and the other was shouting and beating on the door with a tin tray. They appeared quite happy. Poirot added to the noise by beating hard on the door himself.

A woman looked round the corner of the house. She had on a coloured overall and her hair was untidy.

'Stop it, Ernie,' she said.

'Sha'n't,' said Ernie and continued.

Poirot deserted the doorstep and made for the corner of the house.

'Can't do anything with children, can you?' the woman said.

Poirot thought you could, but forbore to say so.

He was beckoned round to the back door.

'I keep the front bolted up, sir. Come in, won't you?'

Poirot passed through a very dirty scullery into an almost more dirty kitchen.

'She wasn't killed here,' said the woman. 'In the parlour.'

Poirot blinked slightly.

'That's what you're down about, isn't it? You're the foreign gentleman from up at Summerhayes?'

'So you know all about me?' said Poirot. He beamed. 'Yes, indeed, Mrs –'

'Kiddle. My husband's a plasterer. Moved in four months ago, we did. Been living with Bert's mother before . . . Some folks said: "You'd never go into a house where there's been a murder, surely?" – but what I said was, a house is a house, and better than a back sitting-room and sleeping on two chairs. Awful, this 'ousing shortage, isn't it? And anyway *we*'ve never been troubled 'ere. Always say they *walk* if they've been murdered, but she doesn't! Like to see where it happened?'

Feeling like a tourist being taken on a conducted tour, Poirot assented.

Mrs Kiddle led him into a small room over-burdened with a heavy Jacobean suite. Unlike the rest of the house, it showed no signs of ever having been occupied.

'Down on the floor she was and the back of her head split open. Didn't half give Mrs Elliot a turn. She's the one what found her – she and Larkin who comes from the Co-op with the bread. But the money was took from upstairs. Come along up and I'll show you where.'

Mrs Kiddle led the way up the staircase and into a bedroom which contained a large chest of drawers, a big brass bed, some chairs, and a fine assembly of baby clothes, wet and dry.

'Right here it was,' said Mrs Kiddle proudly.

Poirot looked round him. Hard to visualize that this rampant stronghold of haphazard fecundity was once the well-scrubbed domain of an elderly woman who was house-proud. Here Mrs McGinty had lived and slept.

'I suppose this isn't her furniture?'

'Oh no. Her niece over in Cullavon took away all that.'

There was nothing left here of Mrs McGinty. The Kiddles had come and conquered. Life was stronger than death.

From downstairs the loud fierce wail of a baby arose.

'That's the baby woken up,' said Mrs Kiddle unnecessarily.

She plunged down the stairs and Poirot followed her.

There was nothing here for him.

He went next door.

II

'Yes, sir, it was me found her.'

Mrs Elliot was dramatic. A neat house, this, neat and prim. The only drama in it was Mrs Elliot's, a tall gaunt dark-haired woman, recounting her one moment of glorious living.

'Larkin, the baker, he came and knocked at the door. "It's Mrs McGinty," he said, "we can't make her hear. Seems she might have been taken bad." And indeed I thought she might. She wasn't a young woman, not by any means. And palpitations she'd had, to my certain knowledge. I thought she might have had a stroke. So I hurried over, seeing as there were only the two men, and naturally they wouldn't like to go into the bedroom.'

Poirot accepted this piece of propriety with an assenting murmur.

'Hurried up the stairs, I did. *He* was on the landing, pale as death he was. Not that I ever thought at the time – well, of course, then I didn't know what had happened. I knocked on the door loud and there wasn't any answer, so I turned the handle and I went in. The whole place messed about – and the board in the floor up. "It's robbery," I said. "But where's the poor soul herself?" And then we thought to look in the sitting-room. *And there she was . . .* Down on the floor with her poor head stove in. Murder! I saw at once what it was – murder! Couldn't be anything else! Robbery and murder! Here in Broadhinny. I screamed and I screamed! Quite a job they had with me. Come over all faint, I did. They had to go and get me brandy from the Three Ducks. And even then I was all of a shiver for hours and hours. "Don't you take on so, mother," that's what the sergeant said to me when he came. "Don't you take on so. You go home and make yourself a nice cup of tea." And so I did. And when Elliot came home, "Why, whatever's happened?" he says, staring at me. Still all of a tremble I was. Always was sensitive from a child.'

Poirot dexterously interrupted this thrilling personal narrative.

'Yes, yes, one can see that. And when was the last time you had seen poor Mrs McGinty?'

'Must have been the day before, when she'd stepped out into the back garden to pick a bit of mint. I was just feeding the chickens.'

'Did she say anything to you?'

'Just good afternoon and were they laying any better.'

'And that's the last time you saw her? You didn't see her on the day she died?'

'No. I saw *Him* though.' Mrs Elliot lowered her voice. 'About eleven o'clock in the morning. Just walking along the road. Shuffling his feet the way he always did.'

Poirot waited, but it seemed that there was nothing to add.

He asked:

'Were you surprised when the police arrested him?'

'Well, I was and I wasn't. Mind you, I'd always thought he was a bit daft. And no doubt about it, these daft ones do turn nasty, sometimes. My uncle had a feeble-minded boy, and he could go very nasty sometimes – as he grew up, that was. Didn't know his strength. Yes, that Bentley was daft all right, and I shouldn't be surprised if they don't hang him when it comes to it, but sends him to the asylum instead. Why, look at the place he hid the money. No one would hide money in a place like that unless he wanted it to be found. Just silly and simple like, that's what he was.'

'Unless he wanted it found,' murmured Poirot. 'You did not, by any chance, miss a chopper – or an axe?'

'No, sir, I did *not*. The police asked me that. Asked all of us in the cottages here. It's a mystery still what he killed her with.'

III

Hercule Poirot walked towards the post office.

The murderer had wanted the money found, but he had not wanted the weapon to be found. For the money would point to James Bentley and the weapon would point to – whom?

He shook his head. He had visited the other two cottages. They had been less exuberant than Mrs Kiddle and less dramatic than Mrs Elliot. They had said in effect that Mrs McGinty was a very respectable woman who kept herself to herself, that she had a niece over at Cullavon, that nobody but the said niece ever came to see her, that nobody, so far as they knew, disliked her or bore a grudge against her, that was it true that there was a petition being got up for James Bentley and would they be asked to sign it?

'I get nowhere – nowhere,' said Poirot to himself. 'There is nothing – no little gleam. I can well understand the despair of Superintendent Spence. But it should be different for *me*. Superintendent Spence, he is a good and painstaking police officer, but me, I am Hercule Poirot. For *me*, there should be illumination!'

One of his patent leather shoes slopped into a puddle and he winced.

He was the great, the unique Hercule Poirot, but he was also a very old man and his shoes were tight.

He entered the post office.

The right-hand side was given to the business of His Majesty's mails. The left-hand side displayed a rich assortment of varied merchandise, comprising sweets, groceries, toys, hardware, stationery, birthday cards, knitting wool and children's underclothes.

Poirot proceeded to a leisurely purchase of stamps.

The woman who bustled forward to attend to him was middle-aged with sharp, bright eyes.

'Here,' said Poirot to himself, 'is undoubtedly the brains of the village of Broadhinny.'

Her name, not inappropriately, was Mrs Sweetiman.

'And twelve pennies,' said Mrs Sweetiman, deftly extracting them from a large book. 'That's four and tenpence altogether. Will there be anything more, sir?'

She fixed a bright eager glance at him. Through the door at the back a girl's head showed listening avidly. She had untidy hair and a cold in the head.

'I am by way of being a stranger in these parts,' said Poirot solemnly.

'That's right, sir,' agreed Mrs Sweetiman. 'Come down from London, haven't you?'

'I expect you know my business here as well as I do,' said Poirot with a slight smile.

'Oh no, sir, I've really no idea,' said Mrs Sweetiman in a wholly perfunctory manner.

'Mrs McGinty,' said Poirot.

Mrs Sweetiman shook her head.

'That was a sad business – a shocking business.'

'I expect you knew her well?'

'Oh I did. As well as anyone in Broadhinny, I should say. She'd always pass the time of day with me when she came in here for any little thing. Yes, it was a terrible tragedy. And not settled yet, or so I've heard people say.'

'There is a doubt – in some quarters – as to James Bentley's guilt.'

'Well,' said Mrs Sweetiman, 'it wouldn't be the first time the police got hold of the wrong man – though I wouldn't say they had in this case. Not that I should have thought it of him really. A shy, awkward sort of fellow, but not dangerous or so you'd think. But there, you never know, do you?'

Poirot hazarded a request for notepaper.

'Of course, sir. Just come across the other side, will you?'

Mrs Sweetiman bustled round to take her place behind the left-hand counter.

'What's difficult to imagine is, who it could have been if it wasn't Mr Bentley,' she remarked as she stretched up to a top shelf for notepaper and envelopes. 'We do get some nasty tramps along here sometimes, and it's possible one of these might have found a window unfastened and got in that way. But he wouldn't go leaving the money behind him, would he? Not after doing murder to get it – and pound notes anyway, nothing with numbers or marked. Here you are, sir, that's a nice blue Bond, and envelopes to match.'

Poirot made his purchase.

'Mrs McGinty never spoke of being nervous of anyone, or afraid, did she?' he asked.

'Not to me, she didn't. She wasn't a nervous woman. She'd stay late sometimes at Mr Carpenter's – that's Holmeleigh at the top of the hill. They often have people to dinner and stopping with them, and Mrs McGinty would go there in the evening sometimes to help wash up, and she'd come down the hill in the dark, and that's more than I'd like to do. Very dark it is – coming down that hill.'

'Do you know her niece at all – Mrs Burch?'

'I know her just to speak to. She and her husband come over sometimes.'

'They inherited a little money when Mrs McGinty died.'

The piercing dark eyes looked at him severely.

'Well, that's natural enough, isn't it, sir? You can't take it with you, and it's only right your own flesh and blood should get it.'

'Oh yes, oh yes, I am entirely in agreement. Was Mrs McGinty fond of her niece?'

'Very fond of her, I think, sir. In a quiet way.'

'And her niece's husband?'

An evasive look appeared in Mrs Sweetiman's face.

'As far as I know.'

'When did you see Mrs McGinty last?'

Mrs Sweetiman considered, casting her mind back.

'Now let me see, when was it, Edna?' Edna, in the doorway, sniffed unhelpfully. 'Was it the day she died? No, it was the day before – or the day before that again? Yes, it was a Monday. That's right. She was killed on the Wednesday. Yes, it was Monday. She came in to buy a bottle of ink.'

'She wanted a bottle of ink?'

'Expect she wanted to write a letter,' said Mrs Sweetiman brightly.

'That seems probable. And she was quite her usual self, then? She did not seem different in any way?'

'N-no, I don't think so.'

The sniffing Edna shuffled through the door into the shop and suddenly joined in the conversation.

'She was different,' she asserted. 'Pleased about something – well – not quite pleased – excited.'

'Perhaps you're right,' said Mrs Sweetiman. 'Not that I noticed it at the time. But now that you say so – sort of spry, she was.'

'Do you remember anything she said on that day?'

'I wouldn't ordinarily. But what with her being murdered and the police and everything, it makes things stand out. She didn't say anything about James Bentley, that I'm quite sure. Talked about the Carpenters a bit and Mrs Upward – places where she worked, you know.'

'Oh yes, I was going to ask you whom exactly she worked for here.'

Mrs Sweetiman replied promptly:

'Mondays and Thursdays she went to Mrs Summerhayes at Long Meadow. That's where you are staying, isn't it?'

'Yes,' Poirot sighed, 'I suppose there is not anywhere else to stay?'

'Not right in Broadhinny, there isn't. I suppose you aren't very comfortable at Long Meadows? Mrs Summerhayes is a nice lady but she doesn't know the first thing about a house. These ladies don't who come back from foreign parts. Terrible mess there always was there to clean up, or so Mrs McGinty used to say. Yes, Monday afternoons and Thursday mornings

Mrs Summerhayes, then Tuesday mornings Dr Rendell's and afternoons Mrs Upward at Laburnums. Wednesday was Mrs Wetherby at Hunter's Close and Friday Mrs Selkirk – Mrs Carpenter she is now. Mrs Upward's an elderly lady who lives with her son. They've got a maid, but she's getting on, and Mrs McGinty used to go once a week to give things a good turn out. Mr and Mrs Wetherby never seem to keep any help long – she's rather an invalid. Mr and Mrs Carpenter have a beautiful home and do a lot of entertaining. They're all very nice people.'

It was with this final pronouncement on the population of Broadhinny that Poirot went out into the street again.

He walked slowly up the hill towards Long Meadows. He hoped devoutly that the contents of the bulged tin and the bloodstained beans had been duly eaten for lunch and had not been saved for a supper treat for him. But possibly there were other doubtful tins. Life at Long Meadows certainly had its dangers.

It had been, on the whole, a disappointing day.

What had he learned?

That James Bentley had a friend. That neither he nor Mrs McGinty had had any enemies. That Mrs McGinty had looked excited two days before her death and had bought a bottle of ink –

Poirot stopped dead . . . Was that a fact, a tiny fact at last?

He had asked idly, what Mrs McGinty should want with a bottle of ink, and Mrs Sweetiman had replied, quite seriously, that she supposed she wanted to write a letter.

There was significance there – a significance that had nearly escaped him because to him, as to most people, writing a letter was a common everyday occurrence.

But it was not so to Mrs McGinty. Writing a letter was to Mrs McGinty such an uncommon occurrence that she had to go out and buy a bottle of ink if she wanted to do so.

Mrs McGinty, then, hardly ever wrote letters. Mrs Sweetiman, who was the postmistress, was thoroughly cognisant of the fact. But Mrs McGinty had written a letter two days before her death. To whom had she written and why?

It might be quite unimportant. She might have written to her niece – to an absent friend. Absurd to lay such stress on a simple thing like a bottle of ink.

But it was all he had got and he was going to follow it up.

A bottle of ink . . .

CHAPTER 8

I

'A letter?' Bessie Burch shook her head. 'No, I didn't get any letter from auntie. What should she write to me about?'

Poirot suggested: 'There might have been something she wanted to tell you.'

'Auntie wasn't much of a one for writing. She was getting on for seventy, you know, and when she was young they didn't get much schooling.'

'But she could read and write?'

'Oh, of course. Not much of a one for reading, though she liked her *News of the World* and her *Sunday Comet*. But writing came a bit difficult always. If she'd anything to let me know about, like putting us off from coming to see her, or saying she couldn't come to us, she'd usually ring up Mr Benson, the chemist next door, and he'd send the message in. Very obliging that way, he is. You see, we're in the area, so it only costs twopence. There's a call-box at the post office in Broadhinny.'

Poirot nodded. He appreciated the fact that twopence was better than twopence ha'penny. He already had a picture of Mrs McGinty as the spare and saving kind. She had been, he thought, very fond of money.

He persisted gently:

'But your aunt did write to you sometimes, I suppose?'

'Well, there were cards at Christmas.'

'And perhaps she had friends in other parts of England to whom she wrote?'

'I don't know about that. There was her sister-in-law, but she died two years ago and there was a Mrs Birdlip – but she's dead too.'

'So, if she wrote to someone, it would be most likely in answer to a letter she had received?'

Again Bessie Burch looked doubtful.

'I don't know who'd be writing to her, I'm sure . . . Of course,' her face brightened, 'there's always the Government.'

Poirot agreed that in these days, communications from what Bessie loosely referred to as 'the Government' were the rule, rather than the exception.

'And a lot of fandangle it usually is,' said Mrs Burch. 'Forms to fill in, and a lot of impertinent questions as shouldn't be asked of any decent body.'

'So Mrs McGinty might have got some Government communication that she had to answer?'

'If she had, she'd have brought it along to Joe, so as he could help her with it. Those sort of things fussed her and she always brought them to Joe.'

'Can you remember if there were any letters among her personal possessions?'

'I couldn't say rightly. I don't remember anything. But then the police took over at first. It wasn't for quite a while they let me pack her things and take them away.'

'What happened to those things?'

'That chest over there is hers – good solid mahogany, and there's a wardrobe upstairs, and some good kitchen stuff. The rest we sold because we'd no room for them.'

'I meant her own personal things.' He added: 'Such things as brushes and combs, photographs, toilet things, clothes . . .'

'Oh, them. Well, tell you the truth, I packed them in a suitcase and it's still upstairs. Didn't rightly know what to do with them. Thought I'd take the clothes to the jumble sale at Christmas, but I forgot. Didn't seem nice to take them to one of those nasty second-hand clothes people.'

'I wonder – might I see the contents of that suitcase?'

'Welcome, I'm sure. Though I don't think you'll find anything to help you. The police went through it all, you know.'

'Oh I know. But, all the same –'

Mrs Burch led him briskly into a minute back bedroom, used, Poirot judged, mainly for home dressmaking. She pulled out a suitcase from under the bed and said:

'Well, here you are, and you'll excuse me stopping, but I've got the stew to see to.'

Poirot gratefully excused her, and heard her thumping downstairs again. He drew the suitcase towards him and opened it.

A waft of mothballs came out to greet him.

With a feeling of pity, he lifted out the contents, so eloquent in their revelation of a woman who was dead. A rather worn long black coat. Two woollen jumpers. A coat and skirt. Stockings. No underwear (presumably Bessie Burch had taken those for her own wear). Two pairs of shoes wrapped up in newspaper. A brush and comb, worn but clean. An old dented silver-backed mirror. A photograph in a leather frame of a wedding pair dressed in the style of thirty years ago – a picture of Mrs McGinty and her husband presumably. Two picture post-cards of Margate. A china dog. A recipe torn out of a paper for making vegetable marrow jam. Another piece dealing with 'Flying Saucers' on a sensational note. A third clipping dealt with Mother Shipton's prophecies. There was also a Bible and a Prayer Book.

There were no handbags, or gloves. Presumably Bessie Burch had taken these, or given them away. The clothes here, Poirot judged, would have been too small for the buxom Bessie. Mrs McGinty had been a thin, spare woman.

He unwrapped one of the pairs of shoes. They were of quite good quality and not much worn. Decidedly on the small side for Bessie Burch.

He was just about to wrap them up neatly again when his eye was caught by the heading on the piece of newspaper.

It was the *Sunday Comet* and the date was November 19th.

Mrs McGinty had been killed on November 22nd.

This then was the paper she had bought on the Sunday preceding her death. It had been lying in her room and Bessie Burch had used it in due course to wrap up her aunt's things.

Sunday, November 19th. And on *Monday* Mrs McGinty had gone into the post office to buy a bottle of ink . . .

Could that be because of something she had seen in Sunday's newspaper?

He unwrapped the other pair of shoes. They were wrapped in the *News of the World* of the same date.

He smoothed out both papers and took them over to a chair where he sat down to read them. And at once he made a discovery. On one page of the *Sunday Comet*, something had been cut out. It was a rectangular piece out of the middle page. The space was too big for any of the clippings he had found.

He looked through both newspapers, but could find nothing else of interest. He wrapped them round the shoes again and packed the suitcase tidily.

Then he went downstairs.

Mrs Burch was busy in the kitchen.

'Don't suppose you found anything?' she said.

'Alas, no.' He added in a casual voice: 'You do not remember if there was a cutting from a newspaper in your aunt's purse or in her handbag, was there?'

'Can't remember any. Perhaps the police took it.'

But the police had not taken it. That Poirot knew from his study of Spence's notes. The contents of the dead woman's handbag had been listed, no newspaper cutting was among them.

'*Eh bien*,' said Hercule Poirot to himself. 'The next step is easy. It will be either the wash-out – or else, at last, I advance.'

II

Sitting very still, with the dusty files of newspaper in front of him, Poirot told himself that his recognition of the significance of the bottle of ink had not played him false.

The *Sunday Comet* was given to romantic dramatizations of past events.

The paper at which Poirot was looking was the *Sunday Comet* of Sunday, November 19th.

At the top of the middle page were these words in big type:

WOMEN VICTIMS OF
BYGONE TRAGEDIES
WHERE ARE THESE
WOMEN NOW?

Below the caption were four very blurred reproductions of photographs clearly taken many years ago.

The subjects of them did not look tragic. They looked, actually, rather ridiculous, since nearly all of them were dressed in the style of a bygone day, and nothing is more ridiculous than the fashions of yesterday – though in another thirty years or so their charm may have reappeared, or at any rate be once more apparent.

Under each photo was a name.

Eva Kane, the 'other woman' in the famous Craig Case.
Janice Courtland, the 'tragic wife' whose husband was a fiend in human form.
Little Lily Gamboll, tragic child product of our overcrowded age.
Vera Blake, unsuspecting wife of a killer.

And then came the question in bold type again:

WHERE ARE THESE
WOMEN NOW?

Poirot blinked and set himself to read meticulously the somewhat romantic prose which gave the life stories of these dim and blurry heroines.

The name of Eva Kane he remembered, for the Craig Case had been a very celebrated one. Alfred Craig had been Town Clerk of Parminster, a conscientious, rather nondescript little man, correct and pleasant in his behaviour. He had had the misfortune to marry a tiresome and temperamental wife. Mrs Craig ran him into debt, bullied him, nagged him, and suffered from nervous maladies that unkind friends said were entirely imaginary. Eva Kane was the young nursery governess in the house. She was nineteen, pretty, helpless and rather simple. She fell desperately in love with Craig and he with her. Then one day the neighbours heard that Mrs Craig had been 'ordered abroad' for her health. That had been Craig's story. He took her up to London, the first stage of the journey, by car late one evening, and 'saw her off' to the South of France. Then he returned to Parminster and at intervals mentioned how his wife's health was no better by her accounts of it in letters. Eva Kane remained behind to housekeep for him, and tongues soon started wagging. Finally, Craig received news of his wife's death abroad. He went away and returned a week later, with an account of the funeral.

In some ways, Craig was a simple man. He made the mistake

of mentioning where his wife had died, a moderately well-known resort on the French Riviera. It only remained for someone who had a relative or friend living there to write to them, discover that there had been no death or funeral of anyone of that name and, after a period of rank gossip, to communicate with the police.

Subsequent events can be briefly summarized.

Mrs Craig had not left for the Riviera. She had been cut in neat pieces and buried in the Craig cellar. And the autopsy of the remains showed poisoning by a vegetable alkaloid.

Craig was arrested and sent for trial. Eva Kane was originally charged as an accessory, but the charge was dropped, since it appeared clear that she had throughout been completely ignorant of what had occurred. Craig in the end made a full confession and was sentenced and executed.

Eva Kane, who was expecting a child, left Parminster and, in the words of the *Sunday Comet*:

> *Kindly relatives in the New World offered her a home. Changing her name, the pitiful young girl, seduced in her trusting youth by a cold-blooded murderer, left these shores for ever, to begin a new life and to keep for ever locked in her heart and concealed from her daughter the name of her father.*
>
> '*My daughter shall grow up happy and innocent. Her life shall not be tainted by the cruel past. That I have sworn. My tragic memories shall remain mine alone.*'
>
> *Poor frail trusting Eva Kane. To learn, so young, the villainy and infamy of man. Where is she now? Is there, in some Mid-western town, an elderly woman, quiet and respected by her neighbours, who has, perhaps, sad eyes . . . And does a young woman, happy and cheerful, with children, perhaps, of her own, come and see 'Momma', telling her of all the little rubs and grievances of daily life – with no idea of what past sufferings her mother has endured?*

'Oh la la!' said Hercule Poirot. And passed on to the next Tragic Victim.

Janice Courtland, the 'tragic wife', had certainly been unfortunate in her husband. His peculiar practices referred to in such a guarded way as to rouse instant curiosity, had been suffered by her for eight years. Eight years of martyrdom, the *Sunday Comet* said firmly. Then Janice made a friend. An idealistic and unworldly young man who, horrified by a scene between husband and wife that he had witnessed by accident, had thereupon assaulted the husband with such vigour that the latter had crashed in his skull on a sharply-edged marble fire surround. The jury had found that provocation had been intense, that the young idealist had had no intention of killing, and a sentence of five years for manslaughter was given.

The suffering Janice, horrified by all the publicity the case had brought her, had gone abroad 'to forget'.

> *Has she forgotten?* asked the *Sunday Comet*. *We hope so. Somewhere, perhaps, is a happy wife and mother to whom those years of nightmare suffering silently endured, seem now only like a dream . . .*

'Well, well,' said Hercule Poirot and passed on to Lily Gamboll, the tragic child product of our overcrowded age.

Lily Gamboll had, it seemed, been removed from her overcrowded home. An aunt had assumed responsibility for Lily's life. Lily had wanted to go to the pictures, aunt had said 'No.' Lily Gamboll had picked up the meat chopper which was lying conveniently on the table and had aimed a blow at her aunt with it. The aunt, though autocratic, was small and frail. The blow killed her. Lily was a well-developed and muscular child for her twelve years. An approved school had opened its doors and Lily had disappeared from the everyday scene.

> *By now she is a woman, free again to take her place in our civilization. Her conduct, during her years of confinement and probation, is said to have been exemplary. Does not this show that it is not the child, but the system, that we must blame? Brought up in ignorance, little Lily was the victim of her environment.*
>
> *Now, having atoned for her tragic lapse, she lives somewhere, happily, we hope, a good citizen and a good wife and mother. Poor little Lily Gamboll.*

Poirot shook his head. A child of twelve who took a swing at her aunt with a meat chopper and hit her hard enough to kill her was not, in his opinion, a nice child. His sympathies were, in this case, with the aunt.

He passed on to Vera Blake.

Vera Blake was clearly one of those women with whom everything goes wrong. She had first taken up with a boyfriend who turned out to be a gangster wanted by the police for killing a bank watchman. She had then married a respectable tradesman who turned out to be a receiver of stolen goods. Her two children had likewise, in due course, attracted the attention of the police. They went with Mamma to department stores and did a pretty line in shoplifting. Finally, however, a 'good man' had appeared on the scene. He had offered tragic Vera a home in the Dominions. She and her children should leave this effete country.

> From henceforward a New Life awaited them. At last, after long years of repeated blows from Fate, Vera's troubles are over.

'I wonder,' said Poirot sceptically. 'Very possibly she will find she has married a confidence trickster who works the liners!'

He leant back and studied the four photographs. Eva Kane with tousled curly hair over her ears and an enormous hat, held a bunch of roses up to her ear like a telephone receiver. Janice Courtland had a cloche hat pushed down over her ears and a waist round her hips. Lily Gamboll was a plain child with an adenoidal appearance of open mouth, hard breathing and thick spectacles. Vera Blake was so tragically black and white that no features showed.

For some reason Mrs McGinty had torn out this feature, photographs and all. Why? Just to keep because the stories interested her? He thought not. Mrs McGinty had kept very few things during her sixty-odd years of life. Poirot knew that from the police reports of her belongings.

She had torn this out on the Sunday and on the Monday she had bought a bottle of ink and the inference was that she, who never wrote letters, was about to write a letter. If it had been a business letter, she would probably have asked Joe Burch to help her. So it had not been business. It had been – what?

Poirot's eyes looked over the four photographs once again.

Where, the *Sunday Comet* asked, *are these women now?*

One of them, Poirot thought, might have been in Broadhinny last November.

III

It was not until the following day that Poirot found himself tête-à-tête with Miss Pamela Horsefall.

Miss Horsefall couldn't give him long, because she had to rush away to Sheffield, she explained.

Miss Horsefall was tall, manly-looking, a hard drinker and smoker, and it would seem, looking at her, highly improbable that it was her pen which had dropped such treacly sentiment in the *Sunday Comet.* Nevertheless it was so.

'Cough it up, cough it up,' said Miss Horsefall impatiently to Poirot. 'I've got to be going.'

'It is about your article in the *Sunday Comet.* Last November. The series about Tragic Women.'

'Oh, *that* series. Pretty lousy, weren't they?'

Poirot did not express an opinion on that point. He said:

'I refer in particular to the article on Women Associated with Crime that appeared on November 19th. It concerned Eva Kane, Vera Blake, Janice Courtland and Lily Gamboll.'

Miss Horsefall grinned.

'*Where are these tragic women now*? I remember.'

'I suppose you sometimes get letters after the appearance of these articles?'

'You bet I do! Some people seem to have nothing better to do than write letters. Somebody "once saw the murderer Craig walking down the street." Somebody would like to tell me "the story of her life, far more tragic than anything I could ever imagine."'

'Did you get a letter after the appearance of that article from a Mrs McGinty of Broadhinny?'

'My dear man, how on earth should I know? I get buckets of letters. How should I remember one particular name?'

'I thought you might remember,' said Poirot, 'because a few days later Mrs McGinty was murdered.'

'Now you're talking.' Miss Horsefall forgot to be impatient

to get to Sheffield, and sat down astride a chair. 'McGinty – McGinty . . . I do remember the name. Conked on the head by her lodger. Not a very exciting crime from the point of view of the public. No sex appeal about it. You say the woman wrote to me?'

'She wrote to the *Sunday Comet*, I think.'

'Same thing. It would come on to me. And with the murder – and her name being in the news – surely I should remember –' she stopped. 'Look here – it wasn't from Broadhinny. It was from Broadway.'

'So you do remember?'

'Well, I'm not sure . . . But the name . . . Comic name, isn't it? McGinty! Yes – atrocious writing and quite illiterate. If I'd only realized . . . But I'm sure it came from Broadway.'

Poirot said: 'You say yourself the writing was bad. Broadway and Broadhinny – they could look alike.'

'Yes – might be so. After all, one wouldn't be likely to know these queer rural names. McGinty – yes. I do remember definitely. Perhaps the murder fixed the name for me.'

'Can you remember what she said in her letter?'

'Something about a photograph. She knew where there was a photograph like in the paper – and would we pay her anything for it and how much?'

'And you answered?'

'My dear man, we don't want anything of that kind. We sent back the standard reply. Polite thanks but nothing doing. But as we sent it to Broadway – I don't suppose she'd ever get it.'

'*She knew where there was a photograph . . .*'

Into Poirot's mind there came back a remembrance. Maureen Summerhayes' careless voice saying, 'Of course she snooped round a bit.'

Mrs McGinty had snooped. She was honest, but she liked to know about things. And people kept things – foolish, meaningless things from the past. Kept them for sentimental reasons, or just overlooked them and didn't remember they were there.

Mrs McGinty had seen an old photograph and later she had recognized it reproduced in the *Sunday Comet*. And she had wondered if there was any money in it . . .

He rose briskly. 'Thank you, Miss Horsefall. You will pardon me, but those notes on the cases that you wrote, were they accurate? I notice, for instance, that the year of the Craig trial is given wrongly – it was actually a year later than you say. And in the Courtland case, the husband's name was Herbert, I seem to remember, not Hubert. Lily Gamboll's aunt lived in Buckinghamshire, not Berkshire.'

Miss Horsefall waved a cigarette.

'My dear man. No point in accuracy. Whole thing was a romantic farrago from beginning to end. I just mugged up the facts a bit and then let fly with a lot of hou ha.'

'What I am trying to say is that even the characters of your heroines are not, perhaps, quite as represented.'

Pamela let out a neighing sound like a horse.

''Course they weren't. What do *you* think? I've no doubt that Eva Kane was a thorough little bitch, and not an injured innocent at all. And as for the Courtland woman, why did she suffer in silence for eight years with a sadistic pervert? Because he was rolling in money, and the romantic boy-friend hadn't any.'

'And the tragic child, Lily Gamboll?'

'I wouldn't care to have her gambolling about *me* with a meat chopper.'

Poirot ticked off on his fingers.

'They left the country – they went to the New World – abroad – "to the Dominions" – "to start a New Life." And there is nothing to show, is there, that they did not, subsequently, come back to this country?'

'Not a thing,' agreed Miss Horsefall. 'And now – I really must fly –'

Later that night Poirot rang up Spence.

'I've been wondering about you, Poirot. Have you got anything? Anything at all?'

'I have made my inquiries,' said Poirot grimly.

'Yes?'

'And the result of them is this: *The people who live in Broadhinny are all very nice people.*'

'What do you mean by that, M. Poirot?'

'Oh, my friend, consider. "Very nice people." That has been, before now, a motive for murder.'

CHAPTER 9

I

'All very nice people,' murmured Poirot as he turned in at the gate of Crossways, near the station.

A brass plate in the doorpost announced that Dr Rendell, M.D., lived there.

Dr Rendell was a large cheerful man of forty. He greeted his guest with definite *empressement*.

'Our quiet little village is honoured,' he said, 'by the presence of the great Hercule Poirot.'

'Ah,' said Poirot. He was gratified. '*You* have, then, heard of me?'

'Of course we have heard of you. Who hasn't?'

The answer to that would have been damaging to Poirot's self-esteem. He merely said politely: 'I am fortunate to find you at home.'

It was not particularly fortunate. It was, on the contrary, astute timing. But Dr Rendell replied heartily:

'Yes. Just caught me. Surgery in a quarter of an hour. Now what can I do for you? I'm devoured with curiosity to know what you're doing down here. A rest cure? Or have we crime in our midst?'

'In the past tense – not the present.'

'Past? I don't remember –'

'Mrs McGinty.'

'Of course. Of course. I was forgetting. But don't say you're concerned with that – at this late date?'

'If I may mention this to you in confidence, I am employed by the defence. Fresh evidence on which to lodge an appeal.'

Dr Rendell said sharply: 'But what fresh evidence can there be?'

'That, alas, I am not at liberty to state –'

'Oh, quite – please forgive me.'

'But I have come across certain things which are, I may say – very curious – very – how shall I put it? – suggestive? I came to you, Dr Rendell, because I understand that Mrs McGinty occasionally was employed here.'

'Oh yes, yes – she was – What about a drink? Sherry? Whisky? You prefer sherry? So do I.' He brought two glasses and, sitting down by Poirot, he went on: 'She used to come once a week to do extra cleaning. I've got a very good housekeeper – excellent – but the brasses – and scrubbing the kitchen floor – well, my Mrs Scott can't get down on her knees very well. Mrs McGinty was an excellent worker.'

'Do you think that she was a truthful person?'

'Truthful? Well, that's an odd question. I don't think I could say – no opportunity of knowing. As far as I know she was quite truthful.'

'If then she made a statement to anyone, you think that statement would probably be true?'

Dr Rendell looked faintly disturbed.

'Oh, I wouldn't like to go as far as that. I really know so little about her. I could ask Mrs Scott. She'd know better.'

'No, no. It would be better not to do that.'

'You're arousing my curiosity,' said Dr Rendell genially. 'What was it she was going around saying? Something a bit libellous, was it? Slanderous, I suppose I mean.'

Poirot merely shook his head. He said: 'You understand, all this is extremely hush hush at present. I am only at the very commencement of my investigation.'

Dr Rendell said rather drily:

'You'll have to hurry a bit, won't you?'

'You are right. The time at my disposal is short.'

'I must say you surprise me . . . We've all been quite sure down here that Bentley did it. There didn't seem any doubt possible.'

'It seemed an ordinary sordid crime – not very interesting. That is what you would say?'

'Yes – yes, that sums it up very fairly.'

'You knew James Bentley?'

'He came to see me professionally once or twice. He was nervous about his own health. Coddled by his mother, I fancy. One sees that so often. We've another case in point here.'

'Ah, indeed?'

'Yes. Mrs Upward. Laura Upward. Dotes upon that son of hers. She keeps him well tied to her apron-strings. He's a clever fellow – not quite as clever as he thinks himself, between you and me – but still definitely talented. By way of being a budding playwright is our Robin.'

'They have been here long?'

'Three or four years. Nobody has been in Broadhinny very long. The original village was only a handful of cottages, grouped round Long Meadows. You're staying there, I understand?'

'I am,' said Poirot without undue elation.

Dr Rendell appeared amused.

'Guest House indeed,' he said. 'What that young woman knows about running a Guest House is just nothing at all. She's lived in India all her married life with servants running round all over the place. I bet you're uncomfortable. Nobody ever stays long. As for poor old Summerhayes, he'll never make anything of this market gardening stunt he's trying to run. Nice fellow – but not an idea of the commercial life – and the commercial life it's got to be nowadays if you want to keep your head above water. Don't run away with the idea that I heal the sick. I'm just a glorified form-filler and signer of certificates. I like the Summerhayes, though. She's a charming creature, and though Summerhayes has a devilish temper and is inclined to be moody, he's one of the old gang. Out of the top drawer all right. You should have known old Colonel Summerhayes, a regular tartar, proud as the devil.'

'That was Major Summerhayes' father?'

'Yes. There wasn't much money when the old boy died and of course there have been death duties to cripple these people, but they're determined to stick to the old place. One doesn't know whether to admire them, or whether to say "Silly fools."'

He looked at his watch.

'I must not keep you,' said Poirot.

'I've got a few minutes still. Besides, I'd like you to meet my wife. I can't think where she is. She was immensely interested to hear you were down here. We're both very crime-minded. Read a lot about it.'

'Criminology, fiction, or the Sunday papers?' asked Poirot smiling.

'All three.'

'Do you descend as low as the *Sunday Comet*?'

Rendell laughed.

'What would Sunday be without it?'

'They had some interesting articles about five months ago. One in particular about women who had been involved in murder cases and the tragedy of their lives.'

'Yes, I remember the one you mean. All a lot of hooey, though.'

'Ah, you think that?'

'Well of course the Craig case I only know from reading about it, but one of the others – Courtland case, I can tell you *that* woman was no tragic innocent. Regular vicious bit of goods. I know because an uncle of mine attended the husband. He was certainly no beauty, but his wife wasn't much better. She got hold of that young greenhorn and egged him on to murder. Then he goes to prison for manslaughter and she goes off, a rich widow, and marries someone else.'

'The *Sunday Comet* did not mention that. Do you remember whom she married?'

Rendell shook his head.

'Don't think I ever heard the name, but someone told me that she'd done pretty well for herself.'

'One wondered in reading the article where those four women were now,' mused Poirot.

'I know. One may have met one of them at a party last week. I bet they all keep their past pretty dark. You'd certainly never recognize any of 'em from those photographs. My word, they looked a plain lot.'

The clock chimed and Poirot rose to his feet. 'I must detain you no longer. You have been most kind.'

'Not much help, I'm afraid. The mere man barely knows what his charlady looks like. But half a second, you must meet the wife. She'd never forgive me.'

He preceded Poirot out into the hall, calling loudly:

'Shelagh – Shelagh –'

A faint answer came from upstairs.

'Come down here. I've got something for you.'

A thin fair-haired pale woman ran lightly down the stairs.

'Here's M. Hercule Poirot, Shelagh. What do you think of that?'

'Oh,' Mrs Rendell appeared to be startled out of speaking. Her very pale blue eyes stared at Poirot apprehensively.

'Madame,' said Poirot, bowing over her head in his most foreign manner.

'We heard that you were here,' said Shelagh Rendell. 'But we didn't know –' She broke off. Her light eyes went quickly to her husband's face.

'It is from him she takes the Greenwich time,' said Poirot to himself.

He uttered a few florid phrases and took his leave.

An impression remained with him of a genial Dr Rendell and a tongue-tied, apprehensive Mrs Rendell.

So much for the Rendells, where Mrs McGinty had gone to work on Tuesday mornings.

II

Hunter's Close was a solidly built Victorian house approached by a long untidy drive overgrown with weeds. It had not originally been considered a big house, but was now big enough to be inconvenient domestically.

Poirot inquired of the foreign young woman who opened the door for Mrs Wetherby.

She stared at him and then said: 'I do not know. Please to come. Miss Henderson perhaps?'

She left him standing in the hall. It was in an estate agent's phrase 'fully furnished' – with a good many curios from various parts of the world. Nothing looked very clean or well dusted.

Presently the foreign girl reappeared. She said: 'Please to come,' and showed him into a chilly little room with a large desk. On the mantelpiece was a big and rather evil-looking copper coffee pot with an enormous hooked spout like a large hooked nose.

The door opened behind Poirot and a girl came into the room.

'My mother is lying down,' she said. 'Can I do anything for you?'

'You are Miss Wetherby?'

'Henderson. Mr Wetherby is my stepfather.'

She was a plain girl of about thirty, large and awkward. She had watchful eyes.

'I was anxious to hear what you could tell me about Mrs McGinty who used to work here.'

She stared at him.

'Mrs McGinty? But she's dead.'

'I know that,' said Poirot gently. 'Nevertheless, I would like to hear about her.'

'Oh. Is it for insurance or something?'

'Not for insurance. It is a question of fresh evidence.'

'Fresh evidence. You mean – her death?'

'I am engaged,' said Poirot, 'by the solicitors for the defence to make an inquiry on James Bentley's behalf.'

Staring at him, she asked: 'But didn't he do it?'

'The jury thought he did. But juries have been known to make a mistake.'

'Then it was really someone else who killed her?'

'It may have been.'

She asked abruptly: 'Who?'

'That,' said Poirot softly, 'is the question.'

'I don't understand at all.'

'No? But you can tell me something about Mrs McGinty, can't you?'

She said rather reluctantly:

'I suppose so . . . What do you want to know?'

'Well – to begin with – what did you think of her?'

'Why – nothing in particular. She was just like anybody else.'

'Talkative or silent? Curious or reserved? Pleasant or morose? A nice woman, or – not a very nice woman?'

Miss Henderson reflected.

'She worked well – but she talked a lot. Sometimes she said rather funny things . . . I didn't – really – like her very much.'

The door opened and the foreign help said:

'Miss Deirdre, your mother say: please to bring.'

'My mother wants me to take this gentleman upstairs to her?'

'Yes please, thank you.'

Deirdre Henderson looked at Poirot doubtfully.

'Will you come up to my mother?'

'But certainly.'

Deirdre led the way across the hall and up the stairs. She said inconsequently: 'One does get so very tired of foreigners.'

Since her mind was clearly running on her domestic help and not on the visitor, Poirot did not take offence. He reflected that Deirdre Henderson seemed a rather simple young woman – simple to the point of gaucheness.

The room upstairs was crowded with knick-knacks. It was the room of a woman who had travelled a good deal and who had been determined wherever she went to have a souvenir of the place. Most of the souvenirs were clearly made for the delight and exploitation of tourists. There were too many sofas and tables and chairs in the room, too little air and too many draperies – and in the midst of it all was Mrs Wetherby.

Mrs Wetherby seemed a small woman – a pathetic small woman in a large room. That was the effect. But she was not really quite so small as she had decided to appear. The 'poor little me' type can achieve its result quite well, even if really of medium height.

She was reclining very comfortably on a sofa and near her were books and some knitting and a glass of orange juice and a box of chocolates. She said brightly:

'You *must* forgive me not getting up, but the doctor does so insist on my resting every day, and everyone scolds me if I don't do what I'm told.'

Poirot took her extended hand and bowed over it with the proper murmur of homage.

Behind him, uncompromising, Deirdre said: 'He wants to know about Mrs McGinty.'

The delicate hand that had lain passively in his tightened and he was reminded for a moment of the talon of a bird. Not really a piece of delicate Dresden china – a scratchy predatory claw . . .

Laughing slightly, Mrs Wetherby said:

'How ridiculous you are, Deirdre darling. Who is Mrs McGinty?'

'Oh, Mummy – you do remember really. She worked for us. You know, the one who was murdered.'

Mrs Wetherby closed her eyes, and shivered.

'Don't, darling. It was all so horrid. I felt nervous for weeks afterwards. Poor old woman, but so *stupid* to keep money under the floor. She ought to have put it in the bank. Of course I remember all that – I'd just forgotten her *name*.'

Deirdre said stolidly:

'He wants to know about her.'

'Now do sit down, M. Poirot. I'm quite devoured by curiosity. Mrs Rendell just rang up and she said we had a very famous criminologist down here, and she described you. And then, when that idiot Frieda described a visitor, I felt sure it must be you, and I sent down word for you to come up. Now tell me, what *is* all this?'

'It is as your daughter says, I want to know about Mrs McGinty. She worked here. She came to you, I understand, on Wednesdays. And it was on a Wednesday she died. So she had been here that day, had she not?'

'I suppose so. Yes, I suppose so. I can't really tell now. It's so long ago.'

'Yes. Several months. And she did not say anything that day – anything special?'

'That class of person always talks a lot,' said Mrs Wetherby with distaste. 'One doesn't really listen. And anyway, she couldn't tell she was going to be robbed and killed that night, could she?'

'There is cause and effect,' said Poirot.

Mrs Wetherby wrinkled her forehead.

'I don't see what you mean.'

'Perhaps I do not see myself – not yet. One works through darkness towards light . . . Do you take in the Sunday papers, Mrs Wetherby?'

Her blue eyes opened very wide.

'Oh yes. Of course. We have the *Observer* and the *Sunday Times*. Why?'

'I wondered. Mrs McGinty took the *Sunday Comet* and the *News of the World*.'

He paused but nobody said anything. Mrs Wetherby sighed and half closed her eyes. She said:

'It was all very upsetting. That horrible lodger of hers. I don't think really he can have been quite right in the head. Apparently he was quite an educated man, too. That makes it worse, doesn't it?'

'Does it?'

'Oh yes – I do think so. Such a brutal crime. A meat chopper. Ugh!'

'The police never found the weapon,' said Poirot.

'I expect he threw it in a pond or something.'

'They dragged the ponds,' said Deirdre. 'I saw them.'

'Darling,' her mother sighed, 'don't be morbid. You know how I hate thinking of things like that. My head.'

Fiercely the girl turned on Poirot.

'You mustn't go on about it,' she said. 'It's bad for her. She's frightfully sensitive. She can't even read detective stories.'

'My apologies,' said Poirot. He rose to his feet. 'I have only one excuse. A man is to be hanged in three weeks' time. If he did not do it –'

Mrs Wetherby raised herself on her elbow. Her voice was shrill.

'But of course he did it,' she cried. 'Of course he did.'

Poirot shook his head.

'I am not so sure.'

He left the room quickly. As he went down the stairs, the girl came after him. She caught up with him in the hall.

'What do you mean?' she asked.

'What I said, mademoiselle.'

'Yes, but –' She stopped.

Poirot said nothing.

Deirdre Henderson said slowly:

'You've upset my mother. She hates things like that – robberies and murders and – and violence.'

'It must, then, have been a great shock to her when a woman who had actually worked here was killed.'

'Oh yes – oh yes, it was.'

'She was prostrated – yes?'

'She wouldn't hear anything about it . . . We – I – we try to – to spare her things. All the beastliness.'

'What about the war?'

'Luckily we never had any bombs near here.'

'What was your part in the war, mademoiselle?'

'Oh, I did VAD work in Kilchester. And some driving for the WVS I couldn't have left home, of course. Mother needed me. As it was, she minded my being out so much. It was all very difficult. And then servants – naturally mother's never done any housework – she's not strong enough. And it was so difficult to get anyone at all. That's why Mrs McGinty was such a blessing. That's when she began coming to us. She was a splendid worker. But of course nothing – anywhere – is like it used to be.'

'And do you mind that so much, mademoiselle?'

'I? Oh no.' She seemed surprised. 'But it's different for mother. She – she lives in the past a lot.'

'Some people do,' said Poirot. His visual memory conjured up the room he had been in a short time before. There had been a bureau drawer half pulled out. A drawer full of odds and ends – a silk pin-cushion, a broken fan, a silver coffee pot – some old magazines. The drawer had been too full to shut. He said softly: 'And they keep things – memories of old days – the dance programme, the fan, the photographs of bygone friends, even the menu cards and the theatre programmes because, looking at these things, old memories revive.'

'I suppose that's it,' said Deirdre. 'I can't understand it myself. I never keep anything.'

'You look forwards, not back?'

Deirdre said slowly:

'I don't know that I look anywhere . . . I mean, today's usually enough, isn't it?'

The front door opened and a tall, spare, elderly man came into the hall. He stopped dead as he saw Poirot.

He glanced at Deirdre and his eyebrows rose in interrogation.

'This is my stepfather,' said Deirdre. 'I – I don't know your name?'

'I am Hercule Poirot,' said Poirot with his usual embarrassed air of announcing a royal title.

Mr Wetherby seemed unimpressed.

He said, 'Ah,' and turned to hang up his coat.

Deirdre said:

'He came to ask about Mrs McGinty.'

Mr Wetherby remained still for a second, then he finished his adjustment of the coat on the peg.

'That seems to me rather remarkable,' he said. 'The woman met her death some months ago and, although she worked here, we have no information concerning her or her family. If we had done we should already have given it to the police.'

There was finality in his tone. He glanced at his watch.

'Lunch, I presume, will be ready in a quarter of an hour.'

'I'm afraid it may be rather late today.'

Mr Wetherby's eyebrows rose again.

'Indeed? Why, may I ask?'

'Frieda has been rather busy.'

'My dear Deirdre, I hate to remind you, but the task of running the household devolves on you. I should appreciate a little more punctuality.'

Poirot opened the front door and let himself out. He glanced over his shoulder.

There was cold dislike in the gaze that Mr Wetherby gave his stepdaughter. There was something very like hate in the eyes that looked back at him.

CHAPTER 10

Poirot left his third call until after luncheon. Luncheon was under-stewed oxtail, watery potatoes, and what Maureen hoped optimistically might turn out to be pancakes. They were very peculiar.

Poirot walked slowly up the hill. Presently, on his right, he would come to Laburnums, two cottages knocked into one and remodelled to modern taste. Here lived Mrs Upward and that promising young playwright, Robin Upward.

Poirot paused a moment at the gate to pass a hand over his moustaches. As he did so a car came twisting slowly down the hill and an apple core directed with force struck him on the cheek.

Startled, Poirot let out a yelp of protest. The car halted and a head came through the window.

'I'm so sorry. Did I hit you?'

Poirot paused in the act of replying. He looked at the rather noble face, the massive brow, the untidy billows of grey hair and a chord of memory stirred. The apple core, too, assisted his memory.

'But surely,' he exclaimed, 'it is Mrs Oliver.'

It was indeed that celebrated detective-story writer.

Exclaiming, 'Why, it's M. Poirot,' the authoress attempted to extract herself from the car. It was a small car and Mrs Oliver was a large woman. Poirot hastened to assist.

Murmuring in an explanatory voice, 'Stiff after the long drive,'

Mrs Oliver suddenly arrived out on the road, rather in the manner of a volcanic eruption.

Large quantities of apples came, too, and rolled merrily down the hill.

'Bag's burst,' explained Mrs Oliver.

She brushed a few stray pieces of half-consumed apple from the jutting shelf of her bust and then shook herself rather like a large Newfoundland dog. The last apple, concealed in the recesses of her person, joined its brothers and sisters.

'Pity the bag burst,' said Mrs Oliver. 'They were Cox's. Still I suppose there will be lots of apples down here in the country. Or aren't there? Perhaps they all get sent away. Things are so odd nowadays, I find. Well, how are you, M. Poirot? You don't live here, do you? No, I'm sure you don't. Then I suppose it's murder? Not my hostess, I hope?'

'Who is your hostess?'

'In there,' said Mrs Oliver, nodding her head. 'That's to say if that's a house called Laburnums, half-way down the hill on the left side after you pass the church. Yes, that must be it. What's she like?'

'You do not know her?'

'No, I've come down professionally, so to speak. A book of mine is being dramatized – by Robin Upward. We're supposed to sort of get together over it.'

'My felicitations, madame.'

'It's not like that at all,' said Mrs Oliver. 'So far it's pure *agony*. Why I ever let myself in for it I don't know. My books bring me in quite enough money – that is to say the bloodsuckers take most of it, and if I made more, they'd take more, so I don't overstrain myself. But you've no idea of the agony of having your characters taken and made to say things that they never would have said, and do things that they never would have done. And if you protest, all they say is that it's "good theatre". That's all Robin Upward thinks of. Everyone says he's very clever. If he's so clever I don't see why he doesn't write a play of his own and leave my poor unfortunate Finn alone. He's not even a Finn any longer. He's become a member of the Norwegian Resistance Movement.' She ran her hands through her hair. 'What have I done with my hat?'

Poirot looked into the car.

'I think, madame, that you must have been sitting on it.'

'It does look like it,' agreed Mrs Oliver, surveying the wreckage. 'Oh well,' she continued cheerfully, 'I never liked it much. But I thought I might have to go to church on Sunday, and although the Archbishop has said one needn't, I still think that the more old-fashioned clergy expect one to wear a hat. But tell me about your murder or whatever it is. Do you remember *our* murder?'

'Very well indeed.'

'Rather fun, wasn't it? Not the actual murder – I didn't like that at all. But afterwards. Who is it this time?'

'Not so picturesque a person as Mr Shaitana. An elderly charwoman who was robbed and murdered five months ago. You may have read about it. Mrs McGinty. A young man was convicted and sentenced to death –'

'And he didn't do it, but you know who did, and you're going to prove it,' said Mrs Oliver rapidly. 'Splendid.'

'You go too fast,' said Poirot with a sigh. 'I do not yet know who did it – and from there it will be a long way to prove it.'

'Men are so slow,' said Mrs Oliver disparagingly. 'I'll soon tell you who did it. Someone down here, I suppose? Give me a day or two to look round, and I'll spot the murderer. A woman's intuition – that's what you need. I was quite right over the Shaitana case, wasn't I?'

Poirot gallantly forbode to remind Mrs Oliver of her rapid changes of suspicion on that occasion.

'You men,' said Mrs Oliver indulgently. 'Now if a woman were the head of Scotland Yard –'

She left this well-worn theme hanging in the air as a voice hailed them from the door of the cottage.

'Hallo,' said the voice, an agreeable light tenor. 'Is that Mrs Oliver?'

'Here I am,' called Mrs Oliver. To Poirot she murmured: 'Don't worry. I'll be very discreet.'

'No, no, madame. I do not want you to be discreet. *On the contrary.*'

Robin Upward came down the path and through the gate. He was bareheaded and wore very old grey flannel trousers and a disreputable sports coat. But for a tendency to embonpoint, he would have been good looking.

'Ariadne, my precious!' he exclaimed and embraced her warmly.

He stood away, his hands on her shoulders.

'My dear, I've had the most marvellous idea for the second act.'

'Have you?' said Mrs Oliver without enthusiasm. 'This is M. Hercule Poirot.'

'Splendid,' said Robin. 'Have you got any luggage?'

'Yes, it's in the back.'

Robin hauled out a couple of suitcases.

'Such a bore,' he said. 'We've no proper servants. Only old Janet. And we have to spare her all the time. That's such a nuisance don't you think? How heavy your cases are. Have you got bombs in them?'

He staggered up the path, calling out over his shoulder:

'Come in and have a drink.'

'He means you,' said Mrs Oliver, removing her handbag, a book, and a pair of old shoes from the front seat. 'Did you actually say just now that you wanted me to be *indiscreet?*'

'The more indiscreet the better.'

'I shouldn't tackle it that way myself,' said Mrs Oliver, 'but it's *your* murder. I'll help all I can.'

Robin reappeared at the front door.

'Come in, come in,' he called. 'We'll see about the car later. Madre is dying to meet you.'

Mrs Oliver swept up the path and Hercule Poirot followed her.

The interior of Laburnums was charming. Poirot guessed that a very large sum of money had been spent on it, but the result was an expensive and charming simplicity. Each small piece of cottage oak was a genuine piece.

In a wheeled chair by the fireplace of the living-room Laura Upward smiled a welcome. She was a vigorous looking woman of sixty-odd, with iron-grey hair and a determined chin.

'I'm delighted to meet you, Mrs Oliver,' she said. 'I expect you hate people talking to you about your books, but they've been an enormous solace to me for years – and especially since I've been such a cripple.'

'That's very nice of you,' said Mrs Oliver, looking uncomfortable and twisting her hands in a schoolgirlish way. 'Oh, this is

M. Poirot, an old friend of mine. We met by chance just outside here. Actually I hit him with an apple core. Like William Tell – only the other way about.'

'How d'you do, M. Poirot. Robin.'

'Yes, Madre?'

'Get some drinks. Where are the cigarettes?'

'On that table.'

Mrs Upward asked: 'Are you a writer, too, M. Poirot?'

'Oh, no,' said Mrs Oliver. 'He's a detective. You know. The Sherlock Holmes kind – deerstalkers and violins and all that. And he's come here to solve a murder.'

There was a faint tinkle of broken glass. Mrs Upward said sharply: 'Robin, do be careful.' To Poirot she said: 'That's very interesting, M. Poirot.'

'So Maureen Summerhayes was right,' exclaimed Robin. 'She told me some long rigmarole about having a detective on the premises. She seemed to think it was frightfully funny. But it's really quite serious, isn't it?'

'Of course it's serious,' said Mrs Oliver. 'You've got a criminal in your midst.'

'Yes, but look here, who's been murdered? Or is it someone that's been dug up and it's all frightfully hush hush?'

'It is not hush hush,' said Poirot. 'The murder, you know about it already.'

'Mrs Mc – something – a charwoman – last autumn,' said Mrs Oliver.

'Oh!' Robin Upward sounded disappointed. 'But that's all over.'

'It's not over at all,' said Mrs Oliver. 'They arrested the wrong man, and he'll be hanged if M. Poirot doesn't find the real murderer in time. It's all frightfully exciting.'

Robin apportioned the drinks.

'White Lady for you, Madre.'

'Thank you, my dear boy.'

Poirot frowned slightly. Robin handed drinks to Mrs Oliver and to him.

'Well,' said Robin, 'here's to crime.'

He drank.

'She used to work here,' he said.

'Mrs McGinty?' asked Mrs Oliver.

'Yes. Didn't she, Madre?'

'When you say work here, she came one day a week.'

'And odd afternoons sometimes.'

'What was she like?' asked Mrs Oliver.

'Terribly respectable,' said Robin. 'And maddeningly tidy. She had a ghastly way of tidying up everything and putting things into drawers so that you simply couldn't guess where they were.'

Mrs Upward said with a certain grim humour:

'If somebody didn't tidy things away at least one day a week, you soon wouldn't be able to move in this small house.'

'I know, Madre, I know. But unless things are left where I put them, I simply can't work at all. My notes get all disarranged.'

'It's annoying to be as helpless as I am,' said Mrs Upward. 'We have a faithful old maid, but it's all she can manage just to do a little simple cooking.'

'What is it?' asked Mrs Oliver. 'Arthritis?'

'Some form of it. I shall have to have a permanent nurse-companion soon, I'm afraid. Such a bore. I like being independent.'

'Now, darling,' said Robin. 'Don't work yourself up.'

He patted her arm.

She smiled at him with sudden tenderness.

'Robin's as good as a daughter to me,' she said. 'He does everything – and thinks of everything. No one could be more considerate.'

They smiled at each other.

Hercule Poirot rose.

'Alas,' he said. 'I must go. I have another call to make and then a train to catch. Madame, I thank you for your hospitality. Mr Upward, I wish all success to the play.'

'And all success to you with your murder,' said Mrs Oliver.

'Is this really serious, M. Poirot?' asked Robin Upward. 'Or is it a terrific hoax?'

'Of course it isn't a hoax,' said Mrs Oliver. 'It's deadly serious. He won't tell me who the murderer is, but he knows, don't you?'

'No, no, madame,' Poirot's protest was just sufficiently unconvincing. 'I told you that as yet, no, I do not know.'

'That's what you said, but I think you do know really . . . But you're so frightly secretive, aren't you?'

Mrs Upward said sharply:

'Is this really true? It's not a joke?'

'It is not a joke, madame,' said Poirot.

He bowed and departed.

As he went down the path he heard Robin Upward's clear tenor voice:

'But Ariadne, darling,' he said, 'it's all very well, but with that moustache and everything, how *can* one take him seriously? Do you really mean he's *good*?'

Poirot smiled to himself. Good indeed!

About to cross the narrow lane, he jumped back just in time.

The Summerhayes' station wagon, lurching and bumping, came racing past him. Summerhayes was driving.

'Sorry,' he called. 'Got to catch train.' And faintly from the distance: 'Covent Garden . . .'

Poirot also intended to take a train – the local train to Kilchester, where he had arranged a conference with Superintendent Spence.

He had time, before catching it, for just one last call.

He went to the top of the hill and through gates and up a well-kept drive to a modern house of frosted concrete with a square roof and a good deal of window. This was the home of Mr and Mrs Carpenter. Guy Carpenter was a partner in the big Carpenter Engineering Works – a very rich man who had recently taken to politics. He and his wife had only been married a short time.

The Carpenters' front door was not opened by foreign help, or an aged faithful. An imperturbable manservant opened the door and was loath to admit Hercule Poirot. In his view Hercule Poirot was the kind of caller who is left outside. He clearly suspected that Hercule Poirot had come to sell something.

'Mr and Mrs Carpenter are not at home.'

'Perhaps, then, I might wait?'

'I couldn't say when they will be in.'

He closed the door.

Poirot did not go down the drive. Instead he walked round the corner of the house and almost collided with a tall young woman in a mink coat.

'Hallo,' she said. 'What the hell do you want?'

Poirot raised his hat with gallantry.

'I was hoping,' he said, 'that I could see Mr or Mrs Carpenter. Have I the pleasure of seeing Mrs Carpenter?'

'I'm Mrs Carpenter.'

She spoke ungraciously, but there was a faint suggestion of appeasement behind her manner.

'My name is Hercule Poirot.'

Nothing registered. Not only was the great, the unique name unknown to her, but he thought that she did not even identify him as Maureen Summerhayes' latest guest. Here, then, the local grape vine did not operate. A small but significant fact, perhaps.

'Yes?'

'I demand to see either Mr or Mrs Carpenter, but you, madame, will be the best for my purpose. For what I have to ask is of domestic matters.'

'We've got a Hoover,' said Mrs Carpenter suspiciously.

Poirot laughed.

'No, no, you misunderstand. It is only a few questions that I ask about a domestic matter.'

'Oh, you mean one of these domestic questionnaires. I do think it's absolutely idiotic –' She broke off. 'Perhaps you'd better come inside.'

Poirot smiled faintly. She had just stopped herself from uttering a derogatory comment. With her husband's political activities, caution in criticizing Government activities was indicated.

She led the way through the hall and into a good-sized room giving on to a carefully tended garden. It was a very new-looking room, a large brocaded suite of sofa and two wing-chairs, three or four reproductions of Chippendale chairs, a bureau, a writing desk. No expense had been spared, the best firms had been employed, and there was absolutely no sign of individual taste. The bride, Poirot thought, had been what? Indifferent? Careful?

He looked at her appraisingly as she turned. An expensive and good-looking young woman. Platinum blonde hair, carefully applied make-up, but something more – wide cornflower blue eyes – eyes with a wide frozen stare in them – beautiful drowned eyes.

She said – graciously now, but concealing boredom:

'Do sit down.'

He sat. He said:

'You are most amiable, madame. These questions now that I wish to ask you. They relate to a Mrs McGinty who died – was killed that is to say – last November.'

'Mrs McGinty? I don't know what you mean?'

She was glaring at him. Her eyes hard and suspicious.

'You remember Mrs McGinty?'

'No, I don't. I don't know anything about her.'

'You remember her murder? Or is murder so common here that you do not even notice it?'

'Oh, the *murder*? Yes, of course. I'd forgotten what the old woman's name was.'

'Although she worked for you in this house?'

'She didn't. I wasn't living here then. Mr Carpenter and I were only married three months ago.'

'But she did work for you. On Friday mornings, I think it was. You were then Mrs Selkirk and you lived in Rose Cottage.'

She said sulkily:

'If you know the answers to everything I don't see why you need to ask questions. Anyway, what's it all about?'

'I am making an investigation into the circumstances of the murder.'

'Why? What on earth for? Anyway, why come to me?'

'You might know something – that would help me.'

'I don't know anything at all. Why should I? She was only a stupid old charwoman. She kept her money under the floor and somebody robbed and murdered her for it. It was quite disgusting – beastly, the whole thing. Like things you read in the Sunday papers.'

Poirot took that up quickly.

'Like the Sunday papers, yes. Like the *Sunday Comet*. You read, perhaps, the *Sunday Comet*?'

She jumped up, and made her way, blunderingly, towards the opened French windows. So uncertainly did she go that she actually collided with the window frame. Poirot was reminded of a beautiful big moth, fluttering blindly against a lamp shade.

She called: 'Guy – Guy!'

A man's voice a little way away answered:

'Eve?'

'Come here quickly.'

A tall man of about thirty-five came into sight. He quickened his pace and came across the terrace to the window. Eve Carpenter said vehemently:

'There's a man here – a foreigner. He's asking me all sorts of questions about that horrid murder last year. Some old charwoman – you remember? I *hate* things like that. You know I do.'

Guy Carpenter frowned and came into the drawing-room through the window. He had a long face like a horse, he was pale and looked rather supercilious. His manner was pompous.

Hercule Poirot found him unattractive.

'May I ask what all this is about?' he asked. 'Have you been annoying my wife?'

Hercule Poirot spread out his hands.

'The last thing I should wish is to annoy so charming a lady. I hoped only that, the deceased woman having worked for her, she might be able to aid me in the investigations I am making.'

'But – what are these investigations?'

'Yes, ask him that,' urged his wife.

'A fresh inquiry is being made into the circumstances of Mrs McGinty's death.'

'Nonsense – the case is over.'

'No, no, there you are in error. It is not over.'

'A fresh inquiry, you say?' Guy Carpenter frowned. He said suspiciously: 'By the police? Nonsense – you're nothing to do with the police.'

'That is correct. I am working independently of the police.'

'It's the Press,' Eve Carpenter broke in. 'Some horrid Sunday newspaper. He said so.'

A gleam of caution came into Guy Carpenter's eye. In his position he was not anxious to antagonize the Press. He said, more amicably:

'My wife is very sensitive. Murders and things like that upset her. I'm sure it can't be necessary for you to bother her. She hardly knew this woman.'

Eve said vehemently:

'She was only a stupid old charwoman. I told him so.'

She added:

'And she was a frightful liar, too.'

'Ah, that is interesting.' Poirot turned a beaming face from one to the other of them. 'So she told lies. That may give us a very valuable lead.'

'I don't see how,' said Eve sulkily.

'The establishment of motive,' said Poirot. 'That is the line I am following up.'

'She was robbed of her savings,' said Carpenter sharply. 'That was the motive of the crime.'

'Ah,' said Poirot softly. 'But was it?'

He rose like an actor who had just spoken a telling line.

'I regret if I have caused madame any pain,' he said politely. 'These affairs are always rather unpleasant.'

'The whole business was distressing,' said Carpenter quickly. 'Naturally my wife didn't like being reminded of it. I'm sorry we can't help you with any information.'

'Oh, but you have.'

'I beg your pardon?'

Poirot said softly:

'*Mrs McGinty told lies.* A valuable fact. What lies, exactly, did she tell, madame?'

He waited politely for Eve Carpenter to speak. She said at last:

'Oh, nothing particular. I mean – I can't remember.'

Conscious perhaps, that both men were looking at her expectantly, she said:

'Stupid things – about people. Things that couldn't be true.'

Still there was a silence, then Poirot said:

'I see – she had a dangerous tongue.'

Eve Carpenter made a quick movement.

'Oh no – I didn't mean as much as that. She was just a gossip, that was all.'

'Just a gossip,' said Poirot softly.

He made a gesture of farewell.

Guy Carpenter accompanied him out into the hall.

'This paper of yours – this Sunday paper – which is it?'

'The paper I mentioned to madame,' replied Poirot carefully, 'was the *Sunday Comet.*'

He paused. Guy Carpenter repeated thoughtfully:

'The *Sunday Comet*. I don't very often see that, I'm afraid.'

'It has interesting articles sometimes. And interesting illustrations . . .'

Before the pause could be too long, he bowed, and said quickly:

'Au revoir, Mr Carpenter. I am sorry if I have – disturbed you.'

Outside the gate, he looked back at the house.

'I wonder,' he said. 'Yes, I wonder . . .'

CHAPTER 11

Superintendent Spence sat opposite Hercule Poirot and sighed.

'I'm not saying you haven't got anything, M. Poirot,' he said slowly. 'Personally, I think you have. But it's thin. It's terribly thin!'

Poirot nodded.

'By itself it will not do. There must be more.'

'My sergeant or I ought to have spotted that newspaper.'

'No, no, you cannot blame yourself. The crime was so obvious. Robbery with violence. The room all pulled about, the money missing. Why should there be significance to you in a torn newspaper amongst the other confusion.'

Spence repeated obstinately:

'I should have got that. And the bottle of ink –'

'I heard of that by the merest chance.'

'Yet it meant something to you – why?'

'Only because of that chance phrase about writing a letter. You and I, Spence, we write so many letters – to us it is such a matter of course.'

Superintendent Spence sighed. Then he laid out on the table four photographs.

'These are the photos you asked me to get – the original photos that the *Sunday Comet* used. At any rate they're a little clearer than the reproductions. But upon my word, they're not much to go upon. Old, faded – and with women the hair-do makes a difference. There's nothing definite in any of them to go upon like ears or a profile. That *cloche* hat and that arty hair and the roses! Doesn't give you a chance.'

'You agree with me that we can discard Vera Blake?'

'I should think so. If Vera Blake was in Broadhinny, everyone would know it – telling the sad story of her life seems to have been her speciality.'

'What can you tell me about the others?'

'I've got what I could for you in the time. Eva Kane left the country after Craig was sentenced. And I can tell you the name she took. It was Hope. Symbolic, perhaps?'

Poirot murmured:

'Yes, yes – the romantic approach. "*Beautiful Evelyn Hope is dead.*" A line from one of your poets. I dare say she thought of that. Was her name Evelyn, by the way?'

'Yes, I believe it was. But Eva was what she was known as always. And by the way, M. Poirot, now that we're on the subject, the police opinion of Eva Kane doesn't quite square with this article here. Very far from it.'

Poirot smiled.

'What the police think – it is not evidence. But it is usually a very sound guide. What did the police think of Eva Kane?'

'That she was by no means the innocent victim that the public thought her. I was quite a young chap at the time and remember hearing it discussed by my old Chief and Inspector Traill who was in charge of the case. Traill believed (no evidence, mind you) that the pretty little idea of putting Mrs Craig out of the way was all Eva Kane's idea – and that she not only thought of it, but she did it. Craig came home one day and found his little friend had taken a short cut. She thought it would all pass off as natural death, I dare say. But Craig knew better. He got the wind up and disposed of the body in the cellar and elaborated the plan of having Mrs Craig die abroad. Then, when the whole thing came out, he was frantic in his assertions that he'd done it alone, that Eva Kane had known nothing about it. Well,' Superintendent Spence shrugged his shoulders, 'nobody could prove anything else. The stuff was in the house. Either of them could have used it. Pretty Eva Kane was all innocence and horror. Very well she did it, too: a clever little actress. Inspector Traill had his doubts – but there was nothing to go upon. I'm giving you that for what it's worth, M. Poirot. It's not evidence.'

'But it suggests the possibility that one, at least, of these "tragic women" was something more than a tragic woman – that she was a murderess and that, if the incentive was strong enough, she might murder again . . . And now the next one, Janice Courtland, what can you tell me about her?'

'I've looked up the files. A nasty bit of goods. If we hanged Edith Thompson we certainly ought to have hanged Janice Courtland. An unpleasant pair, she and her husband, nothing to choose between them, and she worked on that young man until she had him all up in arms. But all the time, mark you, there was a rich man in the background, and it was to marry him she wanted her husband out of the way.'

'Did she marry him?'

Spence shook his head.

'No idea.'

'She went abroad – and then?'

Spence shook his head.

'She was a free woman. She'd not been charged with anything. Whether she married, or what happened to her, we don't know.'

'One might meet her at a cocktail party any day,' said Poirot, thinking of Dr Rendell's remark.

'Exactly.'

Poirot shifted his gaze to the last photograph.

'And the child? Lily Gamboll?'

'Too young to be charged with murder. She was sent to an approved school. Good record there. Was taught shorthand and typing and was found a job under probation. Did well. Last heard of in Ireland. I think we could wash her out, you know, M. Poirot, same as Vera Blake. After all, she'd made good, and people don't hold it against a kid of twelve for doing something in a fit of temper. What about washing her out?'

'I might,' said Poirot, 'if it were not for the chopper. It is undeniable that Lily Gamboll used a chopper on her aunt, and the unknown killer of Mrs McGinty used something that was said to be like a chopper.'

'Perhaps you're right. Now, M. Poirot, let's have your side of things. Nobody's tried to do you in, I'm glad to see.'

'N-no,' said Poirot, with a momentary hesitation.

'I don't mind telling you I've had the wind up about you once or twice since that evening in London. Now what are the possibilities amongst the residents of Broadhinny?'

Poirot opened his little notebook.

'Eva Kane, if she is still alive, would be now approaching sixty. Her daughter, of whose adult life our *Sunday Comet* paints such a touching picture, would be now in the thirties. Lily Gamboll would also be about that age. Janice Courtland would now be not far short of fifty.'

Spence nodded agreement.

'So we come to the residents of Broadhinny, with especial reference to those for whom Mrs McGinty worked.'

'That last is a fair assumption, I think.'

'Yes, it is complicated by the fact that Mrs McGinty did occasional odd work here and there, but we will assume for the time being that she saw whatever she did see, presumably a photograph, at one of her regular "houses".'

'Agreed.'

'Then as far as age goes, that gives us as possibles – first the Wetherbys where Mrs McGinty worked on the day of her death. Mrs Wetherby is the right age for Eva Kane and she has a daughter of the right age to be Eva Kane's daughter – a daughter said to be by a previous marriage.'

'And as regards the photograph?'

'*Mon cher*, no positive identification from that is possible. Too much time has passed, too much water, as you say, has flowed from the waterworks. One can but say this: Mrs Wetherby has been, decidedly, a pretty woman. She has all the mannerisms of one. She seems much too fragile and helpless to do murder, but then that was, I understand, the popular belief about Eva Kane. How much actual physical strength would have been needed to kill Mrs McGinty is difficult to say without knowing exactly what weapon was used, its handle, the ease with which it could be swung, the sharpness of its cutting edge, etcetera.'

'Yes, yes. Why we never managed to find that – but go on.'

'The only other remarks I have to make about the Wetherby household are that Mr Wetherby could make himself, and I fancy does make himself, very unpleasant if he likes. The daughter is fanatically devoted to her mother. She hates her stepfather. I do not remark on these facts. I present them, only for consideration. Daughter might kill to prevent mother's past coming to stepfather's ears. Mother might kill for same reason. Father might kill to prevent "scandal" coming out. More murders have been committed for respectability than one would believe possible! The Wetherbys are "nice people".'

Spence nodded.

'If – I say if – there is anything in this *Sunday Comet* business, then the Wetherbys are clearly the best bet,' he said.

'Exactly. The only other person in Broadhinny who would fit in age with Eva Kane is Mrs Upward. There are two arguments against Mrs Upward, as Eva Kane, having killed Mrs McGinty. First, she suffers from arthritis, and spends most of her time in a wheeled chair –'

'In a book,' said Spence enviously, 'that wheeled chair business would be phoney, but in real life it's probably all according to Cocker.'

'Secondly,' continued Poirot, 'Mrs Upward seems of a dogmatic and forceful disposition, more inclined to bully than to coax, which does not agree with the accounts of our young Eva. On the other hand, people's characters do develop and self-assertiveness is a quality that often comes with age.'

'That's true enough,' conceded Spence. 'Mrs Upward – not impossible but unlikely. Now the other possibilities. Janice Courtland?'

'Can, I think, be ruled out. There is no one in Broadhinny the right age.'

'Unless one of the younger women is Janice Courtland with her face lifted. Don't mind me – just my little joke.'

'There are three women of thirty-odd. There is Deirdre Henderson. There is Dr Rendell's wife, and there is Mrs Guy Carpenter. That is to say, any one of these *could* be Lily Gamboll or alternatively Eva Kane's daughter as far as age goes.'

'And as far as possibility goes?'

Poirot sighed.

'Eva Kane's daughter may be tall or short, dark or fair – we have no guide to what she looks like. We have considered Deirdre

Henderson in that role. Now for the other two. First of all I will tell you this: Mrs Rendell is afraid of something.'

'Afraid of you?'

'I think so.'

'That might be significant,' said Spence slowly. 'You're suggesting that Mrs Rendell might be Eva Kane's daughter *or* Lily Gamboll. Is she fair or dark?'

'Fair.'

'Lily Gamboll was a fair-haired child.'

'Mrs Carpenter is also fair-haired. A most expensively made-up young woman. Whether she is actually good-looking or not, she has very remarkable eyes. Lovely wide-open dark-blue eyes.'

'Now, Poirot –' Spence shook his head at his friend.

'Do you know what she looked like as she ran out of the room to call her husband? I was reminded of a lovely fluttering moth. She blundered into the furniture and stretched her hands out like a blind thing.'

Spence looked at him indulgently.

'Romantic, that's what you are, M. Poirot,' he said. 'You and your lovely fluttering moths and wide-open blue eyes.'

'Not at all,' said Poirot. 'My friend Hastings, *he* was romantic and sentimental, me never! Me, I am severely practical. What I am telling you is that if a girl's claims to beauty depend principally on the loveliness of her eyes, then, no matter how short-sighted she is, she will take off her spectacles and learn to feel her way round even if outlines are blurred and distance hard to judge.'

And gently, with his forefinger, he tapped the photograph of the child Lily Gamboll in the thick disfiguring spectacles.

'So that's what you think? Lily Gamboll?'

'No, I speak only of what might be. At the time Mrs McGinty died Mrs Carpenter was not yet Mrs Carpenter. She was a young war widow, very badly off, living in a labourer's cottage. She was engaged to be married to the rich man of the neighbourhood – a man with political ambitions and a great sense of his own importance. If Guy Carpenter had found out that he was about to marry, say, a child of low origin who had obtained notoriety by hitting her aunt on the head with a chopper, or alternatively the daughter of Craig, one of the most notorious criminals of the century – prominently placed in your Chamber of Horrors – well, one asks would he have gone through with it? You say perhaps, if he loved the girl, *yes*! But he is not quite that kind of man. I would put him down as selfish, ambitious, and a man very nice in the manner of his reputation. I think that if young Mrs Selkirk, as she was then, was anxious to achieve the match she would have been very very anxious that no hint of an unfortunate nature got to her fiancé's ears.'

'I see, you think it's her, do you?'

'I tell you again, *mon cher, I do not know.* I examine only possibilities. Mrs Carpenter was on her guard against me, watchful, alarmed.'

'That looks bad.'

'Yes, yes, but it is all very difficult. Once I stayed with some friends in the country and they went out to do the shooting. You know the way it goes? One walks with the dogs and the guns, and the dogs, they put up the game – it flies out of the woods, up into the air and you go bang bang. That is like us. It is not only one bird we put up, perhaps, there are other birds in the covert. Birds, perhaps, with which we have nothing to do. But the birds themselves do not know that. We must make very sure, *cher ami*, which is *our* bird. During Mrs Carpenter's widowhood, there may have been indiscretions – no worse than that, but still inconvenient. Certainly there must be some reason why she says to me quickly that Mrs McGinty was a liar!'

Superintendent Spence rubbed his nose.

'Let's get this clear, Poirot. What *do* you really think?'

'What I think does not matter. I must *know*. And as yet, the dogs have only just gone into the covert.'

Spence murmured: 'If we could get anything at all definite. One really suspicious circumstance. As it is, it's all theory and rather far-fetched theory at that. The whole thing's thin, you know, as I said. *Does* anyone really murder for the reasons we've been considering?'

'That depends,' said Poirot. 'It depends on a lot of family circumstances we do not know. But the passion for respectability is very strong. These are not artists or Bohemians. Very nice people live in Broadhinny. My postmistress said so. And nice people like to preserve their niceness. Years of happy married life, maybe, no suspicion that you were once a notorious figure in one of the most sensational murder trials, no suspicion that your child is the child of a famous murderer. One might say "I would rather die than have my husband know!" Or "I would rather die than have my daughter discover who she is!" And then you would go on to reflect that it would be better, perhaps, if Mrs McGinty died . . .'

Spence said quietly:

'So you think it's the Wetherbys.'

'No. They fit the best, perhaps, but that is all. In actual character, Mrs Upward is a more *likely* killer than Mrs Wetherby. She has determination and willpower and she fairly dotes on her son. To prevent his learning of what happened before she married his father and settled down to respectable married bliss, I think she might go far.'

'Would it upset him so much?'

'Personally I do not think so. Young Robin has a modern sceptical point of view, is thoroughly selfish, and in any case is less devoted, I should say, to his mother than she to him. He is not another James Bentley.'

'Granting Mrs Upward *was* Eva Kane, her son Robin wouldn't kill Mrs McGinty to prevent the fact coming out?'

'Not for a moment, I should say. He would probably capitalize on it. Use the fact for publicity for his plays! I can't see Robin Upward committing a murder for respectability, or devotion, or in fact for anything but a good solid gain to Robin Upward.'

Spence sighed. He said: 'It's a wide field. We may be able to get something on the past history of these people. But it will take time. The war has complicated things. Records destroyed – endless opportunities for people who want to cover their traces doing so by means of other people's identity cards, etc., especially after "incidents" when nobody could know which corpse was which! If we could concentrate on just *one* lot, but you've got so many possibles, M. Poirot.'

'We may be able to cut them down soon.'

Poirot left the superintendent's office with less cheerfulness in his heart than he had shown in his manner. He was obsessed as Spence was, by the urge of time. If only he could have *time* . . .

And farther back still was the one teasing doubt – was the edifice he and Spence had built up really sound? Supposing, after all, that James Bentley *was* guilty . . .

He did not give in to that doubt, but it worried him.

Again and again he had gone over in his mind the interview he had had with James Bentley. He thought of it now whilst he waited on the platform at Kilchester for his train to come in. It had been market day and the platform was crowded. More crowds were coming in through the barriers.

Poirot leaned forward to look. Yes, the train was coming at last. Before he could right himself he felt a sudden hard purposeful shove in the small of his back. It was so violent and so unexpected that he was taken completely unawares. In another second he would have fallen on the line under the incoming train, but a man beside him on the platform caught hold of him in the nick of time, pulling him back.

'Why, whatever came over you?' he demanded. He was a big burly Army sergeant. 'Taken queer? Man, you were nearly under the train.'

'I thank you. I thank you a thousand times.' Already the crowd was milling round them, boarding the train, others leaving it.

'All right now? I'll help you in.'

Shaken, Poirot subsided on to a seat.

Useless to say 'I was pushed,' but he *had* been pushed. Up till that very evening he had gone about consciously on his guard, on the alert for danger. But after talking with Spence, after Spence's bantering inquiry as to whether any attempt on his life had been made, he had insensibly regarded the danger as over or unlikely to materialize.

But how wrong he had been! Amongst those he had interviewed in Broadhinny one interview had achieved a result. Somebody had been afraid. Somebody had sought to put an end to his dangerous resuscitation of a closed case.

From a call-box in the station at Broadhinny, Poirot rang up Superintendent Spence.

'It is you, *mon ami*? Attend, I pray. I have news for you. Splendid news. *Somebody has tried to kill me . . .*'

He listened with satisfaction to the flow of remarks from the other end.

'No, I am not hurt. But it was a very near thing . . . Yes, under a train. No, I did not see who did it. But be assured, my friend, *I shall find out*. We know now – that we are on the right track.'

CHAPTER 12

I

The man who was testing the electric meter passed the time of day with Guy Carpenter's superior manservant, who was watching him.

'Electricity's going to operate on a new basis,' he explained. 'Graded flat rate according to occupancy.'

The superior butler remarked sceptically:

'What you mean is it's going to cost more like everything else.'

'That depends. Fair shares for all, that's what I say. Did you go in to the meeting at Kilchester last night?'

'No.'

'Your boss, Mr Carpenter, spoke very well, they say. Think he'll get in?'

'It was a near shave last time, I believe.'

'Yes. A hundred and twenty-five majority, something like that. Do you drive him in to these meetings, or does he drive himself?'

'Usually drives himself. Likes driving. He's got a Rolls Bentley.'

'Does himself well. Mrs Carpenter drive too?'

'Yes. Drives a lot too fast, in my opinion.'

'Women usually do. Was she at the meeting last night too? Or isn't she interested in politics?'

The superior butler grinned.

'Pretends she is, anyway. However, she didn't stick it out last night. Had a headache or something and left in the middle of the speeches.'

'Ah!' The electrician peered into the fuse boxes. 'Nearly done now,' he remarked. He put a few more desultory questions as he collected his tools and prepared to depart.

He walked briskly down the drive, but round the corner from the gateway he stopped and made an entry in his pocket book.

'C. Drove home alone last night. Reached home 10.30 (approx.). Could have been at Kilchester Central Station time indicated. Mrs C. left meeting early. Got home only ten minutes before C. Said to have come home by train.'

It was the second entry in the electrician's book. The first ran:

'Dr R. Called out on case last night. Direction of Kilchester. Could have been at Kilchester Central Station at time indicated. Mrs R. alone all evening in house(?) After taking coffee in, Mrs Scott, housekeeper, did not see her again that night. Has small car of her own.'

II

At Laburnums, collaboration was in process.

Robin Upward was saying earnestly:

'You do see, don't you, what a wonderful line that is? And if we really get a feeling of sex antagonism between the chap and the girl it'll pep the whole thing up enormously!'

Sadly, Mrs Oliver ran her hands through her windswept grey hair, causing it to look as though swept not by wind but by a tornado.

'You do see what I mean, don't you, Ariadne darling?'

'Oh, I see what you *mean*,' said Mrs Oliver gloomily.

'But the main thing is for you to feel really happy about it.'

Nobody but a really determined self-deceiver could have thought that Mrs Oliver looked happy.

Robin continued blithely:

'What I feel is, here's that wonderful young man, parachuted down –'

Mrs Oliver interrupted:

'He's sixty.'

'Oh *no*!'

'He is.'

'I don't *see* him like that. Thirty-five – not a day older.'

'But I've been writing books about him for thirty years, and he was at least thirty-five in the first one.'

'But, darling, if he's sixty, you can't have the tension between him and the girl – what's her name? Ingrid. I mean, it would make him just a nasty old man!'

'It certainly would.'

'So you see, he *must* be thirty-five,' said Robin triumphantly.

'Then he can't be Sven Hjerson. Just make him a Norwegian young man who's in the Resistance Movement.'

'But darling Ariadne, the whole *point* of the play is Sven Hjerson. You've got an enormous public who simply *adore* Sven Hjerson, and who'll flock to see Sven Hjerson. He's *box office*, darling!'

'But people who read my books *know* what he's like! You can't invent an entirely new young man in the Norwegian Resistance Movement and just *call* him Sven Hjerson.'

'Ariadne darling, I *did* explain all that. It's not a *book*, darling, it's a *play*. And we've just got to have glamour! And if we get this tension, this antagonism between Sven Hjerson and this – what's-her-name? – Karen – you know, all against each other and yet really frightfully attracted –'

'Sven Hjerson never cared for women,' said Mrs Oliver coldly.

'But you *can't* have him a *pansy*, darling. Not for *this* sort of play. I mean it's not green bay trees or anything like *that*. It's thrills and murders and clean open-air fun.'

The mention of open air had its effect.

'I think I'm going out,' said Mrs Oliver abruptly. 'I need air. I need air *badly*.'

'Shall I come with you?' asked Robin tenderly.

'No, I'd rather go alone.'

'Just as you like, darling. Perhaps you're right. I'd better go and whip up an egg nog for Madre. The poor sweet is feeling just a teeny weeny bit left out of things. She *does* like attention, you know. And you'll think about that scene in the cellar, won't you? The whole thing is coming really wonderfully well. It's going to be the most tremendous success. I *know* it is!'

Mrs Oliver sighed.

'But the main thing,' continued Robin, 'is for you to feel happy about it!'

Casting a cold look at him, Mrs Oliver threw a showy military cape which she had once bought in Italy about her ample shoulders and went out into Broadhinny.

She would forget her troubles, she decided, by turning her mind to the elucidation of real crime. Hercule Poirot needed help. She would take a look at the inhabitants of Broadhinny, exercise her woman's intuition which had never failed, and tell Poirot who the murderer was. Then he would only have to get the necessary evidence.

Mrs Oliver started her quest by going down the hill to the post office and buying two pounds of apples. During the purchase, she entered into amicable conversation with Mrs Sweetiman.

Having agreed that the weather was very warm for the time of year, Mrs Oliver remarked that she was staying with Mrs Upward at Laburnums.

'Yes, I know. You'll be the lady from London that writes the murder books? Three of them I've got here now in Penguins.'

Mrs Oliver cast a glance over the Penguin display. It was slightly overlaid by children's waders.

'*The Affair of the Second Goldfish*,' she mused, 'that's quite a good one. *The Cat it was Who Died* – that's where I made a blowpipe a foot long and it's really six feet. Ridiculous that a blowpipe should be that size, but someone wrote from a museum to tell me so. Sometimes I think there are people who only read books in the hope of finding mistakes in them. What's the other one of them? Oh! *Death of a Débutante* – that's frightful tripe! I made sulphonal soluble in water and it isn't, and the whole thing is wildly impossible from start to finish. At least eight people die before Sven Hjerson gets his brainwave.'

'Very popular they are,' said Mrs Sweetiman, unmoved by this interesting self-criticism. 'You wouldn't believe! I've never read any myself, because I don't really get time for reading.'

'You had a murder of your own down here, didn't you?' said Mrs Oliver.

'Yes, last November that was. Almost next door here, as you might say.'

'I hear there's a detective down here, looking into it?'

'Ah, you mean the little foreign gentleman up at Long Meadows? He was in here only yesterday and –'

Mrs Sweetiman broke off as another customer entered for stamps.

She bustled round to the post office side.

'Good morning, Miss Henderson. Warm for the time of year today.'

'Yes, it is.'

Mrs Oliver stared hard at the tall girl's back. She had a Sealyham with her on a lead.

'Means the fruit blossom will get nipped later!' said Mrs Sweetiman, with gloomy relish. 'How's Mrs Wetherby keeping?'

'Fairly well, thank you. She hasn't been out much. There's been such an east wind lately.'

'There's a very good picture on at Kilchester this week, Miss Henderson. You ought to go.'

'I thought of going last night, but I couldn't really bother.'

'It's Betty Grable next week – I'm out of 5s. books of stamps. Will two 2s. 6d. ones do you?'

As the girl went out, Mrs Oliver said:

'Mrs Wetherby's an invalid, isn't she?'

'That's as may be,' Mrs Sweetiman replied rather acidly. 'There's *some* of us as hasn't the time to lay by.'

'I do so agree with you,' said Mrs Oliver. 'I tell Mrs Upward that if she'd only make more of an effort to use her legs it would be better for her.'

Mrs Sweetiman looked amused.

'She gets about when she wants to – or so I've heard.'

'Does she now?'

Mrs Oliver considered the source of information.

'Janet?' she hazarded.

'Janet Groom grumbles a bit,' said Mrs Sweetiman. 'And you can hardly wonder, can you? Miss Groom's not so young herself and she has the rheumatism cruel bad when the wind's in the east. But archititis, it's called, when it's the gentry has it, *and* invalid chairs and what not. Ah well, I wouldn't risk losing the use of my legs, I wouldn't. But there, nowadays even if you've got a chilblain you run to the doctor with it so as to get your money's worth out of the National Health. Too much of this health business we've got. Never did you any good thinking how bad you feel.'

'I expect you're right,' said Mrs Oliver.

She picked up her apples and went out in pursuit of Deirdre Henderson. This was not difficult, since the Sealyham was old and fat and was enjoying a leisurely examination of tufts of grass and pleasant smells.

Dogs, Mrs Oliver considered, were always a means of introduction.

'What a darling!' she exclaimed.

The big young woman with the plain face looked gratified.

'He *is* rather attractive,' she said. 'Aren't you, Ben?'

Ben looked up, gave a slight wiggle of his sausage-like body, resumed his nasal inspection of a tuft of thistles, approved it and proceeded to register approval in the usual manner.

'Does he fight?' asked Mrs Oliver. 'Sealyhams do very often.'

'Yes, he's an awful fighter. That's why I keep him on the lead.'

'I thought so.'

Both women considered the Sealyham.

Then Deirdre Henderson said with a kind of rush:

'You're – you're Ariadne Oliver, aren't you?'

'Yes. I'm staying with the Upwards.'

'I know. Robin told us you were coming. I must tell you how much I enjoy your books.'

Mrs Oliver, as usual, went purple with embarrassment.

'Oh,' she murmured unhappily. 'I'm very glad,' she added gloomily.

'I haven't read as many of them as I'd like to, because we get books sent down from the Times Book Club and Mother doesn't like detective stories. She's frightfully sensitive and they keep her awake at night. But I adore them.'

'You've had a real crime down here, haven't you?' said Mrs Oliver. 'Which house was it? One of these cottages?'

'That one there.'

Deirdre Henderson spoke in a rather choked voice.

Mrs Oliver directed her gaze on Mrs McGinty's former dwelling, the front doorstep of which was at present occupied by two unpleasant little Kiddles who were happily torturing a cat. As Mrs Oliver stepped forward to remonstrate, the cat escaped by a firm use of its claws.

The eldest Kiddle, who had been severely scratched, set up a howl.

'Serves you right,' said Mrs Oliver, adding to Deirdre Henderson:

'It doesn't *look* like a house where there's been a murder, does it?'

'No, it doesn't.'

Both women seemed to be in accord about that.

Mrs Oliver continued:

'An old charwoman, wasn't it, and somebody robbed her?'

'Her lodger. She had some money – under the floor.'

'I see.'

Deirdre Henderson said suddenly:

'But perhaps it wasn't him after all. There's a funny little man down here – a foreigner. His name's Hercule Poirot –'

'Hercule Poirot? Oh yes, I know all about him.'

'Is he really a detective?'

'My dear, he's frightfully celebrated. And terribly clever.'

'Then perhaps he'll find out that he didn't do it after all.'

'Who?'

'The – the lodger. James Bentley. Oh, I do hope he'll get off.'

'Do you? Why?'

'Because I don't want it to be him. I never wanted it to be him.'

Mrs Oliver looked at her curiously, startled by the passion in her voice.

'Did you know him?'

'No,' said Deirdre slowly, 'I didn't *know* him. But once Ben got his foot caught in a trap and he helped me to get him free. And we talked a little . . .'

'What was he like?'

'He was dreadfully lonely. His mother had just died. He was frightfully fond of his mother.'

'And you are very fond of yours?' said Mrs Oliver acutely.

'Yes. That made me understand. Understand what he felt, I mean. Mother and I – we've just got each other, you see.'

'I thought Robin told me that you had a stepfather.'

Deirdre said bitterly: 'Oh yes, I've got a *step*father.'

Mrs Oliver said vaguely: 'It's not the same thing, is it, as one's own father. Do you remember your own father?'

'No, he died before I was born. Mother married Mr Wetherby when I was four years old. I – I've always hated him. And Mother –' She paused before saying: 'Mother's had a very sad life. She's had no sympathy or understanding. My stepfather is a most unfeeling man, hard and cold.'

Mrs Oliver nodded, and then murmured:

'This James Bentley doesn't sound at all like a criminal.'

'I never thought the police would arrest *him*. I'm sure it must have been some tramp. There are horrid tramps along this road sometimes. It must have been one of them.'

Mrs Oliver said consolingly:

'Perhaps Hercule Poirot will find out the truth.'

'Yes, perhaps –'

She turned off abruptly into the gateway of Hunter's Close.

Mrs Oliver looked after her for a moment or two, then drew a small notebook from her handbag. In it she wrote: '*Not* Deirdre Henderson,' and underlined the *not* so firmly that the pencil broke.

III

Half-way up the hill she met Robin Upward coming down it with a handsome platinum-haired young woman.

Robin introduced them.

'This is the wonderful Ariadne Oliver, Eve,' he said. 'My dear, I don't know *how* she does it. Looks so benevolent, too, doesn't she? Not at all as though she wallowed in crime. This is Eve Carpenter. Her husband is going to be our next Member. The present one, Sir George Cartwright, is quite gaga, poor old man. He jumps out at young girls from behind doors.'

'Robin, you mustn't invent such terrible lies. You'll discredit the Party.'

'Well, why should *I* care? It isn't my Party. I'm a Liberal. That's the only Party it's possible to belong to nowadays, really small and select, and without a chance of getting in. I adore lost causes.'

He added to Mrs Oliver:

'Eve wants us to come in for drinks this evening. A sort of party for you, Ariadne. You know, meet the lion. We're all terribly terribly thrilled to have you here. Can't you put the scene of your next murder in Broadhinny?'

'Oh do, Mrs Oliver,' said Eve Carpenter.

'You can easily get Sven Hjerson down here,' said Robin. 'He can be like Hercule Poirot, staying at the Summerhayes' Guest House. We're just going there now because I told Eve, Hercule Poirot is just as much a celebrity in his line as you are in yours, and she says she was rather rude to him yesterday, so she's going to ask him to the party too. But seriously, dear, do make your next murder happen in Broadhinny. We'd all be so thrilled.'

'Oh do, Mrs Oliver. It would be such fun,' said Eve Carpenter.

'Who shall we have as murderer and who as victim,' asked Robin.

'Who's your present charwoman?' asked Mrs Oliver.

'Oh my dear, not *that* kind of murder. So dull. No, I think Eve here would make rather a nice victim. Strangled, perhaps, with her own nylon stockings. No, that's been done.'

'I think *you'd* better be murdered, Robin,' said Eve. 'The coming playwright, stabbed in country cottage.'

'We haven't settled on a murderer yet,' said Robin. 'What about my Mamma? Using her wheeled chair so that there wouldn't be footprints. I think that would be lovely.'

'She wouldn't want to stab you, though, Robin.'

Robin considered.

'No, perhaps not. As a matter of fact I was considering her strangling *you*. She wouldn't mind doing that half as much.'

'But I want *you* to be the victim. And the person who kills you can be Deirdre Henderson. The repressed plain girl whom nobody notices.'

'There you are, Ariadne,' said Robin. 'The whole plot of your next novel presented to you. All you'll have to do is work in a few false clues, and – of course – do the actual writing. Oh, goodness, what terrible dogs Maureen does have.'

They had turned in at the gate of Long Meadows, and two Irish wolfhounds had rushed forward, barking.

Maureen Summerhayes came out into the stableyard with a bucket in her hand.

'Down, Flyn. Come here, Cormic. Hallo. I'm just cleaning out Piggy's stable.'

'We know that, darling,' said Robin. 'We can smell you from here. How's Piggy getting along?'

'We had a terrible fright about him yesterday. He was lying down and he didn't want his breakfast. Johnnie and I read up all the diseases in the Pig Book and couldn't sleep for worrying about him, but this morning he was frightfully well and gay and absolutely charged Johnnie when Johnnie came in with his food. Knocked him flat, as a matter of fact. Johnnie had to go and have a bath.'

'What exciting lives you and Johnnie lead,' said Robin.

Eve said: 'Will you and Johnnie come in and have drinks with us this evening, Maureen?'

'Love to.'

'To meet Mrs Oliver,' said Robin, 'but actually you can meet her now. This is she.'

'Are you really?' said Maureen. 'How thrilling. You and Robin are doing a play together, aren't you?'

'It's coming along splendidly,' said Robin. 'By the way, Ariadne, I had a brainwave after you went out this morning. About casting.'

'Oh, casting,' said Mrs Oliver in a relieved voice.

'I know just the right person to play Eric. Cecil Leech – he's playing in the Little Rep at Cullenquay. We'll run over and see the show one evening.'

'We want your P.G.,' said Eve to Maureen. 'Is he about? I want to ask him tonight, too.'

'We'll bring him along,' said Maureen.

'I think I'd better ask him myself. As a matter of fact I was a bit rude to him yesterday.'

'Oh! Well, he's somewhere about,' said Maureen vaguely. 'In the garden, I think – Cormic – Flyn – those damned dogs –' She dropped the bucket with a clatter and ran in the direction of the duck pond, whence a furious quacking had arisen.

CHAPTER 13

Mrs Oliver, glass in hand, approached Hercule Poirot towards the end of the Carpenters' party. Up till that moment they had each of them been the centre of an admiring circle. Now that a good deal of gin had been consumed, and the party was going well, there was a tendency for old friends to get together and retail local scandal, and the two outsiders were able to talk to each other.

'Come out on the terrace,' said Mrs Oliver, in a conspirator's whisper.

At the same time she pressed into his hand a small piece of paper.

Together they stepped out through the French windows and walked along the terrace. Poirot unfolded the piece of paper.

'Dr Rendell,' he read.

He looked questioningly at Mrs Oliver. Mrs Oliver nodded vigorously, a large plume of grey hair falling across her face as she did so.

'He's the murderer,' said Mrs Oliver.

'You think so? Why?'

'I just know it,' said Mrs Oliver. 'He's the *type*. Hearty and genial, and all that.'

'Perhaps.'

Poirot sounded unconvinced.

'But what would you say was his motive?'

'Unprofessional conduct,' said Mrs Oliver. 'And Mrs McGinty knew about it. But whatever the reason was, you can be quite sure it was him. I've looked at all the others, and he's the one.'

In reply, Poirot remarked conversationally:

'Last night somebody tried to push me on to the railway line at Kilchester station.'

'Good gracious. To kill you, do you mean?'

'I have no doubt that was the idea.'

'And Dr Rendell was out on a case, I know he was.'

'I understand – yes – that Dr Rendell *was* out on a case.'

'Then that settles it,' said Mrs Oliver with satisfaction.

'Not quite,' said Poirot. 'Both Mr and Mrs Carpenter were in Kilchester last night and came home separately. Mrs Rendell may have sat at home all the evening listening to her wireless or she may not – no one can say. Miss Henderson often goes to the pictures in Kilchester.'

'She didn't last night. She was at home. She told me so.'

'You cannot believe all you are told,' said Poirot reprovingly. 'Families hang together. The foreign maid, Frieda, on the other hand, *was* at the pictures last night, so she cannot tell us who was or was not at home at Hunter's Close! You see, it is not so easy to narrow things down.'

'I can probably vouch for our lot,' said Mrs Oliver. 'What time did you say this happened?'

'At nine thirty-five exactly.'

'Then at any rate Laburnums has got a clean bill of health. From eight o'clock to half-past ten, Robin, his mother, and I were playing poker patience.'

'I thought possibly that you and he were closeted together doing the collaboration?'

'Leaving Mamma to leap on a motor bicycle concealed in the shrubbery?' Mrs Oliver laughed. 'No, Mamma was under our eye.' She sighed as sadder thoughts came to her. 'Collaboration,' she said bitterly. 'The whole thing's a nightmare! How would *you* like to see a big black moustache stuck on to Superintendent Battle and be told it was *you*.'

Poirot blinked a little.

'But it is a nightmare, that suggestion!'

'Now you know what I suffer.'

'I, too, suffer,' said Poirot. 'The cooking of Madame Summerhayes, it is beyond description. It is not cooking at all. And the draughts, the cold winds, the upset stomachs of the cats, the long hairs of the dogs, the broken legs of the chairs, the terrible, terrible bed in which I sleep' – he shut his eyes in remembrance of agonies – 'the tepid water in the bathroom, the holes in the stair carpet, and the coffee – words cannot describe to you the fluid which they serve to you as coffee. It is an affront to the stomach.'

'Dear me,' said Mrs Oliver. 'And yet, you know, she's awfully nice.'

'Mrs Summerhayes? She is charming. She is quite charming. That makes it much more difficult.'

'Here she comes now,' said Mrs Oliver.

Maureen Summerhayes was approaching them.

There was an ecstatic look on her freckled face. She carried a glass in her hand. She smiled at them both with affection.

'I think I'm a bit tiddly,' she announced. 'Such lots of lovely gin. I do like parties! We don't often have one in Broadhinny. It's because of you both being so celebrated. I wish *I* could write books. The trouble with me is, I can't do *anything* properly.'

'You are a good wife and mother, madame,' said Poirot primly.

Maureen's eyes opened. Attractive hazel eyes in a small freckled face. Mrs Oliver wondered how old she was. Not much more than thirty, she guessed.

'Am I?' said Maureen. 'I wonder. I love them all terribly, but is that enough?'

Poirot coughed.

'If you will not think me presumptuous, madame. A wife who truly loves her husband should take great care of his stomach. It is important, the stomach.'

Maureen looked slightly affronted.

'Johnnie's got a wonderful stomach,' she said indignantly. 'Absolutely flat. Practically not a stomach at all.'

'I was referring to what is put inside it.'

'You mean my cooking,' said Maureen. 'I never think it matters much *what* one eats.'

Poirot groaned.

'Or what one wears,' said Maureen dreamily. 'Or what one does. I don't think *things* matter – not really.'

She was silent for a moment or two, her eyes alcoholically hazy, as though she was looking into the far distance.

'There was a woman writing in the paper the other day,' she said suddenly. 'A really stupid letter. Asking what was best to do – to let your child be adopted by someone who could give it every advantage – *every advantage*, that's what she said – and she meant a good education, and clothes and comfortable surroundings – or whether to keep it when you couldn't give it advantages of any kind. I think that's stupid – *really* stupid. If you can just give a child enough to eat – that's all that matters.'

She stared down into her empty glass as though it were a crystal.

'*I* ought to know,' she said. 'I was an adopted child. My mother parted with me and I had every advantage, as they call it. And it's always hurt – always – always – to know that you weren't really wanted, that your mother could let you go.'

'It was a sacrifice for your good, perhaps,' said Poirot.

Her clear eyes met his.

'I don't think that's ever true. It's the way they put it to themselves. But what it boils down to is that they can, really, get on without you . . . And it hurts. I wouldn't give up *my* children – not for all the advantages in the world!'

'I think you're quite right,' said Mrs Oliver.

'And I, too, agree,' said Poirot.

'Then that's all right,' said Maureen cheerfully. 'What are we arguing about?'

Robin, who had come along the terrace to join them, said:

'Yes, what are you arguing about?'

'Adoption,' said Maureen. 'I don't like being adopted, do you?'

'Well, it's much better than being an orphan, don't you think so, darling? I think we ought to go now, don't you, Ariadne?'

The guests left in a body. Dr Rendell had already had to hurry away. They walked down the hill together talking gaily with that extra hilarity that a series of cocktails induces.

When they reached the gate of Laburnums, Robin insisted that they should all come in.

'Just to tell Madre all about the party. So boring for her, poor sweet, not to have been able to go because her leg was playing her up. But she so hates being left out of things.'

They surged in cheerfully and Mrs Upward seemed pleased to see them.

'Who else was there?' she asked. 'The Wetherbys?'

'No, Mrs Wetherby didn't feel well enough, and that dim Henderson girl wouldn't come without her.'

'She's really rather pathetic, isn't she?' said Shelagh Rendell.

'I think almost pathological, don't you?' said Robin.

'It's that mother of hers,' said Maureen. 'Some mothers really do almost eat their young, don't they?'

She flushed suddenly as she met Mrs Upward's quizzical eye.

'Do I devour you, Robin?' Mrs Upward asked.

'Madre! Of course not!'

To cover her confusion Maureen hastily plunged into an account of her breeding experiences with Irish wolfhounds. The conversation became technical.

Mrs Upward said decisively:

'You can't get away from heredity – in people as well as dogs.'

Shelagh Rendell murmured:

'Don't you think it's environment?'

Mrs Upward cut her short.

'No, my dear, I don't. Environment can give a veneer – no more. It's what's bred in people that counts.'

Hercule Poirot's eyes rested curiously on Shelagh Rendell's flushed face. She said with what seemed unnecessary passion:

'But that's cruel – unfair.'

Mrs Upward said: 'Life is unfair.'

The slow lazy voice of Johnnie Summerhayes joined in.

'I agree with Mrs Upward. Breeding tells. That's been my creed always.'

Mrs Oliver said questioningly: 'You mean things are handed down. Unto the third or fourth generation –'

Maureen Summerhayes said suddenly in her sweet high voice:

'But that quotation goes on: "And show mercy unto thousands."'

Once again everybody seemed a little embarrassed, perhaps at the serious note that had crept into the conversation.

They made a diversion by attacking Poirot.

'Tell us all about Mrs McGinty, M. Poirot. Why didn't the dreary lodger kill her?'

'He used to mutter, you know,' said Robin. 'Walking about in the lanes. I've often met him. And really, definitely, he looked frightfully queer.'

'You must have some reason for thinking he didn't kill her, M. Poirot. Do tell us.'

Poirot smiled at them. He twirled his moustache.

'If he didn't kill her, who did?'

'Yes, who did?'

Mrs Upward said drily: 'Don't embarrass the man. He probably suspects one of us.'

'One of us? Oo!'

In the clamour Poirot's eyes met those of Mrs Upward. They were amused and – something else – challenging?

'He suspects one of us,' said Robin delightedly. 'Now then, Maureen,' he assumed the manner of a bullying K.C., 'Where were you on the night of the – what night *was* it?'

'November 22nd,' said Poirot.

'On the night of the 22nd?'

'Gracious, I don't know,' said Maureen.

'Nobody could know after all this time,' said Mrs Rendell.

'Well, I can,' said Robin. 'Because I was broadcasting that night. I drove to Coalport to give a talk on Some Aspects of the Theatre. I remember because I discussed Galsworthy's charwoman in the Silver Box at great length and the next day Mrs McGinty was killed and I wondered if the charwoman in the play had been like her.'

'That's right,' said Shelagh Rendell suddenly. 'And I remember now because you said your mother would be all alone because it was Janet's night off, and I came down here after dinner to keep her company. Only unfortunately I couldn't make her hear.'

'Let me think,' said Mrs Upward. 'Oh! Yes, of course. I'd gone to bed with a headache and my bedroom faces the back garden.'

'And next day,' said Shelagh, 'when I heard Mrs McGinty had been killed, I thought, "Oo! I might have passed the murderer in the dark" – because at first we all thought it must have been some tramp who broke in.'

'Well, I still don't remember what I was doing,' said Maureen. 'But I do remember the next morning. It was the baker told us. "Old Mrs McGinty's been done in," he said. And there I was, wondering why she hadn't turned up as usual.'

She gave a shiver.

'It's horrible really, isn't it?' she said.

Mrs Upward was still watching Poirot.

He thought to himself: 'She is a very intelligent woman – and a ruthless one. Also selfish. In whatever she did, she would have no qualms and no remorse . . .'

A thin voice was speaking – urging, querulous.

'Haven't you got *any* clues, M. Poirot?'

It was Shelagh Rendell.

Johnnie Summerhayes' long dark face lit up enthusiastically.

'That's it, clues,' he said. 'That's what I like in detective stories. Clues that mean everything to the detective – and nothing to you – until the end when you fairly kick yourself. Can't you give us one little clue, M. Poirot?'

Laughing, pleading faces turned to him. A game to them all

(or perhaps not to one of them?). But murder wasn't a game – murder was dangerous. You never knew.

With a sudden brusque movement, Poirot pulled out four photographs from his pocket.

'You want a clue?' he said. '*Voilà!*'

And with a dramatic gesture he tossed them down on the table.

They clustered round, bending over, and uttering ejaculations.

'*Look!*'

'What frightful frumps!'

'Just look at the roses. "*Rowses, rowses, all the way!*"'

'My dear, that *hat!*'

'What a frightful child!'

'But who are they?'

'Aren't fashions ridiculous?'

'That woman must really have been rather good-looking once.'

'But why are they clues?'

'Who are they?'

Poirot looked slowly round at the circle of faces.

He saw nothing other than he might have expected to see.

'You do not recognize any of them?'

'Recognize?'

'You do not, shall I say, remember having seen any of those photographs before? But yes – Mrs Upward? You recognize something, do you not?'

Mrs Upward hesitated.

'Yes – I think –'

'Which one?'

Her forefinger went out and rested on the spectacled child-like face of Lily Gamboll.

'You have seen that photograph – when?'

'Quite recently . . . Now where – no, I can't remember. But I'm sure I've seen a photograph just like that.'

She sat frowning, her brows drawn together.

She came out of her abstraction as Mrs Rendell came to her.

'Goodbye, Mrs Upward. I do hope you'll come to tea with me one day if you feel up to it.'

'Thank you, my dear. If Robin pushes me up the hill.'

'Of course, Madre. I've developed the most tremendous muscles pushing that chair. Do you remember the day we went to the Wetherbys and it was so muddy –'

'Ah!' said Mrs Upward suddenly.

'What is it, Madre?'

'Nothing. Go on.'

'Getting you up the hill again. First the chair skidded and then I skidded. I thought we'd never get home.'

Laughing, they took their leave and trooped out.

Alcohol, Poirot thought, certainly loosens the tongue.

Had he been wise or foolish to display those photographs? Had that gesture also been the result of alcohol?

He wasn't sure.

But, murmuring an excuse, he turned back.

He pushed open the gate and walked up to the house. Through the open window on his left he heard the murmur of two voices. They were the voices of Robin and Mrs Oliver. Very little of Mrs Oliver and a good deal of Robin.

Poirot pushed the door open and went through the right-hand door into the room he had left a few moments before. Mrs Upward was sitting before the fire. There was a rather grim look on her face. She had been so deeply in thought that his entry startled her.

At the sound of the apologetic little cough he gave, she looked up sharply, with a start.

'Oh,' she said. 'It's you. You startled me.'

'I am sorry, madame. Did you think it was someone else? Who did you think it was?'

She did not answer that, merely said:

'Did you leave something behind?'

'What I feared I had left was danger.'

'Danger?'

'Danger, perhaps, to you. Because you recognized one of those photographs just now.'

'I wouldn't say recognized. All old photographs look exactly alike.'

'Listen, madame. Mrs McGinty also, or so I believe, recognized one of those photographs. *And Mrs McGinty is dead.*'

With an unexpected glint of humour in her eye, Mrs Upward said:

'*Mrs McGinty's dead. How did she die? Sticking her neck out just like I.* Is that what you mean?'

'Yes. If you know anything – anything at all, tell it to me now. It will be safer so.'

'My dear man, it's not nearly so simple as that. I'm not at all sure that I do know anything – certainly nothing as definite as a *fact*. Vague recollections are very tricky things. One would have to have some idea of how and where and when, if you follow what I mean.'

'But it seems to me that you already have that idea.'

'There is more to it than that. There are various factors to be taken into consideration. Now it's no good your rushing me, M. Poirot. I'm not the kind of person who rushes into decisions. I've a mind of my own, and I take time to make it up. When I come to a decision, I act. But not till I'm ready.'

'You are in many ways a secretive woman, madame.'

'Perhaps – up to a point. Knowledge is power. Power must only be used for the right ends. You will excuse my saying that you don't perhaps appreciate the pattern of our English country life.'

'In other words you say to me, "You are only a damned foreigner."'

Mrs Upward smiled slightly.

'I shouldn't be as rude as that.'

'If you do not want to talk to me, there is Superintendent Spence.'

'My dear M. Poirot. Not the police. Not at this stage.'

He shrugged his shoulders.

'I have warned you,' he said.

For he was sure that by now Mrs Upward remembered quite well exactly when and where she had seen the photograph of Lily Gamboll.

CHAPTER 14

I

'Decidedly,' said Hercule Poirot to himself the following morning, 'the spring is here.'

His apprehensions of the night before seemed singularly groundless.

Mrs Upward was a sensible woman who could take good care of herself.

Nevertheless in some curious way, she intrigued him. He did not at all understand her reactions. Clearly she did not want him to. She had recognized the photograph of Lily Gamboll and she was determined to play a lone hand.

Poirot, pacing a garden path while he pursued these reflections, was startled by a voice behind him.

'M. Poirot.'

Mrs Rendell had come up so quietly that he had not heard her. Since yesterday he had felt extremely nervous.

'*Pardon*, madame. You made me jump.'

Mrs Rendell smiled mechanically. If he were nervous, Mrs Rendell, he thought, was even more so. There was a twitching in one of her eyelids and her hands worked restlessly together.

'I – I hope I'm not interrupting you. Perhaps you're busy.'

'But no, I am not busy. The day is fine. I enjoy the feeling of spring. It is good to be outdoors. In the house of Mrs Summerhayes there is always, but always, the current of air.'

'The current –'

'What in England you call a draught.'

'Yes. Yes, I suppose there is.'

'The windows, they will not shut and the doors they fly open all the time.'

'It's rather a ramshackle house. And of course, the Summer-hayes are so badly off they can't afford to do much to it. I'd let it go if I were them. I know it's been in their family for hundreds of years, but nowadays you just can't cling on to things for sentiment's sake.'

'No, we are not sentimental nowadays.'

There was a silence. Out of the corner of his eye, Poirot

watched those nervous white hands. He waited for her to take the initiative. When she did speak it was abruptly.

'I suppose,' she said, 'that when you are, well, investigating a thing, you'd always have to have a pretext?'

Poirot considered the question. Though he did not look at her, he was perfectly aware of her eager sideways glance fixed on him.

'As you say, madame,' he replied non-committally. 'It is a convenience.'

'To explain your being there, and – and asking things.'

'It might be expedient.'

'Why – why are you really here in Broadhinny, M. Poirot?'

He turned a mild surprised gaze on her.

'But, my dear lady, I told you – to inquire into the death of Mrs McGinty.'

Mrs Rendell said sharply:

'I know that's what you say. But it's ridiculous.'

Poirot raised his eyebrows.

'Is it?'

'Of course it is. Nobody believes it.'

'And yet I assure you, it is a simple fact.'

Her pale blue eyes blinked and she looked away.

'You won't tell me.'

'Tell you – what, madame?'

She changed the subject abruptly again, it seemed.

'I wanted to ask you – about anonymous letters.'

'Yes,' said Poirot encouragingly as she stopped.

'They're really always lies, aren't they?'

'They are sometimes lies,' said Poirot cautiously.

'Usually,' she persisted.

'I don't know that I would go as far as saying that.'

Shelagh Rendell said vehemently:

'They're cowardly, treacherous, *mean* things!'

'All that, yes, I would agree.'

'And you wouldn't ever believe what was said in one, would you?'

'That is a very difficult question,' said Poirot gravely.

'I wouldn't. I wouldn't believe anything of that kind.'

She added vehemently:

'I know why you're down here. And it isn't true, I tell you, it isn't true.'

She turned sharply and walked away.

Hercule Poirot raised his eyebrows in an interested fashion.

'And now what?' he demanded of himself. 'Am I being taken up the garden walk? Or is this the bird of a different colour?'

It was all, he felt, very confusing.

Mrs Rendell professed to believe that he was down here for a reason other than that of inquiring into Mrs McGinty's death. She had suggested that that was only a pretext.

Did she really believe that? Or was she, as he had just said to himself, leading him up the garden walk?

What had anonymous letters got to do with it?

Was Mrs Rendell the original of the photograph that Mrs Upward had said she had 'seen recently'?

In other words, was Mrs Rendell Lily Gamboll? Lily Gamboll, a rehabilitated member of society, had been last heard of in Eire. Had Dr Rendell met and married his wife there, in ignorance of her history? Lily Gamboll had been trained as a stenographer. Her path and the doctor's might easily have crossed.

Poirot shook his head and sighed.

It was all perfectly possible. But he had to be sure.

A chilly wind sprang up suddenly and the sun went in.

Poirot shivered and retraced his steps to the house.

Yes, he had to be sure. If he could find the actual weapon of the murder –

And at that moment, with a strange feeling of certainty – he *saw it*.

II

Afterwards he wondered whether, subconsciously, he had seen and noted it much earlier. It had stood there, presumably, ever since he had come to Long Meadows . . .

There on the littered top of the bookcase near the window.

He thought: 'Why did I never notice that before?'

He picked it up, weighed it in his hands, examined it, balanced it, raised it to strike –

Maureen came in through the door with her usual rush, two dogs accompanying her. Her voice, light and friendly, said:

'Hallo, are you playing with the sugar cutter?'

'Is that what it is? A sugar cutter?'

'Yes. A sugar cutter – or a sugar hammer – I don't know what exactly is the right term. It's rather fun, isn't it? So childish with the little bird on top.'

Poirot turned the implement carefully in his hands. Made of much ornamented brass, it was shaped like an adze, heavy, with a sharp cutting edge. It was studded here and there with coloured stones, pale blue and red. On top of it was a frivolous little bird with turquoise eyes.

'Lovely thing for killing anyone, wouldn't it be?' said Maureen conversationally.

She took it from him and aimed a murderous blow at a point in space.

'Frightfully easy,' she said. 'What's that bit in the Idylls of the King? *"'Mark's way,' he said, and clove him to the brain."* I should think you could cleave anyone to the brain with this all right, don't you?'

Poirot looked at her. Her freckled face was serene and cheerful.

She said:

'I've told Johnnie what's coming to him if I get fed up with him. I call it the wife's best friend!'

She laughed, put the sugar hammer down and turned towards the door.

'What did I come in here for?' she mused. 'I can't remember . . . Bother! I'd better go and see if that pudding needs more water in the saucepan.'

Poirot's voice stopped her before she got to the door.

'You brought this back with you from India, perhaps?'

'Oh no,' said Maureen. 'I got it at the B. and B. at Christmas.'

'B. and B.?' Poirot was puzzled.

'Bring and Buy,' explained Maureen glibly. 'At the Vicarage. You bring things you don't want, and you buy something. Something not too frightful if you can find it. Of course there's practically never anything you really want. I got this and that coffee pot. I like the coffee pot's nose and I liked the little bird on the hammer.'

The coffee pot was a small one of beaten copper. It had a big curving spout that struck a familiar note to Poirot.

'I think they come from Baghdad,' said Maureen. 'At least I think that's what the Wetherbys said. Or it may have been Persia.'

'It was from the Wetherbys' house, then, that these came?'

'Yes. They've got a most frightful lot of junk. I *must* go. That pudding.'

She went out. The door banged. Poirot picked up the sugar cutter again and took it to the window.

On the cutting edge were faint, very faint, discolorations.

Poirot nodded his head.

He hesitated for a moment, then he carried the sugar hammer out of the room and up to his bedroom. There he packed it carefully in a box, did the whole thing up neatly in paper and string, and going downstairs again, left the house.

He did not think that anyone would notice the disappearance of the sugar cutter. It was not a tidy household.

III

At Laburnums, collaboration was pursuing its difficult course.

'But I really don't feel it's right making him a vegetarian, darling,' Robin was objecting. 'Too faddy. And definitely not glamorous.'

'I can't help it,' said Mrs Oliver obstinately. 'He's *always* been a vegetarian. He takes round a little machine for grating raw carrots and turnips.'

'But, Ariadne, precious, *why*?'

'How do I know?' said Mrs Oliver crossly. 'How do I know why I ever thought of the revolting man? I must have been mad! Why a Finn when I know nothing about Finland? Why a vegetarian? Why all the idiotic manerisms he's got? These things just *happen*. You try something – and people seem to like it – and then you go on – and before you know where you are, you've got someone like that maddening Sven Hjerson tied to you for life. And people even write and say how fond you must be of him. Fond of him? If I met that bony, gangling, vegetable-eating Finn in real life, I'd do a better murder than any I've ever invented.'

Robin Upward gazed at her with reverence.

'You know, Ariadne, that might be rather a marvellous idea.

A real Sven Hjerson – and *you* murder him. You might make a Swan Song book of it – to be published after your death.'

'No fear!' said Mrs Oliver. 'What about the money? Any money to be made out of murders I want now.'

'Yes. Yes. There I couldn't agree with you more.'

The harassed playwright strode up and down.

'This Ingrid creature is getting rather tiresome,' he said. 'And after the cellar scene which is really going to be marvellous, I don't quite see how we're going to prevent the next scene from being rather an anti-climax.'

Mrs Oliver was silent. Scenes, she felt, were Robin Upward's headache.

Robin shot a dissatisfied glance at her.

That morning, in one of her frequent changes of mood, Mrs Oliver had disliked her windswept coiffure. With a brush dipped in water she had plastered her grey locks close to her skull. With her high forehead, her massive glasses, and her stern air, she was reminding Robin more and more of a school teacher who had awed his early youth. He found it more and more difficult to address her as darling, and even flinched at 'Ariadne'.

He said fretfully:

'You know, I don't feel a bit in the mood today. All that gin yesterday, perhaps. Let's scrap work and go into the question of casting. If we can get Denis Callory, of course it will be too marvellous, but he's tied up in films at the moment. And Jean Bellews for Ingrid would be just right – and she *wants* to play it which is so nice. Eric – as I say, I've had a brainwave for Eric. We'll go over to the Little Rep tonight, shall we? And you'll tell me what you think of Cecil for the part.'

Mrs Oliver agreed hopefully to this project and Robin went off to telephone.

'There,' he said returning. 'That's all fixed.'

IV

The fine morning had not lived up to its promise. Clouds had gathered and the day was oppressive with a threat of rain. As Poirot walked through the dense shrubberies to the front door of Hunter's Close, he decided that he would not like to live in this hollow valley at the foot of the hill. The house itself was closed in by trees and its walls suffocated in ivy. It needed, he thought, the woodman's axe.

(The *axe?* The sugar cutter?)

He rang the bell and after getting no response, rang it again.

It was Deirdre Henderson who opened the door to him. She seemed surprised.

'Oh,' she said, 'it's you.'

'May I come in and speak to you?'

'I – well, yes, I suppose so.'

She led him into the small dark sitting-room where he had waited before. On the mantelpiece he recognized the big brother of the small coffee pot on Maureen's shelf. Its vast hooked nose seemed to dominate the small Western room with a hint of Eastern ferocity.

'I'm afraid,' said Deirdre in an apologetic tone, 'that we're rather upset today. Our help, the German girl – she's going. She's only been here a month. Actually it seems she just took this post to get over to this country because there was someone she wanted to marry. And now they've fixed it up, and she's going straight off tonight.'

Poirot clicked his tongue.

'Most inconsiderate.'

'It is, isn't it? My stepfather says it isn't legal. But even if it isn't legal, if she just goes off and gets married, I don't see what one can do about it. We shouldn't even have known she *was* going if I hadn't found her packing her clothes. She would just have walked out of the house without a word.'

'It is, alas, not an age of consideration.'

'No,' said Deirdre dully. 'I suppose it's not.'

She rubbed her forehead with the back of her hand.

'I'm tired,' she said. 'I'm very tired.'

'Yes,' said Poirot gently. 'I think you may be very tired.'

'What was it you wanted, M. Poirot?'

'I wanted to ask you about a sugar hammer.'

'A sugar hammer?'

Her face was blank, uncomprehending.

'An instrument of brass, with a bird on it, and inlaid with blue and red and green stones.' Poirot enunciated the description carefully.

'Oh yes, I know.'

Her voice showed no interest or animation.

'I understand it came from this house?'

'Yes. My mother bought it in the bazaar at Baghdad. It's one of the things we took to the Vicarage sale.'

'The Bring and Buy sale, that is right?'

'Yes. We have a lot of them here. It's difficult to get people to give money, but there's usually something you can rake up and send.'

'So it was here, in this house, until Christmas, and then you sent it to the Bring and Buy sale? Is that right?'

Deirdre frowned.

'Not the Christmas Bring and Buy. It was the one before. The Harvest Festival one.'

'The Harvest Festival – that would be – when? October? September?'

'The end of September.'

It was very quiet in the little room. Poirot looked at the girl and she looked back at him. Her face was mild, expressionless, uninterested. Behind the blank wall of her apathy, he tried to guess what was going on. Nothing, perhaps. Perhaps she was, as she had said, just tired . . .

He said, quietly, urgently:

'You are quite sure it was the Harvest Festival Sale? Not the Christmas one?'

'Quite sure.'

Her eyes were steady, unblinking.

Hercule Poirot waited. He continued to wait . . .

But what he was waiting for did not come.

He said formally:

'I must not keep you any longer, mademoiselle.'

She went with him to the front door.

Presently he was walking down the drive again.

Two divergent statements – statements that could not possibly be reconciled.

Who was right? Maureen Summerhayes or Deirdre Henderson?

If the sugar cutter had been used as he believed it had been used, the point was vital. The Harvest Festival had been the end of September. Between then and Christmas, on November

22nd, Mrs McGinty had been killed. Whose property had the sugar cutter been at the time?

He went to the post office. Mrs Sweetiman was always helpful and she did her best. She'd been to both sales, she said. She always went. You picked up many a nice bit there. She helped, too, to arrange things beforehand. Though most people brought things with them and didn't send them beforehand.

A brass hammer, rather like an axe, with coloured stones and a little bird? No, she couldn't rightly remember. There was such a lot of things, and so much confusion and some things snatched up at once. Well, perhaps she did remember something like that – priced at five shillings it had been, and with a copper coffee pot, but the pot had got a hole in the bottom – you couldn't use it, only for ornament. But she couldn't remember when it was – some time ago. Might have been Christmas, might have been before. She hadn't been noticing . . .

She accepted Poirot's parcel. Registered? Yes.

She copied down the address; he noticed just a sharp flicker of interest in her keen black eyes as she handed him the receipt.

Hercule Poirot walked slowly up the hill, wondering to himself.

Of the two, Maureen Summerhayes, scatter-brained, cheerful, inaccurate, was the more likely to be wrong. Harvest or Christmas, it would be all one to her.

Deirdre Henderson, slow, awkward, was far more likely to be accurate in her identification of times and dates.

Yet there remained that irking question.

Why, after his questions, hadn't she asked him *why he wanted to know?* Surely a natural, an almost inevitable, question?

But Deirdre Henderson hadn't asked it.

CHAPTER 15

I

'Someone rang you up,' called Maureen from the kitchen as Poirot entered the house.

'Rang me up? Who was that?'

He was slightly surprised.

'Don't know, but I jotted the number down on my ration book.'

'Thank you, Madame.'

He went into the dining-room and over to the desk. Amongst the litter of papers he found the ration book lying near the telephone and the words – Kilchester 350.

Raising the receiver of the telephone, he dialled the number.

Immediately a woman's voice said:

'Breather and Scuttle.'

Poirot made a quick guess.

'Can I speak to Miss Maude Williams?'

There was a moment's interval and then a contralto voice said:

'Miss Williams speaking.'

'This is Hercule Poirot. I think you rang me.'

'Yes – yes, I did. It's about the property you were asking me about the other day.'

'The property?' For a moment Poirot was puzzled. Then he realized that Maude's conversation was being overheard. Probably she had telephoned him before when she was alone in the office.

'I understand you, I think. It is the affair of James Bentley and Mrs McGinty's murder.'

'That's right. Can we do anything in the matter for you?'

'You want to help. You are not private where you are?'

'That's right.'

'I understand. Listen carefully. You really want to help James Bentley?'

'Yes.'

'Would you resign your present post?'

There was no hesitation.

'Yes.'

'Would you be willing to take a domestic post? Possibly with not very congenial people?'

'Yes.'

'Could you get away at once? By tomorrow, for instance?'

'Oh yes, M. Poirot. I think that could be managed.'

'You understand what I want you to do. You would be a domestic help – to live in. You can cook?'

A faint amusement tinged the voice.

'Very well.'

'Bon Dieu, what a rarity! Now listen, I am coming into Kilchester at once. I will meet you in the same café where I met you before, at lunch time.'

'Yes, certainly.'

Poirot rang off.

'An admirable young woman,' he reflected. 'Quick-witted, knows her own mind – perhaps, even, she can cook . . .'

With some difficulty he disinterred the local telephone directory from under a treatise on pigkeeping and looked up the Wetherbys' number.

The voice that answered him was that of Mrs Wetherby.

''Allo? 'Allo? It is M. Poirot – you remember, Madame –'

'I don't think I –'

'M. Hercule Poirot.'

'Oh yes – of course – do forgive me. Rather a domestic upset today –'

'It is for that reason exactly I rang you up. I am desolated to learn of your difficulties.'

'So ungrateful – these foreign girls. Her fare paid over here, and everything. I do so hate ingratitude.'

'Yes, yes. I do indeed sympathize. It is monstrous – that is why I hasten to tell you that I have, perhaps, a solution. By the merest chance I know of a young woman wanting a domestic post. Not, I fear, fully trained.'

'Oh, there's no such thing as training nowadays. Will she cook – so many of them won't cook.'

'Yes – yes – she cooks. Shall I then send her to you – at least on trial? Her name is Maude Williams.'

'Oh, please do, M. Poirot. It's most kind of you. Anything would be better than nothing. My husband is so particular and gets so annoyed with dear Deirdre when the household doesn't go smoothly. One can't expect men to understand how difficult everything is nowadays – I –'

There was an interruption. Mrs Wetherby spoke to someone entering the room, and though she had placed her hand over the receiver Poirot could hear her slightly muffled words.

'It's that little detective man – knows of someone to come in to replace Frieda. No, not foreign – English, thank goodness. Very kind of him, really, he seems quite concerned about me. Oh, darling, don't make objections. What does it *matter*? You know the absurd way Roger goes on. Well, I think it's very kind – and I don't suppose she's too awful.'

The asides over, Mrs Wetherby spoke with the utmost graciousness.

'Thank you very much, M. Poirot. We are most grateful.'

Poirot replaced the receiver and glanced at his watch.

He went to the kitchen.

'Madame, I shall not be in to lunch. I have to go to Kilchester.'

'Thank goodness,' said Maureen. 'I didn't get to that pudding in time. It had boiled dry. I think it's really all right – just a little scorched perhaps. In case it tasted rather nasty I thought I would open a bottle of those raspberries I put up last summer. They seem to have a bit of mould on top but they say nowadays that that doesn't matter. It's really rather good for you – practically penicillin.'

Poirot left the house, glad that scorched pudding and near-penicillin were not to be his portion today. Better – far better – eat macaroni and custard and plums at the Blue Cat than the improvisations of Maureen Summerhayes.

II

At Laburnums a little friction had arisen.

'Of course, Robin, you never seem to remember anything when you are working on a play.'

Robin was contrite.

'Madre, I am most terribly sorry. I'd forgotten all about it's being Janet's night out.'

'It doesn't matter at all,' said Mrs Upward coldly.

'Of course it matters. I'll ring up the Rep and tell them we'll go tomorrow night instead.'

'You'll do nothing of the sort. You've arranged to go tonight and you'll go.'

'But really –'

'That's settled.'

'Shall I ask Janet to go out another night?'

'Certainly *not*. She hates to have her plans disarranged.'

'I'm sure she wouldn't really mind. Not if I put it to her –'

'You'll do nothing of the sort, Robin. Please don't go upsetting Janet. And don't go on about it. I don't care to feel I'm a tiresome old woman spoiling other people's pleasure.'

'Madre – sweetest –'

'That's enough – you go and enjoy yourselves. I know who I'll ask to keep me company.'

'Who?'

'That's my secret,' said Mrs Upward, her good humour restored. 'Now stop fussing, Robin.'

'I'll ring up Shelagh Rendell –'

'I'll do my own ringing up, thank you. It's all settled. Make the coffee before you go, and leave it by me in the percolator ready to switch on. Oh, and you might as well put out an extra cup – in case I have a visitor.'

CHAPTER 16

Sitting at lunch in the Blue Cat, Poirot finished outlining his instructions to Maude Williams.

'So you understand what it is you have to look for?'

Maude Williams nodded.

'You have arranged matters with your office?'

She laughed.

'My auntie's dangerously ill! I sent myself a telegram.'

'Good. I have one more thing to say. Somewhere, in that village, we have a murderer at large. That is not a very safe thing to have.'

'Warning me?'

'Yes.'

'I can take care of myself,' said Maude Williams.

'That,' said Hercule Poirot, 'might be classed under the heading of Famous Last Words.'

She laughed again, a frank amused laugh. One or two heads at near tables turned around to look at her.

Poirot found himself appraising her carefully. A strong, confident young woman, full of vitality, keyed up and eager to attempt a dangerous task. Why? He thought again of James

Bentley, his gentle defeated voice, his lifeless apathy. Nature was indeed curious and interesting.

Maude said:

'You're *asking* me to do it, aren't you? Why suddenly try to put me off?'

'Because if one offers a mission, one must be exact about what it involves.'

'I don't think I'm in any danger,' said Maude confidently.

'I do not think so at the moment. You are unknown in Broadhinny?'

Maude considered.

'Ye-es. Yes, I should say so.'

'You have been there?'

'Once or twice – for the firm, of course – only once recently – that was about five months ago.'

'Who did you see? Where did you go?'

'I went to see an old lady – Mrs Carstairs – or Carlisle – I can't remember her name for sure. She was buying a small property near here, and I went over to see her with some papers and some queries and a surveyor's report which we'd got for her. She was staying at that Guest House sort of place where you are.'

'Long Meadows?'

'That was it. Uncomfortable-looking house with a lot of dogs.'

Poirot nodded.

'Did you see Mrs Summerhayes, or Major Summerhayes?'

'I saw Mrs Summerhayes, I suppose it was. She took me up to the bedroom. The old pussy was in bed.'

'Would Mrs Summerhayes remember you?'

'Don't suppose so. Even if she did, it wouldn't matter, would it? After all, one changes one's job quite often these days. But I don't suppose she even looked at me. Her sort don't.'

There was a faint bitterness in Maude Williams' voice.

'Did you see anyone else in Broadhinny?'

Maude said rather awkwardly:

'Well, I saw Mr Bentley.'

'Ah, you saw Mr Bentley. By accident.'

Maude wriggled a little in her chair.

'No, as a matter of fact, I'd sent him a p.c. Telling him I was coming that day. Asked him if he'd meet me as a matter of fact.

Not that there was anywhere to go. Dead little hole. No café or cinema or anything. 'S a matter of fact we just talked in the bus stop. While I was waiting for my bus back.'

'That was before the death of Mrs McGinty?'

'Oh yes. But not much before, though. Because it was only a few days later that it was in all the newspapers.'

'Did Mr Bentley speak to you at all of his landlady?'

'I don't think so.'

'And you spoke to no one else in Broadhinny?'

'Well – only Mr Robin Upward. I've heard him talk on the wireless. I saw him coming out of his cottage and I recognized him from his pictures and I did ask him for his autograph.'

'And he gave it to you?'

'Oh yes, he was ever so nice about it. I hadn't my book with me, but I'd got an odd sheet of notepaper, and he whipped out his fountain pen and wrote it at once.'

'Do you know any of the other people in Broadhinny by sight?'

'Well, I know the Carpenters, of course. They're in Kilchester a lot. Lovely car they've got, and she wears lovely clothes. She opened a Bazaar about a month ago. They say he's going to be our next M.P.'

Poirot nodded. Then he took from his pocket the envelope that he always carried about with him. He spread the four photographs on the table.

'Do you recognize any of – what's the matter?'

'It was Mr Scuttle. Just going out of the door. I hope he didn't see you with me. It might seem a bit odd. People are talking about you, you know. Saying you've been sent over from Paris – from the Sooretay or some name like that.'

'I am Belgian, not French, but no matter.'

'What's this about these photographs?' She bent over, studying them closely. 'Rather on the old-fashioned side, aren't they?'

'The oldest is thirty years ago.'

'Awfully silly, old-fashioned clothes look. Makes the women look such fools.'

'Have you seen any of them before?'

'D'you mean do I recognize any of the women, or do you mean have I seen the pictures?'

'Either.'

'I've an idea I've seen that one.' Her finger rested against Janice Courtland in her cloche hat. 'In some paper or other, but I can't remember when. That kid looks a bit familiar, too. But I can't remember when I saw them; some time ago.'

'All those photographs appeared in the *Sunday Comet* on the Sunday before Mrs McGinty died.'

Maude looked at him sharply.

'And they've got something to do with it? That's why you want me to –'

She did not finish the sentence.

'Yes,' said Hercule Poirot. 'That is why.'

He took something else from his pocket and showed it to her. It was the cutting from the *Sunday Comet*.

'You had better read that,' he said.

She read it carefully. Her bright golden head bent over the flimsy bit of newsprint.

Then she looked up.

'So that's who they are? And reading this has given you ideas?'

'You could not express it more justly.'

'But all the same I don't see –' She was silent a moment, thinking. Poirot did not speak. However pleased he might be with his own ideas, he was always ready to hear other people's ideas too.

'You think one or other of these people is in Broadhinny?'

'It might be, might it not?'

'Of course. Anyone may be anywhere . . .' She went on, placing her finger on Eva Kane's pretty simpering face: 'She'd be quite old now – about Mrs Upward's age.'

'About that.'

'What I was thinking was – the sort of woman she was – there must be several people who'd have it in for her.'

'That is a point of view,' said Poirot slowly. 'Yes, it is a point of view.' He added: 'You remember the Craig case?'

'Who doesn't?' said Maude Williams. 'Why, he's in Madame Tussaud's! I was only a kid at the time, but the newspapers are always bringing him up and comparing the case with other cases. I don't suppose it will ever be forgotten, do you?'

Poirot raised his head sharply.

He wondered what brought that sudden note of bitterness into her voice.

CHAPTER 17

Feeling completely bewildered, Mrs Oliver was endeavouring to cower in the corner of a very minute theatrical dressing-room. Not being the figure to cower, she only succeeded in bulging. Bright young men, removing grease paint with towels, surrounded her and at intervals pressed warm beer upon her.

Mrs Upward, her good humour completely restored, had speeded their departure with good wishes. Robin had been assiduous in making all arrangements for her comfort before departure, running back a couple of times after they were in the car to see that all was as it should be.

On the last occasion he came back grinning.

'Madre was just ringing off on the telephone, and the wicked old thing still won't tell me who she was ringing up. But I bet I know.'

'I know, too,' said Mrs Oliver.

'Well, who do you say?'

'Hercule Poirot.'

'Yes, that's my guess, too. She's going to pump him. Madre does like having her little secrets, doesn't she? Now darling, about the play tonight. It's very important that you tell me honestly just what you think of Cecil – and whether he's your idea of Eric . . .'

Needless to say, Cecil Leech had not been at all Mrs Oliver's idea of Eric. Nobody, indeed, could have been more unlike. The play itself she had enjoyed, but the ordeal of 'going round afterwards' was fraught with its usual terrors.

Robin, of course, was in his element. He had Cecil (at least Mrs Oliver supposed it was Cecil) pinned against the wall and was talking nineteen to the dozen. Mrs Oliver had been terrified of Cecil and much preferred somebody called Michael who was talking to her kindly at the moment. Michael, at least, did not expect her to reciprocate, in fact Michael seemed to prefer a monologue. Somebody called Peter made occasional incursions on the conversation, but on the whole it resolved itself into a stream of faintly amusing malice by Michael.

'– too sweet of Robin,' he was saying. 'We've been urging him to come and see the show. But of course he's completely under that terrible woman's thumb, isn't he? Dancing attendance. And really Robin is brilliant, don't you think so? Quite quite brilliant. He shouldn't be sacrificed on a Matriarchal altar. Women can be awful, can't they? You know what she did to poor Alex Roscoff? All over him for nearly a year and then discovered that he wasn't a Russian émigré at all. Of course he had been telling her some very tall stories, but quite amusing, and we all knew it wasn't true, but after all why should one care? – and then when she found out he was just a little East End tailor's son, she dropped him, my dear. I mean, I do hate a snob, don't you? Really Alex was thankful to get away from her. He said she could be quite frightening sometimes – a little queer in the head, he thought. Her rages! Robin dear, we're talking about your wonderful Madre. Such a shame she couldn't come tonight. But it's marvellous to have Mrs Oliver. All those delicious murders.'

An elderly man with a deep bass voice grasped Mrs Oliver's hand and held it in a hot, sticky grasp.

'How can I ever thank you?' he said in tones of deep melancholy. 'You've saved my life – saved my life many a time.'

Then they all came out into the fresh night air and went across to the Pony's Head, where there were more drinks and more stage conversation.

By the time Mrs Oliver and Robin were driving homeward, Mrs Oliver was quite exhausted. She leaned back and closed her eyes. Robin, on the other hand, talked without stopping.

'– and you do think that might be an idea, don't you?' he finally ended.

'What?'

Mrs Oliver jerked open her eyes.

She had been lost in a nostalgic dream of home. Walls covered with exotic birds and foliage. A deal table, her typewriter, black coffee, apples everywhere . . . What bliss, what glorious and solitary bliss! What a mistake for an author to emerge from her secret fastness. Authors were shy, unsociable creatures, atoning for their lack of social aptitude by inventing their own companions and conversations.

'I'm afraid you're tired,' said Robin.

'Not really. The truth is I'm not very good with people.'

'I adore people, don't you?' said Robin happily.

'No,' said Mrs Oliver firmly.

'But you must. Look at all the people in your books.'

'That's different. I think trees are much nicer than people, more restful.'

'I need people,' said Robin, stating an obvious fact. 'They stimulate me.'

He drew up at the gate of Laburnums.

'You go in,' he said. 'I'll put the car away.'

Mrs Oliver extracted herself with the usual difficulty and walked up the path.

'The door's not locked,' Robin called.

It wasn't. Mrs Oliver pushed it open and entered. There were no lights on, and that struck her as rather ungracious on the hostess's part. Or was it perhaps economy? Rich people were so often economical. There was a smell of scent in the hall, something rather exotic and expensive. For a moment Mrs Oliver wondered if she were in the right house, then she found the light switch and pressed it down.

The light sprang up in the low oak-beamed square hall. The door into the sitting-room was ajar and she caught sight of a foot and leg. Mrs Upward, after all, had not gone to bed. She must have fallen asleep in her chair, and since no lights were on, she must have been asleep a long time.

Mrs Oliver went to the door and switched on the lights in the sitting-room.

'We're back –' she began and then stopped.

Her hand went up to her throat. She felt a tight knot there, a desire to scream that she could not put into operation.

Her voice came out in a whisper:

'Robin – Robin . . .'

It was some time before she heard him coming up the path, whistling, and then she turned quickly and ran to meet him in the hall.

'Don't go in there – don't go in. Your mother – she – she's dead – I think – she's been killed . . .'

CHAPTER 18

I

'Quite a neat bit of work,' said Superintendent Spence.

His red countryman's face was angry. He looked across to where Hercule Poirot sat gravely listening.

'Neat and ugly,' he said. 'She was strangled,' he went on. 'Silk scarf – one of her own silk scarves, one she'd been wearing that day – just passed around the neck and the ends crossed – and pulled. Neat, quick, efficient. The thugs did it that way in India. The victim doesn't struggle or cry out – pressure on the carotid artery.'

'Special knowledge?'

'Could be – need not. If you were thinking of doing it, you could read up the subject. There's no practical difficulty. 'Specially with the victim quite unsuspicious – and she *was* unsuspicious.'

Poirot nodded.

'Someone she knew.'

'Yes. They had coffee together – a cup opposite her and one opposite the – guest. Prints had been wiped off the guest's cup very carefully but lipstick is more difficult – there were still faint traces of lipstick.'

'A woman, then?'

'You expected a woman, didn't you?'

'Oh yes. Yes, that was indicated.'

Spence went on:

'Mrs Upward recognized one of those photographs – the photograph of Lily Gamboll. So it ties up with the McGinty murder.'

'Yes,' said Poirot. 'It ties up with the McGinty murder.'

He remembered Mrs Upward's slightly amused expression as she had said:

'Mrs McGinty's dead. How did she die?
Sticking her neck out, just like I.'

Spence was going on:

'She took an opportunity that seemed good to her – her son and Mrs Oliver were going off to the theatre. She rang up the person concerned and asked that person to come and see her. Is that how you figure it out? She was playing detective.'

'Something like that. Curiosity. She kept her knowledge to herself, but she wanted to find out more. She didn't in the least realize what she was doing might be dangerous.' Poirot sighed. 'So many people think of murder as a game. It is not a game. I told her so. But she would not listen.'

'No, we know that. Well, that fits in fairly well. When young Robin started off with Mrs Oliver and ran back into the house his mother had just finished telephoning to someone. She wouldn't say who to. Played it mysterious. Robin and Mrs Oliver thought it might be *you*.'

'I wish it had been,' said Hercule Poirot. 'You have no idea to whom it was that she telephoned?'

'None whatever. It's all automatic round here, you know.'

'The maid couldn't help you in any way?'

'No. She came in about half-past ten – she has a key to the back door. She went straight into her own room which leads off the kitchen and went to bed. The house was dark and she assumed that Mrs Upward had gone to bed and that the others had not yet returned.'

Spence added:

'She's deaf and pretty crotchety as well. Takes very little notice of what goes on – and I imagine does as little work as she can with as much grumbling as possible.'

'Not really an old faithful?'

'Oh no! She's only been with the Upwards a couple of years.'

A constable put his head round the door.

'There's a young lady to see you, sir,' he said. 'Says there's something perhaps you ought to know. About last night.'

'About last night? Send her in.'

Deirdre Henderson came in. She looked pale and strained and, as usual, rather awkward.

'I thought perhaps I'd better come,' she said. 'If I'm not interrupting you or anything,' she added apologetically.

'Not at all, Miss Henderson.'

Spence rose and pushed forward a chair. She sat down on it squarely in an ungainly schoolgirlish sort of way.

'Something about last night?' said Spence encouragingly. 'About Mrs Upward, you mean?'

'Yes, it's true, isn't it, that she was murdered? I mean the post said so and the baker. Mother said of course it couldn't be true –' She stopped.

'I'm afraid your mother isn't quite right there. It's true enough. Now, you wanted to make a – to tell us something?'

Deirdre nodded.

'Yes,' she said. 'You see, *I* was there.'

A difference crept into Spence's manner. It was, perhaps, even more gentle, but an official hardness underlay it.

'You were there,' he said. 'At Laburnums. At what time?'

'I don't know exactly,' said Deirdre. 'Between half-past eight and nine, I suppose. Probably nearly nine. After dinner, anyway. You see, she telephoned to me.'

'Mrs Upward telephoned to you?'

'Yes. She said Robin and Mrs Oliver were going to the theatre in Cullenquay and that she would be all alone and would I come along and have coffee with her.'

'And you went?'

'Yes.'

'And you – had coffee with her?'

Deirdre shook her head.

'No, I got there – and I knocked. But there wasn't any answer. So I opened the door and went into the hall. It was quite dark and I'd seen from outside that there was no light in the sitting-room. So I was puzzled. I called "Mrs Upward" once or twice but there was no answer. So I thought there must be some mistake.'

'What mistake did you think there could have been?'

'I thought perhaps she'd gone to the theatre with them after all.'

'Without letting you know?'

'That did seem queer.'

'You couldn't think of any other explanation?'

'Well, I thought perhaps Frieda might have bungled the original message. She does get things wrong sometimes. She's a foreigner.

She was excited herself last night because she was leaving.'

'What did you do, Miss Henderson?'

'I just went away.'

'Back home?'

'Yes – that is, I went for a walk first. It was quite fine.'

Spence was silent for a moment or two, looking at her. He was looking, Poirot noticed, at her mouth.

Presently he roused himself and said briskly:

'Well, thank you, Miss Henderson. You were quite right to come and tell us this. We're much obliged to you.'

He got up and shook hands with her.

'I thought I ought to,' said Deirdre. 'Mother didn't want me to.'

'Didn't she now?'

'But I thought I'd better.'

'Quite right.'

He showed her out and came back.

He sat down, drummed on the table and looked at Poirot.

'No lipstick,' he said. 'Or is that only this morning?'

'No, it is not only this morning. She never uses it.'

'That's odd, nowadays, isn't it?'

'She is rather an odd kind of girl – undeveloped.'

'And no scent, either, as far as I could smell. That Mrs Oliver says there was a distinct smell of scent – expensive scent, she says – in the house last night. Robin Upward confirms that. It wasn't any scent his mother uses.'

'This girl would not use scent, I think,' said Poirot.

'I shouldn't think so either,' said Spence. 'Looks rather like the hockey captain from an old-fashioned girls' school – but she must be every bit of thirty, I should say.'

'Quite that.'

'Arrested development, would you say?'

Poirot considered. Then he said it was not quite so simple as that.

'It doesn't fit,' said Spence frowning. 'No lipstick, no scent. And since she's got a perfectly good mother, and Lily Gamboll's mother was done in in a drunken brawl in Cardiff when Lily Gamboll was nine years old, I don't see how she can be Lily Gamboll. *But* – Mrs Upward telephoned her to come there last night – you can't get away from that.' He rubbed his nose. 'It isn't straightforward going.'

'What about the medical evidence?'

'Not much help there. All the police surgeon will say definitely is that she was probably dead by half-past nine.'

'So she may have been dead when Deirdre Henderson came to Laburnums?'

'Probably was if the girl is speaking the truth. Either she *is* speaking the truth – or else she's a deep one. Mother didn't want her to come to us, she said. Anything there?'

Poirot considered.

'Not particularly. It is what mother would say. She is the type, you comprehend, that avoids unpleasantness.'

Spence sighed.

'So we've got Deirdre Henderson – on the spot. Or else someone who came there before Deirdre Henderson. A woman. A woman who used lipstick and expensive scent.'

Poirot murmured: 'You will inquire –'

Spence broke in.

'I'm inquiring! Just tactfully for the moment. We don't want to alarm anyone. What was Eve Carpenter doing last night? What was Shelagh Rendell doing last night? Ten to one they were just sitting at home. Carpenter, I know, had a political meeting.'

'Eve,' said Poirot thoughtfully. 'The fashions in names change, do they not? Hardly ever, nowadays, do you hear of an Eva. It has gone out. But Eve, it is popular.'

'She can afford expensive scent,' said Spence, pursuing his own train of thought.

He sighed.

'We've got to get at more of her background. It's so convenient to be a war widow. You can turn up anywhere looking pathetic and mourning some brave young airman. Nobody likes to ask you questions.

He turned to another subject.

'That sugar hammer or what-not you sent along – I think you've hit the bull's-eye. It's the weapon used in the McGinty murder. Doctor agrees it's exactly suitable for the type of blow. And there has been blood on it. It was washed, of course – but they don't realize nowadays that a microscopic amount of blood will give a reaction with the latest reagents. Yes, it's human blood all right. And that again ties up with the Wetherbys and the Henderson girl. Or doesn't it?'

'Deirdre Henderson was quite definite that the sugar hammer went to the Harvest Festival Bring and Buy.'

'And Mrs Summerhayes was equally positive it was the Christmas one?'

'Mrs Summerhayes is never positive about anything,' said Poirot gloomily. 'She is a charming person, but she has no order or method in her composition. But I will tell you this – I who have lived at Long Meadows – the doors and the windows they are always open. Anyone – anyone at all, could come and take something away and later come and put it back and neither Major Summerhayes nor Mrs Summerhayes would notice. If it is not there one day, she thinks that her husband has taken it to joint a rabbit or to chop wood – and he, he would think she had taken it to chop dogmeat. In that house nobody uses the right implements – they just seize what is at hand and leave it in the wrong place. And nobody remembers anything. If I were to live like that I should be in a continual state of anxiety – but they – they do not seem to mind.'

Spence sighed.

'Well – there's one good thing about all this – they won't execute James Bentley until this business is all cleared up. We've forwarded a letter to the Home Secretary's office. It gives us what we've been wanting – time.'

'I think,' said Poirot, 'that I would like to see Bentley again – now that we know a little more.'

II

There was little change in James Bentley. He was, perhaps, rather thinner, his hands were more restless – otherwise he was the same quiet, hopeless creature.

Hercule Poirot spoke carefully. There had been some fresh evidence. The police were re-opening the case. There was, therefore, hope . . .

But James Bentley was not attracted by hope.

He said:

'It will be all no good. What more can they find out?'

'Your friends,' said Hercule Poirot, 'are working very hard.'

'My friends?' He shrugged his shoulders. 'I have no friends.'

'You should not say that. You have, at the very least, two friends.'

'Two friends? I should like to know who they are.'

His tone expressed no wish for the information, merely a weary disbelief.

'First, there is Superintendent Spence –'

'Spence? Spence? The police superintendent who worked up the case against me? That's almost funny.'

'It is not funny. It is fortunate. Spence is a very shrewd and conscientious police officer. He likes to be very sure that he has got the right man.'

'He's sure enough of that.'

'Oddly enough, he is not. That is why, as I said, he is your friend.'

'That kind of a friend!'

Hercule Poirot waited. Even James Bentley, he thought, must have some human attributes. Even James Bentley could not be completely devoid of ordinary human curiosity.

And true enough, presently James Bentley said:

'Well, who's the other?'

'The other is Maude Williams.'

Bentley did not appear to react.

'Maude Williams? Who is she?'

'She worked in the office of Breather & Scuttle.'

'Oh – that Miss Williams.'

'*Précisément*, that Miss Williams.'

'But what's it got to do with her?'

There were moments when Hercule Poirot found the personality of James Bentley so irritating that he heartily wished that he could believe Bentley guilty of Mrs McGinty's murder. Unfortunately the more Bentley annoyed him, the more he came round to Spence's way of thinking. He found it more and more difficult to envisage Bentley's murdering anybody. James Bentley's attitude to murder would have been, Poirot felt sure, that it wouldn't be much good anyway. If cockiness, as Spence insisted, was a characteristic of murderers, Bentley was certainly no murderer.

Containing himself, Poirot said:

'Miss Williams interests herself in this affair. She is convinced you are innocent.'

'I don't see what she can know about it.'

'She knows *you*.'

James Bentley blinked. He said, grudgingly:

'I suppose she does, in a way, but not well.'

'You worked together in the office, did you not? You had, sometimes, meals together?'

'Well – yes – once or twice. The Blue Cat Café, it's very convenient – just across the street.'

'Did you never go for walks with her?'

'As a matter of fact we did, once. We walked up on the downs.'

Hercule Poirot exploded.

'*Ma foi*, is it a crime that I seek to drag from you? To keep the company with a pretty girl, is it not natural? Is it not enjoyable? Can you not be pleased with yourself about it?'

'I don't see why,' said James Bentley.

'At your age it is natural and right to enjoy the company of girls.'

'I don't know many girls.'

'*Ça se voit!* But you should be ashamed of that, not smug! You knew Miss Williams. You had worked with her and talked with her and sometimes had meals with her, and once went for a walk on the downs. And when I mention her, you do not even remember her name!'

James Bentley flushed.

'Well, you see – I've never had much to do with girls. And she isn't quite what you'd call a lady, is she? Oh very nice – and all that – but I can't help feeling that Mother would have thought her common.'

'It is what *you* think that matters.'

Again James Bentley flushed.

'Her hair,' he said. 'And the kind of clothes she wears – Mother, of course, was old-fashioned –'

He broke off.

'But you found Miss Williams – what shall I say – sympathetic?'

'She was always very kind,' said James Bentley slowly. 'But she didn't – really – *understand*. Her mother died when she was only a child, you see.'

'And then you lost your job,' said Poirot. 'You couldn't get another. Miss Williams met you once at Broadhinny, I understand?'

James Bentley looked distressed.

'Yes – yes. She was coming over there on business and she sent me a post-card. Asked me to meet her. I can't think why. It isn't as if I knew her at all well.'

'But you did meet her?'

'Yes. I didn't want to be rude.'

'And you took her to the pictures or a meal?'

James Bentley looked scandalized.

'Oh no. Nothing of that kind. We – er – just talked whilst she was waiting for her bus.'

'Ah, how amusing that must have been for the poor girl!'

James Bentley said sharply:

'I hadn't got any money. You must remember that. I hadn't any money at all.'

'Of course. It was a few days before Mrs McGinty was killed, wasn't it?'

James Bentley nodded. He said unexpectedly:

'Yes, it was on the Monday. She was killed on Wednesday.'

'I'm going to ask you something else, Mr Bentley. Mrs McGinty took the *Sunday Comet*?'

'Yes, she did.'

'Did you ever see her *Sunday Comet*?'

'She used to offer it sometimes, but I didn't often accept. Mother didn't care for that kind of paper.'

'So you didn't see that week's *Sunday Comet*?'

'No.'

'And Mrs McGinty didn't speak about it, or about anything in it?'

'Oh yes, she did,' said James Bentley unexpectedly. 'She was full of it!'

'Ah la la. So she was full of it. And what did she say? Be careful. This is important.'

'I don't remember very well now. It was all about some old

murder case. Craig, I think it was – no, perhaps it wasn't Craig. Anyway, she said somebody connected with the case was living in Broadhinny now. Full of it, she was. I couldn't see why it mattered to her.'

'Did she say who it was – in Broadhinny?'

James Bentley said vaguely:

'I think it was that woman whose son writes plays.'

'She mentioned her by name?'

'No – I – really it's so long ago –'

'I implore you – try to think. You want to be free again, do you not?'

'Free?' Bentley sounded surprised.

'Yes, free.'

'I – yes – I suppose I do –'

'Then *think! What did Mrs McGinty say?*'

'Well – something like – "so pleased with herself as she is and so proud. Not so much to be proud of if all's known." And then, "You'd never think it was the same woman to look at the photograph." But of course it had been taken years ago.'

'But what made you sure that it was Mrs Upward of whom she was speaking?'

'I really don't know . . . I just formed the impression. She had been speaking of Mrs Upward – and then I lost interest and didn't listen, and afterwards – well, now I come to think of it, I don't really know who she was speaking about. She talked a lot you know.'

Poirot sighed.

He said: 'I do not think myself that it was Mrs Upward of whom she spoke. I think it was somebody else. It is preposterous to reflect that if you are hanged it will be because you do not pay proper attention to the people with whom you converse . . . Did Mrs McGinty speak much to you of the houses where she worked, or the ladies of those houses?'

'Yes, in a way – but it's no good asking me. You don't seem to realize, M. Poirot, that I had my own life to think of at the time. I was in very serious anxiety.'

'Not in so much serious anxiety as you are now! Did Mrs McGinty speak of Mrs Carpenter – Mrs Selkirk she was then – or of Mrs Rendell?'

'Carpenter has that new house at the top of the hill and a big car, hasn't he? He was engaged to Mrs Selkirk – Mrs McGinty was always very down on Mrs Selkirk. I don't know why. "Jumped up," that's what she used to call her. I don't know what she meant by it.'

'And the Rendells?'

'He's the doctor, isn't he? I don't remember her saying anything particular about them.'

'And the Wetherbys?'

'I do remember what she said about them. "No patience with her fusses and her fancies," that's what she said. And about him, "Never a word, good or bad, out of him."' He paused. 'She said – it was an unhappy house.'

Hercule Poirot looked up. For a second James Bentley's voice had held something that Poirot had not heard in it before. He was not repeating obediently what he could recall. His mind, for a very brief space, had moved out of its apathy. James Bentley was thinking of Hunter's Close, of the life that went on there, of whether or not it was an unhappy house. James Bentley was thinking objectively.

Poirot said softly:

'You knew them? The mother? The father? The daughter?'

'Not really. It was the dog. A Sealyham. It got caught in a trap. She couldn't get it undone. I helped her.'

There was again something new in Bentley's tone. 'I helped her,' he had said, and in those words was a faint echo of pride.

Poirot remembered what Mrs Oliver had told him of her conversation with Deirdre Henderson.

He said gently:

'You talked together?'

'Yes. She – her mother suffered a lot, she told me. She was very fond of her mother.'

'And you told her about yours?'

'Yes,' said James Bentley simply.

Poirot said nothing. He waited.

'Life is very cruel,' said James Bentley. 'Very unfair. Some people never seem to get any happiness.'

'It is possible,' said Hercule Poirot.

'I don't think she had had much. Miss Wetherby.'

'Henderson.'

'Oh yes. She told me she had a stepfather.'

'Deirdre Henderson,' said Poirot. 'Deirdre of the Sorrows. A pretty name – but not a pretty girl, I understand?'

James Bentley flushed.

'*I* thought,' he said, 'she was rather good-looking . . .'

CHAPTER 19

'Now just you listen to me,' said Mrs Sweetiman.

Edna sniffed. She had been listening to Mrs Sweetiman for some time. It had been a hopeless conversation, going round in circles. Mrs Sweetiman had said the same thing several times, varying the phraseology a little, but even that not much. Edna had sniffed and occasionally blubbered and had reiterated her own two contributions to the discussion: first, that she couldn't ever! Second, that Dad would skin her alive, he would.

'That's as may be,' said Mrs Sweetiman, 'but murder's murder, and what you saw you saw, and you can't get away from it.'

Edna sniffed.

'And what you did ought to do –'

Mrs Sweetiman broke off and attended to Mrs Wetherby, who had come in for some knitting pins and another ounce of wool.

'Haven't seen you about for some time, ma'am,' said Mrs Sweetiman brightly.

'No, I've been very far from well lately,' said Mrs Wetherby. 'My heart, you know.' She sighed deeply. 'I have to lie up a great deal.'

'I heard as you've got some help at last,' said Mrs Sweetiman. 'You'll want dark needles for this light wool.'

'Yes. Quite capable as far as she goes, and cooks not at all badly. But her manners! And her appearance! Dyed hair and the most unsuitable tight jumpers.'

'Ah,' said Mrs Sweetiman. 'Girls aren't trained proper to service nowadays. My mother, she started at thirteen and she got up at a quarter to five every morning. Head housemaid she was when she finished, and three maids under her. And she trained them proper, too. But there's none of that nowadays – girls aren't trained nowadays, they're just educated, like Edna.'

Both women looked at Edna, who leant against the post office counter, sniffing and sucking a peppermint, and looking particularly vacant. As an example of education, she hardly did the educational system credit.

'Terrible about Mrs Upward, wasn't it?' continued Mrs Sweetiman conversationally, as Mrs Wetherby sorted through various coloured needles.

'Dreadful,' said Mrs Wetherby. 'They hardly dared tell me. And when they did, I had the most frightful palpitations. I'm so sensitive.'

'Shock to all of us, it was,' said Mrs Sweetiman. 'As for young Mr Upward, he took on something terrible. Had her hands full with him, the authoress lady did, until the doctor came and gave him a seddytiff or something. He's gone up to Long Meadows now as a paying guest, felt he couldn't stay in the cottage – and I don't know as I blame him. Janet Groom, she's gone home to her niece and the police have got the key. The lady what writes the murder books has gone back to London, but she'll come down for the inquest.'

Mrs Sweetiman imparted all this information with relish. She prided herself on being well informed. Mrs Wetherby, whose desire for knitting needles had perhaps been prompted by a desire to know what was going on, paid for her purchase.

'It's most upsetting,' she said. 'It makes the whole village so *dangerous*. There must be a maniac about. When I think that my own dear daughter was out that night, that she herself might have been attacked, perhaps killed.' Mrs Wetherby closed both eyes and swayed on her feet. Mrs Sweetiman watched her with interest, but without alarm. Mrs Wetherby opened her eyes again, and said with dignity:

'This place should be patrolled. No young people should go about after dark. And all doors should be locked and bolted. You know that up at Long Meadows, Mrs Summerhayes never locks *any* of her doors. Not even at *night*. She leaves the back door and the drawing-room window open so that the dogs and cats can get in and out. I myself consider that is absolute madness, but she says they've always done it and that if burglars want to get in, they always can.'

'Reckon there wouldn't be much for a burglar to take up at Long Meadows,' said Mrs Sweetiman.

Mrs Wetherby shook her head sadly and departed with her purchase.

Mrs Sweetiman and Edna resumed their argument.

'It's no good your setting yourself up to know best,' said Mrs Sweetiman. 'Right's right and murder's murder. Tell the truth and shame the devil. That's what I say.'

'Dad would skin me alive, he would, for sure,' said Edna.

'I'd talk to your Dad,' said Mrs Sweetiman.

'I couldn't ever,' said Edna.

'Mrs Upward's dead,' said Mrs Sweetiman. 'And you saw something the police don't know about. You're employed in the post office, aren't you? You're a Government servant. You've got to do your duty. You've got to go along to Bert Hayling –'

Edna's sobs burst out anew.

'Not to Bert, I couldn't. However could I go to Bert? It'd be all over the place.'

Mrs Sweetiman said rather hesitantly:

'There's that foreign gentleman –'

'Not a foreigner, I couldn't. Not a foreigner.'

'No, maybe you're right there.'

A car drew up outside the post office with a squealing of brakes.

Mrs Sweetiman's face lit up.

'That's Major Summerhayes, that is. You tell it all to him and he'll advise you what to do.'

'I couldn't ever,' said Edna, but with less conviction.

Johnnie Summerhayes came into the post office, staggering under the burden of three cardboard boxes.

'Good morning, Mrs Sweetiman,' he said cheerfully. 'Hope these aren't overweight?'

Mrs Sweetiman attended to the parcels in her official capacity. As Summerhayes was licking the stamps, she spoke.

'Excuse me, sir, I'd like your advice about something.'

'Yes, Mrs Sweetiman?'

'Seeing as you belong here, sir, and will know best what to do.'

Summerhayes nodded. He was always curiously touched by the lingering feudal spirit of English villages. The villagers knew little of him personally, but because his father and his grandfather and many great-great-grandfathers had lived at Long Meadows, they regarded it as natural that he should advise and direct them when asked so to do.

'It's about Edna here,' said Mrs Sweetiman.

Edna sniffed.

Johnnie Summerhayes looked at Edna doubtfully. Never, he thought, had he seen a more unprepossessing girl. Exactly like a skinned rabbit. Seemed half-witted too. Surely she couldn't be in what was known officially as 'trouble'. But no, Mrs Sweetiman would not have come to him for advice in that case.

'Well,' he said kindly, 'what's the difficulty?'

'It's about the murder, sir. The night of the murder. Edna saw something.'

Johnnie Summerhayes transferred his quick dark gaze from Edna to Mrs Sweetiman and back again to Edna.

'What did you see, Edna?' he said.

Edna began to sob. Mrs Sweetiman took over.

'Of course we've been hearing this and that. Some's rumour and some's true. But it's said definite as that there were a lady there that night who drank coffee with Mrs Upward. That's so, isn't it, sir?'

'Yes, I believe so.'

'I know as that's true, because we had it from Bert Hayling.'

Albert Hayling was the local constable whom Summerhayes knew well. A slow-speaking man with a sense of his own importance.

'I see,' said Summerhayes.

'But they don't know, do they, who the lady is? Well, Edna here *saw* her.'

Johnnie Summerhayes looked at Edna. He pursed his lips as though to whistle.

'You saw her, did you, Edna? Going in – or coming out?'

'Going in,' said Edna. A faint sense of importance loosened her tongue. 'Across the road I was, under the trees. Just by the turn of the lane where it's dark. I saw her. She went in at the gate and up to the door and she stood there a bit, and then – and then she went in.'

Johnnie Summerhayes' brow cleared.

'That's all right,' he said. 'It was Miss Henderson. The police know all about that. She went and told them.'

Edna shook her head.

'It wasn't Miss Henderson,' she said.

'It wasn't – then who was it?'

'I dunno. I didn't see her face. Had her back to me, she had, going up the path and standing there. But it wasn't Miss Henderson.'

'But how do you know it wasn't Miss Henderson if you didn't see her face?'

'Because she had fair hair. Miss Henderson's is dark.'

Johnnie Summerhayes looked disbelieving.

'It was a very dark night. You'd hardly be able to see the colour of anyone's hair.'

'But I did, though. That light was on over the porch. Left like that, it was, because Mr Robin and the detective lady had gone out together to the theatre. And she was standing right under it. A dark coat she had on, and no hat, and her hair was shining fair as could be. I saw it.'

Johnnie gave a slow whistle. His eyes were serious now.

'What time was it?' he asked.

Edna sniffed.

'I don't rightly know.'

'You know about what time,' said Mrs Sweetiman.

'It wasn't nine o'clock. I'd have heard the church. And it was after half-past eight.'

'Between half-past eight and nine. How long did she stop?'

'I dunno, sir. Because I didn't wait no longer. And I didn't hear nothing. No groans or cries or nothing like that.'

Edna sounded slightly aggrieved.

But there would have been no groans and no cries. Johnnie Summerhayes knew that. He said gravely:

'Well, there's only one thing to be done. The police have got to hear about this.'

Edna burst into long sniffling sobs.

'Dad'll skin me alive,' she whimpered. 'He will, for sure.'

She cast an imploring look at Mrs Sweetiman and bolted into the back room. Mrs Sweetiman took over with competence.

'It's like this, sir,' she said in answer to Summerhayes' inquiring glance. 'Edna's been behaving very foolish like. Very strict her Dad is, maybe a bit over strict, but it's hard to say what's best nowadays. There's a nice young fellow over to Cullavon and he and Edna have been going together nice and steady, and her Dad was quite pleased about it, but Reg he's on the slow side, and you know what girls are. Edna's taken up lately with Charlie Masters.'

'Masters? One of Farmer Cole's men, isn't he?'

'That's right, sir. Farm labourer. And a married man with two children. Always after the girls, he is, and a bad fellow in every way. Edna hasn't got any sense, and her Dad, he put a stop to it. Quite right. So, you see, Edna was going into Cullavon that night to go to the pictures with Reg – at least that's what she told her Dad. But really she went out to meet this Masters. Waited for him, she did, at the turn of the lane where it seems they used to meet. Well, he didn't come. Maybe his wife kept him at home, or maybe he's after another girl, but there it is. Edna waited but at last she gave up. But it's awkward for her, as you can see, explaining what she was doing there, when she ought to have taken the bus into Cullavon.'

Johnnie Summerhayes nodded. Suppressing an irrelevant feeling of wonder that the unprepossessing Edna could have sufficient sex appeal to attract the attention of two men, he dealt with the practical aspect of the situation.

'She doesn't want to go to Bert Hayling about it,' he said with quick comprehension.

'That's right, sir.'

Summerhayes reflected rapidly.

'I'm afraid the police have got to know,' he said gently.

'That's what I told her, sir,' said Mrs Sweetiman.

'But they will probably be quite tactful about – er – the circumstances. Possibly she mayn't have to give evidence. And what she tells them, they'll keep to themselves. I could ring up Spence and ask him to come over here – no, better still, I'll take young Edna into Kilchester with me in my car. If she goes to the police station there, nobody here need know anything about it. I'll just ring them up first and warn them we're coming.'

And so, after a brief telephone call, the sniffing Edna, buttoned firmly into her coat and encouraged by a pat on the back from Mrs Sweetiman, stepped into the station wagon and was driven rapidly away in the direction of Kilchester.

CHAPTER 20

Hercule Poirot was in Superintendent Spence's office in Kilchester. He was leaning back in a chair, his eyes closed and the tips of his fingers just touching each other in front of him.

The superintendent received some reports, gave instructions to a sergeant, and finally looked across at the other man.

'Getting a brainwave, M. Poirot?' he demanded.

'I reflect,' said Poirot. 'I review.'

'I forgot to ask you. Did you get anything useful from James Bentley when you saw him?'

Poirot shook his head. He frowned.

It was indeed of James Bentley he had been thinking.

It was annoying, thought Poirot with exasperation, that on a case such as this where he had offered his services without reward, solely out of friendship and respect for an upright police officer, that the victim of circumstances should so lack any romantic appeal. A lovely young girl, now, bewildered and innocent, or a fine upstanding young man, also bewildered, but whose 'head is bloody but unbowed,' thought Poirot, who had been reading a good deal of English poetry in an anthology lately. Instead, he had James Bentley, a pathological case if there ever was one, a self-centred creature who had never thought much of anyone but himself. A man ungrateful for the efforts that were being made to save him – almost, one might say, uninterested in them.

Really, thought Poirot, one might as well let him be hanged since he does not seem to care . . .

No, he would not go quite as far as that.

Superintendent Spence's voice broke into these reflections.

'Our interview,' said Poirot, 'was, if I might say so, singularly unproductive. Anything useful that Bentley might have remembered he did not remember – what he did remember is so vague and uncertain that one cannot build upon it. But at any rate it seems fairly certain that Mrs McGinty was excited by the article in the *Sunday Comet* and spoke about it to Bentley with special reference to "someone connected with the case," living in Broadhinny.'

'With which case?' asked Superintendent Spence sharply.

'Our friend could not be sure,' said Poirot. 'He said, rather doubtfully, the Craig case – but the Craig case being the only one he had ever heard of, it would, presumably, be the only one he could remember. But the "someone" was a woman. He even quoted Mrs McGinty's words. Someone who had "not so much to be proud of if all's known."'

'*Proud?*'

'*Mais oui,*' Poirot nodded his appreciation. 'A suggestive word, is it not?'

'No clue as to who the proud lady was?'

'Bentley suggested Mrs Upward – but as far as I can see for no real reason!'

Spence shook his head.

'Probably because she was a proud masterful sort of woman – outstandingly so, I should say. But it couldn't have been Mrs Upward, because Mrs Upward's dead, and dead for the same reason as Mrs McGinty died – because she recognized a photograph.'

Poirot said sadly: 'I warned her.'

Spence murmured irritably:

'Lily Gamboll! So far as age goes, there are only two possibilities, Mrs Rendell and Mrs Carpenter. I don't count the Henderson girl – she's got a background.'

'And the others have not?'

Spence sighed.

'You know what things are nowadays. The war stirred up everyone and everything. The approved school where Lily Gamboll was, and all its records, were destroyed by a direct hit. Then take people. It's the hardest thing in the world to check on people. Take Broadhinny – the only people in Broadhinny we know anything about are the Summerhayes family, who have been there for three hundred years, and Guy Carpenter, who's one of the engineering Carpenters. All the others are – what shall I say – fluid? Dr Rendell's on the Medical Register and we know where he trained and where he's practised, but we don't know his home background. His wife came from near Dublin. Eve Selkirk, as she was before she married Guy Carpenter, was a pretty young war widow. Anyone can be a pretty young war widow. Take the Wetherbys – they seem to have floated round the world, here, there and everywhere. Why? Is there a reason? Did he embezzle from a bank? Or did they occasion a scandal? I don't say we can't dig up about people. We can – but it takes time. The people themselves won't help you.'

'Because they have something to conceal – but it need not be murder,' said Poirot.

'Exactly. It may be trouble with the law, or it may be a humble origin, or it may be common or garden scandal. But whatever it is, they've taken a lot of pains to cover up – and that makes it difficult to uncover.'

'But not impossible.'

'Oh no. Not impossible. It just takes time. As I say, if Lily Gamboll is in Broadhinny, she's *either* Eve Carpenter or Shelagh Rendell. I've questioned them – just routine – that's the way I put it. They say they were both at home – alone. Mrs Carpenter was the wide-eyed innocent, Mrs Rendell was nervous – but then she's a nervous type, you can't go by that.'

'Yes,' said Poirot thoughtfully. 'She is a nervous type.'

He was thinking of Mrs Rendell in the garden at Long Meadows. Mrs Rendell had received an anonymous letter, or so she said. He wondered, as he had wondered before, about that statement.

Spence went on:

'And we have to be careful – because even if one of them *is* guilty, the other is innocent.'

'And Guy Carpenter is a prospective Member of Parliament and an important local figure.'

'That wouldn't help him if he was guilty of murder or accessory to it,' said Spence grimly.

'I know that. But you have, have you not, to be *sure*?'

'That's right. Anyway, you'll agree, won't you, that it lies between the two of them?'

Poirot sighed.

'No – no – I would not say that. There are other possibilities.'

'Such as?'

Poirot was silent for a moment, then he said in a different, almost casual tone of voice:

'Why do people keep photographs?'

'Why? Goodness knows! Why do people keep all sorts of things – junk – trash, bits and pieces. They do – that's all there is to it!'

'Up to a point I agree with you. Some people keep things. Some people throw everything away as soon as they have done with it. That, yes, it is a matter of temperament. But I speak now especially of photographs. Why do people keep, in particular, *photographs*?'

'As I say, because they just don't throw things away. Or else because it reminds them –'

Poirot pounced on the words.

'Exactly. *It reminds them.* Now again we ask – why? *Why* does a woman keep a photograph of herself when young? And I say that the first reason is, essentially, vanity. She has been a pretty girl and she keeps a photograph of herself to remind her of what a pretty girl she was. It encourages her when her mirror tells her unpalatable things. She says, perhaps, to a friend, "That was me when I was eighteen . . ." and she sighs . . . You agree?'

'Yes – yes, I should say that's true enough.'

'Then that is reason No. 1. Vanity. Now reason No. 2. Sentiment.'

'That's the same thing?'

'No, no, not quite. Because this leads you to preserve not only your own photograph but that of someone else . . . A picture of your married daughter – when she was a child sitting on a hearthrug with tulle round her.'

'I've seen some of those,' Spence grinned.

'Yes. Very embarrassing to the subject sometimes, but mothers like to do it. And sons and daughters often keep pictures of their mothers, especially, say, if their mother died young. "That was my mother as a girl."'

'I'm beginning to see what you're driving at, Poirot.'

'And there is possibly, a *third* category. Not vanity, not sentiment, not love – perhaps *hate* – what do you say?'

'Hate?'

'Yes. To keep a desire for revenge alive. Someone who has injured you – you might keep a photograph to remind you, might you not?'

'But surely that doesn't apply in this case?'

'Does it not?'

'What are you thinking of?'

Poirot murmured:

'Newspaper reports are often inaccurate. The *Sunday Comet* stated that Eva Kane was employed by the Craigs as a nursery governess. Was that actually the case?'

'Yes, it was. But we're working on the assumption that it's Lily Gamboll we're looking for.'

Poirot sat up suddenly very straight in his chair. He wagged an imperative forefinger at Spence.

'Look. Look at the photograph of Lily Gamboll. She is not pretty – no! Frankly, with those teeth and those spectacles she is hideously ugly. Then nobody has kept that photograph for the first of our reasons. No woman would keep that photo out of vanity. If Eve Carpenter or Shelagh Rendell, who are both good-looking women, especially Eve Carpenter, had this photograph of themselves, they would tear it in pieces quickly in case somebody should see it!'

'Well, there is something in that.'

'So reason No. 1 is out. Now take sentiment. Did anybody love Lily Gamboll at that age? The whole point of Lily Gamboll is that they did not. She was an unwanted and unloved child. The person who liked her best was her aunt, and her aunt died under the chopper. So it was not sentiment that kept this picture. And revenge? Nobody hated her either. Her murdered aunt was a lonely woman without a husband and with no close friends. Nobody had hate for the little slum child – only pity.'

'Look here, M. Poirot, what you're saying is that *nobody* would have kept that photo.'

'Exactly – that is the result of my reflections.'

'But somebody did. Because Mrs Upward had seen it.'

'*Had she?*'

'Dash it all. It was you who told me. She said so herself.'

'Yes, she said so,' said Poirot. 'But the late Mrs Upward was, in some ways, a secretive woman. She liked to manage things her own way. I showed the photographs, and she recognized one of them. But then, for some reason, she wanted to keep the identification to herself. She wanted, let us say, to deal with a certain situation in the way she fancied. And so, being very quick-witted, she deliberately pointed to the *wrong* picture. Thereby keeping her knowledge to herself.'

'But why?'

'Because, as I say, she wanted to play a lone hand.'

'It wouldn't be blackmail? She was an extremely wealthy woman, you know, widow of a North Country manufacturer.'

'Oh no, not blackmail. More likely beneficence. We'll say that she quite liked the person in question, and that she didn't want to give their secret away. But nevertheless she was *curious*. She intended to have a private talk with that person. And whilst doing so, to make up her mind whether or not that person had had anything to do with the death of Mrs McGinty. Something like that.'

'Then that leaves the other three photos in?'

'Precisely. Mrs Upward meant to get in touch with the person in question at the first opportunity. That came when her son and Mrs Oliver went over to the Repertory Theatre at Cullenquay.'

'*And she telephoned to Deirdre Henderson.* That puts Deirdre Henderson right back in the picture. And her mother!'

Superintendent Spence shook his head sadly at Poirot.

'You do like to make it difficult, don't you, M. Poirot?' he said.

CHAPTER 21

Mrs Wetherby walked back home from the post office with a gait surprisingly spry in one habitually reported to be an invalid.

Only when she had entered the front door did she once more shuffle feebly into the drawing-room and collapse on the sofa.

The bell was within reach of her hand and she rang it.

Since nothing happened she rang it again, this time keeping her finger on it for some time.

In due course Maude Williams appeared. She was wearing a flowered overall and had a duster in her hand.

'Did you ring, madam?'

'I rang twice. When I ring I expect someone to come at once. I might be dangerously ill.'

'I'm sorry, madam. I was upstairs.'

'I know you were. You were in my room. I heard you overhead. And you were pulling the drawers in and out. I can't think why. It's no part of your job to go prying into my things.'

'I wasn't prying. I was putting some of the things you left lying about away tidily.'

'Nonsense. All you people snoop. And I won't have it. I'm feeling very faint. Is Miss Deirdre in?'

'She took the dog for a walk.'

'How stupid. She might know I would need her. Bring me an egg beaten up in milk and a little brandy. The brandy is on the sideboard in the dining-room.'

'There are only just the three eggs for breakfast tomorrow.'

'Then someone will have to go without. Hurry, will you? Don't stand there looking at me. And you're wearing far too much make-up. It isn't suitable.'

There was a bark in the hall and Deirdre and her Sealyham came in as Maude went out.

'I heard your voice,' said Deirdre breathlessly. 'What have you been saying to her?'

'Nothing.'

'She looked like thunder.'

'I put her in her place. Impertinent girl.'

'Oh, Mummy darling, must you? It's so difficult to get anyone. And she does cook well.'

'I suppose it's of no importance that she's insolent to *me*! Oh well, I shan't be with you much longer.' Mrs Wetherby rolled up her eyes and took some fluttering breaths. 'I walked too far,' she murmured.

'You oughtn't to have gone out, darling. Why didn't you tell me you were going?'

'I thought some air would do me good. It's so stuffy. It doesn't matter. One doesn't really want to live – not if one's only a trouble to people.'

'You're not a trouble, darling. I'd die without you.'

'You're a good girl – but I can see how I weary you and get on your nerves.'

'You don't – you don't,' said Deirdre passionately.

Mrs Wetherby sighed and let her eyelids fall.

'I – can't talk much,' she murmured. 'I must just lie still.'

'I'll hurry up Maude with the egg nog.'

Deirdre ran out of the room. In her hurry she caught her elbow on a table and a bronze god bumped to the ground.

'So clumsy,' murmured Mrs Wetherby to herself, wincing.

The door opened and Mr Wetherby came in. He stood there for a moment. Mrs Wetherby opened her eyes.

'Oh, it's you, Roger?'

'I wondered what all the noise was in here. It's impossible to read quietly in this house.'

'It was just Deirdre, dear. She came in with the dog.'

Mr Wetherby stooped and picked up the bronze monstrosity from the floor.

'Surely Deirdre's old enough not to knock things down the whole time.'

'She's just rather awkward.'

'Well, it's absurd to be awkward at her age. And can't she keep that dog from barking?'

'I'll speak to her, Roger.'

'If she makes her home here, she must consider our wishes and not behave as though the house belonged to her.'

'Perhaps you'd rather she went away,' murmured Mrs Wetherby. Through half-closed eyes she watched her husband.

'No, of course not. Of course not. Naturally her home is with us. I only ask for a little more good sense and good manners.' He added: 'You've been out, Edith?'

'Yes. I just went down to the post office.'

'No fresh news about poor Mrs Upward?'

'The police still don't know who it was.'

'They seem to be quite hopeless. Any motive? Who gets her money?'

'The son, I suppose.'

'Yes – yes, then it really seems as though it must have been one of these tramps. You should tell this girl she's got to be careful about keeping the front door locked. And only to open it on the chain when it gets near dusk. These men are very daring and brutal nowadays.'

'Nothing seems to have been taken from Mrs Upward's.'

'Odd.'

'Not like Mrs McGinty,' said Mrs Wetherby.

'Mrs McGinty? Oh! the charwoman. What's Mrs McGinty got to do with Mrs Upward?'

'She did work for her, Roger.'

'Don't be silly, Edith.'

Mrs Wetherby closed her eyes again. As Mr Wetherby went out of the room she smiled to herself.

She opened her eyes with a start to find Maude standing over her, holding a glass.

'Your egg nog, madam,' said Maude.

Her voice was loud and clear. It echoed too resonantly in the deadened house.

Mrs Wetherby looked up with a vague feeling of alarm.

How tall and unbending the girl was. She stood over Mrs Wetherby like – 'like a figure of doom,' Mrs Wetherby thought to herself – and then wondered why such extraordinary words had come into her head.

She raised herself on her elbow and took the glass.

'Thank you, Maude,' she said.

Maude turned and went out of the room.

Mrs Wetherby still felt vaguely upset.

CHAPTER 22

I

Hercule Poirot took a hired car back to Broadhinny.

He was tired because he had been thinking. Thinking was always exhausting. And his thinking had not been entirely satisfactory. It was as though a pattern, perfectly visible, was woven into a piece of material and yet, although he was holding the piece of material, he could not see what the pattern was.

But it was all there. That was the point. It was all there. Only it was one of those patterns, self-coloured and subtle, that are not easy to perceive.

A little way out of Kilchester his car encountered the Summerhayes' station wagon coming in the opposite direction. Johnnie was driving and he had a passenger. Poirot hardly noticed them. He was still absorbed in thought.

When he got back to Long Meadows, he went into the drawing-room. He removed a colander full of spinach from the most comfortable chair in the room and sat down. From overhead came the faint drumming of a typewriter. It was Robin Upward, struggling with a play. Three versions he had already torn up, so he told Poirot. Somehow, he couldn't concentrate.

Robin might feel his mother's death quite sincerely, but he remained Robin Upward, chiefly interested in himself.

'Madre,' he said solemnly, 'would have wished me to go on with my work.'

Hercule Poirot had heard many people say much the same thing. It was one of the most convenient assumptions, this knowledge of what the dead would wish. The bereaved had never any doubt about their dear ones' wishes and those wishes usually squared with their own inclinations.

In this case it was probably true. Mrs Upward had had great faith in Robin's work and had been extremely proud of him.

Poirot leaned back and closed his eyes.

He thought of Mrs Upward. He considered what Mrs Upward had really been like. He remembered a phrase that he had once heard used by a police officer.

'We'll take him apart and see what makes him tick.'

What had made Mrs Upward tick?

There was a crash, and Maureen Summerhayes came in. Her hair was flapping madly.

'I can't think what's happened to Johnnie,' she said. 'He just went down to the post office with those special orders. He ought to have been back hours ago. I want him to fix the henhouse door.'

A true gentleman, Poirot feared, would have gallantly offered to fix the henhouse door himself. Poirot did not. He wanted to go on thinking about two murders and about the character of Mrs Upward.

'And I can't find that Ministry of Agriculture form,' continued Maureen. 'I've looked everywhere.'

'The spinach is on the sofa,' Poirot offered helpfully.

Maureen was not worried about spinach.

'The form came last week,' she mused. 'And I must have put it somewhere. Perhaps it was when I was darning that pullover of Johnnie's.'

She swept over to the bureau and started pulling out the drawers. Most of the contents she swept on to the floor ruthlessly. It was agony to Hercule Poirot to watch her.

Suddenly she uttered a cry of triumph.

'Got it!'

Delightedly she rushed from the room.

Hercule Poirot sighed and resumed meditation.

To arrange, with order and precision –

He frowned. The untidy heap of objects on the floor by the bureau distracted his mind. What a way to look for things!

Order and method. That was the thing. Order and method.

Though he had turned sideways in his chair, he could still see the confusion on the floor. Sewing things, a pile of socks, letters, knitting wool, magazines, sealing wax, photographs, a pullover –

It was insupportable!

Poirot rose, went across to the bureau and with quick deft movements began to return the objects to the open drawers.

The pullover, the socks, the knitting wool. Then, in the next drawer, the sealing wax, the photographs, the letters.

The telephone rang.

The sharpness of the bell made him jump.

He went across to the telephone and lifted the receiver.

''Allo, 'allo, 'allo,' he said.

The voice that spoke to him was the voice of Superintendent Spence.

'Ah! it's you, M. Poirot. Just the man I want.'

Spence's voice was almost unrecognizable. A very worried man had given place to a confident one.

'Filling me up with a lot of fandangle about the wrong photograph,' he said with reproachful indulgence. 'We've got some new evidence. Girl at the post office in Broadhinny. Major

Summerhayes just brought her in. It seems she was standing practically opposite the cottage that night and she saw a woman go in. Some time after eight-thirty and before nine o'clock. And it wasn't Deirdre Henderson. It was a woman with fair hair. That puts us right back where we were – it's definitely between the two of them – Eve Carpenter and Shelagh Rendell. The only question is – which?'

Poirot opened his mouth but did not speak. Carefully, deliberately, he replaced the receiver on the stand.

He stood there staring unseeingly in front of him.

The telephone rang again.

''Allo! 'Allo! 'Allo!'

'Can I speak to M. Poirot, please?'

'Hercule Poirot speaking.'

'Thought so. Maude Williams here. Post office in a quarter of an hour?'

'I will be there.'

He replaced the receiver.

He looked down at his feet. Should he change his shoes? His feet ached a little. Ah well – no matter.

Resolutely Poirot clapped on his hat and left the house.

On his way down the hill he was hailed by one of Superintendent Spence's men just emerging from Laburnums.

'Morning, M. Poirot.'

Poirot responded politely. He noticed that Sergeant Fletcher was looking excited.

'The Super sent me over to have a thorough check up,' he explained. 'You know – any little thing we might have missed. Never know, do you? We'd been over the desk, of course, but the Super got the idea there might be a secret drawer – must have been reading spy stuff. Well, there wasn't a secret drawer. But after that I got on to the books. Sometimes people slip a letter into a book they're reading. You know?'

Poirot said that he knew. 'And you found something?' he asked politely.

'Not a letter or anything of that sort, no. But I found something interesting – at least *I* think it's interesting. Look here.'

He unwrapped from a piece of newspaper an old and rather decrepit book.

'In one of the bookshelves it was. Old book, published years ago. But look here.' He opened it and showed the flyleaf. Pencilled across it were the words: *Evelyn Hope.*

'Interesting, don't you think? That's the name, in case you don't remember –'

'The name that Eva Kane took when she left England. I do remember,' said Poirot.

'Looks as though when Mrs McGinty spotted one of those photos here in Broadhinny, it was our Mrs Upward. Makes it kind of complicated, doesn't it?'

'It does,' said Poirot with feeling. 'I can assure you that when you go back to Superintendent Spence with this piece of information he will pull out his hair by the roots – yes, assuredly by the roots.'

'I hope it won't be as bad as that,' said Sergeant Fletcher.

Poirot did not reply. He went on down the hill. He had ceased to think. Nothing anywhere made sense.

He went into the post office. Maude Williams was there looking at knitting patterns. Poirot did not speak to her. He went to the stamp counter. When Maude had made her purchase, Mrs Sweetiman came over to him and he bought some stamps. Maude went out of the shop.

Mrs Sweetiman seemed preoccupied and not talkative. Poirot was able to follow Maude out fairly quickly. He caught her up a short distance along the road and fell into step beside her.

Mrs Sweetiman, looking out of the post office window, exclaimed to herself disapprovingly. 'Those foreigners! All the same, every manjack of 'em. Old enough to be her grandfather, he is!'

II

'*Eh bien*,' said Poirot, 'you have something to tell me?'

'I don't know that it's important. There was somebody trying to get in at the window of Mrs Wetherby's room.'

'When?'

'This morning. *She'd* gone out, and the girl was out with the dog. Old frozen fish was shut up in his study as usual. I'd have been in the kitchen normally – it faces the other way like the study – but actually it seemed a good opportunity to – you understand?'

Poirot nodded.

'So I nipped upstairs and into Her Acidity's bedroom. There was a ladder against the window and a man was fumbling with the window catch. She's had everything locked and barred since the murder. Never a bit of fresh air. When the man saw me he scuttled down and made off. The ladder was the gardener's – he'd been cutting back the ivy and had gone to have his elevenses.'

'Who was the man? Can you describe him?'

'I only got the merest glimpse. By the time I got to the window he was down the ladder and gone, and when I first saw him he was against the sun, so I couldn't see his face.'

'You are sure it *was* a man?'

Maude considered.

'Dressed as a man – an old felt hat on. It *might* have been a woman, of course . . .'

'It is interesting,' said Poirot. 'It is very interesting . . . Nothing else?'

'Not yet. The junk that old woman keeps! Must be dotty! She came in without me hearing this morning and bawled me out for snooping. I shall be murdering her next. If anyone asks to be murdered that woman does. A really nasty bit of goods.'

Poirot murmured softly:

'Evelyn Hope . . .'

'What's that?' She spun round on him.

'So you know that name?'

'Why – yes . . . It's the name Eva Whatsername took when she went to Australia. It – it was in the paper – the *Sunday Comet*.'

'The *Sunday Comet* said many things, but it did not say that. The police found the name written in a book in Mrs Upward's house.'

Maude exclaimed:

'Then it *was* her – and she *didn't* die out there . . . Michael was right.'

'Michael?'

Maude said abruptly:

'I can't stop. I'll be late serving lunch. I've got it all in the oven, but it will be getting dried up.'

She started off at a run. Poirot stood looking after her.

At the post office window, Mrs Sweetiman, her nose glued to the pane, wondered if that old foreigner had been making suggestions of a certain character . . .

III

Back at Long Meadows, Poirot removed his shoes, and put on a pair of bedroom slippers. They were not *chic*, not in his opinion *comme il faut* – but there must be relief.

He sat down on the easy-chair again and began once more to think. He had by now a lot to think about.

There were things he had missed – little things.

The pattern was all there. It only needed cohesion.

Maureen, glass in hand, talking in a dreamy voice – asking a question . . . Mrs Oliver's account of her evening at the Rep. Cecil? Michael? He was almost sure that she had mentioned a Michael – Eva Kane, nursery governess to the Craigs –

Evelyn Hope . . .

Of course! Evelyn Hope!

CHAPTER 23

I

Eve Carpenter came into the Summerhayes' house in the casual way that most people did, using any door or window that was convenient.

She was looking for Hercule Poirot and when she found him she did not beat about the bush.

'Look here,' she said. 'You're a detective, and you're supposed to be good. All right, I'll hire you.'

'Suppose I am not for hire. *Mon Dieu*, I am not a taxicab!'

'You're a private detective and private detectives get paid, don't they?'

'It is the custom.'

'Well, that's what I'm saying. I'll pay you. I'll pay you well.'

'For what? What do you want me to do?'

Eve Carpenter said sharply:

'Protect me against the police. They're crazy. They seem to

think I killed the Upward woman. And they're nosing round, asking me all sorts of questions – ferreting out things. I don't like it. It's driving me mental.'

Poirot looked at her. Something of what she said was true. She looked many years older than when he had first seen her a few weeks ago. Circles under her eyes spoke of sleepless nights. There were lines from her mouth to her chin, and her hand, when she lit a cigarette, shook badly.

'You've got to stop it,' she said. 'You've got to.'

'Madame, what can I do?'

'Fend them off somehow or other. Damned cheek! If Guy was a man he'd stop all this. He wouldn't let them persecute me.'

'And – he does nothing?'

She said sullenly:

'I've not told him. He just talks pompously about giving the police all the assistance possible. It's all right for *him*. He was at some ghastly political meeting that night.'

'And you?'

'I was just sitting at home. Listening to the radio actually.'

'But, if you can prove that –'

'How can I prove it? I offered the Crofts a fabulous sum to say they'd been in and out and seen me there – the damned swine refused.'

'That was a very unwise move on your part.'

'I don't see why. It would have settled the business.'

'You have probably convinced your servants that you did commit the murder.'

'Well – I'd paid Croft anyway for –'

'For what?'

'Nothing.'

'Remember – you want my help.'

'Oh! It was nothing that matters. But Croft took the message from her.'

'From Mrs Upward?'

'Yes. Asking me to go down and see her that night.'

'And you say you didn't go?'

'Why should I go? Damned dreary old woman. Why should I go and hold her hand? I never dreamed of going for a moment.'

'When did this message come?'

'When I was out. I don't know exactly when – between five and six, I think. Croft took it.'

'And you gave him money to forget he had taken that message. Why?'

'Don't be idiotic. I didn't want to get mixed up in it all.'

'And then you offer him money to give you an alibi? What do you suppose he and his wife think?'

'Who cares what they think?'

'A jury may care,' said Poirot gravely.

She stared at him.

'You're not serious?'

'I am serious.'

'They'd listen to servants – and not to me?'

Poirot looked at her.

Such crass rudeness and stupidity! Antagonizing the people who might have been helpful. A short-sighted stupid policy. Short-sighted –

Such lovely wide blue eyes.

He said quietly:

'Why don't you wear glasses, madame? You need them.'

'What? Oh, I do sometimes. I did as a child.'

'And you had then a plate for your teeth.'

She stared.

'I did, as a matter of fact. Why all this?'

'The ugly duckling becomes a swan?'

'I was certainly ugly enough.'

'Did your mother think so?'

She said sharply:

'I don't remember my mother. What the hell are we talking about anyway? Will you take on the job?'

'I regret I cannot.'

'Why can't you?'

'Because in this affair I act for James Bentley.'

'James Bentley? Oh, you mean that half-wit who killed the charwoman. What's he got to do with the Upwards?'

'Perhaps – nothing.'

'Well, then! Is it a question of money? How much?'

'That is your great mistake, madame. You think always in

terms of money. You have money and you think that only money counts.'

'I haven't always had money,' said Eve Carpenter.

'No,' said Poirot. 'I thought not.' He nodded his head gently. 'That explains a good deal. It excuses some things . . .'

II

Eve Carpenter went out the way she had come, blundering a little in the light as Poirot remembered her doing before.

Poirot said softly to himself: 'Evelyn Hope . . .'

So Mrs Upward had rung up both Deirdre Henderson *and* Evelyn Carpenter. Perhaps she had rung up someone else. Perhaps –

With a crash Maureen came in.

'It's my scissors now. Sorry lunch is late. I've got three pairs and I can't find one of them.'

She rushed over to the bureau and the process with which Poirot was well acquainted was repeated. This time, the objective was attained rather sooner. With a cry of joy, Maureen departed.

Almost automatically, Poirot stepped over and began to replace the things in the drawer. Sealing wax, notepaper, a work basket, photographs –

Photographs . . .

He stood staring at the photograph he held in his hand.

Footsteps rushed back along the passage.

Poirot could move quickly in spite of his age. He had dropped the photograph on the sofa, put a cushion on it, and had himself sat on the cushion, by the time that Maureen re-entered.

'Where the hell've I put a colander full of spinach –'

'But it is there, madame.'

He indicated the colander as it reposed beside him on the sofa.

'So that's where I left it.' She snatched it up. 'Everything's behind today . . .' Her glance took in Hercule Poirot sitting bolt upright.

'What on earth do you want to sit there for? Even on a cushion, it's the most uncomfortable seat in the room. All the springs are broken.'

'I know, madame. But I am – I am admiring that picture on the wall.'

Maureen glanced up at the oil painting of a naval officer complete with telescope.

'Yes – it's good. About the only good thing in the house. We're not sure that it isn't a Gainsborough.' She sighed. 'Johnnie won't sell it, though. It's his great-great and I think a few more greats, grandfather and he went down with his ship or did something frightfully gallant. Johnnie's terribly proud of it.'

'Yes,' said Poirot gently. 'Yes, he has something to be proud about, your husband!'

III

It was three o'clock when Poirot arrived at Dr Rendell's house.

He had eaten rabbit stew and spinach and hard potatoes and a rather peculiar pudding, not scorched this time. Instead, 'The water got in,' Maureen had explained. He had drunk half a cup of muddy coffee. He did not feel well.

The door was opened by the elderly housekeeper Mrs Scott, and he asked for Mrs Rendell.

She was in the drawing-room with the radio on and started up when he was announced.

He had the same impression of her that he had had the first time he saw her. Wary, on her guard, frightened of him, or frightened of what he represented.

She seemed paler and more shadowy than she had done. He was almost certain that she was thinner.

'I want to ask you a question, madame.'

'A question? Oh? Oh yes?'

'Did Mrs Upward telephone to you on the day of her death?'

She stared at him. She nodded.

'At what time?'

'Mrs Scott took the message. It was about six o'clock, I think.'

'What was the message? To ask you to go there that evening?'

'Yes. She said that Mrs Oliver and Robin were going into Kilchester and she would be all alone as it was Janet's night out. Could I come down and keep her company.'

'Was any time suggested?'

'Nine o'clock or after.'

'And you went?'

'I meant to. I really meant to. But I don't know how it was, I fell fast asleep after dinner that night. It was after ten when I woke up. I thought it was too late.'

'You did not tell the police about Mrs Upward's call?'

Her eyes widened. They had a rather innocent childlike stare.

'Ought I to have done? Since I didn't go, I thought it didn't matter. Perhaps, even, I felt rather guilty. If I'd gone, she might have been alive now.' She caught her breath suddenly. 'Oh, I hope it wasn't like that.'

'Not quite like that,' said Poirot.

He paused and then said:

'*What are you afraid of, madame?*'

She caught her breath sharply.

'Afraid? I'm not afraid.'

'But you are.'

'What nonsense. What – what should I be afraid of?'

Poirot paused for a moment before speaking.

'I thought perhaps you might be afraid of *me* . . .'

She didn't answer. But her eyes widened. Slowly, defiantly, she shook her head.

CHAPTER 24

I

'This way to Bedlam,' said Spence.

'It is not as bad as that,' said Poirot soothingly.

'That's what you say. Every single bit of information that comes in makes things more difficult. Now you tell me that Mrs Upward rang up *three* women. Asked them to come that evening. Why three? Didn't she know herself which of them was Lily Gamboll? Or isn't it a case of Lily Gamboll at all? Take that book with the name of Evelyn Hope in it. It suggests, doesn't it, that Mrs Upward and Eva Kane are one and the same.'

'Which agrees exactly with James Bentley's impression of what Mrs McGinty said to him.'

'I thought he wasn't sure.'

'He was not sure. It would be impossible for James Bentley to be sure of anything. He did not listen properly to what Mrs McGinty was saying. Nevertheless, if James Bentley had an impression that Mrs McGinty was talking about Mrs Upward, it may very well be true. Impressions often are.'

'Our latest information from Australia (it was Australia she went to, by the way, not America) seems to be to the effect that the "Mrs Hope" in question died out there twenty years ago.'

'I have already been told that,' said Poirot.

'You always know everything, don't you, Poirot?'

Poirot took no notice of this gibe. He said:

'At the one end we have "Mrs Hope" deceased in Australia – and at the other?'

'At the other end we have Mrs Upward, the widow of a rich North Country manufacturer. She lived with him near Leeds, and had a son. Soon after the son's birth, her husband died. The boy was inclined to be tubercular and since her husband's death she lived mostly abroad.'

'And when does this saga begin?'

'The saga begins four years after Eva Kane left England. Upward met his wife somewhere abroad and brought her home after the marriage.'

'So actually Mrs Upward *could* be Eva Kane. What was her maiden name?'

'Hargraves, I understand. But what's in a name?'

'What indeed. Eva Kane, or Evelyn Hope, may have died in Australia – but she may have arranged a convenient decease and resuscitated herself as Hargraves and made a wealthy match.'

'It's all a long time ago,' said Spence. 'But supposing that it's true. Supposing she kept a picture of herself and supposing that Mrs McGinty saw it – then one can only assume that *she* killed Mrs McGinty.'

'That could be, could it not? Robin Upward was broadcasting that night. Mrs Rendell mentions going to the cottage that evening, remember, and not being able to make herself heard. According to Mrs Sweetiman, Janet Groom told her that Mrs Upward was not really as crippled as she made out.'

'That's all very well, Poirot, but the fact remains that *she herself* was killed – after recognizing a photograph. Now you want to make out that the two deaths are not connected.'

'No, no. I do not say that. They are connected all right.'

'I give it up.'

'Evelyn Hope. There is the key to the problem.'

'Evelyn Carpenter? Is that your idea? *Not* Lily Gamboll – but Eva Kane's daughter! But surely she wouldn't kill her own mother.'

'No, no. This is not matricide.'

'What an irritating devil you are, Poirot. You'll be saying next that Eva Kane and Lily Gamboll, and Janice Courtland *and* Vera Blake are *all* living in Broadhinny. All four suspects.'

'We have more than four. Eva Kane was the Craigs' nursery governess, remember.'

'What's that got to do with it?'

'Where there is a nursery governess, there must be children – or at least a child. What happened to the Craig children?'

'There was a girl and a boy, I believe. Some relative took them.'

'So there are two more people to take into account. Two people who might have kept a photograph for the third reason I mentioned – revenge.'

'I don't believe it,' said Spence.

Poirot sighed.

'It has to be considered, all the same. I think I know the truth – though there is one fact that baffles me utterly.'

'I'm glad something baffles you,' said Spence.

'Confirm one thing for me, *mon cher* Spence. Eva Kane left the country before Craig's execution, that is right?'

'Quite right.'

'And she was, at that time, expecting a child?'

'Quite right.'

'*Bon Dieu*, how stupid I have been,' said Hercule Poirot. 'The whole thing is simple, is it not?'

It was after that remark that there was very nearly a third murder – the murder of Hercule Poirot by Superintendent Spence in Kilchester Police Headquarters.

II

'I want,' said Hercule Poirot, 'a personal call. To Mrs Ariadne Oliver.'

A personal call to Mrs Oliver was not achieved without difficulties. Mrs Oliver was working and could not be disturbed. Poirot, however, disregarded all denials. Presently he heard the authoress's voice.

It was cross and rather breathless.

'Well, what is it?' said Mrs Oliver. 'Have you got to ring me up just now? I've thought of a most wonderful idea for a murder in a draper's shop. You know, the old-fashioned kind that sells combinations and funny vests with long sleeves.'

'I do not know,' said Poirot. 'And anyway what I have to say to you is far more important.'

'It couldn't be,' said Mrs Oliver. 'Not to *me*, I mean. Unless I get a rough sketch of my idea jotted down, it will *go*!'

Hercule Poirot paid no attention to this creative agony. He asked sharp imperative questions to which Mrs Oliver replied somewhat vaguely.

'Yes – yes – it's a little Repertory Theatre – I don't know its name . . . Well, one of them was Cecil Something, and the one I was talking to was Michael.'

'Admirable. That is all I need to know.'

'But why Cecil and Michael?'

'Return to the combinations and the long-sleeved vests, madame.'

'I can't think why you don't arrest Dr Rendell,' said Mrs Oliver. 'I would, if I were the Head of Scotland Yard.'

'Very possibly. I wish you luck with the murder in the draper's shop.'

'The whole idea has gone now,' said Mrs Oliver. 'You've ruined it.'

Poirot apologized handsomely.

He put down the receiver and smiled at Spence.

'We go now – or at least I will go – to interview a young actor whose Christian name is Michael and who plays the less important parts in the Cullenquay Repertory Theatre. I pray only that he is the right Michael.'

'Why on earth –'

Poirot dexterously averted the rising wrath of Superintendent Spence.

'Do you know, *cher ami*, what is a *secret de Polichinelle*?'

'Is this a French lesson?' demanded the superintendent wrathfully.

'A *secret de Polichinelle* is a secret that everyone can know. For this reason the people who do not know it never hear about it – for if everyone thinks you know a thing, nobody tells you.'

'How I manage to keep my hands off you I don't know,' said Superintendent Spence.

CHAPTER 25

The inquest was over – a verdict had been returned of murder by a person or persons unknown.

After the inquest, at the invitation of Hercule Poirot, those who had attended it came to Long Meadows.

Working diligently, Poirot had induced some semblance of order in the long drawing-room. Chairs had been arranged in a neat semi-circle, Maureen's dogs had been excluded with difficulty, and Hercule Poirot, a self-appointed lecturer, took up his position at the end of the room and initiated proceedings with a slightly self-conscious clearing of the throat.

'Messieurs et Mesdames –'

He paused. His next words were unexpected and seemed almost farcical.

'Mrs McGinty's dead. How did she die?
Down on her knees just like I.
Mrs McGinty's dead. How did she die?
Holding her hand out just like I.
Mrs McGinty's dead. How did she die?
Like this . . .'

Seeing their expressions, he went on:

'No, I am not mad. Because I repeat to you the childish rhyme of a childish game, it does not mean that I am in my second childhood. Some of you may have played that game as children. Mrs Upward had played it. Indeed she repeated it to me – with a difference. She said: "*Mrs McGinty's dead. How did she die? Sticking her neck out just like I.*" That is what she said – and that is what she did. She stuck her neck out – and so she also, like Mrs McGinty, died . . .

'For our purpose we must go back to the beginning – to Mrs McGinty – down on her knees scrubbing other people's houses. Mrs McGinty was killed, and a man, James Bentley, was arrested, tried and convicted. For certain reasons, Superintendent Spence, the officer in charge of the case, was not convinced of Bentley's guilt, strong though the evidence was. I agreed with him. I came down here to answer a question. "How did Mrs McGinty die? *Why* did she die?"

'I will not make you the long and complicated histories. I will say only that as simple a thing as a bottle of ink gave me a clue. In the *Sunday Comet*, read by Mrs McGinty on the Sunday before her death, four photographs were published. You know all about those photographs by now, so I will only say that Mrs McGinty recognized one of those photographs as a photograph she had seen in one of the houses where she worked.

'She spoke of this to James Bentley though he attached no importance to the matter at the time, nor indeed afterwards. Actually he barely listened. But he had the impression that Mrs McGinty had seen the photograph in Mrs Upward's house and that when she referred to a woman who need not be so proud if all was known, she was referring to Mrs Upward. We cannot depend on that statement of his, but she certainly used that phrase about pride and there is no doubt that Mrs Upward *was* a proud and imperious woman.

'As you all know – some of you were present and the others will have heard – I produced those four photographs at Mrs Upward's house. I caught a flicker of surprise and recognition in Mrs Upward's expression and taxed her with it. She had to admit it. She said that she "had seen one of the photographs somewhere but she couldn't remember where". When asked which photograph, she pointed to a photograph of the child Lily Gamboll. But that, let me tell you, *was not the truth*. For reasons of her own, Mrs Upward wanted to keep her recognition to herself. She pointed to the wrong photograph to put me off.

'But one person was not deceived – the *murderer*. One person *knew* which photograph Mrs Upward had recognized. And here I will not beat to and fro about the bush – the photograph in question was that of Eva Kane – a woman who was accomplice, victim or possibly leading spirit in the famous Craig Murder Case.

'On the next evening Mrs Upward was killed. She was killed for the same reason that Mrs McGinty was killed. Mrs McGinty stuck her hand out, Mrs Upward stuck her neck out – the result was the same.

'Now before Mrs Upward died, three women received telephone calls. Mrs Carpenter, Mrs Rendell, and Miss Henderson. All three calls were a message from Mrs Upward asking the person in question to come and see her that evening. It was her servant's night out and her son and Mrs Oliver were going into Cullenquay. It would seem, therefore, that she wanted a private conversation with each of these three women.

'Now why *three* women? Did Mrs Upward know *where* she had seen the photograph of Eva Kane? Or did she know she had seen it but could not remember where? Had these three women anything in common? Nothing, it would seem, but their *age*. They were all, roughly, in the neighbourhood of thirty.

'You have, perhaps, read the article in the *Sunday Comet*. There is a truly sentimental picture in it of Eva Kane's daughter in years to come. The women asked by Mrs Upward to come and see her were all of the right age to be Eva Kane's daughter.

'So it would seem that living in Broadhinny was a young woman who was the daughter of the celebrated murderer Craig and of his mistress Eva Kane, and it would also seem that that young woman would go to any lengths to prevent that fact being known. Would go, indeed, to the length of twice committing murder. For when Mrs Upward was found dead, there were two coffee cups on the table, both used, and on the visitor's cup faint traces of lipstick.

'Now let us go back to the three women who received telephone messages. Mrs Carpenter got the message but says she did not go to Laburnums that night. Mrs Rendell meant to go, but fell asleep in her chair. Miss Henderson *did* go to Laburnums but the house was dark and she could not make anyone hear and she came away again.

'That is the story these three woman tell – but there is conflicting evidence. There is that second coffee cup with lipstick on it, and an outside witness, the girl Edna, states positively that she saw a fair-haired woman go *in* to the house. There is also the evidence of scent – an expensive and exotic scent which Mrs Carpenter uses alone of those concerned.'

There was an interruption. Eve Carpenter cried out:

'It's a lie. It's a wicked cruel lie. It wasn't me! I never went there! I never went near the place. Guy, can't you do something about these lies?'

Guy Carpenter was white with anger.

'Let me inform you, M. Poirot, that there is a law of slander and all these people present are witnesses.'

'Is it slander to say that your wife uses a certain scent – and also, let me tell you, a certain lipstick?'

'It's ridiculous,' cried Eve. 'Absolutely ridiculous! *Anyone* could go splashing my scent about.'

Unexpectedly Poirot beamed on her.

'*Mais oui*, exactly! Anyone could. An obvious, not very subtle thing to do. Clumsy and crude. So clumsy that, as far as I was concerned, it defeated its object. It did more. It gave me, as the phrase goes, ideas. Yes, it gave me ideas.

'Scent – and traces of lipstick on a cup. But it is so easy to remove lipstick from a cup – I assure you every trace can be wiped off quite easily. Or the cups themselves could be removed and washed. Why not? There was no one in the house. But that was not done. I asked myself why? And the answer seemed to be a deliberate stress on femininity, an underlining of the fact that it was a *woman's* murder. I reflected on the telephone calls to those three women – all of them had been *messages*. In no case had the recipient herself spoken to Mrs Upward. So perhaps it was *not* Mrs Upward who had telephoned. It was someone who was anxious to involve a *woman* – *any* woman – in the crime. Again I asked why? And there can only be one answer – that it was not a woman who killed Mrs Upward – but a *man*.'

He looked round on his audience. They were all very still. Only two people responded.

Eve Carpenter said with a sigh: 'Now you're talking sense!'

Mrs Oliver, nodding her head vigorously, said: 'Of course.'

'So I have arrived at this point – a *man* killed Mrs Upward and a *man* killed Mrs McGinty! What man? The reason for the murder must still be the same – it all hinges on a photograph. In whose possession was that photograph? That is the first question. And why was it kept?'

'Well, that is perhaps not so difficult. Say that it was kept originally for sentimental reasons. Once Mrs McGinty is – removed, the photograph need not be destroyed. But after the second murder, it is different. This time the photograph has definitely been connected with the murder. The photograph is now a dangerous thing to keep. Therefore you will all agree, it is sure to be destroyed.'

He looked round at the heads that nodded agreement.

'But, for all that, the photograph was *not* destroyed! No, it was not destroyed! I know that – because I found it. I found it a few days ago. I found it in this house. In the drawer of the bureau that you see standing against the wall. I have it here.'

He held out the faded photograph of a simpering girl with roses.

'Yes,' said Poirot. 'It is Eva Kane. And on the back of it are written two words in pencil. Shall I tell you what they are? "*My mother*" . . .'

His eyes, grave and accusing, rested on Maureen Summerhayes. She pushed back the hair from her face and stared at him with wide bewildered eyes.

'I don't understand. I never –'

'No, Mrs Summerhayes, you do not understand. There can be only two reasons for keeping this photograph after the second murder. The first of them is an innocent sentimentality. *You* had no feeling of guilt and so you could keep the photograph. You told us yourself, at Mrs Carpenter's house one day, that you were an adopted child. I doubt whether you have ever known what your real mother's name was. But somebody else knew. Somebody who has all the pride of family – a pride that makes him cling to his ancestral home, a pride in his ancestors and his lineage. That man would rather die than have the world – and his children – know that Maureen Summerhayes is the daughter of the murderer Craig and of Eva Kane. That man, I have said, would rather die. But that would not help, would it? So instead let us say that we have here a man who is prepared to kill.'

Johnnie Summerhayes got up from his seat. His voice, when he spoke, was quiet, almost friendly.

'Rather a lot of nonsense you're talkin', aren't you? Enjoying yourself spouting out a lot of theories? Theories, that's all they are! Saying things about my wife –'

His anger broke suddenly in a furious tide.

'You damned filthy swine –'

The swiftness of his rush across the floor took the room unawares. Poirot skipped back nimbly and Superintendent Spence was suddenly between Poirot and Summerhayes.

'Now, now, Major Summerhayes, take it easy – take it easy –'

Summerhayes recovered himself, shrugged, said:

'Sorry. Ridiculous really! After all – *anyone* can stick a photograph in a drawer.'

'Precisely,' said Poirot. 'And the interesting thing about this photograph is that it has no fingerprints on it.'

He paused, then nodded his head gently.

'But it should have had,' he said. 'If Mrs Summerhayes kept it, she would have kept it innocently, and so her fingerprints *should* have been on it.'

Maureen exclaimed:

'I think you're mad. I've never seen that photograph in my life – except at Mrs Upward's that day.'

'It is fortunate for you,' said Poirot, 'that I know that you are speaking the truth. The photograph was put into that drawer *only a few minutes before I found it there*. Twice that morning the contents of that drawer were tumbled on to the ground, twice I replaced them; the first time the photograph was *not* in the drawer, the second time it *was*. It had been placed there during that interval – *and I know by whom*.'

A new note crept into his voice. He was no longer a ridiculous little man with an absurd moustache and dyed hair, he was a hunter very close to his quarry.

'The crimes were committed by a *man* – they were committed for the simplest of all reasons – for money. In Mrs Upward's house there was a book found and on the flyleaf of that book is written

Evelyn Hope. Hope was the name Eva Kane took when she left England. If her real name was Evelyn then in all probability she gave the name of Evelyn to her child when it was born. *But Evelyn is a man's name as well as a woman's.* Why had we assumed that Eva Kane's child was a girl? Roughly because the *Sunday Comet* said so! But actually the *Sunday Comet* had not said so in so many words, it had assumed it because of a romantic interview with Eva Kane. But Eva Kane left England *before* her child was born – so nobody could say what the sex of the child would be.

'That is where I let myself be misled. By the romantic inaccuracy of the Press.

'Evelyn Hope, Eva Kane's *son*, comes to England. He is talented and he attracts the attention of a very rich woman who knows nothing about his origin – only the romantic story he chooses to tell her. (A very pretty little story it was – all about a tragic young ballerina dying of tuberculosis in Paris!)

'She is a lonely woman who has recently lost her own son. The talented young playwright takes her name by deed poll.

'*But your real name is Evelyn Hope, isn't it, Mr Upward?*'

Robin Upward cried out shrilly:

'Of course it isn't! I don't know what you're talking about.'

'You really cannot hope to deny it. There are people who know you under that name. The name Evelyn Hope, written in the book, is in your handwriting – the same handwriting as the words "my mother" on the back of this photograph. Mrs McGinty saw the photograph and the writing on it when she was tidying your things away. She spoke to you about it after reading the *Sunday Comet*. Mrs McGinty assumed that it was a photograph of *Mrs Upward* when young, since she had no idea Mrs Upward was not your real mother. But you knew that if once she mentioned the matter so that it came to Mrs Upward's ears, it would be the end. Mrs Upward had quite fanatical views on the subject of heredity. She would not tolerate for a moment an adopted son who was the son of a famous murderer. Nor would she forgive your lies on the subject.

'So Mrs McGinty had at all costs to be silenced. You promised her a little present, perhaps, for being discreet. You called on her the next evening on your way to broadcast – and you killed her! *Like this . . .*'

With a sudden movement, Poirot seized the sugar hammer from the shelf and whirled it round and down as though to bring it crashing down on Robin's head.

So menacing was the gesture that several of the circle cried out.

Robin Upward screamed. A high terrified scream.

He yelled: 'Don't . . . don't . . . It was an accident. I swear it was an accident. I didn't mean to kill her. I lost my head. I swear I did.'

'You washed off the blood and put the sugar hammer back in this room where you had found it. But there are new scientific methods of determining blood stains – and of bringing up latent fingerprints.'

'I tell you I never meant to kill her . . . It was all a mistake . . . And anyway it isn't my fault . . . I'm not responsible. It's in my blood. I can't help it. You can't hang me for something that isn't my fault . . .'

Under his breath Spence muttered: 'Can't we? You see if we don't!'

Aloud he spoke in a grave official voice:

'I must warn you, Mr Upward, that anything you say . . .'

CHAPTER 26

'I really don't see, M. Poirot, how ever you came to suspect Robin Upward.'

Poirot looked complacently at the faces turned towards him.

He always enjoyed explanations.

'I ought to have suspected him much sooner. The clue, such a simple clue, was the sentence uttered by Mrs Summerhayes at the cocktail party that day. She said to Robin Upward: "I don't like being adopted, do you?" Those were the revealing two words. *Do you?* They meant – they could only mean – that Mrs Upward was not Robin's own mother.

'Mrs Upward was morbidly anxious herself that no one should know that Robin was not her own son. She had probably heard too many ribald comments on brilliant young men who live with and upon elderly women. And very few people did know – only the small theatrical *coterie* where she had first come across Robin. She had few intimate friends in this country, having lived abroad so long, and she chose in any case to come and settle down here far away from her own Yorkshire. Even when she met friends of the old days, she did not enlighten them when they assumed that this Robin was the same Robin they had known as a little boy.

'But from the very first something had struck me as not quite natural in the household at Laburnums. Robin's attitude to Mrs Upward was not that of either a spoiled child, or of a devoted son. It was the attitude of a protégé to a *patron*. The rather fanciful title of Madre had a theatrical touch. And Mrs Upward, though she was clearly very fond of Robin, nevertheless unconsciously treated him as a prized possession that she had bought and paid for.

'So there is Robin Upward, comfortably established, with "Madre's" purse to back his ventures, and then into his assured world comes Mrs McGinty who has recognized the photograph that he keeps in a drawer – the photograph with "my mother" written on the back of it. His mother, who he has told Mrs Upward was a talented young ballet dancer who died of tuberculosis! Mrs McGinty, of course, thinks that the photograph is of Mrs Upward when young, since she assumes as a matter of course that Mrs Upward is Robin's own mother. I do not think that actual blackmail ever entered Mrs McGinty's mind, but she did hope, perhaps, for a "nice little present," as a reward for holding her tongue about a piece of bygone gossip which would not have been pleasant for a "proud" woman like Mrs Upward.

'But Robin Upward was taking no chances. He purloins the sugar hammer, laughingly referred to as a perfect weapon for murder by Mrs Summerhayes, and on the following evening, he stops at Mrs McGinty's cottage on his way to broadcast. She takes him into the parlour, quite unsuspicious, and he kills her. He knows where she keeps her savings – everyone in Broadhinny seems to know – and he fakes a burglary, hiding the money outside the house. Bentley is suspected and arrested. Everything is now safe for clever Robin Upward.

'But then, suddenly, I produce four photographs, and Mrs Upward recognizes the one of Eva Kane as being identical with a photograph of Robin's ballerina mother! She needs a little time to think things out. Murder is involved. Can it be possible that Robin —? No, she refuses to believe it.

'What action she would have taken in the end we do not know. But Robin was taking no chances. He plans the whole *mise en scène*. The visit to the Rep on Janet's night out, the telephone calls, the coffee cup carefully smeared with lipstick taken from Eve Carpenter's bag, he even buys a bottle of her distinctive perfume. The whole thing was a theatrical scene setting with prepared props. Whilst Mrs Oliver waited in the car, Robin ran back twice into the house. The murder was a matter of seconds. After that there was only the swift distribution of the "props". And with Mrs Upward dead, he inherited a large fortune by the terms of her will, and no suspicion could attach to him since it would seem quite certain that a *woman* had committed the crime. With three women visiting the cottage that night, one of them was almost sure to be suspected. And that, indeed, was so.

'But Robin, like all criminals, was careless and over confident. Not only was there a book in the cottage with his original name scribbled in it, but he also kept, for purposes of his own, the fatal photograph. It would have been much safer for him if he had destroyed it, but he clung to the belief that he could use it to incriminate someone else at the right moment.

'He probably thought then of Mrs Summerhayes. That may be the reason he moved out of the cottage and into Long Meadows. After all, the sugar hammer was hers, and Mrs Summerhayes was, he knew, an adopted child and might find it hard to prove she was not Eva Kane's daughter.

'However, when Deirdre Henderson admitted having been on the scene of the crime, he conceived the idea of planting the photograph amongst *her* possessions. He tried to do so, using a ladder that the gardener had left against the window. But Mrs Wetherby was nervous and had insisted on all the windows being kept locked, so Robin did not succeed in his purpose. He came straight back here and put the photograph in a drawer which, unfortunately for him, I had searched only a short time before.

'I knew, therefore, that the photograph had been planted, and I knew by whom – by the only person in the house – that person who was typing industriously over my head.

'Since the name Evelyn Hope had been written on the flyleaf

of the book from the cottage, Evelyn Hope must be either Mrs Upward – or Robin Upward . . .

'The name Evelyn had led me astray – I had connected it with Mrs Carpenter since her name was Eve. *But Evelyn was a man's name as well as a woman's.*

'I remembered the conversation Mrs Oliver had told me about at the Little Rep in Cullenquay. The young actor who had been talking to her was the person I wanted to confirm my theory – the theory that Robin was not Mrs Upward's own son. For by the way he had talked, it seemed clear that he knew the real facts. And his story of Mrs Upward's swift retribution on a young man who had deceived her as to his origins was suggestive.

'The truth is that I ought to have seen the whole thing very much sooner. I was handicapped by a serious error. I believed that I had been deliberately pushed with the intention of sending me on to a railway line – and that the person who had done so was the murderer of Mrs McGinty. Now Robin Upward was practically the only person in Broadhinny who could *not* have been at Kilchester station at that time.'

There was a sudden chuckle from Johnnie Summerhayes.

'Probably some old woman with a basket. They do shove.'

Poirot said:

'Actually, Robin Upward was far too conceited to fear me at all. It is a characteristic of murderers. Fortunately, perhaps. For in this case there was very little evidence.'

Mrs Oliver stirred.

'Do you mean to say,' she demanded incredulously, 'that Robin murdered his mother whilst I sat outside in the car, and that I hadn't the least idea of it? There wouldn't have been time!'

'Oh yes, there would. People's ideas of time are usually ludicrously wrong. Just notice some time how swiftly a stage can be reset. In this case it was mostly a matter of props.'

'Good theatre,' murmured Mrs Oliver mechanically.

'Yes, it was pre-eminently a theatrical murder. All very much contrived.'

'And I sat there in the car – and hadn't the least idea!'

'I am afraid,' murmured Poirot, 'that your woman's intuition was taking a day off . . .'

CHAPTER 27

'I'm not going back to Breather & Scuttle,' said Maude Williams. 'They're a lousy firm anyway.'

'And they have served their purpose.'

'What do you mean by that, M. Poirot?'

'Why did you come to this part of the world?'

'I suppose being Mr Knowall, you think you know?'

'I have a little idea.'

'And what is this famous idea.'

Poirot was looking meditatively at Maude's hair.

'I have been very discreet,' he said. 'It has been assumed that the woman who went into Mrs Upward's house, the fair-haired woman that Edna saw, was Mrs Carpenter, and that she has denied being there simply out of fright. Since it was Robin Upward who killed Mrs Upward, her presence has no more significance than that of Miss Henderson. But all the same I do not think she *was* there. I think Miss Williams, that the woman Edna saw was *you*.'

'Why me?'

Her voice was hard.

Poirot countered with another question.

'Why were you so interested in Broadhinny? Why, when you went over there, did you ask Robin Upward for an autograph – you are not the autograph-hunting type. What did you know about the Upwards? Why did you come to this part of the world in the first place? How did you know that Eva Kane died in Australia and the name she took when she left England?'

'Good at guessing, aren't you? Well, I've nothing to hide, not really.'

She opened her handbag. From a worn notecase she pulled out a small newspaper cutting frayed with age. It showed the face that Poirot by now knew so well, the simpering face of Eva Kane.

Written across it were the words, *She killed my mother.*

Poirot handed it back to her.

'Yes, I thought so. Your real name is Craig?'

Maude nodded.

'I was brought up by some cousins – very decent they were. But I was old enough when it all happened not to forget. I used to think about it a good deal. About *her*. She was a nasty bit of goods all right – children know! My father was just – weak. And besotted by her. But he took the rap. For something, I've always believed, that *she* did. Oh yes, I know he's an accessory after the fact – but it's not quite the same thing, is it? I always meant to find out what had become of *her*. When I was grown up, I got detectives on to it. They traced her to Australia and finally reported that she was dead. She'd left a son – Evelyn Hope he called himself.

'Well, that seemed to close the account. But then I got pally with a young actor chap. He mentioned someone called Evelyn Hope who'd come from Australia, but who now called himself Robin Upward and who wrote plays. I was interested. One night Robin Upward was pointed out to me – and he was with his *mother*. So I thought that, after all, Eva Kane *wasn't* dead. Instead, she was queening it about with a packet of money.

'I got myself a job down here. I was curious – and a bit more than curious. All right, I'll admit it, I thought I'd like to get even with her in some way . . . When you brought up all this business about James Bentley, I jumped to the conclusion that it was Mrs Upward who'd killed Mrs McGinty. Eva Kane up to her tricks again. I happened to hear from Michael West that Robin Upward and Mrs Oliver were coming over to this show at the Cullenquay Rep. I decided to go to Broadhinny and beard the woman. I meant – I don't quite know what I meant. I'm telling you everything – I took a little pistol I had in the war with me. To frighten her? Or more? Honestly, I don't know . . .

'Well, I got there. There was no sound in the house. The door was unlocked. I went in. You know how I found her. Sitting there dead, her face all purple and swollen. All the things I'd been thinking seemed silly and melodramatic. I knew that I'd never, really, want to kill anyone when it came to it . . . But I did realize that it might be awkward to explain what I'd been doing in the house. It was a cold night and I'd got gloves on, so I knew I hadn't left any fingerprints, and I didn't think for a moment anyone had seen me. That's all.' She paused and added abruptly: 'What are you going to do about it?'

'Nothing,' said Hercule Poirot. 'I wish you good luck in life, that is all.'

EPILOGUE

Hercule Poirot and Superintendent Spence were celebrating at the *La Vieille Grand'mère*.

As coffee was served Spence leaned back in his chair and gave a deep sigh of repletion.

'Not at all bad grub here,' he said approvingly. 'A bit Frenchified, perhaps, but after all where *can* you get a decent steak and chips nowadays?'

'I had been dining here on the evening you first came to me,' said Poirot reminiscently.

'Ah, a lot of water under the bridge since then. I've got to hand it to you, M. Poirot. You did the trick all right.' A slight smile creased his wooden countenance. 'Lucky that young man didn't realize how very little evidence we'd really got. Why, a clever counsel would have made mincemeat of it! But he lost his head completely, and gave the show away. Spilt the beans and incriminated himself up to the hilt. Lucky for us!'

'It was not entirely luck,' said Poirot reprovingly. 'I played him, as you play the big fish! He thinks I take the evidence against Mrs Summerhayes seriously – when it is not so, he suffers the reaction and goes to pieces. And besides, he is a coward. I whirl the sugar hammer and he thinks I mean to hit him. Acute fear always produces the truth.'

'Lucky you didn't suffer from Major Summerhayes' reaction,' said Spence with a grin. 'Got a temper, he has, *and* quick on his feet. I only got between you just in time. Has he forgiven you yet?'

'Oh yes, we are the firmest friends. And I have given Mrs Summerhayes a cookery book and I have also taught her personally how to make an omelette. *Bon Dieu*, what I suffered in that house!'

He closed his eyes.

'Complicated business, the whole thing,' ruminated Spence, uninterested in Poirot's agonized memories. 'Just shows how true the old saying is that everyone's got something to hide. Mrs Carpenter, now, had a narrow squeak of being arrested for murder. If ever a woman acted guilty, she did, and all for what?'

'*Eh bien*, what?' asked Poirot curiously.

'Just the usual business of a rather unsavoury past. She had been a taxi dancer – and a bright girl with plenty of men friends! She wasn't a war widow when she came and settled down in Broadhinny. Only what they call nowadays an "unofficial wife". Well, of course all that wouldn't do for a stuffed shirt like Guy Carpenter, so she'd spun him a very different sort of tale. And she was frantic lest the whole thing would come out once we started poking round into people's origins.'

He sipped his coffee, and then gave a low chuckle.

'Then take the Wetherbys. Sinister sort of house. Hate and malice. Awkward frustrated sort of girl. And what's behind that? Nothing sinister. Just money! Plain £.s.d.'

'As simple as that!'

'The girl has the money – quite a lot of it. Left her by an aunt. So mother keeps tight hold of her in case she should want to marry. And stepfather loathes her because *she* has the dibs and pays the bills. I gather he himself has been a failure at anything he's tried. A mean cuss – and as for Mrs W., she's pure poison dissolved in sugar.'

'I agree with you.' Poirot nodded his head in a satisfied fashion. 'It is fortunate that the girl has money. It makes her marriage to James Bentley much more easy to arrange.'

Superintendent Spence looked surprised.

'Going to marry James Bentley? Deirdre Henderson? Who says so?'

'I say so,' said Poirot. 'I occupy myself with the affair. I have, now that our little problem is over, too much time on my hands. I shall employ myself in forwarding this marriage. As yet, the two concerned have no idea of such a thing. But they are attracted. Left to themselves, nothing would happen – but they have to reckon with Hercule Poirot. You will see! The affair will march.'

Spence grinned.

'Don't mind sticking your fingers in other people's pies, do you?'

'*Mon cher*, that does not come well from you,' said Poirot reproachfully.

'Well, you've got me there. All the same, James Bentley is a poor stick.'

'Certainly he is a poor stick! At the moment he is positively aggrieved because he is not going to be hanged.'

'He ought to be down on his knees with gratitude to you,' said Spence.

'Say, rather, to you. But apparently he does not think so.'

'Queer cuss.'

'As you say, and yet at least two women have been prepared to take an interest in him. Nature is very unexpected.'

'I thought it was Maude Williams you were going to pair off with him.'

'He shall make his choice,' said Poirot. 'He shall – how do you say it? – award the apple. But I think that it is Deirdre Henderson that he will choose. Maude Williams has too much energy and vitality. With her he would retire even farther into his shell.'

'Can't think why either of them should want him!'

'The ways of nature are indeed inscrutable.'

'All the same, you'll have your work cut out. First bringing him up to the scratch – and then prising the girl loose from poison puss mother – she'll fight you tooth and claw!'

'Success is on the side of the big battalions.'

'On the side of the big moustaches, I suppose you mean.'

Spence roared. Poirot stroked his moustache complacently and suggested a brandy.

'I don't mind if I do, M. Poirot.'

Poirot gave the order.

'Ah,' said Spence, 'I knew there was something else I had to tell you. You remember the Rendells?'

'Naturally.'

'Well, when we were checking up on him, something rather odd came to light. It seems that when his first wife died in Leeds where his practice was at that time, the police there got some rather nasty anonymous letters about him. Saying, in effect, that he'd poisoned her. Of course people do say that sort of thing. She'd been attended by an outside doctor, reputable man, and he seemed to think her death was quite above board. There was nothing to go upon except the fact that they'd mutually insured their lives in each other's favour, and people do do that . . . Nothing for us to go upon, as I say, and yet – I wonder? What do *you* think?'

Poirot remembered Mrs Rendell's frightened air. Her mention of anonymous letters, and her insistence that she did not believe anything they said. He remembered, too, her certainty that his inquiry about Mrs McGinty was only a pretext.

He said, 'I should imagine that it was not only the police who got anonymous letters.'

'Sent them to her, too?'

'I think so. When I appeared in Broadhinny, she thought I was on her husband's track, and that the McGinty business was a pretext. Yes – and he thought so, too . . . That explains it! It was Dr Rendell who tried to push me under the train that night!'

'Think he'll have a shot at doing this wife in, too?'

'I think she would be wise not to insure her life in his favour,' said Poirot drily. 'But if he believes we have an eye on him he will probably be prudent.'

'We'll do what we can. We'll keep an eye on our genial doctor, and make it clear we're doing so.'

Poirot raised his brandy glass.

'To Mrs Oliver,' he said.

'What put her into your head suddenly?'

'Woman's intuition,' said Poirot.

There was silence for a moment, then Spence said slowly: 'Robin Upward is coming up for trial next week. You know, Poirot, I can't help feeling doubtful –'

Poirot interrupted him with horror.

'*Mon Dieu!* You are not now doubtful about Robin Upward's guilt, are you? Do not say you want to start over again.'

Superintendent Spence grinned reassuringly.

'Good Lord, no. *He's* a murderer all right!' He added: 'Cocky enough for anything!'

THE CASE OF THE RICH WOMAN

I

The name of Mrs Abner Rymer was brought to Mr Parker Pyne. He knew the name and he raised his eyebrows.

Presently his client was shown into the room.

Mrs Rymer was a tall woman, big-boned. Her figure was ungainly and the velvet dress and the heavy fur coat she wore did not disguise the fact. The knuckles of her large hands were pronounced. Her face was big and broad and highly coloured. Her black hair was fashionably dressed, and there were many tips of curled ostrich in her hat.

She plumped herself down on a chair with a nod. 'Good-morning,' she said. Her voice had a rough accent. 'If you're any good at all you'll tell me how to spend my money!'

'Most original,' murmured Mr Parker Pyne. 'Few ask me that in these days. So you really find it difficult, Mrs Rymer?'

'Yes, I do,' said the lady bluntly. 'I've got three fur coats, a lot of Paris dresses and such like. I've got a car and a house in Park Lane. I've had a yacht but I don't like the sea. I've got a lot of those high-class servants that look down their nose at you. I've travelled a bit and seen foreign parts. And I'm blessed if I can think of anything more to buy or do.' She looked hopefully at Mr Pyne.

'There are hospitals,' he said.

'What? Give it away, you mean? No, that I won't do! That money was worked for, let me tell you, worked for hard. If you think I'm going to hand it out like so much dirt – well, you're mistaken. I want to spend it; spend it and get some good out of it. Now, if you've got any ideas that are worthwhile in that line, you can depend on a good fee.'

'Your proposition interests me,' said Mr Pyne. 'You do not mention a country house.'

'I forgot it, but I've got one. Bores me to death.'

'You must tell me more about yourself. Your problem is not easy to solve.'

'I'll tell you and willing. I'm not ashamed of what I've come from. Worked in a farmhouse, I did, when I was a girl. Hard work it was too. Then I took up with Abner – he was a workman in the mills near by. He courted me for eight years, and then we got married.'

'And you were happy?' asked Mr Pyne.

'I was. He was a good man to me, Abner. We had a hard struggle of it, though; he was out of a job twice, and children coming along. Four we had, three boys and a girl. And none of them lived to grow up. I dare say it would have been different if they had.' Her face softened; looked suddenly younger.

'His chest was weak – Abner's was. They wouldn't take him for the war. He did well at home. He was made foreman. He was a clever fellow, Abner. He worked out a process. They treated him fair, I will say; gave him a good sum for it. He used that money for another idea of his. That brought in money hand over fist. It's still coming in.

'Mind you, it was rare fun at first. Having a house and a tip-top bathroom and servants of one's own. No more cooking and scrubbing and washing to do. Just sit back on your silk cushions in the drawing-room and ring the bell for tea – like any countess might! Grand fun it was, and we enjoyed it. And then we came up to London. I went to swell dressmakers for my clothes. We went to Paris and the Riviera. Rare fun it was.'

'And then,' said Mr Parker Pyne.

'We got used to it, I suppose,' said Mrs Rymer. 'After a bit it didn't seem so much fun. Why, there were days when we didn't even fancy our meals properly – us, with any dish we fancied to choose from! As for baths – well, in the end, one bath a day's enough for anyone. And Abner's health began to worry him. Paid good money to doctors, we did, but they couldn't do anything. They tried this and they tried that. But it was no use. He died.' She paused. 'He was a young man, only forty-three.'

Mr Pyne nodded sympathetically.

'That was five years ago. Money's still rolling in. It seems wasteful not to be able to do anything with it. But as I tell you, I can't think of anything else to buy that I haven't got already.'

'In other words,' said Mr Pyne, 'your life is dull. You are not enjoying it.'

'I'm sick of it,' said Mrs Rymer gloomily. 'I've no friends. The new lot only want subscriptions, and they laugh at me behind my back. The old lot won't have anything to do with me. My rolling up in a car makes them shy. Can you do anything or suggest anything?'

'It is possible that I can,' said Mr Pyne slowly. 'It will be difficult, but I believe there is a chance of success. I think it's possible I can give you back what you have lost – your interest in life.'

'How?' demanded Mrs Rymer curtly.

'That,' said Mr Parker Pyne, 'is my professional secret. I never disclose my methods beforehand. The question is, will you take a chance? I do not guarantee success, but I do think there is a reasonable possibility of it.

'I shall have to adopt unusual methods, and therefore it will be expensive. My charges will be one thousand pounds, payable in advance.'

'You can open your mouth all right, can't you?' said Mrs Rymer appreciatively. 'Well, I'll risk it. I'm used to paying top price. Only, when I pay for a thing, I take good care that I get it.'

'You shall get it,' said Mr Parker Pyne. 'Never fear.'

'I'll send you the cheque this evening,' said Mrs Rymer, rising. 'I'm sure I don't know why I should trust you. Fools and their money are soon parted, they say. I dare say I'm a fool. You've got nerve, to advertise in all the papers that you can make people happy!'

'Those advertisements cost me money,' said Mr Pyne. 'If I could not make my words good, that money would be wasted. I *know* what causes unhappiness, and consequently I have a clear idea of how to produce an opposite condition.'

Mrs Rymer shook her head doubtfully and departed, leaving a cloud of expensive mixed essences behind her.

The handsome Claude Luttrell strolled into the office. 'Something in my line?'

Mr Pyne shook his head. 'Nothing so simple,' he said. 'No, this is a difficult case. We must, I fear, take a few risks. We must attempt the unusual.'

'Mrs Oliver?'

Mr Pyne smiled at the mention of the world-famous novelist. 'Mrs Oliver,' he said, 'is really the most conventional of all of us. I have in mind a bold and audacious coup. By the way, you might ring up Dr Antrobus.'

'Antrobus?'

'Yes. His services will be needed.'

II

A week later Mrs Rymer once more entered Mr Parker Pyne's office. He rose to receive her.

'This delay, I assure you, has been necessary,' he said. 'Many things had to be arranged, and I had to secure the services of an unusual man who had to come half-across Europe.'

'Oh!' She said it suspiciously. It was constantly present in her mind that she had paid out a cheque for a thousand pounds and the cheque had been cashed.

Mr Parker Pyne touched a buzzer. A young girl, dark, Oriental looking, but dressed in white nurse's kit, answered it.

'Is everything ready, Nurse de Sara?'

'Yes. Doctor Constantine is waiting.'

'What are you going to do?' asked Mrs Rymer with a touch of uneasiness.

'Introduce you to some Eastern magic, dear lady,' said Mr Parker Pyne.

'Mrs Rymer followed the nurse up to the next floor. Here she was ushered into a room that bore no relation to the rest of the house. Oriental embroideries covered the walls. There were divans with soft cushions and beautiful rugs on the floor. A man was bending over a coffee-pot. He straightened as they entered.

'Doctor Constantine,' said the nurse.

The doctor was dressed in European clothes, but his face was swarthy and his eyes were dark and oblique with a peculiarly piercing power in their glance.

'So this is my patient?' he said in a low, vibrant voice.

'I'm not a patient,' said Mrs Rymer.

'Your body is not sick,' said the doctor, 'but your soul is weary. We of the East know how to cure that disease. Sit down and drink a cup of coffee.'

Mrs Rymer sat down and accepted a tiny cup of the fragrant brew. As she sipped it the doctor talked.

'Here in the West, they treat only the body. A mistake. The body is only the instrument. A tune is played upon it. It may be a sad, weary tune. It may be a gay tune full of delight. The last is what we shall give you. You have money. You shall spend it and enjoy. Life shall be worth living again. It is easy – easy – so easy . . .'

A feeling of languor crept over Mrs Rymer. The figures of the doctor and the nurse grew hazy. She felt blissfully happy and very sleepy. The doctor's figure grew bigger. The whole world was growing bigger.

The doctor was looking into her eyes. 'Sleep,' he was saying. 'Sleep. Your eyelids are closing. Soon you will sleep. You will sleep. You will sleep . . .'

Mrs Rymer's eyelids closed. She floated with a wonderful great big world . . .

III

When her eyes opened it seemed to her that a long time had passed. She remembered several things vaguely – strange, impossible dreams; then a feeling of waking; then further dreams. She remembered something about a car and the dark, beautiful girl in a nurse's uniform bending over her.

Anyway, she was properly awake now, and in her own bed.

At least, was it her own bed? It felt different. It lacked the delicious softness of her own bed. It was vaguely reminiscent of days almost forgotten. She moved, and it creaked. Mrs Rymer's bed in Park Lane never creaked.

She looked round. Decidedly, this was not Park Lane. Was it a hospital? No, she decided, not a hospital. Nor was it a hotel. It was a bare room, the walls an uncertain shade of lilac. There was a deal wash-stand with a jug and basin upon it. There was a deal chest of drawers and a tin trunk. There were unfamiliar clothes hanging on pegs. There was the bed covered with a much-mended quilt and there was herself in it.

'Where *am* I?' said Mrs Rymer.

The door opened and a plump little woman bustled in. She had red cheeks and a good-humoured air. Her sleeves were rolled up and she wore an apron.

'There!' she exclaimed. 'She's awake. Come in, doctor.'

Mrs Rymer opened her mouth to say several things – but they remained unsaid, for the man who followed the plump woman into the room was not in the least like the elegant, swarthy Doctor Constantine. He was a bent old man who peered through thick glasses.

'That's better,' he said, advancing to the bed and taking up Mrs Rymer's wrist. 'You'll soon be better now, my dear.'

'What's been the matter with me?' demanded Mrs Rymer.

'You had a kind of seizure,' said the doctor. 'You've been unconscious for a day or two. Nothing to worry about.'

'Gave us a fright you did, Hannah,' said the plump woman. 'You've been raving too, saying the oddest things.'

'Yes, yes, Mrs Gardner,' said the doctor repressively. 'But we musn't excite the patient. You'll soon be up and about again, my dear.'

'But don't you worry about the work, Hannah.' said Mrs Gardner. 'Mrs Roberts has been in to give me a hand and we've got on fine. Just lie still and get well, my dear.'

'Why do you call me Hannah?' said Mrs Rymer.

'Well, it's your name,' said Mrs Gardner, bewildered.

'No, it isn't. My name is Amelia. Amelia Rymer. Mrs Abner Rymer.'

The doctor and Mrs Gardner exchanged glances.

'Well, just you lie still,' said Mrs Gardner.

'Yes, yes; no worry,' said the doctor.

They withdrew. Mrs Rymer lay puzzling. Why did they call her Hannah, and why had they exchanged that glance of amused incredulity when she had given them her name? Where was she and what had happened?

She slipped out of bed. She felt a little uncertain on her legs, but she walked slowly to the small dormer window and looked out – on a farmyard! Completely mystified, she went back to bed. What was she doing in a farmhouse that she had never seen before?

Mrs Gardner re-entered·the room with a bowl of soup on a tray.

Mrs Rymer began her questions. 'What am I doing in this house?' she demanded. 'Who brought me here?'

'Nobody brought you, my dear. It's your home. Leastways, you've lived here for the last five years – and me not suspecting once that you were liable to fits.'

'*Lived* here! *Five* years?'

'That's right. Why, Hannah, you don't mean that you still don't remember?'

'I've never lived here! I've never seen you before.'

'You see, you've had this illness and you've forgotten.'

'I've never lived here.'

'But you have, my dear.' Suddenly Mrs Gardner darted across to the chest of drawers and brought to Mrs Rymer a faded photograph in a frame.

It represented a group of four persons: a bearded man, a plump woman (Mrs Gardner), a tall, lank man with a pleasantly sheepish grin, and somebody in a print dress and apron – herself!

Stupefied, Mrs Rymer gazed at the photograph. Mrs Gardner put the soup down beside her and quietly left the room.

Mrs Rymer sipped the soup mechanically. It was good soup, strong and hot. All the time her brain was in a whirl. Who was mad? Mrs Gardner or herself? One of them must be! But there was the doctor too.

'I'm Amelia Rymer,' she said firmly to herself. 'I know I'm Amelia Rymer and nobody's going to tell me different.'

She had finished the soup. She put the bowl back on the tray. A folded newspaper caught her eye and she picked it up and looked at the date on it, October 19. What day had she gone to Mr Parker Pyne's office? Either the fifteenth or the sixteenth. Then she must have been ill for three days.

'That rascally doctor!' said Mrs Rymer wrathfully.

All the same, she was a shade relieved. She had heard of cases where people had forgotten who they were for years at a time. She had been afraid some such thing had happened to her.

She began turning the pages of the paper, scanning the columns idly, when suddenly a paragraph caught her eye.

Mrs Abner Rymer, widow of Abner Rymer, the 'button shank' king, was removed yesterday to a private home for mental cases. For the past two days she has persisted in declaring she was not herself, but a servant girl named Hannah Moorhouse.

'Hannah Moorhouse! So that's it,' said Mrs Rymer. 'She's me and I'm her. Kind of double, I suppose. Well, we can soon put *that* right! If that oily hypocrite of a Parker Pyne is up to some game or other –'

But at this minute her eye was caught by the name Constantine staring at her from the printed page. This time it was a headline.

DR CONSTANTINE'S CLAIM

At a farewell lecture given last night on the eve of his departure for Japan, Dr Claudius Constantine advanced some startling theories. He declared that it was possible to prove the existence of the soul by transferring a soul from one body to another. In the course of his experiments in the East he had, he claimed, successfully effected a double transfer – the soul of a hypnotized body A being transferred to a hypnotized body B and the soul of body B to the soul of body A. On recovering from the hypnotic sleep, A declared herself to be B, and B thought herself to be A. For the experiment to succeed, it was necessary to find two people with a great bodily resemblance. It was an undoubted fact that two people resembling each other were en rapport. *This was very noticeable in the case of twins, but two strangers, varying widely in social position, but with a marked similarity of feature, were found to exhibit the same harmony of structure.*

Mrs Rymer cast the paper from her. 'The scoundrel! The black scoundrel!'

She saw the whole thing now! It was a dastardly plot to get hold of her money. This Hannah Moorhouse was Mr Pyne's tool – possibly an innocent one. He and that devil Constantine had brought off this fantastic coup.

But she'd expose him! She'd show him up! She'd have the law on him! She'd tell everyone –

Abruptly Mrs Rymer came to a stop in the tide of her indignation. She remembered the first paragraph. Hannah Moorhouse had not been a docile tool. She had protested; had declared her individuality. And what had happened?

'Clapped into a lunatic asylum, poor girl,' said Mrs Rymer.

A chill ran down her spine.

A lunatic asylum. They got you in there and they never let you get out. The more you said you were sane, the less they'd believe you. There you were and there you stayed. No, Mrs Rymer wasn't going to run the risk of that.

The door opened and Mrs Gardner came in.

'Ah, you've drunk your soup, my dear. That's good. You'll soon be better now.'

'When was I taken ill?' demanded Mrs Rymer.

'Let me see. It was three days ago – on Wednesday. That was the fifteenth. You were took bad about four o'clock.'

'Ah!' The ejaculation was fraught with meaning. It had been just about four o'clock when Mrs Rymer had entered the presence of Doctor Constantine.

'You slipped down in your chair,' said Mrs Gardner. "Oh!" you says. "Oh!" just like that. And then: "I'm falling asleep," you says in a dreamy voice. "I'm falling asleep." And fall asleep you did, and we put you to bed and sent for the doctor, and here you've been ever since.'

'I suppose,' Mrs Rymer ventured, 'there isn't any way you could know who I am – apart from my face, I mean.'

'Well, that's a queer thing to say,' said Mrs Gardner. 'What is there to go by better than a person's face, I'd like to know? There's your birthmark, though, if that satisfies you better.'

'A birthmark?' said Mrs Rymer, brightening. She had no such thing.

'Strawberry mark just under the right elbow,' said Mrs Gardner. 'Look for yourself, my dear.'

'This will prove it,' said Mrs Rymer to herself. She knew that she had no strawberry mark under the right elbow. She turned back the sleeve of her nightdress. The strawberry mark was there.

Mrs Rymer burst into tears.

IV

Four days later Mrs Rymer rose from her bed. She had thought out several plans of action and rejected them.

She might show the paragraph in the paper to Mrs Gardner and explain. Would they believe her? Mrs Rymer was sure they would not.

She might go to the police. Would they believe her? Again she thought not.

She might go to Mr Pyne's office. That idea undoubtedly pleased her best. For one thing, she would like to tell that oily scoundrel what she thought of him. She was debarred from putting this plan into operation by a vital obstacle. She was at present in Cornwall (so she had learned), and she had no money for the journey to London. Two and fourpence in a worn purse seemed to represent her financial position.

And so, after four days, Mrs Rymer made a sporting decision. For the present she would accept things! She was Hannah Moorhouse. Very well, she would be Hannah Moorhouse. For the present she would accept that role, and later, when she had saved sufficient money, she would go to London and beard the swindler in his den.

And having thus decided, Mrs Rymer accepted her role with perfect good temper, even with a kind of sardonic amusement. History was repeating itself indeed. This life reminded her of her girlhood. How long ago that seemed!

V

The work was a bit hard after her years of soft living, but after the first week she found herself slipping into the ways of the farm.

Mrs Gardner was a good-tempered, kindly woman. Her husband, a big, taciturn man, was kindly also. The lank, shambling man of the photograph had gone; another farmhand came in his stead, a good-humoured giant of forty-five, slow of speech and thought, but with a shy twinkle in his blue eyes.

The weeks went by. At last the day came when Mrs Rymer had enough money to pay her fare to London. But she did not go. She put it off. Time enough, she thought. She wasn't easy in her mind about asylums yet. That scoundrel, Parker Pyne, was clever. He'd get a doctor to say she was mad and she'd be clapped away out of sight with no one knowing anything about it.

'Besides,' said Mrs Rymer to herself, 'a bit of a change does one good.'

She rose early and worked hard. Joe Welsh, the new farmhand, was ill that winter, and she and Mrs Gardner nursed him. The big man was pathetically dependent on them.

Spring came – lambing time; there were wild flowers in the hedges, a treacherous softness in the air. Joe Welsh gave Hannah a hand with her work. Hannah did Joe's mending.

Sometimes, on Sundays, they went for a walk together. Joe was a widower. His wife had died four years before. Since her death he had, he frankly confessed it, taken a drop too much.

He didn't go much to the Crown nowadays. He bought himself some new clothes. Mr and Mrs Gardner laughed.

Hannah made fun of Joe. She teased him about his clumsiness. Joe didn't mind. He looked bashful but happy.

After spring came summer – a good summer that year. Everyone worked hard.

Harvest was over. The leaves were red and golden on the trees.

It was October eighth when Hannah looked up one day from a cabbage she was cutting and saw Mr Parker Pyne leaning over the fence.

'You!' said Hannah, alias Mrs Rymer. 'You . . .'

It was some time before she got it all out, and when she had said her say, she was out of breath.

Mr Parker Pyne smiled blandly. 'I quite agree with you,' he said.

'A cheat and a liar, that's what you are!' said Mrs Rymer, repeating herself. 'You with your Constantines and your hypnotizing, and that poor girl Hannah Moorhouse shut up with – loonies.'

'No,' said Mr Parker Pyne, 'there you misjudge me. Hannah Moorhouse is not in a lunatic asylum, because Hannah Moorhouse never existed.'

'Indeed?' said Mrs Rymer. 'And what about the photograph of her that I saw with my own eyes?'

'Faked,' said Mr Pyne. 'Quite a simple thing to manage.'

'And the piece in the paper about her?'

'The whole paper was faked so as to include two items in a natural manner which would carry conviction. As it did.'

'That rogue, Doctor Constantine!'

'An assumed name – assumed by a friend of mine with a talent for acting.'

Mrs Rymer snorted. 'Ho! And I wasn't hypnotized either, I suppose?'

'As a matter of fact, you were not. You drank in your coffee a preparation of Indian hemp. After that, other drugs were administered and you were brought down here by car and allowed to recover consciousness.'

'Then Mrs Gardner has been in it all the time?' said Mrs Rymer.

Mr Parker Pyne nodded.

'Bribed by you, I suppose! Or filled up with a lot of lies!'

'Mrs Gardner trusts me,' said Mr Pyne. 'I once saved her only son from penal servitude.'

Something in his manner silenced Mrs Rymer on that tack. 'What about the birthmark!' she demanded.

Mr Pyne smiled. 'It is already fading. In another six months it will have disappeared altogether.'

'And what's the meaning of all this tomfoolery? Making a fool of me, sticking me down here as a servant – me with all that good money in the bank. But I suppose I needn't ask. You've been helping yourself to it, my fine fellow. That's the meaning of all this.'

'It is true,' said Mr Parker Pyne, 'that I did obtain from you, while you were under the influence of drugs, a power of attorney and that during your – er – absence, I have assumed control of your financial affairs, but I can assure you, my dear madam, that apart from that original thousand pounds, no money of yours has found its way into my pocket. As a matter of fact, by judicious investments your financial position is actually improved.' He beamed at her.

'Then why –?' began Mrs Rymer.

'I am going to ask you a question, Mrs Rymer,' said Mr Parker Pyne. 'You are an honest woman. You will answer me honestly, I know. I am going to ask you if you are happy.'

'Happy! That's a pretty question! Steal a woman's money and ask her if she's happy. I like your impudence!'

'You are still angry,' he said. 'Most natural. But leave my misdeeds out of it for the moment. Mrs Rymer, when you came to my office a year ago today, you were an unhappy woman. Will you tell me that you are unhappy now? If so, I apologize, and you are at liberty to take what steps you please against me. Moreover, I will refund the thousand pounds you paid me. Come, Mrs Rymer, are you an unhappy woman now?'

Mrs Rymer looked at Mr Parker Pyne, but she dropped her eyes when she spoke at last.

'No,' she said. 'I'm not unhappy.' A tone of wonder crept into her voice. 'You've got me there. I admit it. I've not been as happy as I am now since Abner died. I – I'm going to marry a man who works here – Joe Welsh. Our banns are going up next Sunday; that is, they *were* going up next Sunday.'

'But now, of course, everything is different.'

Mrs Rymer's face flamed. She took a step forward.

'What do you mean, different? Do you think that if I had all the money in the world it would make me a lady? I don't want to be a lady, thank you; a helpless good-for-nothing lot they are. Joe's good enough for me and I'm good enough for him. We suit each other and we're going to be happy. As you for, Mr Nosey Parker, you take yourself off and don't interfere with what doesn't concern you!'

Mr Parker Pyne took a paper from his pocket and handed it to her. 'The power of attorney,' he said. 'Shall I tear it up? You will assume control of your own fortune now, I take it.'

A strange expression came over Mrs Rymer's face. She thrust back the paper.

'Take it. I've said hard things to you – and some of them you deserved. You're a downy fellow, but all the same I trust you. Seven hundred pounds I'll have in the bank here – that'll buy us a farm we've got our eye on. The rest of it – well, let the hospitals have it.'

'You cannot mean to hand over your entire fortune to hospitals?'

'That's just what I do mean. Joe's a dear, good fellow, but he's weak. Give him money and you'd ruin him. I've got him off the drink now, and I'll keep him off it. Thank God, I know my own mind. I'm not going to let money come between me and happiness.'

'You are a remarkable woman,' said Mr Pyne slowly. 'Only one woman in a thousand would act as you are doing.'

'Then only one woman in a thousand's got sense,' said Mrs Rymer.

'I take my hat off to you,' said Mr Parker Pyne, and there was an unusual note in his voice. He raised his hat with solemnity and moved away.

'And Joe's never to know, mind!' Mrs Rymer called after him.

She stood there with the dying sun behind her, a great blue-green cabbage in her hands, her head thrown back and her shoulders squared. A grand figure of a peasant woman, outlined against the setting sun . . .

DEAD MAN'S FOLLY

To Peggy and Humphrey Trevelyan

I

It was Miss Lemon, Poirot's efficient secretary, who took the telephone call.

Laying aside her shorthand notebook, she raised the receiver and said without emphasis, 'Trafalgar 8137.'

Hercule Poirot leaned back in his upright chair and closed his eyes. His fingers beat a meditative soft tattoo on the edge of the table. In his head he continued to compose the polished periods of the letter he had been dictating.

Placing her hand over the receiver, Miss Lemon asked in a low voice:

'Will you accept a personal call from Nassecombe, Devon?'

Poirot frowned. The place meant nothing to him.

'The name of the caller?' he demanded cautiously.

Miss Lemon spoke into the mouthpiece.

'*Air-raid?*' she asked doubtingly. 'Oh, yes – what was the last name again?'

Once more she turned to Hercule Poirot.

'Mrs Ariadne Oliver.'

Hercule Poirot's eyebrows shot up. A memory rose in his mind: windswept grey hair . . . an eagle profile . . .

He rose and replaced Miss Lemon at the telephone.

'Hercule Poirot speaks,' he announced grandiloquently.

'Is that Mr Hercules Porrot speaking personally?' the suspicious voice of the telephone operator demanded.

Poirot assured her that that was the case.

'You're through to Mr Porrot,' said the voice.

Its thin reedy accents were replaced by a magnificent booming contralto which caused Poirot hastily to shift the receiver a couple of inches farther from his ear.

'M. Poirot, is that really *you*?' demanded Mrs Oliver.

'Myself in person, Madame.'

'This is Mrs Oliver. I don't know if you'll remember me –'

'But of course I remember you, Madame. Who could forget you?'

'Well, people do sometimes,' said Mrs Oliver. 'Quite often, in fact. I don't think that I've got a very distinctive personality. Or perhaps it's because I'm always doing different things to my hair. But all that's neither here nor there. I hope I'm not interrupting you when you're frightfully busy?'

'No, no, you do not derange me in the least.'

'Good gracious – I'm sure I don't want to drive you out of your mind. The fact is, I *need* you.'

'Need me?'

'Yes, at once. Can you take an aeroplane?'

'I do not take aeroplanes. They make me sick.'

'They do me, too. Anyway, I don't suppose it would be any quicker than the train really, because I think the only airport near here is Exeter which is miles away. So come by train. Twelve o'clock from Paddington to Nassecombe. You can do it nicely. You've got three-quarters of an hour if my watch is right – though it isn't usually.'

'But where are you, Madame? What is all this *about*?'

'Nasse House, Nassecombe. A car or taxi will meet you at the station at Nassecombe.'

'But why do you need me? What is all this *about*?' Poirot repeated frantically.

'Telephones are in such awkward places,' said Mrs Oliver. 'This one's in the hall . . . People passing through and talking . . . I can't really hear. But I'm expecting you. Everybody will be *so* thrilled. Goodbye.'

There was a sharp click as the receiver was replaced. The line hummed gently.

With a baffled air of bewilderment, Poirot put back the receiver and murmured something under his breath. Miss Lemon sat with her pencil poised, incurious. She repeated in muted tones the final phrase of dictation before the interruption.

'– allow me to assure you, my dear sir, that the hypothesis you have advanced . . .'

Poirot waved aside the advancement of the hypothesis.

'That was Mrs Oliver,' he said. 'Ariadne Oliver, the detective novelist. You may have read . . .' But he stopped, remembering that Miss Lemon only read improving books and regarded such frivolities as fictional crime with contempt. 'She wants me to go down to Devonshire today, at once, in' – he glanced at the clock – 'thirty-five minutes.'

Miss Lemon raised disapproving eyebrows.

'That will be running it rather fine,' she said. 'For what reason?'

'You may well ask! She did not tell me.'

'How very peculiar. Why not?'

'Because,' said Hercule Poirot thoughtfully, 'she was afraid of being overheard. Yes, she made that quite clear.'

'Well, really,' said Miss Lemon, bristling in her employer's defence. 'The things people expect! Fancy thinking that you'd go rushing off on some wild goose chase like that! An important man like you! I have always noticed that these artists and writers are very unbalanced – no sense of proportion. Shall I telephone through a telegram: *Regret unable leave London*?'

Her hand went out to the telephone. Poirot's voice arrested the gesture.

'*Du tout!*' he said. 'On the contrary. Be so kind as to summon a taxi immediately.' He raised his voice. 'Georges! A few necessities of toilet in my small valise. And quickly, very quickly, I have a train to catch.'

II

The train, having done one hundred and eighty-odd miles of its two hundred and twelve miles journey at top speed, puffed gently and apologetically through the last thirty and drew into Nassecombe station. Only one person alighted, Hercule Poirot. He negotiated with care a yawning gap between the step of the train and the platform and looked round him. At the far end of the train a porter was busy inside a luggage compartment. Poirot picked up his valise and walked back along the platform to the exit. He gave up his ticket and walked out through the booking-office.

A large Humber saloon was drawn up outside and a chauffeur in uniform came forward.

'Mr Hercule Poirot?' he inquired respectfully.

He took Poirot's case from him and opened the door of the car. They drove away from the station over the railway bridge and turned down a country lane which wound between high hedges on either side. Presently the ground fell away on the right and disclosed a very beautiful river view with hills of a misty blue in the distance. The chauffeur drew into the hedge and stopped.

'The River Helm, sir,' he said. 'With Dartmoor in the distance.'

It was clear that admiration was necessary. Poirot made the necessary noises, murmuring *Magnifique!* several times. Actually, Nature appealed to him very little. A well-cultivated neatly arranged kitchen garden was far more likely to bring a murmur of admiration to Poirot's lips. Two girls passed the car, toiling slowly up the hill. They were carrying heavy rucksacks on their backs and wore shorts, with bright coloured scarves tied over their heads.

'There is a Youth Hostel next door to us, sir,' explained the chauffeur, who had clearly constituted himself Poirot's guide to Devon. 'Hoodown Park. Mr Fletcher's place it used to be. The Youth Hostel Association bought it and it's fairly crammed in summer time. Take in over a hundred a night, they do. They're not allowed to stay longer than a couple of nights – then they've got to move on. Both sexes and mostly foreigners.'

Poirot nodded absently. He was reflecting, not for the first time, that seen from the back, shorts were becoming to very few of the female sex. He shut his eyes in pain. Why, oh why, must young women array themselves thus? Those scarlet thighs were singularly unattractive!

'They seem heavily laden,' he murmured.

'Yes, sir, and it's a long pull from the station or the bus stop. Best part of two miles to Hoodown Park.' He hesitated. 'If you don't object, sir, we could give them a lift?'

'By all means, by all means,' said Poirot benignantly. There was he in luxury in an almost empty car and here were these two panting and perspiring young women weighed down with heavy rucksacks and without the least idea how to dress themselves so as to appear attractive to the other sex. The chauffeur started the car and came to a slow purring halt beside the two girls. Their flushed and perspiring faces were raised hopefully.

Poirot opened the door and the girls climbed in.

'It is most kind, please,' said one of them, a fair girl with a foreign accent. 'It is longer way than I think, yes.'

The other girl, who had a sunburnt and deeply flushed face with bronzed chestnut curls peeping out beneath her headscarf, merely nodded her head several times, flashed her teeth, and murmured, *Grazie*. The fair girl continued to talk vivaciously.

'I to England come for two week holiday. I come from Holland. I like England very much. I have been Stratford Avon, Shakespeare Theatre and Warwick Castle. Then I have been Clovelly, now I have seen Exeter Cathedral and Torquay – very nice – I come to famous beauty spot here and tomorrow I cross river, go to Plymouth where discovery of New World was made from Plymouth Hoe.'

'And you, signorina?' Poirot turned to the other girl. But she only smiled and shook her curls.

'She does not much English speak,' said the Dutch girl kindly. 'We both a little French speak – so we talk in train. She is coming from near Milan and has relative in England married to gentleman who keeps shop for much groceries. She has come with friend to Exeter yesterday, but friend has eat veal ham pie not good from shop in Exeter and has to stay there sick. It is not good in hot weather, the veal ham pie.'

At this point the chauffeur slowed down where the road forked. The girls got out, uttered thanks in two languages and proceeded up the left-hand road. The chauffeur laid aside for a moment his Olympian aloofness and said feelingly to Poirot:

'It's not only veal and ham pie – you want to be careful of Cornish pasties too. Put *anything* in a pasty they will, holiday time!'

He restarted the car and drove down the right-hand road which shortly afterwards passed into thick woods. He proceeded to give a final verdict on the occupants of Hoodown Park Youth Hostel.

'Nice enough young women, some of 'em, at that hostel,' he said; 'but it's hard to get them to understand about trespassing. Absolutely shocking the way they trespass. Don't seem to understand that a gentleman's place is *private* here. Always coming through our woods, they are, and pretending that they don't understand what you say to them.' He shook his head darkly.

They went on, down a steep hill through woods, then through big iron gates, and along a drive, winding up finally in front of a big white Georgian house looking out over the river.

The chauffeur opened the door of the car as a tall black-haired butler appeared on the steps.

'Mr Hercule Poirot?' murmured the latter.

'Yes.'

'Mrs Oliver is expecting you, sir. You will find her down at the Battery. Allow me to show you the way.'

Poirot was directed to a winding path that led along the wood with glimpses of the river below. The path descended gradually until it came out at last on an open space, round in shape, with a low battlemented parapet. On the parapet Mrs Oliver was sitting.

She rose to meet him and several apples fell from her lap and rolled in all directions. Apples seemed to be an inescapable *motif* of meeting Mrs Oliver.

'I can't think why I always drop things,' said Mrs Oliver somewhat indistinctly, since her mouth was full of apple. 'How are you, M. Poirot?'

'*Très bien, chère Madame,*' replied Poirot politely. 'And you?'

Mrs Oliver was looking somewhat different from when Poirot had last seen her, and the reason lay, as she had already hinted over the telephone, in the fact that she had once more experimented with her *coiffure*. The last time Poirot had seen her, she had been adopting a windswept effect. Today, her hair, richly blued, was piled upward in a multiplicity of rather artificial little curls in a pseudo Marquise style. The Marquise effect ended at her neck; the rest of her could have been definitely labelled 'country practical,' consisting of a violent yolk-of-egg rough tweed coat and skirt and a rather bilious-looking mustard-coloured jumper.

'I knew you'd come,' said Mrs Oliver cheerfully.

'You could not possibly have known,' said Poirot severely.

'Oh, yes, I did.'

'I still ask myself *why* I am here.'

'Well, I know the answer. Curiosity.'

Poirot looked at her and his eyes twinkled a little. 'Your famous woman's intuition,' he said, 'has, perhaps, for once not led you too far astray.'

'Now, don't laugh at my woman's intuition. Haven't I always spotted the murderer right away?'

Poirot was gallantly silent. Otherwise he might have replied, 'At the fifth attempt, perhaps, and not always then!'

Instead he said, looking round him:

'It is indeed a beautiful property that you have here.'

'This? But it doesn't belong to *me*, M. Poirot. Did you think it did? Oh, no, it belongs to some people called Stubbs.'

'Who are they?'

'Oh, nobody really,' said Mrs Oliver vaguely. 'Just rich. No, I'm down here professionally, doing a job.'

'Ah, you are getting local colour for one of your *chefs-d'oeuvre*?'

'No, no. Just what I said. I'm doing a *job*. I've been engaged to arrange a murder.'

Poirot stared at her.

'Oh, not a real one,' said Mrs Oliver reassuringly. 'There's a big fête thing on tomorrow, and as a kind of novelty there's going to be a Murder Hunt. Arranged by me. Like a Treasure Hunt, you see; only they've had a Treasure Hunt so often that they thought this would be a novelty. So they offered me a very substantial fee to come down and think it up. Quite fun, really – rather a change from the usual grim routine.'

'How does it work?'

'Well, there'll be a Victim, of course. And Clues. And Suspects. All rather conventional – you know, the Vamp and the Blackmailer and the Young Lovers and the Sinister Butler and so on. Half a crown to enter and you get shown the first Clue and you've got to find the Victim, and the Weapon and say Whodunnit and the Motive. And there are Prizes.'

'Remarkable!' said Hercule Poirot.

'Actually,' said Mrs Oliver ruefully, 'it's all much harder to arrange than you'd think. Because you've got to allow for real people being quite intelligent, and in my books they needn't be.'

'And it is to assist you in arranging this that you have sent for me?'

Poirot did not try very hard to keep an outraged resentment out of his voice.

'Oh, *no*,' said Mrs Oliver. 'Of course not! I've done all that. Everything's all set for tomorrow. No, I wanted you for quite another reason.'

'What reason?'

Mrs Oliver's hands strayed upward to her head. She was just about to sweep them frenziedly through her hair in the old familiar gesture when she remembered the intricacy of her hair-do. Instead, she relieved her feelings by tugging at her ear lobes.

'I dare say I'm a fool,' she said. 'But I think there's something wrong.'

CHAPTER 2

There was a moment's silence as Poirot stared at her. Then he asked sharply: 'Something *wrong*? How?'

'I don't know . . . That's what I want *you* to find out. But I've felt – more and more – that I was being – oh! – *engineered* . . . jockeyed along . . . Call me a fool if you like, but I can only say that if there was to be a *real* murder tomorrow instead of a fake one, I shouldn't be surprised!'

Poirot stared at her and she looked back at him defiantly.

'Very interesting,' said Poirot.

'I suppose you think I'm a complete fool,' said Mrs Oliver defensively.

'I have never thought you a fool,' said Poirot.

'And I know what you always say – or look – about intuition.'

'One calls things by different names,' said Poirot. 'I am quite ready to believe that you have noticed something, or heard something, that has definitely aroused in you anxiety. I think it is possible that you yourself may not even know just what it is that you have seen or noticed or heard. You are aware only of the *result*. If I may so put it, you do not know what it is that you know. You may label that intuition if you like.'

'It makes one feel such a fool,' said Mrs Oliver, ruefully, 'not to be able to be *definite*.'

'We shall arrive,' said Poirot encouragingly. 'You say that you have had the feeling of being – how did you put it – jockeyed along? Can you explain a little more clearly what you mean by that?'

'Well, it's rather difficult . . . You see, this is *my* murder, so to speak. I've thought it out and planned it and it all fits in – dovetails. Well, if you know anything at all about writers, you'll know that they can't stand suggestions. People say "Splendid, but wouldn't it be better if so and so did so and so?" or "Wouldn't it be a wonderful idea if the victim was A instead of B? Or the murderer turned out to be D instead of E?" I mean, one wants to say: "All right then, write it yourself if you want it that way!"'

Poirot nodded.

'And that is what has been happening?'

'Not quite . . . That sort of silly suggestion has been made, and then I've flared up, and they've given in, but have just slipped in some quite minor trivial suggestion and because I've made a stand over the other, I've accepted the triviality without noticing much.'

'I see,' said Poirot. 'Yes – it is a method, that . . . Something rather crude and preposterous is put forward – but that is not really the point. The small minor alteration is really the objective. Is that what you mean?'

'That's exactly what I mean,' said Mrs Oliver. 'And, of course, I *may* be imagining it, but I don't think I am – and none of the things seem to matter anyway. But it's got me worried – that, and a sort of – well – *atmosphere*.'

'Who has made these suggestions of alterations to you?'

'Different people,' said Mrs Oliver. 'If it was just *one* person I'd be more sure of my ground. But it's not just one person – although I think it is really. I mean it's one person working through other quite unsuspecting people.'

'Have you an idea as to who that one person is?'

Mrs Oliver shook her head.

'It's somebody very clever and very careful,' she said. 'It might be anybody.'

'Who is there?' asked Poirot. 'The cast of characters must be fairly limited?'

'Well,' began Mrs Oliver. 'There's Sir George Stubbs who owns this place. Rich and plebeian and frightfully stupid outside business, I should think, but probably dead sharp in it. And there's Lady Stubbs – Hattie – about twenty years younger than he is, rather beautiful, but dumb as a fish – in fact, *I* think she's definitely halfwitted. Married him for his money, of course, and doesn't think about anything but clothes and jewels. Then there's Michael Weyman – he's an architect, quite young, and good-looking in a craggy kind of artistic way. He's designing a tennis pavilion for Sir George and repairing the Folly.'

'Folly? What is that – a masquerade?'

'No, it's architectural. One of those little sort of temple things, white, with columns. You've probably seen them at Kew. Then there's Miss Brewis, she's a sort of secretary housekeeper, who runs things and writes letters – very grim and efficient. And then there are the people round about who come in and help. A young married couple who have taken a cottage down by the river – Alec Legge and his wife Sally. And Captain Warburton, who's the Mastertons' agent. And the Mastertons, of course, and old Mrs Folliat who lives in what used to be the lodge. Her husband's people owned Nasse originally. But they've died out, or been killed in wars, and there were lots of death duties so the last heir sold the place.'

Poirot considered this list of characters, but at the moment they were only names to him. He returned to the main issue.

'Whose idea was the Murder Hunt?'

'Mrs Masterton's, I think. She's the local M.P.'s wife, very good at organizing. It was she who persuaded Sir George to have the fête here. You see the place has been empty for so many years that she thinks people will be keen to pay and come in to see it.'

'That all seems straightforward enough,' said Poirot.

'It all *seems* straightforward,' said Mrs Oliver obstinately; 'but it isn't. I tell you, M. Poirot, there's something *wrong*.'

Poirot looked at Mrs Oliver and Mrs Oliver looked back at Poirot.

'How have you accounted for my presence here? For your summons to me?' Poirot asked.

'That was easy,' said Mrs Oliver. 'You're to give away the prizes for the Murder Hunt. Everybody's awfully thrilled. I said I knew you, and could probably persuade you to come and that I was sure your name would be a terrific draw – as, of course, it will be,' Mrs Oliver added tactfully.

'And the suggestion was accepted – without demur?'

'I tell you, everybody was thrilled.'

Mrs Oliver thought it unnecessary to mention that amongst the younger generation one or two had asked 'Who *is* Hercule Poirot?'

'*Everybody?* Nobody spoke against the idea?'

Mrs Oliver shook her head.

'That is a pity,' said Hercule Poirot.

'You mean it might have given us a line?'

'A would-be criminal could hardly be expected to welcome my presence.'

'I suppose you think I've imagined the whole thing,' said Mrs Oliver ruefully. 'I must admit that until I started talking to you I hadn't realized how very little I've got to go upon.'

'Calm yourself,' said Poirot kindly. 'I am intrigued and interested. Where do we begin?'

Mrs Oliver glanced at her watch.

'It's just tea-time. We'll go back to the house and then you can meet everybody.'

She took a different path from the one by which Poirot had come. This one seemed to lead in the opposite direction.

'We pass by the boathouse this way,' Mrs Oliver explained.

As she spoke the boathouse came into view. It jutted out on to the river and was a picturesque thatched affair.

'That's where the Body's going to be,' said Mrs Oliver. 'The body for the Murder Hunt, I mean.'

'And who is going to be killed?'

'Oh, a girl hiker, who is really the Yugoslavian first wife of a young Atom Scientist,' said Mrs Oliver glibly.

Poirot blinked.

'Of course it looks as though the Atom Scientist had killed her – but naturally it's not as simple as that.'

'Naturally not – since *you* are concerned . . .'

Mrs Oliver accepted the compliment with a wave of the hand.

'Actually,' she said, 'she's killed by the Country Squire – and the motive is really rather ingenious – I don't believe many people will get it – though there's a perfectly clear pointer in the fifth clue.'

Poirot abandoned the subtleties of Mrs Oliver's plot to ask a practical question:

'But how do you arrange for a suitable body?'

'Girl Guide,' said Mrs Oliver. 'Sally Legge was going to be it – but now they want her to dress up in a turban and do the fortune telling. So it's a Girl Guide called Marlene Tucker. Rather dumb and sniffs,' she added in an explanatory manner. 'It's quite easy – just peasant scarves and a rucksack – and all she has to do when she hears someone coming is to flop down on the floor and arrange the cord round her neck. Rather dull for the poor kid – just sticking inside that boathouse until she's found, but I've arranged for her to have a nice bundle of comics – there's a clue to the murderer scribbled on one of them as a matter of fact – so it all works in.'

'Your ingenuity leaves me spellbound! The things you think of!'

'It's never difficult to *think* of things,' said Mrs Oliver. 'The trouble is that you think of too many, and then it all becomes too complicated, so you have to relinquish some of them and that *is* rather agony. We go up this way now.'

They started up a steep zig-zagging path that led them back along the river at a higher level. At a twist through the trees they came out on a space surmounted by a small white pilastered temple. Standing back and frowning at it was a young man wearing dilapidated flannel trousers and a shirt of rather virulent green. He spun round towards them.

'Mr Michael Weyman, M. Hercule Poirot,' said Mrs Oliver.

The young man acknowledged the introduction with a careless nod.

'Extraordinary,' he said bitterly, 'the places people *put* things! This thing here, for instance. Put up only about a year ago – quite nice of its kind and quite in keeping with the period of the house. But why *here*? These things were meant to be seen – "situated on an eminence" – that's how they phrased it – with a nice grassy approach and daffodils, et cetera. But here's this poor little devil, stuck away in the midst of trees – not visible from anywhere – you'd have to cut down about twenty trees before you'd even see it from the river.'

'Perhaps there wasn't any other place,' said Mrs Oliver.

Michael Weyman snorted.

'Top of that grassy bank by the house – perfect natural setting. But no, these tycoon fellows are all the same – no artistic sense. Has a fancy for a "Folly," as he calls it, orders one. Looks round for somewhere to put it. Then, I understand, a big oak tree crashes down in a gale. Leaves a nasty scar. "Oh, we'll tidy the place up by putting a Folly there," says the silly ass. That's all they ever think about, these rich city fellows, tidying up! I wonder he hasn't put beds of red geraniums and calceolarias all round the house! A man like that shouldn't be allowed to own a place like this!'

He sounded heated.

'This young man,' Poirot observed to himself, 'assuredly does not like Sir George Stubbs.'

'It's bedded down in concrete,' said Weyman. 'And there's loose soil underneath – so it's subsided. Cracked all up here – it will be dangerous soon . . . Better pull the whole thing down and re-erect it on the top of the bank near the house. That's my advice, but the obstinate old fool won't hear of it.'

'What about the tennis pavilion?' asked Mrs Oliver.

Gloom settled even more deeply on the young man.

'He wants a kind of Chinese pagoda,' he said, with a groan. 'Dragons if you please! Just because Lady Stubbs fancies herself in Chinese coolie hats. Who'd be an architect? Anyone who wants something decent built hasn't got the money, and those who have the money want something too utterly goddam awful!'

'You have my commiserations,' said Poirot gravely.

'George Stubbs,' said the architect scornfully. 'Who does he think he is? Dug himself into some cushy Admiralty job in the safe depths of Wales during the war – and grows a beard to suggest he saw active naval service on convoy duty – or that's what they say. Stinking with money – absolutely stinking!'

'Well, you architects have got to have someone who's got money to spend, or you'd never have a job,' Mrs Oliver pointed out reasonably enough. She moved on towards the house and Poirot and the dispirited architect prepared to follow her.

'These tycoons,' said the latter bitterly, 'can't understand first principles.' He delivered a final kick to the lopsided Folly. 'If the foundations are rotten – everything's rotten.'

'It is profound what you say there,' said Poirot. 'Yes, it is profound.'

The path they were following came out from the trees and the house showed white and beautiful before them in its setting of dark trees rising up behind it.

'It is of a veritable beauty, yes,' murmured Poirot.

'He wants to build a billiard room on,' said Mr Weyman venomously.

On the bank below them a small elderly lady was busy with sécateurs on a clump of shrubs. She climbed up to greet them, panting slightly.

'Everything neglected for years,' she said. 'And so difficult nowadays to get a man who understands shrubs. This hillside should be a blaze of colour in March and April, but very disappointing this year – all this dead wood ought to have been cut away last autumn –'

'M. Hercule Poirot, Mrs Folliat,' said Mrs Oliver.

The elderly lady beamed.

'So this is the great M. Poirot! It *is* kind of you to come and help us tomorrow. This clever lady here has thought out a most puzzling problem – it will be such a novelty.'

Poirot was faintly puzzled by the graciousness of the little lady's manner. She might, he thought, have been his hostess.

He said politely:

'Mrs Oliver is an old friend of mine. I was delighted to be able to respond to her request. This is indeed a beautiful spot, and what a superb and noble mansion.'

Mrs Folliat nodded in a matter-of-fact manner.

'Yes. It was built by my husband's great-grandfather in 1790. There was an Elizabethan house previously. It fell into disrepair and burned down in about 1700. Our family has lived here since 1598.'

Her voice was calm and matter of fact. Poirot looked at her with closer attention. He saw a very small and compact little person, dressed in shabby tweeds. The most noticeable feature about her was her clear china-blue eyes. Her grey hair was closely confined by a hairnet. Though obviously careless of her appearance, she had that indefinable air of being someone which is so hard to explain.

As they walked together towards the house, Poirot said diffidently, 'It must be hard for you to have strangers living here.'

There was a moment's pause before Mrs Folliat answered. Her
voice was clear and precise and curiously devoid of emotion.

'So many things are hard, M. Poirot,' she said.

CHAPTER 3

It was Mrs Folliat who led the way into the house and Poirot
followed her. It was a gracious house, beautifully proportioned.
Mrs Folliat went through a door on the left into a small daintily
furnished sitting-room and on into the big drawing-room beyond,
which was full of people who all seemed, at the moment, to be
talking at once.

'George,' said Mrs Folliat, 'this is M. Poirot who is so kind as
to come and help us. Sir George Stubbs.'

Sir George, who had been talking in a loud voice, swung
round. He was a big man with a rather florid red face and a
slightly unexpected beard. It gave a rather disconcerting effect
of an actor who had not quite made up his mind whether he was
playing the part of a country squire, or of a 'rough diamond' from
the Dominions. It certainly did not suggest the navy, in spite of
Michael Weyman's remarks. His manner and voice were jovial,
but his eyes were small and shrewd, of a particularly penetrating
pale blue.

He greeted Poirot heartily.

'We're so glad that your friend Mrs Oliver managed to persuade
you to come,' he said. 'Quite a brain-wave on her part. You'll be
an enormous attraction.'

He looked round a little vaguely.

'Hattie?' He repeated the name in a slightly sharper tone.
'Hattie!'

Lady Stubbs was reclining in a big arm-chair a little distance
from the others. She seemed to be paying no attention to what
was going on round her. Instead she was smiling down at her
hand which was stretched out on the arm of the chair. She was
turning it from left to right, so that a big solitaire emerald on her
third finger caught the light in its green depths.

She looked up now in a slightly startled childlike way and said, 'How do you do.'

Poirot bowed over her hand.

Sir George continued his introductions.

'Mrs Masterton.'

Mrs Masterton was a somewhat monumental woman who reminded Poirot faintly of a bloodhound. She had a full under-hung jaw and large, mournful, slightly blood-shot eyes.

She bowed and resumed her discourse in a deep voice which again made Poirot think of a bloodhound's baying note.

'This silly dispute about the tea tent has got to be settled, Jim,' she said forcefully. 'They've got to see sense about it. We can't have the whole show a fiasco because of these idiotic women's local feuds.'

'Oh, quite,' said the man addressed.

'Captain Warburton,' said Sir George.

Captain Warburton, who wore a check sports coat and had a vaguely horsy appearance, showed a lot of white teeth in a somewhat wolfish smile, then continued his conversation.

'Don't you worry, I'll settle it,' he said. 'I'll go and talk to them like a Dutch uncle. What about the fortune-telling tent? In the space by the magnolia? Or at the far end of the lawn by the rhododendrons?'

Sir George continued his introductions.

'Mr and Mrs Legge.'

A tall young man with his face peeling badly from sunburn grinned agreeably. His wife, an attractive freckled redhead, nodded in a friendly fashion, then plunged into controversy with Mrs Masterton, her agreeable high treble making a kind of duet with Mrs Masterton's deep bay.

'– *not* by the magnolia – a bottle-neck –'

'– one wants to disperse things – but if there's a queue –'

'– much cooler. I mean, with the sun full on the house –'

'– and the coconut shy can't be too near the house – the boys are so wild when they throw –'

'And this,' said Sir George, 'is Miss Brewis – who runs us all.'

Miss Brewis was seated behind the large silver tea tray.

She was a spare efficient-looking woman of forty-odd, with a brisk pleasant manner.

'How do you do, M. Poirot,' she said. 'I do hope you didn't have too crowded a journey? The trains are sometimes too terrible this time of year. Let me give you some tea. Milk? Sugar?'

'Very little milk, mademoiselle, and four lumps of sugar.' He added, as Miss Brewis dealt with his request, 'I see that you are all in a great state of activity.'

'Yes, indeed. There are always so many last-minute things to see to. And people let one down in the most extraordinary way nowadays. Over marquees, and tents and chairs and catering equipment. One has to keep *on* at them. I was on the telephone half the morning.'

'What about these pegs, Amanda?' said Sir George. 'And the extra putters for the clock golf?'

'That's all arranged, Sir George. Mr Benson at the golf club was most kind.'

She handed Poirot his cup.

'A sandwich, M. Poirot? Those are tomato and these are *paté*. But perhaps,' said Miss Brewis, thinking of the four lumps of sugar, 'you would rather have a cream cake?'

Poirot would rather have a cream cake, and helped himself to a particularly sweet and squelchy one.

Then, balancing it carefully on his saucer, he went and sat down by his hostess. She was still letting the light play over the jewel on her hand, and she looked up at him with a pleased child's smile.

'Look,' she said. 'It's pretty, isn't it?'

He had been studying her carefully. She was wearing a big coolie-style hat of vivid magenta straw. Beneath it her face showed its pinky reflection on the dead-white surface of her skin. She was heavily made up in an exotic un-English style. Dead-white matt skin; vivid cyclamen lips, mascara applied lavishly to the eyes. Her hair showed beneath the hat, black and smooth, fitting like a velvet cap. There was a languorous un-English beauty about the face. She was a creature of the tropical sun, caught, as it were, by chance in an English drawing-room. But it was the eyes that startled Poirot. They had a childlike, almost vacant, stare.

She had asked her question in a confidential childish way, and it was as though to a child that Poirot answered.

'It is a very lovely ring,' he said.

She looked pleased.

'George gave it to me yesterday,' she said, dropping her voice as though she were sharing a secret with him. 'He gives me lots of things. He's very kind.'

Poirot looked down at the ring again and the hand outstretched on the side of the chair. The nails were very long and varnished a deep puce.

Into his mind a quotation came: 'They toil not, neither do they spin . . .'

He certainly couldn't imagine Lady Stubbs toiling or spinning. And yet he would hardly have described her as a lily of the field. She was a far more artificial product.

'This is a beautiful room you have here, Madame,' he said, looking round appreciatively.

'I suppose it is,' said Lady Stubbs vaguely.

Her attention was still on her ring; her head on one side, she watched the green fire in its depths as her hand moved.

She said in a confidential whisper, 'D'you see? It's winking at me.'

She burst out laughing and Poirot had a sense of sudden shock. It was a loud uncontrolled laugh.

From across the room Sir George said: 'Hattie.'

His voice was quite kind but held a faint admonition. Lady Stubbs stopped laughing.

Poirot said in a conventional manner:

'Devonshire is a very lovely county. Do you not think so?'

'It's nice in the daytime,' said Lady Stubbs. 'When it doesn't rain,' she added mournfully. 'But there aren't any nightclubs.'

'Ah, I see. You like nightclubs?'

'Oh, *yes*,' said Lady Stubbs fervently.

'And why do you like nightclubs so much?'

'There is music and you dance. And I wear my nicest clothes and bracelets and rings. And all the other women have nice clothes and jewels, but not as nice as mine.'

She smiled with enormous satisfaction. Poirot felt a slight pang of pity.

'And all that amuses you very much?'

'Yes. I like the casino, too. Why are there not any casinos in England?'

'I have often wondered,' said Poirot, with a sigh. 'I do not think it would accord with the English character.'

She looked at him uncomprehendingly. Then she bent slightly towards him.

'I won sixty thousand francs at Monte Carlo once. I put it on number twenty-seven and it came up.'

'That must have been very exciting, Madame.'

'Oh, it *was*. George gives me money to play with – but usually I lose it.'

She looked disconsolate.

'That is sad.'

'Oh, it does not really matter. George is very rich. It is nice to be rich, don't you think so?'

'Very nice,' said Poirot gently.

'Perhaps, if I was not rich, I should look like Amanda.' Her gaze went to Miss Brewis at the tea table and studied her dispassionately. 'She is very ugly, don't you think?'

Miss Brewis looked up at that moment and across to where they were sitting. Lady Stubbs had not spoken loudly, but Poirot wondered whether Amanda Brewis had heard.

As he withdrew his gaze, his eyes met those of Captain Warburton. The Captain's glance was ironic and amused.

Poirot endeavoured to change the subject.

'Have you been very busy preparing for the fête?' he asked.

Hattie Stubbs shook her head.

'Oh, no, I think it is all very boring – very stupid. There are servants and gardeners. Why should not they make the preparations?'

'Oh, my dear.' It was Mrs Folliat who spoke. She had come to sit on the sofa nearby. 'Those are the ideas you were brought up with on your island estates. But life isn't like that in England these days. I wish it were.' She sighed. 'Nowadays one has to do nearly everything oneself.'

Lady Stubbs shrugged her shoulders.

'I think it is stupid. What is the good of being rich if one has to do everything oneself?'

'Some people find it fun,' said Mrs Folliat, smiling at her. 'I do really. Not all things, but some. I like gardening myself and I like preparing for a festivity like this one tomorrow.'

'It will be like a party?' asked Lady Stubbs hopefully.

'Just like a party – with lots and lots of people.'

'Will it be like Ascot? With big hats and everyone very chic?'

'Well, not quite like Ascot,' said Mrs Folliat. She added gently, 'But you must try and enjoy country things, Hattie. You should have helped us this morning, instead of staying in bed and not getting up until teatime.'

'I had a headache,' said Hattie sulkily. Then her mood changed and she smiled affectionately at Mrs Folliat.

'But I will be good tomorrow. I will do everything you tell me.'

'That's very sweet of you, dear.'

'I've got a new dress to wear. It came this morning. Come upstairs with me and look at it.'

Mrs Folliat hesitated. Lady Stubbs rose to her feet and said insistently:

'You must come. Please. It is a lovely dress. Come *now*!'

'Oh, very well.' Mrs Folliat gave a half-laugh and rose.

As she went out of the room, her small figure following Hattie's tall one, Poirot saw her face and was quite startled at the weariness on it which had replaced her smiling composure. It was as though, relaxed and off her guard for a moment, she no longer bothered to keep up the social mask. And yet – it seemed more than that. Perhaps she was suffering from some disease about which, like many women, she never spoke. She was not a person, he thought, who would care to invite pity or sympathy.

Captain Warburton dropped down in the chair Hattie Stubbs had just vacated. He, too, looked at the door through which the two women had just passed, but it was not of the older woman that he spoke. Instead he drawled, with a slight grin:

'Beautiful creature, isn't she?' He observed with the tail of his eye Sir George's exit through a french window with Mrs Masterton and Mrs Oliver in tow. 'Bowled over old George Stubbs all right. Nothing's too good for her! Jewels, mink, all the rest of it. Whether he realizes she's a bit wanting in the top storey, I've never discovered. Probably thinks it doesn't matter. After all, these financial johnnies don't ask for intellectual companionship.'

'What nationality is she?' Poirot asked curiously.

'Looks South American, I always think. But I believe she comes from the West Indies. One of those islands with sugar and rum and all that. One of the old families there – a creole, I don't mean a half-caste. All very intermarried, I believe, on these islands. Accounts for the mental deficiency.'

Young Mrs Legge came over to join them.

'Look here, Jim,' she said, 'you've got to be on my side. That tent's got to be where we all decided – on the far side of the lawn backing on the rhododendrons. It's the only possible place.'

'Ma Masterton doesn't think so.'

'Well, you've got to talk her out of it.'

He gave her his foxy smile.

'Mrs Masterton's my boss.'

'Wilfred Masterton's your boss. He's the M.P.'

'I dare say, but she should be. She's the one who wears the pants – and don't I know it.'

Sir George re-entered the window.

'Oh, there you are, Sally,' he said. 'We need you. You wouldn't think everyone could get het up over who butters the buns and who raffles a cake, and why the garden produce stall is where the fancy woollens was promised it should be. Where's Amy Folliat? She can deal with these people – about the only person who can.'

'She went upstairs with Hattie.'

'Oh, did she –?'

Sir George looked round in a vaguely helpless manner and Miss Brewis jumped up from where she was writing tickets, and said, 'I'll fetch her for you, Sir George.'

'Thank you, Amanda.'

Miss Brewis went out of the room.

'Must get hold of some more wire fencing,' murmured Sir George.

'For the fête?'

'No, no. To put up where we adjoin Hoodown Park in the woods. The old stuff's rotted away, and that's where they get through.'

'Who get through?'

'Trespassers!' ejaculated Sir George.

Sally Legge said amusedly:

'You sound like Betsy Trotwood campaigning against donkeys.'

'Betsy Trotwood? Who's she?' asked Sir George simply.

'Dickens.'

'Oh, Dickens. I read the *Pickwick Papers* once. Not bad. Not bad at all – surprised me. But, seriously, trespassers are a menace since they've started this Youth Hostel tomfoolery. They come out at you from everywhere wearing the most incredible shirts – boy this morning had one all covered with crawling turtles and things – made me think I'd been hitting the bottle or something. Half of them can't speak English – just gibber at you . . .' He mimicked: '"Oh, plees – yes, haf you – tell me – iss way to ferry?" I say no, it isn't, roar at them, and send them back where they've come from, but half the time they just blink and stare and don't understand. And the girls giggle. All kinds of nationalities, Italian, Yugoslavian, Dutch, Finnish – Eskimos I shouldn't be surprised! Half of them communists, I shouldn't wonder,' he ended darkly.

'Come now, George, don't get started on communists,' said Mrs Legge. 'I'll come and help you deal with the rabid women.'

She led him out of the window and called over her shoulder: 'Come on, Jim. Come and be torn to pieces in a good cause.'

'All right, but I want to put M. Poirot in the picture about the Murder Hunt since he's going to present the prizes.'

'You can do that presently.'

'I will await you here,' said Poirot agreeably.

In the ensuing silence, Alec Legge stretched himself out in his chair and sighed.

'Women!' he said. 'Like a swarm of bees.'

He turned his head to look out of the window.

'And what's it all about? Some silly garden fête that doesn't matter to anyone.'

'But obviously,' Poirot pointed out, 'there are those to whom it does matter.'

'Why can't people have some *sense*? Why can't they *think*? Think of the mess the whole world has got itself into. Don't they realize that the inhabitants of the globe are busy committing suicide?'

Poirot judged rightly that he was not intended to reply to this question. He merely shook his head doubtfully.

'Unless we can do something before it's too late . . .' Alec Legge broke off. An angry look swept over his face. 'Oh, yes,' he said, 'I know what you're thinking. That I'm nervy, neurotic – all the rest of it. Like those damned doctors. Advising rest and change and sea air. All right, Sally and I came down here and took the Mill Cottage for three months, and I've followed their prescription. I've fished and bathed and taken long walks and sunbathed –'

'I noticed that you had sunbathed, yes,' said Poirot politely.

'Oh, this?' Alec's hand went to his sore face. 'That's the result of a fine English summer for once in a way. But what's the *good* of it all? You can't get away from facing truth just by running away from it.'

'No, it is never any good running away.'

'And being in a rural atmosphere like this just makes you realize things more keenly – that and the incredible apathy of the people of this country. Even Sally, who's intelligent enough, is just the same. Why bother? That's what she says. It makes me mad! Why bother?'

'As a matter of interest, why do you?'

'Good God, you too?'

'No, it is not advice. It is just that I would like to know your answer.'

'Don't you see, somebody's got to do something.'

'And that somebody is you?'

'No, no, not me personally. One can't be *personal* in times like these.'

'I do not see why not. Even in "these times" as you call it, one is still a person.'

'But one shouldn't be! In times of stress, when it's a matter of life or death, one can't think of one's own insignificant ills or preoccupations.'

'I assure you, you are quite wrong. In the late war, during a severe air-raid, I was much less preoccupied by the thought of death than of the pain from a corn on my little toe. It surprised me at the time that it should be so. "Think," I said to myself, "at any moment now, death may come." But I was still conscious of my corn – indeed, I felt injured that I should have that to suffer as well as the fear of death. It was *because* I might die that every small personal matter in my life acquired increased importance.

I have seen a woman knocked down in a street accident, with a broken leg, and she has burst out crying because she sees that there is a ladder in her stocking.'

'Which just shows you what fools women are!'

'It shows you what *people* are. It is, perhaps, that absorption in one's personal life that has led the human race to survive.'

Alec Legge gave a scornful laugh.

'Sometimes,' he said, 'I think it's a pity they ever did.'

'It is, you know,' Poirot persisted, 'a form of humility. And humility is valuable. There was a slogan that was written up in your underground railways here, I remember, during the war. "It all depends on *you*." It was composed, I think, by some eminent divine – but in my opinion it was a dangerous and undesirable doctrine. For it is not *true*. Everything does *not* depend on, say, Mrs Blank of Little-Blank-in-the-Marsh. And if she is led to think it does, it will not be good for her character. While she thinks of the part she can play in world affairs, the baby pulls over the kettle.'

'You are rather old-fashioned in your views, I think. Let's hear what your slogan would be.'

'I do not need to formulate one of my own. There is an older one in this country which contents me very well.'

'What is that?'

'"Put your trust in God, and keep your powder dry."'

'Well, well . . .' Alec Legge seemed amused. 'Most unexpected coming from you. Do you know what I should like to see done in this country?'

'Something, no doubt, forceful and unpleasant,' said Poirot, smiling.

Alec Legge remained serious.

'I should like to see every feeble-minded person put out – right out! Don't let them breed. If, for one generation, only the intelligent were allowed to breed, think what the result would be.'

'A very large increase of patients in the psychiatric wards, perhaps,' said Poirot dryly. 'One needs roots as well as flowers on a plant, Mr Legge. However large and beautiful the flowers, if the earthy roots are destroyed there will be no more flowers.' He added in a conversational tone: 'Would you consider Lady Stubbs a candidate for the lethal chamber?'

'Yes, indeed. What's the good of a woman like that? What contribution has she ever made to society? Has she ever had an idea in her head that wasn't of clothes or furs or jewels? As I say, what good is she?'

'You and I,' said Poirot blandly, 'are certainly much more intelligent than Lady Stubbs. But' – he shook his head sadly – 'it is true, I fear, that we are not nearly so ornamental.'

'Ornamental . . .' Alec was beginning with a fierce snort, but he was interrupted by the re-entry of Mrs Oliver and Captain Warburton through the window.

CHAPTER 4

'You must come and see the clues and things for the Murder Hunt, M. Poirot,' said Mrs Oliver breathlessly.

Poirot rose and followed them obediently.

The three of them went across the hall and into a small room furnished plainly as a business office.

'Lethal weapons to your left,' observed Captain Warburton, waving his hand towards a small baize-covered card table. On it were laid out a small pistol, a piece of lead piping with a rusty sinister stain on it, a blue bottle labelled Poison, a length of clothes line and a hypodermic syringe.

'Those are the Weapons,' explained Mrs Oliver, 'and these are the Suspects.'

She handed him a printed card which he read with interest.

Suspects

Estelle Glynne	– a beautiful and mysterious young woman, the guest of
Colonel Blunt	– the local Squire, whose daughter
Joan	– is married to
Peter Gaye	– a young Atom Scientist.
Miss Willing	– a housekeeper.
Quiett	– a butler.
Maya Stavisky	– a girl hiker.
Esteban Loyola	– an uninvited guest.

Poirot blinked and looked towards Mrs Oliver in mute incomprehension.

'A magnificent Cast of Characters,' he said politely. 'But permit me to ask, Madame, what does the Competitor do?'

'Turn the card over,' said Captain Warburton.

Poirot did so.

On the other side was printed:

Name and address ....

Solution:
Name of Murderer: ....
Weapon: ....
Motive: ....
Time and Place: ....
Reasons for arriving at your conclusions: ....
....

'Everyone who enters gets one of these,' explained Captain Warburton rapidly. 'Also a notebook and pencil for copying clues. There will be six clues. You go on from one to the other like a Treasure Hunt, and the weapons are concealed in suspicious places. Here's the first clue. A snapshot. Everyone starts with one of these.'

Poirot took the small print from him and studied it with a frown. Then he turned it upside down. He still looked puzzled. Warburton laughed.

'Ingenious bit of trick photography, isn't it?' he said complacently. 'Quite simple once you know what it is.'

Poirot, who did not know what it was, felt a mounting annoyance.

'Some kind of barred window?' he suggested.

'Looks a bit like it, I admit. No, it's a section of a tennis net.'

'Ah.' Poirot looked again at the snapshot. 'Yes, it is as you say – quite obvious when you have been told what it is!'

'So much depends on how you look at a thing,' laughed Warburton.

'That is a very profound truth.'

'The second clue will be found in a box under the centre of the tennis net. In the box are this empty poison bottle – here, and a loose cork.'

'Only, you see,' said Mrs Oliver rapidly, 'it's a screw-topped bottle, so the *cork* is really the clue.'

'I know, Madame, that you are always full of ingenuity, but I do not quite see –'

Mrs Oliver interrupted him.

'Oh, but of course,' she said, 'there's a story. Like in a magazine serial – a synopsis.' She turned to Captain Warburton. 'Have you got the leaflets?'

'They've not come from the printers yet.'

'But they *promised*!'

'I know. I know. Everyone always promises. They'll be ready this evening at six. I'm going in to fetch them in the car.'

'Oh, good.'

Mrs Oliver gave a deep sigh and turned to Poirot.

'Well, I'll have to tell it you, then. Only I'm not very good at telling things. I mean if I write things, I get them perfectly clear, but if I talk, it always sounds the most frightful muddle; and that's why I never discuss my plots with anyone. I've learnt not to, because if I do, they just look at me blankly and say "– er – yes, but – I don't see what happened – and surely that can't possibly make a book." So damping. And *not* true, because when I write it, it does!'

Mrs Oliver paused for breath, and then went on:

'Well, it's like this. There's Peter Gaye who's a young Atom Scientist and he's suspected of being in the pay of the Communists, and he's married to this girl, Joan Blunt, and his first wife's dead, but she isn't, and she turns up because she's a secret agent, or perhaps not, I mean she may really *be* a hiker – and the wife's having an affair, and this man Loyola turns up either to meet Maya, or to spy upon her, and there's a blackmailing letter which might be from the housekeeper, or again it might be the butler, and the revolver's missing, and as you don't know who the blackmailing letter's to, and the hypodermic syringe fell out at dinner, and after that it disappeared . . .'

Mrs Oliver came to a full stop, estimating correctly Poirot's reaction.

'I know,' she said sympathetically. 'It sounds just a muddle, but it isn't really – not in my head – and when you see the synopsis leaflet, you'll find it's quite clear.

'And, anyway,' she ended, 'the story doesn't really matter, does it? I mean, not to *you*. All you've got to do is to present the prizes – very nice prizes, the first's a silver cigarette case shaped like a revolver – and say how remarkably clever the solver has been.'

Poirot thought to himself that the solver would indeed have been clever. In fact, he doubted very much that there would be a solver. The whole plot and action of the Murder Hunt seemed to him to be wrapped in impenetrable fog.

'Well,' said Captain Warburton cheerfully, glancing at his wrist-watch, 'I'd better be off to the printers and collect.'

Mrs Oliver groaned.

'If they're not done –'

'Oh, they're done all right. I telephoned. So long.'

He left the room.

Mrs Oliver immediately clutched Poirot by the arm and demanded in a hoarse whisper:

'Well?'

'Well – what?'

'Have you found out anything? Or spotted anybody?'

Poirot replied with mild reproof in his tones:

'Everybody and everything seems to me completely normal.'

'Normal?'

'Well, perhaps that is not quite the right word. Lady Stubbs, as you say, is definitely subnormal, and Mr Legge would appear to be rather abnormal.'

'Oh, he's all right,' said Mrs Oliver impatiently. 'He's had a nervous breakdown.'

Poirot did not question the somewhat doubtful wording of this sentence but accepted it at its face value.

'Everybody appears to be in the expected state of nervous agitation, high excitement, general fatigue, and strong irritation, which are characteristic of preparations for this form of entertainment. If you could only indicate –'

'Sh!' Mrs Oliver grasped his arm again. 'Someone's coming.'

It was just like a bad melodrama, Poirot felt, his own irritation mounting.

The pleasant mild face of Miss Brewis appeared round the door.

'Oh, there you are, M. Poirot. I've been looking for you to show you your room.'

She led him up the staircase and along a passage to a big airy room looking out over the river.

'There is a bathroom just opposite. Sir George talks of adding more bathrooms, but to do so would sadly impair the proportions of the rooms. I hope you'll find everything quite comfortable.'

'Yes, indeed.' Poirot swept an appreciative eye over the small bookstand, the reading-lamp and the box labelled 'Biscuits' by the bedside. 'You seem, in this house, to have everything organized to perfection. Am I to congratulate you, or my charming hostess?'

'Lady Stubbs' time is fully taken up in being charming,' said Miss Brewis, a slightly acid note in her voice.

'A very decorative young woman,' mused Poirot.

'As you say.'

'But in other respects is she not, perhaps . . .' He broke off. '*Pardon*. I am indiscreet. I comment on something I ought not, perhaps, to mention.'

Miss Brewis gave him a steady look. She said dryly:

'Lady Stubbs knows perfectly well exactly what she is doing. Besides being, as you said, a very decorative young woman, she is also a very shrewd one.'

She had turned away and left the room before Poirot's eyebrows had fully risen in surprise. So that was what the efficient Miss Brewis thought, was it? Or had she merely said so for some reason of her own? And why had she made such a statement to him – to a newcomer? Because he *was* a newcomer, perhaps? And also because he was a foreigner. As Hercule Poirot had discovered by experience, there were many English people who considered that what one said to foreigners didn't count!

He frowned perplexedly, staring absentmindedly at the door out of which Miss Brewis had gone. Then he strolled over to the window and stood looking out. As he did so, he saw Lady Stubbs come out of the house with Mrs Folliat and they stood for a moment or two talking by the big magnolia tree. Then Mrs Folliat nodded a goodbye, picked up her gardening basket and gloves and trotted off down the drive. Lady Stubbs stood watching her for a moment, then absentmindedly pulled off a magnolia flower, smelt it and began slowly to walk down the path that led through the trees to the river. She looked just once over her shoulder before she disappeared from sight. From behind the magnolia tree Michael Weyman came quietly into view, paused a moment irresolutely and then followed the tall slim figure down into the trees.

A good-looking and dynamic young man, Poirot thought. With a more attractive personality, no doubt, than that of Sir George Stubbs . . .

But if so, what of it? Such patterns formed themselves eternally through life. Rich middle-aged unattractive husband, young and beautiful wife with or without sufficient mental development, attractive and susceptible young man. What was there in that to make Mrs Oliver utter a peremptory summons through the telephone? Mrs Oliver, no doubt, had a vivid imagination, but . . .

'But after all,' murmured Hercule Poirot to himself, 'I am not a consultant in adultery – or in incipient adultery.'

Could there really be anything in this extraordinary notion of Mrs Oliver's that something was wrong? Mrs Oliver was a singularly muddle-headed woman, and how she managed somehow or other to turn out coherent detective stories was beyond him, and yet, for all her muddle-headedness she often surprised him by her sudden perception of truth.

'The time is short – short,' he murmured to himself. '*Is* there something wrong here, as Mrs Oliver believes? I am inclined to think there is. But what? Who is there who could enlighten me? I need to know more, much more, about the people in this house. Who is there who could inform me?'

After a moment's reflection he seized his hat (Poirot never risked going out in the evening air with uncovered head), and hurried out of his room and down the stairs. He heard afar the dictatorial baying of Mrs Masterton's deep voice. Nearer at hand, Sir George's voice rose with an amorous intonation.

'Damned becoming that yashmak thing. Wish I had you in my harem, Sally. I shall come and have my fortune told a good deal tomorrow. What'll you tell me, eh?'

There was a slight scuffle and Sally Legge's voice said breathlessly:

'George, you mustn't.'

Poirot raised his eyebrows, and slipped out of a conveniently adjacent side door. He set off at top speed down a back drive which his sense of locality enabled him to predict would at some point join the front drive.

His manoeuvre was successful and enabled him – panting very slightly – to come up beside Mrs Folliat and relieve her in a gallant manner of her gardening basket.

'You permit, Madame?'

'Oh, thank you, M. Poirot, that's very kind of you. But it's not heavy.'

'Allow me to carry it for you to your home. You live near here?'

'I actually live in the lodge by the front gate. Sir George very kindly rents it to me.'

The lodge by the front gate of her former home . . . How did she really feel about *that*, Poirot wondered. Her composure was so absolute that he had no clue to her feelings. He changed the subject by observing:

'Lady Stubbs is much younger than her husband, is she not?'

'Twenty-three years younger.'

'Physically she is very attractive.'

Mrs Folliat said quietly:

'Hattie is a dear good child.'

It was not an answer he had expected. Mrs Folliat went on:

'I know her very well, you see. For a short time she was under my care.'

'I did not know that.'

'How should you? It is in a way a sad story. Her people had estates, sugar estates, in the West Indies. As a result of an earthquake, the house there was burned down and her parents and brothers and sisters all lost their lives. Hattie herself was at a convent in Paris and was thus suddenly left without any near relatives. It was considered advisable by the executors that Hattie should be chaperoned and introduced into society after she had spent a certain time abroad. I accepted the charge of her.' Mrs Folliat added with a dry smile: 'I can smarten myself up on occasions and, naturally, I had the necessary connections – in fact, the late Governor had been a close friend of ours.'

'Naturally, Madame, I understand all that.'

'It suited me very well – I was going through a difficult time. My husband had died just before the outbreak of war. My elder son who was in the navy went down with his ship, my younger son, who had been out in Kenya, came back, joined the commandos and was killed in Italy. That meant three lots of death duties and this house had to be put up for sale. I myself was very badly off and I was glad of the distraction of having someone young to look after and travel about with. I became very fond of Hattie, all the more so, perhaps, because I soon realized that she was – shall we say – not fully capable of fending for herself? Understand me, M. Poirot, Hattie is *not* mentally deficient, but she *is* what country folk describe as "simple." She is easily imposed upon, over docile, completely open to suggestion. I think myself that it was a blessing that there was practically no money. If she had been an heiress her position might have been one of much greater difficulty. She was attractive to men and being of an affectionate nature was easily attracted and influenced – she had definitely to be looked after. When, after the final winding up of her parents' estate, it was discovered that the plantation was destroyed and there were more debts than assets, I could only be thankful that a man such as Sir George Stubbs had fallen in love with her and wanted to marry her.'

'Possibly – yes – it was a solution.'

'Sir George,' said Mrs Folliat, 'though he is a self-made man and – let us face it – a complete vulgarian, is kindly and fundamentally decent, besides being extremely wealthy. I don't think he would ever ask for *mental* companionship from a wife, which is just as well. Hattie is everything he wants. She displays clothes and jewels to perfection, is affectionate and willing, and is completely happy with him. I confess that I am very thankful that that is so, for I admit that I deliberately influenced her to accept him. If it had turned out badly' – her voice faltered a little – 'it would have been my fault for urging her to marry a man so many years older than herself. You see, as I told you, Hattie is completely suggestible. Anyone she is with at the time can dominate her.'

'It seems to me,' said Poirot approvingly, 'that you made there a most prudent arrangement for her. I am not, like the English, romantic. To arrange a good marriage, one must take more than romance into consideration.'

He added:

'And as for this place here, Nasse House, it is a most beautiful spot. Quite, as the saying goes, out of this world.'

'Since Nasse had to be sold,' said Mrs Folliat, with a faint tremor in her voice, 'I am glad that Sir George bought it. It was requisitioned during the war by the Army and afterwards it might have been bought and made into a guest house or a school, the rooms cut up and partitioned, distorted out of their natural beauty. Our neighbours, the Fletchers, at Hoodown, had to sell their place and it is now a Youth Hostel. One is glad that young people should enjoy themselves – and fortunately Hoodown is late-Victorian, and of no great architectural merit, so that the alterations do not matter. I'm afraid some of the young people trespass on our grounds. It makes Sir George very angry. It's true that they have occasionally damaged the rare shrubs by hacking them about – they come through here trying to get a short cut to the ferry across the river.'

They were standing now by the front gate. The lodge, a small white one-storied building, lay a little back from the drive with a small railed garden round it.

Mrs Folliat took back her basket from Poirot with a word of thanks.

'I was always very fond of the lodge,' she said, looking at it affectionately. 'Merdle, our head gardener for thirty years, used to live there. I much prefer it to the top cottage, though that has been enlarged and modernized by Sir George. It had to be; we've got quite a young man now as head gardener, with a young wife – and these young women must have electric irons and modern cookers and television, and all that. One must go with the times . . .' She sighed. 'There is hardly a person left now on the estate from the old days – all new faces.'

'I am glad, Madame,' said Poirot, 'that you at least have found a haven.'

'You know those lines of Spenser's? "*Sleep after toyle, port after stormie seas, ease after war, death after life, doth greatly please . . .*"'

She paused and said without any change of tone: 'It's a very wicked world, M. Poirot. And there are very wicked people in the world. You probably know that as well as I do. I don't say so before the younger people, it might discourage them, but it's true . . . Yes, it's a very wicked world . . .'

She gave him a little nod, then turned and went into the lodge. Poirot stood still, staring at the shut door.

CHAPTER 5

I

In a mood of exploration Poirot went through the front gates and down the steeply twisting road that presently emerged on a small quay. A large bell with a chain had a notice upon it: 'Ring for the Ferry.' There were various boats moored by the side of the quay. A very old man with rheumy eyes, who had been leaning against a bollard, came shuffling towards Poirot.

'Du ee want the ferry, sir?'

'I thank you, no. I have just come down from Nasse House for a little walk.'

'Ah, 'tis up at Nasse yu are? Worked there as a boy, I did, and my son, he were head gardener there. But I did use to look after the boats. Old Squire Folliat, he was fair mazed about boats. Sail in all weathers, he would. The Major, now, his son, he didn't care for sailing. Horses, that's all he cared about. And a pretty packet went on 'em. That and the bottle – had a hard time with him, his wife did. Yu've seen her, maybe – lives at the Lodge now, she du.'

'Yes, I have just left her there now.'

'Her be a Folliat, tu, second cousin from over Tiverton way. A great one for the garden, she is, all them there flowering shrubs she had put in. Even when it was took over during the war, and the two young gentlemen was gone to the war, she still looked after they shrubs and kept 'em from being over-run.'

'It was hard on her, both her sons being killed.'

'Ah, she've had a hard life, she have, what with this and that. Trouble with her husband, and trouble with the young gentlemen, tu. Not Mr Henry. He was as nice a young gentleman as yu could wish, took after his grandfather, fond of sailing and went into the

Navy as a matter of course, but Mr James, he caused her a lot of trouble. Debts and women it were, and then, tu, he were real wild in his temper. Born one of they as can't go straight. But the war suited him, as yu might say – give him his chance. Ah! There's many who can't go straight in peace who dies bravely in war.'

'So now,' said Poirot, 'there are no more Folliats at Nasse.'

The old man's flow of talk died abruptly.

'Just as yu say, sir.'

Poirot looked curiously at the old man.

'Instead you have Sir George Stubbs. What is thought locally of him?'

'Us understands,' said the old man, 'that he be powerful rich.'

His tone sounded dry and almost amused.

'And his wife?'

'Ah, she's a fine lady from London, she is. No use for gardens, not her. They du say, tu, as her du be wanting up here.'

He tapped his temple significantly.

'Not as her isn't always very nice spoken and friendly. Just over a year they've been here. Bought the place and had it all done up like new. I remember as though 'twere yesterday them arriving. Arrived in the evening, they did, day after the worst gale as I ever remember. Trees down right and left – one down across the drive and us had to get it sawn away in a hurry to get the drive clear for the car. And the big oak up along, that come down and brought a lot of others down with it, made a rare mess, it did.'

'Ah, yes, where the Folly stands now?'

The old man turned aside and spat disgustedly.

'Folly 'tis called and Folly 'tis – new-fangled nonsense. Never was no Folly in the old Folliats' time. Her ladyship's idea that Folly was. Put up not three weeks after they first come, and I've no doubt she talked Sir George into it. Rare silly it looks stuck up there among the trees, like a heathen temple. A nice summerhouse now, made rustic like with stained glass. I'd have nothing against *that*.'

Poirot smiled faintly.

'The London ladies,' he said, 'they must have their fancies. It is sad that the day of the Folliats is over.'

'Don't ee never believe that, sir.' The old man gave a wheezy chuckle. 'Always be Folliats at Nasse.'

'But the house belongs to Sir George Stubbs.'

'That's as may be – but there's still a Folliat here. Ah! Rare and cunning the Folliats are!'

'What do you mean?'

The old man gave him a sly sideways glance.

'Mrs Folliat be living up tu Lodge, bain't she?' he demanded.

'Yes,' said Poirot slowly. 'Mrs Folliat is living at the Lodge and the world is very wicked, and all the people in it are very wicked.'

The old man stared at him.

'Ah,' he said. 'Yu've got something there, maybe.'

He shuffled away again.

'But what have I got?' Poirot asked himself with irritation as he slowly walked up the hill back to the house.

II

Hercule Poirot made a meticulous toilet, applying a scented pomade to his moustaches and twirling them to a ferocious couple of points. He stood back from the mirror and was satisfied with what he saw.

The sound of a gong resounded through the house, and he descended the stairs.

The butler, having finished a most artistic performance, crescendo, forte, diminuendo, rallentando, was just replacing the gong stick on its hook. His dark melancholy face showed pleasure.

Poirot thought to himself: '*A blackmailing letter from the house-keeper – or it may be the butler . . .*' This butler looked as though blackmailing letters would be well within his scope. Poirot wondered if Mrs Oliver took her characters from life.

Miss Brewis crossed the hall in an unbecoming flowered chiffon dress and he caught up with her, asking as he did so:

'You have a housekeeper here?'

'Oh, no, M. Poirot. I'm afraid one doesn't run to niceties of that kind nowadays, except in a really large establishment, of course. Oh, no, I'm the housekeeper – more housekeeper than secretary, sometimes, in this house.'

She gave a short acid laugh.

'So you are the housekeeper?' Poirot considered her thought-fully.

He could not see Miss Brewis writing a blackmailing letter. Now, an anonymous letter – that would be a different thing. He had known anonymous letters written by women not unlike Miss Brewis – solid, dependable women, totally unsuspected by those around them.

'What is your butler's name?' he asked.

'Henden.' Miss Brewis looked a little astonished.

Poirot recollected himself and explained quickly:

'I ask because I had a fancy I had seen him somewhere before.'

'Very likely,' said Miss Brewis. 'None of these people ever seem to stay in any place more than four months. They must soon have done the round of all the available situations in England. After all, it's not many people who can afford butlers and cooks nowadays.'

They came into the drawing-room, where Sir George, looking somehow rather unnatural in a dinner-jacket, was proffering sherry. Mrs Oliver, in iron-grey satin, was looking like an obsolete battleship, and Lady Stubbs' smooth black head was bent down as she studied the fashions in *Vogue*.

Alec and Sally Legge were dining and also Jim Warburton.

'We've a heavy evening ahead of us,' he warned them. 'No bridge tonight. All hands to the pumps. There are any amount of notices to print, and the big card for the Fortune Telling. What name shall we have? Madame Zuleika? Esmeralda? Or Romany Leigh, the Gipsy Queen?'

'The Eastern touch,' said Sally. 'Everyone in agricultural districts hates gipsies. Zuleika sounds all right. I brought my paint box over and I thought Michael could do us a curling snake to ornament the notice.'

'Cleopatra rather than Zuleika, then?'

Henden appeared at the door.

'Dinner is served, my lady.'

They went in. There were candles on the long table. The room was full of shadows.

Warburton and Alec Legge sat on either side of their hostess. Poirot was between Mrs Oliver and Miss Brewis. The latter was engaged in brisk general conversation about further details of preparation for tomorrow.

Mrs Oliver sat in brooding abstraction and hardly spoke.

When she did at last break her silence, it was with a somewhat contradictory explanation.

'Don't bother about me,' she said to Poirot. 'I'm just remembering if there's anything I've forgotten.'

Sir George laughed heartily.

'The fatal flaw, eh?' he remarked.

'That's just it,' said Mrs Oliver. 'There always is one. Sometimes one doesn't realize it until a book's actually in print. And then it's *agony*!' Her face reflected this emotion. She sighed. 'The curious thing is that most people never notice it. I say to myself, "But of course the cook would have been bound to notice that two cutlets hadn't been eaten." But nobody else thinks of it at all.'

'You fascinate me.' Michael Weyman leant across the table. 'The Mystery of the Second Cutlet. Please, please never explain. I shall wonder about it in my bath.'

Mrs Oliver gave him an abstracted smile and relapsed into her preoccupations.

Lady Stubbs was also silent. Now and again she yawned. Warburton, Alec Legge and Miss Brewis talked across her.

As they came out of the dining-room, Lady Stubbs stopped by the stairs.

'I'm going to bed,' she announced. 'I'm very sleepy.'

'Oh, Lady Stubbs,' exclaimed Miss Brewis, 'there's so much to be done. We've been counting on you to help us.'

'Yes, I know,' said Lady Stubbs. 'But I'm going to bed.'

She spoke with the satisfaction of a small child.

She turned her head as Sir George came out of the dining-room.

'I'm tired, George. I'm going to bed. You don't mind?'

He came up to her and patted her on the shoulder affectionately.

'You go and get your beauty sleep, Hattie. Be fresh for tomorrow.'

He kissed her lightly and she went up the stairs, waving her hand and calling out:

'Goodnight, all.'

Sir George smiled up at her. Miss Brewis drew in her breath sharply and turned brusquely away.

'Come along, everybody,' she said, with a forced cheerfulness that did not ring true. 'We've got to *work*.'

Presently everyone was set to their tasks. Since Miss Brewis could not be everywhere at once, there were soon some defaulters. Michael Weyman ornamented a placard with a ferociously magnificent serpent and the words, *Madame Zuleika will tell your Fortune*, and then vanished unobtrusively. Alec Legge did a few nondescript chores and then went out avowedly to measure for the hoop-la and did not reappear. The women, as women do, worked energetically and conscientiously. Hercule Poirot followed his hostess's example and went early to bed.

III

Poirot came down to breakfast on the following morning at nine-thirty. Breakfast was served in pre-war fashion. A row of hot dishes on an electric heater. Sir George was eating a full-sized Englishman's breakfast of scrambled eggs, bacon and kidneys. Mrs Oliver and Miss Brewis had a modified version of the same. Michael Weyman was eating a plateful of cold ham. Only Lady Stubbs was unheedful of the fleshpots and was nibbling thin toast and sipping black coffee. She was wearing a large pale-pink hat which looked odd at the breakfast table.

The post had just arrived. Miss Brewis had an enormous pile of letters in front of her which she was rapidly sorting into piles. Any of Sir George's marked 'Personal' she passed over to him. The others she opened herself and sorted into categories.

Lady Stubbs had three letters. She opened what were clearly a couple of bills and tossed them aside. Then she opened the third letter and said suddenly and clearly:

'Oh!'

The exclamation was so startled that all heads turned towards her.

'It's from Etienne,' she said. 'My cousin Etienne. He's coming here in a yacht.'

'Let's see, Hattie.' Sir George held out his hand. She passed the letter down the table. He smoothed out the sheet and read.

'Who's this Etienne de Sousa? A cousin, you say?'

'I think so. A second cousin. I do not remember him very well – hardly at all. He was –'

'Yes, my dear?'

She shrugged her shoulders.

'It does not matter. It is all a long time ago. I was a little girl.'

'I suppose you wouldn't remember him very well. But we must make him welcome, of course,' said Sir George heartily. 'Pity in a way it's the fête today, but we'll ask him to dinner. Perhaps we could put him up for a night or two – show him something of the country?'

Sir George was being the hearty country squire.

Lady Stubbs said nothing. She stared down into her coffee-cup.

Conversation on the inevitable subject of the fête became general. Only Poirot remained detached, watching the slim exotic figure at the head of the table. He wondered just what was going on in her mind. At that very moment her eyes came up and cast a swift glance along the table to where he sat. It was a look so shrewd and appraising that he was startled. As their eyes met, the shrewd expression vanished – emptiness returned. But that other look had been there, cold, calculating, watchful . . .

Or had he imagined it? In any case, wasn't it true that people who were slightly mentally deficient very often had a kind of sly native cunning that sometimes surprised even the people who knew them best?

He thought to himself that Lady Stubbs was certainly an enigma. People seemed to hold diametrically opposite ideas concerning her. Miss Brewis had intimated that Lady Stubbs knew very well what she was doing. Yet Mrs Oliver definitely thought her half-witted, and Mrs Folliat who had known her long and intimately had spoken of her as someone not quite normal, who needed care and watchfulness.

Miss Brewis was probably prejudiced. She disliked Lady Stubbs for her indolence and her aloofness. Poirot wondered if Miss Brewis had been Sir George's secretary prior to his marriage. If so, she might easily resent the coming of the new régime.

Poirot himself would have agreed wholeheartedly with Mrs Folliat and Mrs Oliver – until this morning. And, after all, could he really rely on what had been only a fleeting impression?

Lady Stubbs got up abruptly from the table.

'I have a headache,' she said. 'I shall go and lie down in my room.'

Sir George sprang up anxiously.

'My dear girl. You're all right, aren't you?'

'It's just a headache.'

'You'll be fit enough for this afternoon, won't you?'

'Yes, I think so.'

'Take some aspirin, Lady Stubbs,' said Miss Brewis briskly. 'Have you got some or shall I bring it to you?'

'I've got some.'

She moved towards the door. As she went she dropped the handkerchief she had been squeezing between her fingers. Poirot, moving quietly forward, picked it up unobtrusively.

Sir George, about to follow his wife, was stopped by Miss Brewis.

'About the parking of cars this afternoon, Sir George. I'm just going to give Mitchell instructions. Do you think that the best plan would be, as you said –?'

Poirot, going out of the room, heard no more.

He caught up his hostess on the stairs.

'Madame, you dropped this.'

He proffered the handkerchief with a bow.

She took it unheedingly.

'Did I? Thank you.'

'I am most distressed, Madame, that you should be suffering. Particularly when your cousin is coming.'

She answered quickly, almost violently.

'I don't want to see Etienne. I don't like him. He's bad. He was always bad. I'm afraid of him. He does bad things.'

The door of the dining-room opened and Sir George came across the hall and up the stairs.

'Hattie, my poor darling. Let me come and tuck you up.'

They went up the stairs together, his arm round her tenderly, his face worried and absorbed.

Poirot looked up after them, then turned to encounter Miss Brewis moving fast, and clasping papers.

'Lady Stubbs' headache –' he began.

'No more headache than my foot,' said Miss Brewis crossly, and disappeared into her office, closing the door behind her.

Poirot sighed and went out through the front door on to the terrace. Mrs Masterton had just driven up in a small car and was directing the elevation of a tea marquee, baying out orders in rich full-blooded tones.

She turned to greet Poirot.

'Such a nuisance, these affairs,' she observed. 'And they will always put everything in the wrong place. No, Rogers! More to the left – *left* – not right! What do you think of the weather, M. Poirot? Looks doubtful to me. Rain, of course, would spoil everything. And we've had such a fine summer this year for a change. Where's Sir George? I want to talk to him about car parking.'

'His wife had a headache and has gone to lie down.'

'She'll be all right this afternoon,' said Mrs Masterton confidently. 'Likes functions, you know. She'll make a terrific toilet and be as pleased about it as a child. Just fetch me a bundle of those pegs over there, will you? I want to mark the places for the clock golf numbers.'

Poirot, thus pressed into service, was worked by Mrs Masterton relentlessly, as a useful apprentice. She condescended to talk to him in the intervals of hard labour.

'Got to do everything yourself, I find. Only way . . . By the way, you're a friend of the Eliots, I believe?'

Poirot, after his long sojourn in England, comprehended that this was an indication of social recognition. Mrs Masterton was in fact saying: 'Although a foreigner, I understand you are One of Us.' She continued to chat in an intimate manner.

'Nice to have Nasse lived in again. We were all so afraid it was going to be a hotel. You know what it is nowadays; one drives through the country and passes place after place with the board up "Guest House" or "Private Hotel" or "Hotel A.A. Fully Licensed." All the houses one stayed in as a girl – or where one went to dances. Very sad. Yes, I'm glad about Nasse and so is poor dear Amy Folliat, of course. She's had such a hard life – but never complains, I will say. Sir George has done wonders for Nasse – and *not* vulgarized it. Don't know whether that's the result of Amy Folliat's influence – or whether it's his own natural good taste. He *has* got quite good taste, you know. Very surprising in a man like that.'

'He is not, I understand, one of the landed gentry?' said Poirot cautiously.

'He isn't even really Sir George – was christened it, I understand. Took the idea from Lord George Sanger's Circus, I suspect. Very amusing really. Of course we never let on. Rich men must be allowed their little snobberies, don't you agree? The funny thing is that in spite of his origins George Stubbs would go down perfectly well anywhere. He's a throwback. Pure type of the eighteenth-century country squire. Good blood in him, I'd say. Father a gent and mother a barmaid, is my guess.'

Mrs Masterton interrupted herself to yell to a gardener.

'Not by that rhododendron. You must leave room for the skittles over to the right. *Right* – not left!'

She went on: 'Extraordinary how they can't tell their left from their right. The Brewis woman is efficient. Doesn't like poor Hattie, though. Looks at her sometimes as though she'd like to murder her. So many of these good secretaries are in love with their boss. Now where do you think Jim Warburton can have got to? Silly the way he sticks to calling himself "Captain." Not a regular soldier and never within miles of a German. One has to put up, of course, with what one can get these days – and he's a hard worker – but I feel there's something rather fishy about him. Ah! Here are the Legges.'

Sally Legge, dressed in slacks and a yellow pullover, said brightly:

'We've come to help.'

'Lots to do,' boomed Mrs Masterton. 'Now, let me see . . .'

Poirot, profiting by her inattention, slipped away. As he came round the corner of the house on to the front terrace he became a spectator of a new drama.

Two young women, in shorts, with bright blouses, had come out from the wood and were standing uncertainly looking up at the house. In one of them he thought he recognized the Italian girl of yesterday's lift in the car. From the window of Lady Stubbs' bedroom Sir George leaned out and addressed them wrathfully.

'You're trespassing,' he shouted.

'Please?' said the young woman with the green headscarf.

'You can't come through here. Private.'

The other young woman, who had a royal blue headscarf, said brightly:

'Please? Nassecombe Quay . . .' She pronounced it carefully. 'It is this way? Please.'

'You're trespassing,' bellowed Sir George.

'Please?'

'*Trespassing!* No way through. You've got to go back. *BACK!* The way you came.'

They stared as he gesticulated. Then they consulted together in a flood of foreign speech. Finally, doubtfully, blue-scarf said:

'Back? To Hostel?'

'That's right. And you take the road – *road* round that way.'

They retreated unwillingly. Sir George mopped his brow and looked down at Poirot.

'Spend my time turning people off,' he said. 'Used to come through the top gate. I've padlocked that. Now they come through the woods, having got over the fence. Think they can get down to the shore and the quay easily this way. Well, they can, of course, much quicker. But there's no right of way – never has been. And they're practically all foreigners – don't understand what you say, and just jabber back at you in Dutch or something.'

'Of these, one is German and the other Italian, I think – I saw the Italian girl on her way from the station yesterday.'

'Every kind of language they talk . . . Yes, Hattie? What did you say?' He drew back into the room.

Poirot turned to find Mrs Oliver and a well-developed girl of fourteen dressed in Guide uniform close behind him.

'This is Marlene,' said Mrs Oliver.

Marlene giggled.

'I'm the horrible Corpse,' she said. 'But I'm not going to have any blood on me.' Her tone expressed disappointment.

'No?'

'No. Just strangled with a cord, that's all. I'd of *liked* to be stabbed – and have lashings of red paint.'

'Captain Warburton thought it might look too realistic,' said Mrs Oliver.

'In a murder I think you *ought* to have blood,' said Marlene sulkily. She looked at Poirot with hungry interest. 'Seen lots of murders, haven't you? So *she* says.'

'One or two,' said Poirot modestly.

He observed with alarm that Mrs Oliver was leaving them.

'Any sex maniacs?' asked Marlene with avidity.

'Certainly not.'

'I like sex maniacs,' said Marlene with relish. 'Reading about them, I mean.'

'You would probably not like meeting one.'

'Oh, I dunno. D'you know what? I believe we've got a sex maniac round here. My granddad saw a body in the woods once. He was scared and ran away, and when he come back it was gone. It was a woman's body. But of course he's batty, my granddad is, so no one listens to what he says.'

Poirot managed to escape and, regaining the house by a circuitous route, took refuge in his bedroom. He felt in need of repose.

CHAPTER 6

Lunch was an early and quickly snatched affair of a cold buffet. At two-thirty a minor film star was to open the fête. The weather, after looking ominously like rain, began to improve. By three o'clock the fête was in full swing. People were paying the admission charge of half a crown in large numbers, and cars were lining one side of the long drive. Students from the Youth Hostel arrived in batches conversing loudly in foreign tongues. True to Mrs Masterton's forecast, Lady Stubbs had emerged from her bedroom just before half-past two, dressed in a cyclamen dress with an enormous coolie-shaped hat of black straw. She wore large quantities of diamonds.

Miss Brewis murmured sardonically:

'Thinks it's the Royal Enclosure at Ascot, evidently!'

But Poirot complimented her gravely.

'It is a beautiful creation that you have on, Madame.'

'It is nice, isn't it,' said Hattie happily. 'I wore it for Ascot.'

The minor film star was arriving and Hattie moved forward to greet her.

Poirot retreated into the background. He wandered around disconsolately – everything seemed to be proceeding in the normal fashion of fêtes. There was a coconut shy, presided over by Sir George in his heartiest fashion, a skittle alley and a hoop-la. There were various 'stalls' displaying local produce of fruit, vegetables, jams and cakes – and others displaying 'fancy objects.' There were 'raffles' of cakes, of baskets of fruit; even, it seemed, of a pig; and a 'Lucky Dip' for children at twopence a go.

There was a good crowd of people by now and an Exhibition of Children's Dancing began. Poirot saw no sign of Mrs Oliver, but Lady Stubbs' cyclamen pink figure showed up amongst the crowd as she drifted rather vaguely about. The focus of attention, however, seemed to be Mrs Folliat. She was quite transformed in appearance – wearing a hydrangea-blue foulard frock and a smart grey hat, she appeared to preside over the proceedings, greeting new arrivals, and directing people to the various side shows.

Poirot lingered near her and listened to some of the conversations.

'Amy, my dear, how are you?'

'Oh, Pamela, how nice of you and Edward to come. Such a long way from Tiverton.'

'The weather's held for you. Remember the year before the war? Cloudburst came down about four o'clock. Ruined the whole show.'

'But it's been a wonderful summer this year. Dorothy! It's *ages* since I've seen you.'

'We felt we *had* to come and see Nasse in its glory. I see you've cut back the berberis on the bank.'

'Yes, it shows the hydrangeas better, don't you think?'

'How wonderful they are. What a blue! But, my dear, you've done wonders in the last year. Nasse is really beginning to look like itself again.'

Dorothy's husband boomed in a deep voice:

'Came over to see the commandant here during the war. Nearly broke my heart.'

Mrs Folliat turned to greet a humbler visitor.

'Mrs Knapper, I am pleased to see you. Is this Lucy? How she's grown!'

'She'll be leaving school next year. Pleased to see you looking so well, ma'am.'

'I'm very well, thank you. You must go and try your luck at

hoop-la, Lucy. See you in the tea tent later, Mrs Knapper. I shall be helping with the teas.'

An elderly man, presumably Mr Knapper, said diffidently:

'Pleased to have you back at Nasse, ma'am. Seems like old times.'

Mrs Folliat's response was drowned as two women and a big beefy man rushed towards her.

'Amy, dear, such *ages*. This looks the *greatest* success! Do tell me what you've done about the rose garden. Muriel told me that you're restocking it with all the new floribundas.'

The beefy man chipped in.

'Where's Marylin Gale –?'

'Reggie's just dying to meet her. He saw her last picture.'

'That her in the big hat? My word, that's some get-up.'

'Don't be stupid, darling. That's Hattie Stubbs. You know, Amy, you really shouldn't let her go round *quite* so like a mannequin.'

'Amy?' Another friend claimed attention. 'This is Roger, Edward's boy. My dear, so nice to have you back at Nasse.'

Poirot moved slowly away and absent-mindedly invested a shilling on a ticket that might win him the pig.

He heard faintly still, the 'So good of you to come' refrain from behind him. He wondered whether Mrs Folliat realized how completely she had slipped into the role of hostess or whether it was entirely unconscious. She was, very definitely this afternoon, Mrs Folliat of Nasse House.

He was standing by the tent labelled '*Madame Zuleika will tell your Fortune for 2s. 6d.*' Teas had just begun to be served and there was no longer a queue for the fortune telling. Poirot bowed his head, entered the tent and paid over his half-crown willingly for the privilege of sinking into a chair and resting his aching feet.

Madame Zuleika was wearing flowing black robes, a gold tinsel scarf wound round her head and a veil across the lower half of her face which slightly muffled her remarks. A gold bracelet hung with lucky charms tinkled as she took Poirot's hand and gave him a rapid reading, agreeably full of money to come, success with a dark beauty and a miraculous escape from an accident.

'It is very agreeable all that you tell me, Madame Legge. I only wish that it could come true.'

'Oh!' said Sally. 'So you know me, do you?'

'I had advance information – Mrs Oliver told me that you were originally to be the "victim," but that you had been snatched from her for the Occult.'

'I wish I *was* being the "body,"' said Sally. 'Much more peaceful. All Jim Warburton's fault. Is it four o'clock yet? I want my tea. I'm off duty from four to half-past.'

'Ten minutes to go, still,' said Poirot, consulting his large old-fashioned watch. 'Shall I bring you a cup of tea here?'

'No, no. I want the break. This tent is stifling. Are there a lot of people waiting still?'

'No. I think they are lining up for tea.'

'Good.'

Poirot emerged from the tent and was immediately challenged by a determined woman and made to pay sixpence and guess the weight of a cake.

A hoop-la stall presided over by a fat motherly woman urged him to try his luck and, much to his discomfiture, he immediately won a large Kewpie doll. Walking sheepishly along with this he encountered Michael Weyman who was standing gloomily on the outskirts near the top of a path that led down to the quay.

'You seem to have been enjoying yourself, M. Poirot,' he said, with a sardonic grin.

Poirot contemplated his prize.

'It is truly horrible, is it not?' he said sadly.

A small child near him suddenly burst out crying. Poirot stooped swiftly and tucked the doll into the child's arm.

'*Voilà*, it is for you.'

The tears ceased abruptly.

'There – Violet – isn't the gentleman kind? Say, Ta, ever so –'

'Children's Fancy Dress,' called out Captain Warburton through a megaphone. 'The first class – three to five. Form up, please.'

Poirot moved towards the house and was cannoned into by a young man who was stepping backwards to take a better aim at a coconut. The young man scowled and Poirot apologized, mechanically, his eye held fascinated by the varied pattern of the young man's shirt. He recognized it as the 'turtle' shirt of Sir George's description. Every kind of turtle, tortoise and sea monster appeared to be writhing and crawling over it.

Poirot blinked and was accosted by the Dutch girl to whom he had given a lift the day before.

'So you have come to the fête,' he said. 'And your friend?'

'Oh, yes, she, too, comes here this afternoon. I have not seen her yet, but we shall leave together by the bus that goes from the gates at five-fifteen. We go to Torquay and there I change to another bus for Plymouth. It is convenient.'

This explained what had puzzled Poirot, the fact that the Dutch girl was perspiring under the weight of a rucksack.

He said: 'I saw your friend this morning.'

'Oh, yes, Elsa, a German girl, was with her and she told me they had tried to get through woods to the river and quay. And the gentleman who owns the house was very angry and made them go back.'

She added, turning her head to where Sir George was urging competitors on at the coconut shy:

'But now – this afternoon, he is very polite.'

Poirot considered explaining that there was a difference between young women who were trespassers and the same young women when they had paid two shillings and sixpence entrance fee and were legally entitled to sample the delights of Nasse House and its grounds. But Captain Warburton and his megaphone bore down upon him. The Captain was looking hot and bothered.

'Have you seen Lady Stubbs, Poirot? Anyone seen Lady Stubbs? She's supposed to be judging this Fancy Dress business and I can't find her anywhere.'

'I saw her, let me see – oh, about half an hour ago. But then I went to have my fortune told.'

'Curse the woman,' said Warburton angrily. 'Where can she have disappeared to? The children are waiting and we're behind schedule as it is.'

He looked round.

'Where's Amanda Brewis?'

Miss Brewis, also, was not in evidence.

'It really is too bad,' said Warburton. 'One's got to have *some* co-operation if one's trying to run a show. Where *can* Hattie be? Perhaps she's gone into the house.'

He strode off rapidly.

Poirot edged his way towards the roped-off space where teas were being served in a large marquee, but there was a long queue waiting and he decided against it.

He inspected the Fancy Goods stall where a determined old lady very nearly managed to sell him a plastic collar box, and finally made his way round the outskirts to a place where he could contemplate the activity from a safe distance.

He wondered where Mrs Oliver was.

Footsteps behind him made him turn his head. A young man was coming up the path from the quay; a very dark young man, faultlessly attired in yachting costume. He paused as though disconcerted by the scene before him.

Then he spoke hesitatingly to Poirot.

'You will excuse me. Is this the house of Sir George Stubbs?'

'It is indeed.' Poirot paused and then hazarded a guess. 'Are you, perhaps, the cousin of Lady Stubbs?'

'I am Etienne de Sousa –'

'My name is Hercule Poirot.'

They bowed to each other. Poirot explained the circumstances of the fête. As he finished, Sir George came across the lawn towards them from the coconut shy.

'De Sousa? Delighted to see you. Hattie got your letter this morning. Where's your yacht?'

'It is moored at Helmmouth. I came up the river to the quay here in my launch.'

'We must find Hattie. She's somewhere about . . . You'll dine with us this evening, I hope?'

'You are most kind.'

'Can we put you up?'

'That also is most kind, but I will sleep on my yacht. It is easier so.'

'Are you staying here long?'

'Two or three days, perhaps. It depends.' De Sousa shrugged elegant shoulders.

'Hattie will be delighted, I'm sure,' said Sir George politely. 'Where *is* she? I saw her not long ago.'

He looked round in a perplexed manner.

'She ought to be judging the children's fancy dress. I can't understand it. Excuse me a moment. I'll ask Miss Brewis.'

He hurried off. De Sousa looked after him. Poirot looked at De Sousa.

'It is some little time since you last saw your cousin?' he asked.

The other shrugged his shoulders.

'I have not seen her since she was fifteen years old. Soon after that she was sent abroad – to school at a convent in France. As a child she promised to have good looks.'

He looked inquiringly at Poirot.

'She is a beautiful woman,' said Poirot.

'And that is her husband? He seems what they call "a good fellow," but not perhaps very polished? Still, for Hattie it might be perhaps a little difficult to find a suitable husband.'

Poirot remained with a politely inquiring expression on his face. The other laughed.

'Oh, it is no secret. At fifteen Hattie was mentally unde-veloped. Feeble minded, do you not call it? She is still the same?'

'It would seem so – yes,' said Poirot cautiously.

De Sousa shrugged his shoulders.

'Ah, well! Why should one ask it of women – that they should be intelligent? It is not necessary.'

Sir George was back, fuming. Miss Brewis was with him, speaking rather breathlessly.

'I've no idea where she is, Sir George. I saw her over by the fortune teller's tent last. But that was at least twenty minutes or half an hour ago. She's not in the house.'

'Is it not possible,' asked Poirot, 'that she has gone to observe the progress of Mrs Oliver's murder hunt?'

Sir George's brow cleared.

'That's probably it. Look here, I can't leave the shows here. I'm in charge. And Amanda's got her hands full. Could *you* possibly have a look round, Poirot? You know the course.'

But Poirot did not know the course. However, an inquiry of Miss Brewis gave him rough guidance. Miss Brewis took brisk charge of De Sousa and Poirot went off murmuring to himself, like an incantation: 'Tennis Court, Camellia Garden, The Folly, Upper Nursery Garden, Boathouse . . .'

As he passed the coconut shy he was amused to notice Sir George proffering wooden balls with a dazzling smile of welcome to the same young Italian woman whom he had driven off that morning and who was clearly puzzled at his change of attitude.

He went on his way to the tennis court. But there was no one there but an old gentleman of military aspect who was fast asleep on a garden seat with his hat pulled over his eyes. Poirot retraced his steps to the house and went on down to the camellia garden.

In the camellia garden Poirot found Mrs Oliver dressed in purple splendour, sitting on a garden seat in a brooding attitude, and looking rather like Mrs Siddons. She beckoned him to the seat beside her.

'This is only the second clue,' she hissed. 'I think I've made them too difficult. Nobody's come yet.'

At this moment a young man in shorts, with a prominent Adam's apple, entered the garden. With a cry of satisfaction he hurried to a tree in one corner and a further satisfied cry announced his discovery of the next clue. Passing them, he felt impelled to communicate his satisfaction.

'Lots of people don't know about cork trees,' he said confidentially. 'Clever photograph, the first clue, but I spotted what it was – section of a tennis net. There was a poison bottle, empty, and a cork. Most of 'em will go all out after the bottle clue – I guessed it was a red herring. Very delicate, cork trees, only hardy in this part of the world. I'm interested in rare shrubs and trees. *Now* where does one go, I wonder?'

He frowned over the entry in the notebook he carried.

'I've copied the next clue but it doesn't seem to make sense.' He eyed them suspiciously. 'You competing?'

'Oh, no,' said Mrs Oliver. 'We're just – looking on.'

'Righty-ho . . . "*When lovely woman stoops to folly*." . . . I've an idea I've heard that somewhere.'

'It is a well-known quotation,' said Poirot.

'A Folly can also be a building,' said Mrs Oliver helpfully. 'White – with pillars,' she added.

'*That's* an idea! Thanks a lot. They say Mrs Ariadne Oliver is down here herself somewhere about. I'd like to get her autograph. You haven't seen her about, have you?'

'No,' said Mrs Oliver firmly.

'I'd like to meet her. Good yarns she writes.' He lowered his voice. 'But they say she drinks like a fish.'

He hurried off and Mrs Oliver said indignantly:

'Really! That's most unfair when I only like lemonade!'

'And have you not just perpetrated the greatest unfairness in helping that young man towards the next clue?'

'Considering he's the only one who's got here so far, I thought he ought to be encouraged.'

'But you wouldn't give him your autograph.'

'That's different,' said Mrs Oliver. 'Sh! Here come some more.'

But these were not clue hunters. They were two women who having paid for admittance were determined to get their money's worth by seeing the grounds thoroughly.

They were hot and dissatisfied.

'You'd think they'd have *some* nice flower-beds,' said one to the other. 'Nothing but trees and more trees. It's not what I call a *garden*.'

Mrs Oliver nudged Poirot, and they slipped quietly away.

'Supposing,' said Mrs Oliver distractedly, 'that *nobody* ever finds my body?'

'Patience, Madame, and courage,' said Poirot. 'The afternoon is still young.'

'That's true,' said Mrs Oliver, brightening. 'And it's half-price admission after four-thirty, so probably lots of people will flock in. Let's go and see how that Marlene child is getting on. I don't really trust that girl, you know. No sense of responsibility. I wouldn't put it past her to sneak away quietly, instead of being a corpse, and go and have tea. You know what people are like about their teas.'

They proceeded amicably along the woodland path and Poirot commented on the geography of the property.

'I find it very confusing,' he said. 'So many paths, and one is never sure where they lead. And trees, trees everywhere.'

'You sound like that disgruntled woman we've just left.'

They passed the Folly and zig-zagged down the path to the river. The outlines of the boathouse showed beneath them.

Poirot remarked that it would be awkward if the murder searchers were to light upon the boathouse and find the body by accident.

'A sort of short cut? I thought of that. That's why the last clue is just a key. You can't unlock the door without it. It's a Yale. You can only open it from the inside.'

A short steep slope led down to the door of the boathouse which was build out over the river, with a little wharf and a storage place for boats underneath. Mrs Oliver took a key from a pocket concealed amongst her purple folds and unlocked the door.

'We've just come to cheer you up, Marlene,' she said brightly as she entered.

She felt slightly remorseful at her unjust suspicions of Marlene's loyalty, for Marlene, artistically arranged as 'the body,' was playing her part nobly, sprawled on the floor by the window.

Marlene made no response. She lay quite motionless. The wind blowing gently through the open window rustled a pile of 'comics' spread out on the table.

'It's all right,' said Mrs Oliver impatiently. 'It's only me and M. Poirot. Nobody's got any distance with the clues yet.'

Poirot was frowning. Very gently he pushed Mrs Oliver aside and went and bent over the girl on the floor. A suppressed exclamation came from his lips. He looked up at Mrs Oliver.

'So . . .' he said. 'That which you expected has happened.'

'You don't mean . . .' Mrs Oliver's eyes widened in horror. She grasped for one of the basket chairs and sat down. 'You can't mean . . . She isn't *dead*?'

Poirot nodded.

'Oh, yes,' he said. 'She is dead. Though not very long dead.'

'But how –?'

He lifted the corner of the gay scarf bound round the girl's head, so that Mrs Oliver could see the ends of the clothes line.

'Just like *my* murder,' said Mrs Oliver unsteadily. 'But *who*? And *why*?'

'That is the question,' said Poirot.

He forebore to add that those had also been her questions.

And that the answers to them could not be her answers, since the victim was not the Yugoslavian first wife of an Atom Scientist, but Marlene Tucker, a fourteen-year-old village girl who, as far as was known, had not an enemy in the world.

CHAPTER 7

Detective-Inspector Bland sat behind a table in the study. Sir George had met him on arrival, had taken him down to the boathouse and had now returned with him to the house. Down at the boathouse a photographic unit was now busy and the fingerprint men and the medical officer had just arrived.

'This do for you here all right?' asked Sir George.

'Very nicely, thank you, sir.'

'What am I to do about this show that's going on, tell 'em about it, stop it, or what?'

Inspector Bland considered for a moment or two.

'What have you done so far, Sir George?' he asked.

'Haven't said anything. There's a sort of idea floating round that there's been an accident. Nothing more than that. I don't think anyone's suspected yet that it's – er – well, murder.'

'Then leave things as they are just for the moment,' decided Bland. 'The news will get round fast enough, I dare say,' he added cynically. He thought again for a moment or two before asking, 'How many people do you think there are at this affair?'

'Couple of hundred I should say,' answered Sir George, 'and more pouring in every moment. People seem to have come from a good long way round. In fact the whole thing's being a roaring success. Damned unfortunate.'

Inspector Bland inferred correctly that it was the murder and not the success of the fête to which Sir George was referring.

'A couple of hundred,' he mused, 'and any one of them, I suppose, could have done it.'

He sighed.

'Tricky,' said Sir George sympathetically. 'But I don't see what reason any one of them could have had. The whole thing seems quite fantastic – don't see who would want to go murdering a girl like that.'

'How much can you tell me about the girl? She was a local girl, I understand?'

'Yes. Her people live in one of the cottages down near the quay. Her father works at one of the local farms – Paterson's, I think.' He added, 'The mother is here at the fête this afternoon. Miss Brewis – that's my secretary, and she can tell you about everything much better than I can – Miss Brewis winkled the woman out and has got her somewhere, giving her cups of tea.'

'Quite so,' said the inspector, approvingly. 'I'm not quite clear yet, Sir George, as to the circumstances of all this. What was the girl doing down there in the boathouse? I understand there's some kind of a murder hunt – or treasure hunt, going on.'

Sir George nodded.

'Yes. We all thought it rather a bright idea. Doesn't seem quite so bright now. I think Miss Brewis can probably explain it all to you better than I can. I'll send her to you, shall I? Unless there's anything else you want to know about first.'

'Not at the moment, Sir George. I may have more questions to ask you later. There are people I shall want to see. You, and Lady Stubbs, and the people who discovered the body. One of them, I gather, is the woman novelist who designed this murder hunt as you call it.'

'That's right. Mrs Oliver. Mrs Ariadne Oliver.'

The inspector's eyebrows went up slightly.

'Oh – her!' he said. 'Quite a best-seller. I've read a lot of her books myself.'

'She's a bit upset at present,' said Sir George, 'naturally, I suppose. I'll tell her you'll be wanting her, shall I? I don't know where my wife is. She seems to have disappeared completely from view. Somewhere among the two or three hundred, I suppose – not that she'll be able to tell you much. I mean about the girl or anything like that. Who would you like to see first?'

'I think perhaps your secretary, Miss Brewis, and after that the girl's mother.'

Sir George nodded and left the room.

The local police constable, Robert Hoskins, opened the door for him and shut it after he went out. He then volunteered a statement, obviously intended as a commentary on some of Sir George's remarks.

'Lady Stubbs is a bit wanting,' he said, 'up *here*.' He tapped his forehead. 'That's why he said she wouldn't be much help. Scatty, that's what she is.'

'Did he marry a local girl?'

'No. Foreigner of some sort. Coloured, some say, but I don't think that's so myself.'

Bland nodded. He was silent for a moment, doodling with a pencil on a sheet of paper in front of him. Then he asked a question which was clearly off the record.

'Who did it, Hoskins?' he said.

If anyone did have any ideas as to what had been going on, Bland thought, it would be P.C. Hoskins. Hoskins was a man of inquisitive mind with a great interest in everybody and everything. He had a gossiping wife and that, taken with his position as local constable, provided him with vast stores of information of a personal nature.

'Foreigner, if you ask me. 'Twouldn't be anyone local. The Tuckers is all right. Nice, respectable family. Nine of 'em all told. Two of the older girls is married, one boy in the Navy, the other one's doing his National Service, another girl's over to a hairdresser's at Torquay. There's three younger ones at home, two boys and a girl.' He paused, considering. 'None of 'em's what you'd call bright, but Mrs Tucker keeps her home nice, clean as a pin – youngest of eleven, she was. She's got her old father living with her.'

Bland received this information in silence. Given in Hoskins' particular idiom, it was an outline of the Tuckers' social position and standing.

'That's why I say it was a foreigner,' continued Hoskins. 'One of those that stop up to the Hostel at Hoodown, likely as not. There's some queer ones among them – and a lot of goings-on. Be surprised, you would, at what I've seen 'em doing in the bushes and the woods! Every bit as bad as what goes on in parked cars along the Common.'

P.C. Hoskins was by this time an absolute specialist on the subject of sexual 'goings-on.' They formed a large portion of his conversation when off duty and having his pint in the Bull and Bear. Bland said:

'I don't think there was anything – well, of that kind. The doctor will tell us, of course, as soon as he's finished his examination.'

'Yes, sir, that'll be up to him, that will. But what I say is, you never know with foreigners. Turn nasty, they can, all in a moment.'

Inspector Bland sighed as he thought to himself that it was not quite as easy as that. It was all very well for Constable Hoskins to put the blame conveniently on 'foreigners.' The door opened and the doctor walked in.

'Done my bit,' he remarked. 'Shall they take her away now? The other outfits have packed up.'

'Sergeant Cottrill will attend to that,' said Bland. 'Well, Doc, what's the finding?'

'Simple and straightforward as it can be,' said the doctor. 'No complications. Garrotted with a piece of clothes line. Nothing could be simpler or easier to do. No struggle of any kind beforehand. I'd say the kid didn't know what was happening to her until it had happened.'

'Any signs of assault?'

'None. No assault, signs of rape, or interference of any kind.'

'Not presumably a sexual crime, then?'

'I wouldn't say so, no.' The doctor added, 'I shouldn't say she'd been a particularly attractive girl.'

'Was she fond of the boys?'

Bland addressed this question to Constable Hoskins.

'I wouldn't say they'd much use for her,' said Constable Hoskins, 'though maybe she'd have liked it if they had.'

'Maybe,' agreed Bland. His mind went back to the pile of comic papers in the boathouse and the idle scrawls on the margin. 'Johnny goes with Kate,' 'Georgie Porgie kisses hikers in the wood.' He thought there had been a little wishful thinking there. On the whole, though, it seemed unlikely that there was a sex angle to Marlene Tucker's death. Although, of course, one never knew . . . There were always those queer criminal individuals, men with a secret lust to kill, who specialized in immature female victims. One of these might be present in this part of the world during this holiday season. He almost believed that it *must* be so – for otherwise he could really see no reason for so pointless a crime. However, he thought, we're only at the beginning. I'd better see what all these people have to tell me.

'What about time of death?' he asked.

The doctor glanced over at the clock and his own watch.

'Just after half-past five now,' he said. 'Say I saw her about twenty past five – she'd been dead about an hour. Roughly, that is to say. Put it between four o'clock and twenty to five. Let you know if there's anything more after the autopsy.' He added: 'You'll get the proper report with the long words in due course. I'll be off now. I've got some patients to see.'

He left the room and Inspector Bland asked Hoskins to fetch Miss Brewis. His spirits rose a little when Miss Brewis came into the room. Here, as he recognized at once, was efficiency. He would get clear answers to his questions, definite times and no muddle-headedness.

'Mrs Tucker's in my sitting-room,' Miss Brewis said as she sat down. 'I've broken the news to her and given her some tea. She's very upset, naturally. She wanted to see the body but I told her it was much better not. Mr Tucker gets off work at six o'clock and was coming to join his wife here. I told them to look out for him and bring him along when he arrives. The younger children are at the fête still, and someone is keeping an eye on them.'

'Excellent,' said Inspector Bland, with approval. 'I think before I see Mrs Tucker I would like to hear what you and Lady Stubbs can tell me.'

'I don't know where Lady Stubbs is,' said Miss Brewis acidly. 'I rather imagine she got bored with the fête and has wandered off somewhere, but I don't expect she can tell you anything more than I can. What exactly is it that you want to know?'

'I want to know all the details of this murder hunt first and of how this girl, Marlene Tucker, came to be taking a part in it.'

'That's quite easy.'

Succinctly and clearly Miss Brewis explained the idea of the murder hunt as an original attraction for the fête, the engaging of Mrs Oliver, the well-known novelist, to arrange the matter, and a short outline of the plot.

'Originally,' Miss Brewis explained, 'Mrs Alec Legge was to have taken the part of the victim.'

'Mrs Alec Legge?' queried the inspector.

Constable Hoskins put in an explanatory word.

'She and Mr Legge have the Lawders' cottage, the pink one

down by Mill Creek. Came here a month ago, they did. Two or three months they got it for.'

'I see. And Mrs Legge, you say, was to be the original victim? Why was that changed?'

'Well, one evening Mrs Legge told all our fortunes and was so good at it that it was decided we'd have a fortune teller's tent as one of the attractions and that Mrs Legge should put on Eastern dress and be Madame Zuleika and tell fortunes at half a crown a time. I don't think that's really illegal, is it, Inspector? I mean it's usually done at these kind of fêtes?'

Inspector Bland smiled faintly.

'Fortune telling and raffles aren't always taken too seriously, Miss Brewis,' he said. 'Now and then we have to – er – make an example.'

'But usually you're tactful? Well, that's how it was. Mrs Legge agreed to help us that way and so we had to find somebody else to do the body. The local Guides were helping us at the fête, and I think someone suggested that one of the Guides would do quite well.'

'Just who was it who suggested that, Miss Brewis?'

'Really, I don't quite know . . . I think it may have been Mrs Masterton, the Member's wife. No, perhaps it was Captain Warburton . . . Really, I can't be sure. But, anyway, it *was* suggested.'

'Is there any reason why this particular girl should have been chosen?'

'N-no, I don't think so. Her people are tenants on the estate, and her mother, Mrs Tucker, sometimes comes to help in the kitchen. I don't know quite why we settled on her. Probably her name came to mind first. We asked her and she seemed quite pleased to do it.'

'She definitely wanted to do it?'

'Oh, yes, I think she was flattered. She was a very moronic kind of girl,' continued Miss Brewis, 'she couldn't have *acted* a part or anything like that. But this was all very simple, and she felt she'd been singled out from the others and was pleased about it.'

'What exactly was it that she had to do?'

'She had to stay in the boathouse. When she heard anyone coming to the door she was to lie down on the floor, put the cord round her neck and sham dead.' Miss Brewis' tones were calm and businesslike. The fact that the girl who was to sham dead had actually been found dead did not at the moment appear to affect her emotionally.

'Rather a boring way for the girl to spend the afternoon when she might have been at the fête,' suggested Inspector Bland.

'I suppose it was in a way,' said Miss Brewis, 'but one can't have everything, can one? And Marlene did enjoy the idea of being the body. It made her feel important. She had a pile of papers and things to read to keep her amused.'

'And something to eat as well?' said the inspector. 'I noticed there was a tray down there with a plate and glass.'

'Oh, yes, she had a big plate of sweet cakes, and a raspberry fruit drink. I took them down to her myself.'

Bland looked up sharply.

'You took them down to her? When?'

'About the middle of the afternoon.'

'What time exactly? Can you remember?'

Miss Brewis considered a moment.

'Let me see. Children's Fancy Dress was judged, there was a little delay – Lady Stubbs couldn't be found, but Mrs Folliat took her place, so that was all right . . . Yes, it must have been – I'm almost sure – about five minutes past four that I collected the cakes and the fruit drink.'

'And you took them down to her at the boathouse yourself. What time did you reach there?'

'Oh, it takes about five minutes to go down to the boathouse – about quarter past four, I should think.'

'And at quarter past four Marlene Tucker was alive and well?'

'Yes, of course,' said Miss Brewis, 'and very eager to know how people were getting on with the murder hunt, too. I'm afraid I couldn't tell her. I'd been too busy with the side show on the lawn, but I did know that a lot of people had entered for it. Twenty or thirty to my knowledge. Probably a good many more.'

'How did you find Marlene when you arrived at the boathouse?'

'I've just told you.'

'No, no, I don't mean that. I mean, was she lying on the floor shamming dead when you opened the door?'

'Oh, no,' said Miss Brewis, 'because I called out just before I got there. So she opened the door and I took the tray in and put it on the table.'

'At a quarter past four,' said Bland, writing it down, 'Marlene Tucker was alive and well. You will understand, I'm sure, Miss Brewis, that that is a very important point. You are quite sure of your times?'

'I can't be exactly sure because I didn't look at my watch, but I had looked at it a short time previously and that's as near as I can get.' She added, with a sudden dawning realization of the inspector's point, 'Do you mean that it was soon after –?'

'It can't have been very long after, Miss Brewis.'

'Oh, dear,' said Miss Brewis.

It was a rather inadequate expression, but nevertheless it conveyed well enough Miss Brewis' dismay and concern.

'Now, Miss Brewis, on your way down to the boathouse and on your way back again to the house, did you meet anybody or see anyone near the boathouse?'

Miss Brewis considered.

'No,' she said, 'I didn't meet anyone. I might have, of course, because the grounds are open to everyone this afternoon. But on the whole, people tend to stay round the lawn and the side shows and all that. They like to go round the kitchen gardens and the greenhouses, but they don't walk through the woodlands as much as I should have thought they would. People tend to herd together very much at these affairs, don't you think so, Inspector?'

The inspector said that that was probably so.

'Though, I think,' said Miss Brewis, with sudden memory, 'that there *was* someone in the Folly.'

'The Folly?'

'Yes. A small white temple arrangement. It was put up just a year or two ago. It's to the right of the path as you go down to the boathouse. There was someone in there. A courting couple, I suspect. Someone was laughing and then someone said, "Hush."'

'You don't know who this courting couple was?'

'I've no idea. You can't see the front of the Folly from the path. The sides and back are enclosed.'

The inspector thought for a moment or two, but it did not seem likely to him that the couple – whoever they were – in the Folly were important. Better find out who they were, perhaps, because they in their turn might have seen someone coming up from or going down to the boathouse.

'And there was no one else on the path? No one at all?' he insisted.

'I see what you're driving at, of course,' said Miss Brewis. 'I can only assure you that I didn't meet anyone. But then, you see, I needn't have. I mean, if there had been anyone on the path who didn't want me to see them, it's the simplest thing in the world just to slip behind some of the rhododendron bushes. The path's ordered on both sides with shrubs and rhododendron bushes. If anyone who had no business to be there heard someone coming along the path, they could slip out of sight in a moment.'

The inspector shifted on to another tack.

'Is there anything you know about this girl yourself, that could help us?' he asked.

'I really know nothing about her,' said Miss Brewis. 'I don't think I'd ever spoken to her until this affair. She's one of the girls I've seen about – I know her vaguely by sight, but that's all.'

'And you know nothing *about* her – nothing that could be helpful?'

'I don't know of any reason why anyone should want to murder her,' said Miss Brewis. 'In fact it seems to me, if you know what I mean, quite impossible that such a thing should have happened. I can only think that to some unbalanced mind, the fact that she was to be the murdered victim might have induced the wish to make her a real victim. But even that sounds very far fetched and silly.'

Bland sighed.

'Oh, well,' he said, 'I suppose I'd better see the mother now.'

Mrs Tucker was a thin, hatchet-faced woman with stringy blonde hair and a sharp nose. Her eyes were reddened with crying, but she had herself in hand now, and was ready to answer the inspector's questions.

'Doesn't seem right that a thing like that should happen,' she said. 'You read of these things in the papers, but that it should happen to our Marlene –'

'I'm very, very sorry about it,' said Inspector Bland gently.

'What I want you to do is to think as hard as you can and tell me if there is anyone who could have had any reason to harm the girl?'

'I've been thinking about that already,' said Mrs Tucker, with a sudden sniff. 'Thought and thought, I have, but I can't get anywhere. Words with the teacher at school Marlene had now and again, and she'd have her quarrels now and again with one of the girls or boys, but nothing serious in any way. There's no one who had a real down on her, nobody who'd do her a mischief.'

'She never talked to you about anyone who might have been an enemy of any kind?'

'She talked silly often, Marlene did, but nothing of that kind. It was all make-up and hair-dos, and what she'd like to do to her face and herself. You know what girls are. Far too young she was, to put on lipstick and all that muck, and her dad told her so, and so did I. But that's what she'd do when she got hold of any money. Buy herself scent and lipsticks and hide them away.'

Bland nodded. There was nothing here that could help him. An adolescent, rather silly girl, her head full of film stars and glamour – there were hundreds of Marlenes.

'What her dad'll say, I don't know,' said Mrs Tucker. 'Coming here any minute he'll be, expecting to enjoy himself. He's a rare shot at the coconuts, he is.'

She broke down suddenly and began to sob.

'If you ask me,' she said, 'it's one of them nasty foreigners up at the Hostel. You never know where you are with foreigners. Nice spoken as most of them are, some of the shirts they wear you wouldn't believe. Shirts with girls on them with these bikinis, as they call them. And all of them sunning themselves here and there with no shirts at all on – it all leads to trouble. That's what I say!'

Still weeping, Mrs Tucker was escorted from the room by Constable Hoskins. Bland reflected that the local verdict seemed to be the comfortable and probably age-long one of attributing every tragic occurrence to unspecified foreigners.

CHAPTER 8

'Got a sharp tongue, she has,' Hoskins said when he returned. 'Nags her husband and bullies her old father. I dare say she's spoke sharp to the girl once or twice and now she's feeling bad about it. Not that girls mind what their mothers say to them. Drops off 'em like water off a duck's back.'

Inspector Bland cut short these general reflections and told Hoskins to fetch Mrs Oliver.

The inspector was slightly startled by the sight of Mrs Oliver. He had not expected anything so voluminous, so purple and in such a state of emotional disturbance.

'I feel awful,' said Mrs Oliver, sinking down in the chair in front of him like a purple blancmange. 'AWFUL,' she added in what were clearly capital letters.

The inspector made a few ambiguous noises, and Mrs Oliver swept on.

'Because, you see, it's *my* murder. I did it!'

For a startled moment Inspector Bland thought that Mrs Oliver was accusing herself of the crime.

'Why I should ever have wanted the Yugoslavian wife of an Atom Scientist to be the victim, I can't imagine,' said Mrs Oliver, sweeping her hands through her elaborate hair-do in a frenzied manner with the result that she looked slightly drunk. 'Absolutely asinine of me. It might just as well have been the second gardener who wasn't what he seemed – and that wouldn't have mattered half as much because, after all, most men can look after themselves. If they can't look after themselves they ought to be able to look after themselves, and in that case I shouldn't have minded so much. Men get killed and nobody minds – I mean, nobody except their wives and sweethearts and children and things like that.'

At this point the inspector entertained unworthy suspicions about Mrs Oliver. This was aided by the faint fragrance of brandy which was wafted towards him. On their return to the house Hercule Poirot had firmly administered to his friend this sovereign remedy for shocks.

'I'm not mad and I'm not drunk,' said Mrs Oliver, intuitively divining his thoughts, 'though I dare say with that man about who thinks I drink like a fish and says everybody says so, you probably think so too.'

'What man?' demanded the inspector, his mind switching from the unexpected introduction of the second gardener into the drama, to the further introduction of an unspecified man.

'Freckles and a Yorkshire accent,' said Mrs Oliver. 'But, as I say, I'm not drunk and I'm not mad. I'm just upset. Thoroughly UPSET,' she repeated, once more resorting to capital letters.

'I'm sure, madam, it must have been most distressing,' said the inspector.

'The awful thing is,' said Mrs Oliver, 'that she *wanted* to be a sex maniac's victim, and now I suppose she was – is – which should I mean?'

'There's no question of a sex maniac,' said the inspector.

'Isn't there?' said Mrs Oliver. 'Well, thank God for that. Or, at least, I don't know. Perhaps she would rather have had it that way. But if he wasn't a sex maniac, why did anybody murder her, Inspector?'

'I was hoping,' said the inspector, 'that you could help me there.'

Undoubtedly, he thought, Mrs Oliver had put her finger on the crucial point. Why should anyone murder Marlene?

'I can't help you,' said Mrs Oliver. 'I can't imagine who could have done it. At least, of course, I can *imagine* – I can imagine anything! That's the trouble with me. I can imagine things now – this minute. I could even make them sound all right, but of course none of them would be true. I mean, she could have been murdered by someone who just likes murdering girls but that's too easy – and, anyway, too much of a coincidence that somebody should be at this fête who wanted to murder a girl. And how would he know that Marlene was in the boathouse? Or she might have known some secret about somebody's love affairs, or she may have seen someone bury a body at night, or she may have recognized somebody who was concealing his identity – or she may have known a secret about where some treasure was buried during the war. Or the man in the launch may have thrown somebody into the river and she saw it from the window of the boathouse – or she may even have got hold of some very important message in secret code and not known what it was herself.'

'Please!' The inspector held up his hand. His head was whirling.

Mrs Oliver stopped obediently. It was clear that she could have gone on in this vein for some time, although it seemed to the inspector that she had already envisaged every possibility, likely or otherwise. Out of the richness of the material presented to him, he seized upon one phrase.

'What did you mean, Mrs Oliver, by the "man in the launch"? Are you just imagining a man in a launch?'

'Somebody told me he'd come in a launch,' said Mrs Oliver. 'I can't remember who. The one we were talking about at breakfast, I mean,' she added.

'Please.' The inspector's tone was now pleading. He had had no idea before what the writers of detective stories were like. He knew that Mrs Oliver had written forty-odd books. It seemed to him astonishing at the moment that she had not written a hundred and forty. He rapped out a peremptory inquiry. 'What *is* all this about a man at breakfast who came in a launch?'

'He didn't come in the launch at breakfast time,' said Mrs Oliver, 'it was a yacht. At least, I don't mean that exactly. It was a letter.'

'Well, what was it?' demanded Bland. 'A yacht or a letter?'

'It was a letter,' said Mrs Oliver, 'to Lady Stubbs. From a cousin in a yacht. And she was frightened,' she ended.

'Frightened? What of?'

'Of him, I suppose,' said Mrs Oliver. 'Anybody could see it. She was terrified of him and she didn't want him to come, and I think that's why she's hiding now.'

'Hiding?' said the inspector.

'Well, she isn't about anywhere,' said Mrs Oliver. 'Everyone's been looking for her. And *I* think she's hiding because she's afraid of him and doesn't want to meet him.'

'Who *is* this man?' demanded the inspector.

'You'd better ask M. Poirot,' said Mrs Oliver. 'Because he spoke to him and I haven't. His name's Estaban – no, it isn't, that was in my plot. De Sousa, that's what his name is, Etienne de Sousa.'

But another name had caught the inspector's attention.

'Who did you say?' he asked. 'Mr Poirot?'

'Yes. Hercule Poirot. He was with me when we found the body.'

'Hercule Poirot . . . I wonder now. Can it be the same man? A Belgian, a small man with a very big moustache?'

'An enormous moustache,' agreed Mrs Oliver. 'Yes. Do you know him?'

'It's a good many years since I met him. I was a young sergeant at the time.'

'You met him on a murder case?'

'Yes, I did. What's *he* doing down here?'

'He was to give away the prizes,' said Mrs Oliver.

There was a momentary hesitation before she gave this answer, but it went unperceived by the inspector.

'And he was with you when you discovered the body,' said Bland. 'H'm, I'd like to talk to him.'

'Shall I get him for you?' Mrs Oliver gathered up her purple draperies hopefully.

'There's nothing more that you can add, madam? Nothing more that you think could help us in any way?'

'I don't think so,' said Mrs Oliver. 'I don't know anything. As I say, I could imagine reasons –'

The inspector cut her short. He had no wish to hear any more of Mrs Oliver's imagined solutions. They were far too confusing.

'Thank you very much, madam,' he said briskly. 'If you'll ask M. Poirot to come and speak to me here I shall be very much obliged to you.'

Mrs Oliver left the room. P.C. Hoskins inquired with interest:

'Who's this Monsieur Poirot, sir?'

'You'd describe him probably as a scream,' said Inspector Bland. 'Kind of music hall parody of a Frenchman, but actually he's a Belgian. But in spite of his absurdities, he's got brains. He must be a fair age now.'

'What about this De Sousa?' asked the constable. 'Think there's anything in that, sir?'

Inspector Bland did not hear the question. He was struck by a fact which, though he had been told it several times, was only now beginning to register.

First it had been Sir George, irritated and alarmed. 'My wife seems to have disappeared. I can't think where she has got to.' Then Miss Brewis, contemptuous: 'Lady Stubbs was not to be found. She'd got bored with the show.' And now Mrs Oliver with her theory that Lady Stubbs was hiding.

'Eh? What?' he asked absently.

Constable Hoskins cleared his throat.

'I was asking you, sir, if you thought there was anything in this business of De Sousa – whoever *he* is.'

Constable Hoskins was clearly delighted at having a specific foreigner rather than foreigners in the mass introduced into the case. But Inspector Bland's mind was running on a different course.

'I want Lady Stubbs,' he said curtly. 'Get hold of her for me. If she isn't about, look for her.'

Hoskins looked slightly puzzled but he left the room obediently. In the doorway he paused and fell back a little to allow Hercule Poirot to enter. He looked back over his shoulder with some interest before closing the door behind him.

'I don't suppose,' said Bland, rising and holding out his hand, 'that you remember me, M. Poirot.'

'But assuredly,' said Poirot. 'It is – now give me a moment, just a little moment. It is the young sergeant – yes, Sergeant Bland whom I met fourteen – no, fifteen years ago.'

'Quite right. What a memory!'

'Not at all. Since you remember me, why should I not remember you?'

It would be difficult, Bland thought, to forget Hercule Poirot, and this not entirely for complimentary reasons.

'So here you are, M. Poirot,' he said. 'Assisting at a murder once again.'

'You are right,' said Poirot. 'I was called down here to assist.'

'Called down to assist?' Bland looked puzzled. Poirot said quickly:

'I mean, I was asked down here to give away the prizes of this murder hunt.'

'So Mrs Oliver told me.'

'She told you nothing else?' Poirot said it with apparent carelessness. He was anxious to discover whether Mrs Oliver had given the inspector any hint of the real motives which had led her to insist on Poirot's journey to Devon.

'Told me nothing else? She never stopped telling me things. Every possible and impossible motive for the girl's murder. She set my head spinning. Phew! What an imagination!'

'She earns her living by her imagination, *mon ami*,' said Poirot dryly.

'She mentioned a man called De Sousa – did she imagine that?'

'No, that is sober fact.'

'There was something about a letter at breakfast and a yacht and coming up the river in a launch. I couldn't make head or tail of it.'

Poirot embarked upon an explanation. He told of the scene at the breakfast table, the letter, Lady Stubbs' headache.

'Mrs Oliver said that Lady Stubbs was frightened. Did you think she was afraid, too?'

'That was the impression she gave me.'

'Afraid of this cousin of hers? Why?'

Poirot shrugged his shoulders.

'I have no idea. All she told me was that he was bad – a bad man. She is, you understand, a little simple. Subnormal.'

'Yes, that seems to be pretty generally known round here. She didn't say why she was afraid of this De Sousa?'

'No.'

'But you think her fear was real?'

'If it was not, then she is a very clever actress,' said Poirot dryly.

'I'm beginning to have some odd ideas about this case,' said Bland. He got up and walked restlessly to and fro. 'It's that cursed woman's fault, I believe.'

'Mrs Oliver's?'

'Yes. She's put a lot of melodramatic ideas into my head.'

'And you think they may be true?'

'Not all of them – naturally – but one or two of them mightn't be as wild as they sounded. It all depends . . .' He broke off as the door opened to re-admit P.C. Hoskins.

'Don't seem able to find the lady, sir,' he said. 'She's not about anywhere.'

'I know that already,' said Bland irritably. 'I told you to find her.'

'Sergeant Farrell and P.C. Lorimer are searching the grounds, sir,' said Hoskins. 'She's not in the house,' he added.

'Find out from the man who's taking admission tickets at the gate if she's left the place. Either on foot or in a car.'

'Yes, sir.'

Hoskins departed.

'And find out when she was last seen and where,' Bland shouted after him.

'So that is the way your mind is working,' said Poirot.

'It isn't working anywhere yet,' said Bland, 'but I've just woken up to the fact that a lady who ought to be on the premises isn't on the premises! And I want to know why. Tell me what more you know about what's-his-name De Sousa.'

Poirot described his meeting with the young man who had come up the path from the quay.

'He is probably still here at the fête,' he said. 'Shall I tell Sir George that you want to see him?'

'Not for a moment or two,' said Bland. 'I'd like to find out a little more first. When did you yourself last see Lady Stubbs?'

Poirot cast his mind back. He found it difficult to remember exactly. He recalled vague glimpses of her tall, cyclamen-clad figure with the drooping black hat moving about the lawn talking to people, hovering here and there; occasionally he would hear that strange laugh of hers, distinctive amongst the many other confused sounds.

'I think,' he said doubtfully, 'it must have been not long before four o'clock.'

'And where was she then, and who was she with?'

'She was in the middle of a group of people near the house.'

'Was she there when De Sousa arrived?'

'I don't remember. I don't think so, at least I did not see her. Sir George told De Sousa that his wife was somewhere about. He seemed surprised, I remember, that she was not judging the Children's Fancy Dress, as she was supposed to do.'

'What time was it when De Sousa arrived?'

'It must have been about half-past four, I should think. I did not look at my watch so I cannot tell you exactly.'

'And Lady Stubbs had disappeared before he arrived?'

'It seems so.'

'Possibly she ran away so as not to meet him,' suggested the inspector.

'Possibly,' Poirot agreed.

'Well, she can't have gone far,' said Bland. 'We ought to be able to find her quite easily, and when we do . . .' He broke off.

'And supposing you don't?' Poirot put the question with a curious intonation in his voice.

'That's nonsense,' said the inspector vigorously. 'Why? What d'you think's happened to her?'

Poirot shrugged his shoulders.

'What indeed! One does not know. All one does know is that she has – disappeared!'

'Dash it all, M. Poirot, you're making it sound quite sinister.'

'Perhaps it *is* sinister.'

'It's the murder of Marlene Tucker that we're investigating,' said the inspector severely.

'But evidently. So – why this interest in De Sousa? Do you think he killed Marlene Tucker?'

Inspector Bland replied irrelevantly:

'It's that woman!'

Poirot smiled faintly.

'Mrs Oliver, you mean?'

'Yes. You see, M. Poirot, the murder of Marlene Tucker doesn't make sense. It doesn't make sense at all. Here's a non-descript, rather moronic kid found strangled and not a hint of any possible motive.'

'And Mrs Oliver supplied you with a motive?'

'With a dozen at least! Amongst them she suggested that Marlene might have a knowledge of somebody's secret love affair, or that Marlene might have witnessed somebody being murdered, or that she knew where a buried treasure was hidden, or that she might have seen from the window of the boathouse some action performed by De Sousa in his launch as he was going up the river.'

'Ah. And which of those theories appeals to you, *mon cher*?'

'I don't know. But I can't help thinking about them. Listen, M. Poirot. Think back carefully. Would you say from your impression of what Lady Stubbs said to you this morning that she was afraid of her cousin's coming because he might, perhaps, know something about her which she did not want to come to the ears of her husband, or would you say that it was a direct personal fear of the man himself?'

Poirot had no hesitation in his reply.

'I should say it was a direct personal fear of the man himself.'

'H'm,' said Inspector Bland. 'Well, I'd better have a little talk with this young man if he's still about the place.'

CHAPTER 9

I

Although he had none of Constable Hoskins' ingrained prejudice against foreigners, Inspector Bland took an instant dislike to Etienne de Sousa. The polished elegance of the young man, his sartorial perfection, the rich flowery smell of his brilliantined hair, all combined to annoy the inspector.

De Sousa was very sure of himself, very much at ease. He also displayed, decorously veiled, a certain aloof amusement.

'One must admit,' he said, 'that life is full of surprises. I arrive here on a holiday cruise, I admire the beautiful scenery, I come to spend an afternoon with a little cousin that I have not seen for years – and what happens? First I am engulfed in a kind of carnival with coconuts whizzing past my head, and immediately afterwards, passing from comedy to tragedy, I am embroiled in a murder.'

He lit a cigarette, inhaled deeply, and said:

'Not that it concerns me in any way, this murder. Indeed, I am at a loss to know why you should want to interview me.'

'You arrived here as a stranger, Mr De Sousa –'

De Sousa interrupted:

'And strangers are necessarily suspicious, is that it?'

'No, no, not at all, sir. No, you don't take my meaning. Your yacht, I understand, is moored in Helmmouth?'

'That is so, yes.'

'And you came up the river this afternoon in a motor launch?'

'Again – that is so.'

'As you came up the river, did you notice on your right a small boathouse jutting out into the river with a thatched roof and a little mooring quay underneath it?'

De Sousa threw back his handsome, dark head and frowned as he reflected.

'Let me see, there was a creek and a small grey tiled house.'

'Farther up the river than that, Mr De Sousa. Set amongst trees.'

'Ah, yes, I remember now. A very picturesque spot. I did not know it was the boathouse attached to this house. If I had done so, I would have moored my boat there and come ashore. When I asked for directions I had been told to come up to the ferry itself and go ashore at the quay there.'

'Quite so. And that is what you did?'

'That is what I did.'

'You didn't land at, or near, the boathouse?'

De Sousa shook his head.

'Did you see anyone at the boathouse as you passed?'

'See anyone? No. Should I have seen anyone?'

'It was just a possibility. You see, Mr De Sousa, the murdered girl was in the boathouse this afternoon. She was killed there, and she must have been killed at a time not very distant from when you were passing.'

Again De Sousa raised his eyebrows.

'You think I might have been a witness to this murder?'

'The murder took place inside the boathouse, but you might have seen the girl – she might have looked out from the window or come out on to the balcony. If you had seen her it would, at any rate, have narrowed the time of death for us. If, when you'd passed, she'd been still alive –'

'Ah. I see. Yes, I see. But why ask *me* particularly? There are plenty of boats going up and down from Helmmouth. Pleasure steamers. They pass the whole time. Why not ask them?'

'We shall ask them,' said the inspector. 'Never fear, we shall ask them. I am to take it, then, that you saw nothing unusual at the boathouse?'

'Nothing whatever. There was nothing to show there was anyone there. Of course I did not look at it with any special attention, and I did not pass very near. Somebody might have been looking out of the windows, as you suggest, but if so I should not have seen that person.' He added in a polite tone, 'I am very sorry that I cannot assist you.'

'Oh, well,' said Inspector Bland in a friendly manner, 'we can't hope for too much. There are just a few other things I would like to know, Mr De Sousa.'

'Yes?'

'Are you alone down here or have you friends with you on this cruise?'

'I have had friends with me until quite recently, but for the last three days I have been on my own – with the crew, of course.'

'And the name of your yacht, Mr De Sousa?'

'The *Espérance*.'

'Lady Stubbs is, I understand, a cousin of yours?'

De Sousa shrugged his shoulders.

'A distant cousin. Not very near. In the islands, you must understand, there is much inter-marrying. We are all cousins of one another. Hattie is a second or third cousin. I have not seen her since she was practically a little girl, fourteen – fifteen.'

'And you thought you would pay her a surprise visit today?'

'Hardly a *surprise* visit, Inspector. I had already written to her.'

'I know that she received a letter from you this morning, but it was a surprise to her to know that you were in this country.'

'Oh, but you are wrong there, Inspector. I wrote to my cousin – let me see, three weeks ago. I wrote to her from France just before I came across to this country.'

The inspector was surprised.

'You wrote to her from France telling her you proposed to visit her?'

'Yes. I told her I was going on a yachting cruise and that we should probably arrive at Torquay or Helmmouth round about this date, and that I would let her know later exactly when I should arrive.'

Inspector Bland stared at him. This statement was at complete variance with what he had been told about the arrival of Etienne de Sousa's letter at the breakfast table. More than one witness had testified to Lady Stubbs having been alarmed and upset and very clearly startled at the contents of the letter. De Sousa returned his stare calmly. With a little smile he flicked a fragment of dust from his knee.

'Did Lady Stubbs reply to your first letter?' the inspector asked.

De Sousa hesitated for a moment or two before he answered, then he said:

'It is so difficult to remember . . . No, I do not think she did. But it was not necessary. I was travelling about, I had no fixed address. And besides, I do not think my cousin, Hattie, is very good at writing letters.' He added: 'She is not, you know, very intelligent, though I understand that she has grown into a very beautiful woman.'

'You have not yet seen her?' Bland put it in the form of a question and De Sousa showed his teeth in an agreeable smile.

'She seems to be most unaccountably missing,' he said. 'No doubt this *espèce de gala* bores her.'

Choosing his words carefully, Inspector Bland said:

'Have you any reason to believe, Mr De Sousa, that your cousin might have some reason for wishing to avoid you?'

'Hattie wish to avoid me? Really, I do not see why. What reason could she have?'

'That is what I am asking you, Mr De Sousa.'

'You think that Hattie has absented herself from this fête in order to avoid me? What an absurd idea.'

'She had no reason, as far as you know, to be – shall we say – afraid of you in any way?'

'Afraid – of *me*?' De Sousa's voice was sceptical and amused. 'But if I may say so, Inspector, what a fantastic idea!'

'Your relations with her have always been quite amicable?'

'It is as I have told you. I have had no relations with her. I have not seen her since she was a child of fourteen.'

'Yet you look her up when you come to England?'

'Oh, as to that, I had seen a paragraph about her in one of your society papers. It mentions her maiden name and that she is married to this rich Englishman, and I think "I must see what the little Hattie has turned into. Whether her brains now work better than they used to do."' He shrugged his shoulders again. 'It was a mere cousinly politeness. A gentle curiosity – no more.'

Again the inspector stared hard at De Sousa. What, he wondered, was going on behind the mocking, smooth façade? He adopted a more confidential manner.

'I wonder if you can perhaps tell me a little more about your cousin? Her character, her reactions?'

De Sousa appeared politely surprised.

'Really – has this anything to do with the murder of the girl in the boathouse, which I understand is the real matter with which you occupy yourself?'

'It might have a connection,' said Inspector Bland.

De Sousa studied him for a moment or two in silence. Then he said with a slight shrug of the shoulders:

'I never knew my cousin at all well. She was a unit in a large family and not particularly interesting to me. But in answer to your question I would say to you that although mentally weak, she was not, as far as I know, ever possessed by any homicidal tendencies.'

'Really, Mr De Sousa, I wasn't suggesting that!'

'Weren't you? I wonder. I can see no other reason for your question. No, unless Hattie has changed very much, she is not homicidal!' He rose. 'I am sure that you cannot want to ask me anything further, Inspector. I can only wish you every possible success in tracking down the murderer.'

'You are not thinking of leaving Helmmouth for a day or two, I hope, Mr De Sousa?'

'You speak very politely, Inspector. Is that an order?'

'Just a request, sir.'

'Thank you. I propose to stay in Helmmouth for two days. Sir George has very kindly asked me to come and stay in the house, but I prefer to remain on the *Espérance*. If you should want to ask me any further questions, that is where you will find me.'

He bowed politely.

P.C. Hoskins opened the door for him, and he went out.

'Smarmy sort of fellow,' muttered the inspector to himself.

'Aah,' said P.C. Hoskins in complete agreement.

'Say she *is* homicidal if you like,' went on the inspector, to himself. 'Why should she attack a nondescript girl? There'd be no sense in it.'

'You never know with the barmy ones,' said Hoskins.

'The question really is, how barmy is she?'

Hoskins shook his head sapiently.

'Got a low I.Q., I reckon,' he said.

The inspector looked at him with annoyance.

'Don't bring out these new-fangled terms like a parrot. I don't care if she's got a high I.Q. or a low I.Q. All I care about is, is she the sort of woman who'd think it funny, or desirable, or necessary, to put a cord round a girl's neck and strangle her? And where the devil *is* the woman, anyway? Go out and see how Frank's getting on.'

Hoskins left obediently, and returned a moment or two later with Sergeant Cottrell, a brisk young man with a good opinion of himself, who always managed to annoy his superior officer. Inspector Bland much preferred the rural wisdom of Hoskins to the smart know-all attitude of Frank Cottrell.

'Still searching the grounds, sir,' said Cottrell. 'The lady hasn't passed out through the gate, we're quite sure of that. It's the second gardener who's there giving out the tickets and taking the admission money. He'll swear she hasn't left.'

'There are other ways of leaving than by the main gate, I suppose?'

'Oh, yes, sir. There's the path down to the ferry, but the old boy down there – Merdell, his name is – is also quite positive that she hasn't left that way. He's about a hundred, but pretty reliable, I think. He described quite clearly how the foreign gentleman arrived in his launch and asked the way to Nasse House. The old man told him he must go up the road to the gate and pay for admission. But he said the gentleman seemed to know nothing about the fête and said he was a relation of the family. So the old man set him on the path up from the ferry through the woods. Merdell seems to have been hanging about the quay all the afternoon so he'd be pretty sure to have seen her ladyship if she'd come that way. Then there's the top gate that leads over the fields to Hoodown Park, but that's been wired up because of trespassers, so she didn't go through there. Seems as though she must be still here, doesn't it?'

'That may be so,' said the inspector, 'but there's nothing to prevent her, is there, from slipping under a fence and going off across country? Sir George is still complaining of trespassing here from the hostel next door, I understand. If you can get in the way the trespassers get in, you can get out the same way, I suppose.'

'Oh, yes, sir, indubitably, sir. But I've talked to her maid, sir. She's wearing' – Cottrell consulted a paper in his hand – 'a dress of cyclamen crêpe georgette (whatever that is), a large black hat, black court shoes with four-inch french heels. Not the sort of things you'd wear for a cross-country run.'

'She didn't change her clothes?'

'No. I went into that with the maid. There's nothing missing – nothing whatever. She didn't pack a suitcase or anything of that kind. She didn't even change her shoes. Every pair's there and accounted for.'

Inspector Bland frowned. Unpleasant possibilities were rising in his mind. He said curtly:

'Get me that secretary woman again – Bruce – whatever her name is.'

II

Miss Brewis came in looking rather more ruffled than usual, and a little out of breath.

'Yes, Inspector?' she said. 'You wanted me? If it isn't urgent, Sir George is in a terrible state and –'

'What's he in a state about?'

'He's only just realized that Lady Stubbs is – well, really missing. I told him she's probably only gone for a walk in the woods or something, but he's got it into his head that something's happened to her. *Quite* absurd.'

'It might not be so absurd, Miss Brewis. After all, we've had one – murder here this afternoon.'

'You surely don't think that Lady Stubbs –? But that's ridiculous! Lady Stubbs can look after herself.'

'Can she?'

'Of course she can! She's a grown woman, isn't she?'

'But rather a helpless one, by all accounts.'

'Nonsense,' said Miss Brewis. 'It suits Lady Stubbs now and then to play the helpless nitwit if she doesn't want to do anything. It takes her husband in, I dare say, but it doesn't take *me* in!'

'You don't like her very much, Miss Brewis?' Bland sounded gently interested.

Miss Brewis' lips closed in a thin line.

'It's not my business either to like or dislike her,' she said.

The door burst open and Sir George came in.

'Look here,' he said violently, 'you've got to do something. Where's Hattie? You've got to find Hattie. What the hell's going on round here I don't know. This confounded fête – some ruddy homicidal maniac's got in here, paying his half-crown and looking like everyone else, spending his afternoon going round murdering people. That's what it looks like to me.'

'I don't think we need take such an exaggerated view as that, Sir George.'

'It's all very well for you sitting there behind the table, writing things down. What I want is my wife.'

'I'm having the grounds searched, Sir George.'

'Why did nobody tell me she'd disappeared? She's been missing a couple of hours now, it seems. I thought it was odd that she didn't turn up to judge the Children's Fancy Dress stuff, but nobody told me she'd really gone.'

'Nobody knew,' said the inspector.

'Well, someone ought to've known. Somebody ought to have noticed.'

He turned on Miss Brewis.

'You ought to have known, Amanda, you were keeping an eye on things.'

'I can't be everywhere,' said Miss Brewis. She sounded suddenly almost tearful. 'I've got so much to see to. If Lady Stubbs chose to wander away –'

'Wander away? Why should she wander away? She'd no reason to wander away unless she wanted to avoid that dago fellow.'

Bland seized his opportunity.

'There is something I want to ask you,' he said. 'Did your wife receive a letter from Mr De Sousa some three weeks ago, telling her he was coming to this country?'

Sir George looked astonished.

'No, of course she didn't.'

'You're sure of that?'

'Oh, quite sure. Hattie would have told me. Why, she was

thoroughly startled and upset when she got his letter this morning. It more or less knocked her out. She was lying down most of the morning with a headache.'

'What did she say to you privately about her cousin's visit? Why did she dread seeing him so much?'

Sir George looked rather embarrassed.

'Blessed if I really know,' he said. 'She just kept saying that he was wicked.'

'Wicked? In what way?'

'She wasn't very articulate about it. Just went on rather like a child saying that he was a wicked man. Bad; and that she wished he wasn't coming here. She said he'd done bad things.'

'Done bad things? When?'

'Oh, long ago. I should imagine this Etienne de Sousa was the black sheep of the family and that Hattie picked up odds and ends about him during her childhood without understanding them very well. And as a result she's got a sort of horror of him. I thought it was just a childish hangover myself. My wife *is* rather childish sometimes. Has likes and dislikes, but can't explain them.'

'You are sure she did not particularize in any way, Sir George?'

Sir George looked uneasy.

'I wouldn't want you to go by – er – what she said.'

'Then she did say something?'

'All right. I'll let you have it. What she said was – and she said it several times – "*He kills people.*"'

CHAPTER 10

I

'He kills people,' Inspector Bland repeated.

'I don't think you ought to take it too seriously,' said Sir George. 'She kept repeating it and saying, "He kills people," but she couldn't tell me who he killed or when or why. I thought myself it was just some queer, childlike memory – trouble with the natives – something like that.'

'You say she couldn't tell you anything definite – do you mean *couldn't*, Sir George – or might it have been *wouldn't*?'

'I don't think . . .' He broke off. 'I don't know. You've muddled me. As I say, I didn't take any of it seriously. I thought perhaps this cousin had teased her a bit when she was a kid – something of that kind. It's difficult to explain to you because you don't know my wife. I am devoted to her, but half the time I don't listen to what she says because it just doesn't make sense. Anyway, this De Sousa fellow couldn't have had anything to do with all this – don't tell me he lands here off a yacht and goes straight away through the woods and kills a wretched Girl Guide in a boathouse! Why should he?'

'I'm not suggesting that anything like that happened,' said Inspector Bland, 'but you must realize, Sir George, that in looking for the murderer of Marlene Tucker the field is a more restricted one than one might think at first.'

'Restricted!' Sir George stared. 'You've got the whole ruddy fête to choose from, haven't you? Two hundred – three hundred – people? Any one of 'em might have done it.'

'Yes, I thought so at first, but from what I've learnt now that's hardly so. The boathouse door has a Yale lock. Nobody could come in from outside without a key.'

'Well, there were three keys.'

'Exactly. One key was the final clue in this Murder Hunt. It is still concealed in the hydrangea walk at the very top of the garden. The second key was in the possession of Mrs Oliver, the organizer of the Murder Hunt. Where is the third key, Sir George?'

'It ought to be in the drawer of that desk where you're sitting. No, the right-hand one with a lot of the other estate duplicates.'

He came over and rummaged in the drawer.

'Yes. Here it is all right.'

'Then you see,' said Inspector Bland, 'what that means? The only people who could have got into the boathouse were first, the person who had completed the Murder Hunt and found the key (which as far as we know, did not happen). Second, Mrs Oliver or some member of the household to whom she may have lent her key, and, third, someone *whom Marlene herself admitted to the room.*'

'Well, that latter point covers pretty well everyone, doesn't it?'

'Very far from it,' said Inspector Bland. 'If I understand the arrangement of this Murder Hunt correctly, when the girl heard anyone approaching the door she was to lie down and enact the part of the Victim, and wait to be discovered by the person who had found the last clue – the key. Therefore, as you must see for yourself, the only people whom she would have admitted, had they called to her from outside and asked her to do so, *were the people who had actually arranged the Murder Hunt.* Any inmate, that is, of this house – that is to say, yourself, Lady Stubbs, Miss Brewis, Mrs Oliver – possibly M. Poirot whom I believe she had met this morning. Who else, Sir George?'

Sir George considered for a moment or two.

'The Legges, of course,' he said. 'Alec and Sally Legge. They've been in it from the start. And Michael Weyman, he's an architect staying here in the house to design a tennis pavilion. And Warburton, the Mastertons – oh, and Mrs Folliat of course.'

'That is all – nobody else?'

'That's the lot.'

'So you see, Sir George, it is not a very wide field.'

Sir George's face went scarlet.

'I think you're talking nonsense – absolute nonsense! Are you suggesting – what you are suggesting?'

'I'm only suggesting,' said Inspector Bland, 'that there's a great deal we don't know as yet. It's possible, for instance, that Marlene, for some reason, came *out* of the boathouse. She may even have been strangled somewhere else, and her body brought back and arranged on the floor. But even if so, whoever arranged her was again someone who was thoroughly cognisant with all the details of the Murder Hunt. We always come back to that.' He added in a slightly changed voice, 'I can assure you, Sir George, that we're doing all we can to find Lady Stubbs. In the meantime I'd like to have a word with Mr and Mrs Alec Legge and Mr Michael Weyman.'

'Amanda.'

'I'll see what I can do about it, Inspector,' said Miss Brewis. 'I expect Mrs Legge is still telling fortunes in the tent. A lot of people have come in with the half-price admission since five o'clock, and all the side shows are busy. I can probably get hold of Mr Legge or Mr Weyman for you – whichever you want to see first.'

'It doesn't matter in what order I see them,' said Inspector Bland.

Miss Brewis nodded and left the room. Sir George followed her, his voice rising plaintively.

'Look here, Amanda, you've got to . . .'

Inspector Bland realized that Sir George depended a great deal upon the efficient Miss Brewis. Indeed, at this moment, Bland found the master of the house rather like a small boy.

Whilst waiting, Inspector Bland picked up the telephone, demanded to be put through to the police station at Helmmouth and made certain arrangements with them concerning the yacht *Espérance*.

'You realize, I suppose,' he said to Hoskins, who was obviously quite incapable of realizing anything of the sort, 'that there's just one perfectly possible place where this damn' woman might be – and that's on board De Sousa's yacht?'

'How d'you make that out, sir?'

'Well, the woman has not been seen to leave by any of the usual exits, she's togged up in a way that makes it unlikely that she's legging it through the fields or woods, but it *is* just possible that she met De Sousa by appointment down at the boathouse and that he took her by launch to the yacht, returning to the fête afterwards.'

'And why would he do that, sir?' demanded Hoskins, puzzled.

'I've no idea,' said the inspector, 'and it's very unlikely that he did. But it's a *possibility*. And if she *is* on the *Espérance*, I'll see to it that she won't get off there without being observed.'

'But if her fair hated the sight of him . . .' Hoskins dropped into the vernacular.

'All we know is that she *said* she did. Women,' said the inspector sententiously, 'tell a lot of lies. Always remember that, Hoskins.'

'Aah,' said Constable Hoskins appreciatively.

II

Further conversation was brought to an end as the door opened and a tall vague-looking young man entered. He was wearing a neat grey flannel suit, but his shirt collar was crumpled and his tie askew and his hair stood up on end in an unruly fashion.

'Mr Alec Legge?' said the inspector, looking up.

'No,' said the young man, 'I'm Michael Weyman. You asked for me, I understand.'

'Quite true, sir,' said Inspector Bland. 'Won't you take a chair?' He indicated a chair at the opposite side of the table.

'I don't care for sitting,' said Michael Weyman, 'I like to stride about. What are all you police doing here anyway? What's happened?'

Inspector Bland looked at him in surprise.

'Didn't Sir George inform you, sir?' he asked.

'Nobody's "informed me," as you put it, of anything. I don't sit in Sir George's pocket all the time. What *has* happened?'

'You're staying in the house, I understand?'

'Of course I'm staying in the house. What's that got to do with it?'

'Simply that I imagined that all the people staying in the house would by now have been informed of this afternoon's tragedy.'

'Tragedy? What tragedy?'

'The girl who was playing the part of the murder victim has been killed.'

'No!' Michael Weyman seemed exuberantly surprised. 'Do you mean really killed? No fakery-pokery?'

'I don't know what you mean by fakery-pokery. The girl's dead.'

'How was she killed?'

'Strangled with a piece of cord.'

Michael Weyman gave a whistle.

'Exactly as in the scenario? Well, well, that does give one ideas.' He strode over to the window, turned rapidly about, and said, 'So we're all under suspicion, are we? Or was it one of the local boys?'

'We don't see how it could possibly have been one of the local boys, as you put it,' said the inspector.

'No more do I really,' said Michael Weyman. 'Well, Inspector, many of my friends call me crazy, but I'm not that kind of crazy. I don't roam around the countryside strangling under-developed spotty young women.'

'You are down here, I understand, Mr Weyman, designing a tennis pavilion for Sir George?'

'A blameless occupation,' said Michael. 'Criminally speaking, that is. Architecturally, I'm not so sure. The finished product will probably represent a crime against good taste. But that doesn't interest you, Inspector. What *does* interest you?'

'Well, I should like to know, Mr Weyman, exactly where you were between quarter past four this afternoon and say five o'clock.'

'How do you tape it down to that – medical evidence?'

'Not entirely, sir. A witness saw the girl alive at a quarter past four.'

'What witness – or mayn't I ask?'

'Miss Brewis. Lady Stubbs asked her to take down a tray of creamy cakes with some fruitade to the girl.'

'Our Hattie asked her that? I don't believe it for a moment.'

'Why don't you believe it, Mr Weyman?'

'It's not like her. Not the sort of thing she'd think of or bother about. Dear Lady Stubbs' mind revolves entirely round herself.'

'I'm still waiting, Mr Weyman, for your answer to my question.'

'Where I was between four-fifteen and five o'clock? Well, really, Inspector, I can't say off-hand. I was about – if you know what I mean.'

'About where?'

'Oh, here and there. I mingled a bit on the lawn, watched the locals amusing themselves, had a word or two with the fluttery film star. Then, when I got sick of it all, I went along to the tennis court and mused over the design for the Pavilion. I also wondered how soon someone would identify the photograph that was the first clue for the Murder Hunt with a section of tennis net.'

'Did someone identify it?'

'Yes, I believe someone did come along, but I wasn't really noticing by then. I got a new idea about the Pavilion – a way of making the best of two worlds. My own and Sir George's.'

'And after that?'

'After that? Well, I strolled around and came back to the house. I strolled down the quay and had a crack with old Merdell, then came back. I can't fix any of the times with any accuracy. I was, as I said, in the first place, *about*! That's all there is to it.'

'Well, Mr Weyman,' said the inspector briskly, 'I expect we can get some confirmation of all this.'

'Merdell can tell you that I talked to him on the quay. But

of course that'll be rather later than the time you're interested in. Must have been after five when I got down there. Very unsatisfactory, isn't it, Inspector?'

'We shall be able to narrow it down, I expect, Mr Weyman.'

The inspector's tone was pleasant, but there was a steely ring in it that did not escape the young architect's notice. He sat down on the arm of a chair.

'Seriously,' he said, 'who can have wanted to murder that girl?'

'You've no ideas yourself, Mr Weyman?'

'Well, off-hand, I'd say it was our prolific authoress, the Purple Peril. Have you seen her imperial purple getup? I suggest that she went a bit off her onion and thought how much better the Murder Hunt would be if there was a *real* body. How's that?'

'Is that a serious suggestion, Mr Weyman?'

'It's the only probability I can think of.'

'There's one other thing I would like to ask you, Mr Weyman. Did you see Lady Stubbs during the course of the afternoon?'

'Of course I saw her. Who could miss her? Dressed up like a mannequin of Jacques Fath or Christian Dior?'

'When did you see her last?'

'Last? I don't know. Striking an attitude on the lawn about half-past three – or a quarter to four perhaps.'

'And you didn't see her after that?'

'No. Why?'

'I wondered – because after four o'clock nobody seems to have seen her. Lady Stubbs has – vanished, Mr Weyman.'

'Vanished! Our Hattie?'

'That surprises you?'

'Yes, it does rather . . . What's she up to, I wonder?'

'D'you know Lady Stubbs well, Mr Weyman?'

'Never met her till I came down here four or five days ago.'

'Have you formed any opinions about her?'

'I should say she knows which side her bread is buttered better than most,' said Michael Weyman dryly. 'A very ornamental young woman and knows how to make the most of it.'

'But mentally not very active? Is that right?'

'Depends what you mean by mentally,' said Michael Weyman. 'I wouldn't describe her as an intellectual. But if you're thinking that she's not all there, you're wrong.' A tone of bitterness came into his voice. 'I'd say she was very much all there. Nobody more so.'

The inspector's eyebrows rose.

'That's not the generally accepted opinion.'

'For some reason she likes playing the dim nitwit. I don't know why. But as I've said before, in my opinion, she's very much all there.'

The inspector studied him for a moment, then he said:

'And you really can't get any nearer to exact times and places between the hours I have mentioned?'

'Sorry.' Weyman spoke jerkily. 'I'm afraid I can't. Rotten memory, never any good about time.' He added, 'Finished with me?'

As the inspector nodded, he left the room quickly.

'And I'd like to know,' said the inspector, half to himself and half to Hoskins, 'what there's been between him and her Ladyship. Either he's made a pass at her and she's turned him down, or there's been some kind of a dust-up.' He went on, 'What would you say was the general opinion round these parts about Sir George and his lady?'

'She's daft,' said Constable Hoskins.

'I know *you* think that, Hoskins. Is that the accepted view?'

'I'd say so.'

'And Sir George – is he liked?'

'He's liked well enough. He's a good sportsman and he knows a bit about farming. The old lady's done a lot to help.'

'What old lady?'

'Mrs Folliat who lives at the Lodge here.'

'Oh, of course. The Folliats used to own this place, didn't they?'

'Yes, and it's owing to the old lady that Sir George and Lady Stubbs have been taken up as well as they have. Got 'em in with the nobs everywhere, she has.'

'Paid for doing so, do you think?'

'Oh, no, not Mrs Folliat.' Hoskins sounded shocked. 'I understand she knew Lady Stubbs before she was married and it was she who urged on Sir George to buy this place.'

'I'll have to talk to Mrs Folliat,' said the inspector.

'Ah, she's a shrewd old lady, she is. If anything is going on, she'd know about it.'

'I must talk to her,' said the inspector. 'I wonder where she is now.'

CHAPTER 11

I

Mrs Folliat was at that moment being talked to by Hercule Poirot in the big drawing-room. He had found her there leaning back in a chair in a corner of the room. She had started nervously when he came in. Then sinking back, she had murmured:

'Oh, it's you, M. Poirot.'

'I apologize, Madame. I disturbed you.'

'No, no. You don't disturb me. I'm just resting, that's all. I'm not as young as I was. The shock – it was too much for me.'

'I comprehend,' said Poirot. 'Indeed, I comprehend.'

Mrs Folliat, a handkerchief clutched in her small hand, was staring up at the ceiling. She said in a voice half-stifled with emotion:

'I can hardly bear to think of it. That poor girl. That poor, poor girl –'

'I know,' said Poirot. 'I know.'

'So young,' said Mrs Folliat; 'just at the beginning of life.' She said again, 'I can hardly bear to think of it.'

Poirot looked at her curiously. She seemed, he thought, to have aged by about ten years since the time early in the afternoon, when he had seen her, the gracious hostess, welcoming her guests. Now her face seemed drawn and haggard with the lines in it clearly marked.

'You said to me only yesterday, Madame, it is a very wicked world.'

'Did I say that?' Mrs Folliat seemed startled. 'It's true . . . Oh, yes, I'm only just beginning to know how true it is.' She added in a low voice, 'But I never thought anything like this would happen.'

Again he looked at her curiously.

'What did you think would happen, then? Something?'

'No, no. I didn't mean that.'

Poirot persisted.

'But you did expect *something* to happen – something out of the usual.'

'You misunderstand me, M. Poirot. I only mean that it's the last thing you would expect to happen in the middle of a fête like this.'   •

'Lady Stubbs this morning also spoke of wickedness.'

'Hattie did? Oh, don't speak of her to me – don't speak of her. I don't want to think about her.' She was silent for a moment or two, and then said, 'What did she say – about wickedness?'

'She was speaking of her cousin. Etienne de Sousa. She said that he was wicked, that he was a bad man. She said, too, that she was afraid of him.'

He watched, but she merely shook her head incredulously.

'Etienne de Sousa – who is he?'

'Of course, you were not at breakfast. I forgot, Mrs Folliat. Lady Stubbs received a letter from this cousin of hers whom she had not seen since she was a girl of fifteen. He told her that he proposed to call upon her today, this afternoon.'

'And did he come?'

'Yes. He arrived here about half-past four.'

'Surely – d'you mean that rather handsome, dark young man who came up the ferry path? I wondered who he was at the time.'

'Yes, Madame, that was Mr De Sousa.'

Mrs Folliat said energetically:

'If I were you I should pay no attention to the things Hattie says.' She flushed as Poirot looked at her in surprise and went on, 'She is like a child – I mean, she uses terms like a child – wicked, good. No half shades. I shouldn't pay any attention to what she tells you about this Etienne de Sousa.'

Again Poirot wondered. He said slowly:

'You know Lady Stubbs very well, do you not, Mrs Folliat?'

'Probably as well as anyone knows her. Possibly even better than her husband really knows her. And if I do?'

'What is she really like, Madame?'

'What a very odd question, M. Poirot.'

'You know, do you not, Madame, that Lady Stubbs cannot be found anywhere?'

Again her answer surprised him. She expressed no concern or astonishment. She said:

'So she has run away, has she? I see.'

'It seems to you quite natural, that?'

'Natural? Oh, I don't know. Hattie is rather unaccountable.'

'Do you think she has run away because she has a guilty conscience?'

'What do you mean, M. Poirot?'

'Her cousin was talking about her this afternoon. He mentioned casually that she had always been mentally subnormal. I think you must know, Madame, that people who are subnormal mentally are not always accountable for their actions.'

'What are you trying to say, M. Poirot?'

'Such people are, as you say, very simple – like children. In a sudden fit of rage they might even kill.'

Mrs Folliat turned on him in sudden anger.

'Hattie was never like that! I won't allow you to say such things. She was a gentle warm-hearted girl, even if she was – a little simple mentally. Hattie would never have killed *anyone*.'

She faced him, breathing hard, still indignant.

Poirot wondered. He wondered very much.

II

Breaking into this scene, P.C. Hoskins made his appearance.

He said in an apologetic manner:

'I've been looking for you, ma'am.'

'Good evening, Hoskins.' Mrs Folliat was once more her poised self again, the mistress of Nasse House. 'Yes, what is it?'

'The inspector's compliments, and he'd be glad to have a word with you – if you feels up to it, that is,' Hoskins hastened to add; noting, as Hercule Poirot had done, the effects of shock.

'Of course I feel up to it.' Mrs Folliat rose to her feet. She followed Hoskins out of the room. Poirot, having risen politely, sat down again and stared up at the ceiling with a puzzled frown.

The inspector rose when Mrs Folliat entered and the constable held the chair for her to sit down.

'I'm sorry to worry you, Mrs Folliat,' said Bland. 'But I imagine that you know all the people in the neighbourhood and I think you may be able to help us.'

Mrs Folliat smiled faintly. 'I expect,' she said, 'that I know everyone round here as well as anyone could do. What do you want to know, Inspector?'

'You knew the Tuckers? The family and the girl?'

'Oh, yes, of course, they've always been tenants on the estate. Mrs Tucker was the youngest of a large family. Her eldest brother was our head gardener. She married Alfred Tucker, who is a farm labourer – a stupid man but very nice. Mrs Tucker is a bit of a shrew. A good housewife, you know, and very clean in the house, but Tucker is never allowed to come anywhere farther than the scullery with his muddy boots on. All that sort of thing. She nags the children rather. Most of them have married and gone into jobs now. There was just this poor child, Marlene, left and three younger children. Two boys and a girl still at school.'

'Now, knowing the family as you do, Mrs Folliat, can you think of any reason why Marlene should have been killed today?'

'No, indeed I can't. It's quite, quite unbelievable, if you know what I mean, Inspector. There was no boyfriend or anything of that kind, or I shouldn't think so. Not that I've ever heard of, anyway.'

'Now what about the people who've been taking part in this Murder Hunt? Can you tell me anything about them?'

'Well, Mrs Oliver I'd never met before. She is quite unlike my idea of what a crime novelist would be. She's very upset, poor dear, by what has happened – naturally.'

'And what about the other helpers – Captain Warburton, for instance?'

'I don't see any reason why he should murder Marlene Tucker, if that's what you're asking me,' said Mrs Folliat composedly. 'I don't like him very much. He's what I call a foxy sort of man, but I suppose one has to be up to all the political tricks and all that kind of thing, if one is a political agent. He's certainly energetic and has worked very hard over this fête. I don't think he *could* have killed the girl, anyway, because he was on the lawn the whole time this afternoon.'

The inspector nodded.

'And the Legges? What do you know about the Legges?'

'Well, they seem a very nice young couple. He's inclined to be what I should call – moody. I don't know very much about him. She was a Carstairs before her marriage and I know some relations of hers very well. They took the Mill Cottage for two months, and I hope they've enjoyed their holiday here. We've all got very friendly together.'

'She's an attractive lady, I understand.'

'Oh, yes, very attractive.'

'Would you say that at any time Sir George had felt that attraction?'

Mrs Folliat looked rather astonished.

'Oh, no, I'm sure there was nothing of that kind. Sir George is really absorbed by his business, and very fond of his wife. He's not at all a philandering sort of man.'

'And there was nothing, you would say, between Lady Stubbs and Mr Legge?'

Again Mrs Folliat shook her head.

'Oh, no, positively.'

The inspector persisted.

'There's been no trouble of any kind between Sir George and his wife, that you know of?'

'I'm sure there hasn't,' said Mrs Folliat, emphatically. 'And I would know if there had been.'

'It wouldn't be, then, as a result of any disagreement between husband and wife that Lady Stubbs has gone away?'

'Oh, no.' She added lightly, 'The silly girl, I understand, didn't want to meet this cousin of hers. Some childish phobia. So she's run away just like a child might do.'

'That's your opinion. Nothing more than that?'

'Oh, no. I expect she'll turn up again quite soon. Feeling rather ashamed of herself.' She added carelessly, 'What's become of this cousin, by the way? Is he still here in the house?'

'I understand he's gone back to his yacht.'

'And that's at Helmmouth, is it?'

'Yes, at Helmmouth.'

'I see,' said Mrs Folliat. 'Well, it's rather unfortunate – Hattie behaving so childishly. However, if he's staying on here for a day or so, we can make her see she must behave properly.'

It was, the inspector thought, a question, but although he noticed it he did not answer it.

'You are probably thinking,' he said, 'that all this is rather beside the point. But you do understand, don't you, Mrs Folliat, that we have to range over rather a wide field. Miss Brewis, for instance. What do you know about Miss Brewis?'

'Well, she's an excellent secretary. More than a secretary. She practically acts as housekeeper down here. In fact, I don't know what they'd do without her.'

'Was she Sir George's secretary before he married his wife?'

'I think so. I'm not quite sure. I've only known her since she came down here with them.'

'She doesn't like Lady Stubbs very much, does she?'

'No,' said Mrs Folliat, 'I'm afraid she doesn't. I don't think these good secretaries ever *do* care for wives much, if you know what I mean. Perhaps it's natural.'

'Was it you or Lady Stubbs who asked Miss Brewis to take cakes and a fruit drink to the girl in the boathouse?'

Mrs Folliat looked slightly surprised.

'I remember Miss Brewis collecting some cakes and things and saying she was taking them along to Marlene. I didn't know anyone had particularly asked her to do it, or arranged about it. It certainly wasn't me.'

'I see. You say you were in the tea tent from four o'clock on. I believe Mrs Legge was also having tea in the tent at that time.'

'Mrs Legge? No, I don't think so. At least I don't remember seeing her there. In fact, I'm quite sure she wasn't there. We'd had a great influx by the bus from Torquay, and I remember looking round the tent and thinking that they must all be summer visitors; there was hardly a face there that I knew. I think Mrs Legge must have come in to tea later.'

'Oh, well,' said the inspector, 'it doesn't matter.' He added smoothly, 'Well, I really think that's all. Thank you, Mrs Folliat, you've been very kind. We can only hope that Lady Stubbs will return shortly.'

'I hope so, too,' said Mrs Folliat. 'Very thoughtless of the dear child giving us all so much anxiety.' She spoke briskly but the animation in her voice was not very natural. 'I'm sure,' said Mrs Folliat, 'that she's *quite* all right. Quite all right.'

At that moment the door opened and an attractive young woman with red hair and a freckled face came in, and said:

'I hear you've been asking for me?'

'This is Mrs Legge, Inspector,' said Mrs Folliat. 'Sally, dear, I don't know whether you've heard about the terrible thing that has happened?'

'Oh, yes! Ghastly, isn't it?' said Mrs Legge. She uttered an exhausted sigh, and sank down in the chair as Mrs Folliat left the room.

'I'm terribly sorry about all this,' she said. 'It seems really unbelievable, if you know what I mean. I'm afraid I can't help you in any way. You see, I've been telling fortunes all the afternoon, so I haven't seen anything of what was going on.'

'I know, Mrs Legge. But we just have to ask everybody the same routine questions. For instance, just where were you between four-fifteen and five o'clock?'

'Well, I went and had tea at four o'clock.'

'In the tea tent?'

'Yes.'

'It was very crowded, I believe?'

'Oh, frightfully crowded.'

'Did you see anyone you knew there?'

'Oh, a few old people, yes. Nobody to speak to. Goodness, how I wanted that tea! That was four o'clock, as I say. I got back to the fortune-telling tent at half-past four and went on with my job. And goodness knows what I was promising the women in the end. Millionaire husbands, film stardom in Hollywood – heaven knows what. Mere journeys across the sea and suspicious dark women seemed too tame.'

'What happened during the half-hour when you were absent – I mean, supposing people wanted to have their fortunes told?'

'Oh, I hung a card up outside the tent. "Back at four-thirty."'

The inspector made a note in his pad.

'When did you last see Lady Stubbs?'

'Hattie? I don't really know. She was quite near at hand when I came out of the fortune-telling tent to go to tea, but I didn't speak to her. I don't remember seeing her afterwards. Somebody told me just now that she's missing. Is that true?'

'Yes, it is.'

'Oh, well,' said Sally Legge cheerfully, 'she's a bit queer in the top storey, you know. I dare say having a murder here has frightened her.'

'Well, thank you, Mrs Legge.'

Mrs Legge accepted the dismissal with promptitude. She went out, passing Hercule Poirot in the doorway.

III

Looking at the ceiling, the inspector spoke.

'Mrs Legge says she was in the tea tent between four and four-thirty. Mrs Folliat says she was helping in the tea tent from four o'clock on but that Mrs Legge was not among those present.' He paused and then went on, 'Miss Brewis says that Lady Stubbs asked her to take a tray of cakes and fruit juice to Marlene Tucker. Michael Weyman says that it's quite impossible Lady Stubbs should have done any such thing – it would be most uncharacteristic of her.'

'Ah,' said Poirot, 'the conflicting statements! Yes, one always has them.'

'And what a nuisance they are to clear up, too,' said the inspector. 'Sometimes they matter but in nine times out of ten they don't. Well, we've got to do a lot of spade work, that's clear.'

'And what do you think now, *mon cher*? What are the latest ideas?'

'I think,' said the inspector gravely, 'that Marlene Tucker saw something she was not meant to see. I think that it was because of what Marlene Tucker saw that she had to be killed.'

'I will not contradict you,' said Poirot. 'The point is what *did* she see?'

'She might have seen a murder,' said the inspector. 'Or she might have seen the person who did the murder.'

'Murder?' said Poirot. 'The murder of whom?'

'What do *you* think, Poirot? Is Lady Stubbs alive or dead?'

Poirot took a moment or two before he replied. Then he said:

'I think, *mon ami*, that Lady Stubbs is dead. And I will tell you *why* I think that. *It is because Mrs Folliat thinks she is dead.* Yes, whatever she may say now, or pretend to think, Mrs Folliat believes that Hattie Stubbs is dead. Mrs Folliat,' he added, 'knows a great deal that we do not.'

CHAPTER 12

Hercule Poirot came down to the breakfast table on the following morning to a depleted table. Mrs Oliver, still suffering from the shock of yesterday's occurrence, was having her breakfast in bed. Michael Weyman had had a cup of coffee and gone out early. Only Sir George and the faithful Miss Brewis were at the breakfast table. Sir George was giving indubitable proof of his mental condition by being unable to eat any breakfast. His plate lay almost untasted before him. He pushed aside the small pile of letters which, after opening them, Miss Brewis had placed before him. He drank coffee with an air of not knowing what he was doing. He said:

'Morning, M. Poirot,' perfunctorily, and then relapsed into his state of preoccupation. At times a few ejaculatory murmurs came from him.

'So incredible, the whole damn' thing. Where *can* she be?'

'The inquest will be held at the Institute on Thursday,' said Miss Brewis. 'They rang up to tell us.'

Her employer looked at her as if he did not understand.

'Inquest?' he said. 'Oh, yes, of course.' He sounded dazed and uninterested. After another sip or two of coffee he said, 'Women are incalculable. What does she think she's doing?'

Miss Brewis pursed her lips. Poirot observed acutely enough that she was in a state of taut nervous tension.

'Hodgson's coming to see you this morning,' she remarked, 'about the electrification of the milking sheds on the farm. And at twelve o'clock there's the –'

Sir George interrupted.

'I can't see anyone. Put 'em all off! How the devil d'you think a man can attend to business when he's worried half out of his mind about his wife?'

'If you say so, Sir George.' Miss Brewis gave the domestic equivalent of a barrister saying 'as your lordship pleases.' Her dissatisfaction was obvious.

'Never know,' said Sir George, '*what* women get into their heads, or what fool things they're likely to do! You agree, eh?' he shot the last question at Poirot.

'*Les femmes?* They are incalculable,' said Poirot, raising his eyebrows and his hands with Gallic fervour. Miss Brewis blew her nose in an annoyed fashion.

'She *seemed* all right,' said Sir George. 'Damn' pleased about her new ring, dressed herself up to enjoy the fête. All just the same as usual. Not as though we'd had words or a quarrel of any kind. Going off without a word.'

'About those letters, Sir George,' began Miss Brewis.

'Damn the bloody letters to hell,' said Sir George, and pushed aside his coffee-cup.

He picked up the letters by his plate and more or less threw them at her.

'Answer them any way you like! I can't be bothered.' He went on more or less to himself, in an injured tone, 'Doesn't seem to be anything I can *do* . . . Don't even know if that police chap's any good. Very soft spoken and all that.'

'The police are, I believe,' said Miss Brewis, 'very efficient. They have ample facilities for tracing the whereabouts of missing persons.'

'They take days sometimes,' said Sir George, 'to find some miserable kid who's run off and hidden himself in a haystack.'

'I don't think Lady Stubbs is likely to be in a haystack, Sir George.'

'If only I could *do* something,' repeated the unhappy husband. 'I think, you know, I'll put an advertisement in the papers. Take it down, Amanda, will you?' He paused a moment in thought. '*Hattie. Please come home. Desperate about you. George.* All the papers, Amanda.'

Miss Brewis said acidly:

'Lady Stubbs doesn't often read the papers, Sir George. She's no interest at all in current affairs or what's going on in the world.' She added, rather cattily, but Sir George was not in the mood to appreciate cattiness, 'Of course you could put an advertisement in *Vogue*. That might catch her eye.'

Sir George said simply:

'Anywhere you think but get on with it.'

He got up and walked towards the door. With his hand on the handle he paused and came back a few steps. He spoke directly to Poirot.

'Look here, Poirot,' he said, '*you* don't think she's dead, do you?'

Poirot fixed his eyes on his coffee-cup as he replied:

'I should say it is far too soon, Sir George, to assume anything of that kind. There is no reason as yet to entertain such an idea.'

'So you do think so,' said Sir George, heavily. 'Well,' he added defiantly, 'I don't! *I* say she's quite all right.' He nodded his head several times with increasing defiance, and went out banging the door behind him.

Poirot buttered a piece of toast thoughtfully. In cases where there was any suspicion of a wife being murdered, he always automatically suspected the husband. (Similarly, with a husband's demise, he suspected the wife.) But in this case he did not suspect Sir George of having done away with Lady Stubbs. From his brief observation of them he was quite convinced that Sir George was devoted to his wife. Moreover, as far as his excellent memory served him (and it served him pretty well), Sir George had been present on the lawn the entire afternoon until he himself had left with Mrs Oliver to discover the body. He had been there on the lawn when they had returned with the news. No, it was not Sir George who was responsible for Hattie's death. That is, if Hattie were dead. After all, Poirot told himself, there was no reason to believe so as yet. What he had just said to Sir George was true enough. But in his own mind the conviction was unalterable. The pattern, he thought, was the pattern of murder – a double murder.

Miss Brewis interrupted his thoughts by speaking with almost tearful venom.

'Men are such fools,' she said, 'such absolute *fools*! They're quite shrewd in most ways, and then they go marrying entirely the wrong sort of woman.'

Poirot was always willing to let people talk. The more people who talked to him, and the more they said, the better. There was nearly always a grain of wheat among the chaff.

'You think it has been an unfortunate marriage?' he demanded.

'Disastrous – quite disastrous.'

'You mean – that they were not happy together?'

'She'd a thoroughly bad influence over him in every way.'

'Now I find that very interesting. What kind of a bad influence?'

'Making him run to and fro at her beck and call, getting expensive presents out of him – far more jewels than one woman could wear. And furs. She's got two mink coats and a Russian ermine. What could any woman want with two mink coats, I'd like to know?'

Poirot shook his head.

'That I would not know,' he said.

'Sly,' continued Miss Brewis. 'Deceitful! Always playing the simpleton – especially when people were here. I suppose because she thought he liked her that way!'

'And did he like her that way?'

'Oh, men!' said Miss Brewis, her voice trembling on the edge of hysteria. 'They don't appreciate efficiency or unselfishness, or loyalty or *any* one of those qualities! Now with a clever, capable wife Sir George would have got somewhere.'

'Got where?' asked Poirot.

'Well, he could take a prominent part in local affairs. Or stand for Parliament. He's a much more able man than poor Mr Masterton. I don't know if you've ever heard Mr Masterton on a platform – a most halting and uninspired speaker. He owes his position entirely to his wife. It's Mrs Masterton who's the power behind the throne. She's got all the drive and the initiative and the political acumen.'

Poirot shuddered inwardly at the thought of being married to Mrs Masterton, but he agreed quite truthfully with Miss Brewis' words.

'Yes,' he said, 'she is all that you say. A *femme formidable*,' he murmured to himself.

'Sir George doesn't seem ambitious,' went on Miss Brewis; 'he seems quite content to live here and potter about and play the country squire, and just go to London occasionally to attend to all his city directorships and all that, but he could make far more of himself than that with *his* abilities. He's really a very remarkable man, M. Poirot. That woman never understood him. She just regards him as a kind of machine for tipping out fur coats and jewels and expensive clothes. If he were married to someone who really appreciated his abilities . . .' She broke off, her voice wavering uncertainly.

Poirot looked at her with a real compassion. Miss Brewis was in love with her employer. She gave him a faithful, loyal and passionate devotion of which he was probably quite unaware and in which he would certainly not be interested. To Sir George, Amanda Brewis was an efficient machine who took the drudgery of daily life off his shoulders, who answered telephone calls, wrote letters, engaged servants, ordered meals and generally made life smooth for him. Poirot doubted if he had ever once thought of her as a woman. And that, he reflected, had its dangers. Women could work themselves up, they could reach an alarming pitch of hysteria unnoticed by the oblivious male who was the object of their devotion.

'A sly, scheming, clever cat, that's what she is,' said Miss Brewis tearfully.

'You say *is*, not *was*, I observe,' said Poirot.

'Of course she isn't dead!' said Miss Brewis, scornfully. 'Gone off with a man, that's what *she's* done! That's her type.'

'It is possible. It is always possible,' said Poirot. He took another piece of toast, inspected the marmalade pot gloomily and looked down the table to see if there were any kind of jam. There was none, so he resigned himself to butter.

'It's the only explanation,' said Miss Brewis. 'Of course *he* wouldn't think of it.'

'Has there – been any – trouble with men?' asked Poirot, delicately.

'Oh, she's been very clever,' said Miss Brewis.

'You mean you have not observed anything of the kind?'

'She'd be careful that I shouldn't,' said Miss Brewis.

'But you think that there may have been – what shall I say? – surreptitious episodes?'

'She's done her best to make a fool of Michael Weyman,' said Miss Brewis. 'Taking him down to see the camellia gardens at this time of year! Pretending she's so interested in the tennis pavilion.'

'After all, that is his business for being here and I understand Sir George is having it built principally to please his wife.'

'She's no good at tennis,' said Miss Brewis. 'She's no good at *any* games. Just wants an attractive setting to sit in, while other people run about and get hot. Oh, yes, she's done her best to make a fool of Michael Weyman. She'd probably have done it too, if he hadn't had other fish to fry.'

'Ah,' said Poirot, helping himself to a very little marmalade, placing it on the corner of a piece of toast and taking a mouthful dubiously. 'So he has other fish to fry, M. Weyman?'

'It was Mrs Legge who recommended him to Sir George,' said Miss Brewis. 'She knew him before she was married. Chelsea, I understand, and all that. She used to paint, you know.'

'She seems a very attractive and intelligent young woman,' said Poirot tentatively.

'Oh, yes, she's very intelligent,' said Miss Brewis. 'She's had a university education and I dare say could have made a career for herself if she hadn't married.'

'Has she been married long?'

'About three years, I believe. I don't think the marriage has turned out very well.'

'There is – incompatibility?'

'He's a queer young man, very moody. Wanders off a lot by himself and I've heard him very bad-tempered with her sometimes.'

'Ah, well,' said Poirot, 'the quarrels, the reconciliations, they are a part of early married life. Without them it is possible that life would be drab.'

'She's spent a good deal of time with Michael Weyman since he's been down here,' said Miss Brewis. 'I think he was in love with her before she married Alec Legge. I dare say it's only a flirtation on her side.'

'But Mr Legge was not pleased about it, perhaps?'

'One never knows with him, he's so vague. But I think he's been even moodier than usual, lately.'

'Did he admire Lady Stubbs, perhaps?'

'I dare say she thought he did. She thinks she only has to hold up a finger for any man to fall in love with her!'

'In any case, if she has gone off with a man, as you suggest, it is not Mr Weyman, for Mr Weyman is still here.'

'It's somebody she's been meeting on the sly, I've no doubt,' said Miss Brewis. 'She often slips out of the house on the quiet and goes off into the woods by herself. She was out the night before last. Yawning and saying she was going up to bed. I caught sight of her not half an hour later slipping out by the side door with a shawl over her head.'

Poirot looked thoughtfully at the woman opposite him. He wondered if any reliance at all was to be placed in Miss Brewis' statements where Lady Stubbs was concerned, or whether it was entirely wishful thinking on her part. Mrs Folliat, he was sure, did not share Miss Brewis' ideas and Mrs Folliat knew Hattie much better than Miss Brewis could do. If Lady Stubbs had run away with a lover it would clearly suit Miss Brewis' book very well. She would be left to console the bereaved husband and to arrange for him efficiently the details of divorce. But that did not make it true, or probable, or even likely. If Hattie Stubbs had left with a lover, she had chosen a very curious time to do so, Poirot thought. For his own part he did not believe she had.

Miss Brewis sniffed through her nose and gathered together various scattered correspondence.

'If Sir George really wants those advertisements put in, I suppose I'd better see about it,' she said. 'Complete nonsense and waste of time. Oh, good morning, Mrs Masterton,' she added, as the door opened with authority and Mrs Masterton walked in.

'Inquest is set for Thursday, I hear,' she boomed. 'Morning, M. Poirot.'

Miss Brewis paused, her hand full of letters.

'Anything I can do for you, Mrs Masterton?' she asked.

'No, thank you, Miss Brewis. I expect you've plenty on your hands this morning, but I do want to thank you for all the excellent work you put in yesterday. You're such a good organizer and such a hard worker. We're all very grateful.'

'Thank you, Mrs Masterton.'

'Now don't let me keep you. I'll sit down and have a word with M. Poirot.'

'Enchanted, Madame,' said Poirot. He had risen to his feet and he bowed.

Mrs Masterton pulled out a chair and sat down. Miss Brewis left the room, quite restored to her usual efficient self.

'Marvellous woman, that,' said Mrs Masterton. 'Don't know what the Stubbses would do without her. Running a house takes some doing nowadays. Poor Hattie couldn't have coped with it. Extraordinary business, this, M. Poirot. I came to ask you what you thought about it.'

'What do you yourself think, Madame?'

'Well, it's an unpleasant thing to face, but I should say we've got some pathological character in this part of the world. Not a native, I hope. Perhaps been let out of an asylum – they're always letting 'em out half-cured nowadays. What I mean is, no one would ever want to strangle that Tucker girl. There couldn't be any motive, I mean, except some abnormal one. And if this man, whoever he is, *is* abnormal I should say he's probably strangled that poor girl, Hattie Stubbs, as well. She hasn't very much sense you know, poor child. If she met an ordinary-looking man and he asked her to come and look at something in the woods she'd probably go like a lamb, quite unsuspecting and docile.'

'You think her body is somewhere on the estate?'

'Yes, M. Poirot, I do. They'll find it once they search around. Mind you, with about sixty-five acres of woodland here, it'll take some finding, if it's been dragged into the bushes or tumbled down a slope into the trees. What they need is bloodhounds,' said Mrs Masterton, looking, as she spoke, exactly like a bloodhound herself. 'Bloodhounds! I shall ring up the Chief Constable myself and say so.'

'It is very possible that you are right, Madame,' said Poirot. It was clearly the only thing one could say to Mrs Masterton.

'Of course I'm right,' said Mrs Masterton; 'but I must say, you know, it makes me very uneasy because the fellow is somewhere about. I'm calling in at the village when I leave here, telling the mothers to be very careful about their daughters – not let 'em go about alone. It's not a nice thought, M. Poirot, to have a killer in our midst.'

'A little point, Madame. How could a strange man have obtained admission to the boathouse? That would need a key.'

'Oh, that,' said Mrs Masterton, 'that's easy enough. She came out, of course.'

'Came out of the boathouse?'

'Yes. I expect she got bored, like girls do. Probably wandered out and looked about her. The most likely thing, I think, is that she actually saw Hattie Stubbs murdered. Heard a struggle or something, went to see and the man, having disposed of Lady Stubbs, naturally had to kill her too. Easy enough for him to take her back to the boathouse, dump her there and come out, pulling the door behind him. It was a Yale lock. It would pull to, and lock.'

Poirot nodded gently. It was not his purpose to argue with Mrs Masterton or to point out to her the interesting fact which she had completely overlooked, that if Marlene Tucker had been killed away from the boathouse, somebody must have known enough about the murder game to put her back in the exact place and position which the victim was supposed to assume. Instead, he said gently:

'Sir George Stubbs is confident that his wife is still alive.'

'That's what he says, man, because he wants to believe it. He was very devoted to her, you know.' She added, rather unexpectedly, 'I like George Stubbs in spite of his origins and his city background and all that, he goes down very well in the county. The worst that can be said about him is that he's a bit of a snob. And after all, social snobbery's harmless enough.'

Poirot said somewhat cynically:

'In these days, Madame, surely money has become as acceptable as good birth.'

'My dear man, I couldn't agree with you more. There's no need for him to be a snob – only got to buy the place and throw his money about, and we'd all come and call! But actually, the man's liked. It's not only his money. Of course Amy Folliat's had something to do with that. She has sponsored them, and mind you, she's got a lot of influence in this part of the world. Why, there have been Folliats here since Tudor times.'

'There have always been Folliats at Nasse House,' Poirot murmured to himself.

'Yes.' Mrs Masterton sighed. 'It's sad, the toll taken by the war. Young men killed in battle – death duties and all that. Then whoever comes into a place can't afford to keep it up and has to sell –'

'But Mrs Folliat, although she has lost her home, still lives on the estate.'

'Yes. She's made the Lodge quite charming too. Have you been inside it?'

'No, we parted at the door.'

'It wouldn't be everybody's cup of tea,' said Mrs Masterton. 'To live at the lodge of your old home and see strangers in possession. But to do Amy Folliat justice I don't think she feels bitter about that. In fact, she engineered the whole thing. There's no doubt she imbued Hattie with the idea of living down here, and got her to persuade George Stubbs into it. The thing, I think, that Amy Folliat couldn't have borne was to see the place turned into a hostel or institution, or carved up for building.' She rose to her feet. 'Well, I must be getting along. I'm a busy woman.'

'Of course. You have to talk to the Chief Constable about bloodhounds.'

Mrs Masterton gave a sudden deep bay of laughter. 'Used to breed 'em at one time,' she said. 'People tell me I'm a bit like a bloodhound myself.'

Poirot was slightly taken aback and she was quick enough to see it.

'I bet you've been thinking so, M. Poirot,' she said.

CHAPTER 13

After Mrs Masterton had left, Poirot went out and strolled through the woods. His nerves were not quite what they should be. He felt an irresistible desire to look behind every bush and to consider every thicket of rhododendron as a possible hiding-place for a body. He came at last to the Folly and, going inside it, he sat down on the stone bench there, to rest his feet which were, as was his custom, enclosed in tight, pointed patent-leather shoes.

Through the trees he could catch faint glimmers of the river and of the wooded banks on the opposite side. He found himself agreeing with the young architect that this was no place to put an architectural fantasy of this kind. Gaps could be cut in the trees, of course, but even then there would be no proper view. Whereas, as Michael Weyman had said, on the grassy bank near the house a Folly could have been erected with a delightful vista right down the river to Helmmouth. Poirot's thoughts flew off at a tangent. Helmmouth, the yacht *Espérance*, and Etienne de Sousa. The whole thing must tie up in some kind of pattern, but what the pattern was he could not visualize. Tempting strands of it showed here and there but that was all.

Something that glittered caught his eye and he bent to pick it up. It had come to rest in a small crack of the concrete base to the temple. He held it in the palm of his hand and looked at it with a faint stirring of recognition. It was a little gold aeroplane charm. As he frowned at it, a picture came into his mind. A bracelet. A gold bracelet hung over with dangling charms. He was sitting once more in the tent and the voice of Madame Zuleika, alias Sally Legge, was talking of dark women and journeys across the sea and good fortune in a letter. Yes, she had had on a bracelet from which depended a multiplicity of small gold objects. One of these modern fashions which repeated the fashions of Poirot's early days. Probably that was why it had made an impression on him. Some time or other, presumably, Mrs Legge had sat here in the Folly, and one of the charms had fallen from her bracelet. Perhaps she had not even noticed it. It might have been yesterday afternoon.

Poirot considered that latter point. Then he heard footsteps outside and looked up sharply. A figure came round to the front of the Folly and stopped, startled, at the sight of Poirot. Poirot looked with a considering eye on the slim, fair young man wearing a shirt on which a variety of tortoise and turtle was depicted. The shirt was unmistakable. He had observed it closely yesterday when its wearer was throwing coconuts.

He noticed that the young man was almost unusually perturbed. He said quickly in a foreign accent:

'I beg your pardon – I did not know –'

Poirot smiled gently at him but with a reproving air.

'I am afraid,' he said, 'that you are trespassing.'

'Yes, I am sorry.'

'You come from the hostel?'

'Yes. Yes, I do. I thought perhaps one could get through the woods this way and so to the quay.'

'I am afraid,' said Poirot gently, 'that you will have to go back the way you came. There is no through road.'

The young man said again, showing all his teeth in a would-be agreeable smile:

'I am sorry. I am very sorry.'

He bowed and turned away.

Poirot came out of the Folly and back on to the path, watching the boy retreat. When he got to the ending of the path, he looked over his shoulder. Then, seeing Poirot watching him, he quickened his pace and disappeared round the bend.

'*Eh bien*,' said Poirot to himself, 'is this a murderer I have seen, or is it not?'

The young man had certainly been at the fête yesterday and had scowled when he had collided with Poirot, and just as certainly therefore he must know quite well that there was no through path by way of the woods to the ferry. If, indeed, he *had* been looking for a path to the ferry he would not have taken this path by the Folly, but would have kept on the lower level near the river. Moreover, he had arrived at the Folly with the air of one who has reached his rendezvous, and who is badly startled at finding the wrong person at the meeting place.

'So it is like this,' said Poirot to himself. 'He came here to meet someone. Who did he come to meet?' He added as an afterthought, 'And why?'

He strolled down to the bend of the path and looked at it where it wound away into the trees. There was no sign of the young man in the turtle shirt now. Presumably he had deemed it prudent to retreat as rapidly as possible. Poirot retraced his steps, shaking his head.

Lost in thought, he came quietly round the side of the Folly, and stopped on the threshold, startled in his turn. Sally Legge was there on her knees, her head bent down to the cracks in the flooring. She jumped up, startled.

'Oh, M. Poirot, you gave me such a shock. I didn't hear you coming.'

'You were looking for something, Madame?'

'I – no, not exactly.'

'You had lost something, perhaps,' said Poirot. 'Dropped something. Or perhaps . . .' He adopted a roguish, gallant air, 'Or perhaps, Madame, it is a rendezvous. I am, most unfortunately, not the person you came to meet?'

She had recovered her aplomb by now.

'Does one ever have rendezvous in the middle of the morning?' she demanded, questioningly.

'Sometimes,' said Poirot, 'one has to have a rendezvous at the only time one can. Husbands,' he added sententiously, 'are sometimes jealous.'

'I doubt if mine is,' said Sally Legge.

She said the words lightly enough, but behind them Poirot heard an undertone of bitterness.

'He's so completely engrossed in his own affairs.'

'All women complain of that in husbands,' said Poirot. 'Especially in English husbands,' he added.

'You foreigners are more gallant.'

'We know,' said Poirot, 'that it is necessary to tell a woman at least once a week, and preferably three or four times, that we love her; and that it is also wise to bring her a few flowers, to pay her a few compliments, to tell her that she looks well in her new dress or new hat.'

'Is that what *you* do?'

'I, Madame, am not a husband,' said Hercule Poirot. 'Alas!' he added.

'I'm sure there's no alas about it. I'm sure you're quite delighted to be a carefree bachelor.'

'No, no, Madame, it is terrible all that I have missed in life.'

'I think one's a fool to marry,' said Sally Legge.

'You regret the days when you painted in your studio in Chelsea?'

'You seem to know all about me, M. Poirot?'

'I am a gossip,' said Hercule Poirot. 'I like to hear all about people.' He went on, 'Do you really regret, Madame?'

'Oh, I don't know.' She sat down impatiently on the seat. Poirot sat beside her.

He witnessed once more the phenomenon to which he was becoming accustomed. This attractive, red-haired girl was about to say things to him that she would have thought twice about saying to an Englishman.

'I hoped,' she said, 'that when we came down here for a holiday away from everything, that things would be the same again . . . But it hasn't worked out like that.'

'No?'

'No. Alec's just as moody and – oh, I don't know – wrapped up in himself. I don't know what's the matter with him. He's so nervy and on edge. People ring him up and leave queer messages for him and he won't tell me *anything*. That's what makes me mad. He won't *tell* me anything! I thought at first it was some other woman, but I don't think it is. Not really . . .'

But her voice held a certain doubt which Poirot was quick to notice.

'Did you enjoy your tea yesterday afternoon, Madame?' he asked.

'Enjoy my tea?' She frowned at him, her thoughts seeming to come back from a long way away. Then she said hastily, 'Oh, yes. You've no idea how exhausting it was, sitting in that tent muffled up in all those veils. It was stifling.'

'The tea tent also must have been somewhat stifling?'

'Oh, yes, it was. However, there's nothing like a cuppa, is there?'

'You were searching for something just now, were you not, Madame? Would it, by any possibility, be this?' He held out in his hand the little gold charm.

'I – oh, yes. Oh, thank you, M. Poirot. Where did you find it?'

'It was here, on the floor, in that crack over there.'

'I must have dropped it some time.'

'Yesterday?'

'Oh, no, not yesterday. It was before that.'

'But surely, Madame, I remember seeing that particular charm on your wrist when you were telling me my fortune.'

Nobody could tell a deliberate lie better than Hercule Poirot. He spoke with complete assurance and before that assurance Sally Legge's eyelids dropped.

'I don't really remember,' she said. 'I only noticed this morning that it was missing.'

'Then I am happy,' said Poirot gallantly, 'to be able to restore it to you.'

She was turning the little charm over nervously in her fingers. Now she rose.

'Well, thank you, M. Poirot, thank you very much,' she said.

Her breath was coming rather unevenly and her eyes were nervous.

She hurried out of the Folly. Poirot leaned back in the seat and nodded his head slowly.

No, he said to himself, no, you did not go to the tea tent yesterday afternoon. It was not because you wanted your tea that you were so anxious to know if it was four o'clock. It was *here* you came yesterday afternoon. Here, to the Folly. *Halfway to the boathouse.* You came here to meet someone.

Once again he heard footsteps approaching. Rapid impatient footsteps. 'And here perhaps,' said Poirot, smiling in anticipation, 'comes whoever it was that Mrs Legge came up here to meet.'

But then, as Alec Legge came round the corner of the Folly, Poirot ejaculated:

'Wrong again.'

'Eh? What's that?' Alec Legge looked startled.

'I said,' explained Poirot, 'that I was wrong again. I am not often wrong,' he explained, 'and it exasperates me. It was not you I expected to see.'

'Whom did you expect to see?' asked Alec Legge.

Poirot replied promptly.

'A young man – a boy almost – in one of these gaily-patterned shirts with turtles on it.'

He was pleased at the effect of his words. Alec Legge took a step forward. He said rather incoherently:

'How do you know? How did – what d'you mean?'

'I am psychic,' said Hercule Poirot, and closed his eyes.

Alec Legge took another couple of steps forward. Poirot was conscious that a very angry man was standing in front of him.

'What the devil did you mean?' he demanded.

'Your friend has, I think,' said Poirot, 'gone back to the Youth Hostel. If you want to see him you will have to go there to find him.'

'So that's it,' muttered Alec Legge.

He dropped down at the other end of the stone bench.

'So that's why you're down here? It wasn't a question of "giving away the prizes." I might have known better.' He turned towards Poirot. His face was haggard and unhappy. 'I know what it must seem like,' he said. 'I know what the whole thing looks like. But it isn't as you think it is. I'm being victimized. I tell you that once you get into these people's clutches, it isn't so easy to get out of them. And I want to get out of them. That's the point. *I want to get out of them*. You get desperate, you know. You feel like taking desperate measures. You feel you're caught like a rat in a trap and there's nothing you can do. Oh, well, what's the good of talking! You know what you want to know now, I suppose. You've got your evidence.'

He got up, stumbled a little as though he could hardly see his way, then rushed off energetically without a backward look.

Hercule Poirot remained behind with his eyes very wide open and his eyebrows rising.

'All this is very curious,' he murmured. 'Curious and interesting. I have the evidence I need, have I? Evidence of what? Murder?'

CHAPTER 14

I

Inspector Bland sat in Helmmouth Police Station. Superintendent Baldwin, a large comfortable-looking man, sat on the other side of the table. Between the two men, on the table, was a black sodden mass. Inspector Bland poked at it with a cautious forefinger.

'That's her hat all right,' he said. 'I'm sure of it, though I don't suppose I could swear to it. She fancied that shape, it seems. So her maid told me. She'd got one or two of them. A pale pink and a sort of puce colour, but yesterday she was wearing the black one. Yes, this is it. And you fished it out of the river? That makes it look as though it's the way we think it is.'

'No certainty yet,' said Baldwin. 'After all,' he added, 'anyone could throw a hat into the river.'

'Yes,' said Bland, 'they could throw it in from the boathouse, or they could throw it in off a yacht.'

'The yacht's sewed up, all right,' said Baldwin. 'If she's there, alive or dead, she's still there.'

'He hasn't been ashore today?'

'Not so far. He's on board. He's been sitting out in a deck-chair smoking a cigar.'

Inspector Bland glanced at the clock.

'Almost time to go aboard,' he said.

'Think you'll find her?' asked Baldwin.

'I wouldn't bank on it,' said Bland. 'I've got the feeling, you know, that he's a clever devil.' He was lost in thought for a moment, poking again at the hat. Then he said, 'What about the body – if there was a body? Any ideas about that?'

'Yes,' said Baldwin, 'I talked to Otterweight this morning. Ex-coastguard man. I always consult him in anything to do with tides and currents. About the time the lady went into the Helm, if she did go into the Helm, the tide was just on the ebb. There is a full moon now and it would be flowing swiftly. Reckon she'd be carried out to sea and the current would take her towards the Cornish coast. There's no certainty where the body would fetch up or if it would fetch up at all. One or two drownings we've had here, we've never recovered the body. It gets broken up, too, on the rocks. Here, by Start Point. On the other hand, it *might* fetch up any day.'

'If it doesn't, it's going to be difficult,' said Bland.

'You're certain in your own mind that she did go into the river?'

'I don't see what else it can be,' said Inspector Bland sombrely. 'We've checked up, you know, on the buses and the trains. This place is a cul-de-sac. She was wearing conspicuous clothes and she didn't take any others with her. So I should say she never left Nasse. Either her body's in the sea or else it's hidden somewhere on the property. What I want now,' he went on heavily, 'is *motive*. And the body of course,' he added, as an afterthought. 'Can't get anywhere until I find the body.'

'What about the other girl?'

'She saw it – or she saw something. We'll get at the facts in the end, but it won't be easy.'

Baldwin in his turn looked up at the clock.

'Time to go,' he said.

The two police officers were received on board the *Espérance* with all De Sousa's charming courtesy. He offered them drinks which they refused, and went on to express a kindly interest in their activities.

'You are farther forward with your inquiries regarding the death of this young girl?'

'We're progressing,' Inspector Bland told him.

The superintendent took up the running and expressed very delicately the object of their visit.

'You would like to search the *Espérance*?' De Sousa did not seem annoyed. Instead he seemed rather amused. 'But why? You think I conceal the murderer or do you think perhaps that I am the murderer myself?'

'It's necessary, Mr De Sousa, as I'm sure you'll understand. A search warrant . . .'

De Sousa raised his hands.

'But I am anxious to co-operate – eager! Let this be all among friends. You are welcome to search where you will in my boat. Ah, perhaps you think that I have here my cousin, Lady Stubbs? You think, perhaps, she has run away from her husband and taken shelter with me? But search, gentlemen, by all means search.'

The search was duly undertaken. It was a thorough one. In the end, striving to conceal their chagrin, the two police officers took leave of Mr De Sousa.

'You have found nothing? How disappointing. But I told you that was so. You will perhaps have some refreshment now. No?'

He accompanied them to where their boat lay alongside.

'And for myself?' he asked. 'I am free to depart? You understand it becomes a little boring here. The weather is good. I should like very much to proceed to Plymouth.'

'If you would be kind enough, sir, to remain here for the inquest – that is tomorrow – in case the Coroner should wish to ask you anything.'

'Why, certainly. I want to do all that I can. But after that?'

'After that, sir,' said Superintendent Baldwin, his face wooden, 'you are, of course, at liberty to proceed where you will.'

The last thing they saw as the launch moved away from the yacht was De Sousa's smiling face looking down on them.

II

The inquest was almost painfully devoid of interest. Apart from the medical evidence and evidence of identity, there was little to feed the curiosity of the spectators. An adjournment was asked for and granted. The whole proceedings had been purely formal.

What followed the inquest, however, was not quite so formal. Inspector Bland spent the afternoon taking a trip in that well-known pleasure steamer, the *Devon Belle*. Leaving Brixwell at about three o'clock, it rounded the headland, proceeded around the coast, entered the mouth of the Helm and went up the river. There were about two hundred and thirty people on board besides Inspector Bland. He sat on the starboard side of the boat, scanning the wooded shore. They came round a bend in the river and passed the isolated grey tiled boathouse that belonged to Hoodown Park. Inspector Bland looked surreptitiously at his watch. It was just quarter-past four. They were coming now close beside the Nasse boathouse. It nestled remote in its trees with its little balcony and its small quay below. There was no sign apparent that there was anyone inside the boathouse, though as a matter of fact, to Inspector Bland's certain knowledge, there *was* someone inside. P.C. Hoskins, in accordance with orders, was on duty there.

Not far from the boathouse steps was a small launch. In the launch were a man and girl in holiday kit. They were indulging in what seemed like some rather rough horseplay. The girl was screaming, the man was playfully pretending he was going to duck her overboard. At that same moment a stentorian voice spoke through a megaphone.

'Ladies and gentlemen,' it boomed, 'you are now approaching the famous village of Gitcham where we shall remain for three-quarters of an hour and where you can have a crab or lobster tea, as well as Devonshire cream. On your right are the grounds of Nasse House. You will pass the house itself in two or three minutes, it is just visible through the trees. Originally the home of Sir Gervase Folliat, a contemporary of Sir Francis Drake who sailed with him in his voyage to the new world, it is now the property of Sir George Stubbs. On your left is the famous Gooseacre Rock. There, ladies and gentlemen, it was the habit to deposit scolding wives at low tide and leave them there until the water came up to their necks.'

Everybody on the *Devon Belle* stared with fascinated interest at the Gooseacre Rock. Jokes were made and there were many shrill giggles and guffaws.

While this was happening, the holidaymaker in the boat, with a final scuffle, did push his lady friend overboard. Leaning over, he held her in the water, laughing and saying, 'No, I don't pull you out till you've promised to behave.'

Nobody, however, observed this with the exception of Inspector Bland. They had all been listening to the megaphone, staring for the first sight of Nasse House through the trees, and gazing with fascinated interest at the Gooseacre Rock.

The holidaymaker released the girl, she sank under water and a few moments later appeared on the other side of the boat. She swam to it and got in, heaving herself over the side with practised skill. Policewoman Alice Jones was an accomplished swimmer.

Inspector Bland came ashore at Gitcham with the other two hundred and thirty passengers and consumed a lobster tea with Devonshire cream and scones. He said to himself as he did so, 'So it *could* be done, and no one would notice!'

III

While Inspector Bland was doing his experiment on the Helm, Hercule Poirot was experimenting with a tent on the lawn at Nasse House. It was, in actual fact, the same tent where Madame Zuleika had told her fortunes. When the rest of the marquees and stands had been dismantled Poirot had asked for this to remain behind.

He went into it now, closed the flaps and went to the back of it. Deftly he unlaced the flaps there, slipped out, relaced them, and plunged into the hedge of rhododendron that immediately backed the tent. Slipping between a couple of bushes, he soon reached a small rustic arbour. It was a kind of summer-house with a closed door. Poirot opened the door and went inside.

It was very dim inside because very little light came in through the rhododendrons which had grown up round it since it had been first placed there many years ago. There was a box there with croquet balls in it, and some old rusted hoops. There were one or two broken hockey sticks, a good many earwigs and spiders, and a round irregular mark on the dust on the floor. At this Poirot looked for some time. He knelt down, and taking a little yard measure from his pocket, he measured its dimensions carefully. Then he nodded his head in a satisfied fashion.

He slipped out quietly, shutting the door behind him. Then he pursued an oblique course through the rhododendron bushes. He worked his way up the hill in this way and came out a short time after on the path which led to the Folly and down from there to the boathouse.

He did not visit the Folly this time, but went straight down the zig-zagging way until he reached the boathouse. He had the key with him and he opened the door and went in.

Except for the removal of the body, and of the tea tray with its glass and plate, it was just as he remembered it. The police had noted and photographed all that it contained. He went over now to the table where the pile of comics lay. He turned them over and his expression was not unlike Inspector Bland's had been as he noted the words Marlene had doodled down there before she died. 'Jackie Blake goes with Susan Brown.' 'Peter pinches girls at the pictures.' 'Georgie Porgie kisses hikers in the wood.' 'Biddy Fox likes boys.' 'Albert goes with Doreen.'

He found the remarks pathetic in their young crudity. He remembered Marlene's plain, rather spotty face. He suspected that boys had not pinched Marlene at the pictures. Frustrated, Marlene had got a vicarious thrill by her spying and peering at her young contemporaries. She had spied on people, she had snooped, and she had seen things. Things that she was not meant to have seen – things, usually, of small importance, but on one occasion perhaps something of more importance? Something of whose importance she herself had had no idea.

It was all conjecture, and Poirot shook his head doubtfully. He replaced the pile of comics neatly on the table, his passion for tidiness always in the ascendent. As he did so, he was suddenly assailed with the feeling of something missing. Something . . . What was it? Something that *ought* to have been there . . . Something . . . He shook his head as the elusive impression faded.

He went slowly out of the boathouse, unhappy and displeased

with himself. He, Hercule Poirot, had been summoned to prevent a murder – and he had not prevented it. It had happened. What was even more humiliating was that he had no real ideas, even now, as to what had actually happened. It was ignominious. And tomorrow he must return to London defeated. His ego was seriously deflated – even his moustaches drooped.

CHAPTER 15

It was a fortnight later that Inspector Bland had a long and unsatisfying interview with the Chief Constable of the County.

Major Merrall had irritable tufted eyebrows and looked rather like an angry terrier. But his men all liked him and respected his judgment.

'Well, well, well,' said Major Merrall. 'What have we got? Nothing that we can act on. This fellow De Sousa now? We can't connect him in any way with the Girl Guide. If Lady Stubbs' body had turned up, that would have been different.' He brought his eyebrows down towards his nose and glared at Bland. 'You think there *is* a body, don't you?'

'What do you think, sir?'

'Oh, I agree with you. Otherwise, we'd have traced her by now. Unless, of course, she'd made her plans very carefully. And I don't see the least indication of that. She'd no money, you know. We've been into all the financial side of it. Sir George had the money. He made her a very generous allowance, but she's not got a stiver of her own. And there's no trace of a lover. No rumour of one, no gossip – and there would be, mark you, in a country district like that.'

He took a turn up and down the floor.

'The plain fact of it is that we don't know. We *think* De Sousa for some unknown reason of his own made away with his cousin. The most probable thing is that he got her to meet him down at the boathouse, took her aboard the launch and pushed her overboard. You've tested that that could happen?'

'Good lord, sir! You could drown a whole boatful of people during holiday time in the river or on the seashore. Nobody'd think anything of it. Everyone spends their time squealing and pushing each other off things. But the thing De Sousa *didn't* know about, was that that girl was in the boathouse, bored to death with nothing to do and ten to one was looking out of the window.'

'Hoskins looked out of the window and watched the performance you put up, and you didn't see him?'

'No, sir. You'd have no idea anyone was in that boathouse unless they came out on the balcony and showed themselves –'

'Perhaps the girl did come out on the balcony. De Sousa realizes she's seen what he's doing, so he comes ashore and deals with her, gets her to let him into the boathouse by asking her what she's doing there. She tells him, pleased with her part in the Murder Hunt, he puts the cord round her neck in a playful manner – and whoooosh . . .' Major Merrall made an expressive gesture with his hands. 'That's that! Okay, Bland; okay. Let's say that's how it happened. Pure guesswork. We haven't got *any* evidence. We haven't got a body, and if we attempted to detain De Sousa in this country we'd have a hornets' nest about our ears. We'll have to let him go.'

'*Is* he going, sir?'

'He's laying up his yacht a week from now. Going back to his blasted island.'

'So we haven't got much time,' said Inspector Bland gloomily.

'There are other possibilities, I suppose?'

'Oh, yes, sir, there are several *possibilities*. I still hold to it that she must have been murdered by somebody who was in on the facts of the Murder Hunt. We can clear two people completely. Sir George Stubbs and Captain Warburton. They were running shows on the lawn and taking charge of things the entire afternoon. They are vouched for by dozens of people. The same applies to Mrs Masterton, if, that is, one can include her at all.'

'Include everybody,' said Major Merrall. 'She's continually ringing me up about bloodhounds. In a detective story,' he added wistfully, 'she'd be just the woman who *had* done it. But, dash it, I've known Connie Masterton pretty well all my life. I just can't see her going round strangling Girl Guides, or disposing of mysterious exotic beauties. Now, then, who else is there?'

'There's Mrs Oliver,' said Bland. 'She devised the Murder

Hunt. She's rather eccentric and she was away on her own for a good part of the afternoon. Then there's Mr Alec Legge.'

'Fellow in the pink cottage, eh?'

'Yes. He left the show fairly early on, or he wasn't seen there. He says he got fed up with it and walked back to his cottage. On the other hand, old Merdell – that's the old boy down at the quay who looks after people's boats for them and helps with the parking – he says Alec Legge passed him going back to the cottage about five o'clock. Not earlier. That leaves about an hour of his time unaccounted for. He says, of course, that Merdell has no idea of time and was quite wrong as to when he saw him. And after all, the old man *is* ninety-two.'

'Rather unsatisfactory,' said Major Merrall. 'No motive or anything of that kind to tie him in?'

'He might have been having an affair with Lady Stubbs,' said Bland doubtfully, 'and she might have been threatening to tell his wife, and he might have done her in, and the girl might have seen it happen –'

'And he concealed Lady Stubbs' body somewhere?'

'Yes. But I'm blessed if I know how or where. My men have searched that sixty-five acres and there's no trace anywhere of disturbed earth, and I should say that by now we've rooted under every bush there is. Still, say he did manage to hide the body, he could have thrown her hat into the river as a blind. And Marlene Tucker saw him and so he disposed of her? That part of it's always the same.' Inspector Bland paused, then said, 'And, of course, there's Mrs Legge –'

'What have we got on her?'

'She wasn't in the tea tent from four to half past as she says she was,' said Inspector Bland slowly. 'I spotted that as soon as I'd talked to her and to Mrs Folliat. Evidence supports Mrs Folliat's statement. And that's the particular, vital half-hour.' Again he paused. 'Then there's the architect, young Michael Weyman. It's difficult to tie him up with it in any way, but he's what I should call a *likely* murderer – one of those cocky, nervy young fellows. Would kill anyone and not turn a hair about it. In with a loose set, I shouldn't wonder.'

'You're so damned respectable, Bland,' said Major Merrall. 'How does he account for his movements?'

'Very vague, sir. Very vague indeed.'

'That proves he's a genuine architect,' said Major Merrall with feeling. He had recently built himself a house near the sea coast. 'They're so vague, I wonder they're alive at all sometimes.'

'Doesn't know where he was or when and there's nobody who seems to have seen him. There *is* some evidence that Lady Stubbs was keen on him.'

'I suppose you're hinting at one of these sex murders?'

'I'm only looking about for what I can find, sir,' said Inspector Bland with dignity. 'And then there's Miss Brewis . . .' He paused. It was a long pause.

'That's the secretary, isn't it?'

'Yes, sir. Very efficient woman.'

Again there was a pause. Major Merrall eyed his subordinate keenly.

'You've got something on your mind about her, haven't you?' he said.

'Yes, I have, sir. You see, she admits quite openly that she was in the boathouse at about the time the murder must have been committed.'

'Would she do that if she was guilty?'

'She might,' said Inspector Bland slowly. 'Actually, it's the best thing she could do. You see, if she picks up a tray with cake and a fruit drink and tells everyone she's taking that for the child down there – well, then, her presence is accounted for. She goes there and comes back and says the girl was alive at that time. We've taken her word for it. But if you remember, sir, and look again at the medical evidence, Dr Cook's time of death is between four o'clock and quarter to five. We've only Miss Brewis' word for it that Marlene was alive at a quarter past four. And there's one curious point that came up about her testimony. She told me that it was Lady Stubbs who told her to take the cakes and fruit drink to Marlene. But another witness said quite definitely that that wasn't the sort of thing that Lady Stubbs would think about. And I think, you know, that they're right there. It's not like Lady Stubbs. Lady Stubbs was a dumb beauty wrapped up in herself and her own appearance. She never seems to have ordered meals or taken an interest in household management or thought of anybody at all except her own handsome self. The more I think of it, the more it seems most unlikely that she *should* have told Miss Brewis to take anything to the Girl Guide.'

'You know, Bland,' said Merrall, 'you've got something there. But what's her motive, if so?'

'No motive for killing the girl,' said Bland; 'but I do think, you know, that she might have a motive for killing Lady Stubbs. According to M. Poirot, whom I told you about, she's head over heels in love with her employer. Supposing she followed Lady Stubbs into the woods and killed her and that Marlene Tucker, bored in the boathouse, came out and happened to see it? Then of course she'd have to kill Marlene too. What would she do next? Put the girl's body in the boathouse, come back to the house, fetch the tray and go down to the boathouse again. Then she's covered her own absence from the fête and we've got *her* testimony, our only reliable testimony on the face of it, *that Marlene Tucker was alive at a quarter past four.*'

'Well,' said Major Merrall, with a sigh, 'keep after it, Bland. Keep after it. What do you think she did with Lady Stubbs' body, if she's the guilty party?'

'Hid it in the woods, buried it, or threw it into the river.'

'The last would be rather difficult, wouldn't it?'

'It depends where the murder was committed,' said the inspector. 'She's quite a hefty woman. If it was not far from the boathouse, she *could* have carried her down there and thrown her off the edge of the quay.'

'With every pleasure steamer on the Helm looking on?'

'It would be just another piece of horse-play. Risky, but possible. But I think it far more likely myself that she hid the body somewhere, and just threw the hat into the Helm. It's possible, you see, that she, knowing the house and grounds well, might know some place where you could conceal a body. She may have managed to dispose of it in the river later. Who knows? That is, of course, if she did it,' added Inspector Bland as an afterthought. 'But, actually, sir, I stick to De Sousa –'

Major Merrall had been noting down points on a pad. He looked up now, clearing his throat.

'It comes to this, then. We can summarize it as follows: we've got five or six people who *could* have killed Marlene Tucker. Some of them are more likely than others, but that's as far as we can go. In a general way, we know *why* she was killed. She was killed because she saw something. But until we know *exactly* what it was she saw – *we don't know who killed her.*'

'Put like that, you make it sound a bit difficult, sir.'

'Oh, it *is* difficult. But we shall get there – in the end.'

'And meantime that chap will have left England – laughing in his sleeve – having got away with two murders.'

'You're fairly sure about him, aren't you? I don't say you're wrong. All the same . . .'

The chief constable was silent for a moment or two, then he said, with a shrug of his shoulders:

'Anyway, it's better than having one of these psychopathic murderers. We'd probably be having a third murder on our hands by now.'

'They do say things go in threes,' said the inspector gloomily.

He repeated that remark the following morning when he heard that old Merdell, returning home from a visit to his favourite pub across the river at Gitcham, must have exceeded his usual potations and had fallen in the river when boarding the quay. His boat was found adrift, and the old man's body was recovered that evening.

The inquest was short and simple. The night had been dark and overcast, old Merdell had had three pints of beer and, after all, he was ninety-two.

The verdict brought in was Accidental Death.

CHAPTER 16

I

Hercule Poirot sat in a square chair in front of the square fireplace in the square room of his London flat. In front of him were various objects that were not square: that were instead violently and almost impossibly curved. Each of them, studied separately, looked as if it could not have any conceivable function in a sane world. They appeared improbable, irresponsible, and wholly fortuitous. In actual fact, of course, they were nothing of the sort.

Assessed correctly, each had its particular place in a particular universe. Assembled in their proper place in their particular universe, they not only made sense, they made a picture. In other words, Hercule Poirot was doing a jigsaw puzzle.

He looked down at where a rectangle still showed improbably shaped gaps. It was an occupation he found soothing and pleasant. It brought disorder into order. It had, he reflected, a certain resemblance to his own profession. There, too, one was faced with various improbably shaped and unlikely facts which, though seeming to bear no relationship to each other, yet did each have its properly balanced part in assembling the whole. His fingers deftly picked up an improbable piece of dark grey and fitted it into a blue sky. It was, he now perceived, part of an aeroplane.

'Yes,' murmured Poirot to himself, 'that is what one must do. The unlikely piece here, the improbable piece there, the oh-so-rational piece that is not what it seems; all of these have their appointed place, and once they are fitted in, *eh bien*, there is an end of the business! All is clear. All is – as they say nowadays – *in the picture*.'

He fitted in, in rapid succession, a small piece of a minaret, another piece that looked as though it was part of a striped awning and was actually the backside of a cat, and a missing piece of sunset that had changed with Turneresque suddenness from orange to pink.

If one knew what to look for, it would be so easy, said Hercule Poirot to himself. But one does not know what to look for. And so one looks in the wrong places or for the wrong things. He sighed vexedly. His eyes strayed from the jigsaw puzzle in front of him to the chair on the other side of the fireplace. There, not half an hour ago, Inspector Bland had sat consuming tea and crumpets (square crumpets) and talking sadly. He had had to come to London on police business and that police business having been accomplished, he had come to call upon M. Poirot. He had wondered, he explained, whether M. Poirot had any ideas. He had then proceeded to explain his own ideas. On every point he outlined, Poirot had agreed with him. Inspector Bland, so Poirot thought, had made a very fair and unprejudiced survey of the case.

It was now a month, nearly five weeks, since the occurrences at Nasse House. It had been five weeks of stagnation and of negation. Lady Stubbs' body had not been recovered. Lady Stubbs, if living, had not been traced. The odds, Inspector Bland pointed out, were strongly against her being alive. Poirot agreed with him.

'Of course,' said Bland, 'the body might not have been washed up. There's no telling with a body once it's in the water. It *may* show up yet, though it will be pretty unrecognizable when it does.'

'There is a third possibility,' Poirot pointed out.

Bland nodded.

'Yes,' he said, 'I've thought of that. I keep thinking of that, in fact. You mean the body's there – at Nasse, hidden somewhere where we've never thought of looking. It could be, you know. It just could be. With an old house, and with grounds like that, there are places you'd never think of – that you'd never know were there.'

He paused a moment, ruminated, and then said:

'There's a house I was in only the other day. They'd built an air-raid shelter, you know, in the war. A flimsy sort of more or less home-made job in the garden, by the wall of the house, and had made a way from it into the house – into the cellar. Well, the war ended, the shelters tumbled down, they heaped it up in irregular mounds and made a kind of rockery of it. Walking through that garden now, you'd never think that the place had once been an air-raid shelter and that there was a chamber underneath. Looks as though it was always *meant* to be a rockery. And all the time, behind a wine bin in the cellar, there's a passage leading into it. That's what I mean. That kind of thing. Some sort of way into some kind of place that no outsider would know about. I don't suppose there's an actual Priest's Hole or anything of that kind?'

'Hardly – not at that period.'

'That's what Mr Weyman says – he says the house was built about 1790 or thereabouts. No reason for priests to hide themselves by that date. All the same, you know, there might be – somewhere, some alteration in the structure – something that one of the family might know about. What do you think, M. Poirot?'

'It is possible, yes,' said Poirot. '*Mais oui*, decidedly it is an idea. If one accepts the possibility, then the next thing is – who would know about it? Anyone staying in the house *might* know, I suppose?'

'Yes. Of course it would let out De Sousa.' The inspector looked dissatisfied. De Sousa was still his preferred suspect. 'As you say, anyone who lived in the house, such as a servant or one of the family, might know about it. Someone just staying in the house would be less likely. People who only came in from outside, like the Legges, less likely still.'

'The person who would certainly know about such a thing, and who could tell you if you asked her, would be Mrs Folliat,' said Poirot.

Mrs Folliat, he thought, knew all there was to know about Nasse House. Mrs Folliat knew a great deal . . . Mrs Folliat had known straight away that Hattie Stubbs was dead. Mrs Folliat knew, before Marlene and Hattie Stubbs died, that it was a very wicked world and that there were very wicked people in it. Mrs Folliat, thought Poirot vexedly, was the key to the whole business. But Mrs Folliat, he reflected, was a key that would not easily turn in the lock.

'I've interviewed the lady several times,' said the inspector. 'Very nice, very pleasant she's been about everything, and seems very distressed that she can't suggest anything helpful.'

Can't or won't? thought Poirot. Bland was perhaps thinking the same.

'There's a type of lady,' he said, 'that you can't force. You can't frighten them, or persuade them, or diddle them.'

No, Poirot thought, you couldn't force or persuade or diddle Mrs Folliat.

The inspector had finished his tea, and sighed and gone, and Poirot had got out his jigsaw puzzle to alleviate his mounting exasperation. For he was exasperated. Both exasperated and humiliated. Mrs Oliver had summoned him, Hercule Poirot, to elucidate a mystery. She had felt that there was something wrong, and there *had* been something wrong. And she had looked confidently to Hercule Poirot, first to prevent it – and he had not prevented it – and, secondly, to discover the killer, and he had *not* discovered the killer. He was in a fog, in the type of fog where there are from time to time baffling gleams of light.

Every now and then, or so it seemed to him, he had had one of those glimpses. And each time he had failed to penetrate farther. He had failed to assess the value of what he seemed, for one brief moment, to have seen.

Poirot got up, crossed to the other side of the hearth, rearranged the second square chair so that it was at a definite geometric angle, and sat down in it. He had passed from the jigsaw of painted wood and cardboard to the jigsaw of a murder problem. He took a notebook from his pocket and wrote in small neat characters:

'Etienne de Sousa, Amanda Brewis, Alec Legge, Sally Legge, Michael Weyman.'

It was physically impossible for Sir George or Jim Warburton to have killed Marlene Tucker. Since it was not physically impossible for Mrs Oliver to have done so, he added her name after a brief space. He also added the name of Mrs Masterton since he did not remember of his own knowledge having seen Mrs Masterton constantly on the lawn between four o'clock and quarter to five. He added the name of Henden, the butler; more, perhaps, because a sinister butler had figured in Mrs Oliver's Murder Hunt than because he had really any suspicions of the dark-haired artist with the gong stick. He also put down 'Boy in turtle shirt' with a query mark after it. Then he smiled, shook his head, took a pin from the lapel of his jacket, shut his eyes and stabbed with it. It was as good a way as any other, he thought.

He was justifiably annoyed when the pin proved to have transfixed the last entry.

'I am an imbecile,' said Hercule Poirot. 'What has a boy in a turtle shirt to do with this?'

But he also realized he must have had some reason for including this enigmatic character in his list. He recalled again the day he had sat in the Folly, and the surprise on the boy's face at seeing him there. Not a very pleasant face, despite the youthful good looks. An arrogant ruthless face. The young man had come there for some purpose. He had come to meet someone, and it followed that that someone was a person whom he could not meet, or did not wish to meet, in the ordinary way. It was a meeting, in fact, to which attention must not be called. A guilty meeting. Something to do with the murder?

Poirot pursued his reflections. A boy who was staying at the

Youth Hostel – that is to say, a boy who would be in that neighbourhood for two nights at most. Had he come there casually? One of the many young students visiting Britain? Or had he come there for a special purpose, to meet some special person? There could have been what seemed a casual encounter on the day of the fête – possibly there had been.

I know a good deal, said Hercule Poirot to himself. I have in my hands many, many pieces of this jigsaw. I have an idea of the *kind* of crime this was – but it must be that I am not looking at it the right way.

He turned a page of his notebook, and wrote:

Did Lady Stubbs ask Miss Brewis to take tea to Marlene? If not, why does Miss Brewis say that she did?

He considered the point. Miss Brewis might quite easily herself have thought of taking cake and a fruit drink to the girl. But if so why did she not simply say so? Why lie about Lady Stubbs having asked her to do so? Could this be because Miss Brewis went to the boathouse *and found Marlene dead?* Unless Miss Brewis was herself guilty of the murder, that seemed very unlikely. She was not a nervous woman nor an imaginative one. If she had found the girl dead, she would surely at once have given the alarm?

He stared for some time at the two questions he had written. He could not help feeling that somewhere in those words there was some vital pointer to the truth that had escaped him. After four or five minutes of thought he wrote down something more.

Etienne de Sousa declares that he wrote to his cousin three weeks before his arrival at Nasse House. Is that statement true or false?

Poirot felt almost certain that it was false. He recalled the scene at the breakfast table. There seemed no earthly reason why Sir George or Lady Stubbs should pretend to a surprise and, in the latter's case, a dismay, which they did not feel. He could see no purpose to be accomplished by it. Granting, however, that Etienne de Sousa had lied, *why* did he lie? To give the impression that his visit had been announced and welcomed? It might be so, but it seemed a very doubtful reason. There was certainly no *evidence* that such a letter had ever been written or received. Was it an attempt on De Sousa's part to establish his *bona fides* – to make his visit appear natural and even expected? Certainly Sir George had received him amicably enough, although he did not know him.

Poirot paused, his thoughts coming to a stop. *Sir George did not know De Sousa. His wife, who did know him, had not seen him.* Was there perhaps something *there?* Could it be possible that the Etienne de Sousa who had arrived that day at the fête was not the real Etienne de Sousa? He went over the idea in his mind, but again he could see no point to it. What had De Sousa to gain by coming and representing himself as De Sousa if he was not De Sousa? In any case, De Sousa did not derive any benefit from Hattie's death. Hattie, as the police had ascertained, had no money of her own except that which was allowed her by her husband.

Poirot tried to remember exactly what she had said to him that morning. 'He is a bad man. He does wicked things.' And, according to Bland, she had said to her husband: 'He kills people.'

There was something rather significant about that, now that one came to examine all the facts. *He kills people.*

On the day Etienne de Sousa had come to Nasse House one person certainly had been killed, possibly two people. Mrs Folliat had said that one should pay no attention to these melodramatic remarks of Hattie's. She had said so very insistently. Mrs Folliat . . .

Hercule Poirot frowned, then brought his hand down with a bang on the arm of his chair.

'Always, always – I return to Mrs Folliat. She is the key to the whole business. If I knew what she knows . . . I can no longer sit in an armchair and just think. No, I must take a train and go again to Devon and visit Mrs Folliat.'

II

Hercule Poirot paused for a moment outside the big wrought-iron gates of Nasse House. He looked ahead of him along the curving drive. It was no longer summer. Golden-brown leaves fluttered gently down from the trees. Near at hand the grassy banks were coloured with small mauve cyclamen. Poirot sighed. The beauty of Nasse House appealed to him in spite of himself. He was not a great admirer of nature in the wild, he liked things trim and neat, yet he could not but appreciate the soft wild beauty of massed shrubs and trees.

At his left was the small white porticoed lodge. It was a fine afternoon. Probably Mrs Folliat would not be at home. She would be out somewhere with her gardening basket or else visiting some friends in the neighbourhood. She had many friends. This was her home, and had been her home for many long years. What was it the old man on the quay had said? 'There'll always be Folliats at Nasse House.'

Poirot rapped gently upon the door of the Lodge. After a few moments' delay he heard footsteps inside. They sounded to his ear slow and almost hesitant. Then the door was opened and Mrs Folliat stood framed in the doorway. He was startled to see how old and frail she looked. She stared at him incredulously for a moment or two, then she said:

'M. Poirot? You!'

He thought for a moment that he had seen fear leap into her eyes, but perhaps that was sheer imagination on his part. He said politely:

'May I come in, Madame?'

'But of course.'

She had recovered all her poise now, beckoned him in with a gesture and led the way into her small sitting-room. There were some delicate Chelsea figures on the mantelpiece, a couple of chairs covered in exquisite petit point, and a Derby tea service stood on the small table. Mrs Folliat said:

'I will fetch another cup.'

Poirot raised a faintly protesting hand, but she pushed the protest aside.

'Of course you must have some tea.'

She went out of the room. He looked round him once more. A piece of needlework, a petit point chair seat, lay on a table with a needle sticking in it. Against the wall was a bookcase with books. There was a little cluster of miniatures on the wall and a faded photograph in a silver frame of a man in uniform with a stiff moustache and a weak chin.

Mrs Folliat came back into the room with a cup and saucer in her hand.

Poirot said, 'Your husband, Madame?'

'Yes.'

Noticing that Poirot's eyes swept along the top of the bookcase as though in search of further photographs, she said brusquely:

'I'm not fond of photographs. They make one live in the past too much. One must learn to forget. One must cut away the dead wood.'

Poirot remembered how the first time he had seen Mrs Folliat she had been clipping with sécateurs at a shrub on the bank. She had said then, he remembered, something about dead wood. He looked at her thoughtfully, appraising her character. An enigmatical woman, he thought, and a woman who, in spite of the gentleness and fragility of her appearance, had a side to her that could be ruthless. A woman who could cut away dead wood not only from plants but from her own life . . .

She sat down and poured out a cup of tea, asking: 'Milk? Sugar?'

'Three lumps if you will be so good, Madame?'

She handed him his cup and said conversationally:

'I was surprised to see you. Somehow I did not imagine you would be passing through this part of the world again.'

'I am not exactly passing through,' said Poirot.

'No?' She queried him with slightly uplifted eyebrows.

'My visit to this part of the world is intentional.'

She still looked at him in inquiry.

'I came here partly to see you, Madame.'

'Really?'

'First of all – there has been no news of the young Lady Stubbs?'

Mrs Folliat shook her head.

'There was a body washed up the other day in Cornwall,' she

said. 'George went there to see if he could identify it. But it was not her.' She added: 'I am very sorry for George. The strain has been very great.'

'Does he still believe that his wife may be alive?'

Slowly Mrs Folliat shook her head.

'I think,' she said, 'that he has given up hope. After all, if Hattie were alive, she couldn't possibly conceal herself successfully with the whole of the Press and the police looking for her. Even if something like loss of memory had happened to her – well, surely the police would have found her by now?'

'It would seem so, yes,' said Poirot. 'Do the police still search?'

'I suppose so. I do not really know.'

'But Sir George has given up hope.'

'He does not say so,' said Mrs Folliat. 'Of course I have not seen him lately. He has been mostly in London.'

'And the murdered girl? There have been no developments there?'

'Not that I know of.' She added. 'It seems a senseless crime – absolutely pointless. Poor child –'

'It still upsets you, I see, to think of her, Madame.'

Mrs Folliat did not reply for a moment or two. Then she said:

'I think when one is old, the death of anyone who is young upsets one out of due proportion. We old folks expect to die, but that child had her life before her.'

'It might not have been a very interesting life.'

'Not from our point of view, perhaps, but it might have been interesting to her.'

'And although, as you say, we old folk must expect to die,' said Poirot, 'we do not really want to. At least *I* do not want to. I find life very interesting still.'

'I don't think that I do.'

She spoke more to herself than him, her shoulders drooped still more.

'I am very tired, M. Poirot. I shall be not only ready, but thankful, when my time comes.'

He shot a quick glance at her. He wondered, as he had wondered before, whether it was a sick woman who sat talking to him, a woman who had perhaps the knowledge or even the certainty of approaching death. He could not otherwise account for the intense weariness and lassitude of her manner. That lassitude, he felt, was not really characteristic of the woman. Amy Folliat, he felt, was a woman of character, energy and determination. She had lived through many troubles, loss of her home, loss of wealth, the deaths of her sons. All these, he felt, she had survived. She had cut away the 'dead wood,' as she herself had expressed it. But there was something now in her life that she could not cut away, that no one could cut away for her. If it was not physical illness he did not see what it could be. She gave a sudden little smile as though she were reading his thoughts.

'Really, you know, I have not very much to live for, M. Poirot,' she said. 'I have many friends but no near relations, no family.'

'You have your home,' said Poirot on an impulse.

'You mean Nasse? Yes –'

'It is *your* home, isn't it, although technically it is the property of Sir George Stubbs? Now Sir George Stubbs has gone to London you rule in his stead.'

Again he saw the sharp look of fear in her eyes. When she spoke her voice held an icy edge to it.

'I don't quite know what you mean, M. Poirot. I am grateful to Sir George for renting me this lodge, but I *do* rent it. I pay him a yearly sum for it with the right to walk in the grounds.'

Poirot spread out his hands.

'I apologize, Madame. I did not mean to offend you.'

'No doubt I misunderstood you,' said Mrs Folliat coldly.

'It is a beautiful place,' said Poirot. 'A beautiful house, beautiful grounds. It has about it a great peace, great serenity.'

'Yes.' Her face lightened. 'We have always felt that. I felt it as a child when I first came here.'

'But is there the same peace and serenity *now*, Madame?'

'Why not?'

'Murder unavenged,' said Poirot. 'The spilling of innocent blood. Until that shadow lifts, there will not be peace.' He added, 'I think you know that, Madame, as well as I do.'

Mrs Folliat did not answer. She neither moved nor spoke. She sat quite still and Poirot had no idea what she was thinking. He leaned forward a little and spoke again.

'Madame, you know a good deal – perhaps everything – about

this murder. You know who killed that girl, you know *why*. You know who killed Hattie Stubbs, you know, perhaps, where her body lies now.'

Mrs Folliat spoke then. Her voice was loud, almost harsh.

'I know nothing,' she said. '*Nothing*.'

'Perhaps I have used the wrong word. You do not know, but I think you *guess*, Madame. I'm quite sure that you guess.'

'Now you are being – excuse me – absurd!'

'It is not absurd – it is something quite different – it is *dangerous*.'

'Dangerous? To whom?'

'To you, Madame. So long as you keep your knowledge to yourself you are in danger. I know murderers better than you do, Madame.'

'I have told you already, I have no knowledge.'

'Suspicions, then –'

'I have no suspicions.'

'That, excuse me, is not true, Madame.'

'To speak out of mere suspicion would be wrong – indeed, wicked.'

Poirot leaned forward. 'As wicked as what was done here just over a month ago?'

She shrank back into her chair, huddled into herself. She half whispered:

'Don't talk to me of it.' And then added, with a long shuddering sigh, 'Anyway, it's over now. Done – finished with.'

'How can you tell that, Madame? I tell you of my own knowledge that it is *never* finished with a murderer.'

She shook her head.

'No. No, it's the end. And, anyway, there is nothing *I* can do. Nothing.'

He got up and stood looking down at her. She said almost fretfully:

'Why, even the police have given up.'

Poirot shook his head.

'Oh, no, Madame, you are wrong there. The police do not give up. And I,' he added, 'do not give up either. Remember that, Madame, I, Hercule Poirot, do not give up.'

It was a very typical exit line.

CHAPTER 17

After leaving Nasse, Poirot went to the village where, by inquiry, he found the cottage occupied by the Tuckers. His knock at the door went unanswered for some moments as it was drowned by the high-pitched tone of Mrs Tucker's voice from inside.

'– And what be yu thinking of, Jim Tucker, bringing them boots of yours on to my nice linoleum? If I've tell ee once I've tell ee a thousand times. Been polishing it all the morning, I have, and now look at it.'

A faint rumbling denoted Mr Tucker's reaction to these remarks. It was on the whole a placatory rumble.

'Yu've no cause to go forgetting. 'Tis all this eagerness to get the sports news on the wireless. Why, 'twouldn't have took ee tu minutes to be off with them boots. And yu, Gary, do ee mind what yu'm doing with that lollipop. Sticky fingers I will not have on my best silver teapot. Marilyn, that be someone at the door, that be. Du ee go and see who 'tis.'

The door was opened gingerly and a child of about eleven or twelve years old peered out suspiciously at Poirot. One cheek was bulged with a sweet. She was a fat child with small blue eyes and a rather piggy kind of prettiness.

''Tis a gentleman, Mum,' she shouted.

Mrs Tucker, wisps of hair hanging over her somewhat hot face, came to the door.

'What is it?' she demanded sharply. 'We don't need . . .' She paused, a faint look of recognition came across her face. 'Why let me see, now, didn't I see you with the police that day?'

'Alas, Madame, that I have brought back painful memories,' said Poirot, stepping firmly inside the door.

Mrs Tucker cast a swift agonized glance at his feet, but Poirot's pointed patent-leather shoes had only trodden the high road. No mud was being deposited on Mrs Tucker's brightly polished linoleum.

'Come in, won't you, sir,' she said, backing before him, and throwing open the door of a room on her right hand.

Poirot was ushered into a devastatingly neat little parlour. It smelt of furniture polish and Brasso and contained a large

Jacobean suite, a round table, two potted geraniums, an elaborate brass fender, and a large variety of china ornaments.

'Sit down, sir, do. I can't remember the name. Indeed, I don't think as I ever heard it.'

'My name is Hercule Poirot,' said Poirot rapidly. 'I found myself once more in this part of the world and I called here to offer you my condolences and to ask you if there had been any developments. I trust the murderer of your daughter has been discovered.'

'Not sight or sound of him,' said Mrs Tucker, speaking with some bitterness. 'And 'tis a downright wicked shame if you ask me. 'Tis my opinion the police don't disturb themselves when it's only the likes of us. What's the police anyway? If they'm all like Bob Hoskins I wonder the whole country isn't a mass of crime. All that Bob Hoskins does is spend his time looking into parked cars on the Common.'

At this point, Mr Tucker, his boots removed, appeared through the doorway, walking on his stockinged feet. He was a large, red-faced man with a pacific expression.

'Police be all right,' he said in a husky voice. 'Got their troubles like anyone else. These here maniacs ar'n't so easy to find. Look the same as you or me, if you take my meaning,' he added, speaking directly to Poirot.

The little girl who had opened the door to Poirot appeared behind her father, and a boy of about eight poked his head round her shoulder. They all stared at Poirot with intense interest.

'This is your younger daughter, I suppose,' said Poirot.

'That's Marilyn, that is,' said Mrs Tucker. 'And that's Gary. Come and say how do you do, Gary, and mind your manners.'

Gary backed away.

'Shy-like, he is,' said his mother.

'Very civil of you, I'm sure, sir,' said Mr Tucker, 'to come and ask about Marlene. Ah, that was a terrible business, to be sure.'

'I have just called upon Mrs Folliat,' said M. Poirot. 'She, too, seems to feel this very deeply.'

'She's been poorly-like ever since,' said Mrs Tucker. 'She's an old lady an't was a shock to her, happening as it did at her own place.'

Poirot noted once more everybody's unconscious assumption that Nasse House still belonged to Mrs Folliat.

'Makes her feel responsible-like in a way,' said Mr Tucker, 'not that 'twere anything to do with her.'

'Who was it that actually suggested that Marlene should play the victim?' asked Poirot.

'The lady from London that writes the books,' said Mrs Tucker promptly.

Poirot said mildly:

'But she was a stranger down here. She did not even know Marlene.'

''Twas Mrs Masterton what rounded the girls up,' said Mrs Tucker, 'and I suppose 'twas Mrs Masterton said Marlene was to do it. And Marlene, I must say, was pleased enough at the idea.'

Once again, Poirot felt, he came up against a blank wall. But he knew now what Mrs Oliver had felt when she first sent for him. Someone had been working in the dark, someone who had pushed forward their own desires through other recognized personalities. Mrs Oliver, Mrs Masterton. Those were the figure-heads. He said:

'I have been wondering, Mrs Tucker, whether Marlene was already acquainted with this – er – homicidal maniac.'

'She wouldn't know nobody like that,' said Mrs Tucker virtuously.

'Ah,' said Poirot, 'but as your husband has just observed, these maniacs are very difficult to spot. They look the same as – er – you and me. Someone may have spoken to Marlene at the fête, or even before it. Made friends with her in a perfectly harmless manner. Given her presents, perhaps.'

'Oh, no, sir, nothing of that kind. Marlene wouldn't take presents from a stranger. I brought her up better than that.'

'But she might see no harm in it,' said Poirot, persisting. 'Supposing it had been some nice lady who had offered her things.'

'Someone, you mean, like young Mrs Legge down at the Mill Cottage.'

'Yes,' said Poirot. 'Someone like that.'

'Give Marlene a lipstick once, she did,' said Mrs Tucker. 'Ever so mad, I was. I won't have you putting that muck on your face, Marlene, I said. Think what your father would say. Well, she says, perky as may be, 'tis the lady down at Lawder's Cottage as give it me. Said as how it would suit me, she did. Well, I said, don't you listen to what no London ladies say. 'Tis all very well for *them*, painting their faces and blacking their eyelashes and everything else. But you're a decent girl, I said, and you wash your face with soap and water until you're a good deal older than what you are now.'

'But she did not agree with you, I expect,' said Poirot, smiling.

'When I say a thing I mean it,' said Mrs Tucker.

The fat Marilyn suddenly gave an amused giggle. Poirot shot her a keen glance.

'Did Mrs Legge give Marlene anything else?' he asked.

'Believe she gave her a scarf or summat – one she hadn't no more use for. A showy sort of thing, but not much quality. I know quality when I see it,' said Mrs Tucker, nodding her head. 'Used to work at Nasse House as a girl, I did. Proper stuff the ladies wore in those days. No gaudy colours and all this nylon and rayon; real good silk. Why, some of their taffeta dresses would have stood up by themselves.'

'Girls like a bit of finery,' said Mr Tucker indulgently. 'I don't mind a few bright colours myself, but I won't have this 'ere mucky lipstick.'

'A bit sharp I was with her,' said Mrs Tucker, her eyes suddenly misty, 'and her gorn in that terrible way. Wished afterwards I hadn't spoken so sharp. Ah, nought but trouble and funerals lately, it seems. Troubles never come singly, so they say, and 'tis true enough.'

'You have had other losses?' inquired Poirot politely.

'The wife's father,' explained Mr Tucker. 'Come across the ferry in his boat from the Three Dogs late at night, and must have missed his footing getting on to the quay and fallen in the river. Of course he ought to have stayed quiet at home at his age. But there, yu can't do anything with the old 'uns. Always pottering about on the quay, he was.'

'Father was a great one for the boats always,' said Mrs Tucker. 'Used to look after them in the old days for Mr Folliat, years and years ago that was. Not,' she added brightly, 'as Father's much loss, as you might say. Well over ninety, he was, and trying in many of his ways. Always babbling some nonsense or other. 'Twas time he went. But, of course, us had to bury him nice – and two funerals running costs a lot of money.'

These economic reflections passed Poirot by – a faint remembrance was stirring.

'An old man – on the quay? I remember talking to him. Was his name –?'

'Merdell, sir. That was my name before I married.'

'Your father, if I remember rightly, was head gardener at Nasse?'

'No, that was my eldest brother. I was the youngest of the family – eleven of us, there were.' She added with some pride, 'There's been Merdells at Nasse for years, but they're all scattered now. Father was the last of us.'

Poirot said softly:

'There'll always be Folliats at Nasse House.'

'I beg your pardon, sir?'

'I am repeating what your old father said to me on the quay.'

'Ah, talked a lot of nonsense, Father did. I had to shut him up pretty sharp now and then.'

'So Marlene was Merdell's granddaughter,' said Poirot. 'Yes, I begin to see.' He was silent for a moment, an immense excitement was surging within him. 'Your father was drowned, you say, in the river?'

'Yes, sir. Took a drop too much, he did. And where he got the money from, I don't know. Of course he used to get tips now and again on the quay helping people with boats or with parking their cars. Very cunning he was at hiding his money from me. Yes, I'm afraid as he'd had a drop too much. Missed his footing, I'd say, getting off his boat on to the quay. So he fell in and was drowned. His body was washed up down at Helmmouth the next day. 'Tis a wonder, as you might say, that it never happened before, him being ninety-two and half blinded anyway.'

'The fact remains that it did *not* happen before –'

'Ah, well, accidents happen, sooner or later –'

'Accident,' mused Poirot. 'I wonder.'

He got up. He murmured:

'I should have guessed. Guessed long ago. The child practically told me –'

'I beg your pardon, sir?'

'It is nothing,' said Poirot. 'Once more I tender you my condolences both on the death of your daughter and on that of your father.'

He shook hands with them both and left the cottage. He said to himself:

'I have been foolish – very foolish. I have looked at everything the wrong way round.'

'Hi – mister.'

It was a cautious whisper. Poirot looked round. The fat child Marilyn was standing in the shadow of the cottage wall. She beckoned him to her and spoke in a whisper.

'Mum don't know everything,' she said. 'Marlene didn't get that scarf off of the lady down at the cottage.'

'Where did she get it?'

'Bought it in Torquay. Bought some lipstick, too, and some scent – Newt in Paris – funny name. And a jar of foundation cream, what she'd read about in an advertisement.' Marilyn giggled. 'Mum doesn't know. Hid it at the back of her drawer, Marlene did, under her winter vests. Used to go into the convenience at the bus stop and do herself up, when she went to the pictures.'

Marilyn giggled again.

'Mum never knew.'

'Didn't your mother find these things after your sister died?'

Marilyn shook her fair fluffy head.

'No,' she said. 'I got 'em now – in my drawer. Mum doesn't know.'

Poirot eyed her consideringly, and said:

'You seem a very clever girl, Marilyn.'

Marilyn grinned rather sheepishly.

'Miss Bird says it's no good my trying for the grammar school.'

'Grammar school is not everything,' said Poirot. 'Tell me, how did Marlene get the money to buy these things?'

Marilyn looked with close attention at a drain-pipe.

'Dunno,' she muttered.

'I think you do know,' said Poirot.

Shamelessly he drew out a half-crown from his pocket and added another half-crown to it.

'I believe,' he said, 'there is a new, very attractive shade of lipstick called "Carmine Kiss."'

'Sounds smashing,' said Marilyn, her hand advanced towards the five shillings. She spoke in a rapid whisper. 'She used to snoop about a bit, Marlene did. Used to see goings-on – you know what. Marlene would promise not to tell and then they'd give her a present, see?'

Poirot relinquished the five shillings.

'I see,' he said.

He nodded to Marilyn and walked away. He murmured again under his breath, but this time with intensified meaning:

'I see.'

So many things now fell into place. Not all of it. Not clear yet by any means – but he was on the right track. A perfectly clear trail all the way if only he had had the wit to see it. That first conversation with Mrs Oliver, some casual words of Michael Weyman's, the significant conversation with old Merdell on the quay, an illuminating phrase spoken by Miss Brewis – the arrival of Etienne de Sousa.

A public telephone box stood adjacent to the village post office. He entered it and rang up a number. A few minutes later he was speaking to Inspector Bland.

'Well, M. Poirot, where are you?'

'I am here, in Nassecombe.'

'But you were in London yesterday afternoon?'

'It only takes three and a half hours to come here by a good train,' Poirot pointed out. 'I have a question for you.'

'Yes?'

'What kind of a yacht did Etienne de Sousa have?'

'Maybe I can guess what you're thinking, M. Poirot, but I assure you there was nothing of that kind. It wasn't fitted up for smuggling if that's what you mean. There were no fancy hidden partitions or secret cubby-holes. We'd have found them if there had been. There was nowhere on it you could have stowed away a body.'

'You are wrong, *mon cher*, that is not what I mean. I only asked what kind of yacht, big or small?'

'Oh, it was very fancy. Must have cost the earth. All very smart, newly painted, luxury fittings.'

'Exactly,' said Poirot. He sounded so pleased that Inspector Bland felt quite surprised.

'What are you getting at, M. Poirot?' he asked.

'Etienne de Sousa,' said Poirot, 'is a rich man. That, my friend, is very significant.'

'Why?' demanded Inspector Bland.

'It fits in with my latest idea,' said Poirot.

'You've got an idea, then?'

'Yes. At last I have an idea. Up to now I have been very stupid.'

'You mean we've all been very stupid.'

'No,' said Poirot, 'I mean specially myself. I had the good fortune to have a perfectly clear trail presented to me, and I did not see it.'

'But now you're definitely on to something?'

'I think so, yes.'

'Look here, M. Poirot —'

But Poirot had rung off. After searching his pockets for available change, he put through a personal call to Mrs Oliver at her London number.

'But do not,' he hastened to add, when he made his demand, 'disturb the lady to answer the telephone if she is at work.'

He remembered how bitterly Mrs Oliver had once reproached him for interrupting a train of creative thought and how the world in consequence had been deprived of an intriguing mystery centring round an old-fashioned long-sleeved woollen vest. The exchange, however, was unable to appreciate his scruples.

'Well,' it demanded, 'do you want a personal call or don't you?'

'I do,' said Poirot, sacrificing Mrs Oliver's creative genius upon the altar of his own impatience. He was relieved when Mrs Oliver spoke. She interrupted his apologies.

'It's splendid that you've rung me up,' she said. 'I was just going out to give a talk on *How I Write My Books*. Now I can get my secretary to ring up and say I am unavoidably detained.'

'But, Madame, you must not let me prevent —'

'It's not a case of preventing,' said Mrs Oliver joyfully. 'I'd have made the most awful fool of myself. I mean, what *can* you say about how you write books? What I mean is, first you've got to think of something, and when you've thought of it you've got to force yourself to sit down and write it. That's all. It would have taken me just three minutes to explain that, and then the Talk would have been ended and everyone would have been very fed up. I can't imagine why everybody is always so keen for authors to *talk* about writing. I should have thought it was an author's business to *write*, not *talk*.'

'And yet it is about how you write that I want to ask you.'

'You can ask,' said Mrs Oliver; 'but I probably shan't know the answer. I mean one just sits down and writes. Half a minute, I've got a frightfully silly hat on for the Talk – and I *must* take it off. It scratches my forehead.' There was a momentary pause and then the voice of Mrs Oliver resumed in a relieved voice, 'Hats are really only a symbol, nowadays, aren't they? I mean, one doesn't wear them for sensible reasons any more; to keep one's head warm, or shield one from the sun, or hide one's face from people one doesn't want to meet. I beg your pardon, M. Poirot, did you say something?'

'It was an ejaculation only. It is extraordinary,' said Poirot, and his voice was awed. 'Always you give me ideas. So also did my friend Hastings whom I have not seen for many, many years. You have given me now the clue to yet another piece of my problem. But no more of all that. Let me ask you instead my question. Do you know an atom scientist, Madame?'

'Do I know an atom scientist?' said Mrs Oliver in a surprised voice. 'I don't know. I suppose I *may*. I mean, I know some professors and things. I'm never quite sure what they actually *do*.'

'Yet you made an atom scientist one of the suspects in your Murder Hunt?'

'Oh, *that*! That was just to be up to date. I mean, when I went to buy presents for my nephews last Christmas, there was nothing but science fiction and the stratosphere and supersonic toys, and so I thought when I started on the Murder Hunt, "Better have an atom scientist as the chief suspect and be modern." After all, if I'd needed a little technical jargon for it I could always have got it from Alec Legge.'

'Alec Legge – the husband of Sally Legge? Is he an atom scientist?'

'Yes, he is. Not Harwell. Wales somewhere. Cardiff. Or Bristol, is it? It's just a holiday cottage they have on the Helm. Yes, so, of course, I *do* know an atom scientist after all.'

'And it was meeting him at Nasse House that probably put the idea of an atom scientist into your head? But his wife is not Yugoslavian.'

'Oh, *no*,' said Mrs Oliver, 'Sally is English as English. Surely you realize *that*?'

'Then what put the idea of the Yugoslavian wife into your head?'

'I really don't know . . . Refugees perhaps? Students? All those foreign girls at the hostel trespassing through the woods and speaking broken English.'

'I see . . . Yes, I see now a lot of things.'

'It's about time,' said Mrs Oliver.

'Pardon?'

'I said it was about time,' said Mrs Oliver. 'That you did see things, I mean. Up to now you don't seem to have done *anything*.' Her voice held reproach.

'One cannot arrive at things all in a moment,' said Poirot, defending himself. 'The police,' he added, 'have been completely baffled.'

'Oh, the police,' said Mrs Oliver. 'Now if a woman were the head of Scotland Yard . . .'

Recognizing this well-known phrase, Poirot hastened to interrupt.

'The matter has been complex,' he said. 'Extremely complex. But now – I tell you this in confidence – but now I arrive!'

Mrs Oliver remained unimpressed.

'I dare say,' she said; 'but in the meantime there have been two murders.'

'Three,' Poirot corrected her.

'Three murders? Who's the third?'

'An old man called Merdell,' said Hercule Poirot.

'I haven't heard of that one,' said Mrs Oliver. 'Will it be in the paper?'

'No,' said Poirot, 'up to now no one has suspected that it was anything but an accident.'

'And it wasn't an accident?'

'No,' said Poirot, 'it was not an accident.'

'Well, tell me who did it – did them, I mean – or can't you over the telephone?'

'One does not say these things over the telephone,' said Poirot.

'Then I shall ring off,' said Mrs Oliver. 'I can't bear it.'

'Wait a moment,' said Poirot, 'there is something else I wanted to ask you. Now, what was it?'

'That's a sign of age,' said Mrs Oliver. 'I do that, too. Forget things –'

'There was something, some little point – it worried me. I was in the boathouse . . .'

He cast his mind back. That pile of comics. Marlene's phrases scrawled on the margin. 'Albert goes with Doreen.' He had had a feeling that there was something lacking – that there was something he must ask Mrs Oliver.

'Are you still there, M. Poirot?' demanded Mrs Oliver. At the same time the operator requested more money.

These formalities completed, Poirot spoke once more.

'Are you still there, Madame?'

'*I'm* still here,' said Mrs Oliver. 'Don't let's waste any more money asking each other if we're there. What is it?'

'It is something very important. You remember your Murder Hunt?'

'Well, of course I remember it. It's practically what we've just been talking about, isn't it?'

'I made one grave mistake,' said Poirot. 'I never read your synopsis for competitors. In the gravity of discovering a murder it did not seem to matter. I was wrong. It did matter. You are a sensitive person, Madame. You are affected by your atmosphere, by the personalities of the people you meet. And these are translated into your work. Not recognizably so, but they are the inspiration from which your fertile brain draws its creations.'

'That's very nice flowery language,' said Mrs Oliver. 'But what exactly do you mean?'

'That you have always known more about this crime than you have realized yourself. Now for the question I want to ask you –

two questions actually; but the first is very important. Did you, when you first began to plan your Murder Hunt, mean the body to be discovered in the boathouse?'

'No, I didn't.'

'Where did you intend it to be?'

'In that funny little summer-house tucked away in the rhodo-dendrons near the house. I thought it was just the place. But then someone, I can't remember who exactly, began insisting that it should be found in the Folly. Well, that, of course, was an *absurd* idea! I mean, anyone could have strolled in there quite casually and come across it without having followed a single clue. People are so stupid. Of course I couldn't agree to *that*.'

'So, instead, you accepted the boathouse?'

'Yes, that's just how it happened. There was really nothing against the boathouse though I still thought the little summer-house would have been better.'

'Yes, that is the technique you outlined to me that first day. There is one thing more. Do you remember telling me that there was a final clue written on one of the "comics" that Marlene was given to amuse her?'

'Yes, of course.'

'Tell me, was it something like' (he forced his memory back to a moment when he had stood reading various scrawled phrases): 'Albert goes with Doreen; Georgie Porgie kisses hikers in the wood; Peter pinches girls in the Cinema?'

'Good gracious me, no,' said Mrs Oliver in a slightly shocked voice. 'It wasn't anything silly like that. No, mine was a perfectly straightforward clue.' She lowered her voice and spoke in mys-terious tones. '*Look in the hiker's rucksack.*'

'*Epatant!*' cried Poirot. '*Epatant!* Of course, the "comic" with that on it would *have* to be taken away. It might have given someone ideas!'

'The rucksack, of course, was on the floor by the body and –'

'Ah, but it is another rucksack of which I am thinking.'

'You're confusing me with all these rucksacks,' Mrs Oliver complained. 'There was only one in my murder story. Don't you want to know what was in it?'

'Not in the least,' said Poirot. 'That is to say,' he added politely, 'I should be enchanted to hear, of course, but –'

Mrs Oliver swept over the 'but.'

'Very ingenious, *I* think,' she said, the pride of authorship in her voice. 'You see, in Marlene's haversack, which was supposed to be the Yugoslavian wife's haversack, if you understand what I mean —'

'Yes, yes,' said Poirot, preparing himself to be lost in fog once more.

'Well, in it was the bottle of medicine containing poison with which the country squire poisoned his wife. You see, the Yugoslavian girl had been over here training as a nurse and she'd been in the house when Colonel Blunt poisoned his first wife for her money. And she, the nurse, had got hold of the bottle and taken it away, and then come back to blackmail him. That, of course, is why he killed her. Does that fit in, M. Poirot?'

'Fit in with what?'

'With your ideas,' said Mrs Oliver.

'Not at all,' said Poirot, but added hastily, 'All the same, my felicitations, Madame. I am sure your Murder Hunt was so ingenious that nobody won the prize.'

'But they did,' said Mrs Oliver. 'Quite late, about seven o'clock. A very dogged old lady supposed to be quite gaga. She got through all the clues and arrived at the boathouse triumphantly, but of course the police were there. So then she heard about the murder, and she was the last person at the whole fête to hear about it, I should imagine. Anyway, they gave her the prize.' She added with satisfaction, 'That horrid young man with the freckles who said I drank like a fish never got farther than the camellia garden.'

'Some day, Madame,' said Poirot, 'you shall tell me this story of yours.'

'Actually,' said Mrs Oliver, 'I'm thinking of turning it into a book. It would be a pity to waste it.'

And it may here be mentioned that some three years later Hercule Poirot read *The Woman in the Wood,* by Ariadne Oliver, and wondered whilst he read it why some of the persons and incidents seemed to him vaguely familiar.

CHAPTER 18

The sun was setting when Poirot came to what was called officially Mill Cottage, and known locally as the Pink Cottage down by Lawder's Creek. He knocked on the door and it was flung open with such suddenness that he started back. The angry-looking young man in the doorway stared at him for a moment without recognizing him. Then he gave a short laugh.

'Hallo,' he said, 'it's the sleuth. Come in, M. Poirot. I'm packing up.'

Poirot accepted the invitation and stepped into the cottage. It was plainly, rather badly furnished. And Alec Legge's personal possessions were at the moment taking up a disproportionate amount of room. Books, papers and articles of stray clothing were strewn all around, an open suitcase stood on the floor.

'The final break-up of the *ménage*,' said Alec Legge. 'Sally has cleared out. I expect you know that.'

'I did not know it, no.'

Alec Legge gave a short laugh.

'I'm glad there's something you don't know. Yes, she's had enough of married life. Going to link up her life with that tame architect.'

'I am sorry to hear it,' said Poirot.

'I don't see why you should be sorry.'

'I am sorry,' said Poirot, clearing off two books and a shirt and sitting down on the corner of the sofa, 'because I do not think she will be as happy with him as she would be with you.'

'She hasn't been particularly happy with me this last six months.'

'Six months is not a lifetime,' said Poirot, 'it is a very short space out of what might be a long happy married life.'

'Talking rather like a parson, aren't you?'

'Possibly. May I say, Mr Legge, that if your wife has not been happy with you it is probably more your fault than hers.'

'She certainly thinks so. Everything's my fault, I suppose.'

'Not everything, but some things.'

'Oh, blame everything on me. I might as well drown myself in the damn' river and have done with it.'

Poirot looked at him thoughtfully.

'I am glad to observe,' he remarked, 'that you are now more perturbed with your own troubles than with those of the world.'

'The world can go hang,' said Mr Legge. He added bitterly, 'I seem to have made the most complete fool of myself all along the line.'

'Yes,' said Poirot, 'I would say that you have been more unfortunate than reprehensible in your conduct.'

Alec Legge stared at him.

'Who hired you to sleuth me?' he demanded. 'Was it Sally?'

'Why should you think that?'

'Well, nothing's happened officially. So I concluded that you must have come down after me on a private job.'

'You are in error,' replied Poirot. 'I have not at any time been sleuthing you. When I came down here I had no idea that you existed.'

'Then how do you know whether I've been unfortunate or made a fool of myself or what?'

'From the result of observation and reflection,' said Poirot. 'Shall I make a little guess and will you tell me if I am right?'

'You can make as many little guesses as you like,' said Alec Legge. 'But don't expect me to play.'

'I think,' said Poirot, 'that some years ago you had an interest and sympathy for a certain political party. Like many other young men of a scientific bent. In your profession such sympathies and tendencies are naturally regarded with suspicion. I do not think you were ever seriously compromised; but I *do* think that pressure was brought upon you to consolidate your position in a way you did not want to consolidate it. You tried to withdraw and you were faced with a threat. You were given a rendezvous with someone. I doubt if I shall ever know that young man's name. He will be for me always *the young man in a turtle shirt*.'

Alec Legge gave a sudden explosion of laughter.

'I suppose that shirt was a bit of a joke. I wasn't seeing things very funny at the time.'

Hercule Poirot continued.

'What with worry over the fate of the world, and the worry over your own predicament, you became, if I may say so, a man almost impossible for any woman to live with happily. You did not confide in your wife. That was unfortunate for you, as I should say that your wife was a woman of loyalty, and that if she had realized how unhappy and desperate you were, she would have been whole-heartedly on your side. Instead of that she merely began to compare you, unfavourably, with a former friend of hers, Michael Weyman.'

He rose.

'I should advise you, Mr Legge, to complete your packing as soon as possible, to follow your wife to London, to ask her to forgive you and to tell her all that you have been through.'

'So that's what you advise,' said Alec Legge. 'And what the hell business is it of yours?'

'None,' said Hercule Poirot. He withdrew towards the door. 'But I am always right.'

There was a moment's silence. Then Alec Legge burst into a wild peal of laughter.

'Do you know,' he said, 'I think I'll take your advice. Divorce is damned expensive. Anyway, if you've got hold of the woman you want, and are then not able to keep her, it's a bit humiliating, don't you think? I shall go up to her flat in Chelsea, and if I find Michael there I shall take hold of him by that hand-knitted pansy tie he wears and throttle the life out of him. I'd enjoy that. Yes, I'd enjoy it a good deal.'

His face suddenly lit up with a most attractive smile.

'Sorry for my filthy temper,' he said, 'and thanks a lot.'

He clapped Poirot on the shoulder. With the force of the blow Poirot staggered and all but fell.

Mr Legge's friendship was certainly more painful than his animosity.

'And now,' said Poirot, leaving Mill Cottage on painful feet and looking up at the darkening sky, 'where do I go?'

CHAPTER 19

The chief constable and Inspector Bland looked up with keen curiosity as Hercule Poirot was ushered in. The chief constable was not in the best of tempers. Only Bland's quiet persistence had caused him to cancel his dinner appointment for that evening.

'I know, Bland, I know,' he said fretfully. 'Maybe he was a little Belgian wizard in his day – but surely, man, his day's over. He's what age?'

Bland slid tactfully over the answer to this question which, in any case, he did not know. Poirot himself was always reticent on the subject of his age.

'The point is, sir, he was *there* – on the spot. And we're not getting anywhere any other way. Up against a blank wall, that's where we are.'

The chief constable blew his nose irritably.

'I know. I know. Makes me begin to believe in Mrs Masterton's homicidal pervert. I'd even use bloodhounds, if there were anywhere to use them.'

'Bloodhounds can't follow a scent over water.'

'Yes. I know what you've always thought, Bland. And I'm inclined to agree with you. But there's absolutely no motive, you know. Not an iota of motive.'

'The motive may be out in the islands.'

'Meaning that Hattie Stubbs knew something about De Sousa out there? I suppose that's reasonably possible, given her mentality. She was simple, everyone agrees on that. She might blurt out what she knew to anyone at any time. Is that the way you see it?'

'Something like that.'

'If so, he waited a long time before crossing the sea and doing something about it.'

'Well, sir, it's possible he didn't know what exactly had become of her. His own story was that he'd seen a piece in some society periodical about Nasse House, and its beautiful *châtelaine*. (Which I have always thought myself,' added Bland parenthetically, 'to be a silver thing with chains, and bits and pieces hung on it that people's grandmothers used to clip on their waistbands – and a good idea, too. Wouldn't be all these silly women for ever leaving their handbags around.) Seems, though, that in women's jargon *châtelaine* means mistress of a house. As I say, that's history and maybe it's true enough, and he *didn't* know where she was or who she'd married until then.'

'But once he did know, he came across post-haste in a yacht in order to murder her? It's far-fetched, Bland, very far-fetched.'

'But it *could* be, sir.'

'And what on earth could the woman know?'

'Remember what she said to her husband. "*He kills people.*"'

'Murder remembered? From the time she was fifteen? And presumably only her word for it? Surely he'd be able to laugh that off?'

'We don't know the facts,' said Bland stubbornly. 'You know yourself, sir, how once one knows *who* did a thing, one can look for evidence *and* find it.'

'H'm. We've made inquiries about De Sousa – discreetly – through the usual channels – and got nowhere.'

'That's just why, sir, this funny old Belgian boy might have stumbled on something. He was in the house – that's the important thing. Lady Stubbs talked to him. Some of the random things she said may have come together in his mind and made sense. However that may be, he's been down in Nassecombe most of today.'

'And he rang you up to ask what kind of a yacht Etienne de Sousa had?'

'When he rang up the first time, yes. The second time was to ask me to arrange this meeting.'

'Well,' the chief constable looked at his watch, 'if he doesn't come within five minutes . . .'

But it was at that very moment that Hercule Poirot was shown in.

His appearance was not as immaculate as usual. His moustache was limp, affected by the damp Devon air, his patent-leather shoes were heavily coated with mud, he limped, and his hair was ruffled.

'Well, so here you are, M. Poirot.' The chief constable shook hands. 'We're all keyed up, on our toes, waiting to hear what you have to tell us.'

The words were faintly ironic, but Hercule Poirot, however damp physically, was in no mood to be damped mentally.

'I cannot imagine,' he said, 'how it was I did not see the truth before.'

The chief constable received this rather coldly.

'Are we to understand that you do see the truth now?'

'Yes, there are details – but the outline is clear.'

'We want more than an outline,' said the chief const...
'We want evidence. Have you got evidence, M. Poirot?'

'I can tell you where to find the evidence.'

Inspector Bland spoke. 'Such as?'

Poirot turned to him and asked a question.

'Etienne de Sousa has, I suppose, left the country?'

'Two weeks ago.' Bland added bitterly, 'It won't be easy to get him back.'

'He might be persuaded.'

'Persuaded? There's not sufficient evidence to warrant an extradition order, then?'

'It is not a question of an extradition order. If the facts are put to him –'

'But *what* facts, M. Poirot?' The chief constable spoke with some irritation. 'What *are* these facts you talk about so glibly?'

'The fact that Etienne de Sousa came here in a lavishly appointed luxury yacht showing that his family is rich, the fact that old Merdell was Marlene Tucker's grandfather (which I did not know until today), the fact that Lady Stubbs was fond of wearing the coolie type of hat, the fact that Mrs Oliver, in spite of an unbridled and unreliable imagination, is, unrealized by herself, a very shrewd judge of character, the fact that Marlene Tucker had lipsticks and bottles of perfume hidden at the back of her bureau drawer, the fact that Miss Brewis maintains that it was Lady Stubbs who asked her to take a refreshment tray down to Marlene at the boathouse.'

'Facts?' The chief constable stared. 'You call those facts? But there's nothing new there.'

'You prefer evidence – definite evidence – such as – Lady Stubbs' body?'

Now it was Bland who stared.

'You have found Lady Stubbs' body?'

'Not actually found it – *but I know where it is hidden*. You shall go to the spot, and when you have found it, then – *then* you will have evidence – all the evidence you need. For only one person could have hidden it there.'

'And who's that?'

Hercule Poirot smiled – the contented smile of a cat who has lapped up a saucer of cream.

n is,' he said softly; 'the *husband*. Sir
.1s wife.'

ible, M. Poirot. We *know* it's impossible.'

oirot, 'it is not impossible at all! Listen, and I

CHAPTER 20

Hercule Poirot paused a moment at the big wrought-iron gates.
He looked ahead of him along the curving drive. The last of the
golden-brown leaves fluttered down from the trees. The cyclamen
were over.

Poirot sighed. He turned aside and rapped gently on the door
of the little white pilastered lodge.

After a few moments' delay he heard footsteps inside, those
slow hesitant footsteps. The door was opened by Mrs Folliat. He
was not startled this time to see how old and frail she looked.

She said, 'M. Poirot? You again?'

'May I come in?'

'Of course.'

He followed her in.

She offered him tea which he refused. Then she asked in a
quiet voice:

'Why have you come?'

'I think you can guess, Madame.'

Her answer was oblique.

'I am very tired,' she said.

'I know.' He went on, 'There have now been three deaths,
Hattie Stubbs, Marlene Tucker, old Merdell.'

She said sharply:

'Merdell? That was an accident. He fell from the quay. He was
very old, half-blind, and he'd been drinking in the pub.'

'It was not an accident. Merdell knew too much.'

'What did he know?'

'He recognized a face, or a way of walking, or a voice –
something like that. I talked to him the day I first came down
here. He told me then all about the Folliat family – about your
father-in-law and your husband, and your sons who were killed

in the war. Only – they were not *both* killed, were they? Your son Henry went down with his ship, but your second son, James, was not killed. He deserted. He was reported at first, perhaps, *Missing believed killed*, and later you told everyone that he *was* killed. It was nobody's business to disbelieve that statement. Why should they?'

Poirot paused and then went on:

'Do not imagine I have no sympathy for you, Madame. Life has been hard for you, I know. You can have had no real illusions about your younger son, but he *was* your son, and you loved him. You did all you could to give him a new life. You had the charge of a young girl, a subnormal but very rich girl. Oh yes, she was rich. You gave out that her parents had lost all their money, that she was poor, and that you had advised her to marry a rich man many years older than herself. Why should anybody disbelieve your story? Again, it was nobody's business. Her parents and near relatives had been killed. A firm of French lawyers in Paris acted as instructed by lawyers in San Miguel. On her marriage, she assumed control of her own fortune. She was, as you have told me, docile, affectionate, suggestible. Everything her husband asked her to sign, she signed. Securities were probably changed and re-sold many times, but in the end the desired financial result was reached. Sir George Stubbs, the new personality assumed by your son, became a rich man and his wife became a pauper. It is no legal offence to call yourself "sir" unless it is done to obtain money under false pretences. A title creates confidence – it suggests, if not birth, then certainly riches. So the rich Sir George Stubbs, older and changed in appearance and having grown a beard, bought Nasse House and came to live where he belonged, though he had not been there since he was a boy. There was nobody left after the devastation of war who was likely to have recognized him. But old Merdell did. He kept the knowledge to himself, but when he said to me slyly that there *would always be Folliats at Nasse House*, that was his own private joke.

'So all had turned out well, or so you thought. Your plan, I fully believe, stopped there. Your son had wealth, his ancestral home, and though his wife was subnormal she was a beautiful and docile girl, and you hoped he would be kind to her and that she would be happy.'

Mrs Folliat said in a low voice:

'That's how I thought it would be – I would look after Hattie and care for her. I never dreamed –'

'You never dreamed – and your son carefully did not tell you, that at the time of the marriage *he was already married.* Oh, yes – we have searched the records for what we knew must exist. Your son had married a girl in Trieste, a girl of the underground criminal world with whom he concealed himself after his desertion. She had no mind to be parted from him, nor for that matter had he any intention of being parted from her. He accepted the marriage with Hattie as a means to wealth, but in his own mind he knew from the beginning what he intended to do.'

'No, no, I do not believe that! I cannot believe it . . . It was that woman – that wicked creature.'

Poirot went on inexorably:

'He meant *murder.* Hattie had no relations, few friends. Immediately on their return to England, he brought her here. The servants hardly saw her that first evening, *and the woman they saw the next morning was not Hattie,* but his Italian wife made up as Hattie and behaving roughly much as Hattie behaved. And there again it might have ended. The false Hattie would have lived out her life as the real Hattie though doubtless her mental powers would have unexpectedly improved owing to what would vaguely be called "new treatment." The secretary, Miss Brewis, already realized that there was very little wrong with Lady Stubbs' mental processes.

'But then a totally unforeseen thing happened. A cousin of Hattie's wrote that he was coming to England on a yachting trip, and although that cousin had not seen her for many years, he would not be likely to be deceived by an impostor.

'It is odd,' said Poirot, breaking off his narrative, 'that though the thought did cross my mind that De Sousa might not be De Sousa, it never occurred to me that the truth lay the other way round – that is to say, that Hattie was not Hattie.'

He went on:

'There might have been several different ways of meeting that situation. Lady Stubbs could have avoided a meeting with a plea of illness, but if De Sousa remained long in England she could hardly have continued to avoid meeting him. And there was already another complication. Old Merdell, garrulous in his old age, used to chatter to his granddaughter. She was probably the only person who bothered to listen to him, and even she dismissed most of what he said because she thought him "batty." Nevertheless, some of the things he said about having seen "a woman's body in the woods," and "Sir George Stubbs being really Mr James" made sufficient impression on her to make her hint about them tentatively to Sir George. In doing so, of course, she signed her own death warrant. Sir George and his wife could take no chances of stories like that getting around. I imagine that he handed her out small sums of hush money, and proceeded to make his plans.

'They worked out their scheme very carefully. They already knew the date when De Sousa was due at Helmmouth. It coincided with the date fixed for the fête. They arranged their plan so that Marlene should be killed and Lady Stubbs "disappear" in conditions which should throw vague suspicion on De Sousa. Hence the reference to his being a "wicked man" and the accusation: "he kills people." Lady Stubbs was to disappear permanently (possibly a conveniently unrecognizable body might be identified at some time by Sir George), and a new personality was to take her place. Actually, "Hattie" would merely resume her own Italian personality. All that was needed was for her to double the parts over a period of a little more than twenty-four hours. With the connivance of Sir George, this was easy. On the day I arrived, "Lady Stubbs" was supposed to have remained in her room until just before teatime. Nobody saw her there except Sir George. Actually, she slipped out, took a bus or a train to Exeter, and travelled from Exeter in the company of another girl student (several travel every day this time of year) to whom she confided her story of the friend who had eaten bad veal and ham pie. She arrives at the hostel, books her cubicle, and goes out to "*explore*." By *tea time*, Lady Stubbs is in the drawing-room. After dinner, Lady Stubbs goes early to bed – but Miss Brewis caught a glimpse of her slipping out of the house a short while afterwards. She spends the night in the hostel, but is out early, and is back at Nasse as Lady Stubbs for breakfast. Again she spends a morning in her room with a "headache," and this time manages to stage an appearance as a "trespasser" rebuffed by Sir George from the window of his wife's room where he pretends to turn and speak to his wife inside that room. The changes of costume were not difficult – shorts and an open shirt under one of the elaborate dresses that Lady Stubbs was fond of wearing. Heavy white make-up for Lady Stubbs with a big coolie hat to shade her face; a gay peasant scarf, sunburned complexion, and bronze-red curls for the Italian girl. No one would have dreamed that those two were the same woman.

'And so the final drama was staged. Just before four o'clock Lady Stubbs told Miss Brewis to take a tea-tray down to Marlene. That was because she was afraid such an idea might occur to Miss Brewis independently, and it would be fatal if Miss Brewis should inconveniently appear at the wrong moment. Perhaps, too, she had a malicious pleasure in arranging for Miss Brewis to be at the scene of the crime at approximately the time it was committed. Then, choosing her moment, she slipped into the empty fortune-telling tent, out through the back and into the summer-house in the shrubbery where she kept her hiker's ruck-sack with its change of costume. She slipped through the woods, called to Marlene to let her in, and strangled the unsuspecting girl then and there. The big coolie hat she threw into the river, then she changed into her hiker dress and make-up, packaged up her cyclamen georgette dress and high-heeled shoes in the rucksack – and presently an Italian student from the youth hostel joined her Dutch acquaintance at the shows on the lawn, and left with her by the local bus as planned. Where she is now I do not know. I suspect in Soho where she doubtless has underworld affiliations of her own nationality who can provide her with the necessary papers. In any case, it is not for an Italian girl that the police are looking, it is for Hattie Stubbs, simple, subnormal, exotic.

'But poor Hattie Stubbs is dead, as you yourself, Madame, know only too well. You revealed that knowledge when I spoke to you in the drawing-room on the day of the fête. The death of Marlene had been a bad shock to you – you had not had the least idea of what was planned; but you revealed very clearly, though I was dense enough not to see it at the time, that when you talked of "Hattie," you were talking of *two different people* – one a woman you disliked who would be "better dead," and against whom you warned me "not to believe a word she said" – the other a girl of whom you spoke in the past tense, and whom you defended with a warm affection. I think, Madame, that you were very fond of poor Hattie Stubbs . . .'

There was a long pause.

Mrs Folliat sat quite still in her chair. At last she roused herself and spoke. Her voice had the coldness of ice.

'Your whole story is quite fantastic, M. Poirot. I really think you must be mad . . . All this is entirely in your head, you have no evidence whatsoever.'

Poirot went across to one of the windows and opened it.

'Listen, Madame. What do you hear?'

'I am a little deaf . . . What should I hear?'

'*The blows of a pick axe* . . . They are breaking up the concrete foundation of the Folly . . . What a good place to bury a body – where a tree has been uprooted and the earth is already disturbed. A little later, to make all safe, concrete over the ground where the body lies, and, on the concrete, erect a Folly . . .' He added gently: 'Sir George's Folly . . . The Folly of the owner of Nasse House.'

A long shuddering sigh escaped Mrs Folliat.

'Such a beautiful place,' said Poirot. 'Only one thing evil . . . The man who owns it . . .'

'I know.' Her words came hoarsely. 'I have always known . . . Even as a child he frightened me . . . Ruthless . . . Without pity . . . And without conscience . . . But he was my son and I loved him . . . I should have spoken out after Hattie's death . . . But he was my son. How could *I* be the one to give him up? And so, because of my silence – that poor silly child was killed . . . And after her, dear old Merdell . . . Where would it have ended?'

'With a murderer it does not end,' said Poirot.

She bowed her head. For a moment or two she stayed so, her hands covering her eyes.

Then Mrs Folliat of Nasse House, daughter of a long line of brave men, drew herself erect. She looked straight at Poirot and her voice was formal and remote.

'Thank you, M. Poirot,' she said, 'for coming to tell me yourself of this. Will you leave me now? There are some things that one has to face quite alone . . .'